A Preface to Chaucer

STUDIES IN MEDIEVAL PERSPECTIVES

A Preface to Chaucer

STUDIES IN

MEDIEVAL PERSPECTIVES

BY D. W. ROBERTSON, JR.

PRINCETON, NEW JERSEY
PRINCETON UNIVERSITY PRESS

ISBN 0-691-01294-6 (paperbound edn.)

ISBN 0-691-06099-1 (clothbound edn.)

First Princeton Paperback Printing, 1969

Second Princeton Paperback Printing, 1970

❖

Publication of this book has been aided
by the Ford Foundation program to support publication,
through university presses, of work in the humanities
and social sciences.

❖

Printed in the United States of America by
Princeton University Press, Princeton, New Jersey

❖

TO THE MEMORY OF
ALAN ROBERTSON
1945–1960

Virtutis gloria merces

PREFACE

"**Mankind**," wrote David Hume, "are so much the same, in all times and places, that history informs us of nothing new or strange in this particular. Its chief use is only to discover the constant and universal principles of human nature." Although political and social historians have long since given up the quest for "human nature," which was, historically speaking, a substitute for Divine Providence, as the primary goal of their researches into the past, their colleagues among literary historians frequently assume that literature is, in whatever time or place, a revelation of "the truth of human passion." If Greek tragedy does not reflect the same passions and emotional difficulties that we ourselves encounter, how can it be made relevant or interesting? If Shakespeare did not grasp universal truths of human nature, wherein does his greatness lie? Chaucer's art, we are told by one recent writer, is "always modern." Does not art transcend time and place? It is not difficult to see that the attitude toward literature implied in these instances may be little more than a romantic projection of the theory of history embraced by Hume and his contemporaries and so brilliantly described by Professor Carl Becker in *The Heavenly City of the Eighteenth Century Philosophers*. There may be, indeed, a "heavenly city" of more recent literary historians.

Suspicions regarding the continuity of human nature in history as a constant have been, perhaps, most vigorously stated by historians of art. Wölfflin's contention that "even the most original talent cannot proceed beyond certain limits which are fixed for it by the date of its birth," and his elaborations of this view, have stimulated an enormous interest in stylistic change. The problem of identifying the source of this change, or even of discovering other changes concomitant with it, is among the most fascinating puzzles of modern cultural history. As Professor Gombrich recently observed, historians and anthropologists "would never accept the idea that man has changed as much within the last three thousand years, a mere hundred generations, as have his art and style."[1] But Professor Gombrich refers here to biological change.

[1] *Art and Illusion* (New York, 1960), p. 22.

vii

There is no evidence to indicate that the hundred generations have produced marked changes in human biological structure. It may be, however, that "human nature" is not altogether a matter of biology, unless we reduce it to a series of relatively simple traits, most of which are shared to a greater or lesser extent by other mammals. Perhaps the distinctive features of human nature are those that arise from the character of human relationships. And these relationships have changed, and changed enormously, with the profound changes that have taken place in the structure of society. The importance of social change as a determining factor in man's psychic constitution has recently been stressed in a brilliant book by J. H. van den Berg, *The Changing Nature of Man*, which sets out to show that "earlier generations lived a different sort of life, and that they were *essentially* different."[2] Some of the ways in which social changes have altered human attitudes since the Middle Ages are suggested in a recent publication in the "Tensions and Technology Series" issued by UNESCO.[3] If, as Professor van den Berg contends, our ancestors were essentially different, we need not assume that they exhibited the same sort of "human nature" which we take for granted. Their "human passions," although not very different from ours biologically, may have been stimulated and elaborated in ways that seem strange to us, and their art, in consequence, may have been appealing in ways that we do not readily understand.

These considerations suggest that the literature of the past may be interesting not because it is "modern," but for exactly the opposite reason: because it is different. Perhaps the history of literary expression may be valuable to us, not because of a monotonous sameness, but because of a refreshing variety of attitude and technique. It is not the purpose of this book to search into the causes of the differences between medieval and modern literature, but simply to describe some of these differences as a background for an approach to the poetry of Chaucer. Essentially, the chapters which follow are concerned with perspectives, with medieval attitudes and opinions which may be thought to account in part for the peculiar character of medieval literature. Intellectual perspec-

[2] (New York, 1961), pp. 7-8.
[3] Jerome F. Scott and R. P. Lynton, *The Community Factor in Modern Technology* (UNESCO, 1952), pp. 13-19.

tive makes just as great a difference in what is understood as does visual perspective in what is seen. Everyone is familiar with optical illusions, for example, in photographs of the surface of the moon, wherein surfaces curve away from the observer at first sight but curve toward him when the image is inverted. In the same way, the "mounds and craters" of literary art can be properly evaluated only if we can see them, at least in momentary glimpses, as they were seen by their creators. Hence the importance of seeking to reconstruct the perspectives of the past, however imperfectly, in our efforts to understand and evaluate its literature.

The specific focus of attention in this book is the poetry of Chaucer. When the work was first planned, a systematic exposition of Chaucer's major poetic works with a gradual development of the background material was contemplated. But it soon became apparent that the result would be a series of volumes as large as this one rather than a single book. It was therefore decided to treat the background materials under the headings represented by the various chapters which follow and to confine the discussions of Chaucer to what amount to a series of final illustrations of the principles adduced. The result is a deductive form of approach which is in many ways unsatisfactory. Convincing analyses of literary texts usually begin with the texts themselves and proceed by what at least appear to be inductive principles to the conclusions which follow. That a procedure of this kind was impossible in the present instance is regrettable, especially since some of the interpretations are unconventional and may hence seem "out of context" to those accustomed to approaching Chaucer's work in another way. It is hoped, however, that the brief and sometimes highly condensed literary illustrations will serve to demonstrate the relevance of the principles adduced and to suggest the possibility of more systematic studies carried out along the lines indicated. Some studies of this kind have been produced or are now in preparation by other scholars.

References to the works of Chaucer, except *Troilus*, are to the edition of F. N. Robinson (Boston, 1957). References to *Troilus* are to the edition of R. K. Root (Princeton, 1945). I am indebted to the following publishers for permission to use printed materials: The Columbia University Press for permission to quote from John Jay Parry, *The Art of Courtly Love* (New York, 1941); Houghton Mifflin Company for permission to quote from F. N. Robinson, *The Works of Geoffrey Chaucer* (Boston, 1957); The University of Chicago Press for permission to use materials from my article, "The Subject of the *De amore* of Andreas Capellanus," *MP*, L (1953), 145-161; The Johns Hopkins University Press for permission to use a revision of my article, "Chaucerian Tragedy," ELH, XIX (1952), 1-37. Occasional variations in punctuation for the sake of emphasis appear in the quotations from Chaucer's text.

The list of illustrations below contains acknowledgments of their sources except where the pictures were made by the author. Since the materials for this book were collected over a number of years in a variety of places, references are sometimes made to more than one edition of a given work, especially where rare early editions are concerned.

The preparation of this book was made practicable by grants from the John Simon Guggenheim Memorial Foundation and from the Princeton University Research Committee. The author is further indebted to librarians both in this country and in England and France whose courtesy enabled him to use rare books and manuscripts. As the list of illustrations indicates, the Bodleian Library and the British Museum were especially helpful in making photographs of illustrated manuscripts. Various parts of the book have been read by my friends Barry Ulanov and Paul A. Olson; and the entire manuscript in its final form was read by Professor J. J. Campbell of Princeton University and Professor R. E. Kaske of the University of Illinois. Although I cannot pretend that all of these readers share all of the views expressed in the following pages, I am indebted to them for many suggestions. I cannot express too strongly my indebtedness to my students and former students at Princeton, some of whose names appear in the footnotes below. I regret that I cannot mention all of them, for without their interest and encouragement this work would not have been undertaken. Some of the basic ideas in this book originated in conversations with my old friend, B. F. Huppé, whose fine study, *Doctrine and Poetry*, forms an excellent introduction to medieval vernacular literature. Finally, my wife, who accompanied me in my wanderings, both geographical and intellectual, while this book was being written, deserves high praise for her unflagging fortitude and patience.

CONTENTS

ILLUSTRATIONS

Following the Index

All photographs of materials in the British Museum are the copyright of the Trustees of the British Museum. NBR = National Buildings Record.

bridge. St. John's College. MS B. 18, fol. 86. Reproduced by permission of the Master and Fellows of St. John's College, Cambridge

49. Horae (French, 14 c.). Oxford. Bodleian Library. MS Douce 62, fol. 43

50, 51. Chartres Cathedral

52. Amiens Cathedral

53. "Amesbury Psalter" (13 c.). Oxford. All Souls College. MS 6, fol. 3

54, 55. Strassburg Cathedral. Photos Giraudon

56. Paris Cathedral

57, 58. Amiens Cathedral

59, 60, 61, 63. Ivory mirror cases. Victoria and Albert Museum. Crown copyright

62. Ivory mirror case. Cambridge. Fitzwilliam Museum. Reproduced by permission of the Syndics of the Fitzwilliam Museum, Cambridge

64. "Ormesby Psalter" (14 c.). Oxford. Bodleian Library. MS Douce 366, fol. 131

65, 66. "Smithfield Decretals" (14 c.). London. British Museum. MS Royal 10 E. IV, fols. 185-185 verso

67. Psalter (ca. 1300). Oxford. Bodleian Library. MS Douce 131, fol. 96 verso

68. *Roman de la rose* (French, 14 c.). London. British Museum. MS Yates Thompson 21, fol. 165

69. *Roman de la rose* (French, ca. 1400). Oxford. Bodleian Library. MS Douce 364, fol. 124 verso

70. Amiens Cathedral

71. *Roman de la rose* (French, 15 c.). Oxford. Bodleian Library. MS Douce 195, fol. 99

72. *Roman de la rose* (French, ca. 1400). Oxford. Bodleian Library. MS Douce 364, fol. 3 verso

73. "Hours of St. Omer" (Flemish, 14 c.). London. British Museum. MS Add. 36684, fol. 69

74. Amiens Cathedral. Photo Marburg

75. Salisbury Cathedral. NBR copyright

76. Wells Cathedral. Copyright Leo Herbert-Felton

77. Beverley Minster. NBR copyright

78. "Ormesby Psalter" (14 c.). Oxford. Bodleian Library. MS Douce 366, fol. 71 verso

79. *Somme le roi* (French). London. British Museum. MS Add. 28162, fol. 7 verso

A Preface to Chaucer

STUDIES IN MEDIEVAL PERSPECTIVES

I · INTRODUCTION: MEDIEVAL AND MODERN ART

𝕬 𝖕𝖗𝖔𝖒𝖎𝖓𝖊𝖓𝖙 art historian has characterized the Middle Ages as an age of "artistry," an age before "art" in the true sense of the word was finally brought to life again in the Renaissance. Although some students of the Middle Ages may feel that this view is prejudiced, it is, nevertheless, in one form or another, widespread; and on the basis of modern aesthetic presuppositions it embodies a large element of truth. There are profound differences between the arts of the Middle Ages and those of modern times, especially if we consider developments subsequent to the beginnings of the romantic movement. To attempt to explain these differences away so as to make what is medieval seem modern is only to prepare false expectations, and we must guard against the very natural tendency of critics to project modern "truths" concerning the nature of beauty and of art on a past which was entirely innocent of these "truths."

Perhaps a better understanding of what is "medieval" can be achieved, and hence a sounder appreciation for it, if we examine some of the differences between the presuppositions of medieval art and those of modern art, suspending, at least for the moment, our desire to make spontaneous judgments of value. Our judgments of value are characteristically dependent on attitudes peculiar to our own place and time. If we universalize these attitudes, as though they were Platonic realities, and assume that they have a validity for all time, we turn history into a mirror which is of significance to us only insofar as we may perceive in it what appear to be foreshadowings of ourselves, but which are, actually, merely reflections of ourselves arising from reconstructions of the evidence based on our own values. And when this happens, history, although it may seem to flatter us with the consoling message, "Thou art the fairest of all," becomes merely an instrument for the cultivation of our own prejudices. We learn nothing from it that we could not learn from the world around us. True, it may seem to have an easy relevance to our own problems, but this relevance is specious and misleading. To form a sound basis for an appreciation of me-

3

dieval art, we must first determine some of the chief differences between those attitudes which underlie modern aesthetic judgments and the corresponding attitudes which underlie medieval aesthetic theory and practice.

Changing attitudes manifest themselves most obviously as differences in style.[1] In the past, it has frequently been customary to consider changes in style in terms of progress, evolution, or organic development.[2] Romanesque sculpture was thought to owe its peculiar features to a lack of skill and craftsmanship on the part of the workmen; Renaissance perspective was thought of, not as a peculiar feature of the style of the period, but as a technical advance setting Renaissance painting far ahead of anything produced in the Middle Ages, and so on. But we are beginning to understand that although technical advances are cumulative, style in the arts, taken in this very general sense, is a feature of the age which produces it. It would be difficult to argue that the Church of the Madeleine in Paris, which illustrates the Empire style, is a great advance over its model, a Temple of Mars in Rome; or that the Chrysler Building in New York City, aside from the technological skills which made it possible, represents an aesthetic advance of great magnitude beyond the Church of the Madeleine. Each style must be allowed its own virtues and potentialities, as well as its limitations; and comparisons between works which represent very different styles, although they may prove stimulating with reference to a given aesthetic theory, are basically unfair when they involve questions of value. The Church of the Madeleine represents an entirely different set of assumptions and ideals, among which may be counted an historical attitude toward antiquity, from that which produced the Temple of Mars. If we wish to understand the integrity and coherence of the Church of the Madeleine we must seek to envisage it, so far as we are able, as it was envisaged by its creators. Stylistic change, like linguistic change, may be thought of as a continuing adaptation of the means of human expression to the needs of a changing cultural environment. And this adaptation in-

[1] The word *style* is used here in its broad historical sense.

[2] The tendency to think of styles in terms of birth, growth, maturity, and decadence imposes arbitrary judgments of value on the artistic productions of certain periods; the concept is therefore avoided in this book. It may be added, moreover, that modern biologists are beginning to issue warnings to the effect that the analogy between cultural evolution and biological evolution is false.

volves new ways of formulating what is "seen" in the world, both concretely and abstractly. The abstract counterparts of visual styles are difficult to describe, and insofar as a style consists of a taste for various kinds of pattern in design, they elude all analysis. But certain very general features of the style of a period may be shown to be characteristic of that period in other ways. And this may be done without conjuring up "Zeitgeists" or other related metaphysical specters.

Modern semanticists like to inform us that our ordinary thought abounds in conventionalized formulas derived from or coexistent with habitual patterns of language. Whether conventionalized modes of thought and expression are, as some semanticists maintain, harmful and somehow scandalous, is a matter for debate. It is certainly true that each age achieves for itself not only a language appropriate to its needs, but also a vocabulary of patterns large and small by means of which it may describe the conventions of its own society and communicate its ideas about those conventions. If we had to begin from scratch with an unpatterned language and without a set of fairly well-established ways of thought derived from our immediate traditions, we should have a very difficult time attempting to describe anything, to formulate any problem in a useful way, or to communicate our descriptions and formulations to anyone else. On the other hand, if we assume that our ancestors, or even our contemporaries in countries whose cultural development has been different from ours, share exactly the same set of intellectual tools that we have developed for ourselves, we shall inevitably find it difficult to understand them. And when difficulties of this kind arise, our natural reaction is to blame the other fellow. He has somehow failed, we assure ourselves, to achieve that degree of culture and sophistication which we so obviously display. Thus if the Romanesque sculptor had been more skilful, we assume, he would have made realistic and humane statues like those of the nineteenth century; and if the medieval painter had known better, he would certainly have availed himself of scientific perspective.[3] Perhaps now that sculpture is no longer realistic, and a great many

[3] The principle that objects seem smaller as their distance from the observer increases was well known in the Middle Ages. E.g., see Alexander Neckam, *De naturis rerum* (London, 1863), pp. 234ff., and Dante, *Paradiso*, 2. 103-104. But medieval artists made very little use of it. Cf. Dagobert Frey, *Gotik und Renaisance* (Augsburg, 1929), p. 10.

painters have deliberately abandoned perspective, these thoughts may be somewhat less reassuring. Perhaps, indeed, our ancestors were justified in their curious modes of expression even when they do not look forward to our own in any obvious way. It may be that art and literature have "languages" made up of conventions of expression which we should learn to "read" just as we learn to read an earlier language or a foreign language.

To go about describing the differences between medieval ways of thought and modern ways of thought in any systematic fashion would require a great deal of minute analysis. No such systematic investigation is contemplated in this book. It will suffice here for purposes of illustration to contrast a dominant medieval convention, the tendency to think in terms of symmetrical patterns, characteristically arranged with reference to an abstract hierarchy, with a dominant modern convention, the tendency to think in terms of opposites whose dynamic interaction leads to a synthesis. These are best described as tendencies; for not all medieval thought necessarily displays an hierarchical pattern, and not all modern thought necessarily involves dynamically opposed contraries. Nevertheless, when we superimpose dynamically interacting opposites upon medieval hierarchies—and there is plenty of evidence to show that we have wished to do this—the result is inevitably a distortion. And it is also true that these two modes of thought produce very different stylistic conventions in art and literature. Admittedly, a contrast between these two conventions can lead only to very crude results, but it will illustrate in very broad terms some basic differences between medieval and modern styles.

The relevance of order as a fundamental principle of medieval iconography was pointed out long ago by Emile Mâle in the opening pages of his great work on religious art in France during the thirteenth century.[4] But the hierarchical pattern, which became most obvious in the Gothic period, had its origins far earlier in Patristic times. If it is obvious in the thought of the Neoplatonic followers of Ammonius, it is equally obvious in the thought and expression of St. Augustine. For example, in his treatise *On Christian Doctrine*, he leads his readers to a conception of God by means of an hierarchical progression (1. 6. 6ff.). In the first place, God must be thought of as a being than which there is nothing better or

[4] *L'art religieux du XIIIe siècle* (Paris, 1923), pp. 7-9.

more sublime. That which is superior in nature may be thought of in two ways, either as something which may be perceived by the bodily senses, or as something accessible only to the understanding. First, those who rely on their senses may think of the sky, or the sun, or the world itself as God. Again, they may rise above anything in the world and think of God as an infinite object shaped in accordance with whatever worldly shape most appeals to them. This is a step upward, certainly, but those who rely on the understanding rather than on the senses may go even farther. They may think of God as being above all mutable things. He must be living, since living beings are superior to lifeless beings. Moreover, since sentient life is superior to insentient life, He must be thought of as sentient, or, indeed, as Life itself. But the life of God must be an immutable life, and, at the same time, it must be a wise life. The wisdom of God must transcend the mutable wisdom of man, so that we must think of God as Wisdom itself. This argument, here briefly paraphrased, must have appealed to St. Augustine's readers as an extremely effective one, since it conforms to a pattern of thought that was natural and familiar to pagans and Christians alike. It is noteworthy that there is no opposition between the bodily senses and the understanding; they represent different ways in which the problem may be approached, and the way of the understanding is superior to, but not opposite to, the way of the senses. The two approaches do not interact dynamically to produce the desired solution. Variations and elaborations of the argument are commonplace in medieval metaphysical systems. The pattern of ascent by degrees is familiar throughout the Middle Ages in works as diverse as St. Bonaventura's *The Mind's Road to God*, Dante's *Divine Comedy*, or Petrarch's *Ascent of Mount Ventoux*. It appears in a wide variety of forms in the work of St. Augustine. Thus, to cite *On Christian Doctrine* again, St. Augustine describes the process by means of which the student of the Bible learns wisdom (2. 7. 9ff.) as a series of ascending steps, of which wisdom is the last. Even evil, in St. Augustine's mind, is subject to the same hierarchical ordering. We find him saying, for example, that "it is brought about as if by a certain secret judgment of God that men who desire evil things are subjected to illusion and deception as a reward for their desires, being mocked and deceived by those lying angels to whom, according to the most beautiful ordering of things, the lowest part of this world is subject by the law of Divine Providence."[5]

By the second half of the twelfth century it was possible to think of rather obvious hierarchies arranged in accordance with systematic degrees in almost all phases of life and thought. To begin with, a moral hierarchy was envisaged in man himself. In its simplest terms this might be expressed as the ascendancy of the reason over the sensuality, or, more elaborately, as the ascendancy of the higher part of the reason, whose function is wisdom, over the lower part of the reason, whose function is knowledge, and the ascendancy of the latter over the motion of the senses.[6] The analogy between this scheme and the hierarchy of Adam, Eve, and the serpent in Genesis suggested a similar hierarchy in the family, where the relationship between husband and wife is sacramentally a reflection of the relationship between Christ and the Church, a relationship which St. Paul had compared with that between the spirit and the flesh.[7] In the state, moreover, the prince was, as John of Salisbury explains in the *Policraticus* (5. 2), the "head" to which the various parts of the commonwealth should be subject in an hierarchical fashion, and of course in actual practice the feudal system was a loose system of hierarchies. The Church was also organized in an hierarchical pattern, and by the thirteenth century the analogy between earthly hierarchies and the celestial hierarchy as described by Dionysius became explicit.[8] The entire creation was sometimes thought of, as it is, for example, in the philosophy of John the Scot, as a hierarchy descending from God to the lowliest of creatures. To illustrate the prevalence of this pattern in theory, in social organization, and in the arts would require many pages. It will suffice here to point out that it existed, and that its existence was a fruitful source of analogies in thought and expression; for once the idea became established, any single hierarchy inevitably

[5] 2. 23. 35. Quotations from *On Christian Doctrine* in this book are from the author's translation (New York: The Liberal Arts Press, 1958).

[6] See St. Augustine, *De Trinitate*, 12. 12; Peter Lombard, *Sententiae*, 2. 24. 6ff. The matter is discussed by O. Lottin, "La doctrine morale des mouvements premiers de l'appetit sensitif aux xiie et xiiie siècles," *Arch. d'hist. doct. et litt. d. m. a.*, vi (1931), 49-173.

[7] Eph. 5. 23-29. The analogy between the hierarchies Christ/Church, husband/wife, spirit/flesh became a fruitful source of literary and artistic imagery.

[8] Cf. Otto von Simson, *The Gothic Cathedral* (New York, 1956), pp. 139-140.

suggested all of the others, and all could be thought of as illustrative of a body of related principles.

In the second canto of the fifth book of Spenser's *Faerie Queene* Artegall meets a giant with a pair of balances who seeks "all things to an equall to restore." After some argument, in which Artegall adduces various analogous hierarchies, Talus throws the giant down from his eminence and drowns him in the sea, also dispersing a "lawlesse multitude" who followed the giant in pursuit of "uncontrolled freedome." But in spite of Talus and his flail, they were to emerge from the "holes and bushes" to which he scattered them, and, by the second half of the eighteenth century, to begin asserting with some success a new order in defiance of the hierarchical systems of the medieval past. They brought with them not only new social and political theories, but also a new art and a new aesthetic. The extent to which the colorful harmonies and deliberate dissonances of romanticism still influence our historical and aesthetic ideals is not commonly realized.[9] The various aesthetic systems that have arisen since art became an entity in itself have a valid application to post-romantic art and literature, but they have little relevance to the art and literature of the pre-romantic past. This difficulty in a simple form is familiar to all teachers of eighteenth-century poetry. Students seem to expect that poetry should be by nature something suitable to the pen of Wordsworth, or Baudelaire, or Eliot, so that they hesitate to acknowledge that Pope's poetry is poetry at all. And the eighteenth century has become a hunting preserve where one seeks to run down "pre-romantics," who wrote, presumably, the only poetry in the period worth reading. That the eighteenth century had a perfectly valid stylistic language of its own has recently been demonstrated in James Sutherland's *Preface to Eighteenth Century Poetry*.[10] That a book of this kind was necessary is a striking testimonial to very general failure on the part of modern students to realize that major

[9] It is probable that the really decisive break in the European tradition should be placed in the last half of the eighteenth century rather than in the Renaissance. Cf. the observations of H. D. F. Kitto, *The Greeks* (Harmondsworth, 1957), p. 108, and, for the visual arts, E. H. Gombrich, *Art and Illusion* (New York, 1960), p. 174.

[10] (Oxford, 1948). Some of the non-romantic features of eighteenth-century poetry as they are described by Professor Sutherland apply equally well to poetry of earlier periods.

alterations in intellectual perspective are necessary if one wishes to form any real appreciation for the art and literature of the pre-romantic past. The statement with which this chapter opens owes part of its validity to the fact that it has been possible to turn the Renaissance into a seeming welter of revolutionary pre-romantic movements. The romantic is a rebel against convention; he feels that rebellion, or at least playful mockery, is a natural prerogative of the artist, if not an artistic obligation. Hence for many years descriptions of the Renaissance were dominated by the notion that during that period humanity arose like an awakening giant, to paraphrase a Soviet textbook, which suddenly cast off the shackles of the medieval Church. It is fairly easy, in pursuance of this line of thought, to think of Rabelais as an atheist, to turn Italian paintings into exemplars of "pure art" celebrating the flesh, and so on. The program has included the discovery of "pre-Renaissance" (i.e., pre-romantic) works in the Middle Ages, among the most famous of which is *Aucasin e Nicolete* as described in the elegant language of Walter Pater.

Romantic criticism, which envisages the artist as a man in dynamic opposition to the conventions of his society, who synthesizes or resolves the tensions thus produced in his art, has sometimes turned medieval artists directly into romantic rebels, without the intervening stage of the Renaissance. They are usually depicted as being rebels against the Church, an institution which many romantics found to be stuffy, oppressive, or downright wicked. Victor Hugo, for example, thought the symbolism of Gothic ornament to be at times foreign or even hostile to Christianity. The more "indecorous" figures on medieval churches were thought to represent a kind of defiance of religious convention. To this conclusion Emile Mâle has written a most emphatic reply, warning that it is necessary to renounce our habit of making "our old artists of the Middle Ages independent and unquiet spirits always eager to throw off the yoke of the Church."[11] The same sort of thing might be said with equal emphasis about medieval poets. To cite only one instance, it has become commonplace to think of the troubadours as rebels in this way, impatient with the restrictions of the Church, and anxious to "throw off the yoke," perhaps with the aid of those early middle-class nonconformists, the Albigensians.

[11] *Op.cit.*, pp. 399-400.

But a careful study of the work of the troubadours shows no evidence of any trace of the distinctive doctrines of the Albigensians with reference to the Trinity, and it is also true that a surprisingly large percentage of them spent their last days in perfectly orthodox monasteries.[12] William IX of Aquitaine may have been intransigent in his amorous affairs and in his relations with ecclesiastical authorities, but his last and most popular song exhibits no trace of rebellion against Christianity. Rebelliousness in the Middle Ages was usually rebelliousness within the limits of the hierarchical ideal. Arnold of Brescia did not wish to destroy the Church; he wished to reform the actual hierarchy in order to make it more harmonious with the ideal. Abelard may have shown the perennial rebelliousness of youth against conventional restraints, but instead of making his lapse with Héloise—if, indeed, anything like what he describes actually took place—a point of departure for an assertion of the individual's right to fulfil his potentialities, he made it the introduction to a treatise on the contemplative life.

The Middle Ages did possess a dialectic, the dialectic of the canonists and the scholastics, but that dialectic did not conform to a pattern of conflict and synthesis. When Abelard set down conflicting opinions of the Fathers in his *Sic et non*, his purpose was neither to cast doubt on their authority nor to suggest that new "compromises" might be made to emerge from their dynamic interaction. He wished instead to suggest that the apparent conflicts might be resolved, by showing, for example, that the same word might be used with different significations in different contexts. In general, the same pattern may be seen in the *quaestiones* of his scholastic successors. Arguments are listed on two sides of a question; the master reaches a decision which he supports, and answers the arguments opposed to it. Typically, the two sides of the problem do not merge to form a new position compounded of their diversity. This fact gives to scholastic discussion a peculiarly "undramatic" quality to those who approach it for the first time. The contrast between this kind of dialectic and the more dynamic pattern familiar today is striking. "Without contraries," wrote William Blake, "is no progression. Attraction and Repulsion, Reason and Energy, Love and Hate, are necessary to human existence."

[12] See Diego Zorzi, *Valori religiosi nella letterature provenzale* (Milan, 1954). Cf. A. Jeanroy, *La poésie lyrique des troubadours* (Toulouse, 1934), I, 134-135.

For Coleridge all creation was the result of the synthesis of dynamically interacting opposites. A tension between opposites is thought of as being necessary to a "progression," to creation, or even to life itself, and this is very different from a desire to reduce contrasts to a state of repose in accordance with the set degrees of a hierarchy.

The romantic is characteristically interested in tensions, in the pursuit of unsatisfied desires, in a dynamic quest which may be, as it is in Goethe's *Faust*, in and of itself regardless of any set goal a means of salvation. Each experience is an avenue to a new one, or, as Tennyson's Ulysses asserts,

> Yet all experience is an arch wherethro'
> Gleams that untravelled world, whose margin fades
> For ever and for ever when I move.

The quest is a lonely one, in which the conventions of society are sources of frustration and corruption. They bring poverty and suffering to Blake's Londoners, pervert the domestic affections of Wordsworth's Michael, and send Byron's Don Juan off to enjoy the natural and unspoiled beauty of love on an island. In an atmosphere of this kind, the artist finds himself no mirror of traditional values, for these are frequently obstacles in his path, but an apostle of human freedom in its purest forms. This is the object of his quest and the goal of his expression.[13] Poetry was for Wordsworth a "spontaneous overflow of powerful feelings," and for Goethe his own work constituted one great "confession." Mr. T. S. Eliot assures us that all art "seeks to metamorphose private failures and disappointments." Artistic expression becomes primarily a kind of self-expression, the unveiling of the sensitive heart. But the search for self-expression of this kind in medieval literature almost always leads to disappointment. Thus the

---

[13] For an extended account of the place of feeling in romantic critical theory, see M. H. Abrams, *The Mirror and the Lamp* (New York, 1958), passim. The critical ideas carefully described and traced in this book furnish an excellent frame of reference for the study of romantic and modern literature. As Marcel Raymond observes in the Foreword to his *From Baudelaire to Surrealism* (New York, 1950), "since romanticism, poetry has followed a very definite line of development." That is, recent styles and fashions in art and literature readily betray their romantic origins. But the aesthetic assumptions which accompany these styles should not be projected on the pre-romantic past.

most distinguished modern student of troubadour poetry, to whom we owe what is still the sanest and most informative introduction to the subject, regretfully concluded that the poets whose works he had studied so carefully were unaware of the cosmic implications of love as they are expressed by more modern poets; instead of all-embracing lyric emotion, he found a system of conventions.[14] Very similar regrets have been expressed over the medieval Latin lyric, which, except on rare occasions, seems oblivious to "the cry of the heart."

As a distinguished historian of medieval art has said, medieval artists were not much concerned to express their private feelings, for artistic expression usually involved "a subordination of the artist's personality to the needs of his patron."[15] It is true that artists sometimes admonished or criticized their patrons. Thus when Pol de Limbourg designed a representation of the *Très riches heures* of Jean de France, Duc de Berry, he included among the cities of the world displayed before Christ by the Adversary a fine representation of his patron's new chateau at Mehun-sur-Yèvre (Fig. 1).[16] Although this picture certainly emphasizes the beauty and grandeur of the new edifice, it is difficult to avoid seeing an implicit warning in it also. What is here done with considerable grace has its counterpart in the moral instruction frequently included in medieval literary works, like that, for example, in Chaucer's "Lak of Stedfastnesse," or, more elaborately, in Gower's *Confessio amantis*. But these examples are hardly illustrative of rebellious self-expression. We learn a great deal in Gower's *Confessio* about the author's concern for the spiritual and political welfare of England, about his regrets concerning deviations from the ideal hierarchies he envisaged, but we learn almost nothing at all, in spite of the title, about the author's cultivation of his own feelings. The standards used for judgment are conservative, not new and revolutionary, and the speaker in the poem is said elsewhere to show "par voie d'essample la sotie de celui qui par amours aime."[17]

[14] Jeanroy, *op.cit.*, II, 96.

[15] Joan Evans, *Art in Mediaeval France* (London, 1948), p. 291.

[16] The three temptations of Christ in the wilderness were conventionally associated with gluttony, vainglory, and avarice, which are also the temptations before which Adam fell. E.g., see Lombard, *Sententiae*, 2. 21. 5. The temptation involving the kingdoms of the world is that of avarice.

[17] From the heading to the "Traitié" in *Works* (Oxford, 1899-1902), I, 379.

He is not even Gower himself, but, like the foolish lover in the *Roman de la rose*, a fiction devised for purposes of exposition.[18] In general, there is little to vitiate the conclusion of a prominent continental scholar to the effect that no poetic is as alien to the notion of "poesia-confessione" in the modern sense as was the medieval poetic.[19]

"The great object of life," wrote Lord Byron, "is sensation, to feel that we exist, even though in pain." Romantic poetry is characteristically designed to arouse, as well as to express, feelings, emotions, sensations. Shelley assures us that "terror, anguish, despair itself, are often the chosen expressions of an approximation to the highest good," and he speaks of poetry as the vehicle for "living impersonations of the truth of human passion." Leigh Hunt says that "poetry is passion," the "ardent subjection of ones-self to emotion." For John Stuart Mill, at least at one stage of his career, "Poetry is feeling confessing itself to itself," or "the thoughts and words in which emotion spontaneously embodies itself." Later on, among the symbolists, for example, the element of self-expression becomes somewhat less spontaneous and the techniques for suggesting emotion are more calculated. Mr. Eliot's "objective correlative" represents a deliberate effort to create "the formula of a particular emotion," not to convey an idea. Perhaps the doctrine of self-expression reached its highest point among the surrealists. How uncharacteristic these attitudes are of medieval thought may be illustrated by a passage from a commentary on the book of Ecclesiasticus, wherein the author, who was probably Robert Holcot, gives us a picture of a young lover who, like the Squire in Chaucer's Franklin's Tale, feels moved to express his secret affection in verse. The verse is not very good verse, but the kind of thing the author thought to be typical of "lyric" emotion is significant. "The Devil," he says, referring to a personage who was in the Middle Ages frequently the *alter ego* of an unsentimental Cupid, "rains ensnaring thoughts upon lechers . . . so that they are troubled by the sickness of carnal love. Whence he who languishes in this way, wishing to express his malady and at the same

---

[18] Cf. the observations of Pierre Col in C. F. Ward, *The Epistles on the Romance of the Rose and other Documents in the Controversy* (Chicago, 1911), pp. 58-59.

[19] Vittore Branca, *Boccaccio Medioevale* (Florence, 1956), pp. 127-128.

time to conceal the name of the darling whom he loves, says subtly in meter,

> Si vertas caput bachi primamque sibille
> Invenies pro quo duco suspiria mille."

That is, our commentator explains, reverse the first syllable of this poem to produce *is*. Similarly, reverse the first syllable of *bachus* to produce *ab*. Now add the ending *-illa* and there appears the name *Isabilla* which identifies the girl "for whom the fool languishes."[20] Holcot is not ridiculing the technique of the poem, which involves a kind of "wit" common even in scriptural commentaries of the period.[21] He is ridiculing the sentiment which produced it. But that sentiment is expressed in a very unsentimental way. To make fun of his lover, Holcot does not have him write something which looks like one of the lesser productions of Edgar Guest, for the simple reason that the direct expression of emotion was not characteristic of his time.

If we except some of the devotional poetry of the later Middle Ages, especially that written under Franciscan influence, and a few scattered pieces here and there from earlier periods, it is safe to say that the function of the medieval poet was not so much to express his personal moods or emotions, his *Sehnsucht* or *Weltschmerz*, as to reflect a reality outside of himself. He might well show the predicament of a lover in a poem without being a lover, and he had, or thought he had, ample precedent in classical Latin poetry for doing just that. As Konrad Burdach explains it, the "nature" he imitated was not what we think of as "nature" but an abstract nature structured by God.[22] Quite frequently the accepted technique involved the use of an enigmatical arrangement of visible things which would serve to call attention to an invisible truth. In other words, a work of art was frequently a problem to be solved, although not always quite so childish a problem as the one we have just quoted. Lactantius wrote, "it is the business of the poet with some gracefulness to change and transfer actual occurrences into other representations by oblique transformations," so that he rep-

---

[20] *Super librum ecclesiastici* (Venice, 1509), fol. 3 verso.

[21] See D. Trapp, o.s.a., "Peter Ceffons of Clairvaux," *Rech. théol. anc. med.*, XXIV (1957), pp. 106 (note 6) and 149.

[22] *Reformation, Renaissance, Humanismus* (Berlin and Leipzig, 1926), p. 166.

resents a "truth veiled with an outward covering and show."[23] This statement was frequently repeated during the Middle Ages, and was used by Petrarch to support his favorite theory that a poet adorns the truth, which has here become a philosophical truth, with veils so that it may be hidden from the unworthy, but to the more ingenious and studious readers, the search for it will be more difficult and the discovery, in consequence, more pleasant.[24] The author of the *Rime* was more interested in our discernment of their philosophical content than he was in our sympathetic response to his real or imagined emotional difficulties.

But this is not to say that medieval art and literature lack emotion, or that they are not "sincere." A twelfth-century writer on love tells us that it is a subject about which only he is worthy to speak "who composes words without in accordance with what the heart says within." It can, he says, neither be learned from books nor from the experience of others.[25] At first glance, this seems to contradict all that we have been saying. But the love that speaks from the heart in this instance is charity, and its expression is not so much a matter of asserting the "self" as a psychological entity as it is a matter of revealing a gift from above. Medieval man, who inherited the implications of Augustine's doctrine of illumination, looked inward, not to find the roots of emotion, but to find God.[26] The last poem of Petrarch's *Rime*, even though many of its images had echoed for hundreds of years in the writings of theologians and poets, is just as "sincere" and just as moving as are the early sonnets. For Petrarch it was undoubtedly the most moving of them all. Its emotional effect rests not so much on the concrete material of the figures as it does on the ideas which those figures convey.

The distinction between a medieval poet who deliberately clothes a truth with a veil and a more modern poet who seeks directly to reveal the non-discursive wisdom of passion finds a rough

[23] *Inst. Div.*, trans. Fletcher, 1. 11.

[24] For a few samples, see Isidore of Seville, *Etymologiae*, 8. 7. 10; Rabanus, *De universo*, PL, 111, col. 419; Petrus Berchorius, *Metamorphosis Ovidiana*, ed. Ghisalberti, *Studij romanzi*, xxiii (1933), p. 87.

[25] *Epistola ad Severinam de caritate*, ed. G. Dumièges (Paris, 1955), p. 45. Cf. Dante, *Purgatorio*, 24. 52-58, where the connotations are similar.

[26] For a typical illustration, see the *Meditationes* attributed to St. Bernard, PL, 184, col. 485.

parallel in Mill's distinction between the work of a "cultivated but
not naturally poetic mind" and the work of "a poet." The first
"desires to convey the thought, and he clothes it in the feelings
which it excites in himself, or which he deems most appropriate to
it. The other merely pours forth the overflowing of his feelings;
and all the thoughts which those feelings suggest are floated promiscuously along the stream." Mill's objection to poetry of the
first type, an objection which still has some currency today, actually constitutes a blanket condemnation of most classical and medieval poetry. Neither Ovid, Horace, nor Virgil may be justly accused
of floating his thoughts promiscuously on a stream of feeling. And
certainly no one would accuse Chrétien de Troyes, Jean de Meun,
Dante, or Chaucer of doing so. Mill was suggesting aesthetic
criteria appropriate to a romantic style, a style formed by a desire
to communicate, or at least to express, the inmost tensions of the
psyche. But these are no suitable criteria to apply to the "artistry"
of pre-romantic poetry, unless, of course, we wish to read that
poetry naïvely in the hope that here and there a purple passage
may seem rewarding.

We have been quick to supply "contraries" for purposes of generating the "tensions" necessary to make our medieval ancestors
seem modern. If we use "the Church" as one pole, a conveniently
nebulous entity,[27] we have a choice among several elements for
the other: "paganism," "obscenity," or simply, "the flesh." Any
of these juxtaposed with "the Church" will produce the much
celebrated "medieval dualism" which flourishes side by side with
the equally celebrated but somewhat discordant "medieval synthesis." Both terms imply a conflict of opposites, unresolved in the
first instance, and "reconciled" in the second. The first of these
poles, "paganism," has been adduced in very diverse forms, depending on the period being studied. The famous theory of A. W.
Schlegel and J. Grimm summed up in the dictum "das Volk
dichtet" has given rise to elaborate theories concerning a substra-

---

[27] The "Church" may mean (1) the body of communicants, (2) the body of
truly faithful communicants, (3) the ecclesiastical hierarchy, (4) a local group of
the ecclesiastical hierarchy (e.g., the officials of a diocese). If one bishop or other
ecclesiastical authority disapproves of something, we should not jump to the conclusion that "the Church" disapproves of it. Although the decrees of Lateran
Councils may be said to represent the opinions of the Church, in actual practice
such decrees sometimes escape local opinion.

tum of pagan folklore underlying the literature of the Middle Ages, and this effort has been amply supplemented by other theories based on assumptions gleaned from Sir James Frazer's *Golden Bough*, a work now happily outmoded in its own field. Scholarship has engaged in a romantic quest for a mysterious realm of pagan superstition and brilliant "Ur-" forms of existing literary works much more glamorous than the texts which survive in our manuscripts. Needless to say, such labors do little more than to demonstrate the tenacity of the romantic imagination in modern times. There is no reason to suppose that the literary activities of English villagers in the Middle Ages were any more significant than are the activities of English villagers today, or that their superstitions were then any more picturesque. More specifically, with the development of modern romantic nationalism in Germany there grew an intense interest in "altgermanische Kultur," a subject about which our knowledge is rather incomplete. Nevertheless, German scholars, abetted by their English-speaking colleagues, eagerly sought out evidence of this early pagan culture in the vernacular literature of the Middle Ages, especially in Old English literature. As a result, Old English poems have frequently been divided into disparate segments, a "pagan" part, said to be "truly poetic," and another part said to be "a sop to Christianity" or a "pious interpolation." The poet is envisaged as a man who is torn between a fascination for the untrammeled freedoms of his pagan inheritance, or what, rather inexplicably, are supposed to be those freedoms, and the confining bonds of Christian morality. In other words, he is transformed into a romantic. Happily, scholarship in this field is now advancing beyond these tendencies, and there is a growing recognition of the integrity and comparative sophistication of Old English culture.[28]

A more refined type of "paganism" appears in the twelfth century, when, as a part of the general intellectual efflorescence of the period, there was a considerable interest in the philosophy, literature, and art of antiquity. At the same time classical elements became prominent in European literature and art so that there is obvious justification for labels like "Romanesque" or "the age of Ovid," although the latter term is too restrictive. At Chartres

[28] See Dorothy Whitelock's brilliant Inaugural lecture, "Changing Currents in Anglo-Saxon Studies" (Cambridge, 1958).

there was a revival of interest in Plato, and this has been hailed as a break with tradition, a deviation toward paganism. In view of St. Augustine's explicit endorsement of Plato and his school,[29] it is difficult to see why this Platonism should be any more "pagan" than the Aristotelianism of the next century, which, at least in the hands of St. Thomas, managed to be largely orthodox. Moreover, it has been shown that the Platonism of the time was far from being "pagan," and one by one those authors who used Platonic formulations *per integumentum* like Bernard Silvestris, Alanus de Insulis, or William of Conches are being reinstated into their position in the normal, and orthodox, stream of Christian thought.[30] Ovid, whose poetry, including the *Remedia amoris* and at times even the *Ars amatoria*, was used for school texts, became a standard authority among perfectly orthodox writers. In the fourteenth century Bishop Bradwardine cites Ovid respectfully as a Platonic philosopher, and he does so without any evidence of "tension." With reference to classical materials in Romanesque art, Dr. Hanns Swarzenski writes that the widespread use of "classical mythology and similar subjects should not be interpreted as a sign of a condescension to worldly mentality, but signifies their acceptance and inclusion in the theocratic programme of the cosmic order."[31] Classical materials in medieval literature and art are thus not a sufficient basis for erecting a "polarity" between "the Church" and paganism. The principles governing what was thought of as the "proper" use of classical literature were widely known and understood.[32] Boccaccio's description of the situation in his own day might well apply two hundred years earlier: "In the days when the Church was just taking root among the pagans, the Christians found it expedient to press hard against the pagan rites and ob-

[29] *On Christian Doctrine*, 2. 40. 60.

[30] See J. M. Parent, *La doctrine de la création dans l'Ecole de Chartres* (Paris and Ottawa, 1938), pp. 23-25; E. Gilson, "La cosmogonie de Bernardus Silvestris," *Arch. d'hist. doct. et litt. d. m. a.*, III (1928), 5-24; R. H. Green, "Alan of Lille's *De planctu naturae*," *Speculum*, XXXI (1956), 649-674. F. M. Cornford once said, *Before and After Socrates* (Cambridge, 1960), p. 65, "Plato and Aristotle are among the greatest fathers of the Christian church." The implications of this statement should be considered well by those who seek heresies among medieval "Platonists" or "Aristotelians."

[31] *Monuments of Romanesque Art* (London, 1954), p. 15.

[32] Bede's opinion on this matter was incorporated into the canon law by Gratian and was widely quoted. E.g., see Richard de Bury, *Philobiblon*, ed. Altamura, 13. 47ff.

servances, colored as men's notions of religion were by the origin and by the very perseverance of paganism. It was a precaution lest readers of pagan literature be caught by the claw of antiquity, and return as a dog to their vomit. But today, by the grace of Christ, our strength is very great; the universally hateful doctrine of paganism has been cast into utter and perpetual darkness, and the Church in triumph holds the fortress of the enemy. Thus there is the very slightest danger in the study and investigation of paganism."[33] When we attribute paganism to medieval authors, we frequently forget how profound the "darkness" described by Boccaccio is; our knowledge of both classical and Germanic paganism is at best rudimentary, even though the romantic paganism of the nineteenth-century parlor may be more familiar.[34] We must avoid projecting this latter-day paganism on antiquity itself and then seeking to trace its "survival" in later periods.

The problem of "obscenity" is closely related to the problem of paganism, since obscene materials in medieval literature and art sometimes have a classical origin. It is well known that medieval artists decorated their churches with "unmentionable" subjects, especially when they set out to depict the vices. The figures of lechery and despair (or wrath) which adorn a capital at Vézelay illustrate well a kind of moral ornament that we should be astonished to find in modern churches (Fig. 2). Similarly, English churches of the fourteenth century contained wall paintings of the vices which, as Professor Tristram describes them, "sometimes resembled some of Chaucer's more pungent passages."[35] Medieval artists did not hesitate to use what we should call "obscenity" to illustrate a moral point. And what is true of medieval artists is, in this instance, equally true of medieval writers. An excellent example is afforded by Thomas Ringstede's use of the story of Priapus "whan the asse hym schente with cri by nighte" in a commentary on the Book of Proverbs. The work is a respectable labor of exegesis. Nevertheless, Ringstede tells the story as it appears in Ovid's

[33] *Gen. deor.*, 15. 9, translated by C. G. Osgood, *Boccaccio on Poetry* (New York, 1956), pp. 123-124.

[34] For example, Venus is a prominent figure in Latin poetry, but we are just beginning to discover what she may have meant to the Romans. See the pioneering study of Robert Schilling, *La religion romaine de Venus* (Paris, 1954).

[35] *English Wall Painting of the Fourteenth Century* (London, 1955), p. 4.

Fasti and even edifies his readers with a quotation which includes the lines

> At deus obscene nimium quoque parte paratus
> Omnibus ad lune lumina risus erat.[36]

The rather amusing rites by means of which Roman women are said to have sought to avoid sterility in connection with this deity are described unblushingly by Ridewal in his commentary on St. Augustine's *City of God*.[37] But neither Ridewal nor Ringstede was aware of the "unseemly mixture of the sacred and profane" which modern critics piously adduce when vernacular authors like Jean de Meun or Boccaccio use "obscene" material for philosophical purposes.[38] It is difficult to see why we should expect vernacular authors to be more reticent than ecclesiastical artists or clerical commentators. The squeamishness about obscenity which modern critics of medieval works evince, either with "pious" indignation or with a sort of triumphant delight, appears first in decisive form in the strictures made by Christine de Pisan concerning the *Roman de la rose*, which, to that lady's dismay, employs vulgar words like *coilles*.[39] But these same "coilles," which were those of Saturn, had frequently appeared with philosophical significance in the sober discussions of the mythographers,[40] and they continued to be illustrated in an unmistakable fashion (Fig. 3). The modern view that such materials represent a romantic assertion of the baser elements of human nature simply overlooks the fact that they were intended to be significant within the framework of Christian morality. Medieval writers were just as capable of a kind of philosophical obscenity as were later writers like Erasmus, Rabelais, Swift, and Sterne. The bare breasts of the mermaids so enticingly revealed on

---

[36] *In proverbia Salomonis* (Paris, 1515), fol. lv. The Renaissance editor attributes this commentary to either Holcot or Thomas Waleys, but Stegmüller, *Repertorium biblicum medii aevi* (Madrid, 1940-1955), no. 8172, identifies it as the work of the English Dominican Thomas Ringstede (d. 1370).

[37] Oxford, Corpus Christi Coll. MS. D. 187, fol. 44.

[38] E.g., see G. Paré, *Les idées et les lettres au XIIIe siècle* (Montreal, 1947), p. 289.

[39] See Ward, *op.cit.*, p. 18.

[40] E.g., Bernard Silvestris, *Comm. super sex libros Eneidos Virg.*, ed., G. Riedel (Greifswald, 1924), p. 10; or Baudri de Bourgueil, *Oeuvres poétiques*, ed. P. Abrahams (Paris, 1926), p. 274.

a capital at Sainte-Eutrope de Saintes,[41] or on a roof boss at Exeter Cathedral (Fig. 4), were designed not to produce dreams of "the breast of the nymph in the brake," but to provoke thought—not to create emotional tensions, but to suggest certain very Christian conclusions.[42] Perhaps the most "shocking" passage in *The Canterbury Tales* is the description of the wooing of Alisoun by "hende Nicholas"; but the technique employed by that eager young clerk is illustrated without qualms in a fourteenth-century devotional manual (Fig. 5), where, of course, it conveys the idea of lechery. Obscene materials, like classical materials, could become a part of "the theocratic programme of the cosmic order."

It is true that neither H. G. Wells nor G. B. Shaw, both of whom regarded Christianity as being stuffy and repressive, would have been likely to hear the story of Priapus from a divine nor to see mermaids looking enticingly at them from ecclesiastical decorations, but the Middle Ages had not yet developed a general consensus about the limits of the "holy." Nor had they made the kind of dramatic opposition between the spirit on the one hand and the flesh on the other which makes a great deal of later Christian thought, centered on the concept of righteousness, seem inhumane. The standard medieval view in this matter—as in so many others —is that stated by St. Augustine. No one, he says, on the authority of Eph. 5. 29, hates his own flesh; those Christians who seem to persecute their flesh, and who do so rightly, do so not for the purpose of destroying it, but to subjugate it in preparation for necessary labors. Those who persecute their flesh perversely as though it were a natural enemy have been misled by the words of St. Paul (Gal. 5. 17): "For the flesh lusteth against the spirit: and the spirit against the flesh, for these are contrary to one another." This is said, St. Augustine explains, because the spirit desires to overcome the evil habit of the flesh, not the flesh itself, so that the flesh may become subjected to it as the natural order requires. The spirit wishes the flesh, which it loves, to be ruled properly, nourished, and cherished "as also Christ does the Church."[43] The "warfare"

---

[41] See Joan Evans, *Cluniac Art of the Romanesque Period* (Cambridge, 1950), fig. 135 *a*.

[42] See below, Ch. III.

[43] *On Christian Doctrine*, I. 24. 24-25. Cf. *Glossa ordinaria*. Pl. 114, col. 599, and the arguments advanced by William of Auvergne, *De tentationibus et resistentijs* in *Opera* (Venice, 1591), pp. 291-292 against the "errorem . . . Mani-

St. Paul describes is thus not a natural state; it is something that arises from sin,[44] in which the ordered hierarchy of created nature is disturbed. Moreover, it does not involve "two mighty opposites," but a superior being and an inferior being whose struggle is like that between a lord and an intransigent vassal, a husband and a disobedient wife, or a rider and a spirited horse. Once the spirit triumphs, it rules with that harmony of virtue which is so vividly portrayed by Veronese (Fig. 6). What appear to be "contraries" in St. Paul were thus thought of as elements in a hierarchy, each good and useful when properly ordered.

It will be seen that this hierarchical solution is much less "puritanical," in the loose sense of that word, than those offered by the leading systems of classical paganism. Socrates regarded the flesh as a prison from which every philosopher seeks to escape in death. But Christianity substituted the "evil habit of the flesh" or the "old man," as St. Paul calls it, for the flesh itself. This was to "die" or be "crucified" at baptism and to be kept in subjection through penance. The Epicureans, or the more sophisticated members of that sect, found that the pleasures of the flesh are risky since they may result in pain. The Stoics treated the flesh with contempt, and Cicero admonishes that pleasure and virtue are incompatible.[45] For the Neopythagoreans, the flesh was something to be transcended.[46] The hierarchical arrangement described by St. Augustine, which prevailed during the Middle Ages except among ascetic extremists and heretics like the Albigensians, should thus be regarded as a philosophical triumph of no mean proportions, and that triumph was made possible by the avoidance of those Manichean contraries which some modern criticism seeks to impose on medieval culture.

What is true in a wider sense of contraries or polarities which we may seek to conjure up between the Church on the one hand and paganism, obscenity, or the flesh on the other, is also true of more

---

cheorum qui duas naturas contrarias in nobis ponunt, alteram bonam, ad bonam semper paratam, alteram vero malam, et ad malam semper paratam."

[44] Cf. St. Augustine, *Enn. in Ps. CXLIII* in *Opera* (Paris, 1836-1838), IV, 2280-2281; and for a vernacular statement of the idea, see *Le cheveler Dé*, ed. K. Urwin, *RLR*, LXVIII (1937), 136ff., lines 809-834. Cf. D. W. Robertson, Jr., "Five Poems by Marcabru," *SP*, LI (1954), 545-555.

[45] *De off.*, 3. 33.

[46] See Jérome Carcopino, *De Pythagore aux Apôtres* (Paris, 1956), p. 57.

specific contraries which form a part of our instinctive habits of thought but which were alien to those of the Middle Ages. Good and evil, for example, were not thought of as "opposite forces." All creation is good to the medieval mind, for "God saw all the things that he had made, and they were good" (Gen. 1. 31). Evil was not an entity in itself, not even a "negation" of the good, but merely a privation of it: "Dicendum est quod malum dicitur defectum boni non negative sed priuatiue."[47] It results from the corrupted will of man, for which he has full responsibility, which places qualities good in themselves in an unnatural order. Lechery, for example, as William of Auvergne explains, is good in a hog, but evil in a man.[48] Similarly, the devil is not the almost invincible rebel envisaged by the romantics, an "opposite" of Christ, but a corrupted angel. He and his cohorts are

> Goddes instrumentz,
> And meenes to doon his comandementz,
> Whan that hym list, upon his creatures,
> In divers art, and in diverse figures.

In the same way, medieval "contraries" like the Church and the Synagogue, the New Law and the Old, Grace and Nature, are not dramatic contraries in the modern sense. The Church is the Synagogue transformed, the New Law is the fulfilment of the Old, and Grace effects a restoration of Nature to something like its original form. Elements such as these cannot be diametrically opposed so as to produce either a "progression" or a "higher synthesis."

This principle applies as well to the "two loves," a favorite realm for reconciliations and syntheses in criticism of Dante, in spite of the fact that what Virgil says about love in the *Purgatorio*

[47] Nicholas Trivet on Boethius, *De cons.*, London, BM, MS Burney 131, fol. 48. The idea is, of course, Patristic. The reluctance of the modern mind to grasp it is vividly illustrated in C. G. Jung's rather desperate argument with the Fathers in *Aion*, Ch. v, printed in *Psyche and Symbol* (New York, 1958), esp. pp. 44ff. Jung attributes to the Fathers a neglect of the real power of evil, a force which no "scientific" psychologist can "gloss over" as they did. He praises the heretical Clementine homilies for seeing "the whole creation in terms of syzygies, or pairs of opposites." What Jung is actually defending is the stylistic configuration of modern thought, not a "scientific" principle.

[48] *De vitiis et peccatis*, in *Opera*, p. 259: ". . . luxuria in porco non est peccatum, neque culpa in eo, immo natura tantum, et opus virtutis generative, quae in eo libera est."

makes such operations clearly impossible.[49] The "two loves" themselves represent a problem which occupied pagan thinkers as well as Christians. Thus for the Pythagoreans true love is not that based on physical desire, but a love directed toward the intelligible rather than the visible world, by means of which the lover raises himself from the world to a realm free from physical suffering and death.[50] The classic Christian definitions of the two loves are those given by St. Augustine in *On Christian Doctrine*: "I call 'charity' the motion of the soul toward the enjoyment of God for His own sake, and the enjoyment of one's self and of one's neighbor for the sake of God; but 'cupidity' is a motion of the soul toward the enjoyment of one's self, one's neighbor, or any corporal thing for the sake of something other than God."[51] The importance of this distinction for Christianity is clear when St. Augustine informs us that "Scripture teaches nothing but charity, nor condemns anything except cupidity, and in this way shapes the minds of men."[52] In other words, charity is the basic lesson of Christianity. It is noteworthy that the Christian definitions imply the idea of the Pythagoreans, for their intelligible world becomes the world of the *invisibilia Dei*. Even if we confine ourselves to the pagan idea, we shall have difficulty in creating a synthesis of the two loves. One loves either the tangible or the intelligible world. It may be possible to move from the tangible to the intelligible, but the two are not opposites; they exist in a relationship of inferior and superior. As for the Christian definition, both loves involve a motion of the spirit toward the enjoyment of something else. A woman may be loved concupiscently with reference to certain physical satisfactions, or charitably with reference to God. But even when these alternatives conflict, they are not contraries. As William of Auvergne puts it, "to desire something and not to consent to the desire are not contraries," or, to put the same idea in another way, "to desire something simply and to desire something else as preferable are not contraries."[53] This being so, it is impossible to "reconcile" or to "synthesize" the two loves.

[49] 17. 91 ff. Love as it is here described may move in one way or another, but it is single, not divided.

[50] See F. Cumont, *After Life in Roman Paganism* (New Haven, 1922), p. 24; and Carcopino, *loc.cit.*, note 46 above.

[51] *On Christian Doctrine*, 3. 10. 16.   [52] *Ibid.*, 3. 10. 15.

[53] *De tentationibus, Opera*, p. 292.

It is possible, however, to move from a cupidinous love to a charitable love, to see the concrete object of enjoyment as a part of or a step toward the enjoyment of the intelligible. This, indeed, is the classic "progression" of Christian literature, but it does not result from the interaction of opposites. St. Paul tells us that the *invisibilia Dei* are to be understood "by the things that are made" (Rom. 1. 20). St. Augustine points out that the beauty of creation should lead a man toward love for the creator—"speciem corporis fabricati sic percurrat oculis, ut in eum qui fabricaverit recurrat affectu"[54]—and advises elsewhere that charity should begin with the love of one's neighbor.[55] The same "progression" leads Boethius in the *Consolation of Philosophy* to discern through wisdom the intelligible good beyond the corporal shadows he has lost. It inspires Fortunatus to visualize Radegunde helping him beyond the fading beauty of the flowers he sends her toward the eternal flowers of Paradise, and it enthrones Beatrice and Laura in the realm of the intelligible. The "Platonic Ladder" in Bembo's famous discourse as recorded by Castiglione has a firm Christian foundation, but that "ladder" is neither a reconciliation nor a synthesis; it is a progression through love—a motion of the soul toward the enjoyment of something else—up the steps of a hierarchy.

If charity represents a harmonious ordering of love with reference to the Divine Order, it may be objected that cupidity, which, as St. Augustine tells us in *The City of God*, creates a Babylonian confusion, has an opposite effect, creating disorder rather than harmony. And since "disorder" is an opposite of "order," perhaps the two loves may at least lead to an opposition. But the disorder resulting from cupidity is a disorder only with reference to nature as it was created; with reference to God, it is a part of the Divine Order and is essentially harmonious with it. This is one of the lessons of the *Consolation* of Boethius. The foolish man who seeks satisfaction in the "false goods" of the world—wealth, power, fame, the pleasures of the senses—is inevitably frustrated as a result of the very order he disregards; but his frustration is itself a part of that order. As Trivet explains in his commentary, "Although it is true that he recedes, with reference to the end, from the order of the divine will in one way, he nevertheless falls

[54] *De libero arbitrio*, 2. 16. 43; cf. St. Gregory, *Moralia*, PL, 76, col. 358.
[55] *In Ioh. Evang.*, 17. 18.

into the order of the divine will in another; for in leaving the order of mercy, he falls into the order of justice."[56] The Divine Order thus includes the sinner as well as the saint; it contains ample provision for both. In this Order "contraries" in the modern sense exist only as the result of false human perspective. They are characteristic of the illusory realm of Fortune, where the eye, unclarified and incapable of discerning the larger whole, finds that confusion so vividly described by Alanus:

> Aspera blandiciis, in lumina nubila, pauper
> Et dives, mansueta ferox, predulcis amara,
> Ridendo plorans, stando uaga, ceca uidendo . . . .[57]

Again, if we look at the origin of the two loves rather than at their results, we shall discover the same sort of hierarchical relationship with reference to an order. The Christian conception of original sin, as it was developed in Patristic texts, has its counterparts in antiquity. Ovid, for example, attributes the confusion which resulted in the flight of Astraea, or Justice, from the earth to man's inordinate *amor habendi*, a formulation which Boethius echoes with implicit Christian significance.[58] In Augustinian terms, this burning desire is *concupiscentia carnis*. Before the Fall, man was gifted with reason to know what is right and a will naturally inclined to desire what was thus known. The beasts, on the other hand, had no reason, and their desires were controlled by a concupiscence necessary both to perpetuate themselves and to perpetuate their species. When man fell, his reason was corrupted and his will was misdirected, so that it became necessary for him to acquire the concupiscence proper to beasts both for his own protection and to insure that he would propagate his kind.[59] This concupiscence, together with a concomitant defect in reason, is the malady of original sin, at least in the Augustinian theology of the Middle Ages. It is not in itself an evil; but in men it represents the corruption of a good which it is the business of wisdom and love to repair. It is a displacement of one kind of desire by another; as Gervais du Bus puts it, in a popular poem, the natural order estab-

[56] London, BM, MS Burney 131, fol. 47 verso. Cf. St. Augustine, *De libero arbitrio*, 39. 24-26; *De musica*, 6. 11. 30.

[57] Alanus, *Anticlaudianus*, ed. Bossuat, 8. 22ff.

[58] *De cons.*, 2 met. 5. Trivet, fol. 26, glosses *amor habendi* as *cupiditas*.

[59] *De gen. ad litt.*, 9. 32. 42.

lished by God was "bestorné" when the Fall took place, so that men became like beasts (Fig. 7).[60] But there is no question of replacing an original good by an unmitigated evil, and there would be little point in trying to reconcile concupiscence, the origin of cupidinous desires, with charity. The effort, where effort was applied, was instead to restore the original condition by heeding that voice which Boethius describes as Lady Philosophy and by following the examples of love offered by Christ and the saints. Man's will had, in effect, descended a step in the hierarchy of nature.

This peculiar "non-dialectic" relationship between the two loves accounts in part for the fact that medieval writers can juxtapose them in more or less extreme forms without seeking to create the jarring effect that such juxtapositions create in us. We may suspect that the same sort of juxtapositions were possible in antiquity. Thus the rape of Phoebe and Hilaria by Castor and Pollux represented on the vault of a Neopythagorean basilica in Rome probably suggested, in terms of physical violence, the ascent of the soul to the heavens;[61] and Sappho's leap, depicted in the apse of the same basilica, was in all likelihood not intended to arouse sympathy for the despair arising from frustrated passion, but to show an advance of the soul toward Apollo and rebirth under the guidance of Eros.[62] A sufficiently remarkable precedent for considering divine love in terms of cupidinous love was afforded Christians by the Canticle of Canticles. The remarks on the subject in the proemium of the commentary on this work ascribed to St. Gregory the Great are instructive: ". . . in this book love is expressed as if in carnal language, so that the mind, stimulated by words it is accustomed to [i.e., rather than being repelled by the unfamiliar language of divine love], may be aroused from its torpor, and through words concerned with a love which is below, may be excited to a love which is above. In this book are mentioned kisses, breasts, cheeks, and thighs. Nor is the Sacred description to be ridiculed on that account, but the greater mercy of God is to be considered; for when He names the members of the body and thus calls to love, it should be noted how wonderfully and mercifully

[60] *Le roman de Fauvel*, ed. Längfors, *SATF* (1914-1919), I, 311ff.

[61] Franz Cumont, *Recherches sur le symbolisme funéraire des Romains* (Paris, 1942), pp. 99ff.

[62] Carcopino, *De Pythagore aux Apôtres*, pp. 10ff., 32-35.

we are treated. For in order that our hearts may be inflamed with sacred love, He extends His words even to wicked love."[63] The two loves are regarded as inferior and superior, and we are to move, at least in the realm of the understanding, from the inferior love to the superior love. To this motion "breasts, cheeks, and thighs" are no impediments. The same principles apply when, in the twelfth century, the Canticle is read as a song in praise of the Blessed Virgin Mary. For example, when William of Newburgh considers the *juncturae femorum* of Cant. 7. 1, he points out that although in men and women this location is shameful, in connection with the Virgin it involves no concupiscence and is virtuous.[64] The imagery of this book became a favorite source for poetic material, and consequently it is not surprising that, on the basis of the example it offered, explicit literary elaborations of both loves should appear in the same context. For example, a thirteenth-century motet contains in the *triplum* a description of a garden of earthly delight where a lover meets his lady; the *duplum*, on the other hand, is a song in praise of Mary.[65] Calling attention to this and other similar pieces, Jacques Handschin suggests that their purpose is to place "worldly love in the perspective of heavenly love," a perspective which "gives us a glimpse of the philosophy of the epoch."[66] Similar combinations appear in the visual arts. For example, the pages of a Flemish Book of Hours of ca. 1300 contain several representations of lovers who are clearly interested in tangible matters (Figs. 8, 9), in spite of the fact that the text is devotional. The principle involved here is exactly analogous with that illustrated on the Beatus page of the St. Albans Psalter. There two knights are shown in combat above the initial, and the marginal comment which accompanies this illustration includes the statement: "We should establish in our spirits all the art which these two warriors contrive with their bodies."[67] That is, what is depicted

[63] *Super cant.*, PL, 79, col. 473.

[64] Cambridge, CUL MS Gg. 4. 16, fol. 60. See now John C. Gorman, S. M., *William of Newburgh's Explanatio* . . . (Fribourg, 1960), pp. 304-305.

[65] Yvonne Rokseth, *Polyphonies du XIIIᵉ siècle* (Paris, 1936-1939), II, no. 36. Cf. nos. 37-46.

[66] "The Summer Canon and its Background," *Musica Disciplina*, v (1951), p. 111.

[67] The page is discussed and transcribed by A. Goldschmidt, *Der Albani-Psalter* (Berlin, 1895), pp. 47-51. See also Otto Pächt, C. R. Dodwell, and Francis

on a fleshly level should be applied on a spiritual level to the warfare against evil. In the same way, the lovers in our illustrations display a corporal passion which should be transferred to the spiritual realm suggested by the text. In this instance, the corporal passion is depicted with a touch of humor; thus in Fig. 8 the horses, which may have been used like the "horse" element in Fig. 7 to suggest the unrestrained flesh, eye each other with an attitude that amusingly parallels that of the lovers, and the ape, a manlike creature without reason, regards the whole scene with approval. In other words, the illustration not only suggests that a transfer to the spiritual realm be made, but reinforces the lesson by making the manifestation of love on a fleshly level appear ridiculous. We may regard the situation in Fig. 6, which would not have appealed to the ape, as the eventuality to be desired. In any event, one love typically suggests the other, and this is the reason that so many literary, theological, and artistic analogies were developed between them. The analogies do not grow out of the parallel development of opposites, but out of the development on two levels of what was essentially the same thing. "The covetise of verray good is naturely iplauntyd in the hertes of men," says Boethius, and Dante echoes the same thought by saying, in the person of Virgil, "Nè creator nè creatura mai . . . fu senza amore." St. Augustine's "motion of the soul toward enjoyment" is common to both charity and cupidity. The motion of the soul toward the enjoyment of a creature may suggest a parallel motion toward the enjoyment of the intelligible, as it does in the Canticle, or it may suggest the absence of the intelligible and its consequences, as it is made to do in the motet. In any event, neither the Canticle, the motet, nor the illustrations discussed above were shocking admixtures of good and evil, nor was any one of them in any sense either an expression of or a generator of dynamic tensions.

In romantic poetry, according to A. W. Schlegel, the love expressed is "a chaos which lies concealed in the very bosom of the ordered universe, and is perpetually striving after new and marvellous births."[68] Implicit in this description is a tension between

Wormald, *The St. Alban's Psalter* (London, 1960), pp. 149-150, 206. Cf. T. S. R. Boase, *English Art 1100-1216* (Oxford, 1953), pp. 101-110.

[68] *A Course of Lectures on Dramatic Art and Literature* (London, 1846), p. 343.

the "order" established by reason and the tumultuous passion of love, a contrast exploited in innumerable modern novels and poems. But to seek this conflict or even this love in medieval literature is to seek the impossible, for love was the tie which bound the spirit to the flesh, the individual to his social order, and the ruler to his subjects. As the trace of the Holy Spirit in the universe, as St. Ailred calls it, it was the force which established order in the elements and harmony in the sidereal heavens. Love was, in short, the bond of all order, not a chaos, and it could conflict with reason only when it was, like the love of Sir Lancelot, misdirected through an erring human will.

The use of an hierarchical mode of thought rather than a pattern of conflict and synthesis during the Middle Ages imparts to the literature of the period a peculiar character which is neither romantic nor modern. Perhaps this fact may become clearer if we consider for a moment Schlegel's contrast between "Grecian" literature and "modern" literature, wherein the description of the latter may be taken to be fairly accurate. "The Grecian ideal of human nature," he wrote, "was perfect unison and proportion between all the powers—a natural harmony. The moderns, on the contrary, have arrived at the consciousness of an internal discord which renders such an ideal impossible; and hence the endeavor of poetry is to reconcile these two worlds between which we find ourselves divided, and to blend them indissolubly together. The impressions of the senses are to be hallowed, as it were, by a mysterious connexion with higher feelings; and the soul, on the other hand, embodies its forebodings, or indescribable intuitions of infinity, in types and symbols borrowed from the visible world."[69] The general configuration familiar in the Middle Ages persists: there are two worlds, and the world of the senses contains "types and symbols" of the other. But the conception of an ordered hierarchy like the "perfect unison and proportion" ascribed to antiquity has disappeared. Instead there is an "internal discord" reflecting a disparity between elements which cannot be reconciled in a rational manner. A synthesis of these elements is to be made by poetry which hallows the impressions of the senses and expresses the indescribable intuitions of the soul. Needless to say, the standard method of "hallowing" the senses among nineteenth-century au-

[69] *Ibid.*, p. 27.

thors involved a liberal use of sentimentality. Moreover, an air of
mystery quite unlike the more intellectual processes of symbolism
and typology familiar in late antiquity and the Middle Ages
shrouds the whole procedure. The world of the intelligible has
become a vague infinite rather than an intellectually conceived
order. It is to be reached, not through a traditional wisdom, but
through a highly personal and distinctly emotional kind of perception, through "indescribable intuitions."

It is inevitable that literary expression based on attitudes of this
kind should be suggestive rather than explicit, not only in its techniques but also in its implications, and that it should subordinate
discursive ideas to mood, emotion, and feeling. The resulting effect
is well described by Conrad in *Heart of Darkness*, where we are
told that Marlow, the narrator, found that "the meaning of an
episode was not inside, like a kernel, but outside, enveloping the
tale which brought it out only as a glow brings out a haze, in the
likeness of one of these misty halos that sometimes are made visible by the spectral illumination of moonshine." When our literary
training has led us to anticipate effects of this kind from figurative
expression, whether in narrative or in poetry, St. Augustine's assertion that hardly anything is conveyed by the figurative language
of the Bible which is not stated elsewhere explicitly comes as something of a shock.[70] But it is nevertheless typical of the general
attitude of medieval exegetes, who, in penetrating the "most
dense mist" which they found to cover most of the Scriptures, customarily used exactly the term Marlow rejects to describe the inner
meaning they sought: *nucleus*. Moreover, medieval discussions of
poetry also employ this term, or one of several synonyms for it,
to describe the truth which they found beneath the "shell" of poetic
fiction.[71] This difference marks one of the most important distinctions between the artistic productions of the Middle Ages and
those of modern times. In medieval art the "mystery" lies on the
surface, in the enigmatic configurations which are presented to the
minds of the audience, and there it is more of a puzzle than a halo.
"You must read," warns Boccaccio, in a discussion of poetry, "you
must persevere, you must sit up nights, you must inquire, and exert

[70] *On Christian Doctrine*, 2. 6. 8.
[71] See D. W. Robertson, Jr., "Some Medieval Literary Terminology," *SP*,
XLVIII (1951), 669ff.

the utmost power of your mind. If one way does not lead to the desired meaning, take another; until if your strength holds out, you will find that clear which at first looked dark."[72] What is here described is an intellectual search for a truth already familiar in other forms. Romantic art makes a more immediate appeal: it "moves" its audience, not to think necessarily, but to feel, and it leaves that audience with a deepened but non-discursive awareness of "the mystery of things." To the modern mind, a work of art which implies an explicit answer to a problem raised seems in bad taste.

Another result of this general difference in attitude is that medieval art and literature are less dramatic than their romantic counterparts. The fact itself has been noticed by the discerning eye of Professor Panofsky. "The Romanesque," he says, "froze the figures into immobility or twisted them into contortions incompatible with the laws of nature. The Gothic preferred to melt them into lyrical self-abandonment; and in neither case would we speak of a 'dramatic' mode of expression."[73] A dramatic mode requires, perhaps, a free revelation of the inner feelings of the personae which is impractical where those personae are restricted in their expression by a generally stylized representation. At least this is true if we use the word *dramatic* in a romantic sense. Thus Freytag, for example, defines the dramatic in terms of "strong motions of the soul" or "inner processes" which manifest themselves in will and action. Dramatic action requires the "outpouring of the power of the will from deep feeling toward the outer world" or the "pouring in" of stimuli from the outer world into "the inner depths of the feeling." Thus drama is basically a matter of feeling, of the inner emotional life of the characters. The content of drama, Freytag assures us, is "always a struggle with strong motions of the soul which the hero carries on against opposing powers."[74] Violent emotional states resulting from a conflict between the will of the protagonist and obstacles of some kind seem to be necessary to our sense of the dramatic. The central importance of the will is also

[72] *Boccaccio on Poetry*, p. 62. Boccaccio adds, referring to Matt. 7. 6, "For we are forbidden by divine command to give that which is holy to dogs, or to cast pearls before swine." This is a sufficiently clear indication of the kind of truth he expected to discover.

[73] *Early Netherlandish Painting* (Cambridge, 1953), I, 21.

[74] *Die Technik des Dramas* (Leipzig, 1898), p. 18.

stressed by Brunetière, who says that "what we ask of the theater, is the spectacle of a will striving towards a goal, and conscious of the means which it employs."[75] He adds that this will must be free.

There are certain general considerations which make the appearance of a mode of this kind unlikely in medieval literature. Stylization in art has its counterpart in the "conventions" of literary expression, already referred to in connection with the troubadours. Even in more complex medieval poetry where verisimilitude has produced an illusion of autobiographical content, like the early poetry of Boccaccio, for example, lovers express themselves in certain set patterns which preclude the kind of effect Freytag would call "dramatic."[76] Perhaps one major difficulty lies in the fact that although freedom of the will, demanded by Brunetièrc as a requisite of dramatic action and certainly implicit in Freytag's discussion, was a major tenet of medieval orthodox philosophy, freedom from the order of Divine Providence was not. Hence the goals that a protagonist set for himself were always seen against an implicit system of values which acted both as a comment on the goals themselves and on any emotional experiences the protagonist might have in seeking them. This fact is probably in part responsible for a lack of interest in "strong motions of the soul" for their own sake in medieval literature. In spite of the conclusions of some modern critics, medieval literary art did not develop the means of analyzing such phenomena. It is, as distinct from romantic or modern literary art, rigorously non-psychological. Literary artists then had no interest in pursuing for their own sakes such problems as "the ruling passion," "the manner in which we associate ideas in a state of excitement," or "the stream of consciousness."

Most commonly, human behavior was thought of in terms of abstractions which retained their individuality without reference to the psychological condition of the subject. The *Psychomachia* of Prudentius may be thought of as typifying a pattern of individual experience in which the virtues triumph over the vices so that a condition of beatitude results. But the virtues and vices involved are not the personal virtues and vices peculiar to any given individual: they retain their generalized forms and serve as exemplary types with reference to which actual individual manifestations

---

[75] *The Law of the Drama* (New York, 1914), p. 73.
[76] See Branca, *Boccaccio Medioevale*, pp. 138-156.

may be judged. Their struggle, whether it is viewed as a struggle among personifications having a sort of independent ideal existence or as a struggle within an individual is hardly dramatic in the sense indicated by Freytag. Similarly, the abstractions which carry out the "action," which is really a kind of disguised exposition, in the *De planctu naturae* and the *Anticlaudianus* of Alanus, although some of them may be seen as attributes of an individual, exist as idealized entities independent of a single personality. Much the same sort of situation prevails in vernacular literature, where elements like those in Prudentius or Alanus are made to reveal the character of an individual decision. Thus in the *Roman de la charrete*, Lancelot engages in an "inner debate" before mounting the cart. But we have no real picture of a "motion of the soul" in terms of emotional states. Instead "love" comes into conflict with "reason" and triumphs. We know, in consequence, that Lancelot's love is unreasonable and that he may be expected to behave foolishly, but we know nothing whatsoever about an inner struggle among emotions peculiar to Lancelot in a given situation. Exactly the same considerations apply to the most celebrated "psychological" poem of the thirteenth century, the *Roman de la rose*. Deduit in this poem is not the peculiar "deduit" of the dreamer; it is the "deduit" of any sensually inclined man. Raison in the same way speaks with the voice of Reason as Reason was conceived in the philosophy of the period; she does not modulate her doctrine in such a way as to represent the peculiar reasoning powers of the dreamer at a given time. He, in fact, fails to understand her and never heeds her admonitions. The fact that the abstractions are felt as beings which inhabit an order independent of the individual is clearly revealed in such figures as Jalosie and Faus-Semblant, who represent jealousy and hypocrisy, conceived as moral attributes, in whatever persons they may appear. The latter is typically in Jean de Meun's mind a friar. But he can represent hypocrisy in any walk of life, the hypocrisy of the evil priest, the false monk, or the foolish lover. If in the "dramatic" conflict of these abstractions Bien celer vanquishes Honte (Fig. 10), this simply means that he who does something he should not may avoid shame by concealing his action (cf. Ecclus. 23. 25-26; Isa. 29. 15). The *Roman* is not a psychological poem at all; it is a description of human actions in terms of abstractions belonging to an objective scheme of moral values whose existence is independent of the psychological state of the dreamer. Its implications are not psychological but moral.

Even when the abstractions used in literary works are derived from medieval "psychology" and have explicit physiological associations, they are used for their moral or philosophical significance rather than for the betrayal of "strong motions of the soul." Thus in the *Vita nuova* of Dante the "spirito de la vita" representing the *vis vitalis* of the heart is made to say, "Ecce deus fortier me, qui veniens dominabitur michi." The "spirito animale" representing the *vis animalis* which rules the senses from the brain observes, "Apparuit iam beatitudo vestra," addressing himself especially to the sight. And the "spirito naturale" or *vis naturalis* which nourishes the body, perhaps from the liver, complains, "Heu miser, quia frequenter impeditus ero deinceps!" But this machinery tells us nothing about the peculiar and specific emotional condition of the speaker; it simply reveals certain aspects of the effects of love on anyone. Dante was not interested in "indescribable intuitions" which demanded this figurative mode of expression. He wished to convey something with poetic license, "ma non sanza ragione alcuna, ma con ragione la quale poi sia possibile d'aprire per prosa." During the later Middle Ages "inner drama" of the kind used by Dante became popular in literature of all types, but it had an explanatory moral purpose. It was not designed to produce an inner conflict which could be shared by the reader through a kind of *Einfühlung*. A typical example is afforded by a description of the effects of sloth in the *Livre de seyntz medicines* of Henry of Lancaster. Sloth counsels delay in confession. It enters through the eyes, and once inside it makes Sin drunk so that it cannot escape, having been "bestournée." When Fear and Shame arrive, they are led by Weak Will to Sloth, who casts them out and remains mistress of the mouth, a strategic position since "Who holds the gate holds the castle."[77] Thus the subject—in this instance Henry—is unable to confess his sins. This "drama" may be a vivid description of the effects of sloth, but it does not afford us a spectacle of the "will" encountering obstacles in a dramatic fashion. The reader is by no means invited to share the feelings experienced by Henry at this juncture. Henry's feelings are not

[77] Ed. Arnould (Oxford, 1940), pp. 58-63.

specifically displayed before us; instead, his condition is described with reference to an objective scheme of moral values.

If we are to respond "dramatically" to the strong emotions described by Freytag or to follow sympathetically the struggling will described by Brunetière, we must share the emotions of the dramatic characters who are set before us. Indeed, the "indescribable intuitions" of romantic literature generally will make little impression upon us unless we can ourselves respond to them sympathetically. And this response requires a vicarious participation in the fictional experience of at least one of the characters in a dramatic context, stimulated either by the fact that the character "heroically" represents some of our most cherished ideals, or by the fact that the character seems to us to be "realistic" and to represent just that peculiar "human condition" in which we find ourselves.[78] Medieval characters are frequently exemplary—either of wise or of unwise action—but medieval authors do not usually invite us to share their experiences. If we turn our attention from medieval mysteries and moralities, which, in spite of "impersonation," remain curiously undramatic, to the first Robin Hood play, *Robin Hood and the Sheriff of Nottingham*, we find a striking difference in effect. The "heroic" proportions of Robin are clearly if crudely established. He defeats Sir Guy of Gisborne, who has promised the sheriff to take him, at archery, at casting the stone, and at wrestling. When the combatants choose swords, Robin is again victorious, overcoming Sir Guy, so to speak, on his own level. He cuts off Sir Guy's head and disguises himself in his clothing. An atmosphere of suspense is created when the sheriff takes Robin's men, including Scarlet and Little John. But Robin comes to the rescue in time and is wily enough to employ a ruse. He presents Sir Guy's head to the sheriff, making him think it is his own, so that the sheriff turns Little John over to him for disposal. Robin, of course, releases him and gives him his bow. In the ensuing battle the sheriff's men are routed, and the sheriff, representing, as it were, the forces of tyrannical authority which impede the freedom of Robin's will, falls pierced by an arrow. In this play, concocted for an illiterate ("folk") audience of the fifteenth century, we are clearly invited

[78] As Focillon points out, *L'art des sculpteurs romans* (Paris, 1931), p. 27, when we think of "realistic" art, we think of "un traitement extrêmement voluntaire et très accentué, et non pas une copie passive du vrai."

to follow the struggling will of the protagonist as it overcomes obstacles set before it, much as we are invited to do the same thing in a modern "western" drama designed for television audiences. Similarly, we read of a naïve Don Quixote making himself a part of the fictional realm of his romances, and of servant girls dreaming of brighter worlds as a result of the same kind of literary inspiration. But in all of these instances the audience involved was unsophisticated. The aesthetic criteria developed among the unpolished folk of the Renaissance did not achieve literate sanction until the eighteenth century, when literature and art began to adjust themselves to wide audiences which required various kinds of vigorous spontaneous appeal.

Thus in Avison's *Essay on Musical Expression* (1752), we learn that "the *Terror* raised by *Musical Expression*, is always of that grateful Kind which arises from an Impression of something terrible to the Imagination, but which is immediately dissipated, by a subsequent Conviction that the Danger is entirely imaginary."[79] At this stage, the concept is still relatively underdeveloped, and the awareness of the fictitious character of the emotion comes as an afterthought—a "subsequent Conviction." A more romantic account of the same process in literary appreciation appears in Thomas Twining's commentary on Aristotle's *Poetics* (1789). Twining is discussing the tragic catharsis: "Pity and terror," he says, "*frequently* excited by such objects and such events in *real life*, as the imitations of the tragic scene set before us, would rather tend to produce apathy than moderation. Nature would struggle against such violent and powerful agitation, and the heart would become callous in its own defense." This "callousness," incidentally, was the favorite explanation of catharsis among Italian critics of the Renaissance after Robortelli's commentary was published (1548), but these early critics had no inkling of the concept with which Twining continues: "It is far otherwise with *fictitious* passion. There, the emotion, though often violent in spite of the consciousness of fiction, is always, more or less, delightful. . . . While it moderates *real* passion by the frequency of similar impressions, it, at the same time, *cherishes* such sympathetic emotions, in a *proper* and *useful* degree, by the delicious feelings which never

[79] Quoted by Thurston Dart, *The Interpretation of Music* (London, 1955), p. 114.

38

fail to accompany the indulgence of them in imitative representation."[80]

To find a conception parallel to this one in the past, it is necessary to turn back to late antiquity and the *De mysteriis* of the school of Iamblichus, where it is said (1. 11) that unexpressed emotions become stronger because they are suppressed, but that they may be relieved and quieted if a means is found to express them moderately and pleasantly. Dramatic representations afford us this opportunity, for the spectacle of the emotions of others enables us to lighten or unburden our own. It is this theory, in effect, which St. Augustine so vehemently attacks in the *Confessions* (3. 2): "Why does a man like to be made sad when viewing doleful and tragical scenes, which yet he himself would by no means suffer? And yet he wishes, as a spectator, to experience from them a sense of grief, and in this very grief his pleasure consists. What is this but a wretched insanity? For a man is more affected by these actions, the less free he is from such affections."[81] The objection is basically ethical, for, as St. Augustine explains, a man who grieves for another in fiction is said to be merciful, but such inconsequential mercy does not lead to any active relief of the suffering. Instead, the spectator applauds the actor for intensifying his passive grief. "In the theatres," he continues, "I sympathized with lovers when they sinfully enjoyed one another, although this was done fictitiously in the play. And when they lost one another, I grieved with them, as if pitying them, and yet had delight in both. But now-a-days I feel more pity for him who delights in wickedness, than for him who is counted as enduring hardships for failing to obtain some pernicious pleasure. . . ." The theory of the *De mysteriis* and St. Augustine's account of his youthful enjoyment of the theater are both consistent with the relatively subjective character of late antique art, which developed illusionistic techniques in the rendering of space in painting and a sense of realistic portraiture in sculpture.

But the significant rôle allotted to vicarious experience in mod-

---

[80] *Aristotle's Treatise on Poetry* (London, 1789), p. 240. Cf. the idea expressed by Lessing in the *Hamburgische Dramaturgie* that the emotions are turned into "virtuous inclinations" by the tragic spectacle. The development of an aesthetic attitude based on "sensibility" during the eighteenth century is discussed by Ernest Tuveson, "The Importance of Shaftesbury," *ELH*, xx (1953), 267-299. See especially pp. 289ff.

[81] Trans. J. G. Pilkington.

ern aesthetics was made possible only when art could be made ethically neutral. In the dramatic theories of Lessing and Twining, as in the earlier theory of the school of Iamblichus, the fictitious emotions aroused by the drama moderate ordinary emotions in an ethically beneficial way. Such emotions, although pleasant, were still not a part of the Beautiful. Thus Schopenhauer sharply distinguished the "interest" aroused by vicarious emotion in a work of art from the "beauty" which he regarded as art's proper function. The desired solution came finally in a masterful philological paper by Jacob Bernays published in the first volume of the *Abhandlungen der historisch-philosophischen Gesellschaft in Breslau* (1857). This essay, entitled "Grundzüge der verlorenen Abhandlung des Aristoteles über Wirkung der Tragödie," was published separately in the same year and reprinted once more in *Zwei Abhandlungen über die Aristotelische Theorie des Drama* in 1880. Its results were incorporated, with some modification, in S. H. Butcher's *Aristotle's Theory of Poetry and Fine Art* (1895), a book which has influenced the minds of generations of English-speaking students and is now available for mass consumption in the United States as an inexpensive "paperback." It is largely through the influence of Bernays that it is now possible to view the release of tensions generated by a work of art of any kind as a "catharsis," and to think of this "catharsis" as a purely aesthetic phenomenon. Bernays was careful, first of all, to assure his readers, with the assistance of a quotation from the inevitable Goethe, that Lessing's interpretation of tragedy as a means of preparing the emotions for virtuous inclinations is impossible, since the drama is not "a Moral House of Correction." His own theory is an account rather of an "ecstatic-hedonistic" or "hedonistic-aesthetic" process. The catharsis clause in Aristotle's definition of tragedy, which I quote in Bernays' language, is to be rendered as follows: "die Tragödie bewirkt durch (Erregung von) Mitleid und Furcht die erleichternde Entladung solcher (mitleidigen und furchtsamen) Gemüthsaffectionen." The inserted phrase "Erregung von" is of special importance, since the pity and fear involved are not those already existing in the spectator, but those aroused by the drama. These two emotions are, as it were, open doors through which the outside world flows into the human personality. The pity the spectator feels for the tragic character, because of that character's force as an exemplar of general human nature, becomes universalized, thus drawing the spectator outside of himself as he becomes identified with the character. And this ecstatic escape from the self into a universalized position is so delightful that the spectator feels no pain at the fictional evils which impend. Similarly, the fear aroused is not a personal fear, but "an ecstatic shudder before the universe." These are the hedonistic emotions properly aroused by tragedy, and once aroused they provide an alleviating unburdening of emotions related to pity and fear. It is noteworthy that this theory involves the almost automatic operation of the feelings; it has nothing to do with ideas of any kind, ethical or otherwise. Moreover, success in obtaining the pleasurable result described depends on the spectator's ability to merge himself with the tragic protagonist. In spite of the careful and resourceful philological skill with which this theory is supported, it probably owes little to Aristotle except its terminology. But it does provide a decisive step forward in the modern development of Art as a separate and peculiar entity with a sanctity and mystical power of its own, free from the trammels of ethical prejudices, or, indeed, from any kind of "utility." In a sense, it is a special fulfilment of the famous dictum of T. Gautier in the Preface to *Mademoiselle de Maupin*: "Il n'y a de vraiment beau que ce qui ne peut servir à rien."

Bernays' theory, which is actually no more than a crystallization of aesthetic ideas which had been current for some time, not only permits but encourages the use of the literature of the past as a mirror for the reader's personality. Since its aims are hedonistic, and it deliberately avoids ethical considerations, the reader, through a process of *Einfühlung*, can legitimately and pleasantly identify himself with characters of all kinds. He can experience Romeo's lust, Hamlet's passion for revenge, or Othello's jealousy, not only without qualms, but with the assurance that what he is doing is aesthetically righteous and just. The eighteenth century found it expedient to change Shakespeare's text in order to make it conform to its own tastes, to make Cordelia retire, for example, "with victory and felicity"; but the nineteenth century could leave the texts alone and still "feel" its own ideals and attitudes in the plays. Since romantic sensibility responded to feelings of all kinds, and did so in a harmless imaginary world, it could easily engage itself in a "dramatic" response to the "motions of the soul" exhibited by

41

evil characters as well as to those of more virtuous characters. As a matter of fact, since evil characters in our earlier literature are more likely to be frustrated in one way or another, they offer more opportunity for emotional tension than do virtuous characters, and are more attractive. Hence, if we read the opening books of *Paradise Lost* "dramatically," Satan becomes a kind of epic Robin Hood whose rebellious rhetoric, considered only for the feeling it expresses, moves us to approve the view of Blake that "Milton was of the Devil's party without knowing it." In the nineteenth century Cain as well as Satan achieved heroic proportions, and in the twentieth both characters have served as inspirations to social revolutionaries. Satan is, as Milton portrays him, a much more readily digestible figure than are many characters in more modern fiction whose feelings we are asked to enjoy. Our increasing interest in psychology for its own sake, an intensified introspectiveness, and a conviction that the business of the artist is in part at least to enable us to respond "ecstatically" to new psychological experiences of all kinds—all these lead us to appreciate aberrations which would have puzzled or amused our ancestors. In William Faulkner's *The Hamlet*, for instance, a work of undeniable artistic merit and considerable moral gravity, we are led to respond sympathetically to an idiot's amorous affection for a cow. A medieval author might have used a situation of this kind for much the same moral purpose that Faulkner implies; but he would have lacked one important asset that Faulkner has at his disposal: the ability to induce us to share, at least momentarily, the feelings of the idiot.

Blake suggested that Milton's sympathies were with Satan without his knowing it, thus introducing a concept which has assisted us more than any other to "modernize" the literature of the past. For we can not only achieve a "dramatic" response to literary characters and an "empathic" response to visual figures; we can also do the same thing with the authors and artists themselves. Having done so, we feel ourselves in a position to comment on their inmost feelings, and even on what we have come to call their "subconscious minds."[82] Once we have made a "dramatic" entry into the "subconscious" of an author, we can attribute to him all of those ideals and attitudes which we ourselves cherish, regardless of the historical context in which the author wrote. Thus Chaucer can be turned

[82] Cf. Abrams, *op.cit.*, pp. 226ff.

into a romantic revolutionary when we have entered into an harmonious emotional response to the doctrines of the wife of Bath, who then becomes an expression of the author's secret longings and "modern" inclinations. It may be quite proper to do this sort of thing with romantic or modern authors whose works are self-revelations arising from tension, but the art of earlier periods does not necessarily have anything at all to do with the reactions of the will of the artist as it struggles against obstacles in its path.

Our ability to sympathize more or less indiscriminately with the more unsavory characters of literature has been facilitated by the weakening of the medieval hierarchy of values, to the extent that good may conflict with good as well as with evil. This fact is strikingly illustrated in the Hegelian theory of tragedy, which maintains that in tragedy two rightful forces come into conflict so that these forces, although essentially just, become wrongs. In the tragic denouement, the resulting distortion of "eternal" justice is righted by processes in the moral order itself.[83] Since the tragic protagonist in a situation of this kind has ample moral justification for his feelings, we can readily sympathize with him and at the same time enjoy the "justice" of the concluding tragic action. We are faced, in the end, with an overwhelming awareness of mystery, which, in its graver aspects, is an essential ingredient of "the tragic view of life." A favorite device, which has been employed by a very distinguished critic, is to assert that a tragic protagonist is "too great" to be evaluated in accordance with the tenets of morality. Hence, if the actions of such a protagonist are very clearly dubious, we can still get around that fact on the grounds of "greatness" and go ahead freely with our vicarious indulgence in his passions. But in the Middle Ages it would have been very difficult to make "opposing forces" out of two aspects of charity. The commonly accepted medieval system of values was not subject, except, perhaps, among the very unlearned, to the kind of initial fragmentation necessary to produce an Hegelian tragic situation, and only persons who shared the character of Chaucer's pardoner thought of themselves as being "above" morality. The outcome of a medieval tragedy is a triumph of Divine Providence, just as the outcome of an early Greek tragedy was a triumph of Dikê; to

[83] Hegel's theory of tragedy is summarized and discussed by A. C. Bradley, *Oxford Lectures on Poetry* (London, 1920), pp. 71 ff.

43

the medieval mind there might be a conflict between "worldly" good and "spiritual" good, but no ultimate conflict in the reasonable order of creation. In medieval tragedy, the manner in which a tragic figure subjects himself to Fortune and thus falls into the order of justice is always clear.[84] He falls in the footsteps of Adam. There are, it is true, a number of ways in which the Fall of Adam may be seen; but it is impossible to regard Adam's initial appetite for "forbidden fruit" as a good, however providential its results may have been.

The general attitude expressed in Hegel's tragic theory finds less philosophical expression in other ways. The romantic emphasis on feeling brought about a new concept of "humanity." Christian philosophers, from St. Augustine to Pico della Mirandola, insist that to be "human" is to be reasonable and to control the passions. Guillaume de Lorris warns us concerning reason

> Que Deus la fist demainement
> A sa semblance e a s'image.

Through her "pooir e seignorie" she guards man from folly. But "reason" for the romantics was associated with conventional restraint laid upon natural human feeling. Hume's theory that morality is based on sympathy and sentiments of humanity, and Rousseau's conviction that truth in literature which seeks to develop a moral lesson results from well representing "les affections naturelles au coeur humain," are foreshadowings of a developing emotionalism in the perception of human values. To be "human" thus became a matter of the free development of the feelings rather than a matter of wisdom, a matter of "nature" rather than a matter of "grace." In this way a great many impulses formerly thought of as "bestial" came to be thought of as being "human," and evil became a result of frustration rather than a result of indulgence. But since traditional morality was not abandoned altogether, it became relatively easy to develop dynamic conflicts between one good and another. Meanwhile, an attitude of this kind toward "natural human inclinations" permits a much more sentimental approach to literary characters than had formerly been possible except among the uneducated. We tend to extend our sympathies spontaneously to characters we think of as being "human," to pity their

---

[84] Cf. the discussion of *Troilus* in the last chapter of this book.

frustrations, and to share their satisfactions with them. Their authors, we are sure, must have shared these feelings also. And we are likely to think of individual artists as Lucio thought of Duke Vincentio: "He had some feeling of the sport; he knew the service, and that instructed him to mercy." Hence it has been possible, for example, to cast a sentimental eye on that unrepentant scoundrel the pardoner in *The Canterbury Tales*, and we have shed many a misguided tear over the "tragedy" of that sweet young thing the prioress, who happens to be immured, like Madame de Cintré, in the restrictions of the contemplative life. These are very suitable reactions for the reader of *Camille* and "The Outcasts of Poker Flat," but they are not at all suitable to the reader of medieval literature. In the Middle Ages the "Whore with the Heart of Gold" and all her numerous sect who so thickly populate contemporary drama had not yet been born, and the kind of reaction with which Germany responded to *The Sorrows of Young Werther* was still inconceivable.

The concept of vicarious experience as a valid aesthetic process, or, rather, the spontaneous inclination to indulge in it now ingrained by the massive techniques of the cinema, affects our ideas of narrative structure as well as those of characterization. A narrative in which we follow the struggling will of the protagonist, as it overcomes obstacles, tends to fall into a pattern. Romantic criticism demanded, in the first place, that a dramatic presentation include "a compendium of whatever is moving and progressive in human life,"[85] omitting the trivial and uninteresting events that clutter up most lives in actual fact. The "progressive" or dynamic aspect of the narrative demands first that we become involved in a problem that "moves" us, and second that the problem be resolved. Hence the classic modern pattern of dramatically effective narrative consists of a "rising" action in which the conflict is developed, a "high point," a "falling action," and a catastrophe. This pattern, first worked out by Freytag,[86] survived in academic circles for many years as the standard configuration of a "plot," and, indeed, when part of this pattern is not present, at least by implication, we are left with a feeling of dramatic disappointment. The rising action or complication enables us to become involved

[85] Schlegel, *Lectures*, pp. 30-31.
[86] *Die Technik des Dramas*, pp. 102ff.

emotionally with the protagonist, and the falling action increases our inner tensions as we move toward the catastrophe which satisfies our desire for comic relief or tragic mystery. The pattern is ideally suited to a story told "for its own sake." Moral or philosophical considerations are perhaps necessary to influence our attitudes toward the characters, unless "realism," "humanity," or some concept of social justice may serve this purpose, but such considerations are not ordinarily introduced as ends in themselves. The narrative is successful if it "moves" us; if it moves us to wonder, it is said to be profound. Since it appeals to the feelings, and since those feelings are fictional, it exists in a world of its own, a world which many of us are inclined to think of as the world of "art" as distinct from the more familiar world of routine affairs.[87] But if a narrative is not designed to introduce only "moving and progressive" elements, if its appeal is intellectual rather than emotional, if it is not intended to induce vicarious emotions at all, there is no reason why it should have a plot structure of this kind. We shall find medieval narratives less unsatisfactory if we deliberately suspend our romantic expectations concerning what a good plot should be. Moreover, we shall find them less crude if we abandon the assumption that they were written "for their own sakes," or, in other words, to stimulate and relieve our emotions—for this is the true aim of a story which is "just a story." Medieval comments on the classics characteristically disregard the emotional appeal we find in them, so that we say that they "disregard the poetry." We allege further that they destroy the poetry by introducing sequential ideas. But they saw in classical narrative exactly what they expected in their own narratives. If it is not what we expect, we should avoid foisting off our expectations on their authors, and seek to understand, as best we can at this distance, what they themselves saw and loved.

Chaucerians may object that if medieval narrative is not dramatic generally, certainly Chaucer's narrative is dramatic. Perhaps it may be worthwhile, therefore, to illustrate more specifically the non-dramatic character of medieval literature in the work of Chaucer. We shall content ourselves at present with a very few brief comments. In the first place, we have suggested that the stylized

[87] Cf. Abrams' illuminating chapter, "The Poem as Heterocosm," *op.cit.*, pp. 272ff.

or conventionalized presentation of strong emotion does not produce an effect suitable to the kind of drama envisaged by Freytag. The manner in which Chaucer's characters "fall in love" illustrates this fact very well. When Arcite sees Emelye in the Knight's Tale, he says "pitously" with a sigh,

> "The fresshe beautee sleeth me sodeynly
> Of hire that rometh in the yonder place,
> And but I have hir mercy and hir grace,
> That I may seen hire atte leeste weye,
> I nam but deed; ther nis namoore to seye."

In short, he will die, he says, if he gets no mercy from the lady. Nicholas in the Miller's Tale expresses exactly the same sentiments:

> And prively he caughte hire by the queynte,
> And seyde, "Ywis, but if ich have my wille,
> For deerne love of thee, lemman, I spille."

Again, in the Man of Law's Tale "Sathan" inspires a young knight to love Custance

> so hoote, of foul affeccioun,
> That verraily hym thoughte he sholde spille.

Aurelius approaches Dorigen in the Franklin's Tale with the plea,

> "Have mercy, sweete, or ye wol do me deye!"

In *Troilus*, Pandarus assures Criseyde that he as well as Troilus will die if she is not merciful:

> "make of this thing an ende,
> Or sle us both at ones . . . ."

If we consider these examples together, it becomes obvious that what we have before us is a convention relevant to the behavior of lovers of a certain type. Walter, in the Clerk's Tale, behaves differently, and Shakespeare, to whom the convention was still familiar, makes the national hero of the Elizabethans observe, "to say to thee that I shall die is true,—but for thy love, by the Lord, no; yet I love thee too." It is clear that the idea of "dying for love" was not calculated to provoke a strong sympathetic response in the reader.

It was not, however, an "empty convention"; for the common assumption that we have "explained" something in medieval art or literature when we say that it is conventional is erroneous. Just as medieval art developed certain conventional ways of indicating the identity of a saint, the character of a vice, or the ramifications of an idea represented by a pagan deity, medieval literature developed a conventional language of narrative or descriptive motifs which were designed to communicate ideas. The area of meaning evoked by the present convention is suggested by Henry of Lancaster, the father of Chaucer's Blanche, who tells us in a discussion of sins of the mouth that "quant n'ose parler a ascune qu jeo quide q'elle seroit daungerouse, jeo envoieroi ascune makerel a qi jeo parleroie molt pitousement et dirroi: 'Jeo ne su qe mort, si vous ne me eidetz,' mes 'Je ne su qe mort, si vous m'eidetz' deusse jeo dire pur dire voir. . . ."[88] In the Knight's Tale, Arcite does die, just at the point where he earns the "mercy" of Emelye. Nicholas manages to enjoy what he has so handily seized upon, but he is very violently "scalded in the towte" as a result. The young knight who attacks Custance meets an appropriate reward. And Aurelius, even though he threatens to "dye of sodeyn deth horrible," and lies bedridden and unable to walk with an unmentionable malady for over two years, has all his pains for nothing. Troilus dies, but he has time, in Chaucer's account, to realize the implications of "dying for love." The theme may be treated with some seriousness, as it is in *Troilus*, or comically, as it is in the Miller's Tale, but it is a theme devised to stimulate thought rather than emotion. When the young man in Guido Faba's *Dictamina rhetorica* writes to his beloved, "non possum aliud nisi de vestra pulcritudine cogitare," we recognize a symptom, or a feigned symptom, of the lover's malady; and when he adds that he must have her grace "sine qua mea mors vita creditur et vita mortua reputatur," we know exactly what he wants and why he wants it.[89] But this desire evokes nothing of the sympathetic emotion we might feel, for example, in contemplating Rodin's "L'éternelle idole."

[88] *Le livre de seyntz medicines*, pp. 21-22. For further illustrations showing the implications of "dying for love," see Jean de Condé, "Li dis Varlet ki ama le femme au bourgois," ed. Scheler, *Dits et contes de Baudoin de Condé et de son fils Jean de Condé* (Brussels, 1866-1867), II, 243ff., and Machaut, "Dit dou Lyon," ed. Hoepffner, *SATF* (1911), lines 949-988.

[89] Ed. A. Gaudenzi, *Il Propugnatore*, n. s. v. 1 (1892), p. 113.

Chaucer's "psychological" analyses, like his direct renditions of emotional states, do not involve the reader personally in the incidents of the plot. Arcite is so overcome by love

> That lene he wex and drye as is a shaft;
> His eyen holwe, and grisly to biholde,
> His hewe falow and pale as asshen colde,
> And solitarie he was and evere allone,
> And waillynge al the nyght, makynge his mone;
> And if he herde song or instrument,
> Thanne wolde he wepe, he myghte nat be stent.
> So feble eek were his spiritz, and so lowe,
> And chaunged so, that no man koude knowe
> His speche nor his voys, though men it herde.
> And in his geere for al the world he ferde,
> Nat oonly lik the loveris maladye
> Of Hereos, but rather lyk manye,
> Engendred of humour malencolik
> Biforen, in his celle fantastik.
> And shortly, turned was al up-so-doun
> Bothe habit and eek disposicioun
> Of hym, this woful lovere, daun Arcite.

It was pointed out long ago by John Livingston Lowes that this is a fairly accurate description of a condition recognized by the physicians of the late Middle Ages.[90] Arcite has not only fallen into "amor qui hereos dicitur," a sufficiently dangerous condition, but he also suffers from a dreaded consequence of this malady, "manye." In mania, the "imaginativa, quae est versus partem anteriori cerebri," is corrupted so that the patient "putat bonum quod non est bonum, et putat honestum, quod non est"—thinks to be good what is not good and considers that virtuous which is not.[91] His inner hierarchy and with it his moral judgment is turned "up-so-doun." We may regard this condition as pathetic, since a malady of the spirit, as Boethius points out, is more terrible than a malady of the flesh; but we are obviously not invited to share it. Palamon's condition differs only in degree, so that in this tale there

[90] *MP*, xi (1914), 491-546.
[91] Bernard of Gordon, *Lilium medicinae* (Lyons, 1574), pp. 208-210.

is no one whose "struggling will" invited us to what Freytag would consider to be a dramatic sympathy.

That the same shortcoming, if we wish to call it that, appears in the Miller's Tale is obvious without elaboration, in spite of the fact that the surface incidents in that tale move with a rapid and logical sequence. But surely, it will be objected, *Troilus* is an exception. Is it? Throughout the first part of the poem, Troilus' will exerts itself hardly at all; the initiative is taken by Pandarus, who manages the complication, woos Criseyde for Troilus, and even, at the crucial moment, throws him in bed with her and strips him to his shirt. All this, moreover, requires, from a purely dramatic point of view, an enormous number of stanzas. Even after Troilus, "sodeynly avysed," begins to act for himself when over a thousand lines of the third book have passed, the dramatic action of the remainder of the poem is slowed down by dramatically inconsequential dialogues and by a long meditation on free will. From a romantic point of view, a point of view entirely justified as an approach to romantic literature, Godwin's judgment of the poem is sound: "Chaucer's poem includes many beauties, many genuine touches of nature, and many strokes of exquisite pathos. It is on the whole, however, written in that style which has unfortunately been imposed upon the world as dignified, classical, and chaste. It is naked of incidents, of ornament, of whatever should most awaken the imagination, astound the fancy, or hurry away the soul. . . . We travel through a work of this sort as we travel over some of the immense downs with which our island is interspersed. All is smooth, or undulates with so gentle a variation as scarcely to be adverted by the sense. But all is homogeneous and tiresome: the mind sinks into a state of aching torpidity; and we feel as if we should never get to the end of our eternal journey."[92] The opening concessions in this statement may be dismissed as a bow to Chaucer's traditional status as a great poet. But if he does not, in his greatest poem, "hurry away the soul," he certainly does so nowhere else. In his own time he was not expected to do so. His art had quite different purposes which were neither romantic nor modern. It has a life and vigor and that sureness of touch which modern critics very naturally call "tension," but these qualities

[92] "Shakespeare and Chaucer Compared," in *Memorials of Shakespeare*, ed. N. Drake (London, 1828), pp. 262-263.

are not dependent on the creation and manipulation of fictional emotions.

To conclude, the medieval world was innocent of our profound concern for tension. We have come to view ourselves as bundles of polarities and tensions in which, to use one formulation, the ego is caught between the omnivorous demands of the id on the one hand, and the more or less irrational restraints of the super-ego on the other. Romantic synthesis has in our day become "adjustment" or "equilibrium." As John Middleton Murry puts it, we demand that poetic expression, which consists of thought charged with an "emotional field," should "not merely thrill but also still our hearts." Nothing seems more natural in the analysis of events than the establishment of a polarity as a coordinate system against which variation of any kind can be measured. We project dynamic polarities on history as class struggles, balances of power, or as conflicts between economic realities and traditional ideals. In our metaphysics we find them operating between Being and Non-being. In architecture we have developed styles involving obvious, rather than concealed, cantilevered or counterbalanced masses, seemingly suspended without support. We demand tensions in literary art— ambiguities, situational ironies, tensions in figurative language, tensions between fact and symbol or between reality and the dream. Our most widely hailed poet, W. B. Yeats, developed an historical and aesthetic system based on conflicting opposites. We have calmed the more violent expression of the early romantics—their "passion," to use William Archer's term, has been restrained—but we have substituted for romantic extravagance a new subjective "realism," which leads to a new intensity. This highly abstract intensity has replaced the romantic infinite. But the medieval world with its quiet hierarchies knew nothing of these things. Its aesthetic, at once a continuation of classical philosophy and a product of Christian teaching, developed artistic and literary styles consistent with a world without dynamically interacting polarities. What some of the aesthetic presuppositions of the Middle Ages were like will be our concern in the next chapter.

II · SOME PRINCIPLES OF MEDIEVAL AESTHETICS

I. THE AESTHETICS OF FIGURATIVE EXPRESSION

𝕴𝖓 𝖛𝖎𝖊𝖜 𝖔𝖋 the thorough and comprehensive collection of materials available in the monumental *Etudes d'esthétique médiévale* by E. de Bruyne (Bruges, 1946), another essay on medieval aesthetics may seem superfluous. But De Bruyne's work, because of his neglect of St. Augustine, is sometimes unbalanced,[1] and because of the very broad field he sought to cover, it was not always possible for him to adduce the context of his materials with sufficient fullness to place them in a useful perspective. In this chapter we shall consider some of the more important contributions of St. Augustine to aesthetic theory and the continuing relevance of his thought to the later Middle Ages. In general, the refinements of the scholastics are here neglected, not because they were not in themselves important, but because they were not immediately relevant to the actual practice of the arts. We shall be concerned with very general principles which may be taken more or less as medieval commonplaces, although some detailed explanation will be necessary to show how those commonplaces arose. The fact that reflections of these commonplaces in literature have not previously been noticed will make some things that are said here seem strange, but it is hoped that sufficient evidence is included to enable the reader to judge for himself the validity of the conclusions.

Much of what St. Augustine said about aesthetic matters had been said before,[2] but his formulations are singularly coherent, and they are harmonious with those basic principles of Christian theology which he left as an inheritance for his medieval successors. The works in which his aesthetic attitudes are stated continued to be copied and read throughout the Middle Ages, when they enjoyed an authority second only to that of the Bible. A conception of what these attitudes were will be easier to formulate if we turn

[1] See the notes by B. F. Huppé, *Doctrine and Poetry* (New York, 1959), pp. 58, 61.
[2] K. Svoboda, *L'esthétique de Saint Augustin* (Brno, 1933), discusses the sources of many of St. Augustine's aesthetic ideas.

our attention first to the theory of figurative expression, since the general pattern which dominates medieval aesthetic ideas of all kinds is most easily discernible there. The most revealing discussion of this subject occurs in the account of scriptural obscurity in *On Christian Doctrine* (2. 6. 7-8). This obscurity, says St. Augustine, was divinely ordained to overcome pride by work, and to prevent the mind from disdaining a thing too easily grasped. It stimulates a desire to learn, and at the same time excludes those who are unworthy from the mysteries of the faith.[3] But it is also pleasant. St. Augustine's account of the manner in which pleasure arises from obscurity reveals an aesthetic attitude which became typically medieval. He begins by calling attention to a general situation which he first describes in literal terms and then in the figurative language of the Canticle of Canticles. There are, he says, holy and perfect men whose example enables the Church to rid of superstitions those who come to it, so that they may be incorporated into it. These faithful and true servants of God, putting aside the burdens of the world, come to the holy laver of baptism, and ascending thence, conceiving by the Holy Spirit, produce a twofold fruit of charity. This fact stated in these literal terms is less pleasing than the same fact revealed in the Scriptures where the Church is being praised as a beautiful woman (Cant. 4. 2): "Thy teeth are as flocks of sheep, that are shorn, which come up from the washing, all with twins, and there is none barren among them." St. Augustine assures us that for a reason he does not understand holy men are more pleasingly described for him as the teeth of the Church, which cut off men from their errors and soften them so that they may be taken into the body of the Church. Moreover, he joyfully recognizes them as sheep, which, having been shorn of the burdens of the world, come up from the washing of baptism bearing the twin loves of charity, the love of God and of one's neighbor for the sake of God. And this is true even though the figurative expres-

---

[3] Cf. Matt. 13. 13, and the much quoted verse from the Sermon on the Mount (Matt. 7. 6): "Give not that which is holy to dogs; neither cast ye your pearls before swine, lest perhaps they trample them under their feet, and turning upon you, they tear you." In connection with this verse, St. Augustine explains, *De sermone Domini in monte*, 2. 20. 69, that it is better for those who attack truth (dogs) and those who despise it (swine) to have to search for what is hidden than to be enabled to attack or to scorn what is open. Cf. the discussion of this subject by John the Scot, *Super ier. cael.*, *PL*, 122, cols. 151-152 and 170.

sion says nothing which is not said in the literal expression. Why it is true is "difficult to say," but no one denies that things are more readily learned through similitudes and that those things which are sought with difficulty are more pleasantly discovered.[4]

If we can avoid the temptation to dismiss this passage as a "typical example of fantastic exegesis"[5] we may learn a great deal from it. First of all, St. Augustine seems unconcerned by the question which most interests the modern aesthetician: why is figurative language pleasant? His answer to this question, insofar as he gives one, is simply that the sense of difficulty overcome is pleasant. He has nothing to say about aesthetic pleasure in itself without reference to the discovery of truth. The reason he has no interest in this matter is clear from his remarks about a poetic passage quoted elsewhere in *On Christian Doctrine* (3. 7. 11):

O Father Neptune, whose aged temples resound,
Wreathed in the noisy sea, from whose beard eternally flows
The vast ocean, and in whose hair the rivers wander . . .

This *siliqua*, or husk, he says, shakes rattling pebbles inside its sweet shell; it is not food for men, but food for swine like that consumed by the prodigal son, who in a far country sought happiness in vain pleasure and empty philosophy.[6] What does it matter, asks St. Augustine, that Neptune here stands for all the world's waters? Neither Neptune nor the ocean is a god to be adored. In other words, the "sweet shell" of figurative language in this instance has no value at all. If it is pleasing, it is misleading because it leads the mind to nothing profitable. We may conclude that for St. Augustine figurative expression is not of any value in itself; it is valuable only as an adjunct to the intellectual search for truth. And the pleasure with which he is concerned is the pleasure arising from the discovery of truth, not the incidental pleasure of the "shell."

[4] For further references to this idea in St. Augustine's work and an enthusiastic if somewhat vague statement of its significance, see H. I. Marrou, *Saint Augustin et la fin de la culture antique* (Paris, 1949), pp. 488-490. The passage from *On Christian Doctrine* is repeated by Rabanus Maurus, *De cler. inst.*, PL, 107, col. 380.

[5] See G. Combès and J. Farges, *Le magistère Chrétien* in *Oeuvres de Saint Augustin*, XI (Paris, 1949), p. 567.

[6] Cf. Huppé, *op.cit.*, p. 14.

This principle undoubtedly accounts for St. Augustine's complacency about what we should think of as the incongruity of the images he adduces from the Canticle. To us a "figure" is a means of inducing a spontaneous emotional perception. But no such emotional response can possibly result from envisaging holy men as the teeth of a beautiful woman, and even if such a response were possible, it would soon be destroyed as we see her biting away the evil from men, chewing them to make them soft, and then digesting them. We are shocked further to find that the "teeth" become sheep, and the situation is not improved when we see the sheep shorn, dipped, and finally blessed with twin lambs. The processes here envisaged are not affectively attractive. To see what St. Augustine saw in the passage, to enjoy it as he undoubtedly did, we shall have to approach it in an entirely different way. First of all, we must abandon our conception that a figurative expression must have an aura of emotional implication which in many instances is its only meaning.

What appealed to St. Augustine was undoubtedly something quite irrelevant to the non-discursive suggestions of the materials used to form the figures. Instead he saw that if the figures are regarded as problems capable of an intellectual solution it is possible to recognize the fact that they conform to an abstract pattern which harmonizes with the pattern of a useful idea. If we begin with the assumption that the woman being addressed is the Church, the idea is not fantastic that her "teeth," which may be seen abstractly as her means of preparing nourishment for herself, are "holy men." Neither is it fantastic to envisage the "shearing" of what are now seen abstractly as "sheep," their bathing, and their fruitfulness as things which conform to a procedure which holy men customarily undergo. Moreover, if the existence of such holy men is thought of as being something extremely desirable, and the pattern of their behavior is a reflection of the highest philosophical truth, we can understand that the discovery of this pattern beneath a puzzling figurative surface may be a source of delight. This is true especially when the idea discovered is not something new but something already known and treasured, for then the pleasure of recognition is added to that of discovery. As St. Augustine says in the *Contra mendacium* (10. 24), "Although we learn things which are said clearly and openly in other places, when these things are dug out of secret places, they are renewed in our comprehension, and being renewed become more attractive." It is important to understand that the affective value of this figurative language lies in what is found beneath the language and not in the concrete materials of the figures.

Moreover, the affective value of what is discovered may be very great indeed, and the process of discovering it may have a profound spiritual significance. In one of his letters (55. 11. 21), St. Augustine asserts that those things which are said figuratively in the Scriptures move and inflame love more than those things which are said literally. When the mind is immersed in terrestrial things, it is slow to be ignited with the fire of divine love, but when it is directed toward similitudes based on corporal things and thence referred to those spiritual things figured in the similitudes, it is excited by the transition from one to the other so that it is carried with a more ardent love toward the peace it seeks. In other words, a figurative expression offers an opportunity to discern the *invisibilia Dei* through "the things that are made," and it has the effect of stimulating love for the *invisibilia*.

To return once more to the passage from the Canticle, it is obvious that St. Augustine was not concerned with any spontaneous associations his experience may have led him to have with teeth and sheep. Teeth do not in themselves suggest holy men. In the same way, shorn and washed ewes with twin lambs are neither empirically nor emotionally connected with human perfection. There is, moreover, no surface consistency between teeth and sheep. But the peculiar configuration of these materials as they are governed by the context does give rise to an abstract pattern which is coherent. The incoherence of the surface materials is almost essential to the formation of the abstract pattern, for if the surface materials—the concrete elements in the figures—were consistent or spontaneously satisfying in an emotional way, there would be no stimulus to seek something beyond them. It follows from these considerations that if the figures were decorative, as they are in much eighteenth-century writing, or if they were spontaneously satisfying to the emotions, as they are in much romantic writing, no such effects as those described by St. Augustine would be possible. It follows also that the concrete materials of the figures do not need to be "realistically" conceived to obtain the effect desired. That is, there is no point in dwelling on the various characteristics of teeth and sheep which have no relevance to the abstraction. This means that when we consider this kind of figurative expression, either in literary art or in the visual arts, neither surface consistency nor "realism" is necessary to its effectiveness.

The aesthetic of figurative expression described by St. Augustine is essentially the aesthetic of what he and his followers in the Middle Ages called *allegoria*: the art of saying one thing to mean another.[7] Although the word *enigma* was conventionally reserved for "obscure allegory," all allegory was thought of as being to some extent enigmatic. Its function in scriptural contexts is described in the Preface to the Canticle ascribed to St. Gregory in terms that clearly reflect the ideas we have just been considering in St. Augustine: "After the human race had been expelled from the joys of Paradise and had entered the pilgrimage of this life, the hearts of men were blind to spiritual understanding. If one says with a human voice to such a blind heart, 'Follow God,' or 'Love God,' as the law demands of him, what is said will be rejected at once, and because of the coldness of infidelity the listener will not grasp what he hears. For this reason, the divine word is spoken by means of certain enigmas to him who is slow and cold, and through the things which are known to him is subtly suggested to him the love which he does not know."[8]

Paradoxically, there is a sense in which "enigmas" are more readily understood than literal statements, for an unusual configuration of "things which are known" stimulates the perception of an abstract unknown. "For allegory serves as a kind of machine to the spirit by means of which it may be raised up to God. Thus when enigmas are set before a man and he recognizes certain things in the words which are familiar to him, he may understand in the sense of the words what is not familiar to him; and by means of earthly words he is separated from the earth. Since he does not abhor what he knows, he may come to understand what he does not know. For the things which are known to us from which allegory

[7] The standard grammatical definition of *allegoria* during the Middle Ages is that given by Isidore of Seville, *Etymologiae*, 1. 37. 22: "Alieniloquium. Aliud enim sonat, et aliud intellegitur."

[8] This passage and the two following are quoted from the Proemium to the commentary on the Canticle of Canticles attributed to St. Gregory the Great, *PL*, 79, cols. 471ff.

is made are clothed in divine doctrine, and, when we recognize the thing by an exterior word, we may come to an interior understanding."[9]

The author leaves no doubt in our minds concerning the location of the referents suggested by the figures. They lie in the spiritual understanding, remote from spontaneous emotional association. We must approach them through the reason, which he considered to be a distinctively "human" faculty: "Thus the sacred Scripture with its words and senses is like a picture with its colors and things pictured. A man would be extremely stupid to confine his attention to the colors and to ignore the things that are depicted. And we, if we embrace only what the words say on the surface and ignore the other senses, are like those who ignore the things depicted and see only the colors. 'The letter kills,' as it is written, 'but the spirit gives life' [2 Cor. 3. 6]; thus the letter covers the spirit as the chaff covers the grain. But to eat the chaff is to be a beast of burden; to eat the grain is to be human. He who uses human reason, therefore, will cast aside the chaff and hasten to eat the grain of the spirit. For this reason it is useful that the mystery be covered in the wrapping of the letter."[10]

In studying this explanation, we should remember that the intelligible—the "grain" which nourishes the interior understanding —is synonymous with the beautiful. Figurative language, whether in the form of similitudes like those discussed by St. Augustine, or in the form of more extended allegory, creates an enigma which challenges the reason to seek an intelligible beauty beneath a surface which is not necessarily beautiful itself.

We have already called attention, in the previous chapter, to a pattern of thought with reference to figurative expression similar to that developed by St. Augustine in the poetic theory of Lactantius. Lactantius was referring to pagan poets, and there was a profound difference, which we shall discuss later, between figurative or allegorical expressions in pagan poetry and similar expressions in the Scriptures. For the moment it is sufficient to notice the similarity between scriptural and poetic expression. St. Augustine suggests that the *aenigmatistae* of Numbers 21. 27 are probably poets, since

[9] St. Paul's distinction between the "exterior" and the "interior" man probably suggested the distinction here.

[10] Cf. St. Augustine, *On Christian Doctrine*, 3. 5. 9.

it is the custom of poets to compose enigmatic fables which are understood to mean something other than what they say.[11] He also defends poets from those who say that they write lies, since a feigned fable which refers to a true *significatio* is not a lie.[12] John the Scot makes explicit the comparison between the obscurity of poetry and that of the Scriptures, pointing out that just as the art of poetry uses "feigned fables and allegorical similitudes" to express moral or physical truth for the purpose of exercising the human mind, in the same way the Scriptures employ figurative expression to lead the mind toward the comprehension of the intelligible.[13] These theoretical considerations were not without practical results. When Lactantius set about writing a poem of his own, *De ave phenice*, he employed poetic enigmas in which truths of the Resurrection are set forth under an obscure surface largely derived from pagan sources.[14] Prudentius, sometimes misleadingly called the first Christian allegorist, used some figurative materials derived from the Scriptures themselves to create the surface of his *Psychomachia*. In these instances the truths involved are not the "moral, physical, and historical" truths of the pagans, but the *invisibilia Dei*, so that, so far as aesthetic matters are concerned, the poems may be thought of as having an effect similar to the effect of figurative passages in the Scriptures. When scriptural figures are used by a poet, they do not lose their original connotations, and the poet requires no special elevation or inspiration to employ them. As a Christian, in fact, he has an obligation to suggest the intelligible to his readers, whether the figures he uses are derived from scriptural or non-scriptural sources. This fact is well illustrated by St. Augustine's advice to Licentius that he should complete his poem on Pyramus and Thisbe by arranging it in such a way as to condemn libidinous love and to praise pure and sincere love, "by which the soul, endowed by discipline and beautiful in

---

[11] *Quaestiones in Numeros*, 45.

[12] *Contra mendacium*, 13. 28. For the concept of the "reasonable lie" in poetic fables as St. Augustine reflects it, see Svoboda, p. 40. And for a similar attitude toward myths, p. 52.

[13] *Super ier. coel.*, PL, 122, col. 146.

[14] For a discussion of the authenticity of this work together with an interpretation based on the literary conventions of Lactantius' time, see E. Rapisarda, *Il carme "De ave phoenice"* (Catania, 1946).

virtue, is joined to the understanding through philosophy."[15] The pagan character of the narrative does not obviate a conclusion, either expressed or implied, which is harmonious with the truths of Christianity.

It is not difficult to cite evidence to show that during the Middle Ages and, indeed, well into the Renaissance, figurative expression in both literary and visual art was designed to lead the mind through exercise to a spiritual understanding. A few instances will suffice here to make the point clear. The preface to the *Anticlaudianus* of Alanus de Insulis, a work of enormous influence,[16] stresses the function of exercise, the ultimate appeal to the reason, and the value of obscurity in excluding the unworthy from an easy approach to holy things:

"For in this work the sweetness of the literal sense will caress the puerile hearing, the moral instruction will fill the perfecting sense, and the sharper subtlety of the allegory will exercise the understanding nearing perfection. But may the approach to this work be barred to those who, following only the sensual motion, do not desire the truth of reason, lest a thing holy be defouled by being offered to dogs, or a pearl trampled by the feet of swine be lost, if the majesty of these things be revealed to the unworthy."[17]

The author quite obviously expected his readers to avoid a spontaneous reaction of the "sensual motion" in reading the work before them. Instead, they were to exercise reason in the search for something holy which lay hidden from the enemies and scorners of truth. A very similar attitude was undoubtedly responsible for the typical manner of presenting the Nativity in Gothic art (Fig. 11). The scene shows neither tenderness nor humanity;[18] its stylized linear technique is not conducive to realistic emotional expression. Mary on her bed looks away from the child, who is placed on an altar between the two animals. The infant is here the Bread of Life, food for the two animals which represent the Jews and the Gentiles, and the scene looks forward to the Sacrifice, the mystery of the Eucharist, and the unity of the Church. The enigmatic

[15] *De ordine*, I. 8. 24. For one use of this story for allegorical purposes during the Middle Ages, see A. Goldschmidt, *Der Albani-Psalter* (Berlin, 1895), pp. 72-73.

[16] See R. Bossuat, ed., *Anticlaudianus* (Paris, 1955), p. 43.

[17] *Ibid.*, p. 56.

[18] Cf. E. Mâle, *L'art religieux du XIIIe siècle* (Paris, 1923), p. 188.

placing of the child in this instance leads to the perception of the underlying ideas. And these ideas, not the relationship between the mother and the child, supply the affective values of the picture.

In the *Roman de la rose* of Jean de Meun it is appropriate that Raison should be the source of instruction on the subject of poetic appreciation. Her own word, she says, sometimes has "autre sen." And if the dreamer will consider the "integumenz" of the poets, he will find there "une grant partie des secrez de philosophie" wherein he should take great delight as well as profit.[19] Here once more the procedure of discovering a reasonable truth beneath an obscure surface is said to be delightful. The fact that the outward attractiveness of a literary work may interfere with the perception of the content as well as of what lies underneath is noticed, with regret, by Watriquet de Couvin, who tells us in "Li dis de la cygoigne" that

> Maintes gens se sont esbaudiz
> D'escouter biaus mos et biaus diz,
> Et moult en ont grant joie en l'eure,
> Mais quant en leur cuers n'en demeure
> Ne sens ne matiere ne glose
> Il n'i profitent nulle chose.[20]

Here the surface delight in the words is regarded as a danger which may interfere with a perception of the meaning, wherein, we may assume, there lies an even greater delight as well as an element of profit. Watriquet also affords us an interesting and significant hypothetical example of the enigmatic in art. In "Li tornois des dames" the poet describes his arrival at the very pleasant château of the Count of Blois. One day after dinner he comes upon a stained glass window depicting a strange tournament between ladies and gentlemen. The ladies are oddly victorious and are making terrible havoc among the gentlemen. Puzzled by what he sees, the poet falls into a deep meditation. In a dream Dame Verité comes to him and explains the picture. The ladies, she says, represent the flesh, which is here engaged in that strife against the spirit, represented by the gentlemen, which was first begun by Adam and Eve. The gentlemen who have been overcome, in

[19] *Roman de la rose,* ed. Langlois, lines 7153ff. The term *integumenz* is discussed in Chapter IV, below.

[20] *Dits de Watriquet de Couvin* (Brussels, 1868), p. 283.

other words, are those who have abandoned themselves to carnal delights and are being made *caitifs* by them. This is the true "glose" of the window.[21] Watriquet's picture, that is, shows the other side of the lesson shown by Veronese (Fig. 6). A picture, like a poem, may have a "glose," and an enigmatic exterior like the one here described is the characteristic method of suggesting it.

When Petrarch develops the poetic theory to which we alluded in the last chapter, it is significant that he adduces, on the authority of St. Gregory, exactly the conception of scriptural obscurity which we have found in St. Augustine: "Following him [i. e., Augustine], Gregory says in his sermons on Ezechiel, 'This obscurity of God's eloquence is of great utility, for it exercises the reason so that it is enlarged by effort, and thus exercised it is able to grasp that which an idle mind could not grasp. It has, moreover, an even greater utility, for the meaning of the Sacred Scriptures, which would become debased if it were open in all places, refreshes us with more sweetness when it is found in certain obscure places, the more the mind has been disciplined by labor in the search for it.' I do not quote all that he and others have said about this matter. But if these things are correctly said about those writings which are set forth for everyone, how much more justly may they be said concerning writings designed for a few? Among poets, therefore . . . a majesty and dignity of style is retained, not that the meaning may be concealed from those who are worthy, but so that, a sweet labor having been proposed, it may provide at once for the reader's memory and delight. For those things are more precious which we seek with difficulty, and are more carefully observed. And it is provided for the less capable, lest in vain they waste themselves away on the surfaces of these things, that, if they are wise, they are deterred from approaching them."[22]

This formulation, with its direct analogy between Augustinian scriptural aesthetics and the aesthetics of poetry, was repeated by

[21] *Ibid.*, pp. 231-271. Specifically, in each case the lady represents the flesh, and the gentlemen "sont les ames / Des chaitis qui vaincre se laissant / A leur charoignes et se paissent / Des deliz et des vanites . . . ."

[22] *Invective contra medicum*, ed. P. G. Ricci (Rome, 1950), pp. 67-70. The idea is expressed succinctly in *Africa*, 9. 96-97:
Quaesitu asperior quo sit sententia, verum
Dulcior inventu.

Boccaccio in the *Genealogie*,[23] a work which became, as Jean Seznec has shown,[24] a standard manual for both painters and poets. But the traditions of medieval art were themselves sufficiently strong to insure the survival of an enigmatic technique of representation even without the influence of Boccaccio. Professor Panofsky demonstrates that in early Netherlandish painting deviations from nature which are retained in a generally naturalistic mode of presentation are indications of an underlying metaphysical idea.[25] Later on, Leonardo could use a departure from historical truth in a devotional painting to call attention to the presence of a spiritual meaning available, after exercise, to the mind of the observer.[26] The delight in the enigmatic which appears in Aldhelm's riddles or in the illuminated initials of insular manuscripts, in Marcabru's poetry or in Romanesque sculpture, in musical configurations of the fourteenth century, and in the emblem books of the Renaissance is not something merely "quaint" and sporadic. It is a manifestation of a fully formed and deeply felt aesthetic theory whose assumptions permeate medieval art and literature generally. The theory may operate in subtle ways; it is easy to mistake its surface application for "crudity" and artistic ineptitude. And we have lost much of our enthusiasm for the abstract truths which its practitioners sought to convey. Nevertheless, the enigmatic figure was one of the most powerful and effective instruments by means of which the medieval artist could fulfill the aims of his art. It enabled him to appeal, first of all, to the reason, and through the reason to the affective values which philosophy and theology pointed to as the highest and most moving values possible to humanity.

All this does not mean, however, that art could not be moving on the surface; it means that whatever surface delight it involves should be referred to another end. This principle may be illustrated in various ways in the writings of St. Augustine. In discussing eloquence, for example, he observes that a distinctive trait of good minds is to love the truth in words and not the words themselves.

[23] See *Boccaccio on Poetry*, ed. and trans. C. G. Osgood (New York, 1956), pp. 61-62.
[24] *The Survival of the Pagan Gods* (New York, 1953), pp. 220, 227, 236, 257-258, 307-308, 312.
[25] *Early Netherlandish Painting* (Cambridge, Mass., 1953), I, 147.
[26] See D. W. Robertson, Jr., *"In foraminibus petrae,"* *Renaissance News*, VII (1954), pp. 92-95.

Nevertheless, it is expedient to use eloquence to appeal to those who do not respond to the truth unless it is stated with some attractiveness.[27] But the "moderate" or pleasing style, used among pagan orators simply to please their auditors, should be used by the Christian orator only so that good customs may be admired and evil customs avoided, or, if the auditors already act virtuously, so that they may do so more zealously and with perseverance.[28] The ornaments of rhetoric, in other words, should please, but they should not please for their own sake. And the "grand" style, by means of which audiences are moved in such a way that they put into practice what they know to be just, is certainly to be used by the Christian orator,[29] but there is here no question of "moving" simply for the sake of "moving." Much the same attitude is revealed in the famous passage in the *Confessions* concerning music (4. 9). Just as it is the "truth in words" and not the outward attractiveness of the words which is of primary importance, so also it is the text of the psalms which is important and not the musical ornamentation of the text. Hence St. Augustine is made uneasy by the possibility that the stimulation of the senses brought about by the music may be misleading. But he feels that so long as the sensation follows the reason, and is not allowed to take precedence over it, the music is to be commended.[30] For then it inflames the heart with piety. Since it has this effect, just as eloquence has the effect of stimulating or confirming virtue, or even of inducing virtuous action, St. Augustine does not hesitate to recommend it, with some reservation inspired by the passionate abandon of Donatist psalm singing, in a letter to Januarius (55. 18. 34). Like eloquence, music is worthy so long as it is the handmaiden of wisdom.

[27] *On Christian Doctrine*, 4. 11. 36.

[28] *Ibid.*, 4. 25. 55.

[29] A vivid instance of St. Augustine's use of the grand style is described, *ibid.*, 4. 24. 53. As if to encourage the use of eloquence, St. Augustine observes, *ibid.*, 4. 20. 41, that all of the devices of the rhetoricians except rhythmic closings (which he himself uses) are to be found in the Scriptures.

[30] What is here stated "autobiographically" might just as well be said in exposition impersonally, although it would then lose some of its effectiveness. In reading this and other parts of the *Confessions* modern readers will treat the book more justly if they relax their interest in autobiographical narrative as a "psychological" phenomenon and devote more attention to what the narrative implies. Dante's observations on this subject, *Convivio*, 1. 2. 14, are very just.

2. THE USE AND ABUSE OF BEAUTY

The philosophical doctrine which underlies these observations concerning eloquence and music, and, indeed, almost all of St. Augustine's central ideas concerning aesthetic matters, is his distinction between those things which are to be *used* and those things which are to be *enjoyed*. If the implications of this doctrine are once understood, much that seems difficult or contradictory in his writing will become clear.[31] To enjoy a thing, he says, is to cling to it with love for its own sake. To use a thing, on the other hand, is to employ a thing with reference to the object which one loves. If a thing is "used" in any other way, it is wasted or abused. But the only proper object of love is God, so that only God is to be enjoyed: "we should use this world and not enjoy it, so that the 'invisible things' of God, 'being understood by the things that are made,' may be seen, that is, so that by means of corporal and temporal things we may comprehend the eternal and spiritual" (cf. Rom. I. 20). Strictly speaking, therefore, it is wrong to enjoy any creature for its own sake. But this limitation is not quite so rigorous as it sounds at first, since St. Augustine goes on to say that "to enjoy" and "to use with joy" are very similar, so that the proper use of a thing may be enjoyable and pleasant.[32] His preliminary reservations about both eloquence and music, which are in themselves pleasant things, are designed, in effect, to insure that they are "used" rather than enjoyed improperly for themselves. When they are so used, they lead toward something which, in St. Augustine's mind, is far more enjoyable than they could possibly be.

It follows that anything beautiful among creatures, whether natural or artificial, is truly beautiful only insofar as it is useful. Thus, as St. Augustine explains in the *De vera religione* (29. 52), the beauty and order of the visible world should be used as a step toward the invisible; and this use is a rational process:

"We should see how far reason may progress from the visible to the invisible, ascending at the same time from the temporal to the

[31] The classic exposition of this doctrine appears in *On Christian Doctrine*, I. 3. 3 to I. 4. 4. Since it is repeated at the beginning of the *Sententiae* of Peter Lombard, it became a commonplace of late medieval thought. The idea itself may owe something to the distinctions made in the third book of Cicero's *De officiis*.

[32] *On Christian Doctrine*, I. 33. 37. An extended discussion of the use of beauty appears in paragraphs 32-37 of the *De vera religione*.

eternal. Then we should not causelessly and vainly consider the beauty of the sky, the order of the stars, the radiance of the light, the alternations of day and night, the monthly course of the moon, the fourfold organization of the year, the fourfold harmony of the elements, the minute force of seeds generating species and numbers, and everything in its kind preserving its proper mode. In considering these things, no empty and transient curiosity is to be exercised, but a step is to be made toward those things which are immortal and which remain always."

The beauties of creation are, as it were, the gestures of Eternal Wisdom (*De libero arbitrio*, 2. 16. 43): "And the Artificer, so to speak, gestures to the spectator of His work concerning the beauty of that work, not that he should cling to it completely, but so that his eyes should scan the corporal beauty of things that are made in such a way that the affection returns to Him who made them."

The analogy between the beauty of the world and the eloquence which adorns a speech came naturally to St. Augustine's mind, since creatures are, in a way, the voice of God. He continues, "Those men who love the things you make before you [O Wisdom!] are like those who, when they hear an eloquent wise speaker and avidly attend to the sweetness of his voice and the aptly placed arrangement of his syllables, lose the meaning of what he is saying in those words which sound as signs of something else. Woe to those who turn away from your Light and cling to their own darkness! As if turning their backs to you, they are fixed spellbound in carnal works as if in your shadow, even though at the same time the things which delight them there still retain something of the reflected glow of your Light. But when shadows are loved, they make the eye of the mind more languid and more inadequate to look upon you."

Speaking of the "numbers" or rational proportions which constitute the beauty of temporal objects in the *De musica* (6. 14. 46), he says that "these, because they are temporal, like a raft in the waves, are neither to be thrown aside as burdensome nor embraced as if they were firmly fixed, but using them well, we shall come to do without them." To summarize, we love that which is beautiful (*ibid.*, 6. 13. 38), but the sensible beauty of creation and artificial beauty, like that of eloquence or music, are attractions to be used, or used with joy, as a means of attaining a beauty that is more properly beautiful and more truly lovable. In general, beauty has exactly the same function that we have seen attributed to figurative expression: it is a means of approaching an underlying truth. And this approach is made, in both instances, through the action of the reason.

A strong didactic element is implicit in this theory, for both the pleasant discovery of what lies beneath the puzzling surface of a figurative expression, and the perception of the invisible reflected in the beauty of created objects, involve a process of learning something which may either be already known in another way or entirely new. In the same way, either the rhetorical or musical adornment of language should assist the didactic purposes of the language. The artist is, in effect, a teacher whose efforts are directed toward the revelation of a truth which is not only beautiful in itself, but which is also the source of all other beauty. The analogy between teaching and the demonstration of beauty is made explicit in the *De catechizandis rudibus*, where St. Augustine is instructing those teachers who are reluctant because they must repeat elementary matters with which they are thoroughly familiar (12. 17). Such teachers are advised to join themselves in a bond of love with those whom they are instructing so that they can share with them the "newness" of what is being said. "Does it not usually happen," he asks, "when we show a great and beautiful prospect, either in the country or in the city, to someone who has never seen it before, and which we, because we have seen it frequently, see without pleasure, that our own delight is renewed in the newness of his?" Having introduced the subject of beauty, St. Augustine hastens to add that "we do not wish those whom we love to wonder and rejoice when they perceive the works of the hands of men, but we wish to lead them to the art and conception of the artist and thence to rise in admiration and praise of God, the Creator of all, and the most fruitful end of love." This hierarchical progression typifies the "use" of beauty.

Whether beauty is used or abused obviously depends on the inclination or "will" of the observer. If he fails to act reasonably, he will refer the beauty of what he sees to his own satisfaction in a material sense rather then to God; that is, he will act in cupidity rather than in charity. The processes by means of which these alternatives are exploited are susceptible to analysis, and, indeed, an elaborate account of them in terms of "numbers" appears in the sixth book of St. Augustine's *De musica*. A few general principles from this very complex source will suffice to serve as background for simpler and more familiar descriptions of the same processes. In the first place, St. Augustine assumes that the human spirit is guided by God "nulla natura interposita," without the intervention of a creature, since the *Verbum Dei* resides in what St. Paul calls the "interior man" (Rom. 7. 22). This reality is not approached through intuition or inspiration but through a rational process analogous with Platonic Recollection. Moreover, the spirit is seen as a principle which animates the body. It is not subjected to the body as material which may be shaped by it, for "omnis materia fabricatore deterior"—all material is less than its fabricator—and the spirit is superior to the body. Its action, in adjusting the body to stimuli it receives, produces sensations. And it forms *phantasiae* or images as a result of this activity, and these may be retained in the memory of sensible things. Sometimes these images are combined to produce *phantasmata* of things not actually perceived. When in the course of its operations the spirit suffers, it does not suffer from the body but from itself as it adjusts itself to the body. It then becomes diminished, for when the spirit turns away from God its Master, to follow its servant the body, it necessarily worsens itself. "For the spirit should be ruled by a superior and should rule an inferior. Only God is superior to it, and only the body is inferior to it, if you consider every spirit as a whole. Just as it cannot be complete without its Lord, it cannot excel without its servant. Just as its Lord is greater than it is, so also is its servant less than it is. This is the reason that when it is attentive to its Lord, it is both greater in itself and its servant is greater through it. But when its Lord is neglected, and it is intent upon its servant which is led by carnal concupiscence, it perceives the motions which that servant communicates to it, and it is lessened" (6. 5. 13). The spirit is therefore most powerful and the body most healthful when the spirit perceives and loves the "numbers" or constituents of beauty which are transmitted to it from God, and which it finds, through a rational motion, in itself. The same beauty may be reflected in creatures, or in the phantasies and phantasms derived from the perception of creatures, but it is there an inferior beauty.

And when the spirit, through an association with the flesh, comes to love this inferior beauty, it becomes contaminated. Its contamination is reinforced by pride, through which the spirit seeks to be without a master, as if imitating but not following God. On the other hand, St. Augustine shows that through prudence, which enables us to distinguish between the eternal and the temporal; temperance, which enables the spirit to free itself from inferior beauty; fortitude, which strengthens the spirit in adversity; and justice, which enables us to preserve the hierarchical order described above, the spirit may achieve peace and harmony with the body in the contemplation of eternal beauty. Since the beautiful is that which is loved, and since love is the lesson of the Scriptures, it is not difficult to understand that St. Augustine regarded the problem of the beautiful as a matter of profound importance.

We should notice that he eliminates what we should call the "imagination" as a source for true beauty. In a letter to Nebridius (7) written at about the same time the *De musica* was being composed, he points out that conceptions like "the eternal" are not derived from the senses and owe nothing to the imaginative faculty. They are, in a Socratic sense, "recollected," since they are retained by the memory from another source. He then divides phantasies into three classes in accordance with whether they originate with the senses, the imagination, or the reason. The first class is made up of images of things actually experienced. The second is made up of imaginary objects and fictions, and the third embraces what we should call abstractions, including things like geometrical figures. The last two classes, the *phantasmata* of the *De musica*, are more deceptive than the first, but the first also is deceptive, since the senses are an unreliable guide to the truth.[33] Hence in his description of the blessed state which the soul seeks in the *De musica* (6. 16. 51), he includes as a condition of that blessedness the elimination of all *phantasmata* from the memory.

The theological importance of a theory which will account for the proper function of the beautiful (or the lovable) in a moral sense is illustrated by the prominence which aesthetic matters have in the tropological description of the Fall of Man which John the

[33] For an account of the deceptiveness of "fantasie" from the fourteenth century, see Jehan le Bel, *Li ars d'amour*, ed. J. Petit (Brussels, 1867-1869), I, 201-203. Cf. Chaucer, Miller's Tale, 3191-3192, 3611-3613; Merchant's Tale, 1577ff.

Scot includes in the *De divisione naturae*. Scotus' exposition shows unmistakable Augustinian influence, and it will help us to understand the significance of certain similar accounts in the work of St. Augustine itself. The passage to be considered includes the famous example of the precious vase.[34] For purposes of tropological analysis, Scotus envisages Paradise as human nature, which includes in a Pauline sense two regions: interior and exterior. The first of these is the man, called νοῦς, who represents the spirit, and in it dwells truth and all good, which is the Word of God—"veritas et omne bonum, quod est Verbum Dei." Hence, this is the habitat of reason. It contains the Tree of Life, called πᾶν, which was placed there by God, and the *fons vitae*, the Fountain of Life, from which flow the four streams of the cardinal virtues. This interior region should be "married" to the exterior region in a manner prefigured by the marriage of Christ and the Church. The exterior region, or the woman, is called αἴσθησις, since it is the region of the corporal senses, and it is a region of falsity and vain phantasies—"falsitatis et vanarum phantasiarum." It contains the Tree of Knowledge of Good and Evil, called γνωστόν, and the serpent, which is illicit delight, *illicita delectatio*. These details should give us no trouble if we remember the convention in accordance with which the spirit is "married" to the flesh and also recall the Augustinian attitude toward phantasies. The allegorical machinery is simply the conventional machinery of spiritual exegesis. To continue with the figure, it is obvious that in a garden of this kind, true beauty and delight are to be found in the inner region, and that whatever impresses the outer region as being beautiful should be referred to the inner region for judgment. But this is not always done, since men are inclined to act effeminately rather than virtuously, and when it is not done, Scotus describes what happens as follows:

"When a phantasy of gold or of some precious material is impressed on the corporal sense, the phantasy seems to that sense beautiful and naturally attractive because it is founded upon a creature which is extrinsically good. But the woman, that is, the carnal sense, is deceived and delighted, failing to perceive hiding beneath this false and fancied [*phantastica*] beauty a malice that

[34] The material in this discussion is derived from *De div. nat.*, PL, 122, cols. 825-829.

is cupidity which is the 'root of all evil' [1 Tim. 6. 10]. 'Whosoever shall look on a woman to lust after her,' Our Lord says
[Matt. 5. 28], 'hath already committed adultery with her in his
heart.' But if He had spoken openly, He might have explained,
whoever impresses the phantasy of feminine beauty on his carnal
sense has already committed adultery in his thought, desiring the
wickedness of libido, which secretly attracts him beneath the imagination of the false beauty of that woman. . . ."

The sudden appearance of the much maligned passage from
Matthew is a little startling here, and it is easy to misinterpret it.
But commenting on this text, Scotus explains that in it *woman*
stands for the sensible beauty of all creatures, and that the libido
implied by *adultery* is a figure for all of the vices, or, that is, for
any kind of cupidinous desire. All error thus begins in the exterior
or aesthetic region of the garden, and through its delight in the
phantasy of a beauty which it falsifies, it may corrupt and pervert
the inner region of the garden, just as Eve successfully tempted
Adam in the Fall. And the allurement of feminine beauty is a
figure for that false "fantastic" attractiveness which once decisively
perverted and, Scotus would say, still perennially perverts the mind
of man.

We should observe that the evil involved in this process of per-
version does not lie in the object. Nor does it necessarily form a
part of the beauty of the object. It lies in the libido, the cupidity,
which Scotus describes as lurking beneath that beauty when it becomes a part of an image formed by the corporal senses. This fact
is clearly illustrated in the example of the precious vase, which we
should now be in a position to understand: "Let us suppose two
men, one a wise man in no way tickled or pricked by the goad of
avarice, but the other stupid, avaricious, everywhere transfixed and
lacerated by the thorns of perverse cupidity. When these two have
been placed in one location, let there be brought a vase made of
refined gold, decorated with precious stones, fashioned in a beautiful shape, fit for royal use. Both look at it, the wise man and the
miser, both receive the image of the vase in the corporal sense,
both place it in the memory and consider it in thought. And the
man who is wise refers the beauty of this vase whose image he considers within himself completely and immediately to the praise of
the Creator of natural things. No allurement of cupidity subverts

him, no poison of cupidity infects his pure mind, no libido contaminates him. But the other, as soon as he takes in the image of the vase, burns with the fire of cupidity. . . ." Instead of referring the beauty of the image he contemplates to God, he plunges into "a most foul pool of cupidity." The location of the difficulty in this hypothetical example which describes the Fall of Man as it is re-enacted by every sinner is of extreme importance. Matters become critical when the image formed by the corporal sense is placed in the memory and considered in thought. If the thought pleasurably contemplates cupidinous satisfaction, the result is evil: the downfall of the reason and the corruption of the garden are distinct possibilities. On the other hand, if the thought refers the beauty of the image to the Creator, all is well. The "man" retains his hierarchical ascendancy over the "woman"; the spirit continues to guide its servant the body; the beauty of the *woman* remains innocent.

It should be sufficiently apparent that the reaction to corporal beauty touches upon some of the most fundamental problems of Christian theology. The fact that Eve saw that the forbidden tree was "fair to the eyes and delightful to behold" is obviously a matter of profound significance. A brief glance at two further tropological analyses of the Fall, both of which occur in the works of St. Augustine, and both of which enjoyed considerable influence during the Middle Ages, will help us to appreciate the urgency of the problem of the beautiful. If we can formulate a general pattern on the basis of these materials in Scotus and St. Augustine, we shall have at our disposal a very valuable medieval commonplace. The simpler of the two accounts in the works of St. Augustine appears in the *De sermone Domini in monte* (1. 12. 33-37). It begins with a quotation of Matt. 5. 27-28: "You have heard that it was said to them of old: Thou shalt not commit adultery [Exod. 20. 14]. But I say to you, that whosoever shall look on a woman," etc. St. Augustine, contrary to prevailing modern opinion, finds the justice of the second command, which warns against sin in the heart, to be greater than the first, which is concerned only with overt action. At the same time, the second confirms and fulfills the first. To lust after a woman and to 'look on a woman to lust after her' are different, since the second implies not only that the observer is tickled by fleshly delight, but also that he has con-sented to this stimulation and is encouraging it. In other words, he has passed through three stages which are involved in the commission of any sin: suggestion, delight (or pleasurable thought), and consent. Only after consent takes place in the mind does the sinner prepare for overt action, a sin "in deed." If sins "in deed" are repeated, the sinner may come to sin "in habit." The suggestion takes place when the attractive object is perceived; the delight arises in the contemplation of the object, or of its image, with a view to fleshly satisfaction; and if this delight is not repressed by the reason, the reason consents to it. This process, St. Augustine explains, is analogous with the process of the Fall. Suggestion enters the senses subtly, like the serpent. There the carnal appetite, or Eve, may take pleasure in what is suggested and cause the reason, or the man, to consent, whereupon he is expelled from Paradise, or, that is, from the light of justice into death. What happens in such instances may be thought of in terms of beauty. All things are beautiful, St. Augustine says, "in their order," a concept which we shall examine presently. But if of our own free choice we descend from a higher beauty, proper to reason, to a lower beauty, proper to the senses, we deserve the penalty which results by virtue of Divine Law.[35] As Scotus does after him, St. Augustine generalizes the *adultery* in the scriptural text to mean the action of any evil cupidity, pointing out that the Scripture frequently uses *fornicatio* to mean any kind of turning away from God.[36] The two accounts differ in their treatment of the serpent, but their general contours are quite similar. Both emphasize the abuse of the beautiful which takes place when the carnal sense is permitted by the reason to react pleasurably to the "woman," and to contemplate it as a potential source of pleasant satisfaction. Needless to say, St. Augustine's formulation exerted considerable influence during

[35] Thus there are three kinds of sin: in the heart, in deed, and in habit; for after consent has led to action, the individual is more than ever sensitive to suggestion, so that the habit of sin readily follows from the initial deed. These are, so to speak, sins in the house, sins outside the gate, and sins in the grave. Christ miraculously cured the first type when He said, to the daughter of Jairus, "Damsel (I say to thee), arise" (Mark 5. 41). He cured the second when He said to the widow's son, "Young man, I say to thee, arise" (Luke 7. 14). And he cured the third when he "cried with a loud voice: Lazarus, come forth" (John 11. 43).

[36] This is not merely a "patristic" concept. For the later Middle Ages, cf. Nicolas de Goran, *In quatuor Evangel.* (Antwerp, 1617), p. 40, where St. Augustine is quoted, and Holcot, *Super librum sapientiae* (Basel, 1586), p. 538.

the Middle Ages. Bede's comment on Matt. 5. 28, which was incorporated into the *Glossa ordinaria*, calls attention to the same three steps, but calls the second *propassio* and the third *passio*, probably because the word *passio* implied an action of the mind contrary to reason.[37] Such *passio*, the *Glossa* tells us, is readily observable in angry men and in lovers.[38]

A somewhat more refined tropological account of the Fall, which follows the same general pattern as the one we have just examined, appears in the *De Trinitate* (12. 12). Here Adam and Eve are made parallel to the two parts of the reason: Adam represents the higher part of the reason whose function is *sapientia*, or wisdom, and Eve represents the lower part of the reason, whose function is *scientia*, or knowledge of things seen. The higher part of the reason is, as it were, "married" to the lower part of the reason, and should dominate it as the husband dominates his wife. In this context, the serpent represents the motion of the senses. It tempts the lower reason which may in turn tempt the higher reason with the "fruit" thus presented to it. The various possibilities here are used to define the gravity of sin in a given instance. Thus if the sin consists merely in the motion of the senses and it is resisted by the lower reason, the sin is "venial." If the lower reason falls and begins to indulge in pleasure of thought—*delectatio cogitationis*—but this pleasure is set aside by the higher reason, the sin is still venial. However, if the higher part of the reason either accepts the "fruit" or allows the lower part of the reason to indulge too long in pleasurable thought, the sin is mortal, the "marriage" between the two parts of the reason is corrupted, and the result is "adultery." This account was incorporated into the *Sententiae* of Peter Lombard (2. 24. 6-13), where it became the basis for a great deal of academic discussion during the Middle Ages.[39] Lombard adds that since the lower part of the reason is closely allied to the

[37] See *On the City of God*, 8. 17, where the idea is derived from Cicero.

[38] *PL*, 92, col. 28; *Glossa ordinaria*, *PL*, 114, col. 94. Cf. St. Gregory, *Moralia*, *PL*, 76, col. 656; Rabanus, *PL*, 107, col. 811; Paschasius Radbertus, *PL*, 120, cols. 247-248.

[39] See O. Lottin, "La doctrine morale des mouvements premiers de l'appetit sensitif aux xiie et xiiiesiècles," *Archives d'hist. doct. et litt. du m. a.*, vi (1931), 49-173. The basic interpretation was expressed in a wide variety of sources. E.g., see Odo of Cluny, *Occupatio*, 2. 167-175; Albericus of London (Mythographus Vaticanus Tertius) ed. G. H. Bode (Cellis, 1834), pp. 182-183; or the account of Gen. 3 in the *Moralisationes* of Nicolas de Lyra.

senses, it may with justice be called "sensuality." Hence it is possible to summarize all three of our tropological interpretations of the Fall as accounts of the interaction of "Reason and Sensuality," so long, that is, as we refrain from emptying them of their content for the sake of a convenient formula. If we look at them together, we see that they have not only a very similar general shape but also one feature in common. All three insist on the critical importance of the second stage in the process, for it is here that the alternative courses of action present themselves. Whether we call "Eve" the exterior man, the stage of "delight" in contemplating the image of an object of desire or wrath, or the lower part of the reason capable of *delectatio cogitationis* does not especially matter. It does matter that the mind should not be allowed to dwell on the "woman," the image of corporal beauty, with a view to pleasurable physical satisfaction. This is an "abuse" or "waste" of such beauty, which should be referred instead to the reason, and specifically to that part of the reason—the *Verbum Dei*, or the higher part—which perceives the Laws of God (rather than those of nature alone), and whose function is wisdom. And this is not simply a principle of "aesthetics" to be applied when considering the uses of eloquence or music. It is relevant there, and indeed relevant to the individual's reaction to beauty of any kind, but it is also one of the most basic principles of Christian philosophy. Where the spirit is concerned, it was felt to be a matter of life and death.

We may well inquire more specifically how the very unromantic business of referring corporal beauty to the reason, or to the higher part of the reason, is to be managed. Two related procedures are evident in the writings of St. Augustine and his medieval successors. The first is an application of the principle we have seen stated in the *De musica* and explained in the *De catechizandis rudibus*: "omnis materia fabricatore deterior"—all material is inferior to its fabricator. Hence the creations of man are inferior to the mind of man, and that mind, together with all other creatures of God, is inferior to God.[40] A work of art should thus lead us to appreciate the conception of the artist, and this, like the beauty of nature itself, should lead us to a contemplation of the immutable beauty

[40] For an application of this principle to knowledge, see *On Christian Doctrine*, 2. 28. 57.

which is its source. This principle is stated succinctly in the Book of Wisdom (13. 5): "a magnitudine enim speciei et creaturae cognoscibiliter poterit creator horum videri." The second procedure is a more concrete development of the same pattern of thought. Since it is the things which are the referents of the words in Scripture which are of signifying force, and not the words themselves, a beautiful object may be taken as a figurative expression representing a principle which forms a part of what, as we shall see, was thought to be the immediate source of created beauty: the Providential Order. Things, as Hugh of St. Victor explains, constitute the "vox Dei ad homines," the voice of God speaking to men.[41] Whether this voice was heard in the things mentioned in Scripture or in the created world itself, which came to be called "the Book of God's work," it was an enigmatic voice. To find

> tongues in trees, books in the running brooks,
> Sermons in stones, and good in everything

requires not only that the fascination of the exterior man for "painted pomp" be set aside, but also that the reason be prepared to ascend from the visible to the invisible.

Some illustration may make these points clear. When Suger was rebuilding the church of St. Denis, he included a new set of bronze doors. On them, he caused to be inscribed some verses, beginning,

> Whoever seeks to exalt the honor of these doors
> Should marvel not at the gold and the expense, but at the
> workmanship;
> The work is nobly luminous, but because it is nobly luminous
> It will illuminate minds that they may travel through true
> lights
> To the True Light where Christ is the True Door.[42]

If we bear in mind as background John the Scot's doctrine of the hierarchy of lights,[43] we shall have no difficulty in finding both

[41] *Didascalicon*, ed. Buttimer, p. 97.

[42] See E. Panofsky, *Abbot Suger* (Princeton, 1946), pp. 46-48. In this instance, I have preferred not to use Professor Panofsky's translation.

[43] For a brief account, see E. Gilson, *History of Christian Philosophy in the Middle Ages* (New York, 1955), pp. 120-122. Cf. the Augustinian doctrine of illumination: *De libero arb.*, 2. 8. 21; 29. 26; *City of God*, 9. 2; *De Trinitate*, 12. 15. 2.

of the principles we have just described in these verses. The "gold and expense," fit objects for pleasurable thought on the part of the "carnal sense," are to be passed over in favor of a consideration of the workmanship. The luminous conception thus revealed should lead us to the True Light and spiritual illumination. Meanwhile, the door of the Church is a "light" or sign of Him who said, "I am the door" (John 10. 9).[44] In this instance, the workmanship which transcends the material is reinforced in its effect by the enigmatic significance of the church door. Again, in speaking of the rear panel of the altar, Suger assures us that although the materials are extremely lavish, the form resulting from the workmanship is so marvelous that one might say, "materiam superbat opus"—the workmanship surpassed the material (Ovid, *Met.*, 2. 5).[45] Those who recognized the quotation would recall that it was originally applied to the doors of the temple of the Sun, and this in turn would suggest once more the familiar *sol iustitiae*, who is Christ. Suger's most famous aesthetic observations are those concerning the precious gems with which he ornamented his church. Noticing that all the gems of Ezech. 28. 13 except the carbuncle are before him, he adds, "When—out of my delight in the beauty of the house of God—the loveliness of the many colored gems has called me away from external cares, and worthy meditation has induced me to reflect, transferring that which is material to that which is immaterial, on the diversity of the sacred virtues: then it seems to me that I see myself dwelling, as it were, in some strange region of the universe which neither exists entirely in the slime of the earth nor entirely in the purity of Heaven; and that, by the grace of God, I can be transported from this inferior to that higher world in an anagogical manner."[46]

This should not be taken as a merely personal statement; it represents the pattern of thought which Suger hoped that all of those who looked on the precious gems which adorned his church would

[44] See John of Garland, *De mysteriis ecclesiae* in F. W. Otto, *Commentarii critici in codicis bibliothecae academiae Gissensis* (Giessen, 1842), p. 132: "Ecclesiae porta Jhesus est." For an excellent illustration of the manner in which this concept is implied, although not overtly indicated, in the structure of an actual Romanesque portal, see Joseph Gantner, *Romanische Plastik* (Vienna, 1948), pp. 26ff.

[45] See Panofsky, *Abbot Suger*, pp. 60-62.

[46] Panofsky's translation, *ibid.*, pp. 62, 64.

follow. First, external cares—the cares of the "exterior man," the "painted pomp" of "envious courts" in Shakespeare's language—must be set aside. Then one proceeds from the material to the immaterial by a "worthy meditation" on the "virtues" of the gems, or, in other words, on their enigmatical significances. We can learn explicitly what these virtues were by consulting a treatise like Bede's *De tabernaculo et vasis ejus*,[47] where we find that they should always appear in the heart of the priest. The onyx, for example, is a red stone with white areas around it representing the ardor of charity or the light of knowledge surrounded by chastity. These and other virtues like them made up what were thought of as "the pleasure of the Paradise of God" referred to in Ezechiel, so that by contemplating them and their multitudinous implications one might ascend "in an anagogical manner" toward that Paradise. Thus by considering either the spiritual significance of a beautiful object or by reflecting on the skill of the ultimate Artificer one might use rather than abuse the beauty of the object.

One further example should suffice. In an effort to establish amicable relations with England, Innocent III at one time sent King John four gold rings adorned with jewels. His intentions regarding the significance of the gift were made unmistakable in an accompanying letter. There he said that he wished the King to understand especially the form, number, material, and color of the gift and to value the "mystery" implied by the gift more highly than the gift itself. The roundness of the rings, he explained, signifies eternity, "which has neither beginning nor end." The royal understanding should thus move from the terrestrial to the celestial, from temporal things to eternal things. The fact that there are four rings suggests the *numerus quadratus* which signifies *constantium mentis*, constancy of mind, neither to be cast down in adversity nor elevated in prosperity. Such constancy is manifested, moreover, by the four cardinal virtues. Gold, the material from which the rings were made, signifies wisdom, a virtue especially appropriate to a king. The green color of the emerald signifies faith, the blue of sapphire signifies hope, the redness of the ruby signifies charity, and the light of the topaz signifies good works. Thus, Innocent wrote, "in the emerald you have what you should believe,

[47] *PL*, 91, esp. cols. 470ff. Bede uses the word "virtues." Panofsky's note, p. 183, on "medicinal and magical qualities" seems to me to be misleading.

in the sapphire what you should hope, in the ruby what you should love, and in the topaz what you should do, so that you 'shall go from virtue to virtue' until 'the God of gods shall be seen in Sion' " (Ps. 83. 8).[48] In effect, the letter invites King John to consider his rings in exactly the same way that Suger considered his precious stones. But such consideration would have required that the "significances" involved be regarded as something more than, mere formulas, as aspects of a very real order of being beneath the material surface of things.

It is clear that Suger was "moved" by the beauty of his gems and that Pope Innocent wished the rings he sent to King John to be "moving" also. But in both instances the motion was deliberately directed in a certain way. Although "motion" in the direction of virtue may seem strange to us today as an aesthetic concept, we must recognize the fact that the use of artistry, whether audible or visible, as a stimulant to the love of God through virtue could be extremely pleasant and satisfying to those who sought to be charitable. When Dante says, therefore, that the purpose of the *Commedia* is moral, and that it is designed to produce practical results,[49] he is not simply concocting an "excuse" for his literary activity; he is expressing, rather, a traditional tenet of Christian aesthetics which he undoubtedly felt very deeply himself and expected his readers to feel also. Again, the same tradition lay behind Petrarch's feeling that Aristotle was a poorer teacher than Cicero: "Ille docet attentius, quid est virtus, urget iste potentius, ut colatur uirtus"— the former teaches more accurately what a virtue is; the latter urges more powerfully that virtue be cultivated.[50] It does us little good to know what virtue is unless we love what we understand to be right: "It is one thing to know and another to love, one thing to understand and another to desire what is understood. Aristotle teaches, I do not deny, what a virtue is. But the reading of Aristotle either lacks entirely, or almost entirely, the verbal goad and

---

[48] The text from Matthew Paris, *Chronica maiora*, is printed by Otto Lehmann-Brockhaus, *Lateinische Schriftquellen zur Kunst in England, Wales, und Schottland* (Munich, 1955-), III, 110-111. It is noteworthy in this example that the "allegories" involved are not literally consistent. The fact that there are four rings suggests the cardinal virtues, but the stones in the rings do not reinforce this idea; they stand instead for the theological virtues plus "good works."

[49] See the close of the Epistle to Can Grande della Scala.

[50] *Contra galli calumnias, Opera* (Basel, 1581), p. 1082.

fire by means of which the mind is inflamed to the love of virtue
and urged to the hatred of vice. He who seeks these things may
find them among the Latins, especially in Cicero and Seneca, and
—a fact that may seem astonishing—in Horace, a poet indeed
thorny in style but most delightful in meaning [*sententiis*]. What
does it profit to know what a virtue is, if being known it is not
loved? Or of what use is it to know what a sin is, if once known it
is not detested?"[51] Here the literary embellishment, the "verbal
goad and fire" of writers in antiquity whom Petrarch admired for
their anticipation of Christian ideas of virtue, has a function very
similar to that of the beauty of Suger's church.

Chaucer, who wrote for one of the most sophisticated courts in
medieval Europe at a time when sophistication implied orthodoxy
in religious matters, at least among the feudal nobility as distinct
from the academic clergy,[52] was thoroughly familiar with the principles we have been discussing. The underlying theological doctrines are explained in the Parson's Tale where there is a familiar
allegorization of the Fall: "The womman thanne saugh that the
tree was good to feedyng, and fair to the eyen, and delitable to the
sighte. She took of the fruyt of the tree, and eet it, and yaf to hire
housbonde, and he eet, and anoon the eyen of hem bothe openeden.
And whan that they knewe that they were naked, they sowed of
fige leves a maner of breches to hiden hire membres. There may
ye seen that deedly synne hath, first, suggestion of the feend, as
sheweth heere by the naddre; and afterward, the delit of the flessh,
as sheweth heere by Eve; and after that, the consentynge of resoun, as sheweth heere by Adam. . . ."[53]

The Fall of Adam, the parson explains, produced concupiscence
of the flesh, the stain of original sin, or "the lawe of oure membres."
All men are subject to its motion. "And after that, a man bi-
thynketh hym wheither he wol doon, or no, thilke thing to which
he is tempted. And thanne, if that a man withstonde and weyve

[51] *De sui ipsius et multorum ignorantia*, ed. Capelli (Paris, 1906), p. 68.

[52] John of Gaunt is said to have at one time patiently explained the orthodox
doctrine of the Eucharist to Wiclif. Dom David Knowles, *The Religious Orders
in England* (Cambridge, 1955), p. 112, calls Chaucer "an excellent example of
the conventional and orthodox party which gained influence during the latter
part of the reign of Richard II." However, I believe that he somewhat under-
estimates the profundity of Chaucer's faith.

[53] *Works*, ed. Robinson, 2 ed., p. 237.

the first entisynge of his flessh and of the feend, thanne is it no synne; and if it so be that he do nat so, thanne feeleth he anoon a flambe of delit. And thanne is it good to be war, and kepen hym wel, or elles he wol falle anon into consentynge of synne; and thanne wol he do it, if he may have tyme and place. . . . And thus is synne acompliced by temptacioun, by delit, and by consentynge. . . ."

We should notice again that the critical moment occurs when the "flambe of delit" accompanies the contemplation of the "fruit," for then a man must "kepen him wel." The parson had already elaborated this point: "This is to seyn, a man shal be very repentaunt for all his synnes that he hath doon in delit of his thoght; for delit is ful perilous. For ther been two maner consentynges: that oon of hem is cleped consentynge of affeccioun, whan a man is moeved to do synne, and deliteth hym longe for to thynke on that synne; and his reson aperceyveth it wel that it is synne agayns the lawe of God, and yet his resoun refreyneth nat his foul delit or talent, though he se wel apertly that it is agayns the reverence of God. . . . For certes, ther is no deedly synne, that it nas first in mannes thought, and after that in his delit, and so forth into consentynge and into dede."[54]

The parson was also aware, as St. Augustine and John the Scot had been before him, that sin involves the subversion of a hierarchy: "And ye shul understonde that in mannes synne is every manere of ordre or ordinaunce turned up-so-doun. For it is sooth that God, and resoun, and sensualitee, and the body of man been so ordeyned that everich of thise foure thynges sholde have lordshipe over that oother; as thus: God sholde have lordshipe over resoun, and resoun over sensualitee, and sensualitee over the body of man. But soothly, whan man synneth, al this ordre or ordinaunce is turned up-so-doun."[55] It is obvious that what is "fair to the eyen, and delitable to the sighte" should not, in accordance with these principles, be turned to the "delit of the flessh" in contemplation, so that the "ordinaunce" of man's nature is in danger of being turned "up-so-doun."

Since Chaucer has left us neither essays nor literary correspondence, we have no explicit statements from him specifically concerning aesthetic matters. Nevertheless, we may find instances in his

[54] *Ibid.*, p. 235.   [55] *Ibid.*, p. 234.

work where an object of beauty is properly treated. For example, in the Clerk's Tale, Walter looks upon the yet unwed Griselda with an eye more to her virtue than to any attributes she may have in common with the young Alisoun of the Miller's Tale:

> Upon Grisilde, this povre creature,
> Ful ofte sithe this markys sette his ye
> As he on huntyng rood paraventure;
> And whan it fil that he myghte hire espye,
> He noght with wantown lookyng of folye
> His eyen caste on hire, but in sad wyse
> Upon hir chiere he wolde hym ofte avyse.
>
> Commendynge in his herte hir wommanhede,
> And eek hir vertu, passynge any wight
> Of so yong age, as wel in chiere as dede.
> For thogh the peple have no greet insight
> In vertu, he considered ful right
> Hir bountee . . . .

We have been prepared beforehand to accept a reaction to Griselda along these lines as something fully justifiable, for she is beautiful both in intention and in deed:

> But for to speke of vertuous beautee,
> Thanne was she oon the faireste under sonne;
> For povreliche yfostred up was she,
> No likerous lust was thurgh hire herte yronne.
> Wel ofter of the welle than of the tonne
> She drank, and for she wolde vertu plese,
> She knew wel labour, but noon ydel ese.

This type of beauty, perceptible to a kind of "insight" with which "the peple" in general are not gifted, was thought to be especially commendable. For example, in his comment on Cant. 4. 1—"How beautiful art thou, my love, how beautiful art thou!"—William of Newburgh, referring to the Blessed Virgin Mary, observes, "Again, in this repetition he shows her to be beautiful within and without: within in intention, without in action. Nor do these words concern corporal beauty, but that beauty which is either within or from within. Corporal beauty is perceived by the corporal eye, but that beauty which is either within or from within is perceived by the divine eye."[56] Walter does not look upon Griselda "to lust after her." His is not, in other words, the "wantown lookyng of folye," which leads to pleasant thought about an object with reference to the corporal sense. Like the beauty of Suger's gems, the beauty of Griselda is for Walter a "vertuous beautee." Like the "corones two" brought to Cecelie and Valerian, it can be seen by no one "but he be chaast and hate vileynye."

These illustrations demonstrate that what St. Augustine would consider to be the "use" of beauty was a fairly common aesthetic principle throughout the Middle Ages. By referring the beauty of sensible objects directly to the Creator, by looking upon the objects as figures, or by doing both, the image of the beautiful might be referred to the reason. Virtue itself might be an object of love when it was discerned either in the writings of the pagan poets or under the surface attractiveness of a human being, and in either case it was aesthetically pleasing. We might summarize these principles simply by saying that the world should be looked upon with the "interior eye" rather than with the "exterior eye" alone, provided, that is, that we do not forget the connotations of these terms. However, the "exterior eye" is in most of us much more active than the other, and illustrations of its operations, which may lead the observer astray, are much more common in medieval literature than are illustrations of the use of beauty. Since it is with the "exterior eye" that modern aesthetics is principally concerned, our taste for interior understanding having considerably declined, even among the devout, we have been inclined to take the materials of these illustrations as being somehow exemplary of proper action, when, in fact, they were designed to show an abuse. It is currently fashionable to associate them with "courtly love," a conception calculated to make medieval literature more harmonious with romantic and post-romantic attitudes, and this concept has been reinforced by resort to various kinds of exoticism: Bulgarian heresies, Albigensian metaphysics, and so on. However,

[56] *In Cant.*, Cambridge, CUL MS Gg. 4. 16, fol. 25. To use Augustinian terms, the beauty that is within or from within may be perceived by the "interior eye" rather than by the "exterior eye," which perceives corporal beauty. Cf. William of Auvergne, *Tractatus de bono et malo*, quoted by Dom Henry Pouillon, "La beauté, propriété transcendentale, chez les scholastiques," *Archives d'hist. doct. et litt. d. m. a.*, XXI (1946), p. 316.

once we understand that after the middle of the twelfth century an iconographic narrative *motif* based on the formulations of St. Augustine, John the Scot, and others concerning the abuse of beauty developed and became conventional, we shall no longer be forced to conclude that a large body of medieval literature represents a philosophical tradition outside of the main stream of medieval culture.

We should recall, in the first place, that the pronouncement of the New Law concerning the subject is phrased in terms of looking on a woman, taken as the type of worldly attractiveness, "to lust after her" (Matt. 5. 28); that the critical juncture in the process occurs when the image or phantasy of the woman is perceived by the corporal sense or the lower part of the reason and impressed on the memory; and that the trouble really begins when this image, because of the stimulus of cupidity or desire, is made the object of delightful thought with a view to sensual satisfaction envisaged as fornication or adultery. Further, if the reason consents to this delight, it is said to suffer a "passion" of a type recognizable among lovers. The whole procedure involves three steps: suggestion, delightful thought, and consent or passion. With these facts in mind, together with an awareness of the symbolic or contextual significance of the terms as they are relevant to the Fall and to the progress of sin in the individual, we should have no trouble in grasping the significance of the definition of "love" in the *De amore* of Andreas Capellanus: "Love is a certain inborn suffering [*passio*] derived from the sight of and excessive meditation upon the beauty of the opposite sex, which causes each one to wish above all things the embraces of the other and by common desire to carry out all of love's precepts in the other's embrace."[57]

This definition may be seen as nothing but a re-statement in terms of "love" of the traditional process of the abuse of beauty. The "love," that is, is not simple desire, but passionate and unreasoning cupidity. The three steps are clearly marked: sight, excessive meditation, and passion. To emphasize the necessity for "immoderate thought," which, as we have seen, is an important and necessary prelude to any real passion, Andreas continues, "That this suffering is inborn I shall show you clearly, because if you will look at the truth and distinguish carefully you will see that it does

[57] Trans. J. J. Parry, *The Art of Courtly Love* (New York, 1941), p. 28. The quotations below are from p. 29.

not arise out of any action; only from the reflection of the mind upon what it sees does this suffering [*passio*] come." He continues his explanation by paraphrasing the scriptural Law: "For when a man sees some woman fit for love and shaped accordingly to his taste, he begins at once to lust after her in his heart; then the more he thinks about her the more he burns with love, until he comes to a fuller meditation." The process of committing "adultery" in the heart is next developed: "Presently, he begins to think about the fashioning of the woman and to differentiate her limbs, to think about what she does, and pry into the secrets of her body, and he desires to put each part of it to its fullest use." In terms of St. Augustine's account in the *De sermone Domini in monte*, the "lover" is now ready for sin "in deed," since the sin has already been committed in the heart. Andreas describes the transition from thought to action: "Then after he has come to this complete meditation, love cannot hold the reins, but he proceeds at once to action; straightway he strives to get a helper and to find an intermediary."[58] Andreas insists, finally, that only an excessive meditation, *immoderata cogitatio*, will suffice to create the passion he describes. The reasons for this stipulation should be sufficiently obvious.

That the implications of this definition and its elaboration were plain to medieval readers is evident from the reactions of Albertanus of Brescia and Jean de Meun. Albertanus, whose writings include the source of Chaucer's Melibee and generally show little tendency to deviate from commonplace orthodoxy, says that Andreas' subject is cupidity and that his definition is a definition of cupidity.[59] Although Christine de Pisan's puritanical squeamishness about the *Roman de la rose* has prevailed in modern times,[60]

[58] The "reins" are a common figure for the restraint of reason or temperance. Cf. Fig. 6, and the discussion in the fifth chapter below.

[59] See the Italian translation of Albertanus' treatise on love printed by F. Selmi, *Dei trattati morali Albertano de Brescia* (Bologna, 1873), pp. 203-204, and the quotation from it in D. W. Robertson, Jr., "The Subject of the *De amore* of Andreas Capellanus," *MP*, L (1953), p. 151. Pietro di Dante, *Commentarium* (Florence, 1846), p. 89, uses Andreas' definition to define the love which condemned those who sinned carnally in the fifth canto of the *Inferno*. Cf. Boccaccio's description of *passio, De gen. deor.*, ed. Romano (Bari, 1951), II, 452-453. F. Schlösser, *Andreas Capellanus* (Bonn, 1959), pp. 100, 180ff., seeks to have Andreas disregard implications of his own words which would have been obvious both to Andreas and to the readers of his text, which, since it was written in Latin, was hardly addressed to an illiterate audience.

[60] The controversy over the *Roman* is discussed below in Chapter IV.

Jean de Meun's treatment of the definition is consistent with what we have seen to be its background. It is paraphrased by Raison (lines 4376ff.) as a description of the kind of love to which, unfortunately, the dreamer has subjected himself. She calls *passio* a "maladie de pensee," which is accurate enough, and goes on, after the definition, to explain that the function of the sexual act is to produce children, and that the accompanying delight was established by Nature to insure the perpetuation of the species, a doctrine, we may observe, that Jean de Meun might have found in St. Augustine's *De Genesi ad litteram*.[61] But, she explains, he who pursues this delight for its own sake, as the dreamer does and as Andreas' definition demands, submits to the "prince de trestouz les vices." In the Middle English translation, the relevant passage reads (lines 4809ff.):

> If love be serched wel and sought
> It is a syknesse of the thought
> Annexed and knet bitwixe tweyne,
> Which male and female, with oo cheyne,
> So frely byndith that they nyll twynne,
> Whether so thereof they leese or wynne.
> The roote springith, thurgh hoot brennyng
> Into disordinat desiryng
> For to kissen and enbrace,
> And at her lust them to solace.
> Of other thyng love recchith nought,
> But setteth her herte and all her thought
> More for delectacioun
> Thon ony procreacioun
> Of other fruyt of engendring;
> Which love to God is not plesyng;
> For of her body fruyt to get
> They yeve no force, they are so set
> Upon delit to pley in feere.

Those who pursue this love

[61] 11. 32. 42: "Hoc ergo amisso statu, corpus eorum [i.e., Eve and Adam] duxit morbidam et mortiferam qualitatem, quae etiam inest pecorum carni, ac per hoc etiam eumdem motum quo fit in pecoribus concumbendi appetitus, ut succedant nascentia morientibus."

> thrall hemsilf, they be so nyce,
> Unto the prince of every vice.
> For of ech synne it is the rote,
> Unlefull lust, though it be sote,
> And of all yvell the racyne . . . .

The "root of all evils" here described is that same *radix malorum* mentioned and described by Albertanus. Neither author says anything about a new and romantic conception of "courtly love." A few instances drawn from literary sources will serve to show that the pattern of action described in the definition, and in the earlier formulations of St. Augustine and John the Scot is a common one in medieval literary texts, where it offered a convenient means of suggesting the abuse of the beauty of creation rather than its use. Numerous examples other than those cited will undoubtedly occur to those familiar with medieval literature.

In the "complainte" of Alisandre which occurs in the first part of Chrétien's *Cligés* (lines 616ff.), the process we have been describing is analyzed in detail. We find Alisandre unable to rest as he engages in "pleasurable thought":

> Tant li delite a remanbrer
> La biauté et la contenance
> Celi, ou n'a point d'esperance,
> Que ja biens l'an doie avenir.

But this "meditation" brings him small comfort, since he knows of no way of gaining the satisfaction it suggests to him. It occurs to him, therefore, that he is being foolish: "An folie ai mon panser mis." Nor does he know of any medicine to cure his "anfermeté" except one which he is hesitant to seek openly. Who is to blame for his condition? Love has wounded him, he thinks. The manner in which Love manages this "wound" in Alisandre's description of it falls into a familiar pattern. He has been wounded through the eye, although the wound itself is in the heart rather than in the eye. For the eye is simply a mirror of the heart through which impressions pass to be judged within, just as light passes through glass. Objects of various colors are transmitted as images by the eye to the heart where they are judged beautiful or not beautiful. In other words, Love acts within, in the heart rather than in the eye. In terms of Andreas' description, it is "inborn"; or in terms of

John the Scot's gardens, cupidity ("Love") lurks in the outer garden beneath the image. What has wounded Alisandre is his desire aroused by a phantasy of Soredamors ("gilded by love"), who becomes a golden arrow in Alisandre's meditation. He thinks of her as the beautiful "arrow" which has passed through his eye into his heart, and he proceeds to consider, one by one, the parts of the arrow which he has seen, and to create *phantasmata* of those parts which he has not seen—

> Bien fust ma dolors alegire,
> Se tot le dart veü eüsse.

The extreme to which the resulting "passion" leads him is revealed later as he spends a sleepless night vainly fondling a shirt which contains a strand of Soredamors' hair. The lady, who has been similarly victimized by "sight," exclaims (475), "Oel! vos m'avez traïe!" Fortunately, in this instance, the lovers do not hasten to obey the precepts of love "in deed," and a reasonable solution to their problem, marriage,[62] is finally proposed by the Queen. The three steps—sight, pleasure of thought, and consent or passion—are obvious in Alisandre's description of his own situation. Indeed, Chrétien is at some pains to describe each of them in detail.

Two features of Chrétien's account of Alisandre's malady deserve comment: its tone, and its poetic embellishment. The fact that materials of this kind in "secular" literature are not expressed in the homiletic tone with which the same materials are expressed in "religious" literature has often led to the impression that the two are unrelated. Chrétien's tone in this instance is light, heightened by some jocular wordplay on love and seasickness (lines 541ff.), not serious like that of the *De sermone Domini in monte*, and he addresses no hortatory expressions to his audience. If he was not preaching, we may ask, why does he use materials of this kind in his romances? The answer to this question is actually very simple, and it does not involve a necessity for setting up a "system" different from and opposed to the tenets of Christian philosophy. As a poet, Chrétien had far more reason to entertain his audience

---

[62] See Peter Lombard, *Sententiae*, 4. 26. 2: "Infirmitas enim incontinentiae, quae est in carne per peccatum mortua, ne cadat in ruinam flagitiorum, excipitur honestate nuptiarum." Cf. the later materials adduced by Gervase Mathew, "Marriage and *Amour Courtois* in Late-Fourteenth-Century England," *Essays Presented to Charles Williams* (Oxford, 1947), pp. 132-133.

than had an ordinary preacher. Although he had no obligation to supply the Word of God to that audience, as had the preacher, he did have, in accordance with traditions concerning poetry handed down from antiquity, an obligation to instruct them as well as to entertain them. And this instruction—the "bread" in his fables, as Boccaccio called it later—was quite naturally derived from the same philosophical traditions employed by the preacher. These were, in fact, the only philosophical traditions which he could expect his audience to use as a basis for inferences concerning his meaning, the only ones with which they were familiar. At the same time, reference to those traditions offered a natural opportunity for satire, comedy, and humor. For these all result from the portrayal of deviations from reasonable behavior presented in such a way that their implications are not immediately serious; and the standards of reasonable behavior were, throughout the Middle Ages, those established by the Church. Sin may be ridiculous as well as pathetic, especially to the unromantic eye.[63] We may conclude, therefore, that the materials of Christian philosophy were a natural asset to any poet, for purposes of both delight and profit. In the example adduced above, we should notice that the character is made to reveal his own foolishness. Alisandre demonstrates his malady in the light of a familiar pattern of Christian thought. This literary device, still employed with remarkable effectiveness in the plays of Shakespeare, was of considerable assistance to authors who sought deliberately to avoid "preaching."

However, the fact that poets employed conventions of Christian philosophy did not insure that their efforts were endorsed wholeheartedly by preachers, even though many of the poets, like Dante and Petrarch, may have regarded the philosophic content of their work with deep seriousness. Certainly Chrétien thought that he was sowing "bone semence" consistent with the New Law of charity in *Le roman de Perceval*. But poetry, no matter how philosophical or how orthodox it may be, is not the Word of God, so that it is not strange to find voices like this one raised against it: "Would he not insult a king who, having set aside the words of the king sent to him by a messenger, listened to the words of some jongleur? Thus you insult God who, neglecting His words, more readily listen to

[63] See Douglas Cole, "Hrotsvitha's Most 'Comic' Play: *Dulcitius*," *SP*, LVII (1960), pp. 601ff. For suggestions of further ironic humor in *Cligés*, see D. W. Robertson, Jr., "Chrétien's *Cligés* and the Ovidian Spirit," *Comp. Lit.*, VII (1955), 32-42.

fables and tirelessly devote your attention to fictions made about Arthur, and about Erec, and about Cligés. We read in the Acts of the Apostles that St. Paul preached from morning until the middle of the night. You had rather stay awake to hear about Perceval. . . . But you say, 'You are not Paul, nor are you like him, and therefore we do not listen to you'. . . . But you should listen to me, for the words that I speak to you are not mine, but God's."[64]

It is significant that the priest, in this condemnation, does not accuse Chrétien, to whose works he obviously refers, of strange doctrines. He is disturbed largely because his audience prefers the more entertaining romances to his sermons. We should add that poets traditionally employed an "integument," an enigmatic mode of expression, which did not by any means make the philosophical content of their poetry either immediately or universally comprehensible. But it is true also that during the thirteenth and fourteenth centuries preachers entered into a sort of competition with the poets by introducing exemplary narratives into their sermons addressed to the people.

In our illustration from *Cligés*, the poetic embellishment is effected not only by a light and humorous tone but also by the use of a classical figure, Cupid, or the God of Love, whose golden arrow is here the beauty of Soredamors which enters into the heart of the lover as a *phantasia*. After the middle of the twelfth century, the desire to find patterns of thought in classical poetry, especially in the poetry of Ovid and Virgil, either analogous with Christian patterns of thought or easily made conformable to such patterns, became more and more evident. At the same time that commentaries on classical texts and manuals of mythography were composed, poets began to make greater use of classical materials for purposes of embellishment. Thus Chrétien's use of Cupid derives from a conception resembling that in the mythographical manual recently attributed to Albericus of London: "Why Love is said to be the son of Venus no one is ignorant, since it is certain that love is born of the desire for pleasure. However, Love is depicted as a boy because the desire [*cupiditas*] for wickedness is foolish,

[64] Odo Tusculanus, *Sermones*, ed. J. B. Pitra, *Analecta novissima Spicilegii Solesmensis* (1885-1888), II, 227.

and because speech is imperfect in lovers as it is in boys. Whence Virgil wrote concerning Dido in love:

She began to speak, but halted in the middle of a word.

He is winged because nothing is lighter or more mutable than lovers are. He carries arrows because these also are uncertain and quick, or, as Remigius has it, because the consciousness of crimes perpetrated goads the mind. However, the golden arrow sends love and the leaden one takes it away, because love is beautiful, like gold, to the lover, but seems a heavy thing, like lead, to one who does not love. . . ."[65]

Perhaps it is no mere coincidence that Soredamors is at one point (lines 1410ff.) hesitant to address Alisandre for fear that she will be able to pronounce only half of his name. In any event, the classical embellishment does not invalidate the philosophical pattern which underlies Alisandre's account of his malady. The "favorable" arrow of Cupid became, in the later Middle Ages, a conventional figure for the phantasy of beauty which enters the heart of the lover through the eye.

A more elaborate poetic integument is used to adorn the procedure necessary for the abuse of beauty in the first part of the *Roman de la rose*. Here the allegorical machinery serves to broaden and deepen the implications of the three familiar steps as well as to confront the reader with an enigmatic surface designed to stimulate thought.[66] The garden of the exterior man in the account of John the Scot here becomes an earthly paradise of Deduit, the fleshly counterpart of the more spiritual garden described later by

---

[65] G. H. Bode, *Scriptores rerum mythicarum* (Cellis, 1834), p. 239. On the identity of "Mythographus Vaticanus Tertius," see E. Rathbone, "Master Alberic of London," *Mediaeval and Renaissance Studies*, 1 (1943), p. 35. The conclusions advanced here have not been universally accepted. Cf. K. O. Elliot and J. P. Elder, "A Critical Edition of the Vatican Mythographers," *TAPA*, LXXVIII (1947), p. 205. The sources of Albericus are discussed by Robertus Raschke, *De Alberico Mythologo* (Breslau, 1912). There are many correspondences between "Albericus" and the commentary on Martianus by Alexander Neckam, so that there is still a possibility that Alexander may have been the author of the treatise in question.

[66] That enigmatic expression was intended is clear from lines 2061-2076; cf. lines 18-20. The following analysis of the *Roman* has much in common with that in an article by C. R. Dahlberg, "Macrobius and the Unity of the *Roman de la rose*," *SP*, LVIII (1961), 573-582.

Jean de Meun (Fig. 12).[67] Admittance to this garden is gained through its porter,[68] Oiseuse, or Idleness, who owes her function partly to Ovid and partly to the principle that idleness is an invitation to the Devil.[69] Since, as Ovid implies in the *Remedia amoris*, Idleness leads to a desire for fleshly delight, she is described in the *Roman* with the mirror and comb which are the conventional Gothic attributes of *luxuria*, and the early illustrators of the poem consistently portray her by copying designs like that used, for exam-

[67] For the chief features of this garden, see D. W. Robertson, Jr., "The Doctrine of Charity in Mediaeval Literary Gardens," *Speculum*, XXVI (1951), 24-49. This article, however, is guilty of "polarities" which I now believe to be misleading. Pierre Col points out the contrast between the garden in Guillaume's part of the *Roman* and the garden described by Genius later in Jean de Meun's continuation, where, he says, Jean "figure si noblement la Trinitey et l'Incarnacion par l'escharboucle et par l'oliue qui prent son acroissement de la rousee de la fontaine." See C. F. Ward, *The Epistles on the Romance of the Rose and Other Documents in the Debate* (Chicago, 1911), p. 61.

[68] Cf. Chaucer, KT, 1940; SNProl., 2-3; ParS.T, 713.

[69] Oiseuse owes her origin ultimately to Ovid, *Rem. amor.*, 139: "otia si tollas, periere Cupidinis arcus." This became a favorite medieval quotation, since it seemed strikingly harmonious with principles of Christian morality. Idleness was regarded as a major enemy of the spirit in the Benedictine Rule, a fact which may have had some economic significance. See R. Latouche, *Les origines de l'économie occidentale* (Paris, 1956), p. 102. Its moral consequences were widely familiar. In the *Architrenius* it is called the nurse of Venus. Holcot, *Heptalogos* (Paris, 1518), sig. e iiii verso, calls it the first cause of lechery, citing St. Bernard as an authority. Richard de Bury, *Philobiblon* (ed. A. Altamura), 15. 9-15, illustrates the typical use of the Ovidian line: "Hic autem amor *philosophia* greco vocabulo nuncupatur, cuius virtutem nulla creata intelligentia comprehendit, quoniam vere creditur bonorum omnium mater esse (Sapientiae VIIe). Estus quippe carnalium viciorum, quasi celicus ros extinguit, dum motus intensus virtutum animalium vires naturalium virtutum remittit, ocio penitus effugato, quo sublato 'periere Cupidinis arcus omnes.' " Cupid's shafts, brought into play by idleness, are here obviously opposed to "philosophy" or what Guillaume called "Raison." A practical illustration of the effect of idleness is afforded by Henry of Lancaster, who tells us in *Le livre de seyntz medicines* (Oxford, 1940), pp. 22-23, that he has frequently said to himself as he lies abed in the morning, "Lesseez moi dormir ou penser en mes amours." That Ovid's words could be paraphrased for the specific purposes of moral theology is shown by Guido Faba, *Summa de viciis et virtutibus*, ed. V. Pini, *Quadrivium*, 1 (1957), 124: "Ocia condecet tollere qui vult luxuriam removere. Quare te modis omnibus exortamur, ut sic circa tuum officium instare debeas et sollicite laborare, ne illecebrosa Venus suis sagittis mortiferis te inuadat, quoniam licet fornicationis labilis sit voluptas, pena tamen non est momentanea sed eterna." Finally, we may observe that Chaucer's second Nun calls idleness the "porter of the gate . . . of delices" whose cultivation invites the attention of "the feend." It is impossible to make Oiseuse an innocent forbear of modern "leisure," as some have sought to do.

ple, in a rose window of Notre Dame de Paris to illustrate that vice (Fig. 13).[70] These attributes, of course, suggest self-love and vanity. Under the auspices of Oiseuse, therefore, the dreamer is well prepared to receive the "suggestion" necessary to begin his fall. He does so at a "fontaine" beneath a pine tree which are the "exterior" counterparts of the *fons vitae* and the Tree of Life which Scotus placed in the "interior" part of the garden.[71] This is, tropologically, the place where Adam and Eve hid *in medio ligni paradisi* (Gen. 3. 8). "Who hides himself from the sight of God," asks St. Augustine, "except he who, having deserted God, now begins to love his own?"[72] And, we may add, who better "loved his own" than Narcissus? The dreamer's well is a well of death, for there Narcissus died in contemplation of his own beauty.

Even without allegorical interpretation the story of Narcissus as it is told in the *Metamorphoses* and summarized by Guillaume (lines 1339ff.) is an obvious example of the folly of self-love.[73] Arnulf of Orléans, whose commentaries on Ovid exerted a very great influence on the thought of the later Middle Ages,[74] says that "Narcissus, indeed, is said to have loved his shadow because he placed his own excellence above all other things. Whence he was turned into a flower, that is, into a useless thing, for he soon perished like a flower."[75] In *Cligés*, Chrétien compares his hero with Narcissus when "in the flower of his age" he first sees Fenice, probably with the implication that what Cligés actually loves is an

[70] The illustrations in the early MSS of the *Roman* and their antecedents are examined by A. Kuhn, "Die Illustration des Rosenromans," *Jahrbuch d. Kunsthist. Sammlungen d. Allerhöchsten Kaiserhauses,* XXXI (1913), 1ff.; see esp. pp. 26-27. For a conventional representation of *luxuria,* see Fig. 68.

[71] These remarks are not intended to imply that John the Scot was a direct source of the *Roman.* The ideas were sufficiently commonplace.

[72] *De genes. contra Manich.,* PL, 34, col. 308.

[73] Thus Hermann Fränkel, *Ovid* (Berkeley and Los Angeles, 1945), p. 85, writes, "The Ovid of the *Metamorphoses* is far from composing parables or preaching sermons; he merely tells fascinating stories; and yet, in so doing, he furnishes material for many a sermon. . . . The words in which Ovid expresses Narcissus' fatal predicament lead very close to a profound truth. Self-love is headed for destruction. Its thirst can never be quenched. . . ." We may doubt that Ovid was merely telling stories.

[74] See F. Ghisalberti, "Mediaeval Biographies of Ovid," *JWCI,* IX (1946), pp. 18-19.

[75] Ed. Ghisalberti (Milan, 1932), p. 181. A very similar interpretation is given in the fourteenth century by Holcot, *Super librum sapientiae* (Basel, 1586), pp. 519-520.

image created within himself, and the self-satisfaction it suggests, rather than Fenice.[76] Medieval authors were not unaware of distinctions of this kind. Thus Jehan le Bel condemns some loves "because the profit and delight on account of which . . . [they] are maintained are not in the persons loved but in the lovers."[77] This is especially true, he says, of love based on delight, "for then the objects of love are not loved, except by chance, but the delight alone is loved."[78] As we see Narcissus in Guillaume's description brooding over his own reflection and dying because he is not able to embrace it, the futility of cherishing a phantasy for the sake of Deduit becomes plain, and Narcissus' plight is an excellent illustration of the danger of *delectatio cogitationis*.

Narcissus engages in this foolishness in a place established by Nature (lines 1433-1434) where many others have perished also (lines 1579ff.). There

> Cupido, li fiz Venus,
> Sema . . . d'Amours la graine,
> Qui toute a teinte la fontaine,
> E fist ses laz environ tendre,
> E ses engins i mist, por prendre
> Damoiseles e damoisiaus,
> Qu'Amours ne viaut autres oisiaus.

The well is thus a bird-snare where *illicita delectatio* or "the desire for pleasure" catches its victims. The figure of the bird-snare is a very old one. Odo of Cluny uses it in the *Occupatio*:

> And just as bait draws flying birds to the snare,
> Wicked appetite draws those moved by its sweetness.
> Fixed in the lime, they cannot stretch their wings;
> They lack devotion to virtue and the wings to fly.
> Hunger for a little morsel makes them hungry forever.[79]

It appears in various forms among the "grotesques" which grace fourteenth-century Psalters and *Horae* (Fig. 24). Sometimes more fortunate (i.e. virtuous) birds escape, after the fashion of the sparrows in Ps. 123. 7: "Our soul hath been delivered as a sparrow

---

[76] Cf. "Chrétien's *Cligés* and the Ovidian Spirit," p. 37.
[77] Jehan le Bel, I, 31; cf. pp. 21-22, 27.
[78] *Ibid.*, II, 134.   [79] 3. 837-841.

out of the snare of the fowlers." The bait in this snare, which may well be the ultimate source for those in the *Occupatio* and the *Roman*, is, according to the *Glossa*, "dulcedo huius vitae"—the sweetness of this life as opposed to the sweetness of the spirit.[80] Neither Narcissus nor the dreamer escapes, but when birds do escape, illustrators show them happy with their young in the nest (Fig. 14).[81] Where did Nature establish this well, and how did it become a snare? As we have seen, love is "inborn": it arises from the contemplation of an image in the mind by the "corporal sense" or by "the lower part of the reason." The well, in other words, is that mirror in the mind where Cupid operates. It has been tainted by Cupid ever since the Fall, when cupidity gained ascendancy over the reason. Thus it is the mirror which medieval artists showed in the hand of *luxuria*, the mirror of Oiseuse, a mirror abused in a wide variety of ways, to the delight of medieval illustrators (Figs. 15, 16).

As the dreamer looks into the well, he finds that he can see the garden through "deus pierres de cristal" (line 1538). These are not the eyes of his beloved, as one romantic account of the poem would have it, but his own eyes, which function in much the same way as in Alisandre's account of his predicament. They transmit colors and forms from outside into the well, just as mirrors do when objects are placed before them. Through them the entire garden is visible to the dreamer—if he turns his head, that is, for they show him only half of it at one time. These, then, are "mirrors" which bring images to the mirror of the mind. As he looks around the garden through them, the dreamer sees many beautiful roses, transient flowers of fleshly beauty to delight him, and from among them he selects for special attention a bud, for the buds

durent tuit frois
A tot le moins deus jourz ou trois.[82]

[80] *PL*, 113, col. 1045. For further documentation and an explanation of the figure as it appears in Chaucer's Prologue to LGW, see B. G. Koonce, "Satan the Fowler," *Mediaeval Studies*, XXI (1959), 176-184.

[81] The symbolism is explained by A. Goldschmidt, *Der Albani-Psalter* (Berlin, 1895), p. 60.

[82] The use of the rose to typify the fading beauty of the flesh was common in the Middle Ages. E.g., see the *Rhythmus* ascribed to Alanus, *PL*, 210, cols. 579-580, and, for the persistence of the tradition, see the very elaborate discussion by F. Picinelli, *Il mondo simbolico* (Venice, 1687), p. 403. Because of the

At this point Cupid, or desire, awaiting just such opportunities, comes into action. His function is to make the dreamer "lust after" what he sees. Guillaume, with a typical thirteenth-century fondness for subdivision, uses five arrows to replace the original golden arrow. Of these, the first is most important: Biauté. It is this which appeals to the "woman" in John the Scot's garden, the "fairness to the eye" which first deceived Eve. Its effectiveness is enhanced by the other arrows which give the dreamer grounds for a conviction that he can reach his "fruit." The lady seems simple, rather than prudent;[83] she is courteous, she accepts his company, and she looks upon him sweetly. Fired with desire, the dreamer longs for the rose, or, that is, to obey the laws of love; but unfortunately the roses of Venus are hedged about with thorns, so that he cannot get at this one immediately. What Guillaume describes, in very revealing detail, is the manner in which "suggestion" operates in the mind. The description is not, however, "psychological" in the modern sense, for what is described is basically a moral process.

The next step is *delectatio cogitationis*. The God of Love, or

---

use of roses in Wisdom 2. 8, these flowers were also associated with *luxuria* and hence with Venus. Thus Baudri de Bourgueil, *Oeuvres poétiques*, ed. P. Abrahams (Paris, 1926), ccvi, lines 435 ff., wrote:

> Philosophia rosas Veneris famularibus addit;
> Ut stipes pungat et folium rubeat:
> Peccatum pungat, rubeat pudibunda libido;
> Mox rosa marcescit, moxque Venus liquefit.

The same idea appears in Albericus ("Myth. Vat. III"), ed. Bode, pp. 228-229, in a discussion of Venus: "Rosae ei adscribuntur. Rosae enim rubent et pingunt; itemque libido ruborem ingerit et pudoris opprobris, pungitque peccati aculeo. Sicut enim rosa delectat quidem, sed celeri motu temporis tollitur; ita et libido." Almost the same words appear in Neckam on Martianus, Oxford, Bodl., MS Digby 221, fol. 37, and in the *Libellus* on the gods by Chaucer's contemporary Thomas Walsingham, Oxford, St. John's Coll., MS 124, fol. 25. Thomas Ringstede, *In prov. Salomonis* (Paris, 1515), fol. xlvii, associates Venus with the passage in Wisdom: "Secundum numen erat Venus . . . . Huius numinis cultores perfecti sunt illi qui dicunt illi Sapientiae secundo, Coronemus nos rosis antequam marcescant."

The dreamer's careful selection of the bud identifies his rose as this one. The rose had not yet developed those connotations which it has in the poetry of Robert Burns. There was, of course, a "good" rose during the Middle Ages, symbolizing charity, martyrdom, or the Blessed Virgin Mary, who was a "rose without spines."

[83] Cf. Matt. 10. 16. The *Glossa*, *PL*, 114, col. 118, refers us to Rabanus on this point, who says, *PL*, 107, cols. 897-898, that the serpent is prudent because he closes his ears to charmers, or, that is, to those who urge the pleasures of the flesh. Hence the "simple" who are not also prudent like the serpent attract the lecherous.

desire, gives the dreamer ample instruction on this point (lines 2233ff.):

> Après t'enjoing en penitence
> Que nuit e jor, senz repentence,
> En amors metes ton penser:
> Toz jorz i pense senz cesser,
> E te membre de la douce eure
> Don la joie tant te demeure.

At night his activity with reference to his *phantasmata* of the rose will resemble that stimulated in Alisandre by the presence of Soredamors' hair in his shirt (lines 2425ff.):

> Tu te coucheras en ton lit,
> Ou tu avras poi de delit,
> Car quant tu cuideras dormir,
> Tu comenceras a fremir,
> A tressaillir, a demener;
> Sor costé t'estovra torner,
> E puis envers, e puis adenz,
> Come ome qui a mal as denz.
> Lors te vendra en remembrance
> E la façon e la semblance
> A cui nule ne s'apareille.
> Si te dirai fiere merveille:
> Tel foiz sera qu'il t'iert avis
> Que tu tendras cele au cler vis
> Entre tes braz trestoute nue,
> Ausi con s'el fust devenue
> Dou tot t'amie e ta compaigne;
> Lors feras chastiaus en Espaigne
> E avras joie de neient
> Tant con tu iras foleiant
> En la pensee delitable
> Ou il n'a que mençonge e fable.

As we shall see, the "pensee delitable" of the dreamer remains a dream, even in the last part of the poem, perhaps with the implication that the pleasure the lover so hotly pursues is, like a dream, transitory and illusory. In *Cligés* the dreams inspired in

Alis by the potion are no more and no less satisfying than the more "real" activities of Cligés. And in Chaucer's *Troilus*, the protagonists find themselves fearful at the height of their delight:

> this was hir mooste feere
> Lest al this thyng but nyce dremes were;
> For which ful ofte ech of hem seyde, "O swete,
> Clippe ich yow thus, or elles I it meete?"

The medieval mind had not yet learned to relish the more refined pleasures discovered by Demetrius in Pierre Louys' *Aphrodite*.

The third step in the fall of Guillaume's lover occurs when he refuses flatly to listen to the voice of Raison, in spite of the fact that

> Deus la fist demainement
> A sa samblance e a s'image,
> E li dona tel avantage
> Qu'ele a pooir e seignorie
> De garder ome de folie . . . .

By disregarding the *Verbum Dei* within himself and disdaining to refer the beauty of the rose to it, rather than to the desire to which he submitted himself, the lover abandons the "interior garden" completely, behaving in the fashion of the man before the precious vase who was "transfixed and lacerated by the thorns of perverse cupidity." He makes of the rose a "saintuaire precieus" in which, in his mind's eye, he hastens to place his staff.

The first part of the *Roman de la rose*, far from being a romantic fantasy or even a "psychological novel," is a philosophical poem of some profundity, adorned with the kind of imagery popular in artistic expressions of all kinds during the first half of the thirteenth century. Jean de Meun's continuation is an elaboration of the themes established in the first part, ornamented with a wealth of "humanistic" and philosophical material, and with satiric glances at the institutions of the society in which he lived. Jean includes, near the end of the poem, an exemplary narrative which repeats in miniature the lesson of Guillaume's garden, perhaps to insure that his conclusion will be seen to be harmonious with the lesson of the work Guillaume began. This narrative places added emphasis on an element in the procedure to which Guillaume simply alludes by using such words as "saintuaire." That element is idolatry.

Before we turn to the exemplary narrative, which is the story of Pygmalion, it would be well to glance briefly at the medieval concept of idolatry, for idolatry was a problem even in a Christian society where no one worshipped "graven images." A brief excerpt from Holcot's discussion of the subject will serve admirably; although written after Jean's poem had been completed, it sums up traditional doctrine very well: "[It is said] in Ecclesiasticus 9. [3], 'Give not the power of thy soul to a woman, lest she enter upon thy strength, and thou be confounded,' and further on [8], 'Turn away thy face from a woman dressed up, and gaze not upon another's beauty.' These women are creatures of whom the letter says [Wisdom, 14. 11], 'because the creatures of God are turned to an abomination,' that is, to God Himself, 'and a temptation to the souls of men, and a snare to the feet of the unwise.' For in this mousetrap David was caught, and this idol also seduced the wisdom of Solomon to the worship of idols as we read in 3 Kings 12 [sc. 11]. These idols are to be fled, and not sought out through curiosity, for as the letter says [Wisd. 14. 12], 'the beginning of fornication is the devising of idols.' For it is impossible for a curious and lascivious man associating with these idols not to be corrupted by them; indeed, a man, diligently seeking out and considering in his thought the beauty of women so that he makes idols for himself, necessarily prepares for his own fall."[84]

An "idol" is thus not always a tangible image of wood or stone; it may be an image in the mind. And such mental images are typically those formed on the basis of feminine beauty, the *phantasmata* of Cupid. Thus the idols of Wisdom 14 and Isaias 44 may be taken as figures for inner idols constructed in the mind by the desire of the idolator.

The story of Pygmalion has been received by modern criticism as being among the more horrid (or fascinating) features of Jean's poem. Paré observes that the story "n'est pas en rapport direct avec l'intrigue, mais elle est en parfaite conformité avec l'atmosphère de sensualité qui baigne toute cette partie et arrive très à point pour illustrer l'hédonisme débridé qui couronne la doctrine morale du

---

[84] *Super librum sapientiae*, pp. 539-540.

Roman."[85] It is thus seen to conform to the sermon of Genius, whose doctrine comes, Paré assures us, "sans doute du naturalisme greco-arabe."[86] Perhaps it is possible, however, to adopt a milder attitude toward an old poet who exerted an enormous influence on writers, some of whom were very wise and quite respectable, like Philippe de Mézières,[87] well down into the Renaissance. If the poem were actually as it is described in modern criticism, Gontier Col would hardly have written of "maistre Jehan de Meun, vray catholique, solennel maistre, et docteur en son temps en saincte theologie, philosophe tresperfont et excellent, sachant tout ce qui a entendement humain est scible, duquel la gloire et renommee vit et viura es aages a venir . . . ."[88] It is possible that Jean was not at all interested in the "intrigue" as a story told for its own sake, that Genius, who was elected to the See of this our little diocese by the God of Love, speaks in character, that the sources of the *Roman* are those usually pointed out and not at all exotic, and, finally, that the conclusion to the poem and the story of Pygmalion are the opposite of "hedonistic."

We are introduced to Pygmalion at that point in the poem where Venus is about to release her burning arrow at the "image" into which the rose has been transformed by the lover's idolatrous passion (Fig. 17). It is noteworthy that what Venus is aiming at is an "image," not a lady, and not a rose. The author finds occasion to compare this image with that of Pygmalion (lines 20785ff.), whose story is then told. Our artisan is said to have been competent in media of all kinds, but he finally made an image of a woman in ivory so beautiful that he fell desperately in love with it. He found a certain consolation in comparing himself with Narcissus, who loved "sa propre figure" (lines 20876-20882). Was he not himself a man who loved "sa propre figure"? Pygmalion, however, found that he had certain advantages over his predecessor. Narcissus could not fondle the image in the water, but Pygmalion's image could be fondled (Fig. 18). Nevertheless, the statue was quite un-

[85] *Les idées et les lettres au XIIIᵉ siècle* (Montreal, 1947), p. 297.

[86] *Ibid.*, p. 285, and note.

[87] Arthur Piaget, *Oton de Grandson, sa vie et ses poésies* (Lausanne, 1941), p. 77, calls Philippe "un des hommes les plus respectables et les plus clairvoyants du temps." On Philippe's use of the *Roman*, see N. Jorga, *Philippe de Mézières* (Paris, 1896), p. 26.

[88] Ward, p. 29.

responsive. Pygmalion dressed it in fine clothes, adorned it with jewels, placed chaplets of fresh flowers on it, played sweet music to it, and even took it to bed with him (Fig. 19). "Ainsinc s'ocit, ainsinc s'afole," observes the poet (line 21065). Finally, Pygmalion prayed to Venus for assistance. As one illustrator envisaged this scene, Venus and the image are both "idols," standing on pedestals in the way idols were conventionally represented in the late Middle Ages (Fig. 20). In this picture, Venus is clearly "de la terre as Sarradins" like the enemies of Christ in late medieval Crucifixions, but this fact hardly implies a "Greco-Arabic" influence. In any event, she answered Pygmalion propitiously, so that when he returned to his image, he was astonished by what he saw (lines 21144ff.):

> "Qu'est-ce?" dist il, "sui je tentez?
> Veille je pas? Nenin, ainz songe;
> Mais, onc ne vi si apert songe.
> Songe! par fei, non faz, ainz veille.
> Don vient donques cete merveille?
> Est ce fantosme ou anemis
> Qui s'est en mon image mis?"

The image replied very sweetly,

> "Ce n'est anemis ne fantosme,
> Douz amis, ainz sui vostre ami."

And after this she did everything he desired.

To the romantic mind, all this undoubtedly sounds very enticing. Pygmalion created an "Impossible She," the white goddess of his imagination, and then was privileged to enjoy her. We readily surround the story with tender sentiments, like those suggested by the work of Falconet (Fig. 21), which led Diderot to exclaim, with reference to the image, "Quelle innocence elle a!"[89] And the miracle of Venus presents no difficulties to one who accepts "a willing suspension of disbelief" or a taste for "the marvellous" in fiction as a part of the natural order of things. But neither Jean de Meun nor his medieval illustrators, in whom we may notice a

[89] See Diderot, *Salons*, ed. J. Seznec and J. Adhémar, 1 (Oxford, 1957), p. 245. In his *Réflexions sur la sculpture* (1768), Falconet himself stressed the importance of "le *sentiment*" as the vivifying principle or "soul" of a work of art.

certain cynicism, when they are compared with their eighteenth-century successor, were addressing themselves to romantic minds. Venus was in their day neither a fairy godmother nor a desert Djinn. She was, among other things, the pleasure of sexual intercourse. If Pygmalion grew so hot in the pursuit of his little phantasm that the pleasure generated by his imagination deprived him of reason and he thought the statue was alive, he was simply doing, perhaps with more decisive irrationality, exactly what Alisandre sought to do with his shirt and what Guillaume's lover did at night when he envisaged his bare rose in bed beside him. Nor is this a modern rationalization of the story. Let us listen once more to the voice of the school of Orléans: "The statue of Pigmalion [was changed] into a living woman. As a matter of fact, Pigmalion, a wonderful artificer, made an ivory statue, and conceiving a love for it began to abuse it as though it were a true woman."[90] The idea still echoes in Froissart:

> Quoique le fol crie et braie
> Et ses dolours li retraie
> Et le vest d'or et de saie,
> Il n'est rien qu'il en extraie
> Fors imagination.[91]

And Lydgate in *Reson and Sensuallyte* (4276-4280) observes concerning Pygmalion,

> Love him made so amerous,
> In Ovide as it ys tolde,
> Al be that yt [i.e. the image] was ded and colde,
> Which made hym selfe for to stryve
> Lyche as hyt hadde ben alyve.

The author of Lydgate's source, *Les échecs amoureux*, was a stout admirer and close student of the *Roman de le rose*, from which he borrowed many details, including, we may assume, this one. That is, so far as Jean de Meun is concerned, Pygmalion did love a "fantosme" and "anemis" within himself to the extent that he abandoned the counsel of reason completely and became just as

[90] From Arnulf's commentary on the *Metamorphoses*, ed. Ghisalberti, p. 223. Arnulf's words on this subject are repeated by Walsingham, fols. 115-115 verso.
[91] "Paradys d'Amours," in *Oeuvres*, ed. A. Scheler (Brussels, 1870-1872), I, 34.

blinded by his passion as was Hrotsvitha's Dulcitius among his pots and pans, or as Chaucer's Januarie was to become at the foot of his pear tree.[92]

The three steps in the abuse of beauty are thus brought home to us once more in the story of Pygmalion: the "suggestion" caused by feminine beauty, the "pensee delitable," and the final corruption of the reason. The story emphasizes the second, with its elaborate description of Pygmalion's antics as he idolizes his image; and the final step as it is developed lends a special emphasis to the irrationality of passion. Jean de Meun's treatment of Pygmalion is thus far less "sensual" in its implications than is Falconet's, for the sculptor seeks to palliate the element of sensuality in the story by means of tenderness and refinement, qualities which have the power to stimulate the warmest compassion in us for what our illiberal and unenlightened ancestors—even among Greeks and Arabs—would have thought of as most irrational behavior. To turn briefly to the conclusion of the *Roman*, if the dreamer's "rose" is an idol image like the image of Pygmalion, this tells us a great deal about the dreamer himself. He too has created an image, an idol in the mind like those described by Holcot, to be given warmth and life by the firebrand of his own concupiscence. And in the end, when his rose has been transformed by the "magic" of his passion, and he has, it seems, almost fulfilled his desire, he awakens. All the insubstantial pageant of fleshly delight fades into the misty recollection of what "un auctor qui ot non Macrobes" defines as a nightmare.[93] Passion, in the sense of the word employed by Andreas Capellanus or in the *Glossa*, requires idolatry, the deliberate cultivation of a phantasm in such a way as to imply a lesser love for God. Hence Jean de Meun's use of words like "sanctuary" and "relic," and hence also the very sound statement by Pierre Col to the effect that such words in the poem serve only to condemn the foolishness of the lover, "Car ung fol amoureux ne pense

[92] Adonis, whom Jean mentions at the end of his account for contrast, was, like Narcissus, changed into a flower, but into a useful flower suggesting the charity of one who flees Venus. See Arnulf, *loc.cit.*

[93] The fact that the dream is, from the point of view of the dreamer, an *insomnium* according to the definition of Macrobius was first pointed out by C. R. Dahlberg, *The Secular Tradition in Chaucer and Jean de Meun* (Princeton Diss., 1953), pp. 137, 183. See also his article "Macrobius and the Unity of the *Roman de la rose*."

a aultre chose que a ce bouton, et est son dieu et la onra comme son dieu."[94] If we have been following the activities of the dreamer in a romantic or "dramatic" fashion, sharing his frustrations and satisfactions, we shall find ourselves immersed, at the close of the poem, in that morass of hedonistic sensuality described by Paré. But this morass is no medieval creation. Jean de Meun's poem is a warning to heed the voice of reason, and to avoid desire that may lead to hypocritical behavior and adultery in the heart. There is no reason to doubt the motive Chaucer advances for translating the *Roman* in the Prologue to *The Legend of Good Women*:

> Ne a trewe lovere oghte me nat to blame,
> Thogh that I speke a fals lovere som shame.
> They oughte rathere with me for to holde,
> For that I of Criseyde wrot or tolde,
> Or of the Rose. What so myn auctour mente,
> Algate, God wot, it was myn entente
> To forthere trouthe in love and it cheryce,
> And to be war fro falsnesse and fro vice
> By swich ensample.

It is unlikely also that he misunderstood what his "auctour mente."

Chaucer's indebtedness to the *Roman* has long been acknowledged,[95] but there is no reason to think that he was fascinated by any "Greco-Arabic" doctrines, nor, indeed, by any kind of Aristotelianism he found in the poem. He does show a deep concern for the traditional principles of Christian philosophy, the kind of philosophy to be found in Boethius, in the *Policraticus*, or in the *Philobiblon*. The *Roman* is a humanistic and poetic expression of ideas which Chaucer could have his parson in the *Tales* state in a straightforward way, but which he, as a court poet, could state most effectively in ways suggested by the *Roman* and by other poems like it. As we have seen, the parson was very much aware of the manner in which things "fair to the eye" may be abused by being contemplated with a view to "delight of the flesh," so that the order of the mind is turned "up-so-doun." Chaucer's poetry contains numerous illustrations of this principle. A few examples will

[94] Ward, p. 60.
[95] See the summary statement by D. S. Fansler, *Chaucer and the "Roman de la Rose"* (New York, 1914), p. 234.

suffice, since, once the principles are understood, the reader will have no difficulty in recognizing the same pattern of action elsewhere.

The operation of "suggestion" is illustrated very vividly in the Knight's Tale. As Palamon and Arcite languish in prison, they observe, in an appropriate garden setting, the beautiful Emelye

> that fairer was to sene
> Than is the lylie upon his stalke grene,
> And fressher than the May with floures newe . . . .

She is suitably crowned to provoke exactly the kind of attention she gets:

> Hir yelow heer was broyded in a tresse
> Bihynde hir bak, a yerde long, I gesse.

Palamon sees her first—

> He cast his eye upon Emelya,
> And therwithal he bleynte and cride, "A!"
> As though he stongen were unto the herte.

As he explains to Arcite,

> "I was hurt right now thurghout myn ye
> Into myn herte, that wol my bane be . . . ."

The object which is "fair to see" thus passes as an "arrow" or image into the heart, where its force sends Palamon to his knees in a prayer to Venus that she may deliver him from prison. Since Venus is conventionally associated with the entangling chains or snares of concupiscence, or with those who "thrall hemsilf" in the words of the *Roman*, this prayer does not lack certain ironic overtones. Arcite's turn comes next, and the effect of beauty is even less wholesome than it was when Palamon suffered it:

> "The fresshe beautee sleeth me sodeynly
> Of hire that rometh in the yonder place,
> And but I have hir mercy and hir grace,
> That I may seen hire atte leeste weye,
> I nam but deed; ther nis namoore to seye."

This reaction leads at once to a passionate dispute between the sworn brothers, for Venus makes all men enemies.[96] Arcite becomes especially irate, condemning all law with a Boethian echo that undercuts what he says even before he has a chance to say it:

> Wostow nat wel the olde clerkes sawe,
> That 'who shal yeve a lovere any lawe?'
> Love is a gretter lawe, by my pan,
> Than may be yeve to any erthely man;
> And therefore positif lawe and swich decree
> Is broken al day for love in ech degree.
> A man moot nedes love, maugre his heed.
> He may nat fleen it, though he sholde be deed,
> Al be she mayde, or wydwe, or elles wyf.

"But what is he that may yeven a lawe to loverys?" asks Boethius in exasperation as he finds himself forced to admit that Orpheus "lokede abakward on Erudyce his wif" when the two were "almest at the termes of the nyght." Orpheus "sette his thoughtes in erthly things" because of his lawless desire and lost "the noble good celestial." Love becomes a "law" unto itself when it abandons all wisdom and reason.[97] Arcite may well swear by his "pan," albeit a trifle inelegantly, for he is making small use of it.

---

[96] Boccaccio identifies Venus in the *Teseida* with the concupiscible passions and Mars with the irascible passions. See the Chiose in Roncaglia's edition (Bari, 1941), p. 417. The manner in which the concupiscible passions move the irascible passions in the course of the lover's malady is described by Bernard of Gordon, *Lilium medicinae* (Lyons, 1574), p. 216.

[97] The story of Orpheus was pregnant with philosophical meaning in antiquity, and undoubtedly had some occult significance for Ovid, who had pronounced Pythagorean and hence "Orphic" tendencies. The early Christians did not allow the story to be forgotten, so that in the early Church the Crucified Christ was regarded as the "true Orpheus," a convention that survives in a twelfth-century hymn. See Hugo Rahner, *Griechische Mythen in christlicher Deutung* (Zürich, 1945), pp. 88-89. By transference, Orpheus could signify the good priest. Hence Berchorius, *Metamorphosis Ovidiana* (Paris, 1515), Lib. x, says, "Orpheus significat predicatorem & divini verbi carminum distatorem: qui de infernis, id est de mundo veniens debet in monte scripture vel religionis sedere carmina & melodiam sacre scripture canere. . . ." Orpheus was said to have been killed by angry women. Berchorius continues, "Mulierum copulam debet fugere & carnis amplexus penitus exhorrere, & contra ipsaram malitias predicare." There was thus a tradition of a successful Orpheus in addition to the Orpheus who looks back. See D. W. Robertson, Jr., "The *Partitura amorosa* of Jean de Savoie," *PQ*, xxxiii (1954), 1-9, and, for an extended example, the Middle English *Sir Orpheo*. Cf. the interpretations recorded by Bukofzer, "Speculative Thinking in Mediaeval Music," *Speculum*, xvii (1942), pp. 174-175. The interpretation indicated by Chaucer's

But instead of bringing Dame Raison on the stage to demonstrate Arcite's foolishness, the Knight achieves the same result by having Arcite tell a fable and then violently misinterpret it:

> We stryve as dide the houndes for the boon;
> They foughte al day, and yet hir part was noon.
> Ther cam a kyte, whil that they were so wrothe
> And baar awey the boon bitwixe hem bothe.

---

gloss to Boethius probably stems from Remigius. He is quoted by Albericus, ed. Bode, pp. 212-213: "Ait enim Euridicen ideo Orphi dictam esse conjugem, quia facundiae comes debet esse discretio. Ipsa vero serpente laesa ad infernum descendit, quum terrenis inhiando commodis veneno iniquitatis ad sinistram partis inflectitur. Sed Orphei carminibus ad superos revocatur, quum loculenta ratione lucri stimulus ad aequitatem reformatur. Sed si respicit, retrahitur ad terrena, nec oranti Orpheo redditur. Nam quum terrenas animus saecularia nimis concupiscit, vix eum aliqua oratio ad statum rectitudinis erigit, quia a Proserpina, id est maxima vitiorum tenetur illecebra." This version is repeated by Walsingham, fol. 111 verso. This author identifies the women who stoned Orpheus, fols. 112, 119, with those "uiuentes muliebriter," or "luxuriosi," who were envious because Orpheus refused to love them but loved men, that is, those "viriliter agentes" or "virtuosos," instead. The women were thus transformed into various figures by Bacchus, that is, by inebriation in vices. A modification of Remigius' interpretation, with minor variations, appears in the commentary on the *Aeneid* by Bernard Silvestris, ed. G. Riedel (Greifswald, 1924), pp. 53-55; in Guillaume de Conches' commentary on Boethius, part of which is printed by Charles Jourdain, *Notices et extraits de MSS de la Bibl. Impér.*, xx (1862), pp. 80-81; and in Nicholas Trivet's commentary on Boethius, MS Burney 131, fols. 48-49. Bernard takes Orpheus to represent a man "sapientem et eloquentem," the son of Apollo, or Sapientia, and Calliope, or Eloquentia. His cithara is "orationem rhetoricam, in qua diversi colores quasi diversi numeri resonant," and by means of this instrument, he moved the lazy, the unstable, and the truculent, or stones, streams, and beasts. Euridice is "naturalis concupiscentia," the "genius" which is born with every man. She wanders in the meadows, or "errat per terrena quae modo virent et statim arescunt et sicut flos feni fit omnis gloria mundi." She is loved by Aristeus, or divine virtue, but fleeing him, is bitten by a serpent—"in pede anguis virus recipit: in sensu boni temporalis delectationem." When she is led off to Hell, or "ad temporalia," her husband pursues her, wishing to extract his concupiscence through wisdom and eloquence from temporal things. This is essentially the interpretation given by William of Conches. Trivet is slightly more specific. He calls Orpheus "pars intellectiua, instrumenta sapientia et eloquentia." Euridice is "pars hominis affectiua." She falls "per sensualitatem" into a Hell of involvement in *temporalia*. If Orpheus looks back, he loses her again. The same general meaning is put in simplified form by Radulphus de Longo Campo in his commentary on the *Anticlaudianus*, Oxford, MS Balliol College 146 B, fol. 150 verso; by John of Garland, *Integumenta ovidiana*, ed. Ghisalberti (Milan, 1933), p. 67, and by a fourteenth-century commentator quoted by Ghisalberti in a note. Radulphus calls Orpheus "racio siue racionalis predicator" and Euridice "caro vel sensualitas." John of Garland's verses run:

Although this *exemplum* clearly shows the futility of wrathful altercation,[98] exactly the kind of altercation the two lovers are engaging in over the phantasm of Emelye, Arcite concludes by setting forth as a doctrine an attitude first experienced by Adam and Eve after the Fall:

> And therfore, at the kynges court, my brother,
> Ech man for hymself, ther is noon other.

The phrase "at the kynges court" may be a bit of glancing satire at English court life in Chaucer's time, but, in any event, Arcite's conclusion shows an inability on his part to follow a logical sequence of thought. As the first part of the poem ends, both lovers cite philosophical principles from Boethius without being able to see their implications.

When we meet Arcite again at the beginning of the second part, his "immoderate thought" has led to the full development of a passion. His condition is

> Nat oonly lik the loveris maladye
> Of Hereos, but rather lyk manye,
> Engendred of humour malencolik,
> Biforen, in his celle fantastik.
> And shortly, turned was al up-so-doun
> Bothe habit and eek disposicioun
> Of hym, this woful lovere, daun Arcite.

The medical language serves only to emphasize the fact that Arcite has undergone the traditional process of suggestion, delightful thought, and passion. The three steps are explicitly defined in the description of the "loveris maladye" given by Arnaldus of Villanova in his treatise *De amore heroico*. After explaining that "heroic love" is not, strictly speaking, a disease, but rather, an accident, Arnaldus continues by saying that "love of this kind, that is, of the

---

> Pratum delicie, coniunx caro, vipera virus,
> Vir ratio, Stix est terra, loquela lira.

The anonymous commentator makes Orpheus a "vir discretus" and Euridice "sensualitas." Neither Chaucer nor those in his audience who recognized his allusion would have failed to see in the "lawless" lover a suggestion of the perennial overthrow of the reason or of wisdom in those not sufficiently "virile" to follow the "true Orpheus."

[98] It is so used by Deschamps, *Oeuvres, SATF*, VII, 133-134.

kind called *heroicus*, consists of vehement and assiduous thought concerning something that is desired, with a prospect of obtaining something apprehended with delight from it. The truth of this description is demonstrated thus. First a thing is fully presented to someone, reaching his apprehension either in itself or through the explanation of someone else, or by means of a simulacrum, or in any other way; and, apprehending something from the form of the said thing, or from its accidents, he conceives it to be delightful. ... And from this it necessarily follows that on account of desires for such a thing, the eager one vigorously retains its impressed form as a phantasm, and making a memory of it thinks of the thing continuously. And from these two [steps] the third arises as a consequence, for it originates when, moved by vehement desire and assiduous thinking, he begins to think of this: in what way and by what devices it may be possible to obtain the thing at will so that he may gain the enjoyment of the noxious delight which he conceives."[99]

As we might expect, the critical activity is the "vehement and assiduous thought," and it is this which must be removed if the "patient" is to be cured;[100] the phantasm must somehow be extracted from the "celle fantastik," for while it is there it corrupts the activity of the *vis aestimativae* and hence disrupts the work of the other two cells which function to discern and to remember.[101] In this way the reasoning powers may become seriously disturbed. Bernard of Gordon, author of the popular fourteenth-century *Lili-*

[99] *Opera* (Basel, 1585), col. 1525. It is instructive to contrast the Arabic view of the cause of this malady. For "daun Constantyn's" opinion, see the *Viaticum* (Leyden, 1510), sig. b iiii, where the difficulty is attributed to the necessity for expelling superfluous humors. This authority says that *hereos* means "delight." The edition here cited is very carelessly printed. A more reliable text of part of the discussion appears in Guibert of Tournai, *De modo addiscendi*, ed. E. Bonifacio (Turin, 1953), p. 193. Bonifacio refers to a text in Rasi, *Opera parva* (1505), which I have not seen.

[100] Arnaldus, *Opera*, col. 1530: "Cum igitur hec furia, suique causa formalis sit intensa cogitatio super delectabile, hoc cum confidentia obtinendi, erit illis directio, & correctiuum oppositum, non in hoc delectabile cogitare, nec sperare ullo modo eius obtentum."

[101] *Ibid.*, col. 1527: "Cum igitur quasi ad imperium aestimatiuae ceterae inclinet virtutes, patet quod superius dicebatur, scilicet quod rationis imperium sensibilium virtutum delusionibus subjugatur erroneis, cum decretum estimationis sustineat, vt informet." Accounts of the functions of the three cells of the brain vary somewhat in medieval sources.

um medicinae, emphasizes the fact that "heroic" love is a *solicitudo melancholica*, and warns that if it is not taken care of quickly, it may lead to mania, or, indeed, to the death of the lover.[102] Arcite is thus well prepared to suffer a "miracle" of Cupid or Venus, and it is not at all surprising, if we take some hints from Boccaccio's notes on the *Teseida* and from the mythographers, that as a devotee of Mars (Wrath), he meets his death through the action of an infernal fury (a wrathful passion) sent up by Pluto (Satan) at the instigation of Saturn (Time, who consumes his "children"), who was, in turn, prompted by Venus (Concupiscence). That is, concupiscence frustrated leads to wrath which in time causes self-destruction (cf. Fig. 68). However that may be, it is significant that the lover's malady as it is envisaged in the late Middle Ages is an extreme form of the pattern of action typical of the abuse of beauty, so that Arcite belongs to the same line of descent as Pygmalion, the dreamer in the *Roman de la rose*, and the cupidinous fool in Scotus' example of the precious vase. To call him a "courtly lover" is simply to obscure him in a very cloudy phantasm. Nor is this phantasm brushed aside if we consider his actions as a satire on "courtly love." Chaucer could not satirize conventions established by a "revolution in love," which later writers ascribe to the eleventh century, for the simple reason that he had never heard of them. He was concerned, moreover, with something far more profound than a set of artificial literary fashions.

An excellent example of the danger of *delectatio cogitationis* is afforded by the story of the old knight Januarie in the Merchant's Tale. Here the mirror visible in representations of Luxuria and described symbolically as the "Well of Narcissus" is pictured in a more literal fashion, and the garden of Deduit becomes an actual garden which shadows forth the ornaments and safeguards which Januarie's imagination conjures up around the phantasm of his little "paradis." Having made it perfectly apparent that, although he talks about the welfare of his "soule," he is actually interested in the "esy and clene" physical delights of marriage, so that like

---

[102] On p. 216 we read, "Amor qui hereos dicitur est solicitude melancholica propter mulieris amorem"; and on p. 217, "Prognosticatio est talis, quod nisi hereosis succurrantur, in maniam cadunt, aut moriuntur." The various cures suggested are designed to remove the "false imagination."

January in the Kalendar he looks both ways (Fig. 22),[103] and having disregarded the voice of reason in the person of Justinus and heeded instead a Placebo who will please the world in the land of the dead rather than "the Lord in the land of the living" (Ps. 114. 9),[104] our old knight follows in the footsteps of Narcissus·

> Heigh fantasye and curious bisynesse
> Fro day to day gan in the soule impresse
> Of Januarie aboute his mariage.
> Many fair shap and many a fair visage
> Ther passeth thurgh his herte nyght be nyght,
> As whoso tooke a mirour, polisshed bryght,
> And sette it in a commune market-place,
> Thanne sholde he se ful many a figure pace
> By his mirour; and in the same wyse
> Gan Januarie inwith his thoght devyse
> Of maydens whiche that dwelten hym bisyde.

Like the dreamer in the *Roman*, he selects a little bud of "fresshe beautee" and "age tendre" as the object of his affections with whom he can lead a life of "ese and hoolynesse" but with particular attention to "ese." Again disregarding Justinus, Januarie prepares for his marriage. His *delectatio cogitationis* is described in unblushing detail, so that our hero even uses the remedies suggested by "daun Constantyne" under the heading, *De paucitate coytus*.[105] As it turns out, they seem to be of small avail, for Januarie is incapable of much more than fancied delight. And in the conclusion of the story we see once again how passion may blind those who abuse beauty not only to reasonable ideas but also to plain visual evidence.[106]

[103] Januarie's delusion that he can have his "paradis" both ways, in the flesh and in the spirit, is vividly illustrated in lines 1637-1652. The names Januarie and May were probably suggested by kalendar illustrations. See Chapter III, below.

[104] The word *Placebo* from the psalm was familiar in fourteenth-century *Horae* and devotional manuals as the first rubric in the Office for the Dead. Chaucer's audience undoubtedly knew that the Lord was to be pleased in the Land of the Living, so that the use of the name Placebo for one who flatters the desires of the flesh has a rather biting irony.

[105] *Viaticum*, sig. K iii-iv, where potions for this deficiency are described.

[106] Both the merchant and that first Chaucerian critic Harry Baily take the story as an attack on women, but this fact is a reflection on their own characters, not on the story.

There is an enormous difference between Januarie and Arcite, and again between either of them and the shadowy figure who moves through the *Roman de la rose*, but these differences should not be allowed to obscure the fact that the actions of all three follow a similar pattern. As far as external circumstances are concerned, the beauty of the world may be abused in an infinite number of ways, and the necessary operations may be carried out by anyone old enough, no matter what his rank or station. The examples already adduced should be sufficient to show the literary importance of the theme. By Chaucer's time, numerous statements of its significance were available in the writings of the Fathers, which continued to be copied and read in the fourteenth century, in treatises on love, and both directly and indirectly in literary texts. Finally, we should not neglect the fact that St. Augustine's distinction between the use and the abuse of beauty is foreshadowed in the Bible itself, not only in Genesis, but more explicitly in Wisdom. With reference to the former, it is said (13. 1, 5): "But all men are vain, in whom there is not the knowledge of God: and who by these good things that are seen, could not understand him that is, neither by attending to the works have acknowledged who was the workman. . . . For by the greatness of the beauty and the creature, the creator of them may be seen, so as to be known thereby." The abuse of beauty is described in terms of idolatry. There is a carpenter who makes an image (13. 11-19; cf. Isa. 44. 12, Jer. 10. 3), there are mariners who pray to a piece of wood (14. 1-14), there is a father who worships an image of his son (14. 15), there are idols of tyrants (14. 16ff.), and there is a potter who creates images in clay (15. 7ff.). Worship of "the shadow of a picture, a fruitless labor, a graven figure with divers colors, the sight whereof enticeth the fool to lust after it" is said to be "the beginning of fornication." All that is necessary to turn these images into images in the mind is the New Law: "whosoever shall look on a woman to lust after her, hath committed adultery with her in his heart." That Law also furnished the typical figure for the idol: *a woman.*

Meanwhile, the characteristic machinery developed in the *Roman de la rose* to set these ideas forth was not without influence on the visual arts, as a series of marginalia in a fourteenth-century Flemish Psalter (Oxford, Bodl., MS Douce 6, Figs. 23-28) demonstrates. Figure 23, which may be said to begin a series, states the theme. The margins show the "inimicos" of Psalm 109 as lovers. At the upper right the God of Love places a wreath on the head of the lady, while the lover, with a gesture that was then erotic rather than avuncular, chucks her under the chin. Both the wreath and the gesture, further examples of which we shall examine later (Figs. 59-63), were common features of amorous imagery in Gothic art. Below, the singing birds (cf. Figs. 8, 9) and amorous dalliance, which includes "chin-chucking" as well as something more obvious, suggest the attractions of Deduit, just as they do when the lover enters the garden in the *Roman*. Figure 24 shows the lover caught in the bird-snare of Cupid, perhaps in consequence of his attention to his hawk in the initial. The next item in the series, which extends over a number of folios with intervening material, appropriately introduces the theme of idolatry as the lover, placing a canopy over her head, kneels before his lady (Fig. 25) as though she were some saint in stone. The rabbit at the top of Fig. 26 indicates what the lover, watching from the side, is actually interested in, a small furry creature of Venus and an object of her "hunt" which owed its popularity as a symbol in part to the fact that a play on words was possible in French involving *con* and *conin*.[107] Below, the lover carries water, perhaps to indicate the "penance" he undertakes for the sake of the rabbit. The "hunt" theme appears again on the right, where, as the lover is about to ascend to his goal, the God of Love hovers above with his arrow in a scene dominated by the fierce lion of youthful desire. In Fig. 27, the hunt appears again at the top while below the God of Love watches the lover offer his wounded heart to the lady. The lover also does his homage to the deity. Finally, in Fig. 28, the lover is seen praying to the lady for the rabbit at the top. She listens to his plea, so that at the bottom of the page the lover, a *miles amoris* with leonine desire, catches the rabbit. What these illustrations imply is simply the road to a position on the lower right in the scene at the left of Fig. 23, a position attained by the abuse of beauty through the wrong kind of reaction to that which is "fair to the eye." The illustrations themselves are not out of place in a devotional manual.

[107] For wordplay on *con, conin,* see Deschamps, *Oeuvres, SATF,* iv, 281, viii, 117.

3. THE NATURE OF BEAUTY

What, we may ask, is this beauty which may be either a snare to the senses or an inspiration to piety? In St. Augustine's treatment of this question, the principle of beauty is the same principle that lends validity to the liberal arts, which were thought to lead the mind in the direction of the intelligible.[108] And in the discussion of the manner in which they function in the *De ordine*, it becomes clear that the arts do so by leading to the perception of "number"[109] (order, proportion, harmony) in creation. The most perfect proportion is equality, which, in its perfect form, resides only with God (*De musica*, 6. 11. 29). It is the persistence of the general attitude implicit in this theory which leads Hugh of St. Victor in the *Didascalicon* to consider the arts to be superior to the materials of the arts. What we would call an "abstraction" is for St. Augustine and for many of his followers a step toward the immutable. Thus in the *De quantitate animae* (8ff.) St. Augustine finds the equilateral triangle, the square, and the circle to be demonstrations of equality. But the equality of the square is greater than that of the triangle, and that of the circle is greater still, so that the circle, the most beautiful of plane figures, most resembles virtue in the soul (16. 27).

In the *De libero arbitrio* (2. 16. 41-44), the specifically aesthetic implications of this attitude are developed in some detail. Anything that is delightful to the flesh through the corporal senses will be found to be rationally ordered (*numerosus*). However, no one is able to judge the presence of "number" in corporal things unless he has within himself certain laws of beauty to which he can refer the "numbers" that he observes outside of himself.[110] Basically, the beauty of the sky, the sea, and the land reflects the ultimate "equal-

---

[108] See Svoboda, p. 30.

[109] The word *numerus* is difficult to translate adequately. F. J. Thonnard in the notes to the edition of the *De musica* in the "Bibliothèque Augustinienne" (Paris, 1947), pp. 513-514, points out that it is used in four ways: (1) in the ordinary mathematical sense, (2) in the sense of rhythm, (3) in the sense of harmony among the parts in physical movement, or, in man, harmony among the various sensible, intellectual, or moral activities, (4) the supreme unity of God, which is the source of mathematical law, beauty, rhythm, and the harmonious activities of nature and of man.

[110] The sixth book of the *De musica* contains a detailed account of the various types of numbers as they operate within the individual.

ity" of the Creator, just as a work of art is formed on the basis of the "numbers" in the mind of the artist. In any kind of beauty, even in the beauty of dancing, we love as beautiful the "proportionate intervals" which are presented to us, and these should rationally be considered as traces of the mind of the Creator. The *De musica* illustrates this principle at length, proceeding from simple proportions, the proportions of metrical feet, which are analyzed in detail,[111] to the ultimate Equality.

Perhaps these principles will be easier to understand, and their specific applications will develop more coherently, if we begin with the ideas which bring the *De musica* to a close and then proceed to more concrete applications. In the last chapter of that work, St. Augustine leads his readers to the theory that the process of creation is itself an ordered development from number in proportion. The terms in which the theory is stated are the technical terms of the treatise, but if we remember the various connotations of "number" and recall that "numbers" not only appear in physical objects but also exist in various ways in the artisan or in the observer, what is said should not be difficult. St. Augustine describes first the techniques by means of which an artisan produces a beautiful (i.e. "numerous") article in wood (6. 17. 57): "Thus the artisan, by means of the rational numbers that are in his art, is able to produce the corporal [i.e., "kinesthetic"] numbers that are implicit in the habitual actions of his craft. He can, by means of these corporal numbers produce overt numbers, those by which he moves his members and to which are relevant the numbers governing intervals of time. He can, further, by means of these overt numbers, produce in wood visible forms rendered numerous by the intervals carved in it. If this is true, cannot the nature of things subject to the least commandment of God produce the wood itself from the earth and the other elements from nothing?"

Nature is superior to any human artisan, and should hence be able to produce "numerous" entities without difficulty. "Indeed, the spatial numbers of a tree [i.e., the harmony of its parts in

<hr>

[111] With one exception, metrical feet all exhibit one of the following ratios when they are divided into arsis and thesis: 1:1, 2:1, 3:2, 4:3. Only the amphibrach shows 3:1, a ratio which skips one and hence is imperfect. Musically, 1:1 is a perfect consonance, 2:1 is an octave, 3:2 a fifth, and 4:3 a fourth.

space] must be preceded by temporal numbers. For there is no kind of vegetable species which does not refer to certain specific dimensions in time for the benefit of its seed. And it takes root and germinates and emerges into the air and unfolds its leaves and strengthens itself and either bears fruit or produces seeds by virtue of the most secret numbers of the plant itself. How much more true is this of the bodies of animals in which the intervals of numbers offer much more evidence of harmonious regularity?"

The very processes of life are thus seen to be controlled by the principle of beauty. But more important still, that principle is the principle of creation itself. "May these things be accomplished among the elements, and the elements themselves not be susceptible to creation from nothing? As if, indeed, anything could be more vile and more abject among them than earth is. Now this element, first of all, has a general corporal form in which may be demonstrated a certain unity and number and order. For every corporal particle, however small, is necessarily extended in length from a single indivisible point [i.e., its first beginning], assumes a third characteristic, width, and is completed in a fourth by height which fills its body. Whence comes this mode of progression from one to four? Whence comes also this equality of parts which is found in length, width, and height? And whence comes that correlation . . . which so operates that the ratio between the length and the point is similar to that between the width and the length and to that between the height and the width? Whence, I ask, do all these things come, except from that eternal and supreme Prince of numbers, of similitude, of equality, and of order? And if we take these things away from earth, it will be nothing. Thus Almighty God made earth, and earth is made from nothing."

The figures 1 to 4 in this description are not geometrical, but in the ancient and medieval sense "musical." That is, let the indivisible point of origin of a particle be represented by 1, its length by 2, its width by 3, and its height by 4.[112] The figure 2 exceeds 1

---

[112] Cf. *De lib. arb.*, 2. 17. 45-47. The *De musica* was not addressed to those already faithful, hopeful, and charitable, but to those who might be led through the language of the arts as they were then understood to appreciate the necessity for these qualities. The peculiar properties of the series 1, 2, 3, 4 as explained in the first book of the *De musica* were undoubtedly set forth in a manner designed to appeal to those educated persons in St. Augustine's audience who were impressed by the fashionable Pythagorean symbolism of late antiquity. Among the

by the same amount that 3 exceeds 2, and so on. For our present purposes, we may look upon the "arithmetical" content of this argument as a poetic figure. What is important is that St. Augustine envisaged both creation and the subsequent processes of nature as harmonious developments governed by the highest principles of beauty.

The temporal harmonies of the created world, which are obvious on every side, are thus reflections of the immutable equality of Heaven (6. 11. 29): "What then are the things above, except those in which resides the supreme, unshaken, immutable, eternal equality? With them there is no time, no mutability; and from them proceed times constructed and ordered and modified in such a way as to imitate eternity, so that the revolution of the heavens returns to the same point and calls back the celestial bodies to the same point, and obeys in days and in months and in years and in lustres and in other sidereal cycles the laws of equality and unity and order. Since earthly things are joined to celestial things, the cycles of their times join together in an harmonious succession as if in universal song."

The "music of the spheres" here suggested is a Christian fulfillment of an idea familiar among Pythagoreans, Platonists, and Stoics in late antiquity. The sidereal cycles were thought to produce a celestial music, sometimes said to be directed by the nine Muses, available only to the ear of wisdom. The Muses became patrons of all intellectual activity. To achieve the wisdom to hear their voices was to achieve immortality.[113] In its Christian form, the idea that temporal cycles are by their very nature reflections of the supreme beauty of eternity occurs elsewhere in St. Augustine's work,[114] and in its later development it was responsible for the

---

Pythagoreans, this series was thought of as an equilateral triangle, the sum of whose elements is 10:

.

. .

. . .

. . . .

The number 10 was thought to embrace all things celestial and terrestrial. A triangle symbolizing it and its series became a common decorative *motif* on pagan funerary monuments. See Franz Cumont, *Recherches sur le symbolisme funéraire des Romains* (Paris, 1942), p. 224.

[113] See the discussion by Cumont, *Recherches*, pp. 258-271.

[114] E.g., *On Christian Doctrine*, 2. 16. 25.

use of cyclic images like the signs of the Zodiac in architectural ornament and painting.[115] Chaucer's reference to the melody

> That cometh of thilke speres thryes thre,
> That welle is of musik and melodye
> In this world here, and cause of armonye

would have thus carried quite specific connotations to his readers.

Creation is not only beautiful in the temporal intervals governed by Nature; there is also a "frozen music" in its spatial relationships. In a discussion of the limitations of the "numbers of judgment" by means of which we determine whether those musical intervals we perceive are pleasing, St. Augustine points out that although our sensory perception is confined to a restricted area by the exigencies of nature, the universe is, nevertheless, a proportionate whole. Its grandeur is not due to any absolute magnitude it may have, but rather to the ratios or intervals that exist among its parts (6. 7. 19): "Thus the world, frequently called 'heaven and earth' in the Divine Scriptures, is, if taken as a whole, something of great extent. If all its parts are diminished in proportion, it remains great. If the parts are augmented, it remains equally great. For in the intervals of time and space, nothing is great in itself, but only as it is compared with something smaller, and nothing is small in itself, but only as it is compared with something greater."

Our perception of the beauty of this proportionate whole is restricted not only by the limitations of our natural sensory faculties, but also by whatever limitations we impose on our reasoning powers by confining them to a literal or sensory view of what we see. These limitations may make many things seem "inordinata et perturbata"—disordered and chaotic—for each one of us is, as it were, tied to the order of things in a specific place determined in accordance with his merits. It is as if each individual were a statue located in a building with large and spacious halls. From his limited vantage he cannot perceive the beauty of which he is himself a part (6. 11. 30). For even the sinner, although he is not himself beautiful, is conducted by that law which he does not wish to follow, and is an integral part of the beauty of the whole.

[115] Cf. E. W. Tristram, *English Wall Painting of the Fourteenth Century* (London, 1955), p. 6.

St. Augustine elaborates this last idea elsewhere. In the *De libero arbitrio*, for example, it is said that "if the soul does not descend to misery except through sin, then our sins are also necessary to the perfection of the universe which God created. . . . Neither the sins in themselves nor the misery in itself is necessary to the perfection of the whole, but it is necessary that the souls in that they are souls sin if they wish to do so, and if they sin, that they be miserable" (3. 9. 26). Similarly, in *On Christian Doctrine*, St. Augustine, as we have seen, can speak of the lowest part of the world which is subject to evil angels "according to the most beautiful order of things." It follows as a first principle of aesthetics that beauty arises from the rational perception of an ordered and proportionate whole, and that the master pattern of such a whole is the created world itself, no matter what its imperfections may seem to be to the carnal eye. A very similar argument was advanced by John the Scot,[116] and it is implicit in the arguments of Boethius in the *Consolation of Philosophy*. Thus we read, in Chaucer's translation (3, m. 9): "Thow, that art althir-fayrest, berynge the faire world in thy thought, formedest this world to the lyknesse semblable of that faire world in thy thought. Thou drawest alle thyng of thy sovereyn ensaumpler and comaundest that this world, parfytly ymakid, have frely and absolut his parfyte parties. Thow byndest the elementis by nombres proporcionables, and the coolde thinges mowen accorde with the hote thinges, and the drye thinges with the moyste; that the fyr, that is purest, fle nat over-heye, ne that the hevynesse drawe nat adoun over-lowe the erthes that ben ploungid in the watris. . . . O Fadir, yyve thou to the thought to steyen up into thi streyte seete; and graunte hym to enviroune the welle of good; and, the lyght ifounde, graunte hym to fycchen the clere syghtes of his corage in the; and skatere thou and tobreke the weyghtes and the cloudes of erthly hevynesse; and schyn thou by thi bryghtnesse, for thou art cleernesse, thow art pesible reste to debonayre folk; thow thiself art bygynnynge, berere, ledere, path and terme; to looke on the, that is our ende."

To follow wisdom rather than one or more of the "false goods" which appeal to the senses is to allow the mind to ascend to God, so that it may discern the fact that all fortune is good; for what appears to be fortune is actually a manifestation of the most beau-

[116] *De div. nat.*, PL, 122, cols. 965 ff.

tiful order of the world established through Providence. In so far as the senses are concerned, therefore, beauty may be implicit, just as it is implicit in a figurative expression.

If the evil angels and the sinners form a part of an ordered whole to whose beauty they contribute, it follows that in general the beauty of the whole is greater than that of any of its parts. This principle is stated explicitly in the *De genesi contra Manichaeos* (1. 21. 32): "For if the single works of God as they are considered by prudent men are found to have praiseworthy measures and numbers and orders constituted in their proper kind, how much more is true of all together, that is, of the universal whole which is filled with these single individuals? Indeed, all beauty evident in parts is much more praiseworthy in the whole than in the part. Thus in the human body, if we commend the eyes alone, the nose alone, the cheeks alone, or only the head, the hands, or the feet, and the other parts alone, how much more do we commend the whole body to which all the members which are beautiful alone contribute their beauty? In the same way, if beautiful hands, which are even praised alone on the body, are separated from the body, do not they themselves lose their grace, and are not the other parts so separated unseemly? Such is the force and power of integrity and unity, that even those things which are good separately please when they come together and join in some kind of whole."

In the *De vera religione* (30. 55) the harmony of the parts with the whole is called *convenientia*, and is said to involve two principles: the similarity of equal parts, and the gradation of unequal parts. The theory itself had some currency during the Middle Ages. Thus in his *Tractatus de bono et malo* William of Auvergne points out that although avarice is a good in itself, it worsens the spirit which it infects; and in the same way, a thing which is beautiful loses its beauty if it is wrongly ordered. An eye may be beautiful, but it is not beautiful if it is placed in the middle of the face. The color red may be beautiful, but it is not beautiful in that part of the eye which should be white, and so on.[117] And Dante says in the *Convivio* (1. 5. 13), "Quella cosa dice l'uomo essere bella cui le parti debitamente si rispondono, per che de la loro armonia resulta piacimento."

[117] See Pouillon, "La beauté" etc., where Guillaume's work is printed in an appendix.

These criteria apply to beauty in the arts as well as to that in nature and in the universe as a whole. For example, St. Augustine illustrates the requirement for the "similarity of equal parts" in the *De ordine* (2. 11. 34) by explaining that a door placed slightly off-center in a building seems to be at fault, and, further, that when the second of three windows in a building is in the center, the other two will seem wrongly placed if they are not at equal distances on either side. And in the *De vera religione* (30. 54), the gradation of unequal parts is shown in another architectural example. If two windows of unequal size are placed side by side, they will seem offensive, but if they are placed one above the other, the result is a gradation which does not offend. If three unequal windows are involved, the largest should exceed the next largest by the same amount as that one exceeds the smallest. But the *ratio* or "reason" in art of this kind, like the technique of the ordinary musician,[118] is based on the artist's memory of past experience concerning what is pleasing. He is not aware of any imitation of divine "numbers." However, as Christianity evolved its own distinctive art forms during the Middle Ages, a conscious effort was made to substitute for those empirical standards in the arts, for which St. Augustine had so little respect, standards based on the science of music as it was developed in the *quadrivium*. The Gothic cathedral was in some instances clearly designed to incorporate proportions suggesting divine harmonies,[119] the tones in vocal and instrumental music were given an aura of philosophical meaning,[120] and, as Petrarch assures us, the Muses of Lady Philosophy were substituted for those eloquent but unwise poetic strumpets with whom Boethius was found consorting at the beginning of the *Consolation*.[121] In its more sophisticated forms, Christian art was an art designed to sug-

[118] Cf. *De mus.*, 1. 6. 11-12.
[119] This thesis is developed by Otto von Simson, *The Gothic Cathedral* (New York, 1956).
[120] See Leo Schrade, "Die Darstellungen der Töne an dem Kapitellen der Abtei-kirche zu Cluni," *Deutsche Vierteljahrschrift f. Litteraturwissenschaft u. Geistes-geschichte*, VII (1929), 229-266. Medieval instrumental and vocal music was developed so as to be "allegorical" in various ways, not so as to produce a "direct communication of the feelings." See Manfred F. Bukofzer, "Speculative Thinking in Mediaeval Music," *Speculum*, XVII (1942), 165-180. This tradition persisted in the Renaissance. See Gretchen L. Finney, "Music: a Book of Knowledge in Renaissance England," *Studies in the Renaissance*, VI (1959), 36-63.
[121] *Invective contra medicum*, ed. P. Ricci (Rome, 1950), p. 36.

gest to the reason those "numbers" which govern the temporal and spatial intervals of creation and reflect, ultimately, the supreme Equality.

Some notion of the importance of music as a study in the medieval curriculum may be gained by a brief glance at Hugh of St. Victor's discussion of it in the *Didascalicon*.[122] He defines music as a "concord of dissimilar things reduced to one." That is, music is the study of those proportions which lead to the perception of an harmonious whole. It is understandable that medieval authorities should sometimes say that music has a place in all the other arts. "There are," Hugh says, "three kinds of music: mundane, human, instrumental. Mundane music exists in the elements, in the planets, in periods of time. In elements it exists in weight, number, measurement; in planets it appears in location, motion, nature; in times it exists in days, in alternations between day and night, in the waxing and waning of the moon, in years, in the alternations of spring, summer, autumn, winter. Human music exists either in the body or in the spirit, or in the relationship between them. In the body it exists in the animation of growth which is proper to all living things; in the humors, whence arises the human complexion. . . . Music in the spirit exists in virtues like justice, piety, and temperance; in powers like reason, wrath, and concupiscence. Music between the body and the spirit is that natural love by which the spirit is joined to the body, not with carnal fetters, but with certain affections directed toward moving the body and endowing it with sensation. According to this love, 'no one hates his own flesh' [Eph. 5. 29]. This music is formed so that the flesh is loved but the spirit is loved more, so that the body may be nourished but virtue remain unimpaired. . . ." In short, the study of music was the study of those aesthetic principles which govern the universe and the activities of man.

A few illustrations may make the pervasive relevance of musical theory clear. The ratio 1:2, or the octave,[123] is said by St. Augustine to represent the concord made possible by Christ between Himself and the inferior nature of man (*On the Trinity*, 4. 3). Christ died once and was resurrected once. But we die two deaths: a death of the spirit and a death of the flesh. In the same way, we undergo

[122] Ed. Buttimer, pp. 32-33.
[123] That is, the octave as expressed on a monochord.

two resurrections: a resurrection at baptism and a final resurrection. Thus there is, in both instances, a ratio of 1:2 or an octave between Christ and man. So far as times are concerned, Sunday is not only the first day of the week, but, counting musically, it is also the octave, and here the octave again recalls the Resurrection, which took place on the Lord's Day. And this meaning is said to have been foreshadowed in the Old Law by the Circumcision, which took place on the eighth day. A numerical calculation also makes an octave of Pentecost.[124] If we project our calculations on a larger scale, the eighth age of the world, following a seventh, which is sometimes made to stand for the age of purification in Purgatory, is eternity; and, in general, seven, which represents temporal things, is followed by an eternal eight.[125] Hence the inscription on the eighth tone as it is carved on a capital of the abbey church of Cluny reads, appropriately, "Octavus sanctos omnes docet esse beatos."[126] Throughout the *terza rima* of Dante's *Commedia*, the ratio 1:2 keeps the underlying lesson of the poem always before our eyes. But the octave had more striking visual results. Octagonal baptismal fonts, symbolizing the harmony which they established between the faithful and Christ, stood in churches and cathedrals throughout Christian Europe during the Middle Ages.[127] There were other forms,[128] but in England the octagonal shape became normal during the thirteenth, fourteenth, and fif-

[124] See the letter to Januarius, *Epist.*, 55. 13. 23 and 15. 28. There is a good discussion by Rahner, *Griechische Mythen*, pp. 106-112. A sermon delivered by a Franciscan during the last decade of the thirteenth century quoted by Beryl Smalley, "John Russell, o.f.m.," *Rech. de théol. anc. méd.*, XXIII (1956), pp. 282-283, demonstrates the harmony of the octave on the Cross: "Nam sicut docet Hugo super Apocalipsim, super illud, *cantabant canticum novum* [Apoc. 5. 9]: in cruce Christi fuit talis cantus, quod ibi erat proportio dupli ad simplum, quia ibi nostra mors destructa est per simplam mortem Christi." The preacher goes on to find the ratio 3:1 on the Cross also, perhaps indicating a relaxation of Patristic musical standards.

[125] E.g., see *Gregorianum*, PL, 193, col. 449, and the sermon of Alanus de Insulis, "In die sancto Pentecostes," PL, 210, col. 218.

[126] The number eight may refer to the beatitudes. See Joan Evans, *Cluniac Art of the Romanesque Period* (Cambridge, 1950), p. 119. But the significance of the ratio remains.

[127] See Mâle, *L'art religieux du XIIIe siècle*, p. 13; Richard Krautheimer, "Introduction to an 'Iconography of Mediaeval Architecture,'" *JWCI*, v (1942), p. 11.

[128] This fact led Francis Bond, *Fonts and Font Covers* (London, 1908), pp. 57-58, to doubt that any of them had any special significance.

teenth centuries.[129] Whether the eight sides of these fonts, or, for that matter, the eight sides of towers and lanterns which had a similar significance, were more appealing to the eye than five sides would have been was a matter of small importance. It was important that a number be suggested which led the mind to contemplate a harmony established by an Artisan whose handiwork in the human heart transcends anything man may do in stone.

Hugh of St. Victor speaks of the harmony between the spirit and the body as "love." A very ancient tradition associates love with harmony, especially with "mundana musica," the concord which governs the elements, the seasons, and the stars. In the invocation at the beginning of the *De rerum natura*, Lucretius attributes this love to Venus, and Ovid does the same thing in the *Fasti* after invoking the "mother of the twin loves" for the month of April. Elsewhere, the same function was attributed to Eros, and the winged loves which appear on pagan funerary monuments are said to represent such music.[130] Among Christians this universal concord was attributed not to Venus but to divine love. The most famous description of it is that which appears in the *Consolation* of Boethius (2 m. 8): "That the world with stable feyth varieth accordable chaungynges; that the contrarious qualites of elementz holden among hemself allyaunce perdurable; that Phebus, the sonne, with his goldene chariet bryngeth forth the rosene day; that the moone hath commaundement over the nyghtes, which nyghtes Esperus, the eve-starre, hath brought; that the see, gredy to flowen, constreyneth with a certein eende his floodes, so that it is nat leveful to strecche his brode termes or boundes uppon the erthes . . . al this accordaunce of thynges is bounde with love, that governeth erthe and see, and hath also comandement to the hevene. And yif this love slakede the bridelis, alle thynges that now loven hem togidres wolden make batayle contynuely, and stryven to fordo the fassoun of this world, the which they now leden in accordable feith by fayre moevynges. This love halt togidres peples joyned with an holy boond, and knytteth sacrement of mariages of chaste loves; and love enditeth lawes to trewe felawes. O weleful were mankynde, yif thilke love that governeth hevene governede yowr corages."

---

[129] See E. Tyrrell-Green, *Baptismal Fonts* (London, 1928), p. 30.
[130] Cumont, *Recherches*, pp. 86-87.

Trivet's unhesitating characterization of the love described in this passage as "divine love"[131] undoubtedly represents a conventional medieval response to it, and, in fact, there is no reason to suspect that Boethius himself did not mean to suggest it, since the "numbers" which govern creation represent the operation of Providence. We may find a more explicitly Christian statement of the same theme in the *Speculum charitatis* of St. Ailred of Rievaulx.[132] The "order of mercy" is a part of the natural harmony of the created world. Sinners in the "order of justice" do not produce a discord, for that is impossible, but they have, as it were, a melody of their own.

To return for a moment to the classical literary precedents, there is an obvious difference between the function of Venus in the Invocation to the *De rerum natura* and her function in the fourth book of the same poem, where she is seen leading young men to what good Epicureans regarded as indiscreet behavior. Again, in the *Fasti*, Venus is the mother of "twin loves," and the poet jokingly brushes aside the implication that he is setting out to write once more in the vein of the *Amores* and the *Ars amatoria*. There are, clearly, two ways to look at Venus, or at least there are two "loves" which may call her Mother. An alternative remains, however, for we may make two Venuses. This solution was developed in late antiquity by the Pythagoreans, who placed the traditional deities in two "hemispheres," one celestial and the other infernal, so as to make pairs, and among these pairs was Venus.[133] As we have seen, the Middle Ages did not attribute "mundana musica" to Venus literally, but the connection between music and Venus was retained for purposes of reading classical texts and as a "philosophical" figure of speech. Both methods of "doubling" Venus were also retained. The Pythagorean method was transmitted to the Middle Ages through the commentary on the *Thebaid* attributed to Lactantius Placidus.[134] Thus Remigius of Auxerre says that

[131] MS Burney 131, fol. 30. Roger of Waltham, *Compendium morale*, Oxford, Bodl., MS Fairfax 4, fols. 33ff., calls the love which "halt togidres peples" a natural bond, since we are born of the same stock and imbued by nature with mutual love. But he goes on to explain that this love can be maintained only in charity.

[132] *PL*, 195, cols. 524-525.

[133] Cumont, *Recherches*, pp. 35ff.

[134] Ed. Jahnke (Leipzig, 1898), pp. 229-230. The possibility that the original parts of this commentary, which enjoyed accretions during the Middle Ages,

"there are two Venuses, one the mother of sensuality and lust . . . the other chaste, who rules over honest and chaste loves."[135] A commentary on the *Fasti* produced during the late eleventh or early twelfth century recognizes that Venus is responsible for both "virtuous love" and "unlawful passion," observing that Ovid considers one Venus to be the mother of both.[136] In another commentary on the same work, the two sons of Venus, perhaps on the basis of a hint from Horace, are called Cupid and Iocus.[137] The two loves produced by Venus, or the two Venuses, are thus seen to correspond to the two kinds of love suggested by the Boethian meter. Bernard Silvestris, in fact, calls the celestial Venus "mundana musica": "We read that there are two Venuses, a legitimate goddess and a goddess of lechery. We say that the legitimate Venus is 'mundana musica,' that is, the equal proportion of worldly things, which some call 'Astrea' and others 'natural justice.' For she is in the elements, in the stars, in times, in animate things. But the shameful Venus, the goddess of sensuality, we call concupiscense of the flesh, which is the mother of all fornication."[138]

The expressions "concupiscense of the flesh" and "mother of all fornication" suggest the Augustinian conception of the malady of original sin, and, indeed, John the Scot had explicitly identified the shameful Venus with that malady.[139] Like her celestial sister, she was frequently associated with music in medieval iconography.[140] Thus there are, in effect, two very different kinds of "melodye"—one the music of the spirit and the flesh in harmony with created nature, and the other the music of the flesh as it seeks inferior satisfactions as a result of its own concupiscence. Both are melodies of love, one a "rational" love, and the other a love whose

---

may have been written as early as the fourth century, is discussed by Paul van de Waestijne, "Les scolies a la 'Thebaide' de Stace," *L'Antiquité Classique*, xix (1950), 150-153.

[135] Quoted by H. Liebeschütz, *Fulgentius metaforalis* (Leipzig, 1926), p. 45. These remarks were elaborated by Albericus, ed. Bode, p. 239, and became a medieval commonplace.

[136] See E. H. Alton, "The Mediaeval Commentators on Ovid's *Fasti*," *Hermathena*, xliv (1926), 136.

[137] Oxford, Bodl., ms Auct. f. 4. 27, fol 8 verso.

[138] Ed. Riedel, p. 9.

[139] *Annotationes in Marcianum*, ed. Lutz, p. 13.

[140] Cf. Folke Nordström, *Virtues and Vices on the Fourteenth-Century Corbels in the Choir of Uppsala Cathedral* (Stockholm, 1956), p. 99.

"ratios" are illogical. The illogical consonances of fleshly love are vividly described by Matthew of Vendôme:

Love is an unjust judge: marrying adverse things
   It causes the natures of things to degenerate.
Opposites are consonant in love: knowledge is ignorant,
   Wrath jokes, honor soils, need is wealthy,
Vile deeds are good, praise reproaches, despair hopes,
   Hope fears, harmful things are profitable, rewards injure . . . .[141]

Music and love are very closely related, and the kind of beauty one sees, or the music one makes or hears, depends upon how one loves. In Chaucer's Knight's Tale, the long speech of Duke Theseus on the "fair chain of love" is, in a sense, an invocation to the celestial Venus, or to *mundana musica*. That Theseus can perceive this love and this music is something decidedly in his favor. But the Venus he invokes is not the lady with the "citole" to whom Palamon had promised to "holden werre alwey with chastitee." Order in the tale is restored with a ceremony that "highte matrimoigne or mariage," and since there is no "jalousie" in it, an essential ingredient of the love of the shipwrecked Venus, we may conclude that it was what Boethius called a "chaste" (i.e., faithful) marriage harmonious with the order Theseus invokes.

In theological terms the melodies of love are the "New Song" of St. Paul's "New Man" and the "Old Song" of the "Old Man," who represents the inherited evil habit of the flesh.[142] These songs, or melodies, are frequently illustrated in the visual arts of the Middle Ages (Figs. 29-38). To consider an early example first, in Fig. 29, from a twelfth-century Psalter, the upper half shows David surrounded by musicians whose harmonies reflect the New Song, while in the lower half a Devil playing a drum leads jongleurs and dancers in the song of the flesh. Another illustration from the same source (Fig. 30) shows a man struggling with a monster while his analogue on the right plays to a dancing girl. The melody he should be, and is not, making is revealed by the

[141] *Tobias*, ed. Mueldner (Göttingen, 1855), p. 53. Cf. Alanus, *De planctu*, PL, 210, col. 455.

[142] Although the two "songs" are a theological commonplace, a convenient source for and introduction to the theme is St. Augustine's sermon *De cantico novo*. The "New Song" is, of course, charity; the "Old Song" is cupidity.

text, *In conspectu angelorum psallam tibi.* Perhaps the most famous representation of this kind is that on a capital at Vézelay, where a jongleur plays to a woman while a devil plays upon her body to show that she responds sensually to the melody.[143] In Fig. 31 the initial shows the bellman who conventionally represents the Art of Music directing his harmony toward God. But in the lower margin the contrasting melody of the flesh is illustrated, and it is accompanied by a singing bird of the kind familiar in the garden of Deduit in the *Roman de la rose* and in Figs. 9 and 23. The same bellman appears in Fig. 32, while the grotesque on the left, playing a bagpipe, steps off toward the female grotesque on the lower right. The bagpipe, also visible in Fig. 15, is, for rather obvious reasons, frequently, although not always, an instrument with which male lovers make melody. It appears in this sense in the lower margin of Fig. 33, while a naked fool, or man without the spiritual clothing of virtue, at the upper right contrasts with the David of the initial, who plays a harp and in consonance with this melody puts down Goliath, the giant of proud worldliness. In Fig. 35 the rabbit, which we have seen in Figs. 26, 27, and 28, serves as a female counterpart to the bagpipe, while a bird sings above. The idea of the "Old" versus the "New" is brought home strikingly in Fig. 36, where the initial for the text *Cantate domini canticum novum* contains three figures singing the New Song. But a contrasting figure on the left, who is obviously an "old" man looks the other way as grotesques below make their own melody. The two melodies could be contrasted in a wide variety of ways and in connection with almost any suitable context. Thus in Fig. 37, a page from a Psalter made for Humphrey de Bohun (ca. 1370), the New Song is sung by some fourteenth-century gentlemen who have successfully made a spiritual journey across the Red Sea under the leadership of Moses while "Mary, the prophetess," using a timbrel, beats time to the melody. Contrasting themes are suggested by the figure to the left of the initial. A two-headed monster produces deciduous leaves which are not the unfading leaves of God's Word. A fool sits idly with crossed hands, and a monster below makes an unseemly melody indeed. These are those who do not cross the Red Sea, probably the *ternistratores* of the *Glossa* who sin in word, thought, and deed. Meanwhile, melody

---

[143] For an illustration, see Paul Deschamps, *Vézelay* (Paris, 1943), pl. 48.

and discord are represented in various ways in the margins. At times, representations of the Old Song are extremely forthright. Thus Fig. 38 depends for its effectiveness on a visual pun, probably suggested by a verbal pun on the word *instrument*. Finally, a "realistic" portrayal of the Old Song is afforded by the "Ymago Luxurie" in Guido Faba's treatise on the vices (Fig. 34). Here the instrumentalist and the lover should be regarded as the same person whose activity is shown in two different ways. The musical idea adds to the representation an element of humor as well as theological and philosophical profundity. To understand art of this kind properly we should abandon the gloomy nineteenth-century attitude that forthright humor and philosophical depth are incompatible. One of the most common iconographic devices for showing deafness to celestial harmony throughout the Gothic period was to represent an ass seated before a harp. This spiritually stupid beast, which amusingly figures those who have ears but hear not because of a lack of spiritual understanding, owes his popularity to a very profound philosophical work, the *Consolation* of Boethius.

Celestial melody may, of course, be contrasted with discord as well as with the melody of the flesh. A splendid example of a contrast of this kind is afforded by a page of the Ormesby Psalter (Fig. 39). The initial shows the familiar bellman accompanied by other musicians who praise God as they should and as the text of the Psalm demands. But the upper and lower margins contain symbols of discord or wrath. The wrestlers in the lower margin represent a very widespread *motif* with this significance.[144] The quarrel in the upper margin is an elaboration of the domestic struggle which represents "discord" on one of the medallions which adorn the façade of Amiens cathedral. The pot and ladle identify the female grotesque as a wife, in this instance a wife with leonine (passionate) propensities. She is shown confronting her goat-footed (lecherous) husband, who is trying to outface her. This domestic conflict is a vivid symbol of the discord which disrupts the harmony of marriage, a melody which should be sustained by a love and

---

[144] It appears in Villard de Honnecourt's Album. See *The Sketchbook of Villard de Honnecourt*, ed. T. Bowie (Bloomington, 1959), pl. 41, or Hahnloser's critical edition, XXVIII. For this *motif* elsewhere in the fourteenth century, see E. W. Tristram, *English Wall Painting of the Fourteenth Century* (London, 1955), p. 96. For an illustration from Paris Cathedral, see Fig. 56.

concord in tune with the notes of the bellman and with the "fair chain of love." Those who, out of fear, are unwilling to undertake the symbolic labors of the musicians are figured by the spiritually weak warrior on the right, who, in accordance with a passage from the *Somme le roi,* is frightened by the horns of a snail.[145] This configuration is a variant of the cowardly warrior who drops his arms in fright before a hare and a hooting owl on the façades of Notre Dame at Paris and the cathedral of Amiens (Figs. 56, 57). He appears again with a grotesque variation in the upper right of Fig. 37, where his stance before the enemy is just as ridiculous as his earlier flight.

Either of the two "songs" might be accompanied by a dance. In Fig. 29 there are some who dance to the Devil's tune. Again the gentlemen who sing the New Song in Fig. 37 join their hands in a dance. Variations on what may be thought of as a New Dance to accompany the New Song and what was actually called the "Old Dance" were common in late medieval art. The former has been well discussed by Professor Tristram,[146] so that it will suffice here to adduce only one further example, a very obvious one from the series which occupies the lower margins of the Queen Mary's Psalter (British Museum MS Royal 2 B VII) beginning on fol. 173 verso and extending, with some interruption, over a considerable number of the following folios. One drawing (Fig. 40) shows an angel leading some saints in a dance. We may assume that the music provided is the harmony of God's love manifested in the created world as *mundana musica,* and that the dance itself represents action appropriately concordant with that melody. A less admirable dance from the same source is shown in Fig. 41, where the bagpipe and drum provide a more earthly melody. This drawing may be compared with the usual illustrations of the dance of Deduit, which is certainly not the "New" dance, in the *Roman de la rose,* of which Fig. 42 is a fair example. We are invited to this dance by Oiseuse, and the music provided, which here involves a bagpipe, leads us to the domination of Cupid and Venus. The term "Old Dance" seems to have been invented by Gautier de Coincy. In his *Theophilus* it is conducted by the Devil, as in Fig. 29:

[145] See Mâle, *L'art religieux du XIII⁰ siècle,* p. 125.
[146] *Op.cit.,* pp. 9-10. Cf. Matt. 11: 16ff., and *Glossa ordinaria, PL,* 114, col. 121. For the song and dance of Fig. 37 specifically, see *PL,* 113, cols. 226, 233.

> Anemis a mout grant puissance
> Et tant seit de la vielle dance
> Qu'a sa dance fait bien baler
> Celz qui plus droit cuident aler.[147]

In *Le sermon en vers de la chasteé as nonains* the dance assumes some of the more obvious amorous connotations we have seen in representations of the Old Song. Gautier engages (lines 407ff.) in a long discourse concerning the merits of virginity and chastity. These virtues are sweeter than the rose, white flowers among "saintes flors de paradis," which should be observed with the eye of the understanding:

> Sachiez de voir: se vous en eles
> Des iex dou cuer bien vous mirez,
> L'anemi tout esbaubirez.
> Mais tant set de la vielle dance,
> S'il voit en vous point d'inconstance,
> De tex pensez voz amenra
> Par quoi mout tost voz sozpenra.[148]

By means of his weapon *concupiscentia carnis*, or Venus, the Enemy may inspire a dance, which, whether it is literally sexual or not, destroys spiritual virginity and chastity. The Old Dance is the dance of fornication, spiritual or physical, and this is the sense in which it appears in the *Roman de la rose* where "Une vieille, que Deus honisse" knows all about it and hence seems, to the eye of worldly wisdom, a good guardian for the rose. The "melody" and "dance" of the Old Man gave depth to the idea of seduction as a "music lesson," as it is, for example, in one of Deschamps' balades (No. MCLXIX):

> Marion, entendez a mi:
> Je vous aim plus que creature,
> Et pour ce d'umble cuer vous pri
> Qu'au dessoubz de vostre sainture
> Me laissez de la turelure
> Et de ma chevrette jouer.

[147] *Les miracles de Nostre Dame*, ed. V. Frederic Koenig (Geneva and Lille, 1955-), I, 159.
[148] Ed. Tauno Nurmela (Helsinki, 1937), pp. 146-147.

> La vous aprandray a dancer
> Au coursault, et faire mains tours.
> —Robin, je n'y sçaroie aler:
> Doint on ainsi parler d'amours?

The *turelure* is, of course, a bagpipe. This theme, not always with a bagpipe, however, remained prominent in art well into the eighteenth century. And there is, perhaps, a dying echo of it in William Holman Hunt's *The Awakened Conscience* (1854).

St. Augustine's association of the beautiful or the lovable with proportionate intervals or with music is thus not alien to the later Middle Ages. Moreover, as we have seen, Gothic art developed convenient means of distinguishing between "true" harmony and what might be called the "illusory" harmony of the flesh, which is mere discord with reference to created nature, but with reference to Divine Providence a part of the Order of Justice. It is not surprising that melody plays an important thematic rôle in Chaucer's poetry. Celestial harmony is described in *The Parliament of Fowls* as the "melodye"

> That cometh of thilke speres thryes thre
> That welle is of musik and melodye
> In this world here, and cause of armonye.

In the same poem, *mundana musica* is attributed to

> Nature, the vicaire of the almyghty Lord,
> That hot, cold, hevy, lyght, moyst, and dreye
> Hath knyt by evene noumbres of acord.

It is probable that this same harmony is that which the dreamer hears when he first enters the garden under African's guidance. We may contrast with it the "swogh" of sighs which permeates the Temple of Venus, and the discord among the birds which results from the "up-so-doun" attitude of the eagles. Sometimes celestial music is reflected in Chaucer's characters. St. Cecelia sings the New Song in her heart:

> And whil the organs maden melodie,
> To God allone in herte thus sang she:
> "O Lord, my soule and eek my body gye
> Unwemmed, lest that it confounded be."

St. Cecelia, it will be remembered, is an exemplar of "leveful bisynesse," the opposite of "ydelnesse" or Oiseuse, who invites one to the song and dance of Deduit. The same melody is reflected in the bird-songs to St. Valentine at the end of the *Parliament*, in the Prologue to the *Legend*, and in the "Complaint of Mars." Much more frequently, however, we find variations of the Old Song, some of which resemble in spirit the more striking representations of the subject in the visual arts. This preponderance might well be expected in *The Canterbury Tales*, since the pilgrims are led away from London, not by the knight as Blake thought, but by the miller, who plays a bagpipe.[149] To cite only two examples, both from the Miller's Tale, if we bear the philosophical and theological implications of music in mind, the humor of the following passage becomes much more than merely dramatic:

> Whan Nicholas had doon thus everideel,
> And thakked hire aboute the lendes weel,
> He kiste hire sweete and taketh his sawtrie,
> And pleyeth faste, and maketh melodie.

That the "melody" of which Nicholas is so fond is not necessarily audible in the ordinary sense is made clear in the development of the tale:

> Withouten wordes mo they goon to bedde,
> Ther as the carpenter is wont to lye.
> Ther was the revel and the melodye!

This is clearly the melody of "mirthe" or Deduit, and it ends appropriately at "the belle of laudes," although in view of Chaucer's attitude toward friars, what the brethren sang "in the chauncel" at the dawn of this *aube* remains amusingly ambiguous. In general, Chaucer's references to melody or harmony are significant and should not be neglected as being merely decorative. Far from being obscure or irrelevant, the connotations of music we have been discussing are always applicable. The question of whether or not a given song or melody is harmonious with the concord of the "speres thryes thre" is in every instance valid. Chaucer not only

---

[149] Cf. the discussion by George F. Jones, *JEGP*, XLVIII (1949), 209-228, and the article by Edward A. Block, "Chaucer's Millers and their Bagpipes," *Speculum*, XXIX (1954), 239-243.

uses specific references to music but also some of the iconological devices which were, in one way or another, related to musical ideas. For example, both the miller's skill at wrestling and the wife of Bath's leonine ways with her husbands are suggestive of the idea of discord. Again, Chaucer was familiar with the implications of the "Old Dance." The worldly-wise physician admonishes governesses of girls in the following terms:

> Thenketh that ye been set in governynges
> Of lordes doghtres, oonly for two thynges:
> Outher for ye han kept youre honestee,
> Or elles ye han falle in freletee
> And knowen wel ynough the olde daunce,
> And han forsaken fully swich meschaunce
> For everemo . . . .

The fact that the wife of Bath and Pandarus are experts in this dance tells us a great deal about their characters. They are not only literally interested in illicit sexual activity, but they are also responsive to a melody which echoes the song of the sirens who tempted Ulysses, the music of the lascivious Venus, and the song of St. Paul's Old Man. When Pandarus says to Criseyde, "lat us daunce," Criseyde suggests as an alternative suitable for a widow that she "bidde and rede on holy seyntes lyves," a kind of activity harmonious with the music of the bellman. The dance she is being invited to engage in is, as events prove, that dance concerning which Pandarus has expert knowledge. In all of these instances, the aesthetic attitudes of the characters are an integral and significant part of their characterization.

The leporine beauty which the lover approaches with his bagpipe does not differ essentially from that which attracts the lover of wisdom. The two are not opposites. Beauty is that which is lovable, and that which is lovable is harmonious, proportionate, or "equal." But to the lover who responds to the notes of "My lief is faren in londe!" these qualities are bound up inseparably with a physical object and are dependent on that object's availability and powers of endurance. Merely physical beauty was sometimes thought of as "false" beauty, and the fact that it soon fades, like the "flower of the field" (Is. 40. 6), or like a rose of Venus, is emphasized again and again. Boethius (3 pr. 6) exclaims, "But the shynynge of thi forme . . . how swyftly passynge is it, and how transitorie! Certes, it is more flyttynge than the mutabilite of floures in the somer seson." Even Petrarch—to whom the general public has been misled into attributing more romantic ideas—dwells on the dangers of such beauty.[150] Nevertheless, feminine beauty could be rationally appreciated, as certain commentaries on the Canticle of Canticles bear witness. Gilbert of Hoiland, for example, had a very respectable idea of feminine charm. "Those breasts," he wrote, "are beautiful which rise up a little and swell moderately, neither too elevated, nor, indeed, level with the rest of the chest. They are as if repressed but not depressed, softly restrained, but not flapping loosely."[151] But these observations were not set forth to awaken Cupid; they illustrate principles of pulpit eloquence. For the lover of wisdom the abstraction which the physical object suggests is more beautiful than the object. Again, with reference to human beauty it was said that charity makes a man beautiful.[152] It is true that charity cannot make a man's features more regular, nor can it raise the fallen breasts of a woman. It lacks those ornaments of dress and feature affected by the followers of the God of Love and the mirrored beauty of Polyphemus or Narcissus. But it does manifest itself in actions from which an inner harmony may be inferred.

In our discussion of figurative expression, we saw that the materials of the figures may or may not be "numerous" or attractive in themselves. Whether they are or not, the fact that the figure leads the mind in the direction of the *invisibilia* means that it leads the mind toward beauty. Again, the abuse of beauty typified by the actions of Scotus' fool before the precious vase, by lovers like Narcissus and Pygmalion, and by musically insensitive characters like Alisoun of Bath and Pandarus, represents a movement away from true beauty toward confusion. St. Augustine, recognizing that everyone loves beauty, tells us that the movement from transitory beauty toward eternal beauty is not difficult (*De musica*, 6. 14. 44): "And what is easier, to love colors, and voices, and delicacies, and roses, and soft gentle bodies? These things are easier for the soul to love, in which it seeks nothing but equality and symmetry, and

[150] *De remediis vtriusque fortunae*, in *Opera* (Basel, 1581), pp. 2-3.
[151] *PL*, 184, col. 163.
[152] See Svoboda, p. 162; St. Bernard, *Serm. in Cant.*, 85.11.

when it considers them a little more diligently, finds hardly a trace or a distant shadow of these qualities there? And is it difficult for the soul to love God, when, although yet wounded and soiled, in thinking of Him it can find nothing unequal, nothing inconsistent, nothing divided in space, nothing varied in time? Does it delight to erect vast monuments and to exert its powers in architectural works, and is it pleased by the numbers in these (I find there nothing else) which are said to be equal or similar because the *ratio* of the art does not deride them? For if it is thus, why does the soul fall away from that most true stronghold of equality to this, and erect earthly scaffoldings from its ruins? This was not the promise of Him who knew not how to deceive. 'For my yoke,' He says, 'is sweet, and my burden light' [Matt. 11. 30]. And the love of this world is more laborious. For that which the soul seeks in it, constancy and eternity, it shall not find. . . ."

When Christian art developed its own styles, they were styles consistent with this attitude, which permitted the artist to point toward a transcendent but objective beauty and to inspire in his audience a love for it. Frequently the medieval artist avoided too obvious a surface *convenientia*, so that the reason might be excited to seek and to discover an equality among the *invisibilia* suggested by the subject matter and the technique. And this is true whether we are considering figurative expression in literature, forms in the visual arts, or rhythmic configurations in music. The demons and monsters of Romanesque churches, the grotesques which appear among the Gothic saints, on misericords or roofs bosses, or in the margins of Psalters, may not be beautiful in themselves, but like the evil angels and the sinners in St. Augustine's hierarchical universe, they contribute through their significances to the ordered beauty of the whole.

It follows from what we have said that in the appreciation of medieval art the attitude of the observer is of primary importance, for no work of art was then self-contained or existed in a "world of its own." For this reason the "pure aesthetics" developed since the early nineteenth century has little validity as an approach to it. St. Augustine says that animals respond to music, but he adds that the wise man may find refreshment in it, and food for meditation.[153]

[153] *De musica*, 1. 4. 5; cf. *On Christian Doctrine*, 2. 16. 26 and 4. 7. 19.

To the more cultivated minds of the Middle Ages artistic works were things designed, through their "numbers," through their figurative devices, or through their very workmanship, to lead the mind toward a beauty which transcends corporal modulations; such works were not merely attractive in themselves, but were intended to lead the mind toward something beyond. Generally, medieval styles were consistent with this aim, as we shall seek to show in the next chapter.

I. THE ROMANESQUE PERIOD

𝕮𝖍𝖆𝖚𝖈𝖊𝖗 wrote during a period characterized by historians of art as "late Gothic." During his lifetime, the English court style in painting acquired features which it is customary to associate with the "International Style," and English architecture developed what has been called its first truly "national" style, the Perpendicular. This seemingly confused situation has no immediate relevance to literature, where such features as pointed arches, linear outlines, or ogees have no place. Nevertheless, there are broader and more general characteristics of the various styles in the visual arts which do have their counterparts in literature. These characteristics will be somewhat easier to grasp if we begin our discussion with the Romanesque period and move more or less chronologically in the direction of Chaucer. In our discussion it will simplify matters if we use the term *Romanesque* to designate the earlier part of the period, and the term *Gothic* to designate the later part of the same period without implying any of the lists of external characteristics customarily used to define these terms.[1] The definitions which re-

[1] In a general sense the word *Romanesque* is now used customarily to designate the period from about the middle of the eleventh century to the early thirteenth century, although architectural historians sometimes include all pre-Gothic medieval art under this heading. The Gothic period, which may be said to overlap later Romanesque, since the spread of the Gothic style was gradual and did not affect all media simultaneously, begins in the middle of the twelfth century and extends into the Renaissance. It is customary to divide Gothic into three periods or phases: (1) from the middle of the twelfth century to ca. 1275; (2) from ca. 1275 to ca. 1350; (3) from ca. 1350 to ca. 1450. In English illumination there seems to be a very marked "shift" between the second and third of these periods. Walter Oakeshott, *The Sequence of English Mediaeval Art* (London, 1950), divides English art into the following "periods": (1) Northumbrian, 650-850; (2) Late Anglo-Saxon, 970-1100; (3) Romanesque, 1100-1200; (4) Early Gothic, 1200-1340; (5) Late Gothic, 1340-1450. In chronological schemes of this kind approximate dates are more useful than rigid divisions. With special reference to French architecture, R. de Lasteyrie, *L'Architecture religieuse en France a l'époque gothique* (Paris, 1926-1927), divided the Gothic period as follows: (1) Transitional stage, 1137-1180; (2) Lanceolate, 1180-1270; (3) Rayonnant, 1270-1400; (4) Flamboyant, 1400-. Some historians now avoid these terms. In spite of the variations which these chronologies reveal, stylistic changes take place with surprising regularity. For example, see the architectural features described by J. Puig y Cadafalch, *Le premier art roman* (Paris, 1928).

sult from these lists usually emphasize the "high points" in the development of each style, suggesting a period of preliminary growth, a mature style consistent with the definition, and a period of decay. It will be more useful for our purposes to consider the period as a whole without resorting to a "wave motion" of this kind and without prejudicing ourselves unnecessarily by thinking any part of it to be "preliminary" on the one hand or "decadent" on the other. Moreover, when we speak of "developments" in this period, we shall imply neither that they are "improvements" nor that they represent a falling away from an established "classic" style. A development in this discussion is simply a change or a series of related changes in time. In some instances the direction of these developments remains more or less constant throughout the period, but this fact does not necessarily imply improvement.

Meanwhile, in discussing Romanesque and Gothic art we shall be forced to seek principles which are sufficiently general to apply to various forms of art in these periods, including literature; these principles, therefore, will not be of much value to historians of the various branches of the visual arts, who have already developed highly sophisticated techniques of stylistic analysis. For the most part, the features of style in the visual arts to which attention is called here have already been discussed by art historians. A few prejudices of the author's own may also appear, however, and the reader who is unfamiliar with art history is urged to study the illustrations carefully and to consult the books referred to in the notes in order to form his own opinions, which may very well differ from the ones here expressed. On the other hand, the author hopes that any historians of art who may consult these pages will view with tolerance the efforts of a non-specialist in the field. The basic assumption of this chapter is that the continuity of medieval styles in the arts is a part of the continuity of medieval culture generally. If this assumption is correct, there may well be other and better ways of demonstrating it.

There are various reasons why it is advantageous for us to begin our discussion with the Romanesque period. In the first place, it is customary to look at Chaucer the other way around, from the point of view of later cultural history. One result of this posture is a more or less constant endeavor to see him as an anticipator of later tendencies and attitudes. Once a few of these anticipations are established and comfortably acclaimed as representing "universal" human values, they begin to appear inconsistent with other elements in his work, and his poetry is reduced to a series of purple passages ensconced in what is, on the whole, a rather disappointing setting. The Melibee and the Parson's Tale, for example, become deadly blemishes, and there are everywhere tedious and digressive materials. On the other hand, if we come to Chaucer through a study of his predecessors, we are in a better position to understand the integrity of his work.

Again, the Romanesque style, in spite of wide variations and distinctive local schools, is the first general European style. Many of its basic features survive throughout the Gothic period with only slight modification. Its origin corresponds roughly with the growth of vernacular literature, with the revival of sculpture, and with the beginnings of a movement to integrate classical materials with European culture in a systematic way. It thus marks a very important stage in the cultural development of Europe. The eleventh century is most significant in economic history as a century of agricultural expansion, made possible by more settled conditions than those of the turbulent centuries which preceded it. Perhaps these conditions afforded sufficient prosperity to permit serious attention to the arts. In any event, there is some justice in the conclusion that the rise of Romanesque art marks the beginning of the immediate cultural tradition in which Chaucer worked. Direct reflections of the literature of the twelfth century are evident in his poetry, but there is no evidence that he had any contact with earlier vernacular traditions in England or in Ireland.

Chaucer was the first English vernacular poet to make extensive use of the classics. In this he reflected a tradition which was already strong in the literature of France and had been developing since the thirteenth century in Italy. Although classical materials had been used in the earlier Middle Ages, especially in the Latin literature of the "Carolingian Renaissance," their extensive use in the vernacular begins in the Romanesque period; and, at the same time, that period witnessed a renewed interest in the visual arts of antiquity. These literary and artistic interests do not represent separate and distinct phenomena, but are a part of a single general movement, so that the treatment of classical materials in art and the treatment of similar materials in literature are mutually illuminating. During the twelfth century, monasteries, churches, and cathedrals sometimes became almost museums, where specimens of sculpture and other works of antique art were preserved, and where they served as models for native artists. Chroniclers called attention to classical monuments, and collectors sought out objects of art for preservation.[2] Although a few Corinthian capitals testify to a desire on the part of medieval artists to copy classical forms directly, in general such forms assumed new features to conform to the characteristics of Romanesque expression; in the same way, in literature, derivatives of the classical epic, like the Old French *Eneas,* were acclimatized to their new cultural environment. This process of transformation involved varying degrees of adjustment in meaning as well as in form. For example, the classical figure of *Terra* nursing the beasts at her breasts was transformed into a figure of *Luxuria,* being gnawed at the breasts or at the crotch by serpents (Fig. 2).[3] Needless to say, under these circumstances there was no valid reason to keep the classical form. *Luxuria* could develop freely in ways designed to emphasize her function without any necessity to remind anyone of her origin. Similarly, Hercules is placed side by side with Samson attacking a lion,[4] in an obvious effort to give him a significance suggested by the parallel. But in this instance, the violence done to traditional meaning is not so severe as at first appears.

Samson attacking a lion is an obvious and well-attested figure for Christ attacking Satan.[5] What, we may ask, has this to do with Hercules? In suggesting that Samson is a figure for Christ do we not widen the gap between him and Hercules still further? Are they not simply related because they were both physically strong? The answers to these questions are not so simple as they seem, for they are affected profoundly by the history of the legend of Hercules.[6] At the close of the fifth century, B.C., the legend offered two alternatives: the hero could be either a brutal villain or a saintly

[2] See Jean Adhémar, *Influences antiques dans l'art du moyen age français* (London, 1939), esp. pp. 45-46, 86, 99ff.
[3] *Ibid.,* pp. 197-200. [4] *Ibid.,* pp. 221-222.
[5] E.g., see *Glossa ordinaria, PL,* 113, col. 531.
[6] For the legend of Hercules and its significance, see F. Cumont, *Recherches sur le symbolisme funéraire des Romains* (Paris, 1942), pp. 294, 415-416, 480-481; and the excellent study by Marcel Simon, *Hercule et le christianisme* (Paris, 1955).

figure. We may see these alternatives in Sophocles and Euripides. In the course of time the Hercules of the type portrayed in the *Alcestis* acquired a profound philosophical significance; he became a warrior against vice whose struggles illustrated ethical doctrines. In Ovid Hercules is a half-human half-divine redeemer, and for the Stoics as represented by Seneca, he was "invictus laboribus, contemptor voluptatis, victor omnium terrarum." In fact, the parallels between the legend of Hercules and the story of the Christian Redeemer are numerous and striking. His cult spread throughout the regions of the Roman Empire until he became a veritable pagan counterpart of Christ. His triumph over death was a promise of immortality celebrated on pagan funerary monuments; and on Christian tombs, the Miracles of Christ sometimes show unmistakable parallels with the Labors of Hercules. The inspiration which a pagan hero could have for Christians because of these resemblances still echoes in Chaucer's Boethius. Having summarized the labors, Boethius adds, "and he diservide eftsones the hevene to ben the pris of his laste travaile." Addressing his readers, Boethius closes his fourth book with the exhortation, "Goth now thanne, ye stronge men, ther as the heye wey of the greet ensaumple [i.e. Hercules] ledith yow. O nyce men! why make ye your bakkes? For the erthe overcomen yeveth the sterres." When Salutati finds Christ suggested in the central figure of the *De laboribus Herculis*, therefore, he is simply continuing a very ancient tradition. And when Chaucer says of Alceste that "Ercules rescued hire . . . and broughte hyre out of helle," we should understand that here too the "erthe" has in some way been "overcomen." But to return to our Romanesque configuration, the double representation is neither a tautology nor an illogical statement, for the actual subject is neither Samson nor Hercules literally conceived, but another victory achieved once, in order that it might be achieved perennially by anyone refusing to "turn his back." The artist has simply added the prophetic voice of antiquity to that of the Old Testament.

There may be similar connections between *Terra* and *Luxuria*, but whether there are or not, Hercules is by no means an isolated example. Among the commonest of the "monsters" in Romanesque sculpture and of the grotesques in Gothic decoration are the sirens and their cousins or alternates the mermaidens (Figs. 43, 44; cf.

Fig. 4). Their history as philosophical beings may well begin with very early Pythagorean glosses on Homer. In any event, for the Pythagoreans Ulysses became a figure for the initiate who, by avoiding the fleshly temptations of the sirens, escaped the circle of necessity and the chain of metamorphosis to reach the stars.[7] The Stoics took the sirens to represent carnal pleasures. For the Neoplatonists there were three kinds of sirens: celestial sirens, infernal sirens, and sirens of generation. Ulysses probably suggested to them a voyager on the sea of generation who avoided its carnal temptations.[8] In view of the currency of ideas similar to these, Ulysses, tied to the mast of his ship and successfully avoiding the sirens, became an appropriate subject for funerary ornamentation (Fig. 45). Christian writers kept the general significance of the symbol but transferred it to a Christian frame of reference. Ulysses tied to the mast became a figure for Christ on the Cross; now the ship is the Church, the wax with which the mariners stop their ears is the teaching of the Scriptures, and the sirens represent lust on the rock of the flesh.[9] The *Physiologus* calls the sirens "delights of this world," or, in later forms, makes them symbols of hypocrisy or some other vice, beautiful maidens at first glance, but disappointing, physically and hence spiritually, in the end.[10] In the twelfth century the ladies were discussed by both mythographers and theologians. The third Vatican mythographer, on the basis of an "etymology" of the name *Ulysses*, makes the man himself a pilgrim, "for wisdom makes men pilgrims among all terrestrial things." The sirens represent corporal pleasures, and the ears of the mariners are stopped with precepts of salvation so that they do not hear the *modulationes* of such pleasures. Tied to the mast, Ulysses hears these melodies, but he is restrained by virtue from their enjoyment so that he moves toward his home in eternal blessedness.[11]

[7] See Jérome Carcopino, *De Pythagore aux Apôtres* (Paris, 1956), pp. 199-201.

[8] See Pierre Courcelle, "Quelques symboles funéraires du neo-platonisme latin," *REA*, XLVI (1944), 80-81.

[9] *Ibid.*, p. 90. Cf. the full discussion by Hugo Rahner, *Griechische Mythen in christlicher Deutung* (Zürich, 1945), pp. 445-466.

[10] E.g., see F. J. Carmody, *Physiologus Latinus, versio B* (Paris, 1939), p. 25, and Florence McCulloch, *Mediaeval Latin and French Bestiaries* (Chapel Hill, 1960), pp. 166ff.

[11] Ed. Bode, *Scriptores rerum mythicarum* (Cellis, 1834), pp. 233-234.

For Honorius of Autun Ulysses is the wise man tied to the Cross of Christ (figuratively) by the fear of God. The island of the sirens is the delight of the mind in worldly things, and the ladies themselves are distinguished by their methods of musical expression. She who sings is avarice, she who plays the pipe is boasting, and she who plucks the lyre is lechery. These are "the three delights which soften the human heart to vice and lead it to the sleep of death."[12] In the fourteenth century Holcot finds Ulysses representative of "the mind in which prudence should dwell," and the sirens to be "corporal evils, which through various pleasures attract those voyaging through the sea of this world to sin."[13] And Berchorius, like Honorius before him, once more associates the sirens with the three basic temptations of humanity.[14] Our Romanesque and Gothic sirens thus retain the general pattern of ideas suggested by their classical models but fit that pattern into a Christian context. The pagan wisdom of Ulysses becomes the wisdom of Christ or of the Christian, and the fleshly temptations of the Pythagoreans and Neoplatonists are made to fit a conventional pattern of Christian theology.

No systematic investigation of the relationship between Romanesque forms and the meanings of their classical antecedents has been made. Since a great deal of the material collected in medieval churches was destroyed by later "zeal," the task would not be an easy one. But it is clear from these examples that Romanesque symbolism does not necessarily make a sharp break with antiquity in every instance. There is no "reconciliation of opposites" in the juxtaposition of Samson and Hercules, no tension between the "Hebraic" and the "Hellenic." In fact, the existence of the juxtaposition is a testimonial to the fact that no such "tension" existed. Again, medieval sirens and mermaidens do not express the "longings" of the artists for the "freedoms" of paganism. They simply reveal the assumption that the wisdom of the ancient Greeks and Romans was "fulfilled" in much the same way that the wisdom of the Hebrews was "fulfilled." Classical influences of this kind were not confined to sculpture. The "harmony of the spheres" decorates the title page of a Reims Pontifical, water basins show scenes from

[12] *Speculum ecclesiae, PL*, 172, cols. 855-857.
[13] *In librum sapientiae* (Basel, 1586), p. 226.
[14] *Reductorium*, s. v. "De sirenibus."

the life of Achilles, a ciborium decorated with scenes from the life of Christ has representations of Achilles and a Centaur on the lid. Such figures, as Dr. Hanns Swarzenski observes, were "charged with Christian meaning."[15] It may be that in many instances the new meaning was a logical development of an old meaning. The Romanesque and Gothic mermaidens are much closer to the spirit of antiquity than are their nineteenth-century relatives in the pages of Matthew Arnold. Meanwhile, the assumption that classical elements in the literature of the period are merely decorative, or are "pagan" in their implications, is completely at variance with the evidence of the visual arts. The kind of interpretation we have suggested for such figures as Venus, Narcissus, and Pygmalion in literature is entirely consistent, on the other hand, with the treatment of these and other classical figures in art. We may, in fact, go so far as to say that one of the most significant features of Romanesque art is its ability to absorb non-scriptural materials, whether from classical or other sources, into the general scheme of Christian reference. The development of philosophical meanings was a primary consideration of Romanesque artists, and this focus of attention on meaning rather than on representation accounts for some of the most striking features of Romanesque style. At the same time, the interest thus displayed in *invisibilia* is entirely consistent with the aesthetic assumptions described in the last chapter. Romanesque art did not seek to exploit the beauty of the visible world, but rather to portray that world in such a way as to call attention to the invisible ideas which lay beneath it.

It is sometimes said that the general characteristics of Romanesque style are due merely to the inept copying of classical models, especially where sculpture is concerned, and it is implied that Romanesque merged into Gothic as artisans developed greater skills. Although it may be true that time is required to develop skills and to allow new technical ideas to be perfected, it is also true that there is a close relation between sculpture and illumination during the Romanesque period, and that the characteristics of Romanesque design are evident in a variety of forms.[16] A lack of technical perfection, therefore, even though it appears in the art

[15] *Monuments of Romanesque Art* (London, 1954), pp. 16-17.

[16] The close relation between sculpture and illumination is described by E. Mâle, *L'art religieuse du XIIe siècle en France*, 2 ed. (Paris, 1924).

of the eleventh and twelfth centuries at times just as it does in the art of any other period, including our own, does not account for the fact that classical forms were not retained. Although it is not often possible to comment with any degree of certainty on the twelfth-century artist's fidelity to his models, for the simple reason that we frequently do not have the models before us, what we know of medieval habits of copying suggests that a considerable deviation from earlier models, whether classical, Byzantine, Celtic, or medieval, was fairly common. It has been shown in connection with architecture that medieval artists of whatever period seldom copied whole configurations. Instead they copied parts, but gave to the parts a new coherence achieved by reshuffling or selection.[17] Even where general outlines were retained, as they sometimes were in illumination, new effects were achieved through adaptations which gave to the copy the peculiar flavor of its own period. This process is vividly illustrated in Dr. Swarzenski's discussion of the three successive versions of the Utrecht Psalter.[18] In general, it is safe to assume that Romanesque stylistic characteristics represent a genuine artistic language, and, further, that Romanesque artists who copied classical models had no antiquarian desire to copy exactly the forms which they saw before them. The form as well as the content required "translation" into a new mode of expression. There is no special reason why we should view this process of translation with regret, as though it would have been better if antiquity had been more faithfully reproduced during the eleventh and twelfth centuries. We certainly do not reproduce it ourselves. The pristine whiteness of modern "classical" architecture and sculpture, for example, creates a chaste effect very unlike that which must have been achieved by the painted originals. Moreover, it should not be forgotten that Romanesque transformations of antique art and literature served to make that art and literature a living part of medieval European culture.

There would be no point in summarizing here all of the features which may be said to distinguish the Romanesque style in all of the

[17] This principle is demonstrated with reference to architecture and to the representation of architecture in sculpture and painting by Richard Krautheimer, "Introduction to an 'Iconography of Mediaeval Architecture,'" *JWCI*, v (1942), pp. 13-14.

[18] *Monuments of Romanesque Art*, pp. 22-35.

various media in which it occurs. However, an examination of such matters as the treatment of the human figure, the development of "monsters," the treatment of space, and the interpretation of action in the visual arts may help to reveal certain underlying attitudes which are also relevant to the interpretation of the literature of the earlier twelfth century. With reference to the treatment of the human figure, it is significant that the Romanesque artist took as little care to reproduce exactly the models he saw around him in "real life" as he did to copy exactly the models left him by antiquity. Although the human figure is sometimes treated with astonishing fidelity to individual details,[19] the parts are not integrated in a natural and "realistic" fashion. Usually little distinction is made between male and female figures except for differences in costume. Two types seem to have been especially fashionable: a squat, dwarfish figure on the one hand, and a narrow, elongated figure on the other. Historians of sculpture are inclined to say that these differences are due to the exigencies of the architectural setting, but this theory has been questioned,[20] and it is true that both types may be found in illumination as well as in sculpture. Whatever the reasons may have been, Romanesque portrayals of the human form do not exhibit any interest either in empirically established canons of proportion or in the kind of geometrical idealizations of such canons favored by the Greeks. In sculpture, if we disregard processional figures, the figure never stands alone as a thing in itself, divorced from its architectural setting, and in illumination it forms a part of a pattern of lines, or of superimposed plane surfaces, which fills the area of design on the page (Fig. 46). We may partly account for the variety of types which appear in Romanesque art by reference to the variety of sources which were available to various artists in various regions, but the fact that the artists showed no more interest than they did in "normalizing" the types available to them on the basis of observation is indicative of a complete lack of interest in the flesh as such, except where such interest has a thematic significance. The evil may be tortured by their own perversity (Fig. 2), or may be torn and gnawed by devilish monsters, but we are not invited to share their torments nor to regard them with what we in the twentieth century would call

[19] Cf. Raymond Rey, *L'art roman et ses origines* (Toulouse, 1945), p. 350.
[20] See J. Gantner, *Romanische Plastik* (Vienna, 1948), p. 127.

147

"sympathetic human understanding." The allurements of the flesh may be suggested by the breasts of the mermaiden, or by the contours of the dancing girl (Fig. 30), but there is no lingering doubt in these portrayals, none of the spirit of Boucher, and no romantic *Sehnsucht*. Romanesque art is innocent of sentimental humanitarianism on the one hand and of sensuality on the other. Usually the very draperies which cover the flesh of men and women, in both sculpture and painting, deny the flesh they are supposed to cover as they fall into whirls and sworls, sometimes reminiscent of the patterns of Celtic art, in accordance with a pattern-making ability of their own which emphasizes the geometrical rather than the "natural" integrity of the figure. In Fig. 46 the symmetrical folds hanging from the knees and shoulders of the Virgin echo each other and the outline of the face, but they do not reveal the plastic shape of the flesh they are supposed to cover.

The appeal of the strange figures which people Romanesque churches, manuscripts, and carvings has nothing to do with "realism," but arises as a result of the imposition of abstract geometrical patterns on the forms represented. In sculpture these patterns seem to be the result of limitations imposed or suggested by the architectural lines. The cubical capitals which were characteristic of the architecture suggested the use of symmetrically arranged figures at the corners, or of balanced patterns within the faces; the tympana seem to impose an hierarchical pattern of figures ascending toward a major figure at the center; the rounded arches suggest a spoke-like arrangement of figures around their circumference, and so on.[21] In illumination the natural articulation of the human figure is sacrificed for the sake of balanced line and symmetrically arranged surfaces. The Virgin of Fig. 46 achieves an "hieratic" or "monumental" appearance by virtue of the stringency with which a geometrical pattern is imposed upon her figure. Her rigorous frontal pose, the balanced arrangement of the arms and knees, the symmetry of the architectural patterns which surround her, all serve to emphasize an abstract pattern of "equality." The lines of the Virgin's crown are repeated in the architectural pattern above her head, not only in general outline, but also in such details as the

[21] Cf. Focillon, *L'art des sculpteurs romans* (Paris, 1931), pp. 18-19, 34-35. The geometrical schemes of Romanesque sculpture are studied in detail by Jurgis Baltrušaitis, *La stylistique dans la sculpture romane* (Paris, 1931). Cf. Rey, *op.cit.*, pp. 346-348.

diagonals at the corners, and the leaves of the lily at the top. These diagonals echo the lines formed by the Virgin's outstretched arms and the similar diagonals formed by the arms of the Child. This geometrical symmetry, which subordinates the parts to an artificially ordered whole, is a step toward the abstract realm of the invisible, which is also governed by an artificial order. Elsewhere, the same kind of order falls on monsters as well as on saints,[22] but this is as it should be, since, as we have seen, all are a part of the beauty of the Divine Order.

Since the order of the whole in Romanesque art is always an artificial rather than a natural order, however, the parts viewed either from the point of view of later art, or from that of "real life," may seem to acquire a kind of autonomy. The "individualizing" or "isolating" tendency which Riegl observed in late antique art[23] pervades Romanesque art as well,[24] and this is true whether we are considering larger units or the representation of the human figure. If we compare a typical Romanesque church with a French Gothic cathedral, the aisles of the former seem to be separated from the main body of the nave as if they were almost distinct rooms, set off by the long "aqueduct" structure of the main arches, and the transept and the choir are separate geometrical entities. From the outside the various parts have an "additive" effect, as though one shaped block had been added to another.[25] Again, when groups of figures appear in sculpture or in illumination, individuals are separated from one another by arcades, nimbuses, mandorolas, or, even in instances where no such mechanical separation occurs, they seem to act independently without reference to each other.[26] In Fig. 46 the Child seems suspended between the Virgin's outstretched knees, and His posture is simply an echo of the Virgin's posture except for a slight turn of the head toward the suppliant nun. He does not look at the nun, and the nun does not actually look toward Him. There is no effort to integrate the group as a whole in a coherent spatial continuum so that they might react

[22] See the elaborate discussion of Baltrušaitis, *op.cit.*, Ch. VII.

[23] *Spätrömische Kunstindustrie* (Vienna, 1927), p. 26 and passim.

[24] Cf. D. Frey, *Gotik und Renaissance* (Augsburg, 1929), p. 39. Here the principle applies to parts of figures as well as to the figures themselves.

[25] Cf. Gantner's discussion, *op.cit.*, pp. 15ff., and Paul Frankl, *The Gothic* (Princeton, 1960), pp. 777f.

[26] Gantner, pp. 92ff.

naturally to one another. In effect, they remain, so far as space and time are concerned, essentially isolated. A disregard for a continuum of this kind is characteristic of the period, so that a single figure may appear in different guises in the same representation,[27] or, as in late antique art, a series of actions by a single person may be either crowded into a single representation or portrayed by repeating his figure within the framework of a single scene (cf. Fig. 89 for a late Gothic example). The same kind of isolation requiring an intellectual act of integration on the part of the observer is common in Romanesque iconology. Thus Dr. Joan Evans calls attention to the "symbolic integration" of the decorations in the apse of Cluny,[28] where the various separate elements have no visual coherence, but a coherence that can be appreciated only with reference to the meanings which may be derived from them. In view of the existence of a pervasive attitude of this kind, it is not surprising that the various parts of the human body should be integrated more in accordance with geometry than with the principles of anatomy. In sculpture, whether in stone or on a smaller scale in bronze or ivory, only the faces and hands are usually in high relief, frequently extending out from the surface to such an extent that they seem independent of the bodies to which they are attached.[29] Generally, the Romanesque artist was more concerned to create a surface pattern of lines and planes governed by an abstract order than he was to produce what we should call "natural" beings like ourselves.

Nevertheless, the curious human figures of Romanesque art are not lifeless.[30] In spite of their abstraction they sometimes have a vivacity and expressiveness, a vigor which is quite unlike the charade-like posturing of personified abstractions in certain eighteenth-century paintings or on the walls of more modern buildings. In sculpture this liveliness is in part due to a tendency to accept an architectural area as a working area and to fill it to the edges. Where a single figure was involved an effort seems to have been made to touch the framing lines in as many places as possible, and the figure is arranged accordingly. In illumination, similar effects

[27] *Ibid.*, p. 59.
[28] *Cluniac Art of the Romanesque Period* (Cambridge, 1950), p. 23.
[29] Cf. Gantner, p. 67.
[30] See Focillon, *op.cit.*, p. 275; Rey, *op.cit.*, pp. 346-347, 351, 379-380.

were achieved within artificially established frames. The result is frequently a linear complex which involves strong diagonal lines as well as curves and erect verticals. So far as facial expression is concerned, Romanesque artists show little of the restraint exhibited by their Gothic successors. The wringing of the hands, which became a standard means of portraying grief, is visible in Fig. 47, but it is accompanied by strong evidence of emotions in the features. The emaciated body of the Crucified in this carving is suggestive of the extreme physical distortion which became popular in the very late Middle Ages, but the artist has not over-emphasized the wounds, and he has done nothing to prettify the figures so as to give them a sentimental appeal. Even the angels, who show no distracting external beauty, echo the sorrow of the mortals. The scene as a whole has a kind of abstract animation designed, like the Alpha and Omega inscribed on the arms of the Cross, to lead the mind toward meditation rather than toward participation in the action.

Perhaps no feature of Romanesque style has elicited more comment than its "monsters." For Mâle, who reacted against ineptly presented symbolic interpretations of their meanings, they were mere designs, some of which were copied from Oriental tapestries and silks.[31] They have been explained as the result of distortions imposed upon animal forms by geometrical patterns.[32] Like the grotesques in Gothic manuscripts, which sometimes exhibit forms obviously descended from Romanesque forms, they have been attributed to the uninhibited fancy of the artists. Finally, there has been a recent tendency to allow the symbolic theory more validity than Mâle was willing to accord it.[33] But these various theories are not, in a given instance, irreconcilable. That is, the source of a figure —Oriental or otherwise foreign—does not prevent that figure from being adjusted to the working area in a typically Romanesque fashion, nor does it prevent elaborations or "flourishes" on the part of the artist. Again, a foreign source, geometrical distortion, and

[31] *L'art rel. du XIIᵉ siècle*, pp. 345ff.

[32] This is the thesis of the book by Baltrušaitis mentioned above.

[33] Joan Evans, *op.cit.*, p. 80. T. S. R. Boase, *English Art 1100-1216* (Oxford, 1953), p. 84, says that he cannot "accept the view, sometimes put forward, that these intricate but whimsical designs are the mere doodling of the cloistered subconscious." He calls them "symbols" and gives a suggestive list of possible and known sources.

fanciful elaboration are not necessarily inconsistent with a symbolic content. To use a simple example, a lion in a manuscript decoration may be based on an earlier artistic tradition rather than on observation of actual lions, and this animal may be stretched into a long vertical to fit the column of an initial, graced with an ornamental fishtail to make a flourish, and even given rudimentary wings; but this lion may nevertheless suggest a demon, a vice, or a vicious person.[34] To reinforce the suggestion that a lion may have "human application" he may be made parallel in some fashion with a human form or given "human" characteristics. Thus in a triple *Quid gloriaris* (Ps. 51) initial (Fig. 48), representing, as a rubric in the lower margin indicates, "victori[a] intellectus," or, more specifically, the victory of the understanding over malice, the intellect is represented by a figure of Christ and the *malitia* of the psalm by a dragon, curved to form the loop of the Q, and by a lion, used to form the tail of the letter. That the lion is symbolic is clear enough at the outset, but the fact that he represents something human is reinforced by the third illustration in the series, where his analogue is a man. Gantner calls attention to a representation of Daniel and the lions, in which the lions have manlike faces, and he observes a general tendency in sculpture to give beasts human countenances.[35] Good illustrations of the mixing of human and animal characteristics are afforded by some Romanesque portrayals of the beasts of the Evangelists, where the lion of St. Mark, the ox of St. Luke, and the eagle of St. John are given animal forms but human postures.

There were several influences at work, in addition to the "sphinxes," centaurs, and sea monsters of classical and Oriental art which helped to create the monsters of the sculptors and illuminators. In the first place various scriptural monsters, of which the "locusts" of the Apocalypse afford a striking but by no means unique example, had to be given completely non-empirical forms if they were to be portrayed at all. Thus a Christian sarcophagus of the third century recently acquired by the British Museum shows the story of Jonah on its side, but the "whales" have dragon heads, front paws, and serpentine tails which terminate in fanlike

[34] It was widely held that to say that a "demon" inhabits a man implies that he is subject to a vice. See Peter Lombard, *Sententiae*, 2. 8. 4.

[35] *Op.cit.*, pp. 107-109 and fig. 42.

fins. In the twelfth century the "asp" of Psalm 57 is illustrated in the St. Alban's Psalter as an animal with a birdlike body, two feet, a tail, and rather long ears. The "furor" of the sinner is shown by depicting a man astride one of these beasts unable to restrain its erratic course.[36]

Again, in accordance with a very venerable Christian idea, which has classical precedents, a man who gives himself up to vices ceases, as it were, to be a man and becomes a beast. In abandoning his reason, he abandons in effect also his upright posture, which, as a symbol of reason, distinguishes him from the animals.[37] This idea receives philosophical expression in the *Consolation* of Boethius (4 pr. 3 and m. 3). In Chaucer's translation we read, "Than betidith it that, yif thou seist a wyght that be transformed into vices, thow ne mayst nat wene that he be a man. For if he be ardaunt in avaryce, and that he be a ravynour by violence of foreyn richesse, thou shalt seyn that he is lik to the wolf; and if he be felonows and withoute reste, and exercise his tonge to chidynges, thow shalt likne hym to the hownd," and so on. The meter continues with the story of Circe. But the vices, we are assured, are even more powerful than Circe was, for they change the heart instead of merely altering the body. Under the influence of ideas of this kind Odo of Cluny tells us that a man may be like a reptile, a quadruped, and a bird. For as he adheres to the earth, he is like a serpent; as he is virtuous simply for praise, he is like a quadruped; and as he imitates the flights of the pious, he is like a bird.[38] Needless to say, an artist wishing to use "imagery" of this kind in the visual arts would have to make the animal qualities explicit. Whereas Boethius leaves Circe's activities on a merely physical level, medieval commentators give her the power to make moral transformations of the kind he said were more miraculous. Thus Bernard Silvestris, speaking of Ulysses' men, says, "Who is more a beast than he who bears an inner bestial nature, nor has anything of a man about him except the form? They are changed into various kinds of beasts: one into a pig, one into a lion, one into a dog, one into a wolf."[39] He goes on to cite Boethius as an authority. Again, he says, "Philosophy

[36] See A. Goldschmidt, *Der Albani-Psalter* (Berlin, 1895), pp. 53-56.
[37] E.g., see St. Augustine, *De Trinitate*, 12. 1, and Cicero, *De nat. deor.*, 2. 56.
[38] *Occupatio*, 3. 1022-1030.
[39] *Comm. super sex libros Eneidos Virgilii*, ed. G. Riedel (Greifswald, 1924), p. 22.

calls the lecherous swine, the fraudulent foxes, the garrulous dogs, the truculent lions, the wrathful boars, the stupid asses."[40] In the fourteenth century Berchorius calls Circe *mundi prosperitas*—worldly prosperity—which makes men drunk with delight or evil concupiscence, and changes them into swine.[41] This type of transformation was regarded as the basic kind of "metamorphosis" implied by the *Metamorphoses* of Ovid, which, in the Middle Ages, was read neither as a series of fairy tales of a kind to astonish children and cottagers with "magic transformations," nor as a series of merely pleasant stories. Thus Arnulf of Orléans says that Ovid's intention was to speak about mutation, not only about external mutation, but also about "mutation which is made within, like that in the soul." Such mutation takes place, he says, when sensuality makes us neglect reason.[42] Radulphus de Longo Campo says that one kind of "ecstasy" is effected by the sensuality; lechery, gluttony, and other carnal vices cause men to degenerate in adulterine habits, "and this is called metamorphosis," the transformation in accordance with which "philosophers" say that some are changed into swine, some into wolves, and so on.[43] Guillaume de Conches, the most influential of the medieval commentators on Boethius, explains that there are three kinds of metamorphosis: natural, like the change of water into ice; magical, in which something that seems to be changed is actually not changed; and moral, in which man conforms to the character of beasts. The last is the most miraculous of these changes.[44] The popularity of Ovid during the twelfth century probably reinforced the artistic validity of an idea, already implicit in Christian philosophy, that a man corrupted in some way by the sensuality might exhibit animal characteristics, or even plantlike features. There were, in other words, intellectual currents prominent during the period which made monsters and grotesques—"metamorphosed" men—reasonable media for the communication of ideas. It is true that analyses of individual specimens are sometimes very difficult to make and convincing accounts

[40] *Ibid.*, p. 62.

[41] *Metamorphosis Ovidiana* (Paris, 1515), Lib. xiv.

[42] F. Ghisalberti, *Arnolfo d'Orléans* (Milan, 1932), pp. 180-181.

[43] Oxford, Balliol College MS 146 b, fol. 100 verso.

[44] Paris, BN, fonds Lat. MS 14380, fol. 87 verso. William says that Ulysses' men undergo a spiritual metamorphosis. Cf. John de Foxton, *Cosmographia*, Cambridge, Trinity College MS R. 15. 21, fol. 53.

of them even more difficult to write, but the general principles which motivated them are fairly clear.

The "philosophical" use of monsters in literature was not uncommon. For example, Odo of Cluny associates the *chimaera* with libido.[45] The third Vatican mythographer gives us an idea of this monster's "appearance." It is depicted, he says, in a triple form, "having, that is, the head of a lion, the belly of a goat, and the tail of a serpent." These parts are said to illustrate the three steps of carnal love, which "invades us ferociously in adolescence like a lion. Then follows the fulfillment of love, designated by the goat, because that animal is most prompt in lechery. Whence Satyrs are depicted with horns of a goat because they are never satisfied with lechery. In the posterior parts it is like a dragon, because after the act, the prick of penance goads the mind."[46] The basic assumption that the sensuality may make men bestial in various ways and the prevalence of this kind of analysis with reference to both classical and scriptural materials made the monster or grotesque a convenient means of depicting the effects of sin. By the thirteenth century lists of beasts associated with various sins had become very elaborate. Thus William of Auvergne's *De vitiis et peccatis* provides a long series of comparisons between sins and various kinds of animals, fish, and birds.[47] The principles in accordance with which monstrous combinations are made are explained further in the fourteenth century, when the grotesque was at the height of its popularity, by Holcot. The Church, he says, has one head, which is Christ. "But regrettably outside of the church there are some monstrous men having two heads and contrary motions. For they have a body of sin joined to the natural body, and the head of this body, which is joined to it by pride, is the Devil. The fiery eyes of this body sparkle with wrath, and its face is lean and sad through envy. The hands are rapacious like the foot of a lion, or like that of an eagle through cupidity and avarice. The belly is porcine through gluttony. The reins are goat-like through lechery, the feet are bear-like through sloth."[48]

[45] *Occupatio*, 3. 608-613.
[46] Bode, *Scriptores*, pp. 252-253; Cf. A. Neckam, *Super Marcianum*, Oxford, Bodl., MS Digby 221, fol. 54 verso, where the same language is used.
[47] *Opera* (Venice, 1591), pp. 273-274.
[48] *Super librum ecclesiastici* (Venice, 1509), fol. 18.

An amusing specimen of a monster of this kind is afforded by Fig. 49. The second head, which is appropriately placed, the lion-like forepaws, and the goatlike feet belie the more pious attitude displayed by the "human" upper parts, and the whole configuration suggests an ironically humorous application of the text above: *Confessio et pulcritudo in conspectu eius.*

Holcot tells us that sinners may be called "monstrous" in many different ways, either because of the excessive magnitude of one sin, or because of the presence of great and weighty sins which are, as it were, contrary to each other. This last principle, which has striking literary as well as visual implications, is explained as follows: "There are, indeed, some vices which, although they are not literally contrary to each other, react in such a way that one commonly decreases as the other increases. Thus pride and lechery are not contrary vices, for they are not of the same species; nevertheless, lechery with its filth naturally corrupts pride. Thus persons found given to lubricity are also found commonly to be sociable and not very proud. In the same way the nobility of pride corrupts lechery, so that there are some men who in proud indignation detest the filth of lechery. But if anyone is found who on the one hand is very lecherous and unclean, and on the other hand is most proud, such a man ought to be reputed monstrous, as being a man by nature, a demon through pride, and a bull through lechery." The specific monster Holcot has in mind is the Minotaur, "the son of Pasiphae the wife of Minos, which she conceived of a bull while her husband was away at war, and this Minotaur was half-bull, half-man (*Met.* 8)."[49] In general, we may conclude that the monster or grotesque was not only consistent with a style which made little attempt to represent observed nature but was also consistent with ideas prominent in the philosophy of medieval Christianity. The enigmatic features of its appearance are consonant with what we have seen in the last chapter to be common medieval aesthetic traditions, since the monster is frequently a kind of visual figurative expression. Finally, the monster or grotesque points toward the fact that the referents of medieval art generally are predominantly abstract rather than concrete.

The treatment of space in Romanesque art is consistent with the abstract nature of its content. If we turn our attention once more

[49] *In librum sapientiae,* p. 697.

to the Etruscan cinerary urn illustrated in Fig. 45, we may notice that the effectiveness of the composition depends not so much on a geometrical arrangement of the parts, like that in Fig. 46, but on a fairly regular rhythmic pattern arranged across the working surface. The lowered right foot of each siren begins a sequence that is continued in the oars of the ship. This rhythm is echoed in the horizontal folds of the sirens' skirts and in the shields above the oars. And the same rhythm appears once more, with a suggestion of irregularity, in the heads of the figures as they are placed against the lower edge of the upper margin. The result is a fairly emphatic horizontal rhythm over the surface of the composition set off by the more rapid and more regular rhythms of the ornamental borders. Beginning with the first siren on the left, and moving toward the right, the heads of the figures gradually ascend, reaching a high point in the head of Ulysses, whose stature is emphasized both because he is considerably larger than his companions and because his figure is undraped. The emphasis falls off again on Ulysses' left, although in this photograph the position of the light source may give undue weight to the prow of the ship which closes the composition. This rhythmic effect is achieved at the expense of spatial rationality, since the spatial relation between the ship and the rock upon which the sirens are seated is hardly possible, and, in spite of the boldness of the relief, the ship itself has no real depth. That is, the representation lacks perspective, and the space which it occupies is an artificial space confined to the working surface. A glance at Falconet's *Pygmalion* (Fig. 21) reveals an entirely different set of stylistic principles. Here the composition is governed by an angle which extends from Pygmalion's right foot to the head of the girl, and down again on her right to the head of the cherub. The lines of this angle, however, are not on a plane that might be envisaged as arising from the front line of the base of the composition, and the latter is itself denied by the overlapping fold of Pygmalion's robe. Moreover, there are major lines of the composition which intersect any plane we might envisage as being established by the governing angle. These arrangements assure the fluidity of the angle itself. Since the head of the cherub is higher than Pygmalion's head, and since the angle does not extend beyond the cherub's head to the base, an impression of unrest is created on the left side of the composition, and this impression is em-

157

phasized by the precarious position of the cherub, whose head extends beyond the base on that side, and by the uneasiness of the outcropping over which he kneels. This compositional unrest, together with the forward inclination of the girl's figure and the tentative position of her unsupported left hand, suggests a forward motion in space toward the kneeling sculptor. We are led to feel that Pygmalion will soon rise to support her in his arms, and this feeling is suggested by the composition itself, without reference to the emotional attitudes of the figures. That is, the composition suggests a continuum of time as well as a continuum of space. It captures a fleeting moment of sensation which will soon vanish in action. An emphasis on the girl is achieved partly by the fact that she is, like Ulysses in Fig. 45, undraped; but unlike Ulysses, she is not larger than ordinary canons of proportion might require. The elevation and the fact that Pygmalion kneels are sufficient to make her the center of the composition. Although the idealized surface texture, the perfection of the figures, and the lack of color create a certain detachment, the space occupied by the figures is essentially the space occupied by the observer, and the impression of imminent motion makes an impression on the observer's sense of the passing of time.

If we disregard such matters as technical proficiency, sureness of touch, and artistic talent, confining our attention exclusively to matters of style, and ask ourselves which of the two works is more advanced, perhaps most of us would unhesitatingly support the work of Falconet. But is our question a legitimate one? We should remember that style is largely a function of attitude and intention. Falconet's purpose was undoubtedly to evoke sentiment, to suggest to his audience a sense of the naïve wonder and trust of the newly awakened girl and of the rapturous astonishment of her creator at a particularly significant moment in time. Although he does not ask us to enter the composition directly, as a romantic artist might, and he does not present us with an illusion of something actually seen in the everyday world, he does ask us to respond to the emotions expressed and to consider them. To make this message of the feelings effective, he gives his figures proportions like our own and places them in a space which we ourselves inhabit, arranging them in such a way that their very positions suggest an immediate emotional fruition transcending the ordinary experiences of which we are capable, and this in turn, realizing as it does one of the most persistent dreams of modern man, becomes a possible object of our contemplation. Turning to the urn, we see at once that although the strength or fortitude of Ulysses is emphasized, there is almost no suggestion of feeling. The sirens, so far as feeling is concerned, are not especially seductive, in spite of their outstretched knees and musical activity. We become aware, in fact, that the music against which Ulysses' companions have closed their ears is envisaged as something abstract. A more modern (but not necessarily more advanced) artist might well prefer nude or semi-nude sirens who could make us "feel" with Ulysses. But underlying the configuration on the urn is an idea, and it is this idea which gives rise to the emotions and feelings evoked rather than the figures themselves. Under these circumstances the immediate suggestion of feeling arising from the figures might well be irrelevant. And the artificial space in which they are set encourages us to seek an objective rather than an immediately subjective significance in their juxtaposition. Instead of suggesting an impending motion, the figures are, as it were, frozen into a rhythmic pattern within a static and timeless space, and the abstract rhythm is a sign pointing toward the abstract beauty of the underlying conception. The differences in style between the urn and Falconet's tableau are thus not matters of "advancement" but of function.

Focillon observes that sculpture either occupies space and limits it away from the observer or occupies a space in common with the observer in which he also participates. Sculpture of the first type "tend au bloc, au dense, à l'epargne des ombres, à la paix de la lumière, à l'unité du mur. Il s'éloigne de nous, il se construit sans nous. L'autre, pour qui l'espace est milieu, a besoin de nous, s'adresse à nous et veut nous rejoindre."[50] As he goes on to point out, Romanesque sculpture belongs to the first type, and we might add that Romanesque illumination displays features that are consistent with it. In other words, we may expect of Romanesque art effects like those visible on the Etruscan urn, but not those produced by Falconet. In early medieval art geometrical pattern plays a more important part than the kind of rhythm displayed on the urn, except, perhaps, in architectural interiors; but we find in the art of the late eleventh and early twelfth centuries a rigor of

[50] *Op.cit.,* p. 25.

limited space which at times even surpasses that of the classical example. In Fig. 47 the working area is defined by the Cross and by the strong framing line. These features serve to create a shallow rectilinear space within which the scene is depicted. The Cross limits the depth of the representation as well as its vertical and lateral extent: there is no space behind it, so that the angel on the left has his left wing pressed flat against the background and extended to fill the working area before him. Again, the angel on the right has his right wing stretched flat above him. Both are in what we should think of as physiologically and aerodynamically unsound positions, but to the artist these considerations were of no weight whatsoever. Nor was he concerned that the little platform on the right has only three legs, all arranged in the same plane. Below the crossbeam the heads of the figures form a diagonal emphasized by the left forearm of the crucified, and this line, like the curves of the drooping figures, contrasts strongly with the rectilinear spirit of the whole. If we allow our eyes to stray from the figures back to the Cross, we may be able to sense in its rectilinear erectness a note of triumph. But this triumph contains no hints of future events in the time-sense of the observer. In spite of the precarious condition of the angels and the improbable balance of the platform, the representation suggests no motion at all. Nothing leads us to anticipate either the further lowering of the Crucified or any action on the part of the angels, the symmetry of whose positions fixes them where they are. In this instance, then, the geometrical arrangement of the composition has an effect very similar to that of the rhythm on the urn. It emphasizes certain features of the scene but brings time to a stop. Again, the space in which the scene is depicted is the space of the Cross and the Crucified, but it is very definitely not the space of the observer, who is not asked to participate in the event, but rather to consider its significance—to understand, perhaps, "the breadth, the length, and height, and depth" [Eph. 3. 18], which things, St. Augustine says, "make up the Cross of Our Lord," in whose sign "the whole action of the Christian is described."[51] There is even less spatial rationality in Fig. 46. The tower at the top stands before the

[51] *On Christian Doctrine*, 2.41.62. Here the "depth" is not the depth of perspective, but the depth of the Cross in the earth. It is interesting that the figure in St. Augustine's mind has only two dimensions in the modern sense.

frame of the picture, but the major architectural frame which extends below and in front of the tower reaches behind the picture frame where it rests on the columns at the side. Again, the Virgin's head appears to be in an area in front of the architectural frame, but her feet, which in view of her posture should be further forward than her head, rest on a platform which is behind the frame at the bottom. The suppliant simply floats in an area before the picture. Here the effect is one of flat surfaces or strips arranged in such a way as to produce a pleasing geometrical pattern without reference to coherent spatial relationships. The picture simply has no depth, and no effort is made to convey any feeling through the expression of the figures. It is not the figures themselves which are important but rather the abstractions which they symbolize, and it is to these abstractions that the symmetry and rigorous surface confinement call our attention. These examples show that a style of this kind is inconsistent with "psychological" depth or with the expression of subjective emotions. The sorrow of the figures in Fig. 47 is clear enough, but it is an abstract sorrow rather than a subjectively felt sorrow. The participants are not convincingly persons "like ourselves"; they occupy a space which is not ours; and their sorrow is significant in an abstract theological realm rather than in the realm of everyday practical experience.

The linear and geometrical complexes of Romanesque art, as we have suggested earlier, do not necessarily suppress a sense of animation. The dancing Isaias of Souillac is only the most famous of a series of strangely animated figures in sculpture, and in the complex interlaced initials of the manuscripts the biting beasts and enmeshed human figures sometimes show a surprising activity. However, this action is confined to the shallow space in which the figures exist; it does not appear as action in the direction of the observer, or as action away from him. It is essentially action in a realm in which the observer cannot participate. When figures are placed at the corners of capitals, as in Fig. 2, the action may extend around the corner so as to produce an effect of movement in two planes. But in such instances the space defined by the figures is a confined space wrapped around the architectural form, and the action does not suggest any breaking away from the architectural lines. Moreover, the actions depicted do not impinge on the observer's time-sense, in the way that the action in Falconet's Pygmalion does. Essentially, "events" in Romanesque art take place in a confined space and time, an area set apart for the representations of symbols which are quite distinct from what we think of as "real" events. In Fig. 46 the nun is placed outside of the frame in an area distinct from that of the representation. The frame is not simply a device to limit the working area, but also a device to separate one kind of symbolic context from another. The suppliant does not worship the actual figures we see before us, but something of which those figures are a symbolic representation. She is not doing something that we may see anyone doing in the literal terms of the picture. That is, what we have before us is not a representation of a nun worshipping the Virgin as she might be seen; nor is it a representation of a nun worshipping a picture of the Virgin as the picture might actually be seen. The action of the suppliant is itself a symbolic action, and she is a symbol of what was considered to be the proper attitude toward the idea conveyed by the framed picture. The frame separates a set of symbols whose referents are theological from a symbol whose referents are literal. In general, the actions displayed in Romanesque art are not imitations of actions actually carried out by individuals, although they may symbolize such actions. Hence they characteristically have nothing to do with the psychological reactions of individuals to their environments. In Fig. 2 the figure that thrusts a sword through its body is not a thing that we may see around us literally, and the action is not a literal action. We see instead an image which suggests the implications of despair. Again, the female figure on the right is not intended as an imitation of a literal action. She typifies instead the pains of lecherous concupiscence which never manifest themselves literally in the way that they are manifested by the sculptor. Even when the actions of figures in art become more lifelike, as they do in the late Middle Ages, they remain symbolic actions in most instances, and the same thing is true of a great deal of Renaissance art (e.g. Fig. 6), in which an illusionistic use of perspective permitted a much more direct appeal to the observer's feelings.

There may be little point in the expression "Romanesque literature," and we should be hard put to make any very clear distinctions between something suggested by that term and "Gothic literature." Nevertheless, there are attitudes evident in Romanesque art which also affected the literature of the period. As an example, let us consider briefly *La chanson de Roland*, since it is well known and is, at the same time, a work of recognized artistic merit. Again, since it is essentially a jongleur's epic, or at least a poem composed for a relatively unlearned audience, it lacks the sophistication which characterizes much of the Latin poetry of the period and hence requires less elaborate discussion. As we have seen, the representation of the human form in Romanesque art shows little interest in the accurate reproduction of nature. Literary characters cannot be restrained by geometrical patterns or given the kind of hieratic symmetry visible in a Romanesque Madonna. Nevertheless, a similar emphasis on the abstract is achieved in other ways. In *Roland* characterization is subordinate to the thematic structure of the poem as a whole, and is rendered in simple, straightforward terms with no attempt at "rounding." The theme of the poem is the conflict between Christendom and paganism expressed in a manner designed to appeal to French *pietas*,[52] and to inspire the zeal of pilgrims and crusaders. For this purpose the instruments chosen are a Christian king of traditional valor and piety with an especial value for French traditions, two faithful vassals whose actions illustrate the kind of tie which should exist between such a king and his subjects, a traitor who exemplifies attitudes and actions to be avoided, and a host of pagans whose villainy is unrelieved by any of the gentler human attributes.

To begin with the traitor, Ganelon is introduced at once, before we have had an opportunity to see him in action, as (178) "Guenes ... ki la traïsun fist." If the narrator were simply telling a story as a story and nothing more, this anticipation of subsequent events might be regarded as an indication of "destiny." But if we look on

---

[52] There is no modern equivalent for the medieval word *pietas* used in its political sense. A valuable body of materials is assembled by Giuseppe de Luca in the introduction to Vol. 1 of *Archivio Italiano per la storia della pietà* (Rome, 1951). The word implied religious piety in the first place, but in addition an inclination to mercy and a readiness to assist widows, the miserable, and the needy. See Alanus, *Anticlaudianus*, ed. Bossuat (Paris, 1955), lines 335-343. Again, the influence of Virgil, whose hero is above all *pius*, suggested that piety involves an awareness of and a feeling of responsibility for the traditions of one's own people. King Alfred's laws, which begin with the Ten Commandments followed by the Two Precepts of Charity and continue with established customs approved by the *witan*, afford an excellent example. Here the two precepts furnish the element of mercy. The French bias of the Roland is obvious and has been most effectively described by A. Pauphilet, *Le legs du moyen âge* (Melun, 1950), pp. 65-89.

the poem not as a story but as a narrative exemplification of a theme, the "anticipation" vanishes, and the line becomes simply a device to indicate the concept for which Ganelon stands. The phrase "ki la traïsun fist" is then a thematic statement to be developed in accordance with the structural materials available in the poem and we are not confronted by the difficulty of having to introduce into its structure what at the time would have been heretical determinism. The theme is consistently maintained. When Roland advises with reference to Marsilie's dubious offer of peace, "Ja mar crerez Marsilie," Ganelon echoes him with "Ja mar crerez bricun," implying an unfavorable comparison between a man who is, on the one hand, Ganelon's own stepson and Charlemagne's most distinguished warrior, and on the other hand a pagan ruler. In the context of the poem, where pagans are little more than devils, such a comparison can suggest nothing but the malice of the speaker.

Malice is a vice traditionally associated with deceit and vainglory, which are, as it were, the roots of treason. Its connotations can best be studied not in the definitions of the theologians but in the text of the fifty-first Psalm, traditionally one of those singled out for illustration by medieval illuminators (Fig. 48):

> Why dost thou glory in malice, thou that art mighty in iniquity?
> All the day long thy tongue hath devised injustice: as a sharp razor, thou hast wrought deceit.
> Thou hast loved malice more than goodness: and iniquity rather than to speak righteousness.
> Thou hast loved all the words of ruin, O deceitful tongue.
> Therefore will God destroy thee forever: he will pluck thee out, and remove thee from thy dwelling place: and thy root out of the land of the living.
> The just shall see and fear, and shall laugh at him and say: Behold the man that made not God his helper.

Deceitfulness and injustice are inconsistent with love, the tie that was thought of as the bond of feudal society. A *vassal* was almost interchangeably an *ami*, or, at times, a *dru*. He was bound, at least in the ideal demanded by feudal theory, by a tie of love to his feudal overlord, and that same tie also bound his lord to him.[53]

[53] See Marc Bloch, *La société féodale: la formation des liens de dépendance* (Paris, 1949), pp. 354-355.

It follows that a vassal was also bound to love his fellow-vassals. If love was the basis for the fellowship of the Church, making it, as it were, "one body" under Christ, the feudal army was also bound by a similar tie, at least in theory. "For love," as John of Salisbury wrote, "is as strong as death [Cant. 8. 6], and that battle-wedge which is bound by the bond of love is not easily broken."[54] A Christian army ranked against heathendom could have no more appropriate unifying principle. But one of Ganelon's earliest acts is to say to Roland, "Jo ne vus aim nïent," and the rift which this statement implies in Charlemagne's following is soon confirmed by a formal *defiance*. Throughout the poem Ganelon is "li fel, li traïtur," and he pursues an unswerving policy of malice toward Roland. At the end, when he receives a traitor's punishment, no sympathy is wasted on him as a human being. In effect, Ganelon is not a human being, but an idea in action, a warning against the danger of personal malice in a society whose integrity depended on personal ties of affection. More generally, he is an echo of the forces represented by Judas, forces which, although evil, provide in a Providential way the machinery for the kind of sacrifice made on the Cross, of which Roland's fall is a distant and peculiarly medieval echo.

Roland himself receives hardly any "characterization" in the modern sense. He is Charlemagne's most worthy vassal, and he acts and speaks accordingly:

> "Pur sun seignor deit hom susfrir destreiz
> E endurer e granz chalz e granz freiz,
> Si·n deit hom perdre e del quir e del peil."

The vassal, as the Manual of Dhuoda explains, should sustain difficulties for his king, just as Joab, Abner, and others did for David;[55] and John of Salisbury repeats the same concept, saying that the knight should shed his blood or give his life if necessary for his companions.[56] Roland's singleminded pursuit of this ideal is what prevents him from blowing his horn at Oliver's request, not pride or rashness. "Kar sunez vostre corn!" Oliver urges. When Roland replies, "Jo fereie que fols; en dulce France en perdreie mun los," he is referring not to a feeling of personal vanity, but to an obliga-

[54] *Policrat.*, 4. 3.   [55] Ed. E. Bondurand (Paris, 1887), p. 91.
[56] *Policrat.*, 6. 8.

tion to his countrymen. This becomes clear in his answer to Oliver's second request:

> "Ne placet Damnedeu
> Que mi parent pur mei seient blasmét,
> Ne France dulce ja cheet en viltét."

And again,

> "Ne placet Damnedeu ne ses angles
> Que ja pur mei perdet sa valur France!"

Roland states once more the doctrine of which he is an exemplification when he addresses his companions:

> "Pur sun seignur deit hom susfrir granz mals
> E endurer e forz freiz e granz chalz,
> Si·n deit hom perdre del sanc e de la char."

That this is essentially a Christian ideal of self-sacrifice, in spite of what may seem to us to be a certain lack of humane restraint, is confirmed in Archbishop Turpin's sermon:

> "Seignurs baruns, Carles nus laissat ci;
> Pur nostre rei devum nus ben murir.
> Chrestïentét aidez a sustenir!
>
> . . . .
>
> Se vos murez, esterez seinz martirs."

Roland's motivation is thus not in any sense of the word "psychological." He is the embodiment of an ideal, not a human being reacting to the stress of an emergency. "Rollant est proz e Oliver est sage," the poet says, but he implies no lack of wisdom in Roland any more than he implies lack of worthiness in Oliver. He adds, "Ambedui unt merveillus vasselage." There is no question of a "tragic weakness" or a "human failing" in Roland. He is the type of the ideal vassal who is willing to sacrifice anything for God, for his king, and for his companions. "This principle, indeed," wrote John of Salisbury, "is to be placed first and implemented in all knighthood, that when faith has been given first to God, then the prince and the state may be served without reservation."[57] This is the idea, the grand doctrine, which won for Roland a place

---

[57] *Ibid.*, 6. 9. Cf. *Le chevaler Dé*, ed. Urwin, *RLR*, LXVIII (1937), lines 15ff.

among the saints in the stained glass of Chartres Cathedral. Meanwhile, he shows abundantly those qualities most obviously lacking in Ganelon. He can disagree with his closest friend, Oliver, without malice and with no lessening of the love that binds them. As a vassal should, he loves his companions, whom he envisages, as they lie fallen on the field, among the eternal flowers of Paradise. As he dies, thinking of his king and of God, the skies darken as they did on the day of the Crucifixion, and when St. Gabriel has accepted Roland's gauntlet, angels bear his soul aloft to Heaven. He is a martyr who has given his last gift of *vasselage*. As an "historical" figure or as a "literal" human being Roland is nothing. He moves not in our world but in a world of abstract values which, to the poet, were eternal. He stands before us like a Romanesque saint, an embodiment of an invisible reality which living human beings can reflect only imperfectly.

Above all the other characters in the poem looms the venerable figure of Charlemagne, "nostre emperere magnes." The problem stated in the opening lines—and the problem of the poem, which is no mere thriller concerning "the adventures of Roland"—is essentially his problem. Spain has been conquered and is in Christian hands, "fors Sarraguce," and this remaining stronghold of heathendom is held by Marsilie, "ki Deu nen aimet." The policy of conquest is illustrated at once in the situation at Cordoba, which has just been taken:

> En la citét nen ad remés paien
> Ne seit ocis u devient chrestïen.

Near the end of the poem, when Saragossa has finally succumbed, the inhabitants, except for the Queen, are either baptized or killed. As for Bramimunde,

> En France dulce iert menee caitive:
> Co voelt li reis, par amur convertisset.

The final act of the poem is her conversion:

> Chrestïene est par veire conoisance.

The emperor is thus a Christian ruler whose function is either the extirpation of pagans or their conversion. But the alternative offered to the pagans, especially if we think of them in terms of the "superior Moslem civilization" currently fashionable among historians, seems, to say the least, barbaric. To do justice to the poem, however, rather than to the pagans, it is necessary to forget history, with which it has very little to do, and to refrain from applying humanitarian concepts to characters who are not human beings. For the saracens who oppose Charlemagne are for the most part no more than personifications of evil, a fact frequently suggested by names like Abisme, Corsablix, Falsaron, Malbien, Malcuid, Malgariz, and so on, and confirmed by the descriptions the poet makes of them. Of Abisme, for example, it is said,

> Plus fel de lui n'out en sa cumpagnie,
> Teches ad males e mult granz felonies,
> Ne creit en Deu, le filz seinte Marie;
> Issi est neirs cume peiz ke est demise.
> Plus aimet il traïsun e murdrie
> Que il ne fesist trestut l'or de Galice,
> Unches nuls hom ne·l vit jüer ne rire,
> Vasselage ad e molt grant estultie;
> Por ço est drud al felun rei Marsilie. . . .

When he sees Abisme, Turpin wishes at once to kill him, for he seems "mult herite." Another, Climborins,

> Fiance prist de Guenelun le cunte,
> Par amistiét l'en baisat en la buche.

Valdabrun took Jerusalem by treason and violated the Temple of Solomon. Baligant, the leader of all heathendom, is ruler of Babylon, whose name suggests, in a Christian context, the very essence of evil. The Saracens, in other words, suffer generally from the same limitations that apply to Ganelon and Roland; they are a part of an abstract configuration, and as such they neither invite nor deserve humanitarian consideration any more than do the suffering sinners (who are more properly sins) in the stones of Romanesque churches. Charlemagne's religious policy in the poem is thus not "inhumane," whatever it may have been in history. It simply demands that evil either be modified or destroyed. Nor is the conversion of Bramimunde through reason and love rather than by force an exception to this principle. The problem at the beginning of the poem was the heathen reign of Marsilie. At the close of the poem, the Queen of Spain, now Juliane, is a Christian, not a pretended Christian, nor a Christian for convenience, but a sincere Christian. Her conversion is properly the last event described, Charlemagne's crowning achievement.

In general, the emperor displays those qualities which are associated with an ideal Christian ruler. A prince, John of Salisbury says, should be a "father and husband" to his subjects, and he should bind them to him with mutual love.[58] "Jo vos aim," Charlemagne assures his men as he leads them into battle against Baligant. His love for Roland is made abundantly clear. A king, says Etienne de Fougères, "obeïr deit le commons voz,"[59] and one of Charlemagne's most characteristic actions is to take counsel with his barons. Nor does he seek to over-rule them when it is decided that Roland should command the rear guard. It is they who decide the course of action to be taken with reference to Marsilie's offer of peace. And, ultimately, they decide the fate of Ganelon. "Reis n'est pas son, ainz est a toz," says Etienne. We see Charlemagne suffering when he knows that Ganelon has betrayed him, restraining his own personal desires and convictions, and, at the end of the poem, we know that he will take up arms against the pagan enemy once more:

"Deus," dist li reis, "si penuse est ma vie!"

But Charlemagne is more than an ideal ruler. His great age and his close association with the Deity give him a patriarchal air. He is warned of impending calamities twice through angelic visions. At one point Gabriel intervenes directly in his battle with Baligant —"Reis magnes, que fais tu?"—so that he can resume it with renewed vigor. The sun itself stands still as he pursues the remnants of Marsilie's forces. These qualities are also suggested in his appearance:

Blanche ad la barbe e tut flurit le chef,
Gent ad le cors e le cuntenant fier.

His actions have an "hieratic" or "monumental" quality suited to his supra-human personality. When he receives Blancandrin's message,

[58] *Ibid.*, 4. 3. For an excellent later expression of the function of love in a feudal kingdom, see *Carmen de bello Lewensi*, ed. C. L. Kingsford (Oxford, 1890), lines 909ff.
[59] *Le livre des manières*, ed. J. Kramer, *AARP*, xxxix (1887), lines 161ff.

Li empereres tent ses mains vers Deu,
Baisset son chef, si cumencet a penser.

We do not see him often, but on three subsequent occasions we find him with his head bowed stroking his white beard and weeping. Like Ganelon and Roland, the emperor is not a "psychological" entity at all; he is a moral being. The depth and fullness of his character is not the depth and fullness of a human personality, but the depth and fullness of an idea.

The structure of the poem is consistent with the demands of the theme. Rychner divides it into four parts: (1) Prelude to Ronceval, (2) Ronceval, (3) Baligant, (4) the Judgment of Ganelon.[60] However, he points out that the structure of *Roland* alone among the chansons de geste approaches a dramatic unity. If we omit the Baligant episode, he maintains, the poem has a rising action, a turning point, and a falling action. For this reason he concludes that the Baligant episode is an accretion, and that the original story must have been more perfectly dramatic. This theory, which is not atypical of modern efforts to find "better stories" in the theoretical "Ur-" forms of medieval narratives, has its temptations; but like other theories of its kind it represents an effort to pursue a feature of nineteenth-century style in times and places utterly foreign to it. To make *La chanson de Roland* "dramatic," it would not only be necessary to omit the Baligant episode; it would be necessary also to make human beings out of its characters and to substitute passions for the ideals which motivate them. The result might do well on television, but it would hardly be a medieval poem. We may as well accept the fact that the author of *Roland* was not writing "drama." The problem of the poem is not the career of Roland, but the problem of paganism and the posture of Christian society with reference to it. By "paganism," moreover, we must understand that the forces of evil in general are implied. The solution suggested stresses the necessity for pious leadership, suffering, self-sacrifice, and unwavering devotion to the cause. Above all, if the forces of justice are to survive, they must find their strength in love. These concepts are developed in feudal terms which demand kingship on the one hand and *vasselage* on the other. The Baligant episode, the conversion of Bramimunde, and the final suggestion

---

[60] *La chanson de geste* (Geneva, 1955), pp. 38ff.

that Charlemagne's vigilance must be perpetual are just as necessary to the poem as is the trial of Ganelon. Finally, a dramatic presentation requires that the audience enter into the personalities of the characters and move freely in their world. But the world of *Roland*, like the confined space of Romanesque sculpture or the flat surface of Romanesque illumination, is a world apart in which the personalities are only shadows of abstractions. It is not intended that the audience identify itself with these shadows, which are means of vivifying an underlying conceptual reality. It is intended that the audience perceive that reality. And it is this abstract reality that is moving in *Roland* rather than the passions of the characters considered as such. If we can grasp the abstractions with sympathy and understanding, we shall have no need for the satisfactions of vicarious participation in the action. What has been called "destiny" in the poem[61] is actually the hand of Providence maintaining that harmony, symmetry, and equality which lies behind the flux of the visible world.

2. THE GOTHIC PERIOD

In spite of rather spectacular surface developments art in the Gothic period does not make any very revolutionary changes in the basic features of Romanesque style. There is a tendency for human figures to become much more lifelike, and for their settings to achieve a greater spatial rationality, but they do not enter the space of the observer and their actions remain largely symbolic rather than literal. A new feeling for linear design and a new rhythm replace Romanesque geometry for a time, but even when this rhythm disappears and the decorative conventions of Gothic art become less insistent late in the period, art is still far from being "realistic." Perhaps the new style can be described partially in terms of certain developments in late medieval culture which had far-reaching effects in realms other than art. Since these developments affected literature as well as art, it will repay us to consider them at some length. They will not, of course, explain Gothic decorative taste. Changes in style, like changes in language, still evade all efforts at explanation. But an awareness of these tendencies may nevertheless be helpful in achieving a preliminary understanding of Gothic style.

[61] *Ibid.,* p. 65.

Speaking very generally, two tendencies are observable in the cultural life of the twelfth century: first, a tendency toward the systematic organization of materials of every kind, and second, a tendency to make this new organization explicit and to make it functional in the attitudes and lives of the people. If we extend our view into the thirteenth century, these two tendencies are seen to be intensified, and in fact do not show signs of serious deterioration until the middle of the fourteenth century. The change that takes place then does not represent a new direction but consists rather of an intensification of the second tendency while the first is neglected, or obscured in over-elaboration. There was no profound change in religion, and the movement toward fragmentation in philosophy did not affect the arts in a significant way until the Renaissance. The new desire for explicit and systematic organization may be illustrated in a great many areas of endeavor during the period that extends roughly from the middle of the twelfth century to the middle of the fourteenth. In theology, for example, a systematic framework of accepted principles, or of problems where principles were uncertain, was provided by the *Sententiae* of Peter Lombard, which rapidly became a standard basic text for study in the schools. The originality of this work does not lie in the realm of ideas, for it consists largely of a series of quotations from Patristic and later authorities. It lies in its style, in the organization of these materials and their presentation in a continuous form to cover all major topics of interest to those seeking to study and to understand the Scriptures. That is, it forms a conceptual framework of *sententiae* which the student might expect to find either explicitly or implicitly in the scriptural text. In *On Christian Doctrine* (2. 9. 14) St. Augustine advises that the student begin by studying the "more open" places of Scripture; the *Sententiae* present in a coherent form the implications of these places and of others as they had been seen by reliable authorities. It is as though Lombard had taken St. Augustine's aesthetic doctrine of *convenientia*—the similarity of equal parts and the gradation of unequal parts—and deliberately set out to implement it in theological exposition. The stylistic significance of the *Sententiae* in this respect may be readily seen if we compare it with the more diffuse treatises of John the Scot, which were still, in the twelfth century, considered to be standard works of theology. The organization of the *Sententiae* greatly facilitated both the further development of systematic theology and the application and exemplification of that theology in pastoral terms.

With reference to the first point, because of the order and scope of the topics discussed, which extended all the way from the attributes of the Deity to the meaning of the sacraments and the implications of Doomsday, the theological student who wished to be inclusive could do no better than to write a commentary on the *Sententiae,* and an enormous number of such commentaries were produced in the theological schools of the later Middle Ages.[62] Perhaps it was as a result of the "system" thus suggested that theology, which had been specifically a preliminary orientation for scriptural study, became, during the second half of the thirteenth century, a discipline in its own right. But the *Sententiae* also contributed to the growth of more practical forms of theology. Among its most important features was the introduction of the system of seven sacraments. Earlier, sacraments and sacramentals were not carefully distinguished, but the seven singled out by Lombard came to be regarded as rites especially established by Christ for the building of His Church under the New Law. After the decisions of the Fourth Lateran Council of 1215 concerning Penance and the Eucharist, it became desirable that a knowledge of these sacraments, together with the entire system (which needed to be understood in connection with the problem of the gravity of sins) be made available through the bishops to every parish priest, and through the priests, if possible, to every communicant. As a result, the bishops of the thirteenth century issued decrees and compiled manuals, like the *Summula* of Peter Quivil, in an effort to educate their clergy in the new doctrines, and there was, in consequence, an enormous growth of pastoral theology. The sacraments together with their attendant theology implied an ordering of the lives of the people in terms of the *invisibilia Dei.* In particular, the mystical significances of baptism, confirmation, marriage, penance, and unction were the concern of every communicant. Chaucer's Parson's Tale, which is an analysis of Penance, affords an excellent example to illustrate both the systematic character of this knowledge and its relevance

[62] A guide to these commentaries is now available. See F. Stegmüller, *Repertorium commentariorum in sententias Petri Lombardi* (Würzburg, 1947), and the supplement by P. V. Doucet, o.f.m. (Florence, 1954).

to the everyday affairs of life. The *Sententiae* and its influence thus illustrate in a striking way the two tendencies we have mentioned.

The same two tendencies—toward a kind of explicit *convenientia* in the organization of materials with an added necessity to impose the results on the life of the times—are readily observable elsewhere. They may represent nothing more than the effort of European society, now relatively free from foreign invasions and inner turbulence, to organize itself in accordance with its own intellectual traditions and to meet the needs of a steadily growing population. In any event, the movement was vigorous and far-reaching. In the "secular" realm, for example, a knight was, until the middle of the twelfth century, a man who had strong personal ties to an overlord, and, above all, a man who fought on horseback with full equipment. During the last half of the twelfth century, although he retained these basic characteristics, a knight was also a member of an "order."[63] Ecclesiastical writers like John of Salisbury and preachers like Alanus de Insulis exerted themselves to see that the implications of this new *ordo* were understood. "Knights are especially instituted," wrote Alanus, "so that they may defend their country and so that they may repel from the Church the injuries of the violent." Those who fight for their own private gain are "fures et raptores" rather than knights. The theme of "appearance and reality" is just as important here as it is, let us say, in the sacrament of Penance:[64] "For external knighthood is a figure for internal knighthood, and without the internal, the external is vain and empty. And just as there are two parts of a man, corporal and spiritual, so there are two swords proper to defense against the various enemies of man: the material, with which injuries are repelled, and the spiritual, with which those things which injure the mind are repelled. Whence it is said, 'Behold, here are two swords' [Luke 22. 38]. The knight should gird on the external one to keep temporal peace safe from violence, and the internal

[63] See Marc Bloch, *La société féodale: les classes et le gouvernement des hommes* (Paris, 1949), p. 49.

[64] An elaborate analysis of the distinction between a feigned appearance and an underlying reality is offered by the *De vera et falsa poenitentia*, which was erroneously attributed to St. Augustine in the twelfth century and used extensively in the treatment of penance in Lombard's *Sententiae*.

one, which is the sword of the Word of God, to restore peace to his own breast."[65]

As time passed, the ceremonies involved in the "ordaining" of a new knight became more and more elaborate, including the symbolic costumes, ritual bath, and night-long vigil described in the fourteenth century by Geoffroi de Charny.[66] Here the ideals of knighthood are organized into a system and developed in ritual form to make them effective.

The desire for more explicit and far-reaching organization made itself felt in almost every aspect of life. The intense administrative activities of twelfth-century monarchs, the development of canon law on the basis of Gratian's successful synthesis of existing traditions, the increasing organizational complexity of the Papal Curia,[67] as it gradually assumed responsibilities that had originally lain in local hands, the reform of the liturgy, with the inclusion of the *elevatio*, which made a direct appeal to the audience,[68] all attest to a new feeling for the functional systematization of traditional materials. That this feeling was not simply a matter of expediency in each separate instance but something more pervasive may be illustrated by the fact that it affected areas in which no sort of emergency may be said to have arisen. For example, it influenced the style of the medieval sermon. During the earlier Middle Ages the sermon was customarily a "postillating" exposition of the text for the day. But as the new theology suggested the need for sermons on special subjects not included in any given lesson, like the seven

---

[65] *De arte praedicatoria*, PL, 210, col. 186. Alanus goes on to say that the knight should arm himself with the breastplate of faith, gird on the sword of God's word, take up the lance of charity, and put on the helmet of salvation. Thus armed, he confronts the triple enemy: the devil, the world, and the flesh.

[66] Geoffroi's treatise is printed in Kervyn van Lettenhove's edition of Froissart, I, 2, 463ff.

[67] See G. Barraclough's stimulating monograph, *Papal Provisions* (Oxford, 1935).

[68] See Sedlmayr, *Die Entstehung der Kathedrale* (Zürich, 1950), pp. 305ff. The matter has been treated by Peter Browe, "Die Elevation in der Messe," *Jahrbuch f. Liturgiewissenschaft*, IX (1929), 20-26. The modern *elevatio* after the consecration was introduced by Odo de Sully, who stipulates in a decree that after the priest says, "Hoc est corpus meum," he should elevate the host "ut possit ab omnibus videri." After the last quarter of the thirteenth century, it was customary to ring the church bell as well as the chime at the *elevatio*, so that those who were forced to remain working in the fields might hear it.

principal vices, two distinct new tendencies are observable in sermon style. Sermons with a new organic and structural unity begin to appear in the twelfth century, and in the thirteenth century the stylized formal sermon appears with its theme, pro-theme, formal division of the theme, and elaborate techniques of development.[69] At the same time, the more popular sermon also begins a new life, and under the leadership of great popular preachers like Jacques de Vitry, and of the Dominicans, who made the technique of the sermon a subject for study, the *exemplum* became an increasingly important part of the preacher's stock in trade. Narrative materials derived from sources of all kinds were used to illustrate theological principles in terms that could readily be understood by popular audiences. If we consider the typical academic sermon, with its tripartite division and systematic linear development of each part, together with the growing taste for exemplary exposition, we have in miniature a sketch of the two tendencies we have been discussing. These tendencies even affected music. The *Magnus liber* of Leonin, composed at the time when Gothic style was beginning to appear in architecture, imposes, with its five rhythmic modes, a new order and, at the same time, a new significance on musical expression.

As a necessary part of the new interest in organization, there developed a new sense of decorum or appropriateness. If materials are to be organized, some basis must be found for determining what elements are equal, what elements are inferior to others, and what elements belong in one category but not in another. Fortunately, one of the most famous manifestations of this new sensitivity concerns the arts. It may be seen as the basis for St. Bernard's famous attack on Cluniac monasticism and Cluniac art in the *Apologia*.[70] The spaciousness and sumptuous decoration of monastic churches seemed to St. Bernard to be wasteful impairments to devotion and to practical charity. He attacked specifically the use of fabulous and symbolic sculpture—"illa ridicula monstruositas, mira quaedam deformis formositas, ac formosa deformitas," as he called it, sin-

[69] Sermon style in the twelfth century is discussed by L. Bourgain, *La chaire française au XIIe siècle* (Paris, 1879), pp. 263-264; and by J. T. Welter, *L'exemplum dans la littérature religieuse et didactique du moyen age* (Paris, 1927), pp. 34-35.

[70] *PL*, 182, esp. cols. 914-916. The fact that St. Bernard's strictures coincide with the beginnings of a new style is emphasized by Otto von Simson, *The Gothic Cathedral* (New York, 1956), pp. 39ff.

gling out for special attention representations of things like apes, lions, centaurs, half-men, tigers, battling knights, hunters, monsters with one head and several bodies or with one body and several heads, quadrupeds with serpentine tails, and so on. His list includes forms that may be seen in manuscripts as early as the Lindisfarne Gospels and as late as fifteenth-century misericords and bosses. These things, he thought, were distracting to the contemplative who should be meditating on the Scriptures: "There is one purpose among bishops, and another among monks. For we know that they, who are under obligation to both the wise and the foolish, must excite the carnal masses to devotion with corporal ornaments because they can not do so with spiritual things. But we who have gone out from the people, and who have also abandoned the precious and beautiful things of the world for Christ, who have judged all beautifully radiant things, all things melodiously delightful, all sweet smelling things, all things savory to the taste, all things pleasing to the touch, and hence all things corporally delightful, to be as so much dung—why, I ask, should we seek to excite devotion in these things?"

Although some allowance must be made for rhetorical overemphasis in this statement,[71] St. Bernard obviously thought that those who have become monks should be able to envisage the realm of the invisible directly, without the intervention of "the things that are made." But he recognized the fact that churches designed for lay audiences could well make use of "corporal ornaments." In other words, he was not expressing a "Puritanical" attitude, as is sometimes suggested,[72] but simply pointing out that things which may be appropriate in one place are not necessarily appropriate in another.

The Gothic decorative arts, to use St. Bernard's contrast, are "episcopal" in that they represent both ordered planning and an effort to appeal to the layman. The principles of *convenientia* in design which St. Augustine had rejected in favor of an abstract "Equality" were themselves employed as a visible step toward that Equality. And the added attractions of stained glass, much

---

[71] See the important discussion by Dom Jean Leclercq, *L'amour des lettres et le désir de dieu* (Paris, 1957), 128ff.

[72] See Franco Simone, "La 'reductio artium ad sacram Scripturam,'" *Convivium* (1949), pp. 919ff.

more brilliant and spectacular than the older Romanesque wall painting, a more realistic sculpture, and decoration with colors and gems marked a deliberate effort to enable the layman to glimpse the order visible to the monk in contemplation. Suger's Church of St. Denis, often associated with the origins of the Gothic style, was not literally "episcopal." But as a center of pilgrimage, and the source of religious inspiration to the lay nobility, it was not by any means a purely monastic church. With a vivid and useful image, Gantner speaks of Romanesque art as a "prayer"—distinct from Gothic art, which is a "sermon."[73] Whether their iconography was understood, or, indeed, whether their handiwork was ever seen, seems often to have made little difference to Romanesque masons. The figures were there, intimately bound up with an architectural scheme significant in the light of eternity, and that was enough. There are traces of this unconcern for "communication" in Gothic art; roof bosses, for example, might be carved with detail that could not possibly be discerned by anyone looking up at them.[74] But the central features of Gothic decoration tended to be conventionally didactic. With its careful organization, under the direct supervision of a bishop or other ecclesiastical authority, and its message for those among the laity who might wish to "read" it, it was a sermon in style as well as in content.

The word *Gothic* suggests above all the style of the great cathedrals at Paris, Chartres, Reims, Amiens, and Beauvais, or the airiness of the Sainte Chapelle where the massive solids and planes of Romanesque have been abandoned completely in favor of stained glass framed in slender verticals of stone. Various theories have been adduced to explain the origin of this astonishing shift in architectural taste, the most recent of which is that developed by Professor Paul Frankl. Here the new features are said to be the result of changes which began in the vaults. Romanesque developed groined vaults erected between transverse arches, but difficulties were encountered in maintaining the lines of the groins during construction. To overcome these difficulties, to facilitate construction generally, and to strengthen the vault structure as a whole, arches were thrown diagonally across the vaults where the lines of the

[73] *Romanische Plastik*, p. 54.

[74] See C. J. P. Cave, *Roof Bosses in Mediaeval Churches* (Cambridge, 1948), pp. 1-4.

groins had run before, and the webs were added later in the quadri-partite structure thus created. What we know as the Gothic style in building resulted from the gradual adaptation of the piers and other features of the structure to the implications of these new vaults.[75] Whereas formerly the lines of the transverse arches had been carried down the piers to produce a "frontal" effect, the diago-nal ribs implied shafts set diagonally on the piers to support them. From an aesthetic point of view, the older style tended to divide the areas between the transverse arches into separate blocks of space whose boundaries were emphasized by the frontal lines on the piers, producing the "additive" effect generally characteristic of the style. The new diagonally set verticals on the piers, produced, on the other hand, a "divisive" effect, which introduced a new feeling of horizontal continuity throughout the structure.[76] This theory, which carries considerable conviction in its original form as opposed to this very brief summary, seems to imply a new interest in line as an organizing feature of architectural interiors.

Architectural theory during the late twelfth century was based on Vitruvius, who set up, among the basic principles of architecture, order, eurythmy, and symmetry. Order involves the use of mod-ules derived from the work itself to give the members "due meas-ure" and to make them agree with the proportions of the whole structure. Eurythmy lies in the suitable proportions of the mem-bers to make them correspond. And symmetry means not the cor-respondence of parts on opposite sides of a line, but the commensur-ability of the parts and the harmonious relation of the parts to the whole. Symmetry, for example, may be obtained by the use of a module.[77] In addition to using modules, Gothic builders developed geometrical methods of transferring plans to the actual construction

[75] Frankl, *op.cit.*, p. 825. The idea that the ribs actually "carry" after the mortar has set has been disputed, but it is probable that medieval masons thought that they did. In any event, they facilitated construction. Kenneth J. Conant, *Carolingian and Romanesque Architecture* (Baltimore, 1959), p. 291, suggests that Suger's vaults at St. Denis "were built up cleverly, arch by arch, between the ribs, with little if any auxiliary falsework." The ribs create, moreover, an appearance of stability.

[76] Frankl, *op.cit.*, pp. 821ff.

[77] A thorough analysis of these and other concepts is given, *ibid.*, pp. 86ff. Hugh of St. Victor, *Didascalicon*, 3. 2, mentions *Vitruvius de architectura* under the heading *De auctoribus artium*.

and further geometrical methods for determining proportions.[78] This emphasis on rational proportion and commensurability suggests quite strongly the Augustinian conception of *convenientia*, and it is not unlikely that this ideal together with its implications had some influence on medieval practice. Vitruvius recommends that architects become familiar with the various arts, and it is likely that medieval architects may have learned something about the arts of the quadrivium as they were understood at the time—if not directly, at least in their contacts with ecclesiastical authorities. It may not be irrelevant to remember that *mundana musica* during the twelfth century was thought to exist among the elements "in weight, number, and measurement," and that "number" in contexts of this kind implies more than simple enumeration. Such music, in its wider sense, was the source of "music in the spirit" which involves the proper hierarchical relationship between the spirit and the flesh.[79] Whether the "symmetry" of the cathedrals was always spontaneously pleasing to the eye may not have been so important as the fact that it might be thought of as having moral or philosophical implications. In any event, the methods of Gothic craftsmen were designed to produce an ordered whole, and the order is explicit and systematic.

We have, unfortunately, little evidence to indicate how medieval observers reacted to the new style. Suger was deeply moved by the light which his new construction at St. Denis afforded, and, as we might expect, this light had for him a symbolic importance.[80] Gervase of Canterbury has left us a series of contrasts between the old choir of Canterbury Cathedral and the new one begun by William of Sens.[81] He does not emphasize light or any other single factor but seeks instead to write a general description of the new interior. He calls attention to the increased height and complexity of the structure and to the generous use of marble shafts, which were to have especial importance in the subsequent development of English architecture.[82] He notes the substitution of ribbed vaults for what were probably earlier groined vaults and detects a new unity in

[78] Frankl, *op.cit.*, pp. 35-54.   [79] See Chapter II, above.

[80] See Erwin Panofsky, *Abbot Suger* (Princeton, 1948), pp. 18-24, 50, 100; Frankl, *op.cit.*, p. 22.

[81] This account is printed and fully discussed by Frankl, pp. 24-35.

[82] See Geoffrey Webb, *Architecture in Britain: The Middle Ages* (Baltimore, 1956), p. 73.

the relationship between the choir and the arms of the transept: "There [in the old structure], a wall, built above the piers, divided the arms of the transept from the choir, but here, not separated from the crossing, they seem to meet in the one keystone in the middle of the great vault that rests on the four main piers."[83] As Frankl points out, this statement calls attention to the "fusion" of areas which, in the former choir, had been separate. Perhaps it might be added that the idea that they meet "in the one keystone" suggests that Gervase had his attention centered on the lines of the ribs as they converge toward the center of the vault and not on the spaces that "interpenetrate." Our responses to Gothic interiors will vary a great deal if, at one moment, we center our attention on the complexes of spaces that are suggested and, at another, we devote our attention instead to the lines suggested by ribs, shafts, and flutings.

It may be that the "restlessness" so often ascribed to the Gothic style is due in part to our modern tendency to think of architecture in terms of "moulded space." If we picture to ourselves the predicament of the tourist with a camera who wishes to obtain in a photograph a general view of a Gothic interior, this point may be made clearer. Impressed by the beauty of the nave with its aisles, the transepts, the radiating chapels, and the span of the vaults, he seeks a convenient location to set up his camera. But there is no position from which all of these things may be seen. To see a Gothic interior spatially it is necessary to move, and, not only to move, but to turn one's head. If our tourist, baffled by the manner in which the piers interfere with his efforts to obtain a diagonal view, compromises by taking up a position at the center of the west end of the nave, his picture will not include a very impressive view of the vaults. To overcome this deficiency, he may find a means to elevate his camera, but if he does so, the result will be a view that hardly anyone ever sees. And whether he does so or not, his picture will show a hall-like room bounded on each side by the piers of the great arches and extending before him with diminishing perspective toward the altar. He may be sensitive to the power of a vista, in which event he may lament with Faust, even though he is facing in the opposite direction, "O, dass kein Flügel mich vom Boden hebt!"

[83] Quoted by Frankl, op.cit., p. 31.

But we may very well suspect that this restless impulse is not an aspect of that perennial sop to current prejudice called "unchanging human nature" but a strictly post-medieval phenomenon. Moreover, the medieval churchgoer had neither a camera nor the desire to encompass in representation a rational continuum of space and time of the kind that a photograph usually seeks to capture[84] Riegl once observed in connection with a late Gothic chapel that "the eye still follows the piers, engaged shafts, and ribs individually, as it was accustomed to do in the Middle Ages, and therefore continues to be distracted from pure appreciation of the free space in between them."[85] This kind of "reading" might be accomplished cinematically, but the result would still not be very satisfactory. If the medieval viewer centered his attention, as Riegl asserts, on the lines of the architecture suggested by the ribs of the vaults and their elaborations, what he saw was a complex of ordered members elaborated with remarkably consistent logic[86] rather than a confusion of interpenetrating spaces vaguely suggestive of the "infinite." The God of the Middle Ages, we might add, may have been ineffable and hence a source of difficulty to metaphysicians, but He was a much more immediate Being than the romantic infinite. The logical consistency of the lines which we may see at any given point in a cathedral is a promise of the logic of those lines which cannot be seen, much in the same way that the operation of Providence as it is seen in particular instances is a promise of its operation elsewhere. The tranquility of the cathedral lies in its obvious linear integration. Heaven, to the medieval mind, was associated with peace, but the peace of the cathedral is linear rather than spatial.

If our tourist with the camera moves outside of the cathedral and seeks to capture the beauty of the exterior, he is likely to find himself baffled again. At Paris, it is true, he can retreat through the traffic across the Place du Parvis Notre-Dame all the way to the Rue de la Cité, or take up a position across the Pont au Double in the Square Viviani. To get a good view of an architectural structure,

[84] Cf. the interesting discussion of Luis Díez del Corral, *The Rape of Europe* (New York, 1959), pp. 217-218.

[85] Quoted by Frankl, *op.cit.*, p. 637.

[86] The logical coherence of the Gothic interior is brilliantly described by E. Panofsky in his lecture *Gothic Architecture and Scholasticism* (New York, 1957), pp. 44ff.

one must find a point at a distance from it of three times its elevation. But in medieval times this was seldom possible. Cathedrals were frequently located among clusters of other buildings which prevented any such view. There are other difficulties, however, some of which are revealed in a criticism of the Gothic style made in the nineteenth century by Kugler: "The exterior, in its basic forms, was a dismembered scaffolding, the individual parts of which could not join to make an effective unit, and, with their projections and their arching masses they . . . concealed themselves and the body of the structure in constant change, affording nowhere a firm, clear picture of the total relationship, nowhere a self-contained and satisfying impression."[87] It is quite possible that medieval builders had no such "self-contained and satisfying impression" in mind. If we move far enough away from a cathedral to gain one, we diminish its grandeur and miss the detail on which the masons lavished so much effort. This fact is emphasized by the sculpture, which is not a form of decoration simply added to the building, but a part of it, carrying out the lines and decorative conventions of the exterior in a sort of spatial halo. The existence of this halo and the indefiniteness of the outlines are further indications that the cathedral should not be regarded as a "moulded form" in space on the outside any more than it should be regarded as "moulded space" on the inside. The outside of a cathedral is also something to be "read" and not something to be grasped in full at a single glance. When the original red, blue, and gold paint was still on the as yet unblackened stone and the sculpture still bore its colors, the effect of such "reading" must have been striking indeed. The order of the lines as the eye moved from one point to another, reinforced by the iconographic order of the sculpture, must have produced the same sort of confidence that we might have in dipping into an authoritative and well-organized book whose implications are multitudinous and profound. It is impossible to gulp down a Gothic work of art at once, and this is true whether we are looking at a building, at a single stained-glass window, at an illumination, or even at the page of a manuscript; but this does not mean that it is "restless" or disorganized. Gothic art may lack any feeling for the presentation of a given space at a given time, all in a single focus, which characterizes more modern art; but a cathe-

[87] Quoted by Frankl, *op.cit.*, pp. 542-543.

dral is nevertheless an ordered whole, and the ordering principles are explicit.

If the cathedral is a triumph of explicit organization, both in its design and in the arrangement of its decorative features, the sculpture which adorns it is, in comparison with Romanesque sculpture, a triumph of restrained exemplification. The figures of the Royal Portal at Chartres (Fig. 50) have been taken to illustrate both a "late Romanesque" and an "early Gothic" style, presumably resembling that of Suger's statues at St. Denis.[88] They are, almost literally, "columns," expressing the ancient idea that "the Saints are the pillars of the Church." Something of their spirit may be suggested by the words of a thirteenth-century preacher in a sermon on St. Lucy. "Four things," he wrote, "are to be observed in columns: beauty, uprightness, height, and firmness. For the beauty of a building consists principally in its columns. Thus the beauty of the Church lies in the Saints."[89] He goes on to explain that St. Lucy deserves to be called a column because she was straight, inclining neither to the right in pride nor to the left in adversity. She was high, her mind soaring above the heavens in contemplation, and she was firm, sustaining the Church. Turning back to the statues, it is clear that "uprightness, height, and firmness" are expressed at the expense of verisimilitude. The female figure is distinguished from her male companions, but the draperies, limited as they are by the columnar form, do not hang very naturally, and their narrow folds are made to conform with the rapid rhythm of the surrounding ornament rather than with any configurations that might be observed in nature. A later step toward a more "realistic" style may be illustrated by the statues on the transepts of the same building (Fig. 51). Here the figures are no longer literal columns. They stand on pedestals and above the head of each is a canopy. This combination of pedestal and canopy became a standard feature of Gothic statuary throughout the period. It serves to give the figures greater freedom of movement than would have been possible in the earlier style, but at the same time it integrates them with the building against which they stand, separating them effectively from the space of the observer. The

[88] See R. de Lasteyrie, *L'architecture religieuse*, ii, 352-356.
[89] Odo Tusculanus, "Sermo de beata Lucia," in J. B. Pitra, *Analecta novissima Spicilegii Solesmensis* (1885-1888), ii, 299-300.

draperies now hang more naturally, with an easy rhythm that is harmonious with the flowing lines of the columns below. But the faces show an obvious stylization, and the figures as they stand holding their attributes before them are clearly not intended as "realistic" portrayals of everyday citizens, although they show a striking verisimilitude as compared with those on the Royal Portal.

Perhaps the reason for this new verisimilitude has best been expressed by Sedlmayr, who calls attention to "an apparent polarity" between architecture and sculpture in the thirteenth century, since the architecture is "idealized" at the same time that the sculpture is "realistic." But this polarity, he explains, is only apparent, for although the architecture may suggest the ordered tranquility of Heaven, the sculpture seeks to bring the Heavenly nearer to the observer.[90] In other words, the greater immediacy of the sculpture represents the same kind of tendency that produced vernacular sermons like those of Maurice de Sully or ritualistic initiations into the order of knighthood. That there was no actual trend toward "realism" for its own sake in Gothic sculpture is apparent from its development elsewhere. We may be impressed by the "classical" look of the famous Visitation at Reims, or by the skilful draperies of the Strassburg Master (Figs. 54, 55), but after the middle of the thirteenth century a more severe stylization begins to set in which harmonizes with the Gothic taste for flowing linearity and pointed finials. The beginnings of this stylization may be seen in the Virgin on the trumeau of the north transept at Paris with her graceful sway away from the vertical lines of the building, the linear cascade of draperies on her right thigh, and the refinement of her features which results from a delicate linearity imposed on a plastic form. Tendencies visible here are intensified in the "Golden Virgin" of Amiens (Fig. 52). Lasteyrie called her a "ravishing young girl,"[91] but she is far from being an actual portrait. Her déhanchement may remind us today of the Knidian Aphrodite and her successors, or, on the other hand, of the natural pose assumed by a young woman with a child on one arm. But we can detect in the line that runs along the Virgin's left side from the tip of her crown to her feet the rhythmic ogee which became a hallmark of Gothic style during the late thirteenth and early fourteenth centuries, a curve which transfixes representations of men and women

[90] *Op.cit.*, p. 245.   [91] *Op.cit.*, II, 402-403.

alike without reference to anything they may or may not be car- rying. This line, the refinement of the features, the graceful curve of the pointing right hand, and the long flowing lines of the drap- eries are consistent with the delicate linearity of the cathedral as a whole. Similar characteristics may be seen in some of the statues at Reims, and, in an even more extreme form, in the Virgin of the choir at Paris. They represent neither aristocratic snobbery nor a perverse disregard for nature, but an effort on the part of the ma- sons to make their figures harmonize with the style of their archi- tectural settings and with the prevailing stylistic feeling of the time. If this effort makes the statues less "realistic," it also creates a sense of detachment from the observer and attachment to the spiritual order of the church as a whole. At Amiens, the fact that the Virgin stands in a Cruciform setting, with the Child at the intersection of the crossed elements, lends a peculiar poignancy to the representa- tion to which greater realism might well have proved a distraction. Stylized Gothic statuary thus represents a compromise between exemplification, which if carried to an extreme would result in naturalism, and the feeling for organization which dominated the expression of the period. The fact that the exemplification is made as explicit as it is in these works without destroying the harmony between the statues and their settings represents a considerable artistic achievement.

The masons of the second half of the thirteenth century did al- low themselves a semi-naturalistic technique in one feature of their carving: the representation of foliage.[92] They disregarded scale, and they arranged their foliage in patterns, so that it represents "nature to advantage dressed," but the foliage sometimes shows an astonishing fidelity to nature in its contours. Perhaps in this in- stance fidelity to linear outline may be thought of as a kind of ac- cident of history, since the natural lines of leaves corresponded for some years with the favored lines of Gothic design. When, later on, masons sought more plastic and less linear effects in their figure representation, the foliage again became stylized, serving as a medium for colored decoration.

In illumination the thirteenth century developed conventions similar to those we find in sculpture. Long linear curves replace

[92] See the attractive little study by N. Pevsner, *The Leaves of Southwell* (Lon- don and New York, 1945).

Romanesque geometry in the treatment of the figures; faces, hands, and feet show a livelier interest in shading; architectural settings become more rational in their arrangement; and the background, instead of being filled in with symmetrical detail, is formed by applying gold leaf, frequently "tooled" or pricked to form glittering patterns of light which set off the deep colors of the figures. The effect of the gold leaf, with the shifting brilliance of its patterns, can be reproduced neither by photography nor by applying gilt paint, which has a granular effect, to photographs, so that the beauty of Gothic illumination must remain hidden from those who do not have access to the original manuscripts. Typically, the "isolating" tendency of earlier painting, although less severe, is retained. The figures do not move in a continuum of rationally conceived space, and they are frequently separated by columns, arches, or other features of the setting. Fig. 53, from the "Amesbury" Psalter,[93] affords a pleasing example. In the original, the path of the descending Dove is much more emphatic than it is in the photograph, continuing the main lines of Mary's figure, so that the configuration on the right, seen as a whole, echoes the ogee that flows from Gabriel's head to his left foot. Although the ogees are not so obvious here as they are in other examples of the style, they still serve to unite the figures in a rhythmic relation which is emphasized by the slender verticals of the columns and echoed in the undulating curves of the arches at the top. The figures themselves are elongated, and, in spite of the shading of the faces, hands, and feet, they are essentially flat. This shading is not "modeling," but a stylized gradation of color arranged in patterns and imposed on a linear drawing. This technique permits a refinement of feature which we have seen to be characteristic of late thirteenth-century sculpture. Again, the draperies are essentially linear and do not give the impression of bodies emerging from the flat surface of the page. Gabriel does not stand on a stage, but on mounds which have no depth but which permit his feet to point downward so as to carry out the curved vertical lines which govern his posture. At the top, the architectural motif, suggestive of two church façades, preserves the geometrical symmetry characteristic of Romanesque backgrounds. The various architectural features are still flat, but

[93] See Margaret Rickert, *Painting in Britain: The Middle Ages* (Baltimore, 1954), pp. 115-116.

their elements are arranged much more rationally than in Fig. 46; there is still no consistency in scale, however, between the large arches under which the two figures stand and the buildings behind them.

Although the figures are much more lifelike than those of Fig. 46, the severely linear conventions of the style prevent the exemplification from being too concrete, so as to destroy the symbolic value of the picture. The picture is not, after all, a picture of anything that could be seen, nor even a literal rendition of anything that ever actually took place. The setting, which serves the same function as the pedestal and canopy convention in Gothic sculpture, is far from being realistic. Within this setting the action is a symbolic action, insofar as it is an action at all. Gabriel's draperies flow behind him as though he were moving forward, and the right foot is extended; but the column which separates the figures is an obvious bar to motion, and the rhythmic relationship between the figures, like that on the Etruscan urn (Fig. 45), effectively "fixes" them in the position in which we see them. They do not actually look at each other, and the gold background does not afford a medium for literal communication between them. Their relation is a symbolic relation, and they are themselves not portraits but symbols, so that Gabriel's "phylactery" bearing the Salutation and the descending Dove of the Holy Spirit are entirely consistent with the rest of the picture. In short, the representation is carefully organized on a flat surface in linear terms to produce exactly the symbolic effect desired, and, at the same time, there is enough verisimilitude in the figures to produce a sense of exemplification.

The various conventions we have seen in architecture, sculpture, and illumination produced a uniformity of expression which had been unknown in the Romanesque period. This uniformity was maintained, perhaps, at the expense of originality, but at the same time, the conventions which determined it made possible a more immediately significant stylistic language than had been previously available. Just as in language itself communication is made possible by a system of conventionally established signs, so also in art conventions make possible the development of ideas and the concise expression of complex meanings. It is important to notice that the new linear conventions of Gothic art fall on the unjust as well as on the just, so that in representations of the Flagellation, for example, the long ogee and the linear refinement of feature may characterize both the Flagellants on the one hand and the figure of Christ on the other. The style thus served as a means for attaining a sort of decorum, a "courtly" elegance which forced the "monsters" of earlier Romanesque art into the background. In Figs. 54 and 55, showing the Church and Synagogue from Strassburg, the Synagogue, with her connotations of the flesh, the Old Law, the "letter," and the earthy, stands hardly less beautiful than the Church across the doorway. To the modern eye with a feeling for the *pathétique*, her broken staff, bowed head, blindfold, and heavy tablets drooping toward the earth may, in fact, make her seem more beautiful than her regal counterpart. She is betrayed, not by any lapse of Gothic elegance, but by the meaning of her attributes.

The staff, blindfold, and tables of the Synagogue are a part of a new and more uniform iconographic language, also illustrated by the book in Mary's hand in the "Amesbury" Annunciation, which developed with the Gothic style. The imagery of the churches, under the influence of the bishops and canons who planned it, became more like that of the liturgy and the sermons addressed to lay audiences. This tendency is already evident in the windows of St. Denis, which displayed "types and antitypes" of a kind which were to become conventional features of medieval decoration. Chaucer's pilgrims would have found them in the windows of Canterbury. What, exactly, are "types and antitypes"? An Old Testament scene is juxtaposed with a New Testament scene to show that one foreshadows the other. It is possible to compile long lists of such parallels,[94] and it is also easy to gain the impression that they are merely mechanical and hence tedious. But this is to miss the whole point of their existence. When St. Paul in Gal. 4 suggests that "by allegory" Sara represents the Church whose children are the faithful, he does not leave the matter there, but uses the history of Sara and Agar to discuss the obligations of his fellow-Christians. The Old Testament "types" are more than foreshadowings of the Gospels; they are historical manifestations of principles set forth in the New Law. Isaac bore a bundle of faggots to his own sacrifice. In Christ's burden of the Cross we may

[94] For a medieval list, see M. R. James, "Pictor in Carmine," *Archaeologia*, xciv (1951), 141-166.

discern the philosophical meaning of this event. But Isaac was an historical figure, a man like ourselves, and we, too, it is suggested, must bear a burden which in one way or another leads to sacrifice. Isaac, in other words, is an historical exemplar whose action suggests something about the inner life and obligation of the observer. In technical language, typology employs allegory to imply tropology, which is its ultimate aim. "Typology" requires careful and systematic organization, it is instructive in an exemplary fashion, and, at the same time, it contains that element of the enigmatic necessary to what the medieval mind considered to be aesthetic appeal. The relationship between the two elements, old and new, is implied rather than stated, but the spiritual meaning for the individual which arises from their combination is something which can result only from the intellectual effort of the observer.

Other features of the new iconographic language are not difficult to find. During the second half of the thirteenth century statues of the Saints reveal an effort to show the dominating virtue of the individual portrayed in dress and countenance, and by the beginning of the fourteenth century each saint was distinguished by an emblem commemorating some distinctive scene or event.[95] Frequently the new conventions are more "decorous" than the old, at least on the surface. For example, the old Romanesque *Luxuria* with her gnawing serpents was replaced by a gracious and "courtly" lady with a mirror and comb. At Paris and Amiens the vices are shown with an element of humor, arising, perhaps, from the fact that since vice is unreasonable it is also ludicrous. The opposite of fortitude, for example, is a man running from a hare and a hooting owl (Figs. 56 and 57). In the thirteenth century more or less standard images for the virtues and the vices were developed, and these were elaborated in a great variety of ways during the later Middle Ages.

Symbolic actions like Lady *Luxuria's* use of her mirror and comb, or the retreat of the youth before the owl, furnished motifs for "secular" as well as for "religious" art, so that both types, which were often not very distinct during the Middle Ages, used a common language. The hawk carried by the lover (Fig. 9) appears in both religious and secular contexts. Thus in the St. Alban's

[95] See Mâle, *L'art rel. du XIIIe siècle* (Paris, 1923), pp. 285-287.

Psalter,[96] an illustration for Psalm 118 shows a figure on the left pointing to a "scene" below and reading the verse (37) "Averte oculos meos [ne videant vanitatem]." The "vanity" he points to, which may not be unrelated to Sir Lancelot's Land of "Gorre," which we shall discuss in the fifth chapter below, contains three parts. On the left a young man with a hawk confronts a girl with a flower in one hand indicating the glory of the flesh which fades "like the flower of the field" (Isa. 40. 6). In her other hand she holds a specimen of *fructus*, which stands for the forbidden "fruit" or enjoyment offered by the daughters of Eve to men, or by the "feminine" lower part of the reason to the "higher" part of the reason. In later versions of the same scene these objects may be replaced by others, the most common of which is a small furry creature which, like the flower, a cousin of the rosebud of Guillame de Lorris, represents the object of the lover's quest. Another pair of lovers stands to the right of these. Here the lover is about to offer the lady some "saint-seducing gold," with the evident implication that she is a prostitute. Still further on the right is a *locus amoenus* consisting of three trees along a river which probably stands for the paradise of earthly delights. The relevance of all this amorous imagery to the verse of the psalm is indicated by St. Ambrose, who wrote concerning it (*Expos. in Ps. CXVIII*, 5. 29): "If you see a woman to lust after her [Matt. 5. 28], death shall enter through the window [cf. Jer. 9. 21]. Therefore, close this window when you see the beauty of a strange woman [cf. Ecclus. 9. 8, 11], lest death should be able to enter. Your eyes should not look upon a strange woman, lest your tongue should utter perverse things [cf. Prov. 23. 33]. Close your window, therefore, lest a way of entrance be made open to death. But also beware a strange window [cf. Ecclus. 21. 26], for from the window of her house a whore enters. She enters from her window when she tempts anyone with the lasciviousness of wanton eyes."

That is, "vanity" lies in the violation of the commandment of

[96] See Otto Pächt, C. R. Dodwell, and Francis Wormald, *The St. Alban's Psalter* (London, 1960), plate 77. Dodwell, pp. 250-251, finds the tripartite configuration discussed here to represent (1) "eternal Eve tempting the soul to sin," (2) cupidity, (3) the Garden of Eden. The present discussion does not follow this analysis, which seems superficial. For the man with the hawk and the lady with the flower, cf. Folke Nordström, *Virtues and Vices on the Fourteenth-Century Corbels of Uppsala Cathedral* (Stockholm, 1956), pp. 95, 97.

Matt. 5. 28, which, as we have seen, has implications which are by no means limited to sexual activity. As Peter of Blois once observed (*Epist.*, 61), with an echo of Ovid (*Met.*, 2. 846-847), "A hair shirt and a hawk do not go well together [*non bene conveniunt*], the affliction of the flesh and the exercise of pleasure." The lover with his hawk is about to set out to abuse beauty. The hawk appears again in a stained-glass window at Bourges which shows the story of the Prodigal Son. The young man sets out on his unfortunate pilgrimage with a hawk on his wrist. Significantly, in the next scene he is welcomed by some harlots, one of whom places a wreath on his head. The young man with a hawk appears in other contexts. He is accompanied by the sign of Taurus, the house of Venus, in the series of "Labors of the Month" at Amiens Cathedral (Fig. 58).[97] Mirror cases display a great deal of amorous imagery of this kind during the later Middle Ages. What better medium was there for the expression of the various activities of the lady with the mirror and the comb than the ivory mirror case? The relationship between mirrors and love had been recognized since antiquity, as a Greek mirror of the second century B.C. carved with a sketch of Venus and Cupid testifies. But the imagery used on medieval mirrors frequently parallels that used on the margins of psalters.

A mirror case from the first half of the fourteenth century (Fig. 59) shows, in the upper left, two young lovers. In the center the lover helps the lady make a chaplet of flowers. The most famous literary elaboration of this motif is the chaplet which the lover provides to gain welcome from the lady in the *Roman de la rose*. It probably derives ultimately from the crown of roses in the second chapter of Wisdom where the vain philosophy of the foolish who wish to use creatures "tanquam in iuventute celeriter" is expressed: "coronemus nos rosis antequam marcescant; nullum pratum sit, quod non pertranseat luxuria nostra: nemo nostrum exors sit luxuriae nostrae." In the lower half of our example a lover leads away a lady who holds in her arm one of the "wigte gent and smale" which are symbols for the center of feminine attractiveness, at least from the young lover's point of view. The central

[97] Taurus was the sign of April, which was associated with Venus by etymology. E.g., see the entry in Huguccio of Pisa's *Derivationes*, Oxford, Bodl., MS Laud Misc. 626, fols. 3 verso and 4, and Isidore, *Etymologiae*, 5. 33. 7.

panel shows not only the chin-chucking motif, some examples of which we saw in the last chapter, but also the more direct approach of "hende Nicholas," which, as we have seen, appears in a devotional manual (Fig. 5). The use of this very obvious gesture in a courtly setting may seem incongruous to us at first, but the ogees in which the figures are fixed represent the outward decorum of the Gothic style; they are no guarantee that the meaning of what is represented would not be shocking to nineteenth-century tastes. In the final scene the lover offers his heart (cf. Fig. 27), as the lady crowns him with the circlet of welcome.

In Fig. 60, a mirror case from the fourteenth century, the central panel at the top shows Cupid transformed into the more decorous-looking Gothic God of Love about to thrust his arrow, the significance of which we have already discussed, at the young man. He holds the hawk of love's hunt on his left wrist, and the lady kneels before him. In the panel on his right a young lover engages in "chin-chucking," while on the other side a lover leads his lady into his presence. Below, a young lover receives the small furry creature, in this instance a dog, from his lady. The wreath-making motif occupies the central panel, and on the right a lover offers homage to his lady. In Fig. 61 we see the hunt of love, the significance of which is emphasized by the dog's pursuit of the rabbit below. A literary echo of this same hunt, which probably owes something ultimately to Ovid's metaphor at the beginning of the *Ars amatoria*, appears in the fabliau "Du chevalier a la robe vermeille," where it is said that the lover

> Et prist son esprevier mué,
> Que il meïsmes ot mué,
> Et maine .II. chienes petiz,
> Qui estoient trestoz fetiz
> Por faire aus chans saillir l'aloe.
> Si com fine amor veut et loe,
> S'est atornez.[98]

An amusing variant is afforded by Fig. 62, where the lover holding the hawk of his hunt chucks the lady under the chin. In her left hand she carries the lure for his hawk to indicate the kind of at-

[98] Montaiglon and Raynaud, *Recueil général des fabliaux* (Paris, 1872-1890), III, 36.

tractiveness for which the mirror was, presumably, to be used. Perhaps a difference in tone may be detected in Fig. 63, a peculiarly striking example of the offer of the heart and the bestowal of the wreath. Behind the lover the horses (cf. Fig. 8) are being held in check and subdued with a scourge. It may be that this example was intended to suggest the kind of love admired by Machaut. It is clear, however, that in the other examples, the "horses," if we may take them figuratively, are not restrained. This is especially true of the mirror case represented in Fig. 59. The flowing lines of the Gothic style lend these pieces an air of elegance, and the treatment of the materials is sometimes light-hearted, if not humorous. But the God of Love and his activities probably lost none of their significance when they were carved on ivory mirrors or caskets for the ladies.

These illustrations may help to show the pervasiveness and the flexibility of the new iconography. To emphasize the fact that it was not confined to either "religious" or "secular" contexts, let us consider two further examples, both from the fourteenth century. A page from the Ormesby Psalter (Fig. 64) shows David kneeling in prayer in the initial which introduces *Domine exaudi orationem meam*. This is, essentially, an aspect of the New Song of praise. At the left of the initial a figure makes a different kind of "melodie" directed toward the earth. And below, a grotesque which is "lion-like" in much the same fashion as is Odo of Cluny's *chimaera*, watches while a young man with a hawk receives a ring from a lady who holds a familiar furry creature, this time a squirrel, in her arm. Her head-dress may be a reflection of Prudentius' *Veterum Cultura Deorum*, for a similar motif from that source was used as an attribute of Idolatry, and, in York Minster, as an attribute of witchcraft.[99] In any event, her relation to the ladies on the mirror cases is clear. The same convention may be illustrated from a book of decretals (Figs. 65, 66), where the religious habit of the gentleman does not prevent him from tickling the lady's chin. We have already encountered many of the motifs of the mirrors in religious contexts (Figs. 5, 8, 9, 23-28), so that this point need be elaborated no further. The stylistic features of Gothic art favored symbolic imagery, since they effectively pre-

[99] See Nordström, *op.cit.*, pp. 36-37.

vented it from being realistic, and the standardization of symbolic conventions permitted their use in a wide variety of situations.

The above examples also serve to illustrate the fact that Gothic representations of what was thought of as unreasonable behavior are generally more elegant than those of the Romanesque period. It may be that Fig. 59 is a trifle shocking, but the other types of activity pictured on mirror cases are easily mistaken for conventional "courtly" pastimes or features of "daily living," when, as a matter of fact, they frequently point in exactly the same direction as the approach of "hende Nicholas." There is no more deceptive feature of Gothic art than its ability to describe unreasonable behavior in elegant and humorous terms, perhaps now and then with a touch of irony. This does not mean, however, that Romanesque forthrightness was abandoned altogether. In ecclesiastical art it may be thrust into the background, but it is still there. A careful examination of Fig. 51, for example, will reveal a figure in the upper left corner which we would not expect to find on a modern church. A more striking example is afforded by Fig. 67, which portrays the Judgment of Solomon. The representation is dominated by the spiritual interpretation of the scriptural narrative. The two harlots, one in red (kneeling) and one in blue (standing) reappear on the balcony above, where the one in blue takes a position on the right and wears a crown to symbolize the New Law of the Church, as opposed to her unsuccessful rival, who is the Old Law or the Synagogue.[100] Although the two devils who sit in the architectural setting on either side are quite definitely guilty of "indecent exposure," this fact in no way detracts from the spirituality of the picture. For they are intended to emphasize the danger of the evils of the "flesh" or the "letter" which militate against the spiritual meaning. Gothic decorum was not modern decorum. The spiritual and the fleshly could be placed side by side without clashing and without producing any "tension." And, on the other hand, the fleshly could be expressed symbolically with a good-natured humor which modern Christian art has seldom had the courage or the confidence to employ, and for which modern secular art lacks the necessary background of values.

Perhaps the most famous literary work of the thirteenth cen-

[100] Cf. *Glossa ordinaria*, *PL*, 113, cols. 582-583.

tury, outside of Italy, where the Gothic style was feebly represented, is the *Roman de la rose*. The various stylistic attitudes we have seen to be characteristic of the art of the period are reflected in the poem, but a failure to recognize them has led to a great deal of disagreement about its actual content. It may seem absurd to speak of an "obvious organization" in the *Roman*, especially in Jean de Meun's continuation, which has a reputation for discursiveness and an inability to stay with the subject. But this reputation rests on the assumption that the subject of the poem is the "story," an account of actions actually carried out. We may safely assume that neither Guillaume de Lorris nor Jean de Meun had a desire to represent actual actions carried out by actual persons in space and time any more than Gothic artists had such a desire. The *Roman* is not a chronicle but a work of fiction. Just as the figures in Gothic art are not photographically conceived as visible beings, neither are the characters in the *Roman* "characters" in the modern sense. The lover is a figure whose actions typify those of a lover, and that is all. He has no personal peculiarities which are irrelevant to this function. The Rose, insofar as she is a human being, and not simply a part of a human being, has absolutely no "character." Some of the abstractions like Faus-Semblant and Jalosie are particularized through exemplification, but they are essentially qualities which appear in human beings of various types, not human beings as such, and not attributes of any peculiar human being. Just as a cathedral is not "organized space" provided as an area for men to act as free agents, but an organization of lines in space constructed to emphasize certain ideas and to facilitate certain symbolic actions, in the same way the organization of the *Roman* is not a framework for literally conceived action, but a vehicle for the development of ideas. The story is of value to the poem only as it permits exemplification, not as a thing in itself. To read the poem for the story is to misread it. Guillaume himself tells us as much at the beginning. The poem, he says, is an account of a dream which is of value in the way that Macrobius suggested that dreams are valuable. On what grounds did Macrobius defend the value of dreams and *narrationes fabulosae*? Simply because they may be useful in philosophical exposition as the dream of Scipio is useful. In this sense a dream is an expository narrative. The subject, Guillaume says, is "l'art d'amors." And this, in the Middle Ages, was a very broad subject with ramifications in theology and philosophy which neither of the two authors considered it wise to neglect. Neither was interested in "telling a story" for its own sake.

Guillaume develops his theme by presenting symbolic actions involving iconographically described characters in an iconographically described setting. Roughly, the action involves subjection to Deduit through Oiseuse; the action of Biauté; homage to Cupid, or wilful desire; the abandonment of Raison; the use of flattery as advocated by Amis; the winning of a kiss with the aid of Venus; and the reaction of Male Bouche, Honte, Peor, and Jalosie. This temporal sequence is hardly a "story"; it is simply the ordinary course of *fol' amour*. Basically, as we have seen, the pattern of Guillaume's poem involves the traditional movement from the stimulation of the senses through delightful thought to passion and consent. Since consent is a normal prelude to action, and since a kiss was commonly thought of as a promise of the "remnant," we may assume that if Guillaume had finished his poem he would have described the plucking of the "rose," although, perhaps, neither quite so precipitously as did the anonymous continuator nor so elaborately as did Jean de Meun.

The significance of the actions described is driven home by the iconographic descriptions, without which the poem would be reduced to a simple statement of a very commonplace idea. A glance at the figures on the outside of the garden of Deduit, for example, will reveal that, stylistically speaking, those which are not merely general descriptions but contain concrete details employ the same basic techniques as those employed in the medallions at Paris and Amiens. We may illustrate this fact by turning to Fig. 68, an illustration of the seven vices in the following order: pride, wrath, lechery, sloth, avarice, envy, and gluttony. Although this is a relatively late illustration which, since it appears in a manuscript of the *Roman*, may have been influenced by the poem itself, that fact is not of significance here since our concern is with technique and not with influence. Self-murdering wrath, lechery with her mirror and comb, and avarice with her bags certainly antedate the poem. In any event, Avarice is dressed in tattered clothes and carries bags. She has exactly the same attributes in the poem, except that there she has only one bag. Envy looks furtively to one side, just as she does in Guillaume's description. The early illustrators of the *Ro-*

man recognized in the poem a technique with which they were were thoroughly familiar. In the poem the description of Vilanie is vague, but it closes with the lines,

> Bien sembloit estre d'afiz pleine
> E fame qui petit seüst
> D'enorer ce qu'ele deüst.

To show this characteristic, the early illustrators used exactly the configuration which identifies the opposite of "Gentleness" as she appears at Paris (Fig. 56, third medallion from the left) and Amiens (Fig. 70). At times, Guillaume uses iconographic detail for implication, just as Falconet (Fig. 21) used spatial and compositional relationships for the same purpose, although in this instance the implication is one of meaning, which was Guillaume's concern, and not one of action in space and time, which was not his concern. Thus Oiseuse carries the mirror and comb of Lechery (Figs. 68, and 13) to suggest that idleness is a prelude to that vice. The details of the garden itself have nothing to do with any conceivable geographical location; they are used to reinforce the meaning of the symbolic action that takes place within it. In view of the structure of the poem and the stylistic devices used to identify the characters and actions, the conclusion that the poem is an autobiographical account of a love affair is absurd. It is entirely possible that Guillaume may have at one time been misled by idleness to pursue the delight of the flesh for its own sake, and that he may have employed a little flattery to seduce a girl and so satisfy his desire. Activity of this kind did not suddenly begin in the Renaissance. But whether he did or not has no relevance to his poem.

In Jean de Meun's continuation, the organization is, if anything, more explicit than that of the earlier part of the poem, and, at the same time, there is a much more thorough effort at exemplification. With reference to the first point, the poem may be seen to fall into well-defined sections devoted to explicit exposition by the principal characters, each of whom, in effect, reveals his or her own nature. The "characters" thus serve as rubrics under which the various ideas and attitudes relevant to the subject of love may be developed. The themes to be elaborated are set forth by Raison (lines 4221ff.) whose Boethian discourse affords the positive ideas against which the subsequent materials in the poem are set. Those of us who have been brought up on romantic poetry or the novels of Dickens may instinctively distrust reason, but Raison speaks with the voice of Patristic authority, Boethius, and Cicero. She is, as it were, Lady Philosophy, who is described by Guillaume as the Image of God. He who seeks Jean de Meun's opinions will find them here, not in the discourses of the other characters, who, with Ciceronian decorum, speak as their natures demand. Raison explains the function of delight in love and the folly of pursuing it for its own sake rather than using it as a stimulus to the perpetuation of the species. She explains the nature of true friendship, condemning any sort of human relationship based on Fortune. Finally, she urges the love of Raison, which is wisdom, as the key to the happy life. If the lover will love Raison, despise the God of Love, or cupidinous desire, and scorn Fortune he will have no difficulty. But the lover abandons Raison and turns to Amis. The discourse of Amis, who is a worldly friend not exactly of the kind advocated by Cicero, is an essay in worldly wisdom. Flattery, hypocrisy, force, deceit, a contempt of marriage, and bribery are strongly urged as proper weapons of a lover. If Raison gives us a wise attitude toward love, Amis furnishes a wily approach to the same subject. To elaborate the ideas set forth by Amis, we are introduced to Faus-Semblant, for, as Amis has indicated, the successful follower of the God of Love must be a "seemer." His "confession" constitutes a long diatribe against those who pretend to be virtuous but who actually devote themselves to the pursuit of an evil cupidity, but since this kind of hypocrisy must accompany the lover until what he actually wants becomes too obvious to conceal any longer, Faus-Semblant aids him in his hunt. A set of worldly-wise instructions for the ladies is furnished by La Vieille, who condemns constancy and advises the use of "love" as a means of gaining wealth. This descendant of Ovid's Dipsas and ancestress of the wife of Bath and Celestina is hardly a spokesman for the author. But the wisdom of Amis and La Vieille is insufficient for purposes of seduction without Venus. As a personification of sexual delight she represents an element which, since the Fall, comes from Nature. The long confession of Nature to Genius, or natural inclination,[101] serves to show

---

[101] See the third Vatican Mythographer in Bode, *op.cit.*, p. 185. Cf. the quotation from Guillaume de Conches in Edouard Jeauneau, "*Integumentum* chez Guillaume de Conches," *Archives d'hist. doct. et litt. d. m. a.*, XXXII (1957), p. 46: "Genius est naturalis concupiscentia."

why Venus operates as she does. Nature's function is to replenish the ravages of death at her forge,[102] but Nature is disturbed, just as she is in the *De planctu naturae* of Alanus, by a fault. Man alone among all creatures violates her laws. She explains at great length that man's actions in this respect have nothing to do with destiny. He acts through his own free will. The heavenly bodies, the elements, plants, animals, and birds all act harmoniously; only man, in spite of the Redemption, acts against Nature and must suffer the consequences. In the course of this confession Nature reveals many of her "wonders" as they were understood in the thirteenth century, doubtless to create an impression of the majesty and dignity of the system which man's willfulness leads him to violate.

To understand this confession it is necessary to remember that Genius, the Father Confessor, is not a Christian priest. One of the illustrators of the *Roman* who depicted the scene shows an awareness of this fact by placing a little idol on an altar in the background (Fig. 69). Genius is not grace; he is merely the inclination of created things to act naturally. Hence Genius is, as it were, the "conscience" of Nature. Since he is not grace, he does not know the solution to Nature's problem: ideas like the mortification of the flesh, the crucifixion of the Old Man, or the value of the sacraments are completely beyond his ken. He absolves Nature, who is obviously not responsible for man's peculiar transgressions, and approaches the God of Love, who, since his dominance at the Fall, has been eager to turn natural inclination to his own purposes and so invests Genius in episcopal robes. Nature is, as it were, the great authority of cupidinous desire and has probably been cited as such ever since the first damsel showed some reluctance. Thus in the "Lai d'Aristote" Alexander's *pucele* threatens to bring Aristotle into subjection through Nature:

> Sire rois, or vos levez main,
> Si verroiz Nature apointier
> Au maistre por lui despointier
> De son sens et de sa clergie.[103]

[102] Nature is usually shown with hammer and anvil completing some. of her work, such as a boy or a bird. On the hammer and anvil, see Alanus, *De planctu naturae, PL,* 210, cols. 445-446.

[103] Henri d'Andeli, *Le lai d'Aristote,* ed. M. Delbrouille (Paris, 1951), lines 254ff.

When Aristotle approaches the girl, he says,

> Tant m'a fet Amors et Nature
> Que de vos partir ne me puis.[104]

And when Aristotle has been duly ridden, Alexander accuses him of having lost his reason and become like a beast:

> Et or vos a mis en tel point
> Qu'il n'a en vos de raison point,
> Ainz vos metez a loi de beste.[105]

But the philosopher attributes his difficulties to Nature:

> M'a desfait Nature en une eure.[106]

Nature is similarly associated with lechery (Venus) by Gervais du Bus in his description of Fauvel's court:

> Après, fu assise Venus,
> Qui prent les gens vestus et nuz:
> Ce est le pechié naturel,
> Qui tous jours est de blancdurel,
> Se viellesce ou mal ou raison
> Ne li fait perdre sa saison.[107]

Nature is in these instances clearly opposed to *sens, clergie,* and *raison*. But if Nature is actually innocent, as we have seen her to be, how does this situation come about? It is the function of Genius' sermon and the events which immediately follow to explain it.

The sermon is an elaboration of the counsel of Gen. 1. 28: "Increase and multiply," for this, in effect, is what Nature does and what Genius urges her to do. All of Jean de Meun's readers were undoubtedly aware of the benefits of multiplication, but they also knew that multiplication could be carried out spiritually as well as literally, so that the number of the faithful in the Church may be "multiplied" through conversion, or the virtues may be "multiplied" within the individual.[108] But Genius sticks to the letter. He describes the garden of the Good Shepherd, the scene of the new

---

[104] *Ibid.*, lines 409-410.   [105] Lines 474-476.   [106] Line 490.
[107] *Le roman de Fauvel*, ed. A. Längfors, *SATF* (1914-1919), ii, 1557ff.
[108] See the discussion by R. P. Miller, "Chaucer's Pardoner, the Scriptural Eunuch, and the Pardoner's Tale," *Speculum*, xxx (1955), 185-186.

Golden Age, which will be, he assures us, the reward of those who follow Nature. He contrasts this garden with the fantastic and misleading garden of Deduit. There can be no question that this garden, with its obvious scriptural iconography, is a figure for Heaven (Fig. 12). Since the loss of the Golden Age, or the state of Nature as it was created,[109] the earth has been very unlike it. The trouble started, Genius says, when Jupiter, who fostered willful rather than natural inclination, castrated his father Saturn (Fig. 3) bringing about the downfall of the Golden Age and eventually producing the Age of Iron. In other words, willful desire, rather than natural desire, is the source of man's difficulties. Jean's readers would not have forgotten that the castration of Saturn led to the birth of Venus. When Genius throws down his torch at the end of his sermon, Venus spreads its flames. That is, the pleasant warmth of Venus which should lead to activities harmonious with Nature is seized upon as the warmth which leads to exactly the kind of desire that causes man to stray from Nature. For when Venus applies her torch, Shame, Fear, and Reason are cast aside (line 20779), and the lover, although he has no interest in "multiplication," is able to take advantage of the resultant heat to win the rose. Neither Nature nor Genius is responsible for this result, over which they have no control. The responsibility rests with Cupid and Venus, with desire and pleasure, to which man voluntarily subjects himself as the lover did at the beginning of the poem. The end of the poem is thus simply an elaborate allegorical account of what Raison says much earlier about the nature and function of desire and pleasure. Nature is innocent, but man, through his erring will, abuses her, making the laws of Nature suit his own cupidinous ends.

The organization of Jean de Meun's continuation is thus far from being discursive or haphazard. The main themes are set by Raison, and the rest of the poem is an elaborate, but not a digressive account of what happens to those who disobey Raison's counsels. The story of the castration of Saturn in Genius' sermon is not a digression, but a narrative exposition of the ideas that are de-

---

[109] The classical "Golden Age" was taken to represent the state of nature before the Fall or the restoration of that condition in the Church of the Faithful. See the excellent discussion by Charles S. Singleton, *Dante Studies 2: Journey to Beatrice* (Cambridge, Mass., 1958), pp. 184-203. Cf. Pietro di Dante, *Commentarium* (Florence, 1846), pp. 295-296.

veloped there, and it is not, by the standards of Gothic taste, an unseemly mixture of the sacred and the profane, as it has been called, any more than Fig. 67 represents such a mixture. The personified abstractions in the poem, like Amis, Nature, and Genius, are its organizing principles. Without Amis and La Vieille it would have been impossible to elaborate the implications of worldly wisdom; without Faus-Semblant, it would have been difficult to show the manifold implications of hypocrisy in the pursuit of cupidinous ends; without Nature, we could not have been shown the implications of the abuse of nature in lustful love, and so on. Moreover, these poetic "rubrics" are arranged in a logical order, the same order, in fact, that was suggested by Guillaume de Lorris in the first part of the poem. The sequence is still a progression: suggestion, pleasurable thought, consent, and deed. But Jean de Meun has added to this framework an exhaustive study of the various principles which it involves.

The configurations we see on the medallions of Paris or Amiens, on mirror cases, or in representations of the vices are to a certain extent exemplary since they represent abstract principles in terms of human action. But the action is typical rather than literal. Persons who lack fortitude do not necessarily run from hares or owls, a man may be avaricious without carrying bags, amorous young ladies do not always go about holding small animals in view, and the slothful do not necessarily carry distaffs in their hands. That is, what we have called "iconographic" descriptions are not directly expressive of human action or of human emotion. Much the same thing may be said of the persons and places in Guillaume's poem. Jean de Meun is just as fond of iconographic detail as was Guillaume, but his continuation of the poem shows a much greater flexibility in the use of exemplary materials. The description of Hunger in lines 10163ff. harmonizes well in its technique with Guillaume's descriptions of personified abstractions, but the materials are derived from Ovid rather than from the traditions of Gothic art. The second part of the *Roman* contains a great deal of classical material of all kinds used for purposes of exemplification. Stories like those of Saturn and Venus, Appius and Virginia, Venus and Adonis, and Pygmalion are told at some length as narrative elaborations and exemplifications of the themes being developed, and significant materials from Ovid's love poetry enrich the speeches of Amis and La Vieille. In the visual arts after about 1160 antique figures were "modernized" in conformity with the new style,[110] and we can see the same tendency in literature. Classical characters who make their appearance in the *Roman* are pretty thoroughly acclimated to the time of the poem itself, not because of a lack of historical sense, but because the poet wished to make them meaningful to his own audience. The God of Love, who is actually Cupid, is only the most striking instance of this transformation (see Figs. 23, 26, 27, 60). He looks very much like a Gothic angel. But other classical figures, both mythological and historical, are treated in the same way and are interpreted accordingly by the illustrators of the poem, who keep them up to date throughout the remainder of the Middle Ages. Thus Venus and Mars, whose indiscretions led them into Vulcan's trap, are shown in Fig. 71 as though they were mere fifteenth-century characters. Jean also borrows exemplary and iconographic materials freely from medieval sources, like the description of Fortune's realm from the *Anticlaudianus* of Alanus, or the materials from the letters of Héloise and Abelard. These materials all had fairly definite connotations in the culture of the time which made their exemplary force apparent. In a few instances actual persons are introduced. In Raison's discourse Charles of Anjou becomes an exemplary figure, and in the confession of Faus-Semblant there are explicit references to William of St. Amour, to the friars, the Beguines, and to specific practices which the author wishes to condemn. In short, Jean reveals a tendency to particularize abstractions in terms of everyday life. But to speak of instances of this kind as "realistic" is not quite accurate, since no realistic detail is included for its own sake. It is used rather to make the principles involved more immediate and striking. Like the "realism" of Gothic art, it is subsumed within a framework of abstract ideas which form, as it were, the medium of the poem.

Guillaume's poem is an excellent example of the kind of surface elegance which we have seen to be a feature of the art of the period. Literary examples of this characteristic of Gothic style are not difficult to find. The "Lai dou Lecheor," for example, in spite of its subject, maintains the same kind of exterior grace we have seen on ivory mirror cases. Writing of this poem, Gaston

[110] Adhémar, *Influences antiques*, pp. 232, 292ff.

Paris observed, "Rien n'est cependant moins 'courtois' que le thème développé ici, et moins conforme à la galanterie chevaleresque. Ce qui est toutefois frappant, dans cette petite pièce, c'est le ton élégant qui y règne."[111] This same elegance is one of the characteristic features of the romances of Chrétien de Troyes and the *Lais* of Marie de France. And wherever it occurs, it poses a serious problem of literary interpretation. Since the actual subject of the "Lai dou Lecheor" is made abundantly plain, it is not difficult to see that the poem is a satire on those who are chivalrous and "virtuous," or "franc et debonere" for an ulterior and rather unworthy purpose. But in instances where the expression is less direct, especially where the reader can find grounds for detecting what he thinks of as romantic or "courtly" love, the satiric intent is in danger of being lost, and things that are elegantly described are assumed to be described with approval. In Guillaume's poem the surface elegance used to describe Oiseuse, Deduit, the God of Love, and their followers in the garden has been a major hindrance to a modern understanding of his intention. But just as the Gothic artist could employ a symbolic technique for a humorous condemnation of evil, presenting his actual materials in the elegant ogees of the prevailing style, so also the literary artist of the Gothic period could maintain a surface elegance and grace, or, in nineteenth-century language, "charm," while depicting in satiric fashion what he regarded as the most dangerous of evils. The problem is somewhat less acute in Jean de Meun's continuation, where the cynical worldliness of Amis, La Vieille, and Faus-Semblant is fairly obvious. Nevertheless, there have been those who would attribute the attitudes of these characters to the author, or who would read *exempla* like the story of Pygmalion literally because of the elegance of the surface narrative. The strange doctrines which result from a misunderstanding of Gothic elegance, both in art and literature, are frequently subsumed under the term "courtly." But there is no evidence whatsoever that medieval feu-

---

[111] "Lais inédits," *Romania*, viii (1879), p. 64. Cf. C. H. Livingston's observation concerning the "Dit du con" in *Le jongleur Gautier le Leu* (Cambridge, Mass., 1951), p. 235: "Ce paradoxe: sujet obscène et ton courtois. . . ." The subsequent discussion misses the point of the poem entirely, for it is a satirical thrust at those who avidly pursue a false goal, not, by any stretch of the imagination, a "hymne païen à la louange de la Vénus physique."

dal courts generally entertained doctrines and attitudes radically at variance with the ordinary traditions of medieval culture.[112]

It is sometimes said that Jean's poem shows the influence of the fabliaux, and hence has a flavor of bourgeois realism.[113] However, the fabliaux are by no means certainly "bourgeois" in origin; in fact, there is considerable evidence to show that they were, like the romances, produced originally for aristocratic audiences.[114] And regardless of their origin, they were certainly written for courtly audiences in the thirteenth century. The fabliaux vary enormously in style, ranging from fairly learned works exhibiting considerable artistry, like the "Lai d'Aristote," of Henri d'Andeli, to relatively unpolished jokes like "Le Male Honte" or "Celle qui se fist foutre sur la fosse de son mari." They also vary a great deal in the matter of "obscenity," a characteristic which modern readers are likely to confuse with "realism." Considering the length of his poem, Jean de Meun is much less "obscene" than some of the more striking of the fabliaux, like that remarkable attack on false modesty "La damoiselle qui ne pooit oïr parler de foutre." Jean offers a very reasonable account of his use of words like *vit* and *coilles*, and this account has nothing to do with "realism." The fabliaux are not actually "realistic" in other ways. Gautier le Leu's "Dit du con" is not a realistic account of actual actions literally carried out, but an emblematic configuration designed as a comment on a popular but unworthy kind of motivation. "Realism" requires realistic characters, but the characters who animate the fabliaux are not, in a modern sense, "realistic" at all. They are, rather, types.[115] Who in the "Lai d'Aristote" is a realistic character? Alexander is the type of the aristocrat who allows himself to be dominated by sensual pleasure, a type criticized by "clerks" of all kinds throughout the Middle Ages. Aristotle is a type of the wise man who allows himself to be tempted and so becomes foolish, a fact which accounts

[112] For good illustrations of courtly tastes, see Tancred Borenius, "The Cycle of the Images in the Castles and Palaces of Henry III," *JWCI*, vi (1943), 40-50. Henry was especially fond of representations of Dives and Lazarus and of the Wheel of Fortune. Scriptural and hagiographical figures are not confined to the ecclesiastical portions of the palaces.

[113] But see Lionel J. Friedman, "Jean de Meung, Antifeminism, and Bourgeois Realism," *MP*, lvii (1959), 13-23.

[114] This is the thesis developed in detail by Per Nykrog, *Les Fabliaux* (Copenhagen, 1957).

[115] Cf. Nykrog, pp. 108-109.

for his frequent appearance with the *pucele* on his back in both ecclesiastical and "secular" art of the late Middle Ages. The fabliaux are realistic only in the sense that pointed satire is realistic; it may make its point in strong terms. But the point is seldom literal. No one expected to find learned men down on all fours saddled and bridled and carrying girls on their backs, although this configuration may well have suggested other things that learned men might do. Jean de Meun does share a fine sense of satiric comedy with the clerical authors of the twelfth-century Latin comedies and with the authors of the fabliaux. But this fact is far from making him a "bourgeois realist" or a realist of any other kind. It simply allies him with a tradition of vigorous expression which may be illustrated in a wide variety of forms from the early part of the period in question (Fig. 2) to the fourteenth century (Fig. 4). The combination of this vigor of statement with Gothic elegance accounts for the style of the final section of the poem, which F. S. Ellis, writing for a generation with different standards of decorum, left untranslated.

3. THE FOURTEENTH CENTURY IN ENGLAND

Developments in style are roughly parallel during the fourteenth century in England, France, and the Low Countries. Nevertheless, there are certain national peculiarities which we should take into account, especially in England. Generally, as a result of Italian influences, the preaching and teaching of the friars, and, above all, because of the continued development of tendencies already apparent in the art of the thirteenth century, there was a greater emphasis on feeling and emotion in painting and sculpture. If feelings are to be portrayed, human beings must be placed in an environment conducive to feeling, and this requires space in which they can move and engage in relationships with other persons and objects. An extreme example will illustrate this point. In Fig. 68 the representation of Envy is sufficiently easy to identify, once the convention of a ragged and shifty-eyed Envy has been established. But the picture does not convey a feeling of envy. We see nothing for Envy to be envious about. She is, in effect, Envy herself rather than an envious person. In Fig. 72, an illustration of the *Roman de la rose* from the fifteenth century, Envy has become an envious person. She still looks out of the corners of her eyes in deference to the iconographic tradition, but she has lost her ragged garments in favor of a haggard countenance to show that her condition is habitual. Her hands suggest that she is muttering an imprecation as she sees the other lady receiving the elaborate attentions of the young gentleman. The picture thus not only conveys the idea of envy; it also gives us an impression of how envy feels in terms of ordinary human experience. This kind of representation requires a spatial continuum rather than an idealized background, and this continuum is afforded by means of perspective.

It has been pointed out that perspective is of two kinds: it may either enclose an area different from that of the observer, as in the paintings of Giotto, or it may suggest a continuation of the space occupied by the observer, as in the paintings of Van Eyck.[116] The very crude beginnings of spatial depth in the painting of England and France during the fourteenth century may be said to represent a tendency toward perspective of the first kind, and its development may be attributed to an effort to represent persons as sentient beings in a manner designed to emphasize an idea. In late English illumination it may be possible to detect a general tendency to provide first a small stage or platform at the feet of the figures, and, later on, with the beginnings of modeling in the faces and figures, to extend this impression of depth to the rest of the picture. The effect of the new sense of depth is peculiarly striking in the rendering of devotional subjects in manuscripts produced in the early fifteenth century, like MS Lat. liturg. f. 2 in the Bodleian Library, where it appears in an emblematic representation of the Wounds of the Sacred Heart (fol. 4 verso) as well as in the treatment of more traditional subjects like St. George (fol. 144 verso).[117] In pictures of this kind we become aware of a more subjective feeling for religious themes than had been common in the preceding century. However, outside of Italy a restlessness in the face of the limitations of flat space was probably felt first in marginal illustra-

[116] On the ideal rather than realistic quality of Giotto's painting, see Max Dvořak, *Kunstgeschichte als Geistesgeschichte* (Munich, 1928), p. 124, and, on the unity of the paintings as it differs from the unity of space and time achieved later, see Frey, *Gotik und Renaissance*, pp. 46-47. The two kinds of perspective are discussed by E. Panofsky, *Early Netherlandish Painting* (Cambridge, Mass., 1953), pp. 3-7.

[117] See Rickert, *Painting in Britain*, pp. 183-184, for a description of this book.

tion, where the artists were free from the conventions of gold leaf backgrounds and Gothic line, and could develop more informal illustrations of ideas in concrete terms. In Fig. 9, for example, from a Flemish MS of around 1300, the artist has faced the problem of an odd spatial relationship and given us what must have been at the time an amusing rear view of the young man. The iconographic details—the hawk and the singing bird—indicate the subject of the picture, but the spatial relationship tends to produce a sense of exemplification. Marginal illustrations frequently reveal a playful awareness of the limitations of the page. Thus in the Hours of St. Omer, from the first half of the fourteenth century, the artist (Fig. 73) shows a pair of hands emerging from the parchment, as though through a hole in it; below, a rabbit which is being pursued emerges from behind one of the linear flourishes which adorn the page. In general, marginal decoration offered a field for experimentation with drawing which could not be indulged in the more conventional illustration of initials. The reduction of symbolic action to more literal terms may be regarded as one of the most significant features of fourteenth-century style. But it should be emphasized that our example in the last paragraph is an extreme one. Perspective was not highly developed in either England or France during the century, and Chaucer may never have seen anything like the effect achieved in Fig. 72. Even in Fig. 1, from the workshop of Pol de Limbourg, which is said to have contributed a great deal to the growth of "Renaissance" attitudes, the perspective is awkward and imperfect.

Although England was subjected to influences from France and the Low Countries throughout the period, and to sporadic influences from Italy, sometimes indirectly through French sources, English style retained certain peculiarities of its own, and, at the same time, produced some highly original characteristics. Perhaps the most consistent feature of English art is its conservatism. But it should be remembered that the imitation of foreign models in an essentially conservative medium sometimes produces highly original effects. This fact is especially obvious in architecture, in which, in the fourteenth century, England produced a "Decorated" style, and, in the second half of the century, the distinctively English style known as "Perpendicular." The rib vaults of Durham Cathedral have long been regarded as forerunners of the Gothic manner, but, in spite of this fact, England did not develop the potentialities of the "broken" or "pointed" arch and the ribbed vault in the same way that they were developed in France. As Jean Bony put it, "England never really gained an idea of what Gothic really meant to the French,"[118] although it might be fairer to say that English architecture retained its own stylistic peculiarities. If we compare Salisbury Cathedral with Amiens, both of which were begun in 1220, certain significant differences emerge, some of which show an English tendency to retain Romanesque characteristics. First of all, the ground-plan of Salisbury is, except for the octagonal forms of the vestry and chapter-house, rigorously rectilinear.[119] As a result, the north porch, the four transepts, and the Lady Chapel seem almost to be separate rooms, distinct from the space occupied by the nave and the choir, and we are confronted with an "additive" effect, similar to that produced by the architecture of the eleventh century. It might be more accurate to say that a plan of this kind conforms to the English tendency to find comfort in small enclosures, shut off to produce a sense of privacy. Even the great hall-like interior of King's College Chapel in Cambridge is broken by a large wooden screen, and, in modern times, the same feeling is expressed in the design of such establishments as Liberty's in London. The great curve of the chevet at Amiens with its rounded chapels, together with the broad shallow transepts, produces a much more unified design. The same kind of difference between the two structures appears on the outside, where Salisbury seems to be made up of separate elements added together to form a whole. Again, if we turn to the interiors (Figs. 74, 75), we notice that at Amiens a strong vertical line runs from the base of each pier to the vaults. At Salisbury this line breaks off at the top of each pier to be resumed rather indecisively between the arches of the triforium. The result is, from the French point of view, "inconsequential," as though the arches of the triforium were added above the main arches without sufficient integration. The rhythm of the clusters of colonnettes in the triforium is much more rapid than

[118] "French Influences on the Origin of English Gothic Architecture," *JWCI*, XII (1949), 14.

[119] Cf. N. Pevsner, *The Englishness of English Art* (London, 1956), pp. 81ff., and Peter Brieger, *English Art: 1216-1307* (Oxford, 1957), p. 6, for a discussion of the English "square east end."

that established in the piers below, and the stories are separated by strong horizontals to produce something very like the "aqueduct" effect of Romanesque interiors. Whereas in the French art of the thirteenth century separate elements are unified by a dominant flowing line, English artists still showed a preference for coordinate elements. One more conservative feature of English architecture appears in the design of façades. Turning again to Figs. 50 and 51, we may notice a much more rapid rhythm in the decorative elements which surround the earlier statues. This rapidity of detail is characteristic of Romanesque façades, like that, for example, of Notre Dame la Grande at Poitiers, where the sculpture above the main arches appears crowded. In English Gothic architecture the crowded effect is ameliorated by a greater rhythmic regularity, but the rhythm is more rapid and confined more to a single surface than it is in French façades. When horizontal elements are crenelated, as they are at Exeter, this rhythm has a very definite martial air.

The first half of the fourteenth century witnessed the development of a new richness of detail in English architecture, and, at the same time, in the work of the court masons at Westminster, the beginnings of the Perpendicular style.[120] The ogee arch, first used on the Eleanor Cross at Northampton, became a common decorative feature, and window-traceries showed a new sense for elaborate decorative pattern. The simple linear ribs of vaults were broken up into decorative designs effected by the application of non-functional liernes between them. In the extension of the choir at Wells, designed by William Joy and begun in 1330 (Fig. 76), the ribs have lost their functional purpose completely, and are simply decorations applied to a pointed barrel vault. Here the rapid sequence of a fairly complex pattern in the vault harmonizes well with the window tracery and with the rhythm of the vertical elements above the arches. There are definite lines from the bottom of each pier to the springing of the vaults, but these lines break up as they flow into the complex rib structure. The whole effect is one of brilliant and ornate elegance which makes earlier interiors like that at Salisbury seem austere by comparison. With reference to French Gothic interiors, like that at Amiens or the nave of St. Denis, on the other hand, the choir at Wells may seem over-elaborate. But the differ-

[120] See the excellent study by Maurice Hastings, *St. Stephen's Chapel* (Cambridge, 1955).

ence is a difference in underlying conception. At Amiens the emphasis is on logical regularity; the structural lines of the building seem to be expressed in the decoration and the whole is integrated in a logical fashion. At Wells the decoration emphasizes pattern or *convenientia* of design, imposed upon a basically logical structure. To use an analogy, whereas Amiens is logical, Wells is both logical and rhetorical, showing the beginnings of an appeal to the observer's sense of satisfying elaboration as well as to his sense of coherence. In other words, the design at Wells is consistent with the general trend we have sketched in fourteenth-century illumination. The appeal of the Wells choir is less abstract and more immediate than the appeal of the Salisbury nave.

The same qualities appear in much of the other decorative work of the period. The "nodding ogee," which makes a rather startling departure from the logic of the pointed arch, is strikingly illustrated on the Percy Tomb at Beverley Minster (Fig. 77). Here the exuberant elaboration of cusps, crockets, and finials, together with the flowing curves, produces an effect of great luxuriance, setting off and intensifying the more abstract appeal of the central figure. The décor and the design as a whole are obviously intended to make a surface appeal to the observer, but they do not interfere with the moving aspects of the underlying concept. Rather, they lead the observer toward a contemplation of the statuary and its significance. It may be that the most elaborate interior of the period was that of St. Stephen's Chapel at Westminster, built originally as a kind of English counterpart to the Sainte Chapelle in Paris. Instead of relying on stained glass as the dominant element of the interior, the designers made extensive use of painting, so that the entire interior surface was adorned with bright colors, gesso work, and murals. The slender lines of the stonework and the emphasis on horizontals, some of which were crenelated, look forward to the Perpendicular style. Hastings suggests that the use of columned panels set in columned arcades combined with nodding ogees must have created diagonal vistas.[121] In any event, the surviving evidence, which includes some fragments of wall painting, suggests that the effect must have been very striking.

The exuberance and luxuriance which characterize the architecture of the period appear also in illumination. The so-called East

[121] *Ibid.*, pp. 86-87.

Anglian manuscripts of the first half of the fourteenth century vary greatly in skill and technique,[122] but they are characterized by an exuberant marginal decoration consisting of elaborate foliage motifs, emblematic scenes in the margins, grotesques, or simply by drawings arranged in narrative or thematic sequences. The drawings in the Queen Mary's Psalter (Figs. 40, 41, 43, 44) reveal a flowing grace and elegance which are also characteristic of much of the wall painting of the period,[123] expressing a conservative reliance on Gothic "sway." In some illuminations the desire to make features conform to Gothic design leads the artist to give eyebrows points at the top.[124] The new decorative elements of the "East Anglian" style may be seen in our reproductions from the Ormesby Psalter, now in the Bodleian (Figs. 39, 64). In this MS the theme of the page is characteristically stated in the initial, and the marginalia either develop ideas which contrast with the theme of the initial, as in the examples referred to above, or parallel it. The latter possibility is illustrated in Fig. 78. Here the initial shows the slaughter of the priests by Doeg. At the bottom the theme of malicious felony is illustrated again in terms of the fable of the Cock and the Fox. The general meaning of this fable is made clear in an illuminated page from the *Somme le roi*, where the Fox with a Cock in his mouth stands beneath the feet of "Equite" as she opposes "Felonie" (Fig. 79). The Fox is thus a symbolic barnyard parallel of the same viciousness which motivated Doeg. Although the animals had more specific connotations in the fourteenth century, to which we shall refer later, the fact that their activity is a kind of echo of the initial should be clear enough. In the same way, the semi-nude *insipiens* prodded on by a devilish grotesque at the left of the initial is another expression of Doeg's irrational passion. The decoration on these pages is not an element which distracts the attention from the text. Rather, it serves to exemplify the theme of the text in terms of traditional iconography and everyday reality.

The grotesques and other figures which abound in the margins of "East Anglian" manuscripts, as a recent writer has pointed out,

[122] For a detailed account of the MSS, see Rickert, *Painting in Britain*, pp. 138ff. A classification of these MSS into three main stylistic groups is made by Otto Pächt, "A Giottesque Episode in English Mediaeval Art," *JWCI*, VI (1943), 53ff.

[123] See E. W. Tristram, *English Wall Painting of the Fourteenth Century* (London, 1955), pp. 8-9.

[124] A good example appears in Cambridge, CUL, MS Dd. 4. 17, fol. 79.

function much in the same way as *exempla* do in sermons.[125] Like
the elaborate rib tracery on the vaults of the period, they serve
the purpose of a more immediate appeal than would have been
possible without them. Fig. 5, from the Taymouth Hours, is icono-
logically obvious: the subject is lechery. But the artist has given
his characters a sense of immediacy by placing them before an
alehouse. If it is possible to speak of "degrees" of exemplification, we may say that this drawing with its familiar setting represents a higher degree than the same general scene on the mirror
case (Fig. 59). In Figs. 65 and 66 from the Smithfield Decretals,
the iconographically significant figures are again given a kind of
stage-setting within which their actions are carried out.

The new style is evident in the principal illuminations of the
manuscripts as well as in marginal illustration. The typical Gothic
illumination is linear, and, so far as features are concerned, inex-
pressive, since the lines which make up the features are adjusted to
the conventions of the style as a whole. During the first half of the
fourteenth century there begin to develop some outward indications of character in the faces portrayed, although the faces so
treated are almost always those of "low" persons. In Fig. 80, again
from the Taymouth Hours, the villainous characters are given
large, coarse features to create a stronger feeling of sympathy for
the suffering Christ. There is no point in calling this device "realistic," as a little reflection will show. But it does make an immediate
appeal to the feelings. The same device appears earlier in Flemish
manuscripts.[126] For purposes of comparison, a French illustration
of the same subject from later in the century (Fig. 81) shows a
more elegant style. The burden seems easy, and everyone involved
is relatively cheerful. Although the Gothic ogee no longer dominates the figures, they retain an air of grace and refinement. Italian
influences directly or indirectly added expressivenes to a number of
conventional scenes. In the Hours of Jeanne d'Evreaux executed
by Jean Pucelle there is a Crucifixion scene in which Mary, instead
of standing in a graceful ogee, faints, while the Centurion, who
stands on the left of the Crucified among the Jews, raises his right
hand to announce "He is truly the Son of God." This configura-

[125] See Lilian M. C. Randall, "Exempla as a Source of Gothic Marginal Illumination," *The Art Bulletin*, xxxix (1957), 97-107.
[126] E.g. London, BM, MS Harley 928, fol. 8, where the villains of the Betrayal
have coarse features.

tion, aside from the "slump," is said to show the influence of Italian models like the Crucifixion of Duccio at Sienna.[127] Although "slumping" Marys appear earlier, the scene as a whole indicates a desire to exploit, at least tentatively, literal as well as symbolic implications of the event. The "slumping Mary" spread rapidly to other countries, including England, where it appears, for example in the Taymouth Hours (Fig. 82). Here the participants are given a little stage in which to move, but they do not occupy it, standing instead at the point at which it joins the abstract background with their feet dangling irrationally above the "terrain." The figure rising from death in the foreground does occupy a space before the Cross, but beyond this the artist shows little interest in depth. The Christ figure retains a Gothic majesty and tranquility, but the slumping figure of Mary and the expressions on the faces of the women convey the element of feeling which we have seen to be characteristic of the period. The extent to which this scene might be developed later is illustrated in Fig. 83 from a Netherlandish manuscript executed late in the fourteenth century. The Centurion has been moved to the right of the Cross so that the wound in the right side may be more plausible, and the space provided by the "stage" is more fully exploited. Perhaps the high point in the development of "slumping" Marys was reached in Roger van der Weyden's Descent from the Cross, now in the Prado, where Mary is reduced to a very commonplace-looking woman indeed who is obviously about to be extremely difficult. The medieval examples, although they reveal an interest in exemplifying Mary's sorrow in concrete terms, show considerably more restraint.

A comparison between Fig. 53 from the "Amesbury" Psalter, and Fig. 84, from the Psalter of Robert de Lisle, will help to emphasize some of the differences between the style of the thirteenth century and that of the first half of the fourteenth century. Both works are greatly reduced in size, especially the later one, which measures nine by fifteen inches in the original, and in neither instance is it possible to photograph the effect of brilliant colors against a background of tooled gold leaf. With reference to the matter of space, the first displays almost no depth, but in the second there is a tentative effort at perspective in the bench upon which the Madonna sits, and a real sense of space between the left

[127] E. Mâle, *L'art rel. de la fin du moyen âge* (Paris, 1925), p. 6.

knee of the Child and the body of the Mother. Again, whereas the architectural motifs above the arches in the earlier picture are simply designs without any actual spatial relation to the arches themselves, in the later one the architectural canopy is consistent with the turrets at the sides, and the only glaring inconsistency in the frame is the vertical element which separates the background of the pinnacles at the top from the area above the arch which contains the angels. In effect, the spiritually celestial is kept separate from the physically celestial. It is true, however, that the Child is suspended above the Virgin's knee as in Fig. 46. Again, although the later example is innocent of any modeling, the draperies are arranged in such a way as to suggest more substantial forms than those of the earlier illumination, and they flow more naturally. Except for the Saint at the lower left, the figures are not restrained in the Gothic ogee. The later picture thus constitutes a step toward the representation of an actual woman as compared with the earlier, but it is only a step. The artist was still not concerned to show us something we might see in the world around us.

So far as decorative elements are concerned, the later picture is considerably more ornate than the earlier. The elaborate foliated crockets, the cusps with foliated finials, and the pinnacles of the turrets at the side are suggestive of the "Decorated" style, while the strong rectilinear areas in which the angels and saints at the sides appear suggest English taste and a hint of the developing Perpendicular manner. The gold background is tooled in flowing lines rather than in the simpler diagonal squares of the "Amesbury" Psalter. The later picture is also more elaborate iconographically. The Virgin not only triumphs over the beasts at her feet, but she also holds a symbolic spray in her hand, while the Child clutches a symbolic goldfinch.[128] It cannot be emphasized too strongly that the more "realistic" features—the "humanity," if you will—of the later picture are an integral part of the same "rhetorical" effect that is conveyed by the more elaborate decoration and iconography. All of these things make an immediate appeal to the feelings, but this appeal is not made for its own sake; it is made to attract the observer to the picture so that he may be led to meditate upon its significance. Decoration and "realism" in

[128] See Herbert Friedmann, *The Symbolic Goldfinch* (Washington, D.C., 1946).

the art of the earlier fourteenth century, like the grotesques which frequently accompany it, have much the same function that *exempla* have in sermons: they attract the audience with a view to leading it toward an underlying concept. Giotto's perspective in Italy represents a different means of achieving the same end.

For reasons which are not clearly understood, there is a distinct stylistic break between the first half of the century and the second. Some features of the style of the latter part of the century seem to be attributable to the Black Death, but not all of them are consistent with this explanation, or, if they are, the consistency has not so far been explained. In any event, the second half of the century taken as a whole showed no diminishing of artistic output. Richard II was one of the most assiduous patrons of the arts among English monarchs, and there were many other noblemen who encouraged artistic work of all kinds, both in England and on the continent. Artists traveled from one country to another, and the interaction of national styles helped to create what is called the International Style, which characterizes European art of the late fourteenth and early fifteenth centuries.[129] England was especially productive in architecture, and toward the end of the century fostered the work of two masons of real distinction, Henry Yevele and William Wynford.[130] Recent research has shown that the break in English architectural style at mid-century was not so abrupt as might have been supposed, and it may be that further study will reveal a similarly even transition elsewhere. The Perpendicular Style, which appears in the east end of Gloucester Cathedral, the rebuilding of which was completed in 1357 (Fig. 85), was probably a court style which had been developing earlier elsewhere. Here strong but thin vertical lines rise up the piers to the springing of the vault, but they are paralleled by other lines which rise through the great arches and the arches of the triforium to form the mullions of the clerestory windows. These vertical lines are intersected by strong horizontals, creating the effect of a light grillwork of tracery over a thin wall. The walls are thus made to har-

[129] The classic description of the International Style is that given by Raimond van Marle, *The Development of the Italian Schools of Painting*, VIII (The Hague, 1926), pp. 1-63. Margaret Rickert, *op.cit.*, pp. 165ff., uses the term to describe English painting generally during the last half of the fourteenth century and the first quarter of the fifteenth.

[130] See John H. Harvey's enthusiastic book, *Henry Yevele* (London, 1944).

monize well with the great east window, whose stained glass com-
memorates English heroism at Crécy (1346) and Calais (1347).
This window, by virtue of the fact that the last bays of the pres-
bytery are flared outward, is six feet wider than the interior itself.
Its tracery divides it into strong vertical and horizontal lines like
those of the walls. Meanwhile, the vault is cut up into a rapid and
complex pattern of ribbing, but two central ribs continue the lines
of the central mullions of the window. The rhythm of the various
elements in this design is even more rapid than that of the choir
at Wells, and the effect, when the weather is fine, is one of great
brilliance. The suggestion of a martial air created by this rhythm
based on strong vertical accents was appropriate to a church containing a royal tomb and what amounts to the largest window ever
constructed to memorialize heroic action. At the same time, the
contrast with the monumentality of the nave, with its huge Nor-
man round piers over thirty feet high, emphasized the elegance
of the design.

The grace and intricacy of detail possible in the Perpendicular
manner are well illustrated in the Neville Screen at Durham
Cathedral (Fig. 86), which was designed and built in London and
shipped to Durham, where it was set up in 1380. It consists of five
octagonal spires, each containing four stages, alternating with four
diagonally set square spires of three stages. The larger spires have
their buttresses terminating in pinnacles which are reached by the
ends of ogee arches at the top of the third stage. The first stage is
closed at the rear. Originally the niches contained alabaster statues.
This work is still basically Gothic in design and conception. Its
purpose is to form a partition, but instead of creating a flat screen
to set off one area from another, the designer, who may have been
Henry Yevele, created a screen of abstract space between the two
areas, suitable as a setting for statuary. Historians of art sometimes refer to the depth of works such as this one as being Baroque
in character, but the term is somewhat misleading, since the space
enclosed by the lines of the structure is not the space of the observer, but a confined space in which the lines of the statuary are set off
by the lines of the framing members. Although the statues which
once adorned this screen have disappeared, this point is illustrated
in contemporary work of the court school like the tomb of Edward III at Westminster Abbey (1377). The bronze weepers as

they stand erectly in their niches (Fig. 87) reflect the perpendicular lines of the decoration. The use of strong vertical lines broken rectilinearly by horizontals is well illustrated in the third figure from the left, said to represent Lionel, Duke of Clarence. A similar rectilinearity may be seen in the statues at Westminster Hall (Fig. 88). The absence of the Gothic ogee as a dominating line for the figures in these instances permits a more lifelike effect than might have been possible earlier in the century, but, at the same time, the dominating rectilinearity lends the figures an aloofness which sets them off from the world of the observer. The delicate openwork of the Neville Screen, but not its Perpendicular manner, reflects a taste that was current in France as well as in England. Pol de Limbourg reflected a similar style, but without ogee arches, in the symbolic representation of the Tree of Life and its accompanying well which appears in the *Tres riches heures* (Fig. 89).

As compared with the Decorated Style, the Perpendicular represents a return to logic. The rectilinear lines produce a sense of stability and ease, permitting the use of slender verticals without an impression of strain or striving for effect. The style was continuously subject to French influences, which contributed to its elegance and refinement. Perhaps the crowning achievement of the fourteenth-century court school in England is Henry Yevele's new nave at Canterbury Cathedral (Fig. 90), which regains, in its logical effectiveness, something of the atmosphere of Amiens. The vertical line is emphasized by the structure of the piers, where three vertical lines rise from the base to the vault broken only by two sets of rings, the upper of which appears on a level with the small capitals at the springing of the arches across the bays. A double ogee molding runs up the piers at either side of these shafts to the apexes of the clerestory windows. The main arcade, which is very tall, is topped by a relatively short triforium and clerestory set off by strong horizontal lines. The aisles at the sides are unusually high, and the light from their windows furnishes the chief source of illumination for the interior. The horizontal theme is set by a rib which runs along the peak of the vault, and this is echoed in the vault itself, in the strings above the arcade and the triforium, and is suggested again rhythmically by the capitals and rings on the shafts of the piers. The tall arcades and aisles show the beginning of a feeling for unity of space in the interior, just as efforts

219

at perspective in the painting of the period also show the beginning of a spatial sense; but these are only beginnings, which would not have been recognized as such by their creators. Chaucer lived in a world in which architecture was not yet "moulded space," in which painting was not yet an extension of the space of the observer, and in which sculpture still occupied a space of its own; but his world nevertheless was far from being naïve or incapable of refinement.

Perhaps the influence of the plague is more apparent in ecclesiastical wall painting of the second half of the century than in the architectural designs of the court school. As Professor Tristram describes it,[131] the iconography of the period includes an emphasis on such subjects as the Last Judgment, the seven sins, and the seven corporal works of mercy. The theme of death is further suggested by representations of the Three Living and the Three Dead. West walls frequently show the torments of the damned. Among the saints, St. Christopher, the patron of man's spiritual pilgrimage, was most common. An excellent example may still be seen at the little church of Wood Eaton near Oxford. It is said that there was a widespread belief that no one would die on the day that he looked at a representation of this saint. Allegorical figures like the Wheel of Fortune and emblematic devotional motifs like the Crown of Thorns around the Sacred Monogram were common. The Wheel of Fortune demonstrates the pervasive influence of the *Consolation* of Boethius, the popularity of which during the later Middle Ages may have been in part the result of the frequent menaces to personal security which the life of the time involved. The emblematic devices suggest a trend toward a more subjective attitude toward religion. The most popular subject of all was the Crucifixion, and this shows a tendency toward a kind of "realism" that appeals to the sensibilities. Tristram calls attention to a painter in Yorkshire, working between 1339 and 1349, who used a living man as a model.[132] It may be doubted that this practice was widespread, but the Crucifixions of the second half of the century stress the pain and pity of the event. Instead of the contorted but relatively tranquil figures of the early part of the century (cf. Fig. 82), there appear figures that are stiff and bloody.

In manuscript illumination English work shows the same gradu-

[131] *English Wall Painting of the Fourteenth Century*, pp. 20-28.
[132] *Ibid.*, p. 9.

al abandonment of a strict linear technique that is apparent on the continent, but the results were quite different. The tradition of the elaborately decorated page established by the "East Anglian" school is continued in the Bohun manuscripts,[133] prepared for Humphrey de Bohun and the members of his family and probably executed in London. An early example (before 1373) is illustrated in Fig. 37. Here the marginalia are generally reminiscent of the East Anglian style, but in the initial the figures are more strongly modeled and they actually occupy the small stage that is provided for them before the gold background. It is true that the Red Sea has been reduced to a mere gesture and that the rough terrain is highly stylized, but the figures are arranged in a variety of positions at different depths and do not seem to be standing either in the air or on each other's feet. A manuscript at Exeter College, Oxford, from roughly the same period, shows a rather different style. The later pages of this book take on a definite Italian air, with flamboyant leaf decoration in the margins, large grotesques, Italianate facial features in the figures, and unpricked gold backgrounds. The page illustrated, however (Fig. 91), has a marked "perpendicular" effect when viewed as a whole. The script is strongly vertical with well-marked horizontal lines above the comparatively flat strokes of the letters (cf. the different effect of the script in Figs. 39, 64, 78), and the architectural setting is marked by tall, thin turrets and pinnacles. A glance at the figures will show that they are not drawn and tinted, like those of the Ormesby Psalter, but painted. Features are modeled with white highlights, occasionally defined by thin lines, but the effort at modeling on such a small scale, which is largely devoted to the faces, sometimes results in over-large heads. The crowded little scenes from the story of Joseph are set against a brilliant pricked gold background, and although there is no real perspective, there is some effort at spatial coherence. In the lower left segment of the initial the figures occupy the space provided for them, although some appear twice in the same scene. The coordination of space and time in painting is still foreign to English art, and was evidently not desired. The figures wear contemporary costumes and are free from the Gothic "sway," but they are still representatives of the abstract values

[133] See M. R. James and E. G. Millar, *The Bohun Manuscripts* (Oxford, 1936), and Rickert, pp. 168-169.

suggested by the narrative rather than literal imitations of events. Their "realism" has an exemplary rather than a photographic purpose.

One further manuscript in the British Museum (Egerton 3277), probably completed for Mary de Bohun after her marriage to Henry of Lancaster in 1380, will suffice for our exploration of this style (Fig. 92). The subject of the initial is the visit of the Marys to the empty tomb and the news of the Resurrection, while the marginalia show the death and funeral of a nobleman. Again the faces are painted rather than drawn. In the upper left quarter of the initial the artist had difficulty with the shadow under the nose of the Mary on the left, which is too pronounced and too long. Elsewhere in the manuscript the same difficulty appears in the treatment of the upper eyelids, made with straight brush strokes, so that some of the faces have a strange heavy-lidded appearance.[134] On the whole, however, the modeling serves its purpose, which is not "realism" but exemplification, and, from a decorative point of view, the enhancement of the jewel-like brilliance of the page. The figures in this example lack the over-large heads frequently characteristic of the style, and they stand in comparatively natural positions, acting as though they were aware of one another. The Marys in the upper left seem to be consulting about the message of the angel, and the disciples clearly express astonishment as they stand about the empty tomb. The only effort at a stage is the small bit of terrain in the lower right quarter, but the modeling, which is extended with some success to the draperies, together with the expressiveness which it makes possible, sets off the figures from their gold background in a manner which must have seemed truly startling to those accustomed to the flat tinted drawings of the first half of the century. It is impossible to convey either in words or by means of photography an adequate impression of the splendor and richness of the more elaborate pages of these manuscripts, with their bright colors and gold leaf. The latter feature appears in the smaller initials in the text and in the marginal decoration as well as in the large initials. Like all Gothic art, these pages are intended for meditation and not for rapid inspection. Neither the text nor the illustrations can be comprehended at a superficial glance.

[134] See Rickert, pl. 150 c.

In the Egerton MS there are frequent small historiated initials, accompanied by grotesques, done in a somewhat more linear style than that of the major illuminations. Typical examples are afforded by Figs. 93, 94, 95, which show Amnon's seduction of Thamar and her subsequent rejection. In Fig. 93, Amnon has followed Jonadab's advice and feigned sickness, asking that Thamar be sent to bring him something to eat. What is actually being fed, a demon of carnal appetite, is suggested by the figures at the top, and a birdlike grotesque with lecherous goat's feet, wings of false piety, and a fierce leonine face on a serpentine neck looks on. In Fig. 94 Amnon throws Thamar upon the bed, much to the dismay of the artist, who, while putting a small furbearer beneath his feet, says, "Je swij trop desconforteie," and looks the other way with his hand before his face. Below, a long-necked grotesque hides his "Old Man" behind him. In Fig. 95 Thamar is rejected to the melody of an ass, while a grotesque at the left assumes a lionlike mask. As these examples show, the marginalia around the initials are not without humor, an element which, as we have seen, was not considered to be inconsistent with piety. In Fig. 94 the introduction of the artist into his own work adds an especially humorous element to the representation. Chaucer was to use a similar device in the Prologue to the *Canterbury Tales* and in the headlink to the Melibee, but, as we see in this instance, the device is not necessarily "realistic."

A noteworthy feature of all of these paintings is their lack of anything approaching "heroic" suggestiveness. An ability to create an effect of modeling does not necessarily imply a desire to anticipate Michelangelo. The angel who rises from the tomb in Fig. 92, aside from his wings, is a slight and humble figure as compared with the sleeping soldiers. Amnon is a lover, but no effort is made to make him look romantic. The same characteristic is evident elsewhere in the art of the period. On the famous Norwich retable the Christ who arises with his victorious banner is a frail man with narrow shoulders and non-muscular arms. And in the painted panel which survives at the Fitzwilliam Museum the Christ who stands before Pilate is a small, humble figure among larger and more vigorous men.[135] In the later fourteenth century

[135] *Ibid.*, plates 159 A and B.

humility, patience, and piety were heroic virtues; no artistic ingenuity was expended on "the glorification of the flesh."

Portrait painting was not practised in France until the second half of the fourteenth century, where the first extant example is the picture of Jean le Bon, painted on canvas stretched over wood about 1359. There are no formal panel portraits in England until the time of Richard II, and neither of the two examples which survive, both of King Richard, can be with certainty attributed to an English artist. The full-length portrait which hangs in Westminster Abbey dates from the last decade of the century, and it may have been done by an artist from France or from northern Europe. The other portrait is the famous Wilton Diptych, now beautifully displayed in its own glass case in the National Gallery (Figs. 97, 98). There has been considerable argument about the date of this work, the possibilities ranging from a time shortly after Richard's coronation to some time after 1400. It has been confidently claimed as an English work, attributed to a French artist, and been said to exhibit marked Italian characteristics. In any event, there is a possibility that it belongs to our period, and if it does, it is certainly one of its most significant masterpieces.[136] On the left King Richard kneels before his patron saints, St. Edmund of East Anglia, St. Edward, and St. John the Baptist. The background is in tooled gold leaf in the Gothic manner and the stage is a "desert" with bare rocks and a forest in the distance at the right. The saints carry their conventional emblems while Richard wears a collar of broomscods (cf. *planta genesta*, "Plantagenet"), a scarlet robe decorated with the same emblem arranged around the badge of the White Hart, and the emblem of the Hart in white. On the right Mary holds the Christ Child and is surrounded by eleven angels, each of whom wears a crown of roses, a collar of broomscods, and the emblem of the White Hart. One carries the banner of the Resurrection, and the nimbus of the Child contains the nails and the Crown of Thorns. The background is again tooled gold, but shows a different pattern from that on the left. The stage is a flowery mead, contrasting with the desert on the other side, and decorated with roses, lilies, daisies, and violets. Richard's hands are stretched forth, neither in an attitude of prayer, nor in an at-

[136] For bibliography, see Martin Davies, *The French School* (National Gallery Catalogue, 1957).

titude of supplication, but as if to receive Christ, Mary's gift to humanity.

The configuration as a whole is highly symbolic in the traditional Gothic manner. In accordance with a well-established Gothic tradition, trees in a representation indicate this world, as contrasted with the next, and the idea of a dark grove as a sign for the kind of *selva oscura* described by Dante is a commonplace.[137] The setting at the left, in short, conveys something of the feeling of Chaucer's line in "Truth," "Her is non hoom, her nis but wildernesse." The angels on the right wear the unfading flowers of Paradise which bloom in Christian literature of all ages: the *Octavius* of Minucius Felix, the poems of Fortunatus, the *Chanson de Roland*, and the Second Nun's Tale. They are surrounded by other flowers which, like Suger's gems, represent virtues: the rose of love and martyrdom, the lily of purity, the daisy of faithful espousal to Christ, and the violet of humility.[138] The Crown of Thorns and the Nails of

[137] Cf. D. W. Robertson, Jr., "The Doctrine of Charity in Mediaeval Literary Gardens," *Speculum*, xxvi (1951), 24ff., and, with special reference to the painting, Francis Wormald, "The Wilton Diptych," *JWCI*, xvii (1954), p. 201.

[138] The rose of martyrdom, which, because of obvious associations, could also imply love or patience, appears in accounts of Ecclus. 24. 18, 39. 17, and 50. 8. E.g., see Rabanus, *PL*, 109, cols. 930, 1041, and 1115. In the last two of these references the lily of chastity is also mentioned. The rose, the lily, and the violet of humility all appear in the same author's commentary on Genesis, *PL*, 107, cols. 589-590, where the source is one of St. Gregory's homilies, *PL*, 76, col. 830. Cf. *De universo*, *PL*, 111, col. 528. The remarks on Cant. 2. 1 in the commentary attributed to Alanus, *PL*, 210, col. 64, include reference to the "viola humilitatis, patientiae rosa, lilium castitatis." Cf. Petrus Riga, *Aurora*, Oxford MS Bodl. 822, fol. 5, where the three flowers have the same meaning. The association of the rose with the Blessed Virgin is explained at length in a sermon attributed to Hugh of St. Victor, *PL*, 187, cols. 1104-1105. The lily appears in Cant. 2. 2, where it is conventionally associated with purity or chastity. See the commentary attributed to St. Gregory, *PL*, 79, cols. 494-495, 501. Cf. Thomas the Cistercian, *PL*, 206, col. 189. The same meaning appears in the scriptural dictionary of Berchorius, *s. v. lilium*, and in Picinelli's *Mondo simbolico* (Venice, 1678), 11. 12 (54). For the violet of humility see *ibid.*, 11. 19 (203). The daisy (OF *consaude*) represents a later development in medieval iconography. Froissart, ed. Scheler, 11, 209-215, says that this flower is impervious to heat, cold, sleet, or wind (i.e., to extremes of Fortune), that it follows the sun, and that it enjoys a kind of immaculate conception "sans semeuse et sans semeur." The referent is clearly Mary. Deschamps, *Oeuvres*, SATF, iii, 379-380, says that the colors of the daisy are green for *seurté* (i.e., steadfast faith), white for *purté*, red for *paour*, and gold for *sens*. Flowers which follow the sun are *solsequia* or *sponsae solis*, which are in Alexander Neckam's *De naturis rerum*, pp. 165-166, symbols in a good sense for faithful espousal to Christ. Picinelli, 11. 13 (100)

the Passion suggest the mortification of the flesh, and the standard of the Resurrection is a promise of immortality. At first, the badges of the White Hart and the broomscods may seem presumptuous on the angels, but these angels may be meant to represent the guardians of the Plantagenets. Their number, eleven, is probably symbolic. Perhaps the suggestion is that when Richard's angel joins them, the perfect number, twelve, will result.[139] Other explanations of some of these details are possible, but, in any event, the picture was clearly intended to convey, and perhaps to encourage, Richard's devotion to Mary.

The style shows strong linear outlines with delicate modeling characterized by the effective use of highlights. Details like the petals of the roses are painted rather than drawn and tinted. Mary is given a touch of the Gothic "sway," but the other figures assume their postures in a fairly natural way, although the kneeling angel immediately on Mary's right, who probably offered the greatest problem to an artist trained in the Gothic style, does not seem to have his left knee on the ground, and his right hand is turned back at an awkward angle. The treatment of space in the left panel is not exceptional. In the panel on the right, however, the left hand of the angel kneeling at Mary's left is convincingly separated from Mary's robe, and the right hand of the angel to whom he turns is well separated both from the head and the robe of the angel in the background. An impression of space is thus very successfully conveyed, and it is probable that this success, at a time when such effects were rare outside of Italy, must have evoked a sense of wonder which enhanced the spirituality of the picture. In spite of this spatial sense, however, with one or two possible exceptions, no one in the picture actually looks at anyone else, and, as a result, the composition has a peculiarly abstract character. But this feature is perhaps desirable in a devotional picture, whose ultimate appeal is in its iconology rather than in its "realism." The grace and elegance of the whole, the Gothic character of both the

---

and (101), associates such flowers with devotion or constant love. Chaucer's Alceste, identified with the daisy, "taughte of fyn lovynge, / And namely of wifhod the lyvynge." These flowers, which are common in early Renaissance painting, could be associated with persons typifying the virtues, or with the Blessed Virgin.

[139] For a different interpretation of the number symbolism, see Tristram, *op.cit.*, p. 56.

style and the iconology, and the lack of Italianate characteristics in the features suggest a French origin, or at least a strong French influence. But it is clear that these panels would not have been possible without that interaction among various national styles which characterized the art of the last part of the fourteenth century.

The artistic milieu in which Chaucer lived and worked was still, in spite of Italian influences, a Gothic world. As compared with the thirteenth century, the fourteenth discovered new techniques in decorative effects, in iconography, and in the representation of nature which enabled artists to appeal to the feelings of their audiences. In illumination, villainous characters begin to have "villainous" features. As modeling replaces tinted drawing, a space in which figures with volume may move begins to develop. In some instances, these figures appear to interact with one another, but in the background the abstract space of ornamental gold leaf has not yet given way to landscapes and interiors, at least not to any appreciable extent in England.[140] Whatever space there is thus remains a closed space which is not shared by the observer. Nothing approaching a camera's eye view is sought either in architecture or in painting, and in England sculptured figures still stand under their Gothic canopies which separate them from the everyday world. Where "realistic" effects are achieved, they either enhance decorative motifs or contribute to the particularization of exemplary action. The figure of Richard II on the Wilton Diptych is that of an actual person, and it may be a reasonable likeness, but that likeness is placed in a situation which no one could possibly see in the world around him. The picture as a whole serves to exemplify an idea, or a series of related ideas, not to portray an external reality. As the fourteenth century progressed, iconology became more complex and original. Established Gothic motifs appear in the margins of psalters and books of Hours, but many new variations upon them also appear, and entirely new motifs are introduced. It is significant that when painting became more "naturalistic" in the next century in Flanders, the new fidelity to nature was accompanied by a concomitant symbolism which pervaded concrete details of all kinds.[141] The richness of significance which

[140] A few exceptions may occur at the end of the century, but these are not typical.
[141] See Panofsky, *Early Netherlandish Painting*, p. 142.

was achieved in this fashion was made possible by the traditions of fourteenth-century art, an art which, in spite of its greater fidelity to nature is still, like the art of the Romanesque period, dominated by ideas.

Although English art was affected by influences from the continent, it remained, throughout the period, essentially conservative. The Virgin placed on the outer gate of Winchester College in the last decade of the fourteenth century (Fig. 96) is obviously a cousin of the Golden Virgin of Amiens and is only distantly related to the imperious Lady by Giovanni Pisano in the Arena Chapel at Padua. As compared with her French predecessor, her features are somewhat fuller and less linear, and her draperies are of thinner material not quite so rigorously disciplined by Gothic line. But her body still sways in the strange detachment of the ogee, and the arch above her now flows in the same graceful curve. Unlike her predecessor at Amiens, she looks down, smiling in the direction of her admirers, and this gesture, which invites them to smile also, typifies the contribution of the later fourteenth century to the Gothic tradition. But the smile of the Winchester Madonna is not a romantic smile. It does not convey the feeling of the artist, but the mercy of Mary for suffering humanity, a theological idea which had been a commonplace of Christian worship for centuries.

4. CHAUCER'S LITERARY BACKGROUND

In Chaucer's literary environment tendencies similar to those we have seen in the visual arts are readily observable. English lyrics of the thirteenth century are frequently characterized by a surface grace, an impersonal tone, and a reliance on conventional figurative expression which together create a stylistic atmosphere very much like that of the sculpture and illumination of the period. An excellent example is afforded by the song to the Virgin, "Of One that is so Fair and Bright,"[142] with its stanzas made up of skilfully interwoven English and Latin lines:

> For on that is so feir ant brist
> *uelud maris stella,*
> bristore then the dai-is list,
> *parens & puella,*

[142] The standard text is that of Carleton Brown, *English Lyrics of the Thirteenth Century* (Oxford, 1932), no. 17.

> i crie the grace of the.
> leuedi, prie thi sone for me
> *tam pia*
> that i mote come to the
> *maria* ....

Here conventionalized figurative devices, not unlike the "attributes" of the Saints in art, such as *maris stella*, the paradox *parens et puella*, or, later on, the play on *eva* and *ave*, supply the ideas which are the basis for the poem's emotional appeal, while the surface is kept with some rigor within the confines of a rather sprightly rhythm. The first person pronouns of lines 5, 6, and 7 give way later on to more general plurals in lines 24 and 26 so that the tone is impersonal rather than "lyrical" in a romantic sense. Emotional expression in these lyrics sometimes closely resembles that seen in contemporary illustrations. For example, in "A Light Is Come to the World"[143] Mary wrings her hands as she stands beside the Cross, just as she does in illuminations:

> Ha isei the rode stonden,
> Hire sone ther-to ibunden;
> Hoe wroinc hire honden
> Bi-heild his suete wunden.

In the fourteenth century the emotional appeal comes more to the surface, and the Crucified may address the reader directly. An early example is afforded by the short poem "Look to Me on the Cross,"[144] which begins,

> Man and wyman, loket to me,
> u michel pine ich tholede for the ....

In "How Crist Spekes tyll Synfull Man of His Gret Mercy,"[145] from the mid-century, the possibilities of this convention are exploited still further:

> Man, thus on rode I hyng for the,
> For-sake thi syn for luf of me,
> Sen I swilk luf the bede;
> Man, I luf the ouer al thing,

[143] *Ibid.*, no. 24.
[144] Brown, *Religious Lyrics of the Fourteenth Century* (Oxford, 1924), no. 4.
[145] *Ibid.*, no. 47. Cf. no. 51.

And for thi luf thus wald I hyng,
My blyssed blode to blede.

The theme of the poem is the boundless mercy of God to those who are penitent, but the idea is made more emphatic by portraying Christ as a suffering human personality. In the second half of the century this effect is intensified by displaying Him as a babe in arms who may talk with His mother, as He does in "Dialogue between the B. V. and her Child,"[146] weep for the sins of humanity, as He does in "Christ Weeps in the Cradle for Man's Sin,"[147] or be greeted with a lullaby, as He is in "A Lullaby to Christ in the Cradle."[148] In "The Christ Child Shivering with Cold,"[149] the dual nature of these portrayals is made strikingly apparent. The Divinity of Christ is evident as well as His humanity, and the cold which the Innocent suffers is not simply the unnecessary affliction of a poor unfortunate, but a part of the Divine Order:

> Cold the taket, i may wel se.
> For loue of man it mot be
> The to suffren wo,
> For bet it is thu suffre this
> Than man for-bere heuene blis—
> Thu most him biyen ther-to.

We are still, in these poems, a very long way from Tiny Tim, but they nevertheless display an increasing sense of the surface attraction of human emotion. This emotion is not an end in itself, however, as it might be said to be in Dickens where emotion constitutes a kind of wisdom. It is used instead to reinforce the basic ideas, much in the same way that modeling and a concomitant rudimentary concession to spatial relationships were used to intensify the traditional themes of Gothic art. Meanwhile, what might be called a "Decorated" style in literature developed which roughly parallels the Decorated Style in architecture. While writers of the court school, like Gower and Chaucer, were imitating and adapting French verse forms, authors in the west and north were reviving, or perhaps, more accurately, elaborating and perfecting the native alliterative tradition. *Pearl*, with its alliteration, rhyme, *concate-*

---

[146] *Ibid.*, no. 56.   [147] *Ibid.*, no. 59.
[148] *Ibid.*, no. 65.   [149] *Ibid.*, no. 75.

natio, and brilliant symbolic landscapes, may be said to mark the high point in this style. It would not be difficult to show the presence of symbolic characters, symbolic actions, and symbolic settings in the poems of the alliterative school, but since Chaucer's poetry is rooted more firmly in continental traditions than it is in those of his native England, it will repay us to glance very briefly at stylistic developments in France and Italy.

In general, French literature of the fourteenth century develops and elaborates stylistic techniques established by the *Roman de la rose*. The tendency to exploit exemplary materials, which we observed in Jean de Meun, becomes increasingly obvious in the works of Jean de Condé and Watriquet de Couvin. Most of the poems of the former are, in fact, "parables" or "examples" based either on narrative materials or on the properties of animals or objects like the cock or the candle. The general tone of these poems may be illustrated in "Li dis de la torche,"[150] which begins,

> A l'example des anciiens
> Se devroit princes terriens
> Gouverner s'il faisoit que sages.

The examples are Alexander, Julius Caesar, Arthur, and Charlemagne, who together will serve as an exemplary "torch" to light the way of the prince. The same kind of interest may be seen in Watriquet's "Li dis de la Nois":[151]

> Li sages Salemons nous moustre
> Par bon example et par vrai moustre,
> C'on doit touzjours son sens moustrer
> Par biaux examples demoustrer. . . .

The example in this instance is a nut, which is compared with a young man. Just as the little nut is protected by leaves, so youth should be guided. If you pick a nut at Pentecost, it is bitter and small; in the same way a youth should be watched until he matures. Taking the bitter shell from a nut is like stripping vices from a youth. The hard shell of a nut is like the body, which should be hard and not soft through sin. The kernel is like the soul, and the

[150] Ed. Scheler, *Dits et contes de Baudouin de Condé et de son fils Jean de Condé* (Brussels, 1866-1867), III, 289ff.
[151] Ed. Scheler (Brussels, 1868), pp. 55-64.

thin skin which covers it is like original sin. Both Jean and Watriquet delight in "explaining" the significance of their materials. In Jean's "Dis d'Entendement" the explanations are given by the person of Entendement, who appears as an elderly guide to the poet. In Watriquet's "Dis de l'iraigne et du crapot," the "gloss" is furnished by Dame Raison. In other instances explanations are furnished by the poets themselves. The same kind of interest in the *significatio* of things and events is observable in Philippe de Vitry's "Le chapel des fleurs de lis,"[152] where the flowers are "moralized" to show the virtues necessary to crusaders. It is significant that an interest in "examples" as a means of exposition is also evident in the Latin writings of the period. Holcot's famous commentary on Sapientia is full of exemplary materials of all kinds: from the Bible, from the classics, from history, from everyday objects and events. Perhaps the most striking illustration of the tendency is the great *Repertorium* of Berchorius, which contains a moralization of the Bible, a scriptural dictionary, a moralization of the *De proprietatibus rerum* of Bartholomew Anglicanus, and a commentary on Ovid's *Metamorphoses*.[153] All of these works furnished abundant materials for the exemplification of moral and theological ideas. "Created things, or the creatures of the world," wrote Berchorius, "constitute a book in which God depicted and described His benevolence, wisdom, and power [i.e., the Trinity]; for, as it is said in Romans 1, 'Invisibilia enim Dei per ea, quae facta sunt, intellecta conspiciuntur.' "[154] The same underlying attitude, transferred to the somewhat less theological but no less moral realm of courtly entertainment, is responsible for the prevailing conception of poetry, which is reflected at the beginning of Watriquet's "Li mireoirs aus princes":[155]

> En cours des rois, des dux, des contes,
> Doit on les biaus diz et les contes
> Et les examples raconter
> Por les bons instruire et donter.

---

[152] See A. Piaget's text in *Romania*, XXVII (1898), 55-92.

[153] There are a number of editions of the works, exclusive of the commentary on Ovid, printed as late as the eighteenth century. The commentary on the *Metamorphoses*, which aroused the laughter of Rabelais, was printed in the Renaissance under the name of Thomas Waleys.

[154] *Opera* (Cologne, 1731-1732), IV, 451.   [155] Ed. Scheler, p. 199.

The use of "examples" brought all sorts of elements from "everyday life" into the realm of poetry, but these elements are no more "realistic" here than they are in the margins of fourteenth-century manuscripts. The attention of the poets and their audiences was directed to the world around them not for its own sake but for the sake of the ideas it suggested.

The longer poems of Machaut display an interest of the kind we might expect in exemplary materials. The pleas in "Le jugement dou Roy de Navarre" furnish good illustrations of "argument by example." In "Le dit dou lyon," the lion becomes an exemplar of the reasonable lover. Various kinds of birds of prey show the natures of various ladies in "Le dit de l'alerion," and there are classical *exempla* in "Le jugement dou Roy de Navarre" and in "La fonteinne amoureuse." But Machaut is much more important as a continuator of the allegorical devices of the *Roman de la rose*, which he not only used, but adapted to suit his own purposes. He does not make intensive use of conventional iconographic descriptions, although good examples of the technique are furnished by the garden in "Le dit de l'alerion," and the fountain in "La fonteinne amoureuse." But he does use Jean de Meun's personified abstractions. The God of Love, Raison, and other familiar figures appear once more, and it has been customary to say on this account that Machaut's poetry is conventional and unoriginal. But this allegation is somewhat unfair. In the first place, the tone of Machaut's poems generally, if we except "Le voir dit," lacks either the quiet irony of Guillaume de Lorris or the more biting satirical mood of Jean de Meun. The personified abstractions are for the most part very gracious and courteous beings, cultivated and good-natured ladies and gentlemen, who have more "personality" than their predecessors in the *Roman*. Their attractiveness is actually not difficult to account for, since Machaut customarily prefers to use Love and his followers to show the characteristics of reasonable love rather than to mock the failings of the kind of foolish love attacked by Jean de Meun. Thus in the "Remede de Fortune" the lover in the poem is taught the nature of true love by Esperance, who, by means of material derived from the *Consolation* of Boethius, offers him true hope based on a recognition of the fact that love should be allied with virtue rather than with Fortune, so that its aims are consonant with the principle that true happiness rests in

God. In "Le dit dou lyon" reasonable love is typified by the lion, who is made to suffer the malicious attacks of false lovers patiently. In "Le dit de l'alerion" the lover is constantly under the guidance of Raison, who is in turn a companion of Amours, rather than an enemy as in the *Roman*:

> Qui sont la gent qui dames gardent
> Et qui le vray amant regardent
> En trés tous ses amoureus fais,
> Et li merissent ses biens fais?
> C'est Amours tout premierement,
> Et Raison qui est hautement
> Trés tout decoste li assise,
> Grace, Pais, Honneur et Franchise,
> Mesure, Foy et Verité,
> Attemprance et Humilité,
> Et tant qu'on ne s'en puet nombrer
> Qui trop ne s'en vuet encombrer.[156]

In "La fonteinne amoureuse" the lover is the young Duc de Berry about to be exiled from his lady. The lady is his wife. Here the instruction is given by Venus, who shows the Judgment of Paris as an element injected by Discorde into the wedding of Peleus and Thetis, implying much the same idea as that developed in Machaut's source, which was the *Ovide moralisé*.[157] The young duke should not allow any inclinations in the direction of the decision of Paris to make him miserable during his exile. Venus thus becomes a kind of fourteenth-century echo of Ovid's *Venus verticordia*. In all of these poems there is an atmosphere of good-nature and reasonableness quite unlike the atmosphere of the *Roman*, and personifications like Amours and Franchise acquire connotations very different from those that surround them there. Meanwhile, the inclusion of musical pieces in graceful forms—like the *lay*, the *complainte*, the *chanson roial*, the *baladelle*, the *balade*, the *chanson baladeé* or *virelai*, and the *rondel*—especially in the "Remede de Fortune," lends this poetry a decorated elegance of a kind that would have been foreign to Jean de Meun. Stylistically speaking, Machaut should be credited with a considerable enrichment of the traditions of love poetry.

Although personified abstractions, the techniques of the dream

---

[156] *Oeuvres*, ed. Hoepffner, II, 322-323.
[157] Ed. C. de Boer (Amsterdam, 1915-1954), Livre XI, lines 1242-2545.

vision, the elaborate use of exemplary materials, and a prevailing
tendency toward musical expression prevent this poetry from approaching anything like "realism" or narrative for the sake of narrative, Machaut does make considerably more effort to provide a
"stage setting" for his characters than Jean de Meun had done
before him. Thus the description of Durbury in "Le jugement dou
Roy de Behaigne" is convincing, but the action is not related in any
detail to its concrete features. Again, "Le jugement dou Roy de
Navarre" opens with a description of portents, wars, corruption,
and, finally, the plague. The last, personified as *la mort*, fiercely
devours everyone within its reach, and the vivid picture of its action prepares us for the reversal of the *jugement* of the King of
Bohemia:

> Quant Dieus vit de sa mansion
> Dou monde la corruption
>
> .   .   .   .
>
> Fist la mort issir de sa cage,
> Pleinne de forsen et de rage,
> Sans frein, sans bride, sans loien,
> Sans foy, sans amour, sans moien,
> Si trés fiere et si orguilleusé,
> Si gloute et si familleuse,
> Que ne se pooit säouler
> Pour riens que peüst engouler.
> Et par tout le munde couroit,
> Tout tuoit et tout acouroit,
> Quanqu'il li venoit a l'encontre,
> N'on ne pooit resister contre.
> Et briefment tant en acoura,
> Tant en occist et devoura,
> Que tous les jours a grans monciaus
> Trouvoit on dames, jouvenciaus,
> Juenes, viels et de toutes guises,
> Gisans mors parmi les eglises;
> Et les gettoit on en grans fosses
> Tous ensamble, et tous mors de boces,
> Car on trouvoit les cimatieres
> Si pleinnes de corps et de bieres

235

Qu'il couvint faire des nouvelles. . . .
Et si ot mainte bonne ville
Qu'on n'i vëoit, ne filz, ne fille,
Femme, n'homme venir n'aler,
N'on n'i trouvoit a qui parler,
Pour ce qu'il estoient tuit mort
De celle mervilleuse mort. . . .[158]

This passage, together with its continuation in the poem, probably represents Machaut's closest approach to "realism." Many of the details must have been based on personal observation or on first-hand accounts by others. But it is significant that Machaut thinks of the plague as an abstraction conveniently personified and released by a just God as a punishment for human corruption. Visual reality is related to an underlying abstract reality, and this in turn is seen as a part of the Divine Order. In the same way, the actual persons who appear in Machaut's poems, like the King of Bohemia, the King of Navarre, or the Duc de Berry, are used as exemplars for the development of thematic ideas. In other words, Machaut was not concerned to show actual persons behaving dramatically in space. His art is governed by ideas. In the general prologue which he set before his collected poems he describes his poetic gifts as consisting of rhetoric (the art of versifying), music, and "Scens." The last is an essential ingredient of fourteenth-century poetry, just as it is an essential element in fourteenth-century art.

Machaut was the dominating poetic influence in France during the remainder of the century. Deschamps regarded him as a master, Froissart imitated him, and the poetry of Oton de Grandson shows a pervasive influence of his work. The poems of Deschamps reveal a somewhat less genial personality, bitter against the evils of his

[158] *Oeuvres*, I, 149-150. Hoepffner's conclusion, p. LXVII, that the "introduction historique," of which I have quoted only a fragment, "reste sans aucune relation avec ce qui fait le véritable sujet du poème," seems to me to be singularly perverse, in view of the nature of the judgment rendered and the fact that the poem is followed by the "Lay de Plour." We may assume that the terrible havoc of *la mort*, which struck the virtuous and the vicious alike, and which deprived many of the survivors of those most dear to them, must have rendered the arguments of "Le jugement dou Roy de Behaigne" somewhat academic. Moreover, the reservations concerning the nature of the love involved in the earlier poem are not revived in the later one, where they would have been irrelevant. Thus the two poems do not contradict each other directly, even though they may seem to do so at first glance.

age and full of moral fervor. The *balades* frequently record personal experience, not in the form of "poetic confession," but in the form of comments on persons and their actions. His poetic ideal as stated in *L'art de dictier* is embraced in the statement: "Tout bon rhetoricien doit parler . . . saigement, briefment, substancieusement et hardiement."[159] We are reminded of Chaucer's Clerk:

> Noght o word spak he moore than was neede,
> And that was seyd in forme and reverence,
> And short and quyk and ful of hy sentence.

Machaut's allegorical bent is easily discernible in Froissart, who imitated his master's themes as well as his techniques. Thus in the "Paradys d'Amours"[160] the poet prays to Morpheus, Juno, and Eolus that he may fall asleep. When he does sleep, he dreams that he is in a garden in May. Plaisance and Esperance lead him to the God of Love, before whom he sings his woes. He is then led to his lady, who asks for a song. When he sings a balade in praise of the marguerite, the lady laughs and crowns him with a chaplet of daisies, saying, "Alons, alons, esbanoyer d'une autre part" as the poet awakens. Here the variation on the themes of the *Roman* is effected by the daisies, which were probably intended to suggest the Blessed Virgin.[161] In any event, the gracious personified abstractions, the elegant poetic forms, and the abstract realm in which the action takes place are all reminiscent of Machaut. So far as love is concerned, Oton de Grandson was a spectacular living exemplar of Machaut's theories concerning the matter, and it was this fact, perhaps, rather than his literary skill, which won him the reputation of being a great poet, "flour of hem that make in France." Oton was a very pious man, an ardent promoter of Philippe de Mézières' chivalric order of the Passion of Jesus Christ,[162] an organization which also affected the ideals of Deschamps.[163] Chaucer may well have known him personally.[164] Oton's lady, celebrated

[159] *Oeuvres*, vii, 267. Cf. the balade "Comment tout homme doit parler selon Rhetorique."

[160] *Oeuvres*, ed. Scheler (Brussels, 1870-1872), i, 1-52.

[161] See the references to Froissart in note 138 above.

[162] See A. Piaget, *Oton de Grandson* (Lausanne, 1941), pp. 75-77.

[163] See N. Jorga, *Philippe de Mézières* (Paris, 1896), pp. 488-489.

[164] Oton had relatives in England, where he spent a great deal of time. See Piaget's sketch of his career, pp. 11ff., and Lucy Toulmin Smith, *Expeditions to Prussia and the Holy Land* (Camden Soc., 1894), p. 309.

in his poetry, was Isabelle of Bavaria, Queen of France. The relation between the poet and his lady is concisely expressed in "Le souhait de Saint Valentin":

> Je vouldroye que je feusse, par m'ame,
> Por homme tel commë elle est pour femme,
> Pareil a lui de tout amendement,
> Et mon cuer fust aussi entierement
> En Dieu servir et faire bonnes euvres,
> Comme le sien est a toutes les heures.[165]

The lady is thus regarded, not as an object of sexual passion, but as a lovable exemplar and inspiration to virtue, a kind of Beatrice or Laura in death to the poet. In effect, Grandson makes Isabelle into a personified abstraction. He rears, so to speak, a Gothic canopy over her head, but he does so from impeccable motives in a manner that must have been both satisfying to the lady and flattering to her husband. There is no special reason why love of this kind should not be called "amour courtoise" or "courtly love," but it would be futile to seek "origins" for it in Andalusia or among the Albigensians. Chaucer reflects this kind of attitude only once, in *The Book of the Duchess*, before his "Ovidian" posture, which is actually a return to the attitudes of Jean de Meun, became firmly established. And even here, the later attitude is clearly foreshadowed. What is especially significant about Grandson's attitude stylistically is that he looked upon another human being much in the same way that one might look on a Gothic statue or illumination —not as an "event" in space and time to be apprehended simply by the senses, but as a being symbolizing or exemplifying a higher reality. It is not improbable that this attitude was quite common in the fourteenth century among relatively cultured people.

The current passion for abstraction is illustrated well in the epistle which Philippe de Mézières addressed to Richard II in 1396. This work, which was designed to persuade Richard to marry Charles' daughter, and, at the same time, to interest him in the Order of the Passion of Jesus Christ, was delivered by Robert the Hermit. The original document survives in the British Museum.[166] Instead of presenting a series of logical arguments, Philippe used

[165] Ed. Piaget, p. 202. [166] MS Royal 20 B. VI.

a thoroughly symbolic approach, involving dreams, symbolic comparisons, *exempla*, and even allegorical gardens. Perhaps the most famous of the examples adduced to persuade Richard to marry is the story of Griselda "escripte per le solempnel docteur & souverain poete maister francois petrac,"[167] adduced with the implication that the proposed French wife would be patient and loving, just as Griselda was. Philippe assures Richard that the story is true, derived from a "cronique autentique." He did not, in other words, think of it as a mere fiction designed to convey an idea, but as a concrete manifestation of the idea in life. The same taste for symbolism is displayed in the decorative frontispiece which adorns the manuscript. Three arched frames display the crown of France, the Crown of Thorns, and the crown of England. Below, the lilies of France on a blue field and the pards of England on a red field are overlaid with the Sacred Monogram. The idea thus displayed is the union of France and England in Christ. It is significant that these symbolic and allegorical devices must have seemed to their author to constitute the most effective persuasion he could use. There is no question either of Philippe's sincerity or of his intelligence. The basic attitudes we have seen in the art and literature of the period were thus a genuine and important part of fourteenth-century intellectual life. The invisible lay always just beneath the visible. To suggest its presence was not only a function of art but also a function of rhetorical persuasion.

Italian literature, like Italian art, maintained its own peculiar characteristics during the later Middle Ages. Among the most significant of these national characteristics was a greater subjectivity and concomitant sensitivity to feeling than was fashionable elsewhere on the continent. Giotto's perspective is a striking illustration of this point. It provoked the unstinting admiration of Boccaccio (*Dec.*, 6. 5), who thought that the paintings of the master were so natural that they might be confused with the things represented. Even a touch of something approaching empathy is observable in Dante, who tells us in the *Purgatorio* (10. 130-134) that he can feel the burden of the proud bent under the weight of their stones just as one feels uncomfortable when he sees a corbel made in the shape of a man:

[167] Fol. 49.

Come per sostentar solaio o tetto,
per mensola talvolta una figura
si vede giunger le ginocchia al petto,

la qual fa del non ver vera rancura
nascere a chi la vede: così fatti
vid' io color, quando, posi ben cura.

These reactions to visual imagery have their literary counterparts. Thus the plight of Paulo and Francesca rouses such strong sympathy in Dante the pilgrim (*Inferno*, 5. 112ff.) that he faints for pity when he has heard their story. Reactions of this kind, however, should not be taken to indicate a weakening of the poet's philosophical position, no matter how strong their appeal may be to the modern reader who looks instinctively for romantic or post-romantic emphasis on feeling in art. With reference to the present instance, we learn in the *Purgatorio* (27) that our pilgrim needed to be purged a little of Paulo's weakness. Many have been misled by Boccaccio's deliberate assumption of a personal point of view to see autobiographical elements in his early poetry and to think of the emotions expressed there as being actually those of the author. The result has been that most accounts of the poet's early life are sensational and novelistic. It is undoubtedly true that this Italian tendency toward subjectivity, or assumed subjectivity, exerted an enormous influence on the art and literature of the Renaissance, when Italian fashions spread northward. It then hastened the development of much more restrained subjective tendencies already operative in France and England. Nevertheless, in the fourteenth century it was still a form of provincialism. A further Italian characteristic shows itself in a preference for the systematic numerical or geometrical organization of materials. We may cite as examples the systematic Aristotelian organization of the sins in the *Inferno* or Boccaccio's careful numerical arrangement of the tales of *The Decameron* into ten groups of ten. But neither of these two peculiarities of Italian art was adopted by Chaucer, who lived in a world much more restrained by Gothic traditions.

There was much, however, that Chaucer could find in Italian literature that was congenial to his taste. In both the *Vita nuova*, which is an elaborate essay on the use of beauty, and the *Commedia* Dante evinced the same kind of passionate interest in the abstract that is characteristic of his French contemporaries. And the *Convivio* not only provided excellent statements of traditional ideals, like that of *gentilesse*; it also furnished some very interesting studies in poetic implication. The *Commedia* employs exemplary and symbolic devices, including iconographic scenery, the techniques of the grotesque, exemplary narratives, and so on, although this fact has been somewhat obscured by modern neglect of the early commentaries on the poem. Petrarch's Laura has much in common, at least in the later poems, with ladies celebrated by Machaut and his successors, and the *Africa* draws upon the traditions of mythography.[168] Boccaccio's poems utilize personified abstractions, exemplary materials, and allegorical devices based on Boethius which are basically similar to the corresponding features of poetry in France, not to mention elaborate iconographic scenery like that which makes up the temples of Mars and Venus in the *Teseida*. Dante, Petrarch, and Boccaccio, that is, were not only Italian; they were also medieval. Petrarch did not actually become "the first modern man" by virtue of an interest in collecting books or because he described an allegorical ascent of Mount Ventoux. The "International Style" in the visual arts during the late Middle Ages has its counterpart in literature, for, in spite of national peculiarities, the writers of England, France, and Italy during the period share many common interests and techniques. It is this fact which made it natural for Chaucer to make extensive use of French and Italian sources. Nevertheless, his style, as we shall see, was distinctively English.

5. CHAUCER AND THE STYLE
OF HIS PERIOD

Chaucer's literary art is, in spite of a surface appeal which gives it significance to readers as diverse in stylistic attitude as Dryden and Blake, distinctly a product of its time. Influences of the *Ro-*

---

[168] The usual contention that Petrarch used mythographic materials in the *Africa* merely for decoration cannot be supported on the grounds that he omitted moralizations in his sources. He was by no means the first poet to use such materials without moralization, and the inclusion of any kind of explanation would have been inconsistent with his own poetic theory which demanded that the truth be "veiled" in poetry. In other words, it would have been strange if Petrarch *had* included moralizations, and, at the same time, there is no reason to suppose that he expected his readers to overlook the common significances of the details he employed.

man de la rose, of more recent French poetry, and of Dante, Boccaccio, and Petrarch are obvious in his work; and, although he gave the materials he borrowed a distinctively English flavor, there is no ground for the assumption that he created a radically new set of stylistic conventions without the emphasis on underlying abstractions that was characteristic of the art and literature of the period. Iconographic descriptions made up of elements to which conventionally established areas of meaning were attached are frequent not only in the formal allegories but also in *The Canterbury Tales*. In *The Book of the Duchess* the Cave of Morpheus, the painted chamber in which the dreamer awakens, and the wood in which the Black Knight is found are clearly artificial settings, having little to do with everyday experience, in which the details are intended to be significant for the thematic development of the poem. As much may be said for the elaborate description of Blanche, which was probably suggested by the stylized portraits in Machaut's "Jugement dou Roy de Behaigne" and "Remede de Fortune." Here the emphasis is not on literal portraiture, which was rare in the art and literature of the period, but on the abstract qualities suggested by the details of the description. Formal mythographical descriptions, which carried with them connotations which had been developing since late antiquity, appear in *The Parliament of Fowls*, *The House of Fame*, and in the Prologue to *The Legend of Good Women*. In *The Canterbury Tales* it will suffice to mention the temples of Mars, Venus, and Diana in the Knight's Tale, and the garden of the Merchant's Tale, which is clearly a variant of the Garden of Deduit in the *Roman de la rose*. But even more significant than the appearance of these formally iconographic descriptions, of which only a few have been mentioned, is Chaucer's tendency to mingle details of an iconographic nature with other details which produce an effect of considerable verisimilitude. We may compare this technique stylistically with that of the marginalia in fourteenth-century manuscripts, where conventional themes from earlier Gothic art are included in representations which seem on the surface to be no more than reflections, sometimes a little fantastic, of "daily life." At the same time, new iconographic motifs appear which are either elaborations of old ones, or details whose meanings are supplied by the contexts in which they appear.

This technique is especially evident in the General Prologue to *The Canterbury Tales*. A few examples will suffice to demonstrate its importance. The miller, who leads the pilgrims out of town, is the very picture of *discordia*:

> Ful byg he was of brawn, end eek of bones.
> That proved wel, for over al ther he cam
> At wrastlynge he wolde have alwey the ram.

The wrestlers who appear on roof bosses, medallions, in the margins of manuscripts and elsewhere (e.g., Fig. 39) were sufficiently commonplace so that few in Chaucer's audience would have been likely to miss the suggestion. Alone it might mean very little, but it is reinforced by the exaggerated coarseness of the miller's features, which, as others have pointed out, suggest gluttony and lechery as well as contentiousness. The "realism" of this physiognomy is consistent with that of Fig. 80, and it should not be taken as a delineation from life. The miller proudly carries a "sword and bokeler," and is a "jangler" and a thief. As if these things were not enough, "A baggepipe koude he blowe and sowne," the instrument so frequently set in contrast with the *concordia* of the New Song in marginal illustration.[169] It is appropriate that this character should thrust himself forward out of order at the conclusion to the Knight's Tale, offer to "quit" the knight, stir up a quarrel with the reeve, and tell a tale whose high point is the "revel and the melodye" of the flesh. If the pilgrimage to Canterbury is a reflection of the manner in which the pilgrimage of life was generally carried out in Chaucer's England, the fact that it follows a drunken wrestler out of town to the tune of a bagpipe is an amusing if slightly bitter comment on contemporary society—a society which, Chaucer must have felt, was far from the amiable concord it should have developed in imitation of "Jerusalem celestial." The reality which underlies the description of the miller is not the reality of an individual, nor even that of a type; it is the harsh reality of discord nourished on gluttony, vainglory, and avarice as seen in one segment of fourteenth-century life. That the manifestation is convincing on the surface is a tribute to Chaucer's artistry, but the fact that the picture as a whole is a combination of convincing detail

---

[169] Details of the miller's physiognomy are discussed by W. C. Curry, *Chaucer and the Mediaeval Sciences* (New York, 1926), pp. 81-89. For the bagpipe, see Edward A. Block, "Chaucer's Millers and their Bagpipes," *Speculum*, xxix (1954), 239-242.

and conventional iconographic motifs is an indication that Chaucer was above all an artist of his own place and time.

Materials from the *Roman de la rose*, which was one of the most widely read vernacular works of the later Middle Ages, were frequently employed by Chaucer for their iconographic value. Two examples appear in the portrait of the prioress. The description begins,

> Ther was also a Nonne, a Prioresse,

with a slight climactic progression from "nun" to "prioress" as if to imply, "She was not simply a nun, but also a prioress." What follows is an amusing anticlimax:

> That of her smylyng was ful symple and coy.

"Smiling" is not exactly what Chaucer's audience would have thought of as the primary attribute of a prioress, however simple and quiet it might be. We are told further that her greatest oath was only "By St. Loy!" the patron saint of goldsmiths, smiths, and carters. The same saint is invoked by the carter in the Friar's Tale, a fact which does not speak well for the elegance of the lady's language. The effect of urbane sarcasm, or *astysmos*, as it was called by the grammarians, is continued when we are told her name:

> And she was cleped Madame Eglentyne.

It may be that Lady Sweetbriar sang her service appropriately, but Chaucer has made that song rhetorically parallel with the lady's not very elegant efforts to "sing" French:

> Ful weel she soong the service dyvyne,
> Entuned in hir nose ful semely,
> And Frenssh she spak ful faire and fetisly,
> After the scole of Stratford atte Bowe,
> For Frenssh of Parys was to hire unknowe.

Again the effect is one of anticlimax, which emphasizes the nun's unsuccessful efforts to make herself a lady of the world.[170] The

---

[170] Skeat's note on this passage contemptuously denies the joke and stoutly defends the lady's French, which is said to be that of the law courts. However, Chaucer was not writing for the law courts. We have the testimony of Froissart that Richard II spoke excellent French. See May McKisack, *The Fourteenth Century* (Oxford, 1959), p. 524. We may assume that he expected his courtiers to do likewise.

iconographic material which follows immediately serves only to re-inforce this effect. It begins, "at mete wel ytaughte was she with alle," and ends, "Ful semely after hir mete she raughte." Are her manners "seemly" for a prioress? They are taken directly from the cynical, worldly-wise instructions of La Vieille in the *Roman de la rose*. Far from being the manners of a great lady, who would doubtless have shown small concern for such trivial matters, or the manners of a prioress, who should have had her heart on the food of the spirit rather than on the ostentatiously "correct" consumption of the food of the flesh, they are the manners of the social climber who wishes to form a reputation for being ladylike. As Chaucer says, she

> peyned hire to countrefete cheere
> Of court, and to been estatlich of manere,
> And to been holden digne of reverence.

There are quite other grounds, which have nothing to do with either French or table manners, upon which a nun is "worthy of reverence." At this point the *allegoria*[171] becomes somewhat more bitter and sarcastic, although it has been the policy of editors to conceal it by misglossing the text. The effect is again achieved by anticlimax. The passage begins,

> But for to speken of hire conscience,
> She was so charitable and so pitous
> She wolde wepe . . .

Since the subject is a nun, whose life is dedicated, presumably, to meditation and devotion, and to charity within the discipline of a rule, the word *conscience* means just what it says, "conscience." The meaning "concern" or "sensibility" was rare in the fourteenth century, if indeed it existed at all; and there is no reason to suppose that it would have occurred to Chaucer's audience at this point with nothing but the context already quoted to go on. The only other alleged instance of it in Chaucer's writings appears in LGW, 1255, where it appears along with "innocence," "pite," and "trouthe," qualities which should aid women in avoiding the wiles of un-scrupulous men. Chaucer was not Trollope, and the ability to judge

---

[171] Medieval rhetoricians considered irony, sarcasm, and *astysmos* to be types of *allegoria*. This matter is discussed in the next chapter.

between right and wrong in one's actions is certainly consistent with this context also. Charity is, of course, necessary to a clear conscience, and pity and tears are signs of an absence of *duritia cordis*, the worst enemy of conscience. We are led quite naturally, therefore, from conscience to charity and tears, but the anticlimax, amusingly enough, arrives once more—

> . . . if that she saugh a mous
> Kaught in a trappe, if it were deed or bledde.

It becomes apparent at once that the concepts of "conscience," "charity," and "pity" are used ironically. To gloss *conscience* "sensibility" so as to make it "fit the context" of what follows as it is seen from a modern point of view is simply to destroy the irony, disregard the humor, and, in short, to take all the life out of the poetry. It is also to engage in unwarranted philological speculation. Chaucer tells us further of the lady's small, spoiled dogs, another courtly affectation, and of her tears if anyone struck one of them or kicked it, concluding with unmistakable sarcasm, "And al was conscience and tendre herte." The nun's conscience is, in effect, consistent with the iconography of her table manners. The sarcastic mood does not slacken with the description of the lady's person. She has a small mouth "softe and reed," and a broad forehead which, in Chaucer's time, was regarded as an indication of stupidity or lack of discretion.[172] But the crowning attribute is the motto on the brooch: *Amor vincit omnia*. It is true that *amor* can mean either charity or cupidity, perhaps even in an echo of Virgil's *Bucolics*, but we have already seen exactly the kind of "charity" of which the prioress was capable. Her *amor* is undoubtedly consistent with the smiles, the French, the table manners, and the soft, red lips: It is not necessary to argue the point, however, for the motto is another echo of the *Roman de la rose*, a piece of literary iconography whose significance is clearly established in that poem, where it forms a part of the argument by means of which Courteisie persuades Bel Acueil to give the lover the "rose." The subsequent action is clear enough, and it has nothing to do with charity. It is not difficult to see that the various attributes of the prioress all point in one direction: she is a peculiarly striking exemplar of false courtesy,

[172] Thus Thomas of Cantimpré's encyclopedia, Cambridge, Trinity College, MS O. I. 34, fol. 5, says that a broad forehead signifies *parvitatem discretionis*.

nourished, in this instance, by an excessive tenderness with respect to the flesh, or, in other words, by sentimentality.

To consider once more the technique of the description, we find that Chaucer has used two bits of iconographic material whose significance had been established by Jean de Meun: the table manners and the motto. To these he added materials of his own with similar implications, in order to form a picture with a certain amount of verisimilitude, and he couched the whole in schemes and tropes designed to emphasize the principal idea. His own materials do not differ in kind from those borrowed. They are essentially "attributes," iconographic details which point toward an abstract reality. Generally, the descriptions of the pilgrims in the Prologue are merely more elaborate manifestations of the techniques employed in the medallions at Paris and Amiens, or of those used in the marginalia of psalters and books of Hours. The action of weeping over a mouse in a trap has the same kind of revealing quality as does, let us say, the action of combing one's hair before a mirror or of running away from a rabbit. It is not something the prioress does on the pilgrimage, not something we see her doing at the Tabard. It is, on the other hand, a typifying action which has nothing specifically to do with the action of *The Canterbury Tales*. She has the dogs with her, but no one, not even the miller, kicks them. We have no occasion to see the nun at table or to hear her French. The details, in other words, have no "dramatic" function; they serve only to enforce an idea. In a very real sense, the prioress is a "grotesque." Her office and habit suggest one "face," while her interest in a kind of courtesy which has nothing to do with habit or office produces another. And like other grotesques, she is humorously, not sentimentally, ambiguous. It follows from these considerations that although the characters in the Prologue have an undeniable verisimilitude, consistent with the increasing interest in verisimilitude in the visual arts, they are in no sense "realistic." The function of the verisimilitude is, first of all, to attract attention, and, ultimately, to show the validity of the underlying abstractions as they manifest themselves in the life of the times.

The use of iconographic details as a means of calling attention to an underlying abstract reality accounts for the surface inconsistency of Chaucer's portraits. Details of biography, action, costume, physiognomy, and manners are sometimes mixed in what seems to be a random order. Chaucer seems unwilling to adopt a consistent "point of view" in his descriptions so as to arrange his materials to form a coherent surface. The reason for this, however, is obvious if we remember that his interest was not in the "surface reality" but in the reality of the idea. The details are arranged, just as they are in Romanesque and Gothic art, with a view to developing the idea and not with a view to rendering a photographic image. Seen in this way, the details in the description of the prioress, from coy smiles to the final motto, have a climactic order, an order which we can find without much difficulty in portraits of other pilgrims. In the description of the knight, for example, the details are used first of all to emphasize the idea of "worthiness." The chivalry, "truth" (in a feudal sense), honor, generosity, and courtesy are here virtues of a worthy man who has known a great deal of crusading warfare in far places. We pass from worthiness to wisdom (not "prudence"), and to the concomitant virtue of humility which is particularized in the good but not "gay" horse, the "bismotered" gypon, and the pilgrimage undertaken devoutly after a warlike enterprise. Since humility is the first of the Christian virtues, the end of the portrait is a fitting climax to the description. The picture that results of a very distinguished knight and warrior riding meekly and unostentatiously "for to doon his pilgrimage" may exhibit little "realism" with reference to fourteenth-century life, but it does represent an ideal that was still very much alive.

The same kind of "characterization" by means of iconographic detail appears throughout Chaucer's work. The word *characterization* is, however, somewhat misleading, since the aim is not to delineate character in a psychological sense but to call attention to abstractions which may manifest themselves in human thought and action. For example, the description of Alisoun in the Miller's Tale begins by calling her "fair." As we read it, we find that although she wears what Dominicans called the colors of holiness— black and white—she makes a vivid animal appeal to each of the five senses. That she is a kind of epitome of those aspects of the world which are "fair" to the senses is made clear at the close of the description. Here the outward holiness is contrasted once more very briefly and humorously with the sensual appeal: "She was a primerole, a piggesnye . . . ." The anticlimax involves a play on the daisy or "day's eye" (*primerole*) and the "pig's eye" (*pig-*

gesnye). The daisy was a symbol both in literature and in art for faithful espousal, but the "pig's eye" suggests once more the object of animal desire, and this is the idea elaborated at the close:

> For any lord to leggen in his bedde,
> Or yet for any good yeman to wedde.

Alisoun is neither a "realistic" reflection of the times nor a "character" in the modern sense; rather, she is an elaborately and amusingly conceived manifestation of the *woman* who is an object of lust. Again, the description of the friar in the Summoner's Tale is little more than a compendium of charges which had been leveled at friars ever since the first protests of William of St. Amour, skillfully adapted to the purposes of a narrative. The iconography is here derived from the pages of ecclesiastical controversy and rests ultimately on the Bible. But what it points to is neither a "typical friar" nor a "character" of any kind, but to the abstraction "Faus-Semblant" as he appears in the habit of a friar. In general, the figurative and descriptive materials which Chaucer uses to describe the personages of his narratives are conventional and derivative rather than original. His originality lies largely in his ability to form new and striking combinations and elaborations of these materials and to place them in contexts suitable to the tastes of his immediate audience. In every instance where derivative materials are employed, whether they come from Scripture, from mythography, or from any other source, a knowledge of their significance as it was understood in the fourteenth century is of the utmost importance to our understanding of his art, just as important, in fact, as a knowledge of Middle English. For the "attributes" with which Chaucer's descriptions are filled constitute a kind of language. To disregard this language is not, as one academic critic has suggested, to disregard something esoteric, but to disregard what Chaucer wrote.

The iconographically described "character" is a close relative of the personified abstraction. Such abstractions are very common in Chaucer's poetry, although their presence is not always obvious at first glance. Among the more obvious figures of this kind are Fortune in *The Book of the Duchess*, Fame in *The House of Fame*, Nature in *The Parliament of Fowls*, and various subsidiary figures like Patience, Riches, Peace, and so on. We should not overlook the fact that the classical deities frequently belong to the same family, and that many of them had belonged there at least since the days of the Romans, who were capable of erecting temples to figures like Mens Bona. During the course of Roman antiquity and later among mythographers from Fulgentius to Boccaccio the principal deities had developed fairly stable abstract significances. Frequently, these were "doublets" with parallel meanings on contrasting levels. Sometimes they were also manifold, embracing a series of unrelated meanings. In a surprising number of instances these meanings correspond with those handed down by Arabic astrologers from antique traditions, indicating that mythographers and astrologers alike represent the continuation of classical ideas. Figures like Venus, Mars, Diana, Saturn, Pluto, and so on were thus in Chaucer's time little more than personified abstractions. They sometimes carried with them whole series of iconographic attributes, so that in more elaborate descriptions they may be thought of as iconographically described abstractions. When Chaucer introduces Pluto and Proserpine in the Merchant's Tale, therefore, we should not assume that he is indulging in "fantasy," however "delightful" that assumption may be to the post-nineteenth-century mind. These characters are just as meaningful as are simpler abstractions like Riches or Peace, although it is true that their significance may not be quite so obvious. The same tale affords examples of abstractions of a more subtle kind. Januarie is advised by Justinus and Placebo, and these "characters" are little more than personifications of Justice and Flattery adapted to the special situation of the narrative. Again, in the Pardoner's Tale, the Old Man who sends the rioters up a crooked way to find Death is probably a personification of St. Paul's "Old Man."[173] The lack of appeal which Griselda and Custance have for most modern readers rests on the fact that they are little more than personified abstractions of Patience and Constancy, without the more "human" characteristics which produce well-rounded and appealing "characters."

It was suggested above that the prioress is in a sense a "grotesque." It is true that Chaucer does not use the kind of obvious grotesque that appears in the first book of Gower's *Vox clamantis*, but the influence of the grotesque in the shaping of his characters is nevertheless unmistakable. It appeared in stained glass, in wood

[173] See the article by R. P. Miller referred to above, note 108.

carving, in wall painting, and even in the decoration of ecclesiastical vessels, as well as in the margins of manuscripts.[174] Much of the grotesque material in wall painting has been effaced, but the technique of the grotesque must have been commonplace to any literate man of affairs in the last half of the fourteenth century. Chaucer's most obvious use of the technique appears in the Nun's Priest's Tale, where the principal character is at once a cock and a human being. In the visual arts, this kind of combination appears quite naturally in grotesque form (Fig. 99). But the story itself is also common in marginal decoration; to the examples already adduced (Figs. 78, 79), we may add, simply to illustrate this point, one more from a Flemish manuscript of the early fourteenth century (Fig. 101). Turning again to the example from the Ormesby Psalter (Fig. 78), which we have seen to be illustrative of the vice of "Felonie," we may discover a more specific meaning if we ask, "Who was Doeg?" Historical figures in the Bible were often given a "typical" meaning so that their immediate relevance might be more apparent, and in this instance the *Glossa ordinaria* tells us that Doeg typifies Antichrist and his followers.[175] Were the felonious men of Antichrist discernible in fourteenth-century society? William of St. Amour suggested that Antichrist was represented in his time by the friars, and this suggestion was repeated in the *Roman de la rose*, where Faus-Semblant is made to say, "Of Antecristes men am I," and in *Piers Plowman*.[176] The charge was a common one in anti-fraternal circles. But what have friars to do with foxes? In the earlier Middle Ages the fox was a frequent symbol for the heretical *seductor* of the faithful.[177] Although the fox is sometimes shown in late medieval art as a bishop to symbolize the false prelate, in many instances the foxy fourteenth-century *seductor* is a friar. Charles V of France had an ebony fox dressed as a Franciscan,[178] and the fox-friar is a common figure on

[174] Tristram, *op.cit.*, pp. 17-18, 98, 104; Maurice Hastings, *op.cit.*, pp. 79-80; Joan Evans, *Art in Mediaeval France* (London, 1948), pp. 204-205.

[175] *PL*, 113, cols. 920-921.

[176] See D. W. Robertson, Jr., and B. F. Huppé, *"Piers Plowman" and Scriptural Tradition* (Princeton, 1951), pp. 229-231.

[177] E.g., see the commentary on the Canticum attributed to St. Gregory, *PL*, 79, col. 500; and *Glossa ordinaria*, *PL*, 114, col. 283.

[178] Joan Evans, *Art in Mediaeval France*, p. 192.

English misericords.[179] It is quite probable, therefore, that the Ormesby fox is a fourteenth-century friar who, like Doeg in the initial, represents the forces of Antichrist. Meanwhile, the cock was a very common figure for the priest or prelate, and had been so ever since the early Middle Ages, so that the configuration in the lower margin of the Ormesby page is an exact echo of the meaning of the initial. The priest is persecuted by a representative of Antichrist, while slothful Malkyn looks on. That Chaucer had something very similar in mind is shown by the fact that he calls his fox "Russel," the name given in an analogue to the Franciscan son of Renart,[180] and there is thus strong evidence that the Nun's Priest's Tale is, if one takes the "fruit" as the teller advises, a story of a priest who falls into the clutches of a friar but escapes just in time when he discovers the essential weakness of the friar's evil nature. This discovery, of course, represents also a discovery of his own weakness which was responsible for making him, as it were, a chicken in the first place, or, in other words, a "grotesque." The tale thus affords a striking example not only of the use of grotesque characters, but also of a common grotesque theme. Chaucer's chickens are amazingly convincing as chickens, and they are, at the same time, amusingly human. But they are far from being "well-rounded" characters; they and their behavior suggest a pattern of abstract principles which manifest themselves in common abuses of the time, abuses which Chaucer does not represent on the surface at all. The verisimilitude of the representation, fantastic as it is if taken literally, is a tribute to Chaucer's ability to make ideas "come to life," to give to airy nothings a local habitation and a name. But no one would call the tale "realistic." Grotesques may exemplify ideas in striking ways, but their technique is about as remote as one can get from a realistic technique.

There are less obvious uses of the technique of the grotesque in Chaucer's poetry, and they account for a great deal of humor. As we have seen, the grotesque is a monster because of unresolved conflicts in his make-up, although these conflicts, it should be emphasized, do not in the Middle Ages necessarily imply "tensions."

[179] Francis Bond, *Wood Carvings in English Churches: Misericords* (London, 1910), pp. 163-166; M. D. Anderson, *Misericords* (Harmondsworth and Baltimore, 1954), pp. 21-22.

[180] See Charles Dahlberg, "Chaucer's Cock and Fox," *JEGP*, LIII (1954), 277-290.

Typically, the grotesque pretends to be one thing but is actually something else, just as the prioress, for example, is a nun superficially but a social climber in her actions and attitudes who is "seemly" in unseemly ways. Much the same sort of discrepancy appears in the character of the monk:

> A Monk ther was, a fair for the maistrie,
> An outridere, that lovede venerie . . . .

As an "outrider" the monk had a legitimate reason for leaving the cloister, but this fact does not justify the kind of generalizations he makes about monks and the value of the contemplative life. Not all monks can be "outriders" and serve the world; if they could there would be no more monks, and Chaucer was far from any Tudor ambitions to turn monasteries into country seats or profitable factories. In any event, the word *venerie* was, and still is, a pun. It is probable that outriders had a reputation for more than one kind of venery, but at this point in the description there is no way of telling whether the monk loved hunting or the act of Venus. Neither pursuit is appropriate to a monk, although a notable and well-liked abbot of the period, William of Clown, was much given to rabbit-hunting,[181] which we may regard literally as the lesser of the two evils. The next line does not enlighten us, but rather intensifies the problem:

> A manly man, to been an abbot able.

A man may be manly in that he is virtuous or manly in that he exercises more literal masculine potentialities. If anything, the following line simply makes the problem more acute:

> Ful many a deyntee hors hadde he in stable.

For although horses are used in hunting, and "dainty" horses, as the parson tells us, indicate pride, the horse, at least since the time of William of Aquitaine,[182] had been a figure for something more dainty than horses usually are. The idea is made explicit, for example, in the Middle English *De clerico et puella*,[183] where, after Clericus has described his lovesickness, Puella replies, in part,

[181] Hamilton Thompson, *The English Clergy* (Oxford, 1947), pp. 168ff.
[182] Ed. Jeanroy (Paris, 1913), pp. 1-3.
[183] Brown, *English Lyrics of the Thirteenth Century*, no. 85.

Yef thou in my boure art take, shame the may bityde.
The is bettere on fote gon, then wycked hors to ryde.

The same figure appears in the fifteenth-century play *Mankind*,[184] where Mercy says to Mankynde,

Yf a man haue an hors, and kepe hym not to hye,
He may then reull hym at hys own dysyre;
Yf he be fede ouer well he wyll dysobey,
And in happe cast his master in the myre.

New-Gyse interrupts, saying,

Ye sey trew, ser; ye are no faytour!
I haue fede my wyff so well tyll sche ys
my master!

The analogy horse/wife (or woman) is clear. Its origin is implicit in Mercy's speech, which is not actually about horses, but about the flesh. The analogy horse/flesh is very old and very common. Thus St. Gregory wrote, "Indeed the horse is the body of any holy soul, which it knows how to restrain from illicit action with the bridle of continence and to release in the exercise of good works with the spur of charity."[185] The same figure is familiar in the Middle English "Debate of the Body and the Soul," and a four-teenth-century commentator on Scripture sums it up succinctly, "Thus *moraliter* our flesh is the horse and the reason spirit is the rider."[186] The transition from "flesh" to "woman" made by New-Gyse is based on a common elaboration of the figure, for which it is sufficient to quote St. Augustine, who says (*De vera religione*, 41. 78), "Let us subjugate this cupidity or flattery or troublesome-ness; let us subjugate this woman, if we are men." The whole complex "woman/horse/flesh" is illustrated vividly in Fig. 6. To return to our "fair" monk, the dainty horses are, to say the least, suspicious. Our suspicions are not put to rest by the account of worldliness which follows. The jangling bells of the bridle suggest an ostentatious but sham restraint, and the monk's contempt for the rule, for labor, and for the traditional condemnation of monks

[184] J. Q. Adams, *Chief Pre-Shakespearean Dramas* (Cambridge, Mass., 1924), p. 309.
[185] *PL*, 76, col. 588.
[186] *In proverbia Salomonis* (Paris, 1515), fol. ix.

out of cloister suggest the vice of inconstancy which is typified on one of the medallions of Amiens Cathedral by a monk leaving his cloister. A similar representation of the same vice appears on the south portal of Chartres Cathedral.[187] Chaucer's monk is a rather elaborate literary elaboration of these figures in which the contrast between the monk's inner nature and his outer habit is sufficiently emphasized to produce a "grotesque" effect. The auctorial comment, "And I seyde his opinion was good," is probably not an indication of naïveté of a fictional *persona*, Chaucer the Pilgrim, but an example of *antiphrasis*, as the following ironic argument suggests—to the effect that the world, as distinct from the spiritual life of the cloister, would be at a loss without the assistance of the monk.

The theme of *venerie* is introduced once more:

> Therefore he was a prikasour aright:
> Grehoundes he hadde as swift as fowel in flight;
> Of prikyng and of huntyng for the hare
> Was al his lust—for no cost wolde he spare.

The logical sequence here should not be overlooked: the Monk disdained the rule and the cloistered life; therefore he was a true "prikasour." The slightly obscene suggestion of "prikyng" is sustained by the fact that this inconstant monk hunts rabbits, which were, as we have seen, associated with the hunt of Venus. To the evidence for this fact already adduced, we may add that one common medieval device for illustrating lechery is to depict a man riding on a goat and either carrying or pursuing a rabbit.[188] Not infrequently he wears a net to show that he is caught in Vulcan's snare (Fig. 100). However, the question of whether the horses were actually nothing but horses and the hares merely hares is irrelevant and has no operational meaning. Chaucer was writing poetry, not history, and the suggestive implications of *venerie* are features of the poetry. They suggest that the monk was, like Esau, a hunter for the sake of the flesh and not a hunter like those of Jer. 16. 16, who were taken as figures of true Christian prelates. Chaucer leaves the sexual overtones of his description vague be-

---

[187] For an illustration showing the inconstant monk of Chartres, see C. R. Morey, *Mediaeval Art* (New York, 1942), fig. 112.

[188] Bond, *Wood Carvings*, pp. 182-183.

cause the point is not simply that the monk is to be thought of as being lecherous. Any monk may be occasionally lecherous, but this one is a deliberate cultivator of the world and the flesh. His inconstancy in this respect is worse than lechery, a sin of the spirit rather than a lapse of the flesh. The obesity, the shameless staring eyes,[189] and the dubious fondness for roast swan properly conclude the picture of a monk whose love of the flesh causes him to be contemptuous of his rule. The description as a whole again reflects the technique of the grotesque, for although the monk's habit indicates one thing, his nature is something very different. Just as the fox lurks beneath the Franciscan robes of the ebony statue owned by Charles V, so also here a very fleshy animal, which, in Boethian terms, is hardly a man at all, lurks beneath the holy habit of our "outrider."

Other instances which echo in one way or another that great original of many medieval grotesques, the scriptural wolf in sheep's clothing, are not difficult to find in Chaucer's poetry. Januarie in the Merchant's Tale with his desire for both "paradis" on earth and "Paradis" above is obviously two-faced, like Janus who sits, as we are told in the Franklin's Tale, "by the fyr with double berd." The two faces of Janus could be interpreted to mean either prudence, which looks before and after,[190] or gluttony and lechery, or other vices.[191] It is clear that our old knight who busies himself in a garden like that of Deduit in the *Roman de la rose*, which is the reverse of those gardens illustrated in Figs. 12 and 89, is not very prudent. In kalendar illustrations January frequently has two faces (Fig. 22), and he sits in some instances "by the fyr" (Fig. 102). The latter configuration suggests old age, and is sometimes used, albeit usually with a feminine figure, to indicate that state in illustrations of the *Roman de la rose* (Fig. 103). Moreover, the sign of January, usually included also in kalendars, is Aquarius, the house of Saturn who is a cold old planet (cf. Knight's Tale, 2443ff.). The idea of a strange union between old January and some fresh spring month as a commentary on marriages between old men and young girls was thus natural, and Deschamps

---

[189] Jehan le Bel, *Li ars d'amour* (Brussels, 1867-1869), ii, 194, says that glowing eyes signify a person "sans vergoigne."

[190] Alexander Neckam, *Super Marcianum*, fol. 49 verso.

[191] E.g., see John of Garland, ed. Paetow (Berkeley, 1927), p. 197.

gives us a picture of a union between old January and young April in his balade "Contre les mariages disproportionés."[192] Chaucer's lady May was probably suggested by the fact that kalendars sometimes show May as a young girl holding flowers (Fig. 105). Her sign is Gemini, and this figure is sometimes shown as a male and female figure together naked, in more or less suggestive postures (Figs. 105, 106); in any event, the month of May was associated with "amoenitas" and *luxuria* (cf. Fig. 107).[193] Gemini, the sign under which Januarie is deceived in the Merchant's Tale (line 2222), is the house of Mercury, lord of eloquence as well as of merchants, and it is May's eloquence which triumphs in the end. That two-faced old Januarie is a grotesque is further indicated by the fact that two-faced characters who are naked of virtue appear elsewhere in marginal illustrations (Fig. 104). Grotesque characters serve to call attention to abstract concepts just as do characters who are described in terms of iconographic attributes, but they have the added spice of humor. Januarie's desire to have his "paradis" both ways is patently ludicrous. He has, as Holcot put it, "two heads with contrary motions," and one of these is an "old man" indeed. It is sometimes difficult to distinguish personified abstractions, iconographically described characters, and grotesques; but this is not a real difficulty, since the divisions are purely arbitrary. In the visual arts, Cupid sometimes appears with claws instead of feet, so that he belongs to all three categories. The fact that the things themselves merge in actual practice is an indication that they all have the same function.

Although Chaucer's characters frequently convey a strong impression of verisimilitude, they are not essentially realistic, and there would have been little point in giving them elaborate realistic settings in which to move. In the dream visions, the settings are clearly iconographic in technique, although some of them may

[192] *Oeuvres*, v, 63. See the note by William Matthews, *MLR*, li (1956), 217-221.

[193] The month of May was traditionally associated with flowers, love, and lechery. See Berchorius, *Opera* (Cologne, 1731-1732), i, 248; ii, 128. It was also, however, the month perpetually established in Paradise before the Fall. In the former sense, cf. the description of the squire in the General Prologue to *The Canterbury Tales*, the description of the squire in the Franklin's Tale, the garden of Emelye, and the garden in which Dorigen meets her young lover. Pandarus also invites Criseyde to perform some "observances" to May. In the Knight's Tale, all of the major events take place in May.

show, like the painted chamber with its stained-glass windows in *The Book of the Duchess*, a certain resemblance to locations actually observed. The framework of *The Canterbury Tales* exhibits a typical Gothic disregard for spatial coherence. The tales are told as though a large group of people riding down a fairly narrow road could hear a story told by one of them. Beyond a few references to place-names no details of the scene are given. Hills, forests, fords, meadows, and other features of the landscape are disregarded, and the pardoner's reference to an alehouse is so vague that efforts have been made to explain it away. The canon and his yeoman come riding up, but otherwise the landscape is empty of people other than the pilgrims themselves. No dogs bark at their heels, and no cattle wander across the road. The pilgrims might just as well be seen moving against a background of gold leaf. Meanwhile, although a coherent temporal sequence from one tale to the next was obviously planned, the reference of Justinus to the wife of Bath in the Merchant's Tale is symptomatic of Chaucer's playful disregard for a rigorous coordination of space and time. A similar lapse in this respect appears in the prologue to the Melibeus, where the use of the word *write* reveals that Chaucer the poet, rather than Chaucer the pilgrim, addresses the remarks about *sentence* to the audience of the tales, rather than to the other pilgrims.[194] Within the tales themselves, settings vary a great deal in the elaborateness with which they are presented. But the most elaborate settings are iconographic rather than realistic. This is true, for example, of the temples in the Knight's Tale, the garden in the Merchant's Tale, the rocks off the coast in the Franklin's Tale, the grove in the Pardoner's Tale, and the yard in the Nun's Priest's Tale. Where details of setting are given elsewhere, they are usually only sufficient to make the action understandable. The arrangement of the carpenter's house in the Miller's Tale is vague, except for the location of the window in John's chamber, which is low enough for the required action. Rather startlingly, Alisoun threatens to "caste a ston" from within, as though she were outside, but this may be an ironic reference to another story of a woman taken in adultery. A more modern writer might have enjoyed de-

---

[194] The use of the verb *write* in the prologue to the Second Nun's Tale, which is not integrated with the tales as a whole by means of dialogue, is probably due to a failure to revise material originally independent of the collection.

scribing the mill in the Reeve's Tale, but the "hopper" is not described for us, and all we know about the dwelling is that it was small and contained the beds, cradle, and staff necessary for the action. Again in the first part of the Canon's Yeoman's Tale, the details of alchemical apparatus, materials, and procedure are not organized as features of a given place at a given time, but are presented in the form of lists, and miscellaneous actions and conversations, arranged so as to develop the idea of "false wisdom." Perhaps *Troilus*, developed from an Italian model, seems to display more carefully worked out settings than those which usually appear in the Tales, but this impression may be due in part to the slowness of the action. We do not actually see much of the festival of Pallas in the first book, and Troilus' chamber is not set before us in detail. The garden described by Pandarus in which Troilus makes his confession to Love is iconographic rather than realistic, and the only setting where many actual details are given is the interior of Pandarus' house. But here Chaucer allows us only sufficient information so that we can understand the manner in which the lovers are secretly united. Generally, Chaucer's lack of concern for "scenery" is analogous with the situation in the visual arts. It is neither a personal peculiarity nor an accident, but a feature of the style of the time.

In what kinds of actions do Chaucer's characters engage? In previous chapters we have called attention to the fact that some of them follow stylized patterns of action for iconographic purposes. Lovers especially are portrayed in such a way as to call attention to the philosophical significance of their actions as we see them "dying" for love, receiving heart-wounds through the eyes, or falling into the "lover's malady." But Chaucer uses many other devices to stylize their actions in order to give them an abstract value. Thus we may recall that Alisandre in Chrétien's *Cligés* foolishly embraces a shirt at night, that the God of Love in the *Roman de la rose* envisages the lover vainly solacing himself with a phantasm of his lady, or that Pygmalion goes to bed with his ivory image. It is not therefore surprising to find Troilus, after Criseyde has left him, complaining, "Save a pilowe, I fynde naught t'enbrace." Pandarus' ruse to bring Troilus and Criseyde together at Deiphebus' house is an echo of Jonadab's ruse to bring Thamar to Amnon,[195] and it probably suggested to the audience certain of the unfortunate implications of the scriptural narrative. The story was not neglected by fourteenth-century illustrators (Figs. 93-95 and 108), so that we may assume that it was not obscure. Again, those subject to the temptations of love are advised by moralists and physicians to avoid solitude,[196] but Arcite is "solitarie" and "evere allone," Damyan retires hastily to bed, Aurelius remains there for over two years ludicrously unable to walk, and Troilus retires at once to his chamber after he has seen Criseyde. The action is still significant in Elizabethan times, when Romeo "private in his chamber pens himself." Sometimes stylization of this kind is productive of humor as well as of significance. When Aleyn and Malyn part in the Reeve's Tale, they do so, as Professor Kaske has shown, in terms of an *aube*.[197]

The more or less stereotyped behavior of Chaucer's lovers has long been recognized, but it is not so often remarked that other characters also behave in ways that suggest abstract principles. Let us consider very briefly the actions of Duke Theseus in the Knight's Tale. Theseus belongs, like most of the other materials in the tale, to the traditions of classical iconography. His reputation as the conquering hero of the *Thebaid* and as a wise leader of a city whose "patron saint" was Minerva,[198] the goddess of wisdom, was firmly established in the Middle Ages. Bernard Silvestris, referring to the story of the rescue of Perotheus from Hell, says that by Theseus we are to understand "a reasonable and virtuous man who descends to the underworld in accordance with the virtuous manner of de-

---

[195] See Charles Muscatine, "The Feigned Illness in Chaucer's *Troilus and Criseyde*," *MLN*, LXIII (1948), 372-377; and D. W. Robertson, Jr., "Chaucerian Tragedy," *ELH*, XIX (1952), 23.

[196] Thus Peter of Blois, Epist. IX, *PL*, 207, col. 26, wrote: "Solitudo, quam desideras, subversio est virtutum. 'Vae soli,' quia, 'si cecideret, non habet sublevantem' (Eccl. 4). Solitudo Amnon fratrem Thamar ad incestuosum sororis suae concubitum provocabit." Cf. Gérard de Liege, ed. Wilmart, *Analecta reginensia* (Vatican, 1933), p. 90, who advises that the third remedy for subjugation to love is to avoid solitude. Cf. the remedies applied by Dorigen's friends, Franklin's Tale, 895ff., and the remedies suggested by Arnaldus of Villanova, *Opera* (Basel, 1585), col. 1530.

[197] "An Aube in the Reeve's Tale," *ELH*, XXVI (1959), 295-310. Cf. *idem.*, "January's 'Aube,' " *MLN*, LXXV (1960), 1-4.

[198] See Boccaccio's note to *Teseida*, 1. 60. 1, in Roncaglia's edition (Bari, 1941), p. 376.

scent."[199] That is, as Bernard has already explained, he is a man who wisely evaluates the relationship between *temporalia* and *invisibilia*.[200] The wisdom of Theseus was, in fact, impressive enough so that in one instance he was used as a figure for Christ.[201]. It would not have been easy for Chaucer to make any abrupt departure from the traditional associations of wisdom and virtue which surrounded this "character"; and, indeed, he shows no inclination to do so. He is introduced as a great conqueror and an exemplar of wisdom and chivalry. At critical points in the narrative Theseus is shown exhibiting mercy, and in all but the first of these instances, which has connotations in the medieval traditions of the *Thebaid*, the mercy of Theseus clearly "tempers justice," so that it is a reflection of the wisdom of the New Law. Theseus states the principle at some length:

> "Fy
> Upon a lord that wol have no mercy,
> But been a leon, bothe in word and dede,
> To hem that been in repentaunce and drede,
> As wel as to a proud despitous man
> That wol mayntene that he first bigan.
> That lord hath litel of discrecioun,
> That in swich cas kan no divisioun,
> But weyeth pride and humblesse after oon."

The "repentaunce" of Palamon and Arcite may be a little dubious, but there is nothing dubious about the principle that justice should be tempered with mercy to those who are repentant, which is the New Law of mercy as opposed to the Old Law of strict jus-

---

[199] *Comm. in sex libros Eneidos*, p. 56.

[200] The four ways of descending to Hell, p. 30, are (1) the way of nature, (2) the way of virtue, (3) the way of vice, (4) the way of artifice. The way of nature is birth into a fallen world, which is common to all. The way of virtue is that of the wise man like Hercules or Orpheus who descends by considering the fragility of worldly things while adhering to *invisibilia*. The way of vice is like that of Euridice, who places her whole confidence in temporal things. Finally, the way of artifice involves necromancy. Theseus' descent is thus a figure for a philosophical attitude toward the world. Cf. Salutati, *De laboribus Herculis*, ed. Ullman (Zurich, 1951), II, 483ff., and Pietro di Dante, *Commentarium*, pp. 11-17.

[201] J. Sauer, *Symbolik des Kirchengebäudes* (Freiburg im Breisgau, 1922), p. 259. The story of Ariadne is involved here. Cf. *Ovide moralisé*, VIII, lines 1395ff.

tice. The decision not to punish the two youths strictly in accordance with the law is followed by another of the same kind to eliminate "mortal bataille" from the tournament.[202] And again at the close of the tale, Theseus, having been advised by his council, urges Emelye to marry Palamon on the grounds that "gentil mercy oghte to passen right." It is quite probable that Chaucer's audience would have seen this same principle operating at the beginning of the tale when Duke Theseus decides to take pity on the ladies in the temple of Clementia, with which the idea of Christian mercy was easily associated.[203] All of these instances reinforce the idea that Theseus is a wise and merciful ruler. The actions are symbolic actions which reinforce the traditional connotations of his character.

But the wisdom of Theseus is emphasized in yet other ways. In his speech on the God of Love which follows his remarks about mercy for those who are repentant, he demonstrates the fact that he recognizes the folly of the kind of love to which Palamon and Arcite have subjected themselves, but he is also aware that a Puritanical attitude toward it should be avoided. This is not "tolerance," that great solvent of modern opinion, but a Boethian recognition of the fact that wretches are to be pitied rather than hated. Again, it is significant that the decision concerning the marriage of Emelye is made in "parlement," as such decisions should be made by a wise ruler, and that the marriage itself was proposed for what were regarded as excellent reasons:

> To have with certein contrees alliaunce,
> And have fully of Thebans obeisaunce.

The establishment of peaceful alliances was said to be one of the just causes for marriage.[204] Both the manner of the decision and the decision itself bespeak the wisdom of the Duke. Again, it is Theseus who delivers the speech on the "faire cheyne of love" which is a

[202] Trial by battle was still an accepted judicial procedure in Chaucer's time, as the career of Oto de Grandson shows, so that we should not quarrel with the tournament itself.

[203] Thus Thomas Ringstede, *In proverbia Salomonis*, fol. xix, observes, "Statius secundum Thebaidem narrat quod in medio civitatis atheniensium erat ara deo clementie consecrata . . . . Moraliter per hanc aram siue per hoc templum si bene respicimus cristum secundum naturam humanam intelligere debemus qui tanta habundat clementia vt nullos recuset volentes ad se quodammodo venire."

[204] Lombard, *Sententiae*, 4.30.3.

résumé of the wisdom of Lady Philosophy with special significance for the subject of marriage.[205]

It may be objected that Theseus was a hunter, and that hunters, like the monk, are not "hooly men." But the fact that Theseus rides out hunting is described explicitly as an act of God's "purveiance," and the hunt itself is conducted under the influence of "Dyane." There had been, since antiquity, two hunts, one the hunt of Venus used as a controlling figure at the beginning of Ovid's *Ars amatoria* and recommended by that lady to Adonis in the tenth book of the *Metamorphoses*, and another more virtuous hunt. Late antique funerary monuments frequently combine representations of the celestial banquet with hunting scenes in which ferocious animals are the object of the quest. In these instances the hunt represents the exercise of virtue necessary to the attainment of the banquet. The motif of the hunt continued to be used in early Christian funerary monuments with the same moral significance given a Christian coloring.[206] Subsequently the hunt for the boar or the hart became a fairly common motif in Christian art, although it is necessary to distinguish among several types of hart-hunts.[207] One of the illustrators of the *Roman de la rose*, wishing to show the virtuous hunt of Adonis for the boar, added by way of contrast a hart-hunt to suggest the less commendable pursuit recommended by Venus (Fig. 109). But the hart, enriched in meaning by associations derived from Psalm 41, the bestiaries, and the legends of St. Eustachius and St. Hubert, could also be concerned in virtuous pursuits. The two contrasting hunts are probably represented in Fig. 110, where, in a *Dixit insipiens* initial, a dog seizes a rabbit. Outside the *insipiens* and his apes indulge in an appropriate song

[205] See the discussion by Paul A. Olson, "A Midsummer Night's Dream and the Meaning of Court Marriage," *ELH*, xxiv (1957), 99ff.

[206] See Cumont, *Recherches*, pp. 438-456.

[207] The hart might be attacked by the evil as well as pursued by the virtuous. Thus a centaur representing the Devil might be shown pursuing the virtuous man or the hart. See R. van Marle, *Iconographie de l'art profane* (La Haye, 1932), II, 108. Again, because of the legends of St. Eustachius and St. Hubert the hart might represent Christ, and this significance is reinforced by the bestiaries. Finally, in the Renaissance, the hart might represent a man pursued and brought down by his passions. See Emile Picot, "Le cerf allégorique dans les tapisseries et les miniatures," *Bulletin de la soc. franç. de reproduction de manuscrits à peintures*, III, 2 (1913), 57ff. Little effort has been made to sort out the various hart hunts which appear in medieval art.

and dance while below, in contrast, two dogs pursue a hart. Ovid had made Diana hunt *fortes feras*, and although he included the hart in the hunt of Venus, it was natural that the more virtuous associations of the hart should cause it to be transferred to the hunt of Diana, especially after the hunt of Venus had centered itself on rabbits, conies, and other small creatures.[208] The virtuous hart-hunt is made explicit in a woodcut of 1525 described by Raimond van Marle which was called "The Hunt of Virtue." Here a man, accompanied by two dogs, which represent desire and thought, pursues a hart.[209] We may thus regard it as almost certain that Theseus' hart-hunt, shaped by Providence, and carried out under the auspices of Diana, is an iconographic action designed to reinforce the attributes of wisdom and virtue which he displays elsewhere in other ways.

There remain to be discussed the first actions in which we see Theseus engaged, his conquest of the Amazons and his marriage to their queen, Ypolita. It must not be forgotten that the conquest of the Amazons was one of the labors of Hercules, for which, as Boethius informs us, he gained immortality. The special significance of this story was suggested by Lactantius, who did not moralize the story but condemned it. He asks (*Div. inst.*, 1. 9. 5) whether he who subdues an Amazon is better than "he who subdues lust, the vanquisher of modesty and fame." Almost as if in answer to this criticism, Amazons were made figures for lust, for, as Salutati puts it when he makes this point, "Nothing, indeed, enervates or makes effeminate and diminishes our virtues [*vires*] more strongly than libido."[210] At first glance, this interpretation may seem to be inconsistent with the picture of the Amazons we find in the *Teseida* (1. 6-7):

> Al tempo che Egeo re d'Attene era,
> fur donne in Scizia crude e dispietate,
> alle qua' forse parea cosa fiera

[208] The two hunts are contrasted in Lydgate's *Reson and Sensualyte*, ed. Sieper, EETS ES 84 (1901), lines 2850ff. and 3711ff. where Diana's hunt is taken as an antidote to idleness. But the hunt of Venus here includes, as it does in Ovid and the *Roman de la rose*, the hart as well as "the konyn and the hare."

[209] *Iconographie*, ii, 108.

[210] *De laboribus*, ii, 364. Cf. Richard Hamilton Green, "Classical Fable and English Poetry in the Fourteenth Century," *Critical Approaches to Medieval Literature* (New York, 1960), pp. 130-131.

esser da' maschi lor signoreggiate;
per che, adunate, con sentenzia altiera
deliberar non esser soggiogate,
ma di voler per lor la signoria;
e trovar modo a fornir loro follia.

E come fer le nepoti di Belo
nel tempo cheto alli novelli sposi,
cosi costor, ciascuna col suo telo
de' maschi suoi li spirti sanguinosi
cacciò, lasciando lor di mortal gielo
tututti freddi, in modi dispettosi;
e'n cotal guisa libere si fero,
ben che poi mantenersi non potero.

But if we recall once more the Pauline traditions underlying Fig. 6, it is not difficult to see that the inversion achieved by these ferocious ladies may be thought of as a triumph of the flesh and that the Amazons are worthy precursors of the wife of Bath. They are, in effect, figures for rampant sensuality or effeminacy. In the *Teseida*, the marriage of Teseo to Ipolita effectively puts an end to the inversion and to the evil custom of the Amazons, who, as the last stanza in Boccaccio's first book indicates, learn to subject themselves to men again without too much hesitation. Chaucer's lines put the matter more decorously and abstractly:

What with his wysdom and his chivalrie,
He conquered al the regne of Femenye . . . .

Wisdom is traditionally the virtue by means of which the "regne of Femenye" is controlled, and the reason, which is the source of wisdom, is traditionally "married" to the sensuality when a proper relationship between the two is maintained. The "marriage" suggested here is suggested once more at the end of the tale, for the marriage of Palamon and Emelye establishes Thebes, the city of Venus and Bacchus, in a position of "obeisance" to Athens, the city of Minerva. The actions of Duke Theseus in the Knight's Tale are thus, like the actions of the figures we see in the visual arts of the fourteenth century, symbolic actions. They are directed toward the establishment and maintenance of those traditional hierarchies which were dear to the medieval mind. They have nothing to do with "psychology" or with "character" in the modern sense, but are instead functions of attributes which are, in this instance, inherited from the traditions of medieval humanistic culture.

In the same way it is not difficult to see without elaborate analysis that Custance's actions in the Man of Law's Tale are symbolic actions which reinforce the idea of constancy, that Griselda's actions in the Clerk's Tale are intended to stress the idea of patience and its attendant virtues, and that Prudence's actions, or speeches, in the Tale of Melibee are intended to develop the idea of prudence as it functions in warding off the attacks of the flesh, the devil, and the world, and in leading the mind toward penance. We should also expect symbolic actions in the Second Nun's Tale, which is a Saint's legend, or in the Prioress' Tale, which is almost a Saint's legend. But when the characters are neither personified abstractions, near-abstractions, nor characters whose attributes are established by traditional associations, the symbolic nature of the action may be more difficult to discern. Nevertheless, it can, I think, be demonstrated even in these instances.

Let us consider as an example the actions of the summoner in the Friar's Tale. It is true that summoners and their masters the archdeacons had been acquiring very dubious reputations for many years before Chaucer wrote, but the specific attributes of the summoner in the tale are nevertheless Chaucer's own creation. The attributes of the other chief character in the tale were well established; his dress,[211] his habitat—"fer in the north contree"—are symbolic. But we need not concern ourselves directly with his actions here. The summoner is, of course, a "false theef," who not only sets snares for lechers whom he can penalize, but also preys upon the innocent. He sneers at conscience, and lives, like the devil, by "extorcions":

> Stomak ne conscience ne knowe I noon;
> I shrewe thise shrifte-fadres everychoon.

What does Chaucer wish us to discern in this unrepentant and actively malicious sinner, who should be interested in the souls of those with whom he deals but is interested instead in their wealth? The dialogue and action following the devil's revelation "I am a

---

[211] D. W. Robertson, Jr., "Why the Devil Wears Green," *MLN*, LXIX (1954), 470-472.

feend," and his statement of an affinity between himself and the summoner all serve to emphasize one idea. Psychologically speaking, we might expect the summoner to be alarmed by the discovery that his newly sworn brother is a fiend, but morally he is quite at home with him, so that he simply observes, "Ye han a mannes shap as wel as I," and asks,

> "Han ye a figure thanne determinat
> In helle, ther ye been in youre estat?"

To this concern for external appearances, the fiend replies that devils may take any shape, so that a devil is far more deceptive than a "lowsy jogelour" who can fool the summoner. But this revelation of devilish craft does not allay the summoner's curiosity about external "shap":

> "Why . . . ryde ye thanne or goon
> In sondry shap, and nat alwey in oon?"

The devil assures him that devils assume shapes suitable to their purposes in taking "preyes." The summoner, still interested in "shap," asks why devils have "al this labour." At this, the devil explains that devils are "Goddes instrumenz" who have all their power from Him. Sometimes they attack the body and not the soul, sometimes they attack both, and sometimes they attack the soul alone. When men withstand them, they are saved, in spite of the devils. Moreover, devils may be servants to holy men. This revelation of Divine power and Divine justice, which should frighten the acknowledged unrepentant sinner even more than that concerning the wiles of devils, does not quench the summoner's curiosity about the outer nature of devils, and he asks, disregarding completely what he has just heard,

> "Make ye yow newe bodies thus alway
> Of elementz?"

The devil, who knows that there is no need to deceive a man who has already thoroughly deceived himself, assures him frankly that he shall learn all about this matter in due time:

> "But o thyng warne I thee—I wol nat jape:
> Thou wolt algates wite how we been shape;
> Thou shalt herafterward, my brother deere,
> Come there thee nedeth nat of me to leere."

And in the face of this warning, the summoner renews his pledge of brotherhood and the two ride off agreeing to share their prey. This little dialogue reveals one thing about the summoner: he has an insatiable curiosity, a truly scientific interest, in *visibilia*; he cannot understand *invisibilia* even when they are patiently and authoritatively explained to him. To him the devil is simply another hunter like himself, a companion who has certain curious potentialities for changing his surface. Just as in the pursuit of his duties he is blind to the spiritual nature of his victims and can see them only as sources of external reward, he is, in a more profound sense, blind to spiritual forces in the world generally. In the language of theology, he is hopelessly "carnal." This, then, is the idea that emerges from the dialogue. Its details all point in that direction, and the resulting picture is not a picture of a "psychological" entity, but a concrete manifestation of a moral concept.

The subsequent action simply reinforces the idea established by the dialogue and develops its implications. When the two "brothers" come upon the carter who curses his horses, cart, and hay because they are stuck in the mire, consigning them all to the devil, the summoner takes him literally, or, that is, externally, and demands his share of the booty. But the fiend correctly points out that what the carter said did not represent his "entente." Just as the summoner could see only the outside of his "brother," so also he can see only the letter and not the spirit of the carter's curse. The lesson, however, does not penetrate, for when the old woman curses the summoner, offering him to "the devel blak and rough of hewe," the devil gains from her the assurance that this is actually her intention unless the summoner repents. But the unrepentant summoner, who has stressed his contempt for conscience, violently and foolishly exclaims that he has no intention of repenting, thus confirming the old woman's gift. Once more he has failed to see the "fruyt" beneath the "chaff," and this time the result is, so far as he is concerned, disastrous. It is clear that the actions in which we see the summoner engaged all point toward the same idea. They are symbolic actions, not actions carried out in space or time for their psychological validity or for the sake of developing "depth" of character. The "depth" of the summoner lies in the profundity of the ideas he is made to represent and not in his "human" characteristics. His actions or statements serve to develop, elaborate, and particularize the implications of a theme.

In the above example, we should notice that there is no "psychological" communication between the two principal characters. The devil's speeches might as well be addressed to the audience as to the summoner, upon whom they have no effect. Characters in Chaucer's narrative tend to react in accordance with their moral natures rather than in accordance with their natures as free psychological entities in a world of free events. For example, in the Knight's Tale Emelye is overjoyed by the victory of Arcite, not because she has been peculiarly attracted by any feature of his personality or appearance, but because

> wommen, as to speken in comune,
> Thei folwen alle the favour of Fortune.

In the Miller's Tale, John the carpenter is duped by Nicolas because the latter is able to take advantage of his extreme avarice. The prospect of being lord of the world with Alisoun, as if he were Noah and she his wife, blinds him to the improbability of the clerk's prediction so that he forgets even the elementary principles of his simple faith. Again, in the Reeve's Tale when "deynous Symkyn" discovers how Aleyn and Malyn have spent the night, he can think of nothing but that "linage" which for him, ludicrously enough, represents "hooly chirches blood that is descended." This dominance of moral character over "psychological" character tends to isolate the personages from one another. And this is true even in the Clerk's Tale where Griselda submits her will completely to Walter's. Her patience and his function as a testing agent render any normal psychological reaction between them impossible. That is, figures are separated or isolated from one another much as they are in Gothic art. In Chaucer's work this feature is not so striking as it is in Jean de Meun's, where the characters are more abstract on the surface. Its presence is nevertheless clearly marked, although a failure to recognize it has sometimes created false problems of interpretation. For example, the pardoner makes it abundantly clear that although he knows the implications of *radix malorum est cupiditas*, cupidity is nevertheless his prime motivation in life. He acknowledges, moreover, that the pardon of Jesus Christ is the only one worth seeking, but then turns to the other pilgrims and offers to sell his wares. Psychologically, this last action is highly improbable. But morally it is perfectly justified, for the pardoner's vice in recognizing the truth but deliberately abusing it is presumption, one of the two aspects of the Sin against the Holy Spirit. His action in offering his wares is undoubtedly described as a crowning indication of the presence of this sin and of the blindness which accompanies it. As such, it is a logical and reasonable narrative development, but, at the same time, it illustrates well the lack of any psychological *rapport* between the pardoner and his audience.

As a result of this kind of isolation, the longer speeches of the characters frequently assume something of the nature of soliloquies, the function of which is to present ideas to the audience rather than to any of the other characters. Thus in the Knight's Tale Arcite's speech concerning his uneasiness at leaving Athens, although he addresses it to his "deere cosyn Palamon," wanders off into a discussion of Providence, Fortune, and man's erring will, which conveys nothing to Palamon but does demonstrate to the audience Arcite's failure to understand the conventional Boethian solution to his problem. Palamon replies "whan that he wiste Arcite was agon," addressing himself to "Arcita, cosyn myn," but actually speaking to no one in particular. His speech, like Arcite's, shows a failure on his part to understand a problem raised by Boethius, but this fact is, or was, communicated to the audience of the poem rather than to anyone in the poem. Similarly, Theseus' remarks about the "god of love" reveal to the audience the basis for his decision concerning the young lovers, but they are completely disregarded by the lovers. The long Boethian discourse of Theseus which begins, "The Firste Moevere of the cause above," contains the solution to the problems raised by the preceding action, and is hence very valuable to the audience of the poem, but it elicits no verbal response from anyone else in the narrative. Sometimes speeches of this kind are explicitly "thoughts" rather than speeches, but these "thoughts," like the soliloquies in Chrétien's narratives or the long speeches in the *Roman de la rose*, are revelations of moral character or statements of principle rather than psychological revelations, so that they serve the same general purposes as speeches of the type we have just discussed. To this type belongs Theseus' meditation on justice and mercy, which, as we have seen, serves to define and to emphasize the nature of his wisdom. One further example from *Troilus* will suffice to demonstrate the value of "mental" soliloquies of this kind. After Criseyde has seen Troilus for the first time as he rides home from battle in Book II, she engages in a long argument with herself about the advisability of reciprocating his love. Significantly, the considerations which she adduces are basically selfish and reveal a "calculating" spirit, consistent with the "loneliness" and "fearfulness" of the lady and her thrill at the notion that the hero's distress "was al for hire." First, she thinks that it would be "honorable" to deal with such a noble man. Moreover, he is a king's son and might disdain her if she resisted, so that it might be more honorable to give in. Again, measure in all things is best, and a moderate indulgence with Troilus, she rationalizes, would be virtuous. The idea that moderate fornication is virtuous would hardly have failed to amuse Chaucer's original audience. She feels that he is no boaster, so that she would be safe in this course of action. What dishonor, then, could come of it? It is obvious here, as elsewhere, that Criseyde thinks of "honor" only in terms of what other people think. Troilus could have anyone because of his station, she continues. It is no wonder that he has chosen her, for, as she thinks,

> I am oon the faireste, out of drede,
> And goodlieste, whoso taketh hede,
> And so men seyn, in al the town of Troie.

Moreover, she will have no husband to worry about. On the other side, Criseyde suddenly becomes fearful, thinking of her potential loss of liberty, the stormy life of love, the possibility of wicked talk, of lover's treason, of the onerousness of pleasing those who "jangle of love," and so on. It is obvious at the end of the meditation that Criseyde will love only when she has decided that to do so will flatter her vanity and further her immediate interests. The monologue thus has the function of revealing her moral nature, and it prepares the way for her later submission to Diomede, which is made on the basis of similar selfish considerations. The frequency with which such soliloquies and semi-soliloquies appear in Chaucer's poetry is another indication of the fact that he is more concerned with the development of ideas than with a literal rendition of events organized in space and time. Above all, they reveal

271

that each character is a discrete moral entity and that the author was concerned to reveal the nature of this entity in each instance rather than to place it in a nexus of dramatic or psychological interactions.

If Chaucer's characters are frequently reflections of a conceptual reality, and the actions of these characters are often more significant as developments in a conceptual realm than as imitations of external life in space and time, it follows that the completed narratives in which they appear can not be structured in accordance with what we ordinarily think of as "plot development." That is, the narratives themselves are significant in an exemplary fashion rather than "for their own sakes," or for our emotional participation in them. There are a few instances in which this fact is clear without further discussion. We may accept it without analysis in connection with the Second Nun's Tale, for example. As Dom Jean Leclercq explains concerning the value of hagiographical legends, as distinct from the *vitae* compiled preparatory to canonization, medieval men were more interested in permanent and universal ideas than in transitory actions, and it is these ideas that are stressed and illustrated in the legends.[212] In two instances in *The Canterbury Tales* the significance of the narrative is partially explained: the Melibee and the Clerk's Tale. In one instance, the Nun's Priest's Tale, the audience is urged to seek the "fruyt" beneath the surface of the story. At the close of *Troilus* there is a clear indication of the direction which interpretation should take, and in *The Book of the Duchess* there is a warning that the ensuing dream will be difficult to interpret. Generally, we may assume that Chaucer was not addressing an audience of blind summoners, and that he hoped that his readers would be more successful in their pursuit of *sentence* than was Harry Baily. The nature of his characters and their actions suggests strongly that his narrative is expository in function, and is not intended as a reflection of literal events. It is true that Chaucer is usually much less explicit than Watriquet or Jean de Condé, and his materials are considerably more complex than those employed by these earlier poets, but we should not forget that he was addressing himself to a very select courtly audience which might be expected to be unusually alert.

[212] See the excellent discussion in *L'amour des lettres et le désir de Dieu* (Paris, 1957), 154-160.

Chaucer's fondness for exemplification generally may be judged by the prominence given to exemplary materials in the *Tales*. That the interpretation of these *exempla* was, in his mind, a matter of profound importance is revealed by the frequency with which the characters in the stories either misinterpret exemplary materials or disregard their significance. We have discussed in another connection Arcite's amusing misinterpretation of the story of the two dogs fighting over a bone, a misinterpretation designed to emphasize the fact that passion has clouded his reason. In the Miller's Tale old John adduces the example of the clerk who walked in the fields looking at the stars and fell into a marle-pit. This story, which may be found in Walter Burley's *Liber de vita et moribus philosophorum* under Thales of Miletus, was used by both Nicole Oresme and Deschamps to show the foolishness of a belief in judicial astrology.[213] But John, in spite of the lesson of his *exemplum*, proceeds to take seriously the highly improbable astrological prediction of "hende Nicolas" and to suffer a fall himself. In the Summoner's Tale the friar includes a series of *exempla* in the little sermon on wrath which he delivers to Thomas. But instead of illustrating the disadvantages of wrath to the wrathful man himself, they show the dangers of associating with wrathful persons, especially those with any power. Thus after the second, on Cambises, the friar says, drawing a false distinction,

> Beth war, therfore, with lordes how ye pleye.
> Syngeth *Placebo*, and 'I shal, if I kan,'
> But if it be unto a povre man.
> To a povre man men sholde his vices telle,
> But nat to a lord, thogh he sholde go to helle.

The *exempla* have no relevance to Thomas, who only becomes more wrathful at what he hears, but they do apply to the friar, who is associating with a wrathful man while he is telling them. He soon has occasion to learn the lesson of his own stories in a striking way, becomes very wrathful himself, and suffers the consequences of "singing *Placebo*" once too often when the lord's squire decides his fate. Again, in the Franklin's Tale when Dorigen

---

[213] See *Contra astrologos*, cap. 2, in H. Pruckner, *Studien zu den astrologischen Schriften des Heinrich von Langenstein* (Leipzig, 1933), pp. 230-231, and Deschamps, *Demonstracions contra sortileges* in *Oeuvres*, SATF, vii, pp. 193-194.

is told by Aurelius that the rocks have been removed from the coast, she indulges in a long exemplary speculation designed to show the virtue of ladies who do away with themselves rather than suffer forceful violation. The irony here arises from the fact that the *exempla* are completely irrelevant to Dorigen's situation. Her assurance in "pley" that she would submit to Aurelius if he removed the rocks from the coast was a clearly intended negative, consistent with the remark,

> Ne shal I nevere been untrewe wyf
> In word ne werk, as fer as I have wit.

Dorigen's interest in her *exempla* arises from the fact that she, like the summoner in the Friar's Tale, takes a figurative statement for a literally intended asseveration.[214] That she is not really concerned about the lesson of her examples is evident from her subsequent behavior. The fact that she goes to Aurelius with the consent of her husband, in spite of the principles adduced in her *exempla*, does not shed a very favorable light on her character. Finally, in the Nun's Priest's Tale, Chantecleer engages in a long exemplary discourse to show that his dream presages adversity, concluding,

> Shortly I seye, as for conclusioun,
> That I shal han of this avisioun
> Adversitee.

As it turns out, he is right. But the beauty of Pertelote and the pleasure she is capable of supplying cause him to disregard the lesson of his own stories, and he suffers the consequences. A similar effect with reference to the tales themselves is achieved on those occasions when Harry Baily sees fit to make any extended remarks about them. He is so preoccupied with his own marital situation that he can think of little else. Hence he wishes that his wife might hear the Clerk's Tale, even though the Clerk has explained that

> This story is seyd, nat for that wyves sholde
> Folwen Griselde as in humylitee . . . .

---

[214] Even if we take the joke as an oath, as most modern critics have done, it was widely held both in antiquity and during the Middle Ages that hasty oaths leading to vicious action are not to be kept. This fact is fully documented in a paper now in preparation by A. C. Gaylord.

He takes the Merchant's Tale as an attack on the "sleightes and subtilitees" of women, which is what the Merchant intended, but the story nevertheless clearly emphasizes Januarie's foolishness. Harry even makes the Melibee a tale about a husband and a wife in spite of the fact that the allegory is transparent and is largely explained in the tale itself. That is, Harry is consistently blind to the *sentence* of what he hears, and this situation was undoubtedly created by Chaucer as a jocular warning to his audience to avoid a similar blindness.

Just as characters within the tales sometimes misinterpret or disregard the implications of the *exempla* they adduce, so also the pilgrims themselves, except for idealized characters like the knight, the clerk, and the parson, or reformed sinners like the canon's yeoman, frequently show a blindness to the implications of their own tales, so that the tales themselves become subtle comments on their narrators. Perhaps this fact is most obvious in the Merchant's Tale, where the merchant's effort to demonstrate the wiles of women only serves to emphasize the foolishness of men of his own kind.[215] Again, the friar tells a tale designed to show the baseness of summoners and hence of the summoner himself. But his accusation involved the contention that summoners are concerned only with *visibilia* and the further allegation that they are unrepentant. A glance at the description of the friar in the General Prologue shows, first of all, that he is guilty of exactly the same kind of blindness to spiritual values that he attributes to summoners. At the same time, his administration of the sacrament of penance is characterized by a complete lack of interest in the spiritual welfare of those who confess to him. If the summoner had habitually chosen the friar as a Father Confessor, it is not difficult to see that his inclination to repent would have been no stronger. Hence the concluding lines of the Friar's Tale serve to comment on the friar himself:

> And prayeth that thise somonours hem repente
> Of hir mysdedes, er that the feend hem hente!

Similarly, the franklin, impressed by the Squire's Tale, sets out to

[215] See Paul A. Olson, "The Merchant's Lombard Knight," *University of Texas Studies in Literature and Language*, III (1961), 259-263; and the further study of the Merchant's Tale by the same author, *ELH*, xxviii (1961), 203-214.

illustrate the principles of *gentilesse*, adducing what he considers to be the noble generosity of a knight, a squire, and a clerk, with the implication that a franklin who can tell a gentle tale can be a gentleman also. But unfortunately for his implication, no one in the tale gives up anything he has any real right to hold, so that no one is actually generous. Thus the knight has abjured sovereignty in marriage so that he has no real authority over Dorigen. He can only threaten her to be silent so as to preserve his superficial honor. The squire bases his claim on the letter rather than on the "entente" of a jocular remark, and the clerk has not removed the rocks but merely calculated the time of a high tide which makes them, if anything, more dangerous than they were before. The franklin's conception of *gentilesse* is thus consistent with the entirely superficial nobility of a wealthy man of the middle class who is "Epicurus owene sone" and is hence, like the summoner in the friar's Tale, blind to anything beneath surface appearances.[216] The employment of this technique enables Chaucer to have his pilgrims tell tales which are consistent with their own moral natures but which, at the same time, contribute to the thematic development of *The Canterbury Tales* as a whole. This rather subtle arrangement is made possible by the fact that the tales have an exemplary force.

The nature of Chaucer's literary art is thus quite different from that of more recent times. We admire psychological profundity, dramatic intensity, well-rounded characters, realism, and well-structured plot development in our own literature, and we naturally ascribe these same characteristics to Chaucer's narrative art in order to express our admiration for it. But such criteria are basically misleading when used in this way. They are inconsistent with fourteenth-century stylistic conventions. No one thought in terms

---

[216] The fourteenth-century attitude toward Epicurus is well summed up by Gower, *Mirour de l'omme*, ed. Macaulay, lines 9529ff.:

> Trop fuist de Foldelit apris
> Uns philosophes de jadys
> Qui Epicurus nom avoit:
> Car ce fuist cil q'a son avis
> Disoit que ly charnels delitz
> Soverain des autres biens estoit.
> Et pour cela trestout laissoit
> Les biens del alme et se donnoit
> A sa caroigne.

of psychology in the fourteenth century any more than he thought in terms of differential calculus or Marxist dialectic. Cultural developments had not yet provided conditions suitable to the growth of a taste for dramatic intensity in the nineteenth-century sense. Realism was alien to the artistic expression of the period generally, and artists showed no interest in the ordering of events in a continuum of space and time shared by the observer, in such a way as to create structures suitable for the vicarious release of tensions. Much the same reservations might be made about the literature of Chaucer's contemporaries, which shares, to a greater or lesser degree, all of the attributes we have seen to be characteristic of Chaucer's art. Yet Chaucer's poetry is very different from that of *Pearl*, or *Piers Plowman*, or *Confessio amantis*. The stamp of his genius is almost unmistakable, and it might be profitable to consider very briefly some of the stylistic characteristics which are peculiar to him.

Perhaps the most obvious distinction which separates Chaucer and Gower on the one hand from the authors of *Pearl*, *Piers Plowman*, and *Sir Gawain* on the other is their greater reliance on the traditions of romance versification, a feature which may well be due to the international associations of the royal court and the tastes for elegance in expression which developed there. French literature had long enjoyed a considerable prestige. Nothing was produced in England or in northern Europe during the thirteenth century in a vernacular language which could equal in elegance or philosophical effectiveness the *Roman de la rose*. Later on, in the fourteenth century, the great poet-musicians Philippe de Vitry and Machaut set the standards for sophisticated literary art in the centers of feudal Europe. It was natural that the more cosmopolitan noblemen of England should seek to rival their French contemporaries on the basis of standards already established in France. Meanwhile, the only effective non-French tradition was that which developed in Italy under the leadership of Dante, Petrarch, and Boccaccio. Petrarch's extravagant defense of things Italian in general and of Italian letters in particular, which may be seen most directly, perhaps, in his controversy with Jean de Hesdin, was effective in producing a growing respect for Italian accomplishment. Italy was beginning to make itself felt also as an arbiter of taste in the visual arts and in music. We can with some justification, therefore, attribute the surface features of Chaucer's verse to a desire to appeal to court tastes. To those accustomed to the smooth flow of French verse the heavy beat of the native alliterative poets, even in its most accomplished expression like that in *Pearl* or *Gawain,* must have sounded crude and provincial. Chaucer had no way of knowing that he would become famous among the early Elizabethans as the first significant poet in English, and the fact that English verse in its later development superficially bears a greater resemblance to Chaucer's than it does to the alliterative verse of some of his contemporaries was an accident of history which he could not have foreseen. Looking back, we may still be inclined to neglect the formative influence of local demand.

If we compare Chaucer and Gower, however, Chaucer's superiority becomes evident at once, but this superiority must be attributed to something more than greater skill and polish. If we discount the rather remarkable achievement of perfecting the decasyllabic line in English, the difference between the two poets is not, strictly speaking, a matter of versification. In the more accomplished passages of his later poetry Chaucer achieves an easy and conversational manner, spiced by the rhythms of vigorous speech. Neither Gower, who spreads relatively long and somewhat "literary" sentences over many rhetorically unbroken octosyllabic lines, nor the alliterative poets, constrained by the regular emphasis of their heavily stressed verses, were capable of the free and rhetorically emphatic rhythms which Chaucer was thus able to produce. The conversational manner allows Chaucer to take constant advantage of the devices of oral rhetoric, and these devices, although they are sometimes the product of a considerable sophistication in rhetorical theory, lend a naturalness and vigor to his language which must have been even more apparent at a time when poetry was customarily delivered orally rather than read alone in the study. We may assume, moreover, that even those who read alone read aloud, or at least allowed themselves an awareness of the sound of what they read as well as of its sense. The modern "silent" reader who is more easily impressed by visual than by auditory effects is not in a position to appreciate the humor and subtlety of Chaucer's verse without deliberate effort. In his own time, however, the conversational tone gave him two distinct advantages over most of his contemporaries: a pleasing variety which dispels monotony, and an enhanced atmosphere of immediacy. The effective rendering of dialogue in verse was a relatively early achievement, appearing, for example, in the romances of Chrétien de Troyes, but the intimacy achieved by a generally conversational tone is distinctly a late fourteenth-century development, related stylistically to the increasing verisimilitude of the visual arts. We may see its growth in Chaucer from *The Book of the Duchess*, which is still influenced by the stylized elegance of Machaut and the French poets, to *The Canterbury Tales*, where some effort is made to adjust the manner of delivery to the status of the pilgrims who tell the tales. This effort falls far short of "realism," but it nevertheless makes a distinct concession to Ciceronian decorum in style as well as in content.[217]

The *Pearl* poet was capable of compressing a wealth of detail into a relatively short passage, but Chaucer far surpasses any of his contemporaries in this respect, especially in *The Canterbury Tales*. We may compare this wealth of significant detail with the technique of such monuments as the Neville Screen or the more elaborate pages of the Bohun manuscripts. It not only represents fine craftsmanship, but, more significantly, it reveals an unusual alertness both to the concrete particularization of the themes being developed and, on the other hand, to the significance of the visible materials which make up the detail. Considering the nature of his poetry, which was concerned primarily with ideas rather than with the affective values of the concrete, Chaucer thus demonstrates an unusually keen intellect, capable not only of grasping abstract concepts, but also of perceiving the significance of concrete materials as manifestations of those concepts. It is one thing to be able to comprehend the formulations of philosophers and theologians or the inherited principles of traditional wisdom in their abstract form, but quite another to be able to see the implications of these concepts in concrete terms. P. W. Bridgman once said that "it requires practice, imagination, and insight to see that the most obvious observations . . . may contain revolutionary implications." We might add that the same qualities are required to see the manifold implications of obvious observations in everyday experience. This is not so much a matter of poetic genius today as it is a matter of intelligence, but whether we call it one or the other, we must grant that

---

[217] Lines 730-736 of the General Prologue constitute, indirectly, a statement of the principles of decorum as described by Cicero, *De officiis*, 1. 28. 97-98.

Chaucer possessed the required quality developed to a very high degree. The picture of Alisoun of Bath as it is revealed in her prologue is made up of commonplace "anti-feminist" materials, some of which are as old as the Bible and Ovid; yet Chaucer has expressed these ideas with such a keen eye for the life around him that scholars have gone looking for an actual woman who might have served as a model among his contemporaries. The pursuit is misdirected, but it is nevertheless a tribute to Chaucer's genius. Much of the detail in *Pearl* or *Piers Plowman* involves symbolic or scriptural materials combined to form pictures of things which cannot be seen in the terms used to describe them, like the colorful forest along the river in *Pearl* or the Castle of Caro in *Piers Plowman*. The same observation might be made about much of the materials in Chaucer's formal allegories. But in some parts of *The Canterbury Tales* the details are immediately recognizable without any loss of significance. This means also that from the point of view of the audience Chaucer's poetry is more difficult than that of his contemporaries. The "poetic veil," as Petrarch and Boccaccio called it, becomes denser as the verisimilitude of the materials which make it up becomes more convincing. The fact that Chaucer was able to create a sense of immediacy without destroying the value of his symbolic material is not only a tribute to him, but also a tribute to his audience. The court of Richard II constituted one of the most demanding and sophisticated audiences in Europe, and we owe that audience a debt of gratitude for making possible the achievements of artists like Henry Yevele and Geoffrey Chaucer. It was their perceptiveness which enabled Chaucer to write "saigement, briefment, substancieusement et hardiement" without losing his audience.

Chaucer differs from his contemporaries not only in the intimacy of his language and the immediacy and variety of the details he employs, but also in his unfailing sense of humor. Contemporaries like Gower and Deschamps thought of him as a sort of English Ovid, not simply because he was an interesting narrator of pleasant stories, but because he was, like Ovid, a *tenerorum lusor amorum* who maintained a lively intellectual awareness of the ridiculous. Chaucer's "Ovidian" air owes a great deal to the traditions of humor which extend from the Ovidian works of the twelfth century through the fabliaux to Jean de Meun and his imitators. Basically, it is the same strain of mockery that we see in Gothic portrayals of the vices and in the grotesques of the late thirteenth and fourteenth centuries. Technically, Chaucer's humor is harmonious with his love for concrete detail and his informal conversational tone. But Chaucer's humor is not altogether a matter of the skilful manipulation of an inherited tradition. Deschamps also admired Chaucer as a philosopher, and Usk praises him for his *sentence*. Chaucer's philosophy gave to his humor a peculiar flavor, for that humor, which is based on the confident acceptance of a Providential order underlying the apparent irrationality of the world and its inhabitants, is sometimes more profound and more persuasive than any "highly serious" discourse couched in the grand style can possibly be. True humor, as distinct from Lucretian glee or a more modern "release of tensions," requires an intellectual approach which permits a sense of detachment, not the detachment of the egoist or of the self-styled sophisticate, but the detachment of a man whose faith is unshaken by the shortcomings of society and whose love for his fellows enables him to regard both their pettiness and his own with a certain equanimity. It is this detachment which sets Chaucer apart from his contemporaries, and, indeed, from most of his successors. The attitude seriously expressed in the second stanza of that Boethian elaboration of John 8. 32 called "A Balade of Good Counsel" goes far to account for the peculiar greatness of Chaucer's art:

> Tempest thee noght al croked to redresse,
> In trust of hir that turneth as a bal:
> Gret reste stant in litel besinesse;
> Be war also to sporne ayeyns an al;
> Stryve not, as doth the crokke with the wal.
> Daunte thyself, that dauntest otheres dede;
> And Trouthe thee shal delivere, it is no drede.

It is, of course, impossible to describe the personal genius of a great poet in a few words, and it is also extremely difficult to say anything very definite about his national characteristics. The latter may be fairly easy to sense, but they remain very difficult to explain. Nevertheless, a few very general conclusions may be reached about Chaucer's "Englishness." In the first place, as we have seen, the one fairly consistent feature of English art is its conservatism.

Conservative tendencies in Chaucer should therefore occasion no surprise. The more "advanced" or, that is, courtly, literature in France during the latter part of the century followed the conventions established by Machaut, and in Italy stylistic devices like the use of perspective in painting and the adoption of a personal attitude in poetry were to develop and spread across the rest of Europe during the Renaissance. But Chaucer, except for some parts of *The Book of the Duchess*, refuses to adopt current French fashions. In that poem there is a humorous informality in the speaker's reaction to the story of Ceys and Alcion that is unlike the general style of Machaut, and the treatment of the Black Knight's love in its early stages lacks completely the idealism of Machaut's treatment of the subject. In the later allegories the humorous element is still more evident. Again, *Troilus* is based on an Italian source, but, as has been pointed out several times, it seems much more "medieval" than Boccaccio's poem; that is, it maintains a sense of detachment which gives the characters and actions the remoteness necessary to Chaucer's emphasis on ideas rather than on feelings. Generally, Chaucer lacks either the easy elegance of Machaut or the assumed subjectivity of the Italians. This does not mean that he is more "medieval," however; it means that he is English.

What Chaucer has instead of these characteristics is, first of all, a taste for the kind of exuberance and vivid exemplification that we have seen to be typical of the "East Anglian" and Bohun manuscripts, or of fourteenth-century English architecture. This exuberant and informal manner is especially evident in some of *The Canterbury Tales*, but it appears elsewhere also: in the amusing picture of Priapus in *The Parliament of Fowls*, in the dialogue between the speaker and the dreamer in *The House of Fame*, and in the picture of the birds who have escaped from the fowler in the Prologue to *The Legend of Good Women*. This list is, of course, merely illustrative. But it does indicate the presence of the same spirit that makes English decoration less formally elegant than French decoration of the same type, and, at the same time, richer in detail than the more "realistic" but cruder decoration of Flemish art.

We have seen in English architecture a tendency to compartmentalize, to prefer a juxtaposition of discrete forms to a lineally integrated whole in the French fashion. The liernes of English vaults create an impression of a roof which is entirely distinct from the walls, and which is not simply a linear continuation of the walls. And English façades exhibit statuary placed in regularly ordered compartments placed across the surface of the building. Admirers of French Gothic have long regarded features such as these with disfavor. But it may be a mistake to consider French fashions as norms against which to compare other national styles which were influenced by them. English medieval art simply lacks what Roger Fry once called "the peculiar rhythmic flow and unity" of French art of the same period. But this does not mean that English art deliberately sought such a unity and failed to achieve it. Rather, it is safe to assume that the English preferred a more conservative manner in which the unity of the whole is implied rather than expressed. In this sense it is also different from Italian art. *The Decameron*, like *The Canterbury Tales*, is a collection of stories, each of which is a discrete entity, but the Italian work is much more rationally ordered than the English. There are ten speakers, each of whom is to tell one tale on each of ten days, and each of whom is to begin a day and set the theme. The establishment of this mathematical order gives the whole an artificially integrated structure, so that the tales of each day have a certain coherence, and there is a systematic progression throughout the whole toward the climax at the hundredth story. A taste for mathematical regularity of this kind was to have profound effects on the subsequent development of Italian art, but there is no such regularity in Chaucer's collection. After the first drawing of straws, the decision concerning who is to tell a tale next is left to the whim of the Host, but even he cannot control the sequence. The miller interrupts to "quit" the knight, and quarrels like that between the miller and the reeve and the friar and the summoner interrupt the sequence. At one point the fortuitous appearance of the canon and his yeoman introduces a new speaker. This does not mean, of course, that Chaucer had no scheme in mind for arranging his stories. But this arrangement is a matter of implicit thematic development and is not the result of any outwardly established system. The unity of the collection as a whole is left implicit rather than explicit.

The same feature is evident in the allegories, where it has given rise to difficulties in critical interpretation. In *The Book of the Duchess*, for example, there is no outward connection between the story of Ceys and Alcion and the subsequent dream vision. Again, in *The Parliament of Fowls*, the connection between the dream of Scipio and the activities of the birds in Nature's garden is implied rather than stated. In *The Legend of Good Women* the elaborate prologue seems to be connected with the tales only by the tenuous thread of the "penance" administered by the God of Love, and the stories themselves, aside from the fact that they are about unfortunate women, do not have any apparent unity. In *The House of Fame* the various parts all concern the same speaker, and they appear in narrative sequence, but otherwise they have little outward connection with one another. We may compare this situation with the arrangement of the pages in one of the great East Anglian psalters, where there is no explicit relationship between the marginalia and the initials. In general, Chaucer's art lacks the formal unity which appears, in various guises, in both French and Italian art, as well as the coherence in space and time which characterizes more modern art. As a result, we have been quick to accuse him of "digressions," sometimes alleging in support what we are pleased to regard as the principles of medieval rhetoric. The passage on free will in the Nun's Priest's Tale, the long meditation on the same subject in *Troilus*, Dorigen's thoughts concerning Providence in the Franklin's Tale—to cite only a few examples—have been condemned as irrelevancies which interrupt the narratives in which they occur. But the fact that elements such as these retain their surface discreteness may be attributed to a feature of English style. The separateness of the parts does not, however, imply the lack of an underlying unity, any more, let us say, than the separateness of "types" from their "antitypes" in medieval art implies such a lack of unity. Significant juxtapositions were an established technique in Gothic art, and English art particularly during the later Middle Ages exhibits a desire to keep the juxtaposed elements separate.

Meanwhile, we have noticed one further characteristic of English art which Chaucer may be said to share. During the second half of the fourteenth century English art fails to show any outward manifestations of the heroic. The "heroes" of *The Canterbury Tales* are Duke Theseus, Constance, Griselda, and St. Cecelia —all figures who are distinguished by virtue rather than by heroic action. It is true that Theseus is a mighty conqueror, but his physical heroism is passed over lightly and his wisdom and mercy are stressed instead. Among the pilgrims to Canterbury a meek knight, a threadbare clerk, and a poor parson stand out as ideal figures. The heroic potentialities of Troilus are undercut whenever they appear. His action on the battlefield is designed either to make an impression on Criseyde or, later on, to seek vengeance and self-destruction. He has no stature as a prince fighting in the defence of his people, and his desire for vengeance ends in frustration. As a lover, he has to be thrown into bed by Pandarus, and his thoughts of forcibly rescuing Criseyde from the Greeks turn out to be empty dreams which he has no power to fulfill. In the allegories the only figure of grand stature is Alceste, and her greatness rests neither on intelligence nor on physical charm, but on the virtues of a faithful wife. Chaucer neither uses outward heroism as a symbol for spiritual heroism nor confuses the two. Most revealing, perhaps, is his picture of himself in the prologue to Sir Thopas. A feeling for the heroic requires a certain inner seriousness about one's own potentialities, perhaps a touch of vanity. But we cannot imagine Chaucer seeking a laurel crown in Rome. The stout little man we see riding silently with downcast eyes toward Canterbury meekly accepting the banter of Harry Baily is above all a man with a keen eye for the distinction between outward grandeur and inner worth. English experience with an old Edward doting on an unworthy woman and a young Richard who could not always achieve those principles of chivalry which he so ardently admired may have made this distinction acutely apparent during Chaucer's lifetime. Whatever the cause, the English of Chaucer's day were not inspired by posturing in the grand manner, and in this matter Chaucer seems to have shared their taste. "Englishness" is an elusive concept, as Professor Pevsner's delightful lectures on *The Englishness of English Art* demonstrate. However, in spite of Chaucer's reliance on continental traditions, he was an English artist in style as well as in his inimitable mastery of the idioms of his own tongue. Just as foreign influences working on a conservative native tradition produced something new but distinctively English in the designs of Henry Yevele, so also the poetry of Chaucer is a unique but very English result of foreign influences, predominantly French, operating on a strong native tradition.

IV · ALLEGORY,
HUMANISM, AND LITERARY THEORY

I. CHRISTIAN ALLEGORY

𝕵𝖓 𝖔𝖚𝖗 𝖉𝖎𝖘𝖈𝖚𝖘𝖘𝖎𝖔𝖓𝖘 of medieval aesthetics and medieval style, we have called attention repeatedly to the abstract quality of medieval art and to the widespread use of iconographic techniques in both art and literature. These distinctive traits were made possible by a pervasive tendency to think in allegorical terms. Although modern criticism demonstrates a fondness for symbolism in poetry and fiction, especially when it may be seen as a structural element, allegory is almost universally regarded with suspicion, if not with contempt. In the Middle Ages, on the other hand, the word *symbolism* was very seldom used, and poetry was thought of as being by nature allegorical. The difference is more than a difference in terminology, however; for the symbolism of modern poetry, which is most typically a vehicle for the expression of mood or emotion, has no counterpart in the Middle Ages; and medieval allegory, which is a vehicle for the expression of traditional ideas, has with a few exceptions no counterpart in modern poetry. Our critical disdain for allegory thus rests partly on the fact that the concept of allegory as it was understood in the Middle Ages has little relevance to modern literature. But it is also based on certain historical assumptions. One of the commonest of these is the notion that a "humanist" is a man who distrusts allegory. Since we are all, of course, "humanists," we feel that we, too, must distrust allegory. But a little reflection will show that our historical assumption leaves something to be desired. Thus if humanists are men who distrust allegory, we shall have to erase the names of Petrarch, Ficino, and Erasmus—all of whom were very fond of allegory—from our rosters of humanism; we shall have to disassociate Edmund Spenser, who thought epics to be allegorical, from the traditions of English humanism; and we shall have to speak of a great many masterpieces of Renaissance painting and sculpture as "anti-humanistic." We shall also have difficulty in explaining why it is that allegorical theory flourished especially during those periods of history which we associate with humanistic tendencies: the Carolingian Renaissance, the Renaissance of the Twelfth Century, and the Renaissance which followed the Middle Ages. In all of these various "Renaissances" men sought to preserve the traditions of the past and to explain them once more in terms suitable to their own contemporaries. Since their effort was directed toward the enrichment of human life on the basis of human experience in the past, we may as well call them "humanists," even if most of them did not resemble very closely the famous Bishop of St. Praxed's. But we should also recognize the fact that one of the most useful instruments they had at their disposal for the expression of traditional ideals in a form harmonious with the experience of their audiences was allegory.

Even more important, perhaps, as a deterrent to our appreciation of allegory is the fact that its presence cannot be detected by modern philological methods. Scientific scholarship insists on confining itself to what a text "actually says." During the Middle Ages, this restriction was sometimes regarded not as a virtue but as a mark of illiteracy. Thus Thomas Usk complains in the Prologue to his *Testament of Love* that "Many men ther ben that, with eres openly sprad, so moche swalowen the deliciousnesse of the jestes and of ryme, by queynt knitting coloures, that of the goodnesse or of the badnesse of the sentence take they litel hede or els none." The "sentence" is what the text implies rather than what it "actually says," and for Usk, as well as for all of his more literate contemporaries, this was its most important feature. A more modern writer, noticing the same deficiency to which Usk called attention in another context, places the blame where it now belongs: "Un certain positivisme historique tue méthodiquement son objet, les yeux fermés."[1] Since Usk's highest praise for his great contemporary Chaucer was to say that "in witte and good reson of sentence he passeth al other makers," we may suspect that in neglecting Chaucer's "sentence" we are neglecting something which was highly valued by his contemporary audience. And "sentence" is, so to speak, the fruit of allegory.

The helplessness of scientific philology as it is now conceived before allegory is very easy to illustrate even where the simplest form of allegory, the trope described by medieval grammarians, is concerned. This trope consists, as Isidore of Seville describes it,

[1] Henri de Lubac, *Exégèse médiévale*, Première Partie (Paris, 1959), p. 661.

of *alieniloquium*. One thing is said by the words, but something else is understood.[2] There are, he says, numerous forms which the figure may take, but seven may be singled out as being most important. They are irony (deriding through praise), antiphrasis, aenigma, charientismos, paroemia (proverbial expression), sarcasm, and astysmos (sarcasm without bitterness). Surely, these tropes should be more evident to modern sophistication than they were to our plodding medieval ancestors! But they are not. For example, modern critics of Lucan almost without exception regard the invocation to Nero in the *Pharsalia* as a panegyric, but medieval commentators from the tenth century to the Renaissance treat the dedication as being ironic. It has recently been suggested that the earlier opinion, which regarded "what the text actually says" with some suspicion was probably correct.[3] To cite a Chaucerian example, it was once held very seriously that the Envoy at the close of the Clerk's Tale is "out of character," since what it "actually says" is inconsistent with the Clerk's obvious attitude toward women. The difficulty lies in the fact that allegory in this sense must rest on an assumed sense of values. When the values upon which such tropes are based are not understood, or when more modern values are assumed for the text, the tropes themselves disappear, and we are left with "literal" statements which all too frequently are said to reveal the ineptness, inconsistency, or the quaint and curious prejudices of their authors. St. Augustine assumes that tropes of this kind are to be found in the Bible.[4] Medieval students undoubtedly learned about them in school, observed their appearance in both sacred and profane texts, and acquired a taste for using them in their own writings. Needless to say, no such tastes are cultivated in our schools today. Unless irony results from an obvious "contrast," or is "situational" or "dramatic," we are very likely to miss it. And once it is missed, there is no way of "proving" that it exists. It is quite unlikely that Defoe would have been misunderstood in *The Shortest Way with the Dissenters* if his audience had been trained in medieval schools.

Yet another prejudice of an historical character assumes that

[2] *Etymologiae*, 1. 37. 22.

[3] Berthe M. Marti, "Lucan's Invocation to Nero in the Light of Mediaeval Commentaries," *Quadrivium*, 1 (1956), 7-18.

[4] *On Christian Doctrine*, 4. 29. 40-41.

allegory~is a medieval invention discarded by a non-allegorical Renaissance when it revived a non-allegorical antiquity. As a matter of fact, medieval allegory as a literary device (as distinct from scriptural allegory) represents a continuation of techniques which had been developing in antiquity since the sixth century B.C.[5] The growth of allegory in the classical world has recently been sketched by Jean Pépin,[6] and although detailed studies have yet to be made, the importance of literary allegory in antiquity cannot now be denied. By the time of imperial Rome, Cumont assures us, "aucun esprit cultivé ne prenait plus les récits de la Fable au sens littéral."[7] Every myth had its physical or moral application, since it was, by definition, a "lying discourse figuring forth a truth." Stoics, Neoplatonists, and Neopythagoreans found their own doctrines in the myths of the poets, assuming that the gods revealed their mysteries in an obscure way and that the discovery of the secrets thus concealed was a source of pleasure as well as of profit. The result of these efforts, however misguided they may have been, was to preserve the literature of the past and to give it a contemporary relevance. That the humanists of the Renaissance did not hesitate to allegorize and even to produce popular manuals of mythography to assist the process has been sufficiently demonstrated by Jean Seznec.[8] It is not, therefore, feasible to cite either antiquity or the Renaissance as generalized precedents for a modern distrust of allegorical methods. As a matter of fact, there is a continuous tradition of allegorical theory and practice extending from the sixth century B.C. well into the eighteenth century. During these centuries, of course, the tradition underwent many modifications, adapting itself to a wide variety of stylistic and cultural changes. The most important of these changes was the introduction of Christianity, which brought with it an allegorical method of its own. During the course of the Middle Ages, literary allegory, although it remained a distinct entity, became closely associated with the allegorical interpretation of the Scriptures. Since it is difficult to understand specifically Christian attitudes toward literary allegory

[5] On the beginning of Greek allegory, see Jérome Carcopino, *De Pythagore aux apôtres* (Paris, 1956), p. 208, note 128.

[6] *Mythe et allégorie* (Paris, 1958), pp. 86-214.

[7] *Recherches sur le symbolisme funéraire des Romains* (Paris, 1942), pp. 2ff.

[8] *The Survival of the Pagan Gods* (New York, 1953).

without some knowledge of scriptural allegory, we shall begin our treatment of the subject with an examination of some of the basic principles of early Christian exegesis.

A taste for allegory among Christians was certainly encouraged by the prophetic books of the Old Testament as well as by the Parables of Christ in the Gospels,[9] but it was more than encouraged by the Epistles of St. Paul, which formed the source and inspiration for the tradition of allegorical exegesis during the Middle Ages.[10] Hence his fame in medieval art as the "miller" who grinds the "grain" of the Prophets to produce the "flour" of the New Law (Fig. 111). It should be emphasized in the first place that Pauline allegory is not simply a modification of the tradition of literary allegory which we have just been discussing, a tradition which did strongly influence Philo and the exegetical practice of the Jews.[11] The frequently repeated allegation that spiritual interpretation in the Fathers and in their medieval successors represents a reflection of "pagan and Jewish" practices is thus without foundation,[12] although it is true, of course, that an allegorical mode of thought was common among pagans, Jews, and Christians in late antiquity. St. Paul's most famous use of allegorical interpretation, which includes, in the Greek original, a form of the word *allegory*,[13] is that which appears in Galatians 4. 22ff.: "For it is written that Abraham had two sons: the one by a bondwoman [Gen. 16. 15], and the other by a freewoman [Gen. 21. 2]. But he who was of the bondwoman, was born according to the flesh: but he of the freewoman was by promise. Which things are said by an allegory. For these are the two testaments: the one from mount Sina, engendering unto bondage, which is Agar: For Sina is a mountain in Arabia which hath affinity to that Jerusalem which now is, and is in bondage with her children. But that Jerusalem which is above, is free: which is our mother. For it is written [Isa. 54. 1]: 'Rejoice, thou barren,

---

[9] On the Parables as allegories, see Pépin, *Mythe et allégorie*, pp. 252-259.

[10] On St. Paul's allegory, see Pépin, *ibid.*, pp. 247-252. On the influence of St. Paul as an exegete during the Middle Ages, see Henri de Lubac, *op.cit.*, pp. 373-383, 668-681.

[11] Pépin, pp. 221-244; Lubac, pp. 391-396.

[12] E.g., see the note by A. Devinck in *Oeuvres de Saint Augustin*, XI (Paris, 1949), pp. 567-568.

[13] The term *allegory* is said to have been used first by a grammarian around 60 B.C. It replaced the ancient term ὑπόνοια. See Pépin, pp. 85ff., Lubac, pp. 373ff.

that bearest not: break forth and cry, thou that travailest not: for many are the children of the desolate, more than of her that hath a husband.' Now we, brethren, as Isaac was, are the children of promise. But as then he that was born according to the flesh, persecuted him that was after the spirit, so also it is now. But what saith the scripture? 'Cast out the bondwoman and her son; for the son of the bondwoman shall not be made heir with the son of the freewoman.' So, then, brethren, we are not the children of the bondwoman but of the free: by the freedom wherewith Christ had made us free."

The word *allegory* here means, as it does among the grammarians, "saying one thing to mean another," but the thing said in the first place is also true. The principle involves neither the analysis of figurative language nor the interpretation of a superficially false fable. The things and events described in the Old Testament remain things and events, but they are nevertheless significant *by an allegory*. They have an application to St. Paul's contemporaries, moreover, not only as these persons may be thought of as belonging to two groups or "generations," but also as the individuals who make up these groups may or may not take advantage of the "freedom" made possible by Christ. For as St. Paul goes on to explain in the following chapter, "freedom" involves a life according to the spirit in charity, wherein there are twelve fruits. That is, the concept "son of the freewoman" implies not only an external division among men, but also an internal obligation of the individual; and the manner in which this obligation is met is obviously relevant to the individual's ultimate destiny.

In St. Paul's view the ability to see the spirit beneath the surface of the Old Testament was made possible only by the teachings of Christ [2 Cor. 3. 12-16]: "Having therefore such hope, we use much confidence: And not as Moses put a veil upon his face, that the children of Israel might not look steadfastly on the face of that which is made void. But their senses were made dull. For, until this present day, the selfsame veil, in the reading of the old testament, remaineth not taken away (because in Christ it is made void). But even until this day, when Moses is read, the veil is upon their heart. But when they shall be converted to the Lord, the veil shall be taken away."

Patristic commentators were naturally anxious that their fellow-

Christians should be able to look beneath the veil, and St. Paul gave them many hints. For example, the crossing of the Red Sea is a figure for baptism, and the rock which furnished water is a figure for Christ (1 Cor. 10. 1-6). Adam also prefigures Christ (Rom. 5. 14). The Epistles not only furnish a series of allegorical interpretations but also a series of figurative concepts which may be used to govern similar interpretations: the "flesh" (used to mean the evil habit of the flesh resulting from the Fall) as contrasted with the "spirit"; the "exterior man" as contrasted with the "interior man"; the "old man" as contrasted with the "new man"; and so on. The use of these concepts strongly suggests that spiritual meanings are to be found in the New Testament as well as in the Old. Moreover, the reference to "fit ministers of the new testament, not in the letter, but in the spirit" (2 Cor. 3. 6) followed by the warning, "the letter killeth, but the spirit quickeneth" made a constant search for spiritual understanding in the sacred texts imperative.

A detailed history of the development of St. Paul's techniques in Patristic and subsequent times would be out of place here, but a few general principles which were of profound importance for the history of medieval exegesis need emphasis. The problem before Christian exegetes was that of interpreting all of the Bible in such a way that it demonstrated the spirit as it was revealed in the acts and teachings of Christ.[14] Moreover, a necessity was felt to develop the implications of the fact that Christ had removed the "veil" from the letter. If the veil were removed, the principles discovered beneath it would obviously have implications for the Church, which sought to maintain its members in "freedom"; for the individual members of the Church, who might be more or less "free"; and for the ultimate destinies of those members with reference to "that Jerusalem which is above." The logic of these various implications is simple enough, and we can see all of them at work in Galatians 4 and 5. In the course of time names were given to these various kinds of implications. Those which referred to the Church were called *allegorical*; those which pertained to the spiritual constitution of the individual were called *tropological*; and those which referred to the afterlife were called *anagogical*. But there is nothing sacrosanct about these terms. St. Augustine,

[14] Cf. Lubac, pp. 318-328.

who was the most profound and influential spiritual exegete in the history of the Church, does not use them. Other terms were sometimes used, and the various kinds of implication were sometimes subdivided in other ways. The terms themselves are a mere convenience; what is important is the pattern of thought which underlies them. The taste for organization characteristic of the thirteenth century produced systematic statements of the various "levels," of which the following was most popular:

> Littera gesta docet, quid credas allegoria,
> Moralis quid agas, quo tendas anagogia.[15]

The danger in formulae of this kind for the modern student, however, is that they encourage him to reduce allegory to a "system." What was felt by the spiritual exegetes of the Middle Ages was not a "system" but a "spiritual understanding" which might be described rather crudely and inadequately in a series of technical terms.

The underlying logic of these spiritual levels is neither strange nor specifically Christian. The wise man at the close of the ninth book of Plato's *Republic* will "look at the city which is within him, and take heed that no disorder occur in it." He will be a ruler, not of an actual city, but of a city which exists "in idea only" patterned after a city "in heaven." These various "cities" correspond roughly with the Christian divisions of spiritual implication. The "inner" one is, as it were, "tropological"; the one "in heaven" is "anagogical"; and the one which for Plato existed "in idea only" may be thought of as analogous with the city implied allegorically in the Old Testament and realized in the Church. In Christian thought, Jerusalem might imply the ordered soul of the faithful, the City of Heaven, or the Church. This comparison is, admittedly, superficial, and it is not intended to provide support for the allegation that St. Paul was a "Platonist." There is a wide disparity between Plato's wisdom and Christian spiritual understanding. But the logic of positing analogous realms within the individual, in society, and in eternity is a fairly natural result of an hierarchical mode of thought which emphasizes the reality of abstract values. The medieval mind moved easily from one realm to another, and was

---

[15] See Lubac, pp. 23ff. The verses are said to have been used first by Augustine of Dacia, ca. 1260.

quick to seize upon and to elaborate analogies among them. It did so, moreover, with a conviction based on faith.

It will appear at once that the various kinds of implications we have suggested may be apprehended with varying degrees of profundity. That is, a tropological meaning may involve a simple description of the moral structure of the individual, it may set forth a fairly commonplace principle of morality, or it may have profound implications for the spiritual life of the individual. All of these various kinds of tropology have their uses, but the profundity of the understanding involved depends in part on the profundity of the author of the comment and in part on the degree of understanding of which the reader is capable. During the Middle Ages, the order in which spiritual implications were developed varied. Sometimes the moral meaning was developed first; at other times it was given only after the allegorical meaning. It has been suggested that the second of these procedures is the more profound,[16] since the morality then takes on a specifically Christian coloring developed from the allegorical meaning, concentrating attention on the inner implications of the principle involved.[17] On the other hand, the order which turns first to tropology may often develop a fairly simple moral meaning, consistent, perhaps, with the needs of elementary instruction. However, it should be emphasized that not every scriptural passage was thought to have a full range of implications. Some passages might apply only to the Church, some only to the individual, some only to the afterlife, and some to only two of these. Again, a given commentator might choose to emphasize only one level throughout his work. This does not mean that he did not "believe in" the others, but simply that he selected his materials for a special purpose.

If we turn once more to the verses quoted above from 2 Cor. 3, we can understand why the process of discerning the spirit beneath the letter was felt to be an aspect of the process of conversion.[18] An historical example illustrating this fact appears in St. Augustine's *Confessions* (6. 4), where the author describes the effect produced on him by the sermons of St. Ambrose, in which the "veil" was removed from the letter so that a spiritual understanding of

[16] This is the procedure followed by St. Gregory in the *Moralia*.
[17] This thesis is developed at length by Lubac, passim.
[18] Cf. Lubac, *Histoire et esprit* (Paris, 1950), p. 392.

the Old Testament was made possible. What appears to most of us to be "irrational" in scriptural allegory seemed to late antique and medieval Christians to be a reasonable and intellectually satisfying elaboration of the philosophy of the New Testament. At the same time, to those who wished earnestly for charity in their hearts nothing could have been more emotionally satisfying than the discovery of principles encouraging charity beneath the somewhat perplexing surfaces of Old Testament texts. The satisfactions of spiritual exegesis were both intellectually and emotionally very genuine, and they were closely associated with the development of faith in the mind. The fact that scientific rationalism and romantic emotionalism seek very different ends should not cause us to close our minds, at least in an historical sense, to the possibilities for fulfillment which allegory offered to our Christian forefathers.

St. Paul provided later exegetes with an example, but not with a very fully worked out theoretical basis for Christian teaching. This lack was gradually supplied in the course of time, and for the Middle Ages the most important single work describing the theoretical principles of exegesis is St. Augustine's *On Christian Doctrine*. It is significant, first of all, because of its insistence on charity as a criterion for determining whether or not a given scriptural passage is figurative. We learn in Matt. 22. 40 that "the whole law and the prophets" depend on the two precepts of charity. St. Augustine concludes, on the basis of this and other assertions like that in 1 Tim. 1. 5, that "Scripture teaches nothing but charity, nor condemns anything except cupidity" (3. 10. 15). It follows that "whatever appears in the divine Word that does not literally pertain to virtuous behavior or the truth of faith you must take to be figurative. Virtuous behavior pertains to the love of God and of one's neighbor; the truth of faith pertains to a knowledge of God and of one's neighbor" (3. 10. 14). A discipline is thus afforded for the exegete. Those passages which promote charity or condemn cupidity are to be left with their literal significance; but all figurative interpretations must promote the love of God and of one's neighbor. If they do not, the interpreter is either deceived or deceiving, and the interpretations are false.

A passage which is figurative is a passage which contains ambiguous signs. A sign is a thing—a word or an object—which is used to signify something else. Thus a scriptural passage may be figurative because it uses figurative language or tropes, or Hebrew names which require interpretation. On the other hand, it may be figurative because the things or actions mentioned in it are used to signify something else. Tropes are common in ordinary speech and in the writings of the pagans, but only the Scriptures, which were inspired by the Holy Spirit, use figurative things. As Hugh of St. Victor, the "Augustinus Secundus" of the twelfth century, put it, "the significance of things is far more excellent than that of words, because the latter is instituted by custom, the former by nature; the latter is the voice of men, the former the voice of God speaking to men."[19] In the example from Galatians quoted above, the bondwoman, the freewoman, and Jerusalem are not figures of speech but things used to stand for other things. St. Augustine assures us that "An ignorance of things makes figurative expression obscure when we are ignorant of the natures of animals, or stones, or plants, or other things which are often used in the Scriptures for purposes of constructing similitudes" (2. 16. 23). In the same way, as he goes on to explain, numbers and things pertaining to music may be significant. A primary aim of the great encyclopedias of the Middle Ages was to furnish the knowledge of things required to understand the Scriptures. Some of them, like the *De universo* of Rabanus, the *De naturis rerum* of Alexander Neckam, or the encyclopedias of Thomas of Cantimpré and Berchorius supply extensive allegorical meanings for the things discussed as well as descriptions of them. But these encyclopedias include, in addition to things mentioned in the Bible, other things which are not found there at all. As the Middle Ages progressed, the idea developed that if things in the Bible are significant, other things are significant also, so that creation itself is an allegorical book revealing beneath the "literal" or visible surfaces of objects "the invisible things of God" (Rom. 1. 20).[20]

The Scriptures thus not only contain figurative words and locutions which are allegorical in the sense that the language of pagan writings may be allegorical; they also include things which are

[19] *Didascalicon*, ed. Buttimer, pp. 96-97; *De script.*, PL, 175, cols. 20-21. Cf. the objection of John of Salisbury to finding spiritual meanings in "liberal" studies, where "not things but words alone are significant" (*Policrat.*, 7. 12).

[20] A special impetus to the development of this view was given by John the Scot. See Lubac, *Exégèse médiévale*, pp. 121-122; cf. Otto von Simson, *The Gothic Cathedral* (New York, 1956), p. 53.

allegorical in a peculiarly Christian way. During the Middle Ages the disciplines of the *trivium* were brought to bear on the literal sense of Scripture which embraced the allegory of words, while the allegory of things was left to the disciplines of the *quadrivium*. Thus after explaining the difference between figurative words and figurative things, Hugh of St. Victor wrote, "A knowledge of words is considered in two ways: that is, in pronunciation and in signification. Grammar pertains to pronunciation alone, dialectic pertains only to signification, and rhetoric pertains to both pronunciation and signification at once. A knowledge of things involves two considerations: that is, form and nature. Form appears in the external disposition of a thing; nature in its interior quality. The form of things is considered either with reference to number, to which arithmetic pertains, or to proportion, to which music pertains, or to dimension, to which geometry pertains, or to motion, to which astronomy pertains. To the interior quality of things, however, physics is relevant."[21]

Needless to say, none of these disciplines has any close counterpart in modern education. There is a very real sense in which medieval education was a preparation for the study of the Bible, and theology itself originally had this end in view.[22] The *trivium* prepared the student to confront the letter of the text; the *quadrivium* was of assistance in understanding its spirit.

Although things which are signs of other things tended to acquire certain fairly well-established values or significations, these significations might appear either *in bono* "in a good sense," or *in malo*, "in an evil sense." Moreover, in many instances a "thing" might have a series of unrelated meanings. St. Augustine describes this situation as follows (3. 25. 36-37): "Thus one thing signifies another and still another in such a way that the second thing signified is contrary to the first, or in such a way that the second thing is entirely different from the first. The things signified are contrary, that is, when one thing is used in a similitude in a good sense and in another place in an evil sense. This is the situation where the

---

[21] *De sacramentis, PL,* 176, col. 185. The term *pronunciation* is used here in its classical sense. See H. I. Marrou, *Saint Augustin et la fin de la culture antique* (Paris, 1938), p. 21.

[22] See G. Paré, A. Brunet, and P. Tremblay, *La renaissance du XII*[e] *siècle* (Paris and Ottawa, 1933), pp. 253ff.

lion is used to signify Christ, when it is said, 'The lion of the tribe of Juda ... has prevailed' [Apoc. 5. 5], but also signifies the Devil, when it is written, 'Your adversary the devil, as a roaring lion, goeth about seeking whom he may devour' [1 Pet. 5. 8]. . . . In the same way other things signify not one thing but more, and not only two diverse things, but sometimes many different things in accordance with the meaning of passages in which they are found."

The first principle, that of contraries, harmonizes generally with the medieval tendency to see things in two distinct ways: in a carnal or worldly sense, and in a spiritual sense. The virtues may be false worldly virtues (vices masquerading as virtues), or true virtues. The pagan gods frequently have "good" significations and "evil" significations, and so on. Generally, a thing of this world suggests a corresponding spiritual thing, and vice versa. It may simplify matters to say that a medieval sign, whether scriptural or not, is very often like a coin with two sides. The second principle emphasizes the fact that a sign is controlled by its context. Although St. Augustine says nothing about it, it is also clear that in exegetical practice a sign could be considerably extended by analogy, so that, for example, values could be assigned to it which would apply either to the Church, to the individual, or to the afterlife. Medieval thought is rich in analogy, and once a figurative context is established, it tends to elaborate itself through comparisons and associations with other contexts. Again, Pauline concepts like the contrast between the Old Man and the New Man furnished patterns for further elaboration. When these principles are understood, the diversity of meanings adduced for scriptural signs in handbooks like the *Distinctiones* of Alanus de Insulis, the *Allegoriae in sacram Scripturam*, or the scriptural dictionary of Berchorius becomes less confusing.

Signs also tend to acquire diverse meanings because, in spiritual exegesis, there is no such thing as a single definitive interpretation. St. Augustine welcomes the resulting diversity of interpretations as a feature of the richness of the sacred writings,[23] but to the modern student it may suggest that the whole matter of allegorical exegesis is in danger of becoming a hopeless chaos of unrelated ideas. Fortunately, certain Patristic interpretations, many of which were in-

[23] *Enn. in Ps. 126*. Cf. *On Christian Doctrine*, 2. 27. 38.

cluded in works of reference like the *Glossa ordinaria,* tended to become standardized. We may assume that after the twelfth century most literate persons were familiar with many of the interpretations which appear in standard glosses, and, directly or indirectly, with other interpretations of the Fathers. Certain works, like the *Moralia* of St. Gregory the Great[24] or St. Augustine's commentary on the Psalms, exerted a continuous influence throughout the Middle Ages, so that many of the interpretations in them became commonplaces. Diversity of interpretation, therefore, did not in the course of time produce such a wide variety of values for "things" that it was impossible to acquire a vocabulary of accepted spiritual significations.

A problem which presents considerable difficulty to the modern student arises from the fact that in actual practice spiritual exegetes do not systematically make use of every detail in the texts before them. Our more or less instinctive literal-mindedness extends to allegory, where we feel more comfortable when every single detail "fits" the general interpretation.[25] For the principle underlying much medieval practice, we may turn to a passage from St. Augustine's *City of God* (16. 2): "Yet not all things which are described as having been done are to be thought of as signifying something; but for the sake of those things which do signify something other things which do not have any signification are included. For the soil is cloven only by the plowshare, but in order that this may be done, the other parts of the plow are necessary also. And only the strings of harps and other such instruments are struck in playing; but in order that they may be plucked, other parts are included in the structure of the instruments which are not struck by those who play, but, being connected with the strings, resound when they are struck. Thus in prophetic history things are said which signify nothing [spiritually], but are, as it were, the frame to which those things which do signify are attached."

A medieval exegete frequently selects only certain details from a context with which to construct his allegory. When we consider that his basic text was often historical, this fact is not surprising.

[24] On the popularity of the *Moralia,* see *Exégèse médiévale,* pp. 537ff.

[25] Patently allegorical forms, like dream visions, for example, present less difficulty in this respect than exemplary narratives. When the latter are ornamented or reinforced with allegorical materials, as they often are, the problem becomes acute.

We may notice that in the passage from Galatians St. Paul refers to only two of Abraham's sons (cf. Gen. 25. 1ff.). We may add that the same kind of selectivity characterizes a great deal of literary interpretation of classical narratives and that medieval authors of narratives may be expected to include in their allegorical works a certain amount of non-significant framework. For the modern interpreter, these facts are disconcerting, and the only solution to the problems they generate seems to be the acquisition of a "feeling" for allegorical technique based on extensive experience with both scriptural and literary allegory.

Our texts so far have referred for the most part to significant things. These things are frequently involved in some kind of action, so that patterns of action or "things done" may be considered significant also.[26] The actions of the Old Testament are frequently thought to look forward to the actions of the New, and these in turn are prophetic of the actions of Christians in the future. The distinction between significant deeds and significant things does not seem to have troubled medieval exegetes. When St. Paul said (1 Cor. 10. 2) "And all in Moses were baptized, in the cloud, and in the sea," implying that the crossing of the Red Sea is a sign of baptism, he was not actually using a method different from that employed in his discussion of Sara and Agar. The types and antitypes of medieval art, discussed in the preceding chapter, are quite legitimate manifestations of allegory whether they depend for their force on significant actions or on significant persons. Most of them, in fact, involve both. There is no point, therefore, in seeking to differentiate between actions which are "allegorical" and things which are "symbolic." Allegory is simply the device of saying one thing to mean another, and its ulterior meaning may rest on things or on actions, or on both together.

What happens to time in spiritual exegesis may also be confusing to the modern reader who is accustomed to arranging his world within a fairly rigorous and superficially rational coordinate system of time and space. It is true that this system is sometimes violated in one way or another by modern authors of fiction for technical reasons, but these violations always presuppose a willingness on the part of the reader to make an imaginative restoration of the rational scheme. The medieval attitude toward time was

[26] Cf. the account of John the Scot in *Exégèse médiévale*, pp. 497-498.

very different from ours.[27] Specifically, an action carried out in the Old Testament may be, spiritually understood, an action described in the New Testament, and the same action, considered tropologically, becomes a potential action in the life of any man.[28] Thus allegory has the effect of reducing the events of the Old Testament, the New Testament, and one's own actions, together with those of contemporaries, to a kind of continuous present. Boethius explains in the *Consolation* that God sees what we regard as the past, the present, and the future simultaneously, since there is no time in Heaven. There is a sense in which the spiritual understanding of Christian allegory produces a similar effect, so that temporal sequence acquires something of the nature of an illusion. Patterns set by the Bible constantly repeat themselves, not in the cyclic form fashionable among modern historical metaphysicians, but continuously. Hence allegory in its general sense makes the scriptural narrative constantly relevant and immediate. The same treatment of time frequently appears in medieval literary texts. The action in the *De planctu naturae*, for example, is an action continuously taking place; men tear Nature's garment at all times in post-lapsarian history. Again, in the familiar Second Shepherd's Play of the Wakefield Cycle, there are references to Christ at a time before Christ is born in the play. The shepherds are, moreover, obviously contemporaries of the play itself who live in an English town. But the distance to the scene of the Nativity is not great for them, either in space or time, simply because the play is not about a discovery of Christ which took place once at a given moment of history, but about the discovery of Christ as any man who saw the play as it was originally produced might make it. The sufferings of the shepherds in a cold and stormy world where masters are oppressive and marriages are inverted are, moreover, not mere "reflections of contemporary life"; they are instead typical of the sufferings under the Old Law which any man may experience before he has discovered for himself what St. Paul calls "the freedom wherewith Christ hath made us free." For the purposes of the play, therefore, the Nativity is a perennial event, both historically and immediately relevant to its audience. It is not a thing

---

[27] For some hints concerning this problem, see Georges Poulet, *Studies in Human Time* (New York, 1959), pp. 3-8.

[28] See the penetrating discussion in *Exégèse médiévale*, pp. 558-571.

cut off from the audience by receding perspectives of rationally measured space and time. The underlying secret of this rather striking literary effect is tropology, at once the simplest and the most profound of the spiritual senses.

What, we may ask, was the attitude of those exegetes who insisted on following St. Paul's allegorical techniques toward the literal or historical sense of the Bible? Turning once more to St. Augustine's *On Christian Doctrine* (3. 5. 9), we find the following stern warning: "At the outset you must be very careful lest you take figurative expressions literally. What the Apostle says pertains to this problem: 'For the letter killeth, but the spirit quickeneth.' That is, when that which is said figuratively is taken as though it were literal, it is understood carnally. Nor can anything more appropriately be called the death of the soul [cf. Rom. 8. 6] than that condition in which the thing which distinguishes us from beasts, which is the understanding, is subjected to the flesh in the pursuit of the letter."[29]

John the Scot assures us that St. Paul's admonition against the letter applies to "all mystical figures, whether in words, or in deeds, or in sensible things" anywhere in the Bible,[30] and it would be possible to amass a long list of similar statements throughout the Middle Ages, many of which refer also to Rom. 7. 6: "But now we are loosed from the law of death wherein we were detained, so that we should serve in newness of spirit, and not in the oldness of the letter." The great scriptural dictionary of Berchorius written in the fourteenth century contains the following observations under the heading *Litera*: "In the third place I say that there are certain literal passages which sensibly conceal the truth and are therefore to be penetrated. These, indeed, are the literal meanings of the antique law, and also historical things expressed literally— those passages, that is, under whose cortex the sense of divine understanding is contained so that they have an interior signification, in spite of the fact that they seem to say something else externally. For just as honey is contained in a honeycomb and is clarified and pressed forth, in the same way the letter contains an inner sense which is to be taken forth and held by right understanding reached through appropriate exposition. For this is the letter that kills,

[29] Cf. *On the Spirit and the Letter*, 6.
[30] *Super ier. coel., PL*, 122, cols. 170-171.

the old letter, since he who follows it according to its external appearance is killed by infidelity and made ancient in vices. The spirit, or the spiritual sense, is to be sought, but the literal, indeed, is to be wholly cast aside."

Berchorius goes on to cite 2 Cor. 3. 6, Rom. 7. 6, and the authority of St. Augustine. His figure of the honeycomb and the honey is a commonplace of exegesis.[31] Moreover, the idea that the letter is "old," "sterile," or "unprofitable" is constantly reiterated by medieval commentators.[32] Condemnations such as these and continual admonitions to the effect that the letter should be "cast aside" have led many modern historians to the conclusion that spiritual exegetes "neglected the literal sense." But nothing could be more mistaken.

The condemnations are directed against the letter only insofar as it is taken without the spirit, and not against the letter itself. To use an analogy, medieval authors condemn the flesh, not because they have forgotten that "no man hates his own flesh," but because they wish to condemn the flesh as it operates without the guidance of the spirit. They condemn women, not because there is anything intrinsically evil about women, but because women may be easily regarded as a source of fleshly rather than spiritual satisfaction. The letter is in this sense like the world itself; it should be used rather than abused. Properly used, it is indispensable, for it leads to spiritual understanding. But abused, or taken for its own sake, it becomes an evil. Far from neglecting the letter, spiritual exegetes from Patristic times onward regarded it as the foundation of spiritual understanding. Just as Christ came to fulfill the law and not to destroy it, so also His teaching "fulfilled" the letter. What was to be "cast aside" was the letter without divine understanding. No one denied the necessity for understanding the literal meaning of the text; in fact, there is an almost unanimous insistence on this point.[33] The Old Testament is a Christian document only when it is "unveiled," and it can be unveiled only in the light of the New. On the façade of Notre Dame de Poitiers two figures may be seen embracing, the Old Law and the New, which, taken together, constitute the foundation of Christian teaching (Fig. 114).

[31] See *Exégèse médiévale*, pp. 599ff.　　[32] *Ibid.*, pp. 439ff.
[33] Cf. Lubac, "Le 'quadruple sens' de l'écriture," *Melanges F. Cavallera* (Toulouse, 1948), pp. 352, 355, and *Exégèse médiévale*, pp. 425-439.

Obviously, if the literal meaning of the Old Testament is not understood, its spiritual implications cannot be understood either.

It is true that medieval students did not have at their disposal modern scientific techniques of historical and philological analysis, so that their conceptions of the history underlying much of the Biblical text and of accuracy in translation and quotation were different from ours; but they did have a keen eye for the subtleties of figurative language and a trained awareness of the nature of logical coherence. The arts of the *trivium* gave them a certain advantage over modern students in these respects. With such tools as they had, they did their best to clarify and explain the literal sense. An interest in the letter does not, in the Middle Ages, imply a neglect of the spirit; and, on the other hand, an interest in allegory does not imply a neglect of the letter. Thus it is possible to cite instances of commentators who devoted much attention to both the letter and the spirit; St. Jerome, St. Thomas Aquinas, Nicolas de Lyra, and, in the Renaissance, Erasmus, all afford excellent illustrations of this point.[34] We should be careful, in short, not to regard the letter and the spirit as modern "opposites" which are mutually exclusive. The letter is an evil only when it is not understood spiritually, but remains the basis for spiritual understanding.

A current fashion has it that the spiritual interpretation of Scripture "declined" after the twelfth century, or after the middle of the thirteenth century, as if, in these late days, St. Paul were little remembered. Since this misapprehension has been popular especially among literary scholars who do not wish to add exegetical materials to the burden of learning which already bends their weary backs, it may be worthwhile to examine it in some detail. St. Thomas assembled the conventions of spiritual exegesis and gave them, with typical Gothic taste, an ordered, logical, and systematic exposition, but this fact does not mean that he was responsible for a change in exegetical fashion. A modern historian writes, "Grâce à son analyse des modes de signification des mots signifiants, et des choses signieés et signifiantes, il donnait décidément à l'exégèse littérale toute sa valeur, et réduisait considérablement l'intérêt des interprétations mystiques du haut Moyen Age."[35]

---

[34] On St. Jerome as an allegorical exegete, see *Exégèse médiévale*, p. 663.
[35] C. Spicq, o.p., *Esquisse d'une histoire de l'exégèse latine au moyen age*

As a matter of fact, St. Thomas gave no new values to literal exegesis, and his discussion of words and things is basically Augustinian.
Furthermore, even if he had belittled the value of the spiritual
interpretation—which he did not—it is doubtful that his influence
was great enough during the later Middle Ages outside of the
Dominican order to effect any appreciable change in exegetical
taste. Again, another historian finds that "the spiritual exposition
receded into the background in the second half of the thirteenth
century," so that in writing spiritual commentaries Bishop Grosseteste "represented the past."[36] If this is true, it must be admitted
that many of Grosseteste's contemporaries and successors "represented the past" in the same way. We might mention, for example,
Hugh of St. Cher (d. 1263), St. Bonaventura, whose great commentary on Luke is especially rich in allegorical conventions, or
Nicolas de Goran (d. 1295). In the fourteenth century Nicolas de
Lyra's influential *Moralitates* is certainly neither literal nor out of
date.

The most celebrated English exegete of the fourteenth century
was Robert Holcot, whose commentary on the Book of Wisdom
has been called "one of the best-sellers of the age."[37] Those who
seek a weakening of the allegorical method in this commentary will
be disappointed. It is true that the work does not have the flavor
of a twelfth-century commentary, and it certainly lacks the force
of Patristic commentaries, but its peculiarities are not due to literalism. At times the *lectiones*, into which the work is divided, contain fairly elaborate allegorical essays. Lectio xxviii, for example,
discusses seven types of spiritual blindness corresponding to the
seven principal vices and to seven exemplars in the Bible. In Lectio
ci there is an elaboration of the figure of *dentes* for *doctores* made
famous by the passage in St. Augustine's *On Christian Doctrine*
concerning the obscurity of Scripture discussed in Chapter 11 above.
Lectio cxxxiii develops another familiar Augustinian figure where-

(Paris, 1944), p. 288. On Spicq's attitude toward scriptural allegory, cf. P.
Dumontier, *Saint Bernard et la Bible* (Paris, 1953), p. 142, note 1.

[36] Beryl Smalley in D. A. Callus, ed., *Robert Grosseteste* (Oxford, 1955), p. 86.

[37] Citations are from the edition printed very badly at Hagenau (1494). On
the popularity of the work, see W. A. Pantin, *The English Church in the Fourteenth Century* (Cambridge, 1955), p. 145.

in the sea is taken to represent the world.[38] A long series of figurative meanings for *aqua* appears in Lectio CXXXVII, and in Lectio CLXXXII there is an extended argument to show that manna should be taken as a figure for the Eucharist. In addition to extended allegorical discussions such as these, there are innumerable incidental uses of allegory. It is noteworthy in this connection that Holcot makes frequent references to the *Moralia* of St. Gregory the Great. The book contains a number of scholastic *quaestiones*, but they by no means dominate it. Thus in Lectio XXI, after explaining in traditional fashion that the roses of Sap. 2. 8 are signs of *luxuria*, Holcot introduces a *dubitatio literalis* which sets forth the problem "Whether simple fornication is a mortal sin." The contrary argument, which is, of course, refuted, is given at length. It may well be a variant of the argument condemned by thirteenth-century English bishops and by Bishop Tempier at Paris;[39] but in any event, it simply adds weight to Holcot's condemnation of the false roses of the text. In the closing section of the book, entitled "On the Study of Sacred Scripture," Holcot explains, quoting Hugh of St. Victor, that "In the refectory of the Sacred Scriptures three tables, or three understandings, are placed: historical, mystical, and moral. The first of these is for the simple, the second for the learned, and the third for both. On the first the food is coarser, on the second more subtle, and on the third sweeter." The "mystical" sense here was probably intended to embrace both allegory and anagogy.[40] The prologue to the book as a whole contains a quotation from the *Didascalicon* (4. 1) reflecting the figure of the honeycomb: "The divine Words are most aptly compared with a honeycomb, for they also because of the simplicity of their expression appear dry on the outside and are filled with sweetness within."

What distinguishes Holcot's commentary is not literalism, but a typically fourteenth-century richness in moralizations. Almost

---

[38] See Henri Rondet, s.j., "Le symbolisme de la mer chez saint Augustin," *Augustinus Magister* (Paris, 1954), II, 691-701.

[39] D. Wilkins, *Concilia Magnae Britanniae et Hiberniae* (London, 1737), I, 577, 636-637, 659; II, 143. Where the thirteenth century is concerned, this work should be used in conjunction with C. R. Cheney, *English Synodalia of the Thirteenth Century* (Oxford, 1941). Cf. Denifle-Chatelain, *Chartularium universitatis Parisiensis*, I, 553.

[40] Cf. Lubac, "Le 'quadruple sens,'" pp. 348-349.

anything is capable of producing a moral lesson. In Lectio IV, for example, Albertus Magnus is cited to the effect that if one throws finely powdered sulphur on a candle which has just been extinguished, it will light again. In the same way, *moraliter*, the flames of delight, once extinguished, are relighted with the sulphur of *luxuria*, for "Sulphur is hot, stinking, and tenacious, and signifies lechery." Elsewhere passages from the *Historia regum Britanniae* of Geoffrey of Monmouth are moralized. There is, in addition, a great deal of moralized natural history. Thus in Lectio IX, for example, we learn that a hyena figures a detractor, and Lectio LXIV is devoted to a moralized account of birds of various kinds. The mythographers are used frequently, so that in Lectio CXL we find, for instance, that Mercury is depicted "with the head of a dog, and a dog is a most sagacious animal, and Mercury is the god of eloquence." Again, Holcot's discussions of Ovidian stories resemble at times those given later by Berchorius. Thus in Lectio XXXVI he says, "Morally, a literate clerk is like Argus." Berchorius describes Argus as a "circumspect prelate."[41] Both authors take Hippomenes in the story of Atalanta's race to represent the Devil, but the three golden apples are given slightly different emphases. Holcot makes them lecherous delight, pride, and avarice (Lectio XIII), which represent a variation of the standard triple temptation of gluttony, vainglory, and avarice.[42] Berchorius places the same temptations in the order avarice, lechery, and pride.[43] In one instance, the story of Alcyone (Lectio CXCI), Berchorius acknowledges that he borrows his interpretation directly from Holcot's commentary.[44]

Holcot was at one time a member of the circle of distinguished scholars gathered together in the household of Richard de Bury.[45] It is of some interest to know what Richard's attitude toward scriptural exegesis may have been, and there is sufficient evidence in the *Philobiblon* to give us more than an inkling. In his attack on the mendicant friars (6. 44-53), Richard deplores their neglect of the Bible in the following highly significant terms: "Holy Scrip-

[41] *Metamorphosis ovidiana* (Paris, 1515), fol. xxiii verso.

[42] See Lombard, *Sententiae*, 2. 21. 5. Holcot's moralization is borrowed word for word in one of the sermons attributed to Thomas Brinton, ed. Sister Mary Aquinas Devlin, O.P. (London, 1954), "Camden Third Series," LXXV, LXXVI, p. 41.

[43] *Op.cit.*, fol. lxxxv recto.   [44] *Ibid.*, fol. lxxxvii verso.

[45] See Pantin, *op.cit.*, pp. 139-140.

ture is not expounded, but altogether set aside, as though it were commonplace and made known to all. Yet hardly any have touched its hem [cf. Matt. 14. 36]; for such is the profundity of its words that it cannot be comprehended by the human understanding, even if it devotes its greatest effort and most profound study to it, as St. Augustine asserts. He who gives himself to it assiduously, if only He who created the spirit of piety will open the door [Col. 4. 3], may extract from its nucleus [*enucleare*] a thousand lessons of moral discipline which will not only be powerful in most recent newness [cf. Rom. 7. 6], but will also refresh the understandings of the auditors with a most savory sweetness."

The reference to St. Augustine probably recalls an Epistle to Volusianus (137. 1. 3), where the relevant passage reads: "For such is the depth of the Christian Scriptures, that even if I were attempting to study them and nothing else from early boyhood to decrepit old age, with the utmost leisure, the most unwearied zeal, and talents greater than I have, I would still daily be making progress in discovering their treasures; not that there is so great difficulty in coming through them to know the things necessary to salvation, but when anyone has accepted these truths with a faith that is indispensable as a foundation of a life of piety and uprightness, so many things which are veiled under manifold shadows of mystery remain to be inquired into by those who are advancing in the study, and so great is the depth of wisdom not only in the words in which these have been expressed, but also in the things themselves, that the experience of the oldest, the ablest, and the most zealous students of Scripture illustrates what Scripture itself has said: 'When a man hath done, then he beginneth' " [Ecclus. 18. 6].[46]

The reference therefore suggests that Richard was urging the friars, some of whom may have been occupied with other matters, to expound the spiritual sense of the Bible. But if there is any doubt about the nature of the reference and its meaning, it is completely dispelled by the language which follows. For the "door" of Colossians is a "door of speech to speak the mystery of Christ," and the "newness" of Romans is, as we have seen, contrasted with the "oldness of the letter" in a passage conventionally used to condemn the practice of taking the letter without the spirit. More-

[46] Trans. by the Rev. J. G. Cunningham.

308

over, the verb *enucleare* is a common means of expressing the
process by which the *nucleus* of the spirit is derived from the *cortex* of the letter. Finally, the "sweetness" of the spiritual sense
is still another exegetical commonplace. In short, there can be no
doubt whatsoever that Richard de Bury, almost a hundred years
after the death of Grosseteste, was strongly urging the friars to
expound the spiritual sense of the Scriptures. To say that Richard,
who moved in the most advanced intellectual circles in England,
"represented the past" in this respect would be absurd. We may add
that the assumption of scriptural allegory had a pervasive influence
on the style of the *Philobiblon*. When Richard accuses the mendicants of producing unlearned preachers, he says (6. 91-95), "Surely, you are plowing in a manner contrary to the law with an ox
and an ass [Deut. 22. 10] when you commit learned and unlearned
alike to the cultivation of the Lord's field. It is written [Job 1. 14],
'The oxes were ploughing, and the asses feeding beside them';
whence it is right for the discreet to preach, but for the simple to
feed themselves in silence through hearing the sacred eloquence."
No one is here literally accused of plowing the soil of medieval
England with teams made up of oxes and asses; rather, Richard
refers to a traditional allegory like that of St. Gregory, who says,
with reference to the passage from Deuteronomy, "Do not associate fools with wise men in preaching, lest he who is incapable
hinder him who is capable."[47] Richard simply carries out this figure
in his interpretation of the passage from Job, and he does so in a
manner that is far from being literal. This is only one instance of a
figurative expression in the *Philobiblon* which would have been
impossible without a background of allegorical exegesis. The texture of the work is richly interwoven with similar figures.

If we turn our attention to France, we find that the most distinguished exegetical writer of the mid-century was Berchorius,
friend of Petrarch and Philippe de Vitry, translator of Livy, and
author of a commentary on the *Metamorphoses* of Ovid. As we
have seen, Berchorius adopted a traditional Patristic attitude toward the literal sense of Scripture. He is the author of a commentary which covers most of the Bible, and also of what is perhaps the
most elaborate scriptural dictionary ever compiled, rich in allegorical meanings of all kinds for things, deeds, and concepts mentioned

---

[47] *Moralia, PL,* 175, col. 537. Cf. 1 Tim. 5. 18-19.

in the Bible. The nature of the commentary may be indicated by quoting a brief passage from the beginning. Discussing creation, Berchorius says, "It seems proper that just as God conducted Himself in the creation of this greater world, so also He conducts Himself in the lesser world, that is, in the creation of man and in the composition of man's moral nature. I say, therefore, that the light is faith, the firmament is hope, and the superior waters are tribulations sent by God. But the inferior waters are temptations born of the flesh. The earth is the body, the herbs and trees are good works, the fruits and seeds are virtues and merits. . . ."[48]

Among meanings for Paradise, Berchorius lists the Glorious Virgin, Holy Church, and the conscience of just men. Throughout the commentary the emphasis is tropological, but this fact by no means detracts from its spiritual nature. The author's moralization of the encyclopedia of Bartholomew Anglicanus reveals much the same kind of taste for discerning the moral significances of things that we found in Holcot. The two authors, in fact, are very similar in style and outlook. Taken together, the works of Berchorius, aside from the translation of Livy, constitute a veritable monument to the allegorical habit of thought as it flourished during the later Middle Ages. Far from indicating a "decline" in spiritual interpretation, they contain almost overwhelming evidence for a keen popular interest in allegorical analysis of both the Book of God's Word and the Book of God's Work,[49] and an astonishing knowledge on the part of the author of the traditions of spiritual interpretation. The same kind of interest is apparent among literary men of the period. The poetic theories of Dante, for whom the allegorical meaning of the Bible was most important,[50] of Mussato, Petrarch, Boccaccio, and Salutati, are all founded on the assumption that the Scriptures are allegorical. And the writings of Philippe de Mézières in France, and of Gower in England, are filled with echoes of traditional allegorical exegesis.[51]

[48] *Opera* (Cologne, 1730-1731), I, I.

[49] The works of Berchorius have been used extensively by historians of art interested in early Renaissance iconology. Literary historians, on the other hand, have neglected them.

[50] See A. Valensin, *Le Christianisme de Dante* (Paris, 1954), p. 32. The notion sometimes expressed that Dante's *De monarchia* was a blow to traditional allegory may be dispelled simply by reading that work carefully.

[51] Philippe's *repraesentatio figurata* for the Feast of the Presentation of the

During the later Middle Ages, the spiritual interpretation was neglected in certain quarters, but this fact is not evidence for its "decline." As we have seen, there is no such thing as a single "definitive" spiritual interpretation of a scriptural passage. It follows that allegorical readings are of no use in scholastic debate, which, to be effective, must confine itself either to the "more open" places in Scripture or to principles that may be adduced therefrom. The avoidance of allegory in technical theology is thus not surprising. The new interest in Aristotle also produced commentaries which proceed by systematically exploiting Aristotelian "causes." But these works are simply exercises with a new tool; their existence, which is certainly not something to be hailed as a great achievement, may be a testimonial to the pedantry of their authors, but it does not necessarily imply that those authors did not believe in spiritual interpretation. Nevertheless, Aristotelian exposition produced a reaction, the beginnings of which may be seen in the protests of William of St. Amour. Toward the close of the Prologue to his *De periculis novissimorum temporum*, William asserts that he is ready to dispute with anyone who attacks his work "not by philosophical and sophistical disputation and altercation, but rather by catholic collation, which alone should take place among servants of God and Christ, according to the teaching of the Apostle, 2. Tim. 2. 14, where it is said, 'Contend thou not in

---

Virgin, which had the approval of many learned authorities in the Papal retinue at Avignon, was, as he explained, specifically designed so that the spectators might be led to see the mysteries of the invisible beneath the actions displayed. The costumes are colored with an eye to traditional scriptural symbolism, and the speeches at times rely on the allegorical interpretation of the Canticle of Canticles. The same author's *Livre de la vertu du sacrament de mariage*, which contains a version of the Griselda story, sets forth a very elaborate allegorical development of the idea of marriage based on conventional treatments of the subject with special reference to the *Soliloquium de Arrha animae* of Hugh of St. Victor. The *Songe du vieil pèlerin* is based on an allegorical elaboration of the Parable of the Talents derived from St. Gregory the Great. On the last work, see Dora M. Bell, *Etude sur le songe du vieil pèlerin de Philippe de Mézières* (Geneva, 1955). An edition of Philippe's works would make certain aspects of late fourteenth-century taste considerably clearer. Gower made extensive use of Petrus Riga's *Aurora* for allegorical purposes. See Paul E. Beichner, "Gower's use of *Aurora* in *Vox Clamantis*," *Speculum*, xxx (1955), p. 589. The *Aurora*, also admired by Salutati, *Epistolario*, iv, 231-232, has been neglected largely because of prejudice against allegory. For an especially blatant expression of this prejudice, see J. de Ghellinck, *L'essor de la littérature latine au XIIe siècle* (Paris, 1946), ii, 215.

words, for it is to no profit but to the subjecting of the hearers.' "[52] "Catholic collation," in William's view, is argument based on "the truth of sacred Scripture." Since he refers with great respect to the *Consolation* of Boethius in a context where almost all other authority rests on Scripture, the Gloss, and the Fathers,[53] we may conclude that his animus was directed against a particular kind of philosophy, not philosophy in general. Among the signs which William lists as means by which false prophets may be distinguished from their true counterparts, the thirty-ninth is that "true apostles neither devote their attention to nor use logical and sophistical reasoning,"[54] a fact which strongly suggests that he was troubled by the scholastic device of reasoning by syllogisms. John of Salisbury had defined philosophy after the manner of Plato and St. Augustine (*City of God*, 8. 1): "If, according to Plato a philosopher is a lover of God, what else, then, is philosophy except the love of Divinity? . . . Indeed, he who in his philosophising either acquires or spreads charity has attained the end of his philosophy."[55] But the study of philosophy "according to Aristotle" led to a position which was rather different. As Boethius of Dacia so aptly and indiscreetly put it, "A syllogistic demonstration leads to knowledge, as it is written in the first part of the *Posterior Analytics*, and faith is not knowledge [*scientia*]."[56] Neither is *scientia* wisdom. Philosophy in both senses persisted throughout the later Middle Ages, and although William officially lost his argument, there were others who objected violently to the rhetoric of Aristotelian logic. Petrarch's contempt for syllogistic reasoning as expressed in the *De sui ipsius et multorum ignorantia* is, to say the least, virulent; and in the Renaissance Erasmus was still complaining, "What is more disparate from the style of the Apostles than that in which those who follow Thomas and Scotus now dispute of things divine?"[57] For the most part, however, the scholastic philosophers employed their own methods for their own purposes, without either coming into conflict with or opposing the

---

[52] Quoted from the text in Vlastimil Kybal, *Mattiae de Janov . . . regulae veteris et novi Testamenti* (Innsbruck, 1908-1913), III, 255-256. William goes on to support his argument by quoting the Glossa. See *PL*, 114, col. 635.

[53] Kybal, p. 259.   [54] *Ibid.*, p. 313.

[55] *Policrat.*, 7. 11.

[56] *De mundi aeternitate*, ed. Géza Sajó (Budapest, 1954), p. 119.

[57] See the discussion in *Ratio verae theologiae*, *Opera* (Basel, 1576), V, 82-83.

traditions of Patristic exegesis.[58] Aristotelian jargon became a convenient academic refuge which was not effectively challenged until the time of Locke.

A more serious kind of neglect of Patristic learning was attributed to students of law. Thus Dante wrote to the Italian cardinals, urging them to study Gregory, Ambrose, Augustine, Dionysius, John of Damascus, and Bede rather than canon law, with the evident implication that they were in danger of spiritual aridity.[59] A similar complaint is registered by Berchorius: "Is it not true that Augustine, Jerome, Ambrose, Origen, and others were doves full of divine learning? . . . But there are today many legists and canonists who vilify such learned ones, and fall upon them with arrows of detraction and calumny."[60] He goes on to say that there are such men at the Papal court. Richard de Bury (*Phil.* II. I-5) makes a similar point concerning civil lawyers: "It may be said of the lucrative skill at positive law that the more usefully it serves the children of this world, the less it assists the children of light to understand the mysteries of the sacred Scriptures and the secret sacraments of the faith, since it especially disposes one to a friendship with the world, by which a man, as James testifies [James 4. 4], is made an enemy of God." For similar reasons Boccaccio places lawyers among the enemies of poetry in the fourteenth book of the *Genealogie.* We may recall also the lawyers of the Prologue to *Piers Plowman* who

[58] Among the very few attacks on spiritual exegesis is that which appears in the *De legibus* of William of Auvergne, *Opera* (Venice, 1591), 46-47. William says that there are four types of non-literal signification in the Bible: (1) when things are done for the purpose of signifying something else, (2) when something is said expressly for the purpose of signifying something else, as in the parables, (3) when a consequence may be applied, in instances, for example, where a literal prohibition may be made spiritual, and (4) when a significance may be made by a similitude in an instance where things are not done for the purpose of signification. William's peculiarity lies in the fact that he would place some passages in class 4 which others would place in class 1. For example, in discussing the story of David and Bathsheba, he says that when David's rather shocking love for Bathsheba is said to be a sign of the love of Christ for the Church, many are offended. He advises using a simile instead in such instances: "Just as David loved Bathsheba, so also etc." William was very partial to rhetorical comparisons of this kind. His views in *De faciebus mundi*, Oxford, ms Bodl. 281, if he is indeed the author, are more conventional.

[59] *Epistolae*, ed. Monti (Milan, 1921), pp. 284-286.

[60] *Opera*, IV, 475.

Plededen for penyes   and poundes the lawe,
And nougt for loue of oure lord   vnlese here lippes onis,

or the very successful and legally learned sergeant of the Prologue
to *The Canterbury Tales*. But we may safely assume that most
poets, artists, and humanists of the fourteenth century had a proper
respect for Patristic learning and for "the mysteries of the sacred
Scriptures" which that learning revealed, and were not deeply
interested either in syllogistic reasoning or the intricacies of the
law.

There seems to have been very little exegetical activity during
the second half of the fourteenth century, but there is no evidence
to indicate that allegorical exposition ceased suddenly to be esteemed
at any time during the Middle Ages. The prologue to the Wiclifite
Bible admonishes its readers to take the four levels of meaning
into account and recommends St. Augustine's *On Christian Doctrine* as an authority on scriptural allegory.[61] In the Renaissance
Erasmus was a staunch defender of the spiritual interpretation.
The words of Scripture, he explains, conceal an underlying mystery: "If anyone handles the surface, and, as it were, the *siliqua*,
what is more hard and more bitter? . . . Dig out the spiritual sense,
for there is nothing more sweet, nothing more succulent."[62] A
spiritual meditation on one little verse is worth more, he affirms,
than the whole Psalter read according to the letter.[63] Among exegetes, he recommends for study those who depart most of all
from the letter, that is, after St. Paul, Origen, Ambrose, Jerome,
and Augustine.[64] His explanation of the function of scriptural obscurity closely parallels that of St. Augustine, whose work *On
Christian Doctrine* is mentioned as an authority.[65] In short, the
opinions of Erasmus on exegetical matters are basically traditional.
It is quite likely that his views were shared by many of his contemporaries, and the works in which he expressed them were extremely influential. The possibility that Chaucer or any other
prominent poet of the fourteenth century could take a literal view

[61] See Margaret Deanesley, *The Lollard Bible* (Cambridge, 1920), pp. 264-
265, and the edition of Forshall and Madden (Oxford, 1850), I, 43-44.

[62] *Opera* (Leyden, 1703-1706), v, 7. On *siliqua*, cf. St. Augustine, *On Christian Doctrine*, 3. 7. 11.

[63] *Opera*, v, 8. Cf. 371ff.   [64] *Ibid.*, v, 8, and 133.

[65] *Ibid.*, v, 1047; cf. 117.

of the Bible is, historically speaking, extremely unlikely. It may be true that allegory did not flourish in scholastic debate, but nothing else of any literary importance flourished there either.

It will help us to understand the traditions of literary allegory in the Middle Ages if we familiarize ourselves with a few terms which were used in both scriptural and literary exposition. One of the most important of these is *sententia*, or, in Middle English, *sentence*, a word with special meanings in rhetoric and scholastic disputation which acquired an exegetical application in the twelfth century.[66] As Hugh of St. Victor explains in the *Didascalicon*, the exposition of a text involves the examination of three things: the *letter*, the *sense*, and the *sentence*.[67] A study of the letter involves the techniques of grammatical analysis. The sense is the obvious or surface meaning of a text, and the sentence is its doctrinal content or "higher" meaning. All texts, by virtue of the fact that they are texts, have a letter to be studied; some have letter and sense alone; some, which are meaningless without interpretation, have only letter and sentence; and some have all three. The purpose of exposition is to arrive at the *sentence*, since a text which has no third level does not require explanation. Following this convention, it became customary after the twelfth century to speak of the import of a text, whether sacred or profane, as its *sentence*. It should be remembered, however, that an older convention used only two terms: *letter* and *sense*. When this convention was employed, as it was down through the sixteenth century at least, the *letter* involves what Hugh called the sense, and the *sense* involves what Hugh called the sentence. Hence *letter* may mean either (1) the grammatical construction of a text, or (2) its obvious meaning. *Sense* may mean either (1) the final meaning of a text achieved through exposition, or (2) the obvious meaning of a text. But *sentence* when used in connection with a text or the interpretation of a text always means its doctrinal implication. In actual practice, the convention being employed in specific instances is almost always clear, so that the disparity in terminology causes little confu-

[66] See Paré, Brunet, and Tremblay, *op.cit.*, pp. 267-274. Cf. pp. 116-119, 228. For these and other terms, cf. D. W. Robertson, Jr., "Some Medieval Literary Terminology," *SP*, XLVIII (1951), 669-692.

[67] Ed. Buttimer, pp. 58, 125. Cf. E. de Bruyne, *Etudes d'esthétique médiévale* (Bruges, 1946), II, 324-329; and Guilbert of Tournai, *De modo addiscendi*, ed. E. Bonifacio (Turin, 1953), p. 90.

sion. The result of allegorical interpretation might be called either *sense* or *sentence*. The latter term was somewhat more popular during the fourteenth century.

Common synonyms for *allegoria* in the twelfth century were *integumentum* and *involucrum*, which, since they have in this connection a very special application, are better left untranslated.[68] Although they were occasionally used in scriptural exegesis, their use was much more widespread in the philosophical analysis of profane texts, which might be either poetic, like the *Aeneid* or the *Metamorphoses*, or philosophical, like the *Timaeus* or the *Consolation* of Boethius. One feature of these terms is especially important to bear in mind. Just as there is no single definitive allegorical interpretation of a scriptural passage, there is also no single definitive interpretation of something said *per integumentum*. The same *integumentum* may cover different underlying ideas, and the same idea may appear under different *integumenta*. Generally, in the twelfth century the terms *integumentum* and *involucrum*, which are synonyms, are applied only to fabulous material, or, that is, to material whose literal meaning is not true, so that, with this restriction in mind, it would be proper to employ them in connection with the Scriptures only when fables, like that of the trees in Judges 9. 8-15, are being discussed. The use of *integumentum* in the twelfth century reveals a very significant fact: the basic method of analyzing philosophical texts which could not be taken literally was identical with the method used to analyze poetic texts. A commentary on the *Aeneid* was just as respectable "philosophically" as a commentary on the *Timaeus*.

Meanwhile, a whole series of figurative terms of scriptural origin were used in connection with both sacred and profane texts, and these terms carried with them the richness of connotation which their origin implies. In Isa. 11. 7 we read that "the lion shall eat straw [*paleus*] like the ox." The Glossa tells us that "the princes of this world and other simple persons are content with the surface of the history, for they do not understand the wheat and the pith, or the inner sense."[69] In Jer. 23. 28, we find the text "What hath the

---

[68] For an excellent discussion of these terms, see Edouard Jeauneau, "L'usage de la notion d'*integumentum* à travers les gloses de Guillaume de Conches," *Archives d'hist. doct. et litt. du m. a.*, xxxii (1957), 35-100.

[69] *PL*, 113, col. 1251. Cf. Isa. 65. 25 and *PL*, 113, cols. 1311-1312.

chaff to do with the wheat, saith the Lord?" The Glossa explains that "the pleasing doctrine of heretics is compared with chaff, for chaff has no pith, nor does it offer refreshment."[70] On the basis of interpretations like these the convention displayed in the prologue to the Canticle of Canticles quoted in Chapter II above developed: "He who uses human reason, therefore, will cast aside the chaff and hasten to eat the grain of the spirit." Again, Jacob's rods, as they are described in Gen. 30. 37, gave rise to a contrast between the *cortex* and an inner *candor*. Thus Rabanus wrote, "What does it mean to place green rods of almond and plane before the eyes of the flock except to offer as example to the people the lives and lessons of the ancient Fathers as they appear throughout the Scriptures? . . . And when from these the bark [*cortex*] of the letter is taken away, the interior whiteness is shown allegorically."[71] It is noteworthy that the meanings of these and similar terms may be extended to other levels. In Matt. 3. 12 it is said that "the chaff he will burn with unquenchable fire." The Glossa explains that here the chaff represents "those who have been imbued with the faith of the sacraments, but are not firm in it."[72] Like other scriptural figures, these carry with them an almost automatic set of analogies. A person who is "chaffy" or has no "pith" exhibits a taste for "chaff" or bran and is destined to be "burned with unquenchable fire." Such a person, moreover, produces the "chaff" of heretical doctrines. There are other terms of this kind, like *fructus, nucleus, farina,* and so on, all of which have considerably more force than mere figures of speech.

2. CHAUCER'S EXEGETES

There are a number of exegetes in Chaucer's *Canterbury Tales,* some casually so and some professionally. Among the more prominent are the wife of Bath, the friar in the Summoner's Tale, the pardoner, and the parson. Of these, the first is hopelessly carnal and literal, the second is an arrant hypocrite, the third is aware of the spirit but defies it, and the last is, from a fourteenth-century point of view, altogether admirable. A very brief discussion of the techniques employed by each will make these points clear. The wife, who is hailed by the pardoner as a "noble prechour" and com-

[70] *PL,* 114, col. 39.   [71] *PL,* 107, col. 603.
[72] *PL,* 114, col. 821.

mended by our "leeve maister" the friar for touching "in scole-matere greet difficultee," begins the little sermon which forms the first part of her prologue by citing "experience," the source of the worldly wisdom of La Vieille in the *Roman de la rose* (12805), as opposed to "auctoritee," as the basis for her knowledge of "wo that is in mariage." Her conclusions turn out to be considerably at variance with those of received authority, which she does not hesi-tate to quote. Where the Scriptures are concerned, her empirical attitude is, as we might expect, a very carnal one.

She begins by attacking two arguments familiar in St. Jerome's *Adversus Jovinianum*: (1) that since Christ went to only one wed-ding, at Cana, no one should marry more than once, (2) that when Christ said to the Samaritan, "that ilke man that now hath thee is noght thyn housbonde," He implied that where there are more marriages than one, a true husband does not exist.[73] With reference to the latter argument, she says,

> What that he mente therby, I kan nat seyn,
> But that I axe, why that the fifthe man
> Was noon housbonde to the Samaritan?

Now it is undoubtedly true that Chaucer here and elsewhere in the prologue was borrowing from the *Adversus Jovinianum*, and that the wife takes up a position somewhat like that of Jovinian whom Jerome called an "Epicurus among Christians." But it is also true that Chaucer does not simply paraphrase this source; the ma-terials are presented in an order different from that in Jerome, and we may assume that Chaucer's arrangement of his materials was purposeful. Moreover, both of the scriptural allusions with which the wife begins had connotations outside of Jerome, which, taken together, serve to heighten the import of what is being said. Chau-cer does not say to his audience, "Confine your associations to the *Adversus Jovinianum*, which I am using here," and that audience did not have before it a modern annotated edition to guide it in its reactions. Alisoun mentions the fact that she has had five hus-bands, calls attention to the marriage at Cana, and then speaks of the Samaritan, who also had five husbands. When Christ says to the Samaritan, "For thou hast had five husbands: and he whom

---

[73] *PL*, 23, col. 282. Cf. St. Augustine, *De nuptiis et concupiscentia*, 1. 9. 10. On the Samaritan, see *PL*, 23, col. 244.

thou now hast, is not thy husband," the woman replies, "Sir, I perceive that thou art a prophet"; but the wife says, in rather startling contrast to her predecessor, "What that he mente therby, I kan nat seyn." Three questions present themselves. Why do the wife and the Samaritan both have five husbands? What does the marriage at Cana have to do with this situation? What, exactly, does the wife, with her reliance on "experience," fail to understand?

To begin with the second question, we must ask ourselves why the marriage at Cana is relevant to the matter of five husbands. The scriptural marriage is still referred to in modern marriage ceremonies as the event by means of which the sacrament was established. The sacrament is, in this instance, a sign of the relationship between Christ and the Church which forms a model for the relationship between husband and wife in Christian marriage.[74] At the same time, in St. Paul's view, it is analogous with the proper relationship between the spirit and the flesh. There is no reason why Chaucer's audience should not have remembered these things, especially since the sacramental character of marriage, which the wife avoids mentioning, is the basis for the argument that men and women should marry only once. Thomas Ringstede, an English exegete of the fourteenth century, asks why second marriages should not be blessed as first marriages are blessed, and answers this question as follows: "The response is, on account of the signification; for the union of a husband and a wife signifies the union of Christ and the Church, so that there should be one wife (the Church) for one husband (Christ). Thus when a woman accepts a second husband, she becomes one wife of two husbands, and the primary signification ceases."[75] But the wife, as she said at the outset, has had five husbands. Since she is quite happy with this situation and sees nothing wrong with it, we may reasonably conclude that she has little regard for the sacramental aspect of marriage. The "spirit" of the institution escapes her completely.

But the marriage at Cana has still further implications, since it was the scene of Christ's first miracle. The water in six jars was transformed into wine. The Glossa tells us in this connection that when Christ is hidden beneath the veil of the Scriptures, they are

[74] Cf. Lombard, *Sententiae*, 4. 25. 5 and 6.
[75] *In proverbia Salomonis* (Paris, 1515), fol. xc.

insipid water; but when the veil is removed, they are inebriating wine.[76] The six jars are sometimes said to represent the six ages of the world, the sixth being the age in which Christ comes. These are not obscure ideas. Pilgrims to Canterbury would have found them expressed on a stained-glass window there, where a representation of the marriage at Cana is accompanied by the inscription:

Hydria metratas capiens est quaelibet aetas:
Lympha dat historiam, vinum notat allegoriam.[77]

A tropological interpretation is given by Nicolas de Goran, who says, "Morally, these nuptials are those between God and the soul. . . . Wine is lacking in these nuptials when the soul lacks internal devotion."[78] When the wife denies the argument that Christ's attendance at one wedding is an indication that a person should marry only once, she not only implies that she disregards the sacrament or spirit of marriage, but also indicates a preference on her own part for the laws of the first five ages, for the "oldness of the letter," for the insipid water of pleasure rather than the wine of spiritual inebriation, and for an undevout condition characteristic of those who are not "married," as all Christians should be, to Christ. These ideas are elaborated further in the treatment of the story of the Samaritan, which gives us an indication of what the wife's five husbands may be said to imply in a poetic sense.

The "five husbands" mentioned in the General Prologue and again at the beginning of the prologue to the tale, together with the hint of an analogy between a lady with five husbands from "biside Bath" and another with five husbands "biside a welle," suggest that the wife's marital condition may be an iconographic device based on the story of the Samaritan. The Samaritan learns to listen to the message of Christ, but the wife is "somdel deef," an attribute which indicates that although she has ears, she hears not (Ps. 113. 14), so that the analogy applies only to the condition of the Samaritan before her conversion. These conclusions are substantiated by the wife's treatment of the scriptural narrative. The

---

[76] *PL*, 114, col. 364.

[77] E. Mâle, *L'art rel. du XIIIᵉ siècle* (Paris, 1923), pp. 196-197. For a fuller account, see Bernard Rackham, *The Ancient Glass of Canterbury Cathedral* (London, 1949), p. 63 and pl. 19.

[78] *In quatuor evang. comm.* (Antwerp, 1617), p. 839.

Glossa contains a long discussion of the dialogue between Christ and the Samaritan, based partly on St. Augustine and partly on St. Gregory,[79] the high points of which are as follows. The Samaritan in her unconverted condition is either the Synagogue or the Church of the Gentiles; Jesus comes at the sixth hour, which is the sixth age. The water of the well, which may be thought of as being analogous with the water in the jars at Cana before its transformation, represents "pleasure from the depths of the world." This is contrasted with the "living water," or grace, which Christ offers. He who drinks of the Samaritan's well "shall thirst again," since sensual delight affords no permanent satisfaction but only whets the appetite. When Christ says, "Go, call thy husband," He means that the Samaritan should call upon her rational understanding, which she has neglected. The five husbands, who are not true husbands, may be the laws of the first five ages, before the coming of Christ and the New Law, in which case what Christ means by saying that "he whom thou now hast, is not thy husband," is that she should turn from the letter to the spirit, so that she may conceive by it spiritual children of virtue. On the other hand, the five husbands may represent the five senses, in which case the husband the Samaritan should have is spiritual understanding. This tropological interpretation is explained by Nicolas de Goran, who wrote, "Mystically, the wife is the inferior part of the reason." The Samaritan is reprehended "because she had five husbands when she gave herself to her five senses in youth, so that they ruled her like husbands."[80] Thus what the wife of Bath fails to understand is the spiritual significance of Christ's words to the Samaritan, just as she has failed to understand the spiritual significance of marriage. Like the Samaritan, she prefers the Old Law to the New, or the law of fallen nature to the law of grace. She drinks the pleasures of the flesh which produce a thirst similar to that which Ovid called down upon Dipsas, a lady who is without doubt one of her literary ancestors. She is dominated by the senses or the flesh rather than by the understanding or the spirit, by oldness rather than by newness. In short, the wife of Bath is a literary personification of rampant "femininity" or carnality, and her exegesis is, in consequence, rigorously carnal and literal. Her disagreement with Christ, there-

---

[79] *PL*, 114, cols. 371ff.
[80] *Op.cit.*, pp. 856-857.

fore, is much more than a simple disagreement with an argument set forth by St. Jerome. These conclusions are fully substantiated by her subsequent essays in exegesis and theology.

Her next reference to the Bible, in fact, is a ludicrous and extremely carnal treatment of Gen. 1. 28:

> But wel I woot, expres, withoute lye,
> God bad us for to wexe and multiplye;
> That gentil text kan I wel understonde.

The wife is obviously not interested in generating children, but simply in the pleasure of the process involved. That the humor of her situation was not missed is evident from the fact that the joke reappears in a fifteenth-century paraphrase of the Ten Commandments, where a wife who enjoys wandering by the way is described. A few passages from this text will illustrate the point:

> For she is so bold off her synne,
> She seith it is but a comyn game;
> Why shuld she than have eny shame,
> Yf she can eny goodly man a-spie,
> Wyth her crokyd instrument encrese and multiplie.
>
> . . . .
>
> She wil be redy with the twynkelyng of an eie,
> And wyth her lytille whetyng-corne to encrese and multeply.
>
> . . . .
>
> But with her prety tytmose to encrece and multeply.
>
> . . . .
>
> And yet som men wille thynk and say that I lie,
> Ther ben so many workars to encrece and multeplye.[81]

The idea was still amusing to Richard Steele in the eighteenth century.[82] Part of the joke arises from the fact that Gen. 1. 28 is a "commandment" only under the Old Law; under the new, marriage is still a good, but it is an indulgence rather than a commandment.[83] Moreover, the spiritual sense of Gen. 1. 28 refers to the multiplication of the faithful in the Church, in the way that saints and good priests bring this about, or, tropologically, to the

---

[81] *Reliquae antiquae*, ed. Wright and Halliwell (London, 1843), ii, 27-28.
[82] *Tatler*, no. 20.
[83] Cf. Lombard, *Sententiae*, 4. 26. 1-3.

multiplication of virtues in the individual.[84] But the wife seems interested only in multiplying her pleasures and her wealth in ways that are hardly virtuous. She goes on to cite Gen. 2. 24, "a man shall leave father and mother, and shall cleave to his wife," neglecting the very obvious implications of this text under the New Law, obvious in this instance because they are supplied by Christ in Matt. 19, which glosses the text with the admonition, "What therefore God hath joined together, let no man put asunder," and some counsel that men should become "eunuchs for the kingdom of heaven." The text is taken up once more by St. Paul, who adds [Eph. 5. 32], "This is a great sacrament, but I speak in Christ and in the Church." Our lady exegete clearly has no interest either in becoming a "eunuch for the kingdom of heaven" or in undertaking marriages which reflect the relation between Christ and the Church; the text from Genesis suggests to her no criticism of "bigamye, or of octogamye." We may say without hesitation that she belongs among those late medieval exegetes for whom the spiritual interpretation has "receded into the background."

She continues with the example of Solomon:

> Lo, heere the wise kyng, daun Solomon;
> I trowe he hadde wyves mo than oon.
> As wolde God it were leveful unto me
> To be refresshed half so ofte as he!
> Which yifte of God hadde he for alle his wyvys!
> No man hath swich that in this world alyve is.
> God woot, this noble kyng, as to my wit,
> The firste nyght had many a myrie fit
> With ech of hem, so wel was hym on lyve.

The "yifte of God" (cf. 1 Cor. 7. 7) Solomon had is readily discernible in 3 Kings 11: "And king Solomon loved many strange women . . . . And he had seven hundred wives as queens, and three hundred concubines: and the women turned away his heart. And when he was now old, his heart was turned away by women to follow strange gods: and his heart was not perfect with the Lord his God. . . ." In fact, the foolishness of Solomon in his old age

---

[84] See R. P. Miller, "Chaucer's Pardoner, the Scriptural Eunuch, and the Pardoner's Tale," *Speculum*, xxx (1955), 185-186.

was proverbial.[85] As Proserpyna observes in the Merchant's Tale,

> He was a lecchour and an ydolastre,
> And in his elde he verray God forsook.

Five husbands of which she has "pyked out the beste / Bothe of here nether purs and of her cheste" have been sufficient to bring the wife to a similar position. In view of the meaning of the six vessels in the story of the marriage at Cana and of the sixth husband which Christ urges the Samaritan to call forth,[86] there is a rather touching irony in the wife's exclamation, "Welcome the sixte, whan that evere he shal!" For what she looks forward to is not the illumination of the sixth age or the advantages of rational understanding, but rather a further opportunity for "refreshment."

The support for her position that Alisoun is able to derive from St. Paul is obtained only by quoting him out of context or by disregarding the obvious implications of what he says. This device, of course, is the simplest means of avoiding the spirit of a text, although it does rely on what that text "actually says" and thus affords superficially credible arguments which may easily entrap the unwary. She points out, on the authority of the Apostle, that she is at liberty to wed, "a Goddes half," wherever she pleases, once her husband is dead. The authority here is 1 Cor. 7. 39 or Rom. 7. 2-6. The first of these runs, "A woman is bound by the law as long as her husband liveth; but if her husband die, she is at liberty: let her marry to whom she will; only in the Lord." The neglected implication here arises from the phrase "only in the Lord." Although the wife quotes it, she has already demonstrated a strong disinclination to marry "in the Lord," so that her neglect of what she herself says is amusingly obvious. Moreover, the text appears in the midst of some earnest counsel to the effect that widows should not remarry, and is, in fact, followed by the following statement in the next verse: "But more blessed shall she be,

[85] For Jerome's view, see *PL*, 23, col. 254. Cf. St. Augustine, *On Christian Doctrine*, 3. 21. 31.

[86] St. Jerome takes the sixth husband to be the man currently married to the Samaritan, but St. Augustine and St. Gregory regard the current false husband as the fifth. That Chaucer was following the latter authorities, probably through the *Glossa ordinaria*, and not St. Jerome on this point, is clear from lines 21-22 of the prologue.

if she so remain, according to my counsel." The parallel text from Romans is even more damaging, or, from a fourteenth-century point of view, revealing: "For the woman that hath a husband, whilst her husband liveth is bound to the law. But if her husband be dead, she is loosed from the law of her husband. Therefore, whilst her husband liveth, she shall be called an adulteress, if she be with another man: but if her husband be dead, she is delivered from the law of her husband; so that she is not an adulteress, if she be with another man. Therefore, my brethren, you also are become dead to the law by the body of Christ; that you may belong to another, who is risen again from the dead, that we may bring forth fruit to God. For when we were in the flesh, the passions of sins, which were by the law, did work in our members to bring forth fruit unto death. But now we are loosed from the law of death wherein we were detained, so that we should serve in newness of spirit, and not in the oldness of the letter."

Alisoun shows no interest in "newness of spirit." Again, she supports her argument about the legality of second marriages by quoting 1 Cor. 7. 9, "For it is better to marry than to be burnt," a text which is followed by the words: "But to them that are married, not I, but the Lord commandeth, that the wife depart not from her husband: And if she depart, that she remain unmarried, or be reconciled to her husband." Needless to say, St. Paul does not recommend marriage as a means of maintaining that fire in which one is "burnt."

St. Augustine observes that "caution must be exercised lest anyone think that those things in the Scriptures which are neither vices nor crimes among the ancients because of the condition of their times may be transferred to our own times and put in practice. Unless he is dominated by cupidity and seeks protection for it in the very Scriptures by means of which it is to be overthrown, no one will do this."[87] Students of Old English literature may remember a similar caution in Aelfric's Preface to Genesis, where a difficulty is recalled concerning the matter of marriage: "Nu þincð me, leof, þæt þæt weorc is swiðe pleolic me oððe ænigum men to underbeginnenne, for þan þe ic ondræde, gif sum dysig man þas boc ræt oððe rædan gehyrð, þæt he wille wenan þæt he mote lybban nu on þære niwan æ swa swa þa ealdan fæderas leofodon þa on þære

[87] *On Christian Doctrine*, 3. 18. 36.

tide ær þan þe seo ealde æ gesett wære, oððe swa swa men leofodon under Moyses æ. Hwilon ic wiste þæt sum mæssepreost, se þe min magister wæs on þam timan, hæfde þa boc Genesis, and he cuðe be dæle Lyden understandan; þa cwæð he be þam heahfædere Iacobe, þæt he hæfde feower wif, twa geswustra and heora twa þinena. Ful soð he sæde, ac he nyste, ne ic þa git, hu micel todal ys betweohx þære ealdan æ and þære niwan."

The wife's references to Lamech, Jacob, and Abraham, who, she says, had more than one wife, reveal the practice which St. Augustine condemns so vigorously and which Aelfric recalls with such distaste. Moreover, these references form a kind of gloss on St. Paul, so that the wife is, in effect, reversing the usual process and glossing the New Law in the "light" of the Old, a ruse which is consistent with the generally "up-so-doun" nature of her character.

Returning to St. Paul, Alisoun regales her audience with a long disquisition on the difference between counsel and precept, which is correct in principle, except that she makes it perfectly clear that she wishes to obey neither. A passage from Timothy is once more used out of context:

> For wel ye knowe, a lord in his houshold,
> He nath nat every vessel al of gold;
> Somme been of tree, and doon hir lord servyse.

The implication is that although the wife herself is not a vessel of gold or silver, she is nevertheless a serviceable wooden vessel. If we turn to the text itself (2 Tim. 2. 20ff.), we find that the vessels of wood and of earth are used to cleanse the more precious vessels, and that the character of a good vessel is very different from the character of our lady of Bath: "But in a great house there are not only vessels of gold and of silver, but also of wood and of earth: and some indeed unto honour, but some unto dishonour. If any man therefore shall cleanse himself from these [vessels of wood and of earth], he shall be a vessel unto honour, sanctified and profitable to the Lord, prepared unto every good work. But flee thou youthful desires, and pursue justice, faith, charity, and peace, with them that call on the Lord out of a pure heart. And avoid foolish and unlearned questions, knowing that they beget strifes.

But the servant of the Lord must not wrangle: but be mild towards all men, ready to teach, patient."

The Glossa explains the usefulness of wooden and earthen vessels as follows: "Just as wooden and earthen vessels are of value for cleansing gold and silver vessels, in the same way, the evil are of profit for the improvement of the good. For the Church is a great house in which there are vessels of gold and silver, that is, good and faithful and holy servants of God, dispersed everywhere and united in spiritual unity, continuing at the same time in the communion of the sacraments. There are also wooden and earthen vessels, that is, those who are in the house in such a way that they are not a part of the structure of the household nor in the peaceful community, but are nevertheless in the same organization with the good."[88] The wife's reference to vessels thus puts her firmly among the evil who are in the Church but not of it. This admission, although inadvertent on her part, reveals a situation that results logically from her contempt of counsel.

After a reference to her proper "yifte," which turns out to be "the beste quoniam myghte be," she turns to a discussion of the perfection of virginity, which she scorns. To illustrate this attitude she cites Matt. 19. 21, maintaining that the admonition to sell what one has and give it to the poor applies only to those who wish to be perfect. Having no desire for perfection, she will take another course:

> I wol bistowe the flour of al myn age
> In the actes and in fruyt of mariage.

That is, she will follow the advice of La Vieille in the *Roman de la rose* (13483ff.):

> Le fruit d'Amours, se fame est sage,
> Cueille en la fleur de son aage,
> Car tant pert de son tens, la lasse,
> Con sanz joïr d'amours en passe.

---

[88] *PL*, 114, col. 635. Although it might appear that the wife is here simply following St. Jerome, the latter does not actually identify the married with wooden vessels (*Adv. Jov.*, 1. 40). He makes the point that the Church does not condemn marriage but simply puts it in its proper place. Referring to the vessels of 2 Tim. 20ff., he asserts that all who cleanse themselves (i.e., whether married or virgin) are made worthy.

The "fruit" these ladies have in mind is clearly neither the "virginity" St. Jerome regarded as the fruit of marriage,[89] nor progeny, nor that spiritual perfection which, regardless of physical condition, may also be called "virginity." Both kinds of virginity are, in effect, dismissed at once. That this conclusion is implied is clear from the discussion of "instruments" which follows.[90] St. Jerome, noting a similar argument to the effect that the members of generation would not have been formed if they were not intended to be used, replied that a Christian should live according to the spirit rather than according to the flesh,[91] a thesis not calculated to appeal to the wife, who avoids mentioning it. Instead, she uses as an argument the principle of the marriage debt (1 Cor. 7. 1-5), and concludes that the instruments in question were made "To purge uryne and eek for engendrure." Aside from the fact that she is clearly not interested in "engendrure," her assertion that a man must use his "sely instrument" to pay his debt omits all mention of the doctrine that the marriage debt was instituted for the purpose of putting down concupiscence so as to avoid fornication. The wife would be the last person to employ her "bele chose" in this way. Neither physical nor spiritual virginity is of any interest to her.

In spite of Christ's maidenhood, and the maidenhood of many a saint, Alisoun will have none of it:

> Lat hem be breed of pured whete-seed
> And lat us wyves hoten barley breed.

The contrast between barley bread and wheaten bread is from the *Adversus Jovinianum*. Jerome asserts that it is better to marry and eat "barley bread" than to be a fornicator and eat *stercus bubulum*.[92] But it is better still to be a virgin and eat wheaten bread. In these terms, we must admit that the wife, if we recall the "other company in youth" of the General Prologue, has occasionally

[89] *PL*, 23, col. 223. Cf. Chaucer, Parson's Tale, 867ff. C. R. Dahlberg, who is preparing a translation of the *Roman de la rose*, informs me in a letter that one MS of the poem (Paris, BN fr. 25526) contains, among its marginalia, representations of women plucking "fruit" in the form of male genitalia. Cf. May's appetite for "fruit" in the Merchant's Tale.

[90] For another fourteenth-century instance of the sophistry concerning "instruments," see Jehan le Bel, *Li ars d'amour*, ed. J. Petit (Brussels, 1867-1869), I, 362.

[91] *PL*, 23, cols. 271-274.

[92] *Ibid.*, col. 229.

shown a rather curious appetite. But she goes on to cite, from the wrong Evangelist, the story of the loaves and the fishes, wherein the five loaves of barley bread had been taken since St. Augustine's memorable exposition as a figure for the hardness of the Old Law.[93] Nicolas de Goran wrote concerning this matter: "By the five loaves the five books of Moses are understood. Moreover, the doctrine of Moses is bitter and hard, and thus the loaves of barley bread are multiplied in order to suggest that the substance of the books of Moses was not to be changed, but that those things which were contained in them as if wrapped up and closed should be through Christ in spiritual understanding extended and multiplied."[94]

In other words, barley bread in this connection suggests the untransformed Old Law, and the wife's assertion concerning it identifies her further with that institution. We may notice, moreover, a further analogy between the five husbands and the five loaves, and an indirect reference in the wife's citation to the concept of "multiplication," first suggested in the quotation of Gen. 1. 28. A brief exposition such as this one cannot do justice to the manner in which Chaucer has carefully interwoven and elaborated the various themes of the prologue.

In conclusion, the wife threatens any husbands she may have with the "tribulation" of 1 Cor. 7. 28. She will bring this about and make her husband her "thral" by asserting the rights granted by the last half of 1 Cor. 7. 4: "And in like manner the husband also hath not power of his own body, but the wife." Her threat, however, disregards the first half of the same verse: "The wife hath not power of her own body, but the husband." Alisoun does not anticipate any effective exercise of mutual rights in this respect; she will grant the validity of only one side of the contract. Finally, her sermon ends with a further principle obtained by blithely disregarding the context of either Eph. 5. 25 or Colos. 3. 19:

> Right thus the Apostel tolde it unto me;
> And bad oure housbondes for to love us weel.
> Al this sentence me liketh every deel.

[93] See Marie Comeau, *Saint Augustin, exégète du quatrième évangile*, 2 ed., (Paris, 1930), pp. 150-151.
[94] *Op.cit.*, p. 873.

Unfortunately the "sentence" of the original would have occurred to almost anyone in Chaucer's courtly audience. In Ephesians we read: "As the Church is subject to Christ, so also let the wives be to their husbands in all things. Husbands, love your wives as Christ also loved the Church." This "sentence" is hardly consistent with the wife's ambition to enslave her husbands, although her disregard for the sacramental character of marriage is consistent with what we have seen to be her attitude from the beginning. In Colossians 3. 18-19, St. Paul admonishes: "Wives, be subject to your husbands, as it behoveth in the Lord. Husbands, love your wives, and be not bitter towards them." These precepts are part of a series designed to show how one should go about stripping off the old man and putting on the new. With this admirable procedure the wife will have nothing to do; in fact, her entire sermon is designed to resist any such rejuvenation. She does her best to subvert the traditional hierarchy of husband over wife as it reflects the hierarchy of Christ over the Church and parallels the hierarchy of the spirit over the flesh, or the "newness of the spirit" over "the oldness of the letter." If we take her as a useful exemplar of a wooden vessel, we can see that the "wo that is in mariage" results from any of these inversions. He who allows his wife to dominate him will be served as the wife of Bath seeks to serve her husbands; he who allows the flesh to dominate the spirit will find it a tyrant like the wife;[95] and, finally, he who disregards the spirit of the Scriptures in favor of experience will find himself enslaved to the Old Law, unredeemed by the "freedom wherewith Christ hath made us free." These ideas and their corollaries must have been what Chaucer had in mind when he wrote the first 162 lines of the wife's prologue. These lines, taken together, afford a humorous example of carnal understanding and its consequences which is, at the same time, a scathing denunciation of such understanding. Alisoun of Bath is not a "character" in the modern sense at all, but an elaborate iconographic figure designed to show the manifold implications of an attitude.[96] She is, in some ways, typically "feminine,"

[95] On submission to a woman as a submission of the reason to the senses, cf. Boccaccio, *Il Corbaccio*, ed. N. Bruscoli (Bari, 1940), p. 205. The idea is a commonplace, however, further instances of which will appear below.

[96] The iconographic and thematic significance of the wife is discussed at length in an unpublished dissertation by Robert S. Haller, "The Old Whore and Mediaeval Thought." A somewhat fuller discussion of the wife's prologue than that in

but the femininity she represents was in Chaucer's day a philosophical rather than a psychological concept. That she still seems feminine to us is a tribute to the justness of the ideas which produced her. Those who grow sentimental over her "human" qualities are, from a fourteenth-century point of view, simply being misled.

The wife's prologue, of which we have examined only the first part, is extremely rich in exegetical materials, and the use made of them is, at least to those of us who are not intimately familiar with the Bible and its commentaries, rather complex. The nature of the exegesis produced by the friar, the pardoner, and the parson may be made clear on the basis of a much more cursory examination. If the wife represents carnality, with reference both to the Scriptures and to life generally, the friar of the Summoner's Tale represents hypocrisy. His motives for preaching in the first place are entirely selfish. He excites the people to spend their money for "trentals" and for the "holy houses" of the friars, where, he says, divine service "is honoured." He leaves church when people have given him "what hem leste," or, in other words, when he has squeezed all he can get out of them. To further his own purposes, he does not hesitate to misrepresent the Word of God. As he says to Thomas,

> I have to day been at youre chirche at messe
> And seyd a sermon after my symple wit,
> Nat al after the text of hooly writ;
> For it is hard to yow, as I suppose,
> And therfore wolde I teche yow al the glose.
> Glosynge is a glorious thyng, certayn,
> For lettre sleeth, so as we clerkes seyn.
> Ther have I taught hem to be charitable,
> And spende hir good ther it is resonable.

these pages will appear in an article now in preparation by the same author. Iconographically, the wife is related to those wives who so mercilessly beat their husbands in English wood carvings. For an illustration, see M. D. Anderson, *Misericords* (Harmondsworth, 1954), plate 43. She also has affinities, because of the inversion she represents, with the lady who bestrides Aristotle in various late medieval media. Both of these other ladies carry scourges, and the Ellesmere illustrator has given one to Alisoun. The wife's deafness relates her to the ass before the harp in Gothic ornament. She has further affinities, because of her attachment to the Old Law, with the Synagogue (Fig. 55). She represents an inversion of all the implications of Fig. 6.

This passage has sometimes been cited as evidence that Chaucer had small use for the allegorical interpretation of the Bible, since he obviously had no use for the "glosynge" of this friar. However, what is here satirized is not the spiritual sense, but its abuse. And this is a very different thing. The friar's errors are, first of all, that he neglects the literal sense completely, substituting for it ideas of his own; and a neglect of the letter, either in this way or in any other, had been condemned by spiritual exegetes ever since Patristic times. Second, charity affords the disciplinary principle which limits spiritual interpretation. The object of the friar's "glosynge" is not to further a love for God and for one's neighbor, but to persuade the people to be "charitable" by giving their wealth to him. That is, the friar's discipline in his preaching is not charity but his own cupidity, which he seeks to conceal under a pretext of holiness. To overlook the fact that Chaucer is here commenting humorously but with some bitterness on the abuse of something which he and his contemporaries valued very highly, and to say that he is condemning the thing itself, is not only to oversimplify the problem, but to miss the point of the satire completely. The same point is made again a little later:

> But herkne, now, Thomas, what I shal seyn.
> I ne have no text of it, as I suppose,
> But I shal fynde it in a maner glose,
> That specially oure sweete Lord Jhesus
> Spak this by freres, whan he seyde thus:
> "Blessed be they that povere in spirit been."

"Poverty of spirit" or humility is a virtue in which our friar is obviously lacking; he has, in fact, just been boasting about how acceptable to God are the prayers of the abstinent, vigilant, continent, and otherwise virtuous friars like himself. Again, the "glose" is a device used by the friar to further the aims of his own cupidity. As an exegete, the friar is a seemingly pious deceiver, whose abuse of allegory is, ultimately, an abuse of Christ.

The pardoner is not only cupidinous himself; he deliberately fosters cupidity in his audience while developing the theme *radix malorum est cupiditas*. He tempts his listeners by assuring them that the proper application of his "relics" will multiply the "beestes" and the "stoor" of his customers, cause them to be unconcerned about the marital infidelities of their spouses, and bring about a "multiplying" of grain. In other words, he appeals to their cupidity and encourages it, at the same time seeking to satisfy his own. He tells entertaining stories so that his words will be more profitable to himself in a material way, but these stories, he assures us, can be moral. And he proceeds to tell a moral story in the development of his theme which actually constitutes a kind of self-portrait. From an exegetical point of view, the expository development which the pardoner applies to his theme is vivid, energetic, and not without subtlety. He subdivides *cupiditas* into three parts: gluttony, gambling, and swearing. The first leads to the death of the spirit (cf. 1 Tim. 5. 6):

> he that haunteth swiche delices
> Is deed, whil that he liveth in tho vices.

The second is the "mooder of lesynges," and the third is a violation of the Second Commandment (640-642). In the sermon itself, these transgressions are not ordered in accordance with any set principles, or at least the principles are not made explicit, probably because Chaucer did not wish the pardoner to seem aware of the implications of what he says for himself. The three sins may, however, be seen as a progression along the road to spiritual death: (1) the submission of the spirit to the flesh in gluttony, foreshadowed, as the pardoner suggests, by the sin of Adam and Eve, (2) the submission to Fortune implied by gambling, and (3) the denial of Christ, which is the "spiritual" implication of violating the Second Commandment.[97] Hence, the three sins reflect the old pattern of the temptations of the flesh, the world, and the Devil, for submission to Fortune is submission to the world, and the denial of Christ is the ultimate aim of the Devil's temptation. All men seek to conquer death, to find, in one way or another, a death for death. For Christians the road to this achievement was foreseen by the prophet Osee [13. 14]: "O death, I will be thy death." As St. Paul explains it [1 Cor. 15. 53ff.], "this corruptible must put on incorruption; and this mortal must put on immortality. And when this mortal hath put on immortality, then shall come to pass the saying that is written: 'Death is swallowed up in victory. O death,

---

[97] Lombard, *Sententiae*, 3. 37. 2. Cf. in English Robert Mannyng, *Handlyng Synne*, EETS OS, 119, lines 647-654. The idea is commonplace.

where is thy victory? O death, where is thy sting?' Now the sting of death is sin: and the power of sin is the law."

Death may be conquered, that is, through the New Man. But there are also those who seek the same goal through the pardoner's three sins. Having allowed the flesh to dominate the spirit, or, in Pauline language, having given themselves up to the counsels of the Old Man, they seek satisfaction in the realm of Fortune and become members of that sect whose "wombe is hir god" and who are "enemys of Cristes croys" [Phil. 3. 18ff.]. But this pursuit leads only to death rather than to the death of death. The rioters of the pardoner's exemplum give themselves up to gluttony in drunkenness, seek the counsel of the Old Man, immerse themselves in a lust for worldly treasure, and, finally, deny the bond of sworn brotherhood which unites them as each makes himself the object of his worship. But the pardoner has given himself up wholeheartedly to the same pursuit. He will do anything to satisfy his flesh, he abuses the Word of God for worldly ends, and he ends his sermon by first calling attention to Christ's pardon and then denying it by offering his wares to the pilgrims. Taken as a whole, the Pardoner's Tale is an excellent illustration of what happens to those who deny the spirit of Christ beneath the letter of the text *radix malorum est cupiditas* and devote themselves to the pursuit of the corporal rather than the intelligible. Their pursuit ends in the denial of the spirit everywhere, and it would be difficult to imagine a more forceful and vivid denunciation of this denial than that which Chaucer has left us in the pardoner's prologue and tale.

It is difficult to see how Chaucer could have more vividly illustrated the abuses of false scriptural interpretation than he has in his accounts of the wife of Bath, the friar of the Summoner's Tale, and the pardoner. If we neglect the standard against which they are drawn—the beauty, the efficacy, and the "sweetness" of the spirit—we shall miss much of the humor of the wife's carnality, the vigor of the satire against deceivers like the friar, and the tremendous force of the Pardoner's Tale. Those who deny the validity of spiritual exegesis in the fourteenth century are in effect implying that the Church was dominated by exegetes like these three. The techniques of modern scriptural criticism had not yet been developed, so that we cannot assume these as an alternative. Chaucer indicates unmistakably that carnality like that of the wife leads to inversions both in the individual and in society, that hypocritical deception like that practiced by the friar puts the practitioner in "a bad odor," and, finally, that in his view those who, like the pardoner, deny the spirit are sterile eunuchs whose life is death.

The Parson's Tale is an excellent specimen of the series of penitential manuals which developed as a result of the decree concerning penance issued by the Fourth Lateran Council. At first such manuals were written chiefly for priests, like the *Summula* of Bishop Peter Quivil, but in time translations and adaptations were compiled for laymen as well.[98] Since their purpose was elementary instruction, they were theological rather than exegetical in character. Nevertheless, the Parson's Tale contains very definite traces of the spiritual interpretation of Scripture. The parson begins by refusing the host's request for a fable:

> Thou getest fable noon ytold for me;
> For Paul, that writeth unto Thymothee,
> Repreveth hem that weyven soothfastnesse,
> And tellen fables and swich wrecchednesse.
> Why sholde I sowen draf out of my fest,
> Whan I may sowen whete, if that me leste?

St. Paul's epistles to Timothy and Titus constitute the classical source of Apostolic instruction concerning preaching.[99] The warnings to Timothy concerning fables were taken during the Middle Ages as applying to fables without any meaning or to fables whose meaning was heretical.[100] When the parson says that he will mingle no chaff with his wheat, he means that he will, as an expositor should, explain his text clearly and straightforwardly. The principle involved here is a commonplace. Holcot, reflecting St. Augustine, explains it as follows: "1 Cor. 15 [37]: 'And that which thou sowest, thou sowest not the body that shall be; but the bare

---

[98] Cf. D. W. Robertson, Jr., "The Cultural Tradition of *Handlyng Synne*," *Speculum*, XXII (1947), pp. 171-172.

[99] Cf. *On Christian Doctrine*, 4. 16. 33.

[100] See 1 Tim. 1. 4ff., where the use of fables is contrasted with "the end of the commandment" which is "charity," and *Glossa major*, PL, 192, cols. 327-329. Again, cf. 1 Tim. 4. 7, and *PL*, 192, col. 348, where the fables condemned are said to be those *sine fructu*. Finally, cf. 2 Tim. 4. 4 and *PL*, 192, col. 379, where the author of vain fables is compared with the "foolish woman" of Prov. 9. 13-18.

grain [as of wheat].' Whence I say that according to Palladius in his Book of Agriculture, a grain sown in its covering of chaff will not as well and quickly germinate as it would if the chaff were removed. In the same way a mystical and obscure teaching will not be so fruitful as a nude one, although it may delight the curious very much more. Thus St. Augustine teaches in *On Christian Doctrine* [4. 8. 22] that expositors in their sermons should elaborate what they have to say first of all in a manner designed chiefly so that they may be understood, at least concerning those things which may be spoken of with clarity. Thus either he who does not understand may be one who is very slow, or there may be some refinement and subtlety in what we wish to say. The reason why what we say is either little understood or slowly understood should not lie in our speech."[101]

In other words, the parson will speak as a preacher or expositor and not as a poet. His sermon is developed from the text of Jer. 6. 16, but it is clear that he does not take it literally. The "olde pathes" become "olde sentences," and among the "weyes espirituels" one good way for those who, like most of the Canterbury Pilgrims, have "mysgoon fro the ryghte wey of Jerusalem celestial" is penance. The sermon thus hinges on a spiritual interpretation. Although its materials belong to the realm of pastoral theology, it contains a lengthy exposition of the most common tropological interpretation of the narrative of the Fall (321ff.), a clear reflection of the spiritual interpretation of the "hundred-fold fruit" of Matt. 13. 8 and 23 (867ff.), and other incidental interpretations of the same kind. The parson thus neither reads his text carnally, abuses the spirit for his own interest, nor denies the validity of the spirit beneath the letter. It is true that most of his authorities are clear on the surface without exposition, and this is as it should be in a manual addressed to laymen; but it is also true that insofar as it is exegetical, it makes no departures from the traditions of Pauline allegory. There are other exegetical materials in *The Canterbury Tales* in addition to those we have discussed, but the examples of the wife, the summoner's friar, the pardoner, and the parson are sufficient to show that in his attitude toward the Scriptures Chaucer had nothing in common with the summoner of the Friar's Tale.

[101] *Super librum Ecclesiastici* (Venice, 1509), 3 verso.

3. CHRISTIAN HUMANISM

The attitude of the Church Fathers toward pagan literature has frequently been characterized as being vacillating and inconsistent, but in view of the circumstances under which they wrote, some of their inconsistency may be seen to be only apparent. In the first place, since the principles of pagan literary allegory were felt to be inferior, as compared with the principles employed by St. Paul, they were attacked. Moreover, pagans used their allegory to support philosophies hostile to Christianity. Hence attacks on pagan allegorizing like that in St. Augustine's *Contra Faustum* (20. 9) were quite natural. In this instance, some of the specific interpretations mentioned with contempt were taken up by later Christian allegorists of pagan literature. But the explanation for this fact is simple: an idea "used" in the service of Christianity is quite different from the same idea "abused" in the service of paganism. Again, Christians insisted on the superiority of the Scriptures over poetic fables as a source for philosophy, as St. Augustine does in *De vera religione* (51. 100), but contrasts of this kind, no matter how violently they are asserted, should not be taken as modern "black or white" oppositions, any more, let us say, than the contrast between the "oldness of the letter" and the "newness of the spirit" should be taken in this way. Elsewhere, St. Augustine is more lenient toward poetic fables. Thus in the *Contra mendacium* (13. 28), he defends Horace's satire based on the fable of the mice (2. 6), and Aesop's fables against the charge that they are lies. And in the *Soliloquiae* (2. 10. 18 and 19) he asserts that a work of art is true insofar as it is false (that is, insofar as it is not literal), and defines a fable as a "lie" composed for utility and delight. The lie in this instance is a superficial lie which covers an underlying truth, not the kind of lie condemned in the *De mendacio*, which results from having one thing in the heart and expressing something else, quite literally, either in words or in other ways. Again, in the *De ordine* (1. 8. 24), he advises his friend Licentius to keep his poem on Pyramus and Thisbe, but to arrange it in such a way that it becomes a poem in praise of divine love. That is, a poetic fable has its uses in Christian hands. St. Augustine's own use of Virgil throughout his writings affords a further illustration of the same principle.[102] It is apparent, therefore, that in St. Augustine's mind a poetic fable was not in and of itself either a good thing or a bad thing. It is also clear that he thought of poems as being allegorical.[103]

St. Jerome's difficulties with pagan literature represent a somewhat different situation, but St. Jerome was not quite so inconsistent in this respect as he has been made out to be. The context in which the "difficulties" are expressed, a letter to Eustochium in which St. Jerome seeks to persuade that lady to abandon the world for the sake of God, should be taken into consideration. The relevant passages (22. 29-30) are worth quoting in full:

"Nor should you desire to seem excellent in discourse, nor witty in making lyric songs in meter. Do not imitate the enervated and delicate affectation which has arisen among matrons, who now with teeth clenched, now with lips wide, with a stuttering tongue cut their words in half, thinking all else rustic, to such a degree does adultery, even of the tongue, please them. For [2 Cor. 6. 14-15] 'What fellowship has light with darkness? And what concord has Christ with Belial?' What has Horace to do with the Psalter? Or Virgil with the Gospels? Or Cicero with the Apostle? Would not your brother be scandalized if he saw you reclining in a temple for idols? And although 'all things are clean to the clean' [Tit. 1. 15], and 'nothing is to be rejected that is received with thanksgiving' [1 Tim. 4. 4], nevertheless, we should not drink at the same time from the chalice of Christ and the chalice of demons. I shall tell you my own story of infelicity.

"When, many years ago, for the sake of the kingdom of heaven [cf. Matt. 19. 12], I castrated myself of home, parents, sister, relatives, and, what is more difficult, of the habit of elegant food, and pressed on in warfare to Jerusalem, I could not go without the library which I had gathered with the greatest diligence and labor at Rome. Thus, miserable creature, about to read Cicero, I fasted; after nights of frequent vigils, after tears, which the memory of past sins drew forth from the depths of my bowels, I took Plautus in my hands. When I returned to myself and began to read the Prophets, I was horrified by their rude style, and, when my

---

[102] See K. H. Schelke, *Virgil in der Deutung Augustins* (Stuttgart, 1939), pp. 158-159, 195.
[103] Cf. *Quaestiones in Numeros*, 45.

blind eyes did not see the light, I did not think my eyes to be at fault, but the sun. While the Old Serpent was thus playing with me, about the middle of Lent, a fever invaded my exhausted and restless body, infused the very marrow, and—what is almost incredible—so wasted my unhappy members that I could hardly cling to my bones. Meanwhile, a funeral was prepared, and the heat of my vital spirit, growing cold, now palpitated only very weakly on the surface of my breast, when, suddenly seized in spirit, I was dragged to a bar of justice where such was the light and such the clear brilliance of those assembled that, prostrated on the ground, I did not dare to look up. Asked about my status, I said I was a Christian. And He who presided said, 'You lie. You are a Ciceronian, not a Christian; *for where thy treasure is, there is thy heart also*' [Matt. 6. 21]. I was speechless, and between the blows —for he ordered me whipped—my conscience tortured me like fire as I muttered to myself the verse [Ps. 6. 6], 'and who shall confess to thee in hell?' Then I began to cry out and to lament [Ps. 56. 2], 'Have mercy on me, O God, have mercy on me.' These words resounded amid the cracking of the whip until those who were present, falling at the knees of the Judge, prayed that he might have mercy on my immaturity, so that a time to repent my error might be granted, but that I should be tortured if I ever again read the books of the pagans. I, constrained by such an injunction, would have promised more, and I began to swear, and taking His name to witness, said, 'Lord, if I have secular books again, if I read them, I deny you.' "

It will be seen that Jerome's error in the first place was not simply that he read secular literature, but that he read it in preference to the Scriptures at a time when he should have been occupied with spiritual matters. Under these circumstances, since it is assumed that he might weaken again, the punishment indicated and the oath taken may not seem extreme. However, it is best to look on this history as an exemplary narrative, embellished with a great deal of rhetorical exaggeration in the classical manner, designed especially for the ears of Eustochium and for others like her, rather than as a piece of psychological self-revelation. In another letter (70), Jerome defends his use of pagan literature in his writings. Among various arguments in defense of his practice, one became more famous than the others. It is based on the text of Deut. 21.

10-13: "If thou go out to fight against thy enemies, and the Lord thy God deliver them into thy hand, and thou lead them away captives, and seest in the number of the captives a beautiful woman, and lovest her and wilt have her to wife, thou shalt bring her into thy house: and she shall shave her hair and pare her nails, and shall put off the raiment wherein she was taken, and shall remain in thy house, and mourn for her father and mother one month: and after that thou shalt go in unto her, and shalt sleep with her, and she shall be thy wife."

"What wonder is it," says Jerome, "if I also wish to make a servant and captive for the Israelites of secular wisdom on account of the attractiveness of its eloquence and the beauty of its members? Or if, whatever dead matter in it of idolatry, voluptuousness, error, or libido having been shaved or pared, I mingle with this most pure body and generate from it domestics for the Lord of Hosts?" This argument, which stems from Origen, became a medieval commonplace.[104] Although the two letters we have quoted seem to be contradictory on the surface, they are actually consistent. The Jerome of the letter to Eustochium read pagan literature without reference to Christ; the Jerome of the letter to Magnus made his pagan learning an adjunct to his Christianity. Secular learning, like the letter of the Old Testament, is an evil taken for itself alone; when, again like the letter, it is a stepping-stone to spiritual understanding, it is a very valuable asset.

A passage from St. Augustine's *On Christian Doctrine* (2. 40. 60), also derived in substance from Origen, was even more influential than St. Jerome's "beautiful captive" in promoting the study of pagan letters during the Middle Ages: "Just as the Egyptians had not only idols and grave burdens which the people of Israel detested and avoided, so also they had vases and ornaments of gold and silver and clothing which the Israelites took with them secretly as they fled, as if to put them to a better use. They did not do this on their own authority but at God's commandment, while the Egyptians unwittingly supplied them with things which they themselves did not use well [Exod. 3. 22; 11. 2; 12. 35]. In the same way all the teachings of the pagans contain not only simulated and superstitious imaginings and grave burdens of unnecessary labor, which each one of us leaving the society of pagans under the leader-

---

[104] See *Exégèse médiévale*, pp. 290ff.

ship of Christ ought to abominate and avoid, but also liberal disciplines more suited to the uses of truth, and some most useful precepts concerning morals. Even some truths concerning the worship of one God are discovered among them. These are, as it were, their gold and silver, which they did not institute themselves but dug up from certain mines of divine Providence, which is everywhere infused, and perversely and injuriously abused in the worship of demons. When the Christian separates himself in spirit from their miserable society, he should take this treasure with him for the just use of the teaching of the Gospel. And their clothing, which is made up of those human institutions which are accommodated to human society and necessary to the conduct of life, should be seized and held to be converted to Christian uses."

Among the many medieval authors who echo this argument, we may mention John the Scot,[105] Rabanus Maurus,[106] Peter of Blois,[107] Alanus de Insulis,[108] Baudri de Bourgueil,[109] John of Salisbury,[110] and Jacques de Vitry.[111] It would be possible to extend this list considerably. Pagan literature was thus cultivated not only for the beauty of its eloquence, which might profitably be imitated for Christian purposes—Goliath was beheaded with his own sword, as St. Jerome points out—but also for whatever useful knowledge and wisdom it might contain. Since the attitudes expressed by St. Jerome and St. Augustine in these instances stimulated the reading of classical texts, they were essentially "humanistic." Certainly, both authors had in mind what they regarded as the cultivation of man's most distinctively human characteristics as well as the benefit of mankind in general.

If there are doubts about this point, it may clarify matters somewhat to show that the attitudes of Petrarch and Erasmus were very much like those of St. Augustine and St. Jerome. Petrarch wrote (*Fam.* 6. 2. 4): "Christ is the true wisdom of God; in order that we may philosophize truly, we must first of all love and worship

---

[105] *De div. nat.*, PL, 122, cols. 723-724.
[106] *De cler. inst.*, PL, 107, col. 404.
[107] Epist. 91, *PL*, 207, col. 286.
[108] *De arte praed.*, PL, 210, col. 180.
[109] *Oeuvres poet.*, ed. P. Abrahams (Paris, 1926), ccxxxviii, lines 121-126.
[110] *Policrat.*, 7. 2.
[111] *Sermo ad scholares*, ed. Pitra, *Anal. nov. Spicilegii Solesmensis* (1885-1888), ii, 366.

Him. We should so live that we are, above all, Christians; thus we should read philosophy, poetry, and history so that the Gospel of Christ echoes in our hearts. With this alone we are learned and happy; without it, the more we study, the less learned and the more miserable we shall become. To it, as to the highest truth, all else is to be referred. Upon it, like an immutable foundation of true learning, human labor may safely build; and studiously gathering other doctrines not contrary to it, we shall incur little blame, for even though they may add little to the ultimate truth, in pursuing them we shall certainly seem to contribute much to the delight of the mind and to a more cultivated life."

In the *Enchiridion* Erasmus informs us that a delight in pagan literature is profitable "if everything is referred to Christ." He adds, addressing prospective young soldiers in the Christian battle, "You love learning properly if you do so for the sake of Christ; and if you are confident of yourself and hope for a great reward in Christ, travel like a bold merchant, journey for a long while among pagan letters, and convert Egyptian wealth for the ornament of the Temple of the Lord."[112] Much the same thing, expressed, perhaps, a little less movingly, could be said in the Middle Ages. The great preacher, Cardinal Jacques de Vitry, said, "All knowledge whatsoever ought to be applied to learning about Christ."[113]

At times the basic doctrine of Christian humanism is stated even more bluntly and emphatically. Thus St. Augustine wrote, "Every good and true Christian should understand that wherever he may find truth, it is his Lord's."[114] A similar very broad view is expressed by John of Salisbury (*Policrat.* 7. 10): "It is probable that all writings are to be read (except those that are forbidden), for not only all things written but all things done are believed to have been instituted for the utility of man, even though they are sometimes abused."[115] We may recognize here an echo of Rom. 15. 4, "For what things soever were written, were written for our learning," and of St. Augustine's distinction between *use* and *abuse*. With reference to the latter, John makes what he means very

---

[112] *Opera*, v, 2-3, and 25.

[113] *Anal. nov. Spic. Sol.*, ii, 360.

[114] *On Christian Doctrine*, 2. 18. 28.

[115] Ed. Webb, i, 194, 281; ii, 93, 130. Cf. Baudri de Bourgueil, *Oeuvres*, ccxxxviii, lines 133-134, and the statement of Peter Ceffons quoted by D. Trapp, o.s.a., "Peter Ceffons of Clairvaux," *Rech. theol. anc. med.*, xxiv (1957), p. 119.

clear by saying in the next chapter, "This is the true and immutable rule for those who philosophize, that anyone should so conduct himself in all reading or teaching, acting or refraining from action, that he promotes charity."[116] That is, just as charity is a limiting principle in the interpretation of Scripture, it should also be a limiting principle in human action generally and in reading or exposition of any kind. If we recall the aesthetic principles explained earlier, we can understand that this limitation by no means excludes aesthetic enjoyment, even though it may not appear "for its own sake."

What Christian humanists sought in pagan literature may be summed up under two headings: eloquence, and wisdom. St. Augustine points out that pagan teachers of rhetoric held that "wisdom without eloquence is of small benefit to states; but eloquence without wisdom is often extremely injurious and profits no one."[117] He goes on to say, "If those who taught the rules of eloquence, in the very books in which they did so, were forced by the power of truth to confess this, being ignorant of that true wisdom which descends from the Father of Lights, how much more ought we, who are the sons and ministers of this wisdom, to think in no other way?" The combination of wisdom and eloquence became a leading humanistic and educational goal of the Middle Ages. Thus Bernard Silvestris says at the beginning of his commentary on the *Aeneid* that the poem "has a twofold utility: first, a skill at writing which may be gained by imitation, and, second, a prudence concerning right action which is gathered from the teaching of examples."[118] Generally, the studies of the *trivium* were said to be designed to teach eloquence; wisdom was learned in the *quadrivium*. The prevalence of this dual ideal in the twelfth century has recently been thoroughly demonstrated,[119] and there is nothing to indicate that it was forgotten during the later Middle Ages. Thus John de Foxton asserts, "There are two kinds of knowledge: wisdom and eloquence. And wisdom is the true understanding of things; eloquence is the knowledge of how to express what is

---

[116] Cf. Guilbert of Tournai, *De modo addiscendi*, p. 185.

[117] *On Christian Doctrine*, 4. 5. 7. Cf. Cicero, *De invent.*, I. I. I.

[118] *Comm. in sex libros Eneidos*, ed. Riedel (Greifswald, 1924), pp. 2-3.

[119] Gabriel Nuchelmans, "Philologia et son mariage avec Mercure jusqu'à la fin du xɪɪᵉ siècle," *Latomus*, xvɪ (1957), 84-107.

known in ornamented language."[120] In the consideration of poetry, this idea harmonized well with the Horatian ideal of "profit and delight"; it thus underlies the criteria set by Harry Baily for the judgment of the tales told by Chaucer's pilgrims.

The problem of discovering eloquence among pagan authors was simple enough, even though its analysis in detail might be complex. Wisdom of a kind easily adapted to Christian uses was also not difficult to find: St. Augustine's well-known admiration for philosophical principles derived from Cicero offers one convenient illustration. The *De amicitia*, the *De senectute*, the *De officiis*, along with the moral essays of Seneca were enormously influential in the development of feudal ideals. Reflections of Cicero and Seneca are clear and obvious in works of political theory like the *Policraticus* of John of Salisbury, or, in the fourteenth century, in the *Compendium morale* of Roger of Waltham.[121] Petrarch's famous dictum that "it seems certain to me that Cicero himself would have been a Christian if he had been able to see Christ or to know the teaching of Christ"[122] represents, in somewhat extreme form, a very common medieval attitude. The poets were also full of sententious sayings easily given a Christian application, so that it was possible to compile useful *florilegia* derived from classical prose and verse. One of the most famous of these, arranged systematically to cover the chief points of moral philosophy, was the *Moralium dogma philosophorum* attributed to Guillaume de Conches.[123] But poetry, when it was neither openly historical nor sententious, required interpretation; and for this purpose allegory was just as useful a preservative in Christian hands as it had been in antiquity. The classical idea that poetic fables, in one way or another, are veils covering underlying truths enjoyed an unbroken tradition throughout the Middle Ages.

Thus Lactantius said that poets "change and transfer actual occurrences into other representations by oblique transformations," forming a veil for an underlying truth. This idea achieved wide currency. It is echoed by Isidore of Seville, who adds that, for this

[120] *Liber cosmographiae*, Cap. 22. d. 2.
[121] Oxford, Bodl., MS Fairfax 4.
[122] *De sui ipsius et multorum ignorantia*, ed. Capelli (Paris, 1906), p. 78.
[123] For a list of such florilegia, see Ph. Delhaye, *Florilegium morale oxoniense* (Louvain and Lille, 1955), p. 21.

reason, Lucan is an historian rather than a poet.[124] Isidore's statement was incorporated by Rabanus in his *De universo*,[125] and by the fourteenth century the idea had become extremely common, although the original restriction to historical truth was abandoned. Thus, in Petrarch's quotation from Lactantius, he is made to say that poets transfer "those things which are true" rather than "actual occurrences."[126] Berchorius cites Rabanus to support his moralization of Ovid.[127] Thomas Waleys, citing Isidore of Seville, says that "beneath all poetic fables there lies something of truth according to the intention of the poet composing the fable. Whence, according to Isidore . . . the office of poets is to describe this truth under a certain covering. Thus some fables have physical exposition, some historical, and some moral."[128] The same theory found expression in many other ways. Thus Theodulf of Orléans defended his reading of Ovid and Virgil by saying that in their poems "although there may be many frivolous things, many truths lie hidden beneath the false covering."[129] John the Scot says that the poetic art "conveys moral or physical doctrine by feigned fables and allegorical similitudes."[130] Baudri de Bourgueil tells us that when poets are read, we should "investigate what lies hidden within."[131] In the *De planctu naturae*, Nature informs the speaker that many authors have described Cupid "sub integumentali involucro aenigmatum," having explained that "the poetic lyre resounds falsely in the superficial cortex of the letter, but within a secret of higher understanding is spoken to the listeners, so that if the shells of exterior falseness are set aside, the reader will find hidden within a sweeter nucleus of truth."[132] Nigellus Wireker expresses a similar theory in the prologue to his *Speculum stultorum*:

> Frequently a little history encloses a
> Great mystery, and precious things are hidden in the lowly.

[124] *Etym.*, 8. 7. 10. [125] *PL*, III, col. 419.
[126] *Invective contra medicum*, ed. Ricci (Rome, 1950), p. 36.
[127] See F. Ghisalberti, "L'Ovidius Moralizatus di Pierre Bersuire," *Studij romanzi*, XXIII (1933), p. 88.
[128] Quoted by Beryl Smalley, "Thomas Waleys, o.p.," *Arch. frat. pred.*, XXIV (1954), p. 100.
[129] *MGH, Poetae*, I, 543. [130] *Super ier. coel.*, *PL*, 122, col. 146.
[131] *Oeuvres*, CCXVI, lines 649-650. [132] *PL*, 210, cols. 451, 454.

John of Salisbury, paraphrasing Bernard Silvestris on the *Aeneid*, finds wisdom in Virgil *sub involucro*,[133] and John of Garland wrote a brief commentary on Ovid called *Integumenta ovidiana*. Jean de Meun, as we have seen, refers to "les integumenz des poetes," and in his defense of poetry Richard de Bury refers to the same theory when he speaks of "the delicate Minerva [i.e., wisdom] secretly lurking beneath the image of pleasure."[134] He goes on to quote Horace on profit and delight in a manner which suggests that, in his mind, Horatian "profit" was synonymous with allegorical truth.[135] It would be possible to cite many more comments which show that the medieval reader expected to find philosophical utility in poetry through allegorical analysis.

The attitude toward poetry was, in this sense, optimistic. Radulphus de Longo Campo says of poetry that it is "a science enclosing in meter or prose serious and illustrious speech. There are three species: history, fable, and argument (or comedy). History is a narration of true things or of things seeming to be true. A fable is a narrative of a thing which is neither true nor seems to be true. An argument is a narration of a thing which may not be true, but which nevertheless seems to be true. Under history fall satire and tragedy. A satire is devoted altogether to the extirpation of vices and the promotion of virtues. A tragedy is a work altogether in contempt of fortune. With reference to a fable or an argument, moreover, although their narration may be fictitious, they nevertheless exhort a contempt of vice and an appetite for virtue. Thus poetry expels vices and promotes virtue, sometimes by history, sometimes by fable, and sometimes by argument."[136]

The predominantly moral nature of poetry is here fully appreciated. Certain other medieval statements about poetry are less sanguine, and, indeed, poetry has always had its enemies. But we should be careful not to misinterpret statements like that of Bernard Silvestris to the effect that poets are "introducers to philosophy"[137] so as to make them seem a kind of damning with faint praise. By "philosophy" Bernard meant the love of God, and by

[133] *Policrat.*, 8. 24.
[134] *Philobiblon*, 13. 16.
[135] This is certainly true of Holcot's use of it, *In lib. sap.* (Basel, 1586), p. 4.
[136] Oxford, Balliol Coll. MS 146 b, fol. 101 verso. On *argumentum* cf. John of Garland, *De arte prosayca metrica et rithmica*, ed. G. Mari, *RF*, XII (1902), 926.
[137] *Comm. super Eneidos*, p. 36.

"poetry" he meant pagan poetry. Thus what he said was, from his point of view, highly complimentary. In the same way, Hugh of St. Victor distinguishes between the arts proper and certain appendages to the arts which "prepare the way toward philosophy." Included among the latter are all the songs of the poets as well as the writings of those "whom we are now accustomed to call philosophers," who present material of brief compass "in long verbal ambiguities."[138] The latter are those philosophers in the Platonic tradition who say things *per involucrum*. The fact that pagan poets and philosophers do not present the naked truth simply and directly is responsible for their "preparatory" character. What they may be found to say, after exposition, may harmonize with the substance of the arts, or may illustrate their conclusions, but such works in themselves are not true philosophy. What this amounts to is a statement in twelfth-century terms of exactly the same kind of reservation about pagan letters that is illustrated very emphatically in St. Jerome's letter to Eustochium, but the attitude does not preclude, any more than it did in the mind of St. Jerome, the general view expressed in the letter to Magnus. Pagan poetry was thought to have an ethical function, but it was not in itself divine philosophy. Elsewhere, Hugh observes that "the pagan philosophers also wrote works concerning ethics in which they described, as it were, certain members of virtue cut off from the body of felicity; but the members of virtue cannot live without the body of God's love."[139] To continue the figure, the members of virtue may, however, introduce the subject. No one expected to find in the pagan poets and philosophers what he could find in the New Testament, but men of all sorts did expect to find ancillary material. Hugh recommends that the arts be studied seriously, but that the poets be read "if time allows," since "at times serious things delight more when mixed with the ludicrous, and rarity makes a good thing precious. Thus we sometimes retain more eagerly a *sentence* found in the midst of a fable. . . ." There is more than a germ here of the literary aesthetic developed in more positive form later by Petrarch, Ficino, and Erasmus.

The fact that there were similarities between the allegory of poetry and the allegory of Scripture, in spite of their essential dif-

[138] *Didascalicon*, 3. 4.
[139] *De scripturis*, PL, 175, cols. 9-10.

ferences, did not escape medieval exegetes and critics. As time passed, habits of thought developed in scriptural exegesis left a strong mark on literary analysis. John the Scot sought, in fact, to explain scriptural allegory by analogy with poetic allegory, suggesting that theology (*sc.* "exegesis") is a kind of poetry.[140] During the later Middle Ages the analogy was usually reversed; defenders of poetry made constant reference to the fact that *alieniloquium* is common to poetry and the Bible, and to the further fact that the Bible does contain, in addition to historical and doctrinal materials, some materials that are obviously fabulous. Perhaps the most widely discussed instance of this comparison is that which appears in Dante's *Convivio* (2. 1). For our purposes, the important point is that the comparison exists, but in order to discuss it, one must take some sort of attitude about its significance. Since there is no standard opinion in the matter a tentative interpretation is involved in the following discussion, although, so far as the main points are concerned, almost any other interpretation would serve as well. In the relevant passage, Dante explains that the exposition of his poetry should be both literal and allegorical. A poetic fable is itself literal, but the sense hidden under the veil of the fable is allegorical. Thus when Ovid says that Orpheus calmed wild beasts and caused trees and stones to be moved by his music, he meant that a wise man through his eloquence can soften hard hearts and move those who are without knowledge and art. "Truly," Dante continues, "the theologians take this sense otherwise than the poets, but since my intention is to follow the poets, I take the allegorical sense in the way the poets use it." What does this distinction mean? The theologians use *allegory* in the specific sense suggested by St. Paul: things and actions under the old dispensation are allegorical foreshadowings of things and actions under the new dispensation. Dante uses instead fabulous things and actions to suggest other things and actions, just as Ovid is said to do in the example. Dante goes on to explain the "moral" meaning with a scriptural illustration: just as Christ took only three others—Peter, James, and John—with Him to the mount of the transfiguration, so also we should have only a few companions in our most secret undertakings. Now it will be seen that this interpretation, which is embarrassingly shallow to anyone familiar with the traditions of exe-

[140] *Super ier. coel., PL,* 122, col. 146.

gesis, is not, technically speaking, tropological. The "moral" might have been derived just as well from a pagan poem, since no specifically Christian truth is involved in it, and, in fact, the lesson produced sounds a little like worldly prudence. This gives us three senses: literal, allegorical, and moral. Although a scriptural illustration is used for the third, it is not specifically theological. Dante has not, up to this point, been concerned with the "four senses" of Scripture, but with poetic allegory of a type that would have been familiar in antiquity.

He goes on, however, to discuss one further level, the "anagogical" or the "spiritual" sense. In this context it seems to me wrong to take the word *anagogico* (i.e., "leading upward") in the specific meaning it has in the famous diptych; it is simply a synonym for "spiritual," used in such a way that it can refer to any or all of the three conventional "higher" meanings. As Dante goes on to explain, in this sense the things mentioned signify "the supernal things of eternal glory," just as the exodus of the people of Israel from Egypt, which actually took place, signifies spiritually the exodus of the soul from sin. This interpretation is tropological, not anagogical; in the letter to Can Grande it is called "moral." But it is most definitely a "spiritual" sense, so that Dante insists that its basis must be literal truth rather than fable. What he has done is to list two modes of fabulous or poetic allegory and to add, as a further possibility in some texts, the kind of allegory found in interpretations of the Scriptures, without meaning to refer to the convention of distinguishing among allegory, tropology, and anagogy. When he says that he is following the allegory of the poets, he means that he is not, at the time, inviting his readers to seek a true history and a spiritual significance in his texts.

Is it possible that a poem which is not directly inspired by the Holy Spirit, even though it is written by a Christian, may contain materials to be understood spiritually? A very significant document bearing on this question is the Preface to the *Anticlaudianus* of Alanus de Insulis, the relevant passage from which is quoted in the last chapter. The account of allegory it contains closely parallels a classical account of scriptural allegory in the *Periarchon* of Origen, which was known to the Middle Ages in a Latin translation.[141] There Origen says that the Scriptures are so written (1)

[141] See the quotation in *Exégèse médiévale*, p. 199.

that the more simple may be edified by the historical sense, (2) that those who have begun to perfect themselves may be edified morally, and (3) that those who have perfected themselves may be led to discern the allegorical significance. That is, a progression is seen from the historical to the moral and thence to the allegorical in terms of "perfection." Alanus says with reference to his poem that the sweetness of the literal sense will caress the puerile ear, that the moral significance will instruct those who are perfecting themselves, and that the allegory will sharpen the understandings of those nearing perfection.[142] The parallel is clear, and it is also clear that the author of the Preface expected his readers to use the same approach to the poem that they were accustomed to use in reading the Bible. Moreover, Alanus, or the author of the Preface if it was not Alanus, goes on to warn off the merely carnal, lest sacred things prostituted before dogs grow vile, or pearls perish beneath the feet of swine, or lest secrets become debased if their majesty is divulged to the unworthy.[143] The references to Matt. 7. 6 and 13. 11-15 indicate that the same kind of spiritual message is implicit in the poem that is implicit in the Scriptures.

Actually, there is nothing very strange about the underlying assumptions of this Preface. If a Christian author uses figurative concepts from the Scriptures, like the various Pauline expressions of "oldness" and "newness" or "marriage" taken in its figurative sense, or, on the other hand, if he employs "things" or "actions" mentioned in the Bible in such a way that their conventional figurative meanings are implied, these concepts, things, and actions will carry their spiritual overtones with them into the poem. The spiritual meanings are not creations of the author of the poem, but represent a common language of the faith. Exactly the same situation prevails in the visual arts, where scriptural imagery carries with it the fruits of traditional spiritual interpretation. The artist or poet may not be very "inspired" in any way, but this fact has nothing to do with his ability to employ scriptural signs significantly. Allegorical imagery from the Scriptures might appear during the Middle Ages in literary works of all kinds, in the lives of the saints, in the poems of the troubadours, in the jocular produc-

---

[142] Ed. Bossuat (Paris, 1955), p. 56.
[143] Cf. *De planctu naturae*, *PL*, 210, col. 445.

tions of clerks, in fabliaux, or, in fact, in ordinary conversation.[144] There is no reason why we should be surprised to find it in Dante's *Commedia*, and no special critical theories are needed to account for its presence there. The *accessus* to the *Commedia* written to Can Grande demands that we seek spiritual understanding in that poem in accordance with the conventional four levels, but there is nothing new or startling about this demand. The pilgrimage described in it is literally a fable, but it nevertheless reflects the scriptural concept of the pilgrimage of the spirit (e.g., 1 Pet. 2. 11), and carries with it many of the connotations of that concept developed in Patristic and later exegesis. Moreover, Dante makes frequent use of things and actions which had acquired very rich areas of spiritual significance. His own holiness is not here in question, any more, let us say, than the holiness of a priest, or the lack of it, has any bearing on the validity of the sacraments he administers.

To return for a moment to the *Convivio*, it is of especial interest to notice that Dante uses a scriptural illustration for his poetically "moral" level. This illustration lends authority to his point, even though it contributes nothing to the theory of exegesis. The same kind of authority was used to defend the study of pagan poetry which could not, strictly speaking, give rise to spiritual understanding. Thus Berchorius posits an analogy between poetry and the Scriptures in the preface to his commentary on Ovid: " 'And they will indeed turn away their hearing from the truth, but will be turned unto fables' [2 Tim. 4. 4] says the planter and waterer of the Christian faith, Paul [1 Cor. 3. 4ff], the Apostle of Jesus Christ. But certainly we may bring forth the additional thought that many fables are to be used as enigmas so that a moral sense may be extracted from them and so that their falsity may be associated with the truth. And indeed the Holy Scripture may be seen to do just this in many passages where it is known to use fables for the demonstration of some truth, as we may see in the Book of Judges in the fable of the trees wishing to elect a king [Ju. 9. 8-15], in the Book of Kings where the thistle wishes his son to take

---

[144] For examples, see D. W. Robertson, Jr., "St. Foy among the Thorns," *MLN*, LXVII (1952), 295-299; "Five Poems of Marcabru," *SP*, LI (1954), 539-560; "The 'Partitura amorosa' of Jean de Savoie," *PQ*, XXXIII (1954), 1-9; "The Doctrine of Charity in Mediaeval Literary Gardens," *Speculum*, XXVI (1951), 43-45.

a wife [4 Kings 14. 9], or in Ezechiel where the eagle is feigned to carry away the marrow of the cedar [Ez. 17]. For thus Scripture uses these and similar fables so that some truth may be extracted from them. The poets who first wrote fables composed them in a similar way. That is, they wished always that through their fictions some truth might be understood."[145]

Berchorius adds that it is permissible, moreover, "to erect and fabricate the Tabernacle of the Law with the treasures of the Egyptians." That is, the Bible shows that although there may be empty fables, like those condemned by St. Paul, it also demonstrates that there is nothing wrong with useful fables, and even pagan fables, if treated properly, may be made useful. A more general comparison between poetry and the Scriptures was made by Petrarch, who wrote to his brother in defense of poetry, "Is it not enough that I affirm theology to be poetry concerning God? To speak of Christ as a lion, as a lamb, or as a worm [Ps. 21. 7]—what is this if not poetry? A thousand such things you would find in the Sacred Scriptures which would take too long to enumerate. Indeed, how else do the parables of the Savior in the Gospels operate except, if I may express it in one word, by *alieniloquium*, which we are accustomed to call 'allegory'? And with words of this kind the whole realm of poetry is clothed."[146]

Boccaccio makes the comparison more explicit by dividing poetic fables into types, each of which has a scriptural analogy. First, there are fables which lack all appearance of truth, like the fables of Aesop. Second, there are those which on the surface mingle truth and fiction. And third, there are fables which are more like history than fiction since they concern things which might have happened. The first type appears in the Bible in fables like that in Judges. The second represents the technique of much of the Old Testament. And the third is like the parables of Christ. Boccaccio adds that there is a fourth type of fiction which contains truth neither on the surface nor underneath, but such fictions are like "the ravings of old women" and have nothing to do with poetry.[147]

The humanistic tradition represented by Dante, Petrarch, and Boccaccio was carried into the fifteenth century by Coluccio Salutati, who also stressed the analogy between poetry and the Bible. To-

[145] *Studij romanzi*, XXIII, 87.   [146] *Familiari*, 10. 4.
[147] *Gen. deor.*, 14. 9.

ward the close of his life Salutati became involved in a controversy over the subject of poetry with a Dominican. The latter wrote a bulky treatise attacking the traditional doctrines of medieval humanism, but not, we must hasten to add, with a view to setting up a humanism of another kind.[148] This treatise provoked a further defense of poetry by Salutati in an epistle. Although the letter is unfinished, it expresses Salutati's critical position very well.[149] After explaining the indebtedness of poetry to the arts generally, and calling attention to its allegorical or "bilingual" character,[150] Salutati observes sadly that the name of poetry is detestable "among the religious."[151] But this should not be true, since, he says, the Scriptures are allegorical in the same way that poetry is allegorical. For authority on this point, he cites Origen, St. Gregory, and St. Peter Damian, exclaiming concerning the Canticle of Canticles, "What is more poetical, and, according to the *cortex*, more amorous and lascivious?" The whole Scripture, he says, is "mystical," and capable of being reduced to an "allegorical understanding." Impatient with his opponent, he urges, "Read and consider those most holy and most learned books of St. Augustine, of which the title is *On Christian Doctrine*." There the reader will find that the Scriptures abound in mystical senses of the same kind as those used by the poets. This argument, which was a commonplace of fourteenth-century humanism, illustrates well the way in which the defense of poetry was based on an assumption of scriptural allegory. If the spiritual interpretation of Scripture was out of date in the fourteenth century, as has been alleged, the humanism of the pe-

---

[148] Now edited by E. Hunt, *Iohannis Dominici lucula noctis* (Notre Dame, Indiana, 1940).

[149] There is another discussion of the same points at the beginning of the *De laboribus Herculis.*

[150] *Epistolario*, ed. Novati (Rome, 1905), IV, 233-234.

[151] Albertino Mussato had been attacked for his poetic interests by a Dominican. See *Epistolae*, pp. 72-74 in *Opera* (Venice, 1636), a volume in which the epistles are paginated separately. The traditional character of Mussato's views is emphasized, but without evidence to speak of, in E. R. Curtius, "Theologische Poetik in italienischen Trecento," *ZfrP*, LX (1940), 1-45. Boccaccio included the friars prominently among the enemies of poetry in the *Genealogie*. On the other hand, Holcot, Trivet, and Thomas Walsingham were Dominicans and Ridewal was a Franciscan. We should therefore not conclude that all friars were anti-humanistic, but it is, at the same time, obvious that some of them developed an attitude toward literature and the arts very much like that of the Puritans of the sixteenth century.

riod, including that of Petrarch, was out of date also. The arguments of the humanists, moreover, represent a clear development of Patristic traditions which are in turn firmly based on the theology of St. Paul. They cannot be dismissed as mere excuses, without resort to a transcendent cynicism which would deny the whole edifice of Christian thought as a mere rationalization on the part of men who were essentially selfish. Boccaccio's expositions in the *Genealogie* and Salutati's analyses of the labors of Hercules afford excellent illustrations of the way in which cultured men of the period approached poetry. We have no obligation to like what they did, but we should at least accord it a certain respect.

Among the arguments adduced against the study of poetry during the Middle Ages, perhaps the most significant were those which are found in the *Summa theologica* of St. Thomas Aquinas. We should understand at the outset that St. Thomas had in mind pagan poetry.. The first argument (1-1. 9. ad 1) appears in a defense of the allegorical character of the Bible, where it is directed against the view that Scripture should not use metaphors, which are proper only to poetry, "the lowest among all the disciplines." St. Thomas replies that poetry uses metaphors for purposes of representation, which is naturally delightful; but the Scriptures use metaphors on account of necessity and utility. This argument was repeated by the Dominican critic of Mussato, who said that poetry uses figurative language "for representation and delight," whereas the Scriptures use metaphor to veil truths so that they may be revealed to the studious but hidden from the unworthy.[152] Actually, St. Thomas's distinction involves simply the difference between figurative expressions used for pleasing ornament or emphasis and figurative expressions used in a Pauline sense. No one expected to find the latter in pagan poetry. The second argument (1-2. 101. 2 ad 2) appears in answer to the proposition that rituals are improper because they are "theatrical and poetical." St. Thomas replies to the effect that poetry contains little truth, whereas ritual, because of the divine mysteries it contains, must use sensible figures. Again, it is obvious that pagan poetry cannot be expected to contain divine mysteries. Mussato's assertion that Virgil should be ranged with the Prophets among "Christians without Christ" is simply an extreme way of putting something which had been held for centuries:

[152] Mussato, *Epistolae*, pp. 72-73.

although poetry does not contain revealed truth, it looks forward to that truth and does contain ancillary truths. St. Thomas, who was aware of his own search for "Egyptian gold" in the works of Aristotle, might well have admitted as much if he had been pressed in another context. But in both instances the context demanded a sharp distinction and a pat conclusion, and, as usual, St. Thomas did not hesitate to supply them. Those Dominicans who pressed his arguments into service against traditional humanism were taking an extreme position which confined all culture to the Scriptures, the exegetes, and the theologians.

Still to be accounted for is the fact that certain commentators on the classics, including the author of the *Ovide moralisé* and Berchorius, sometimes adduce patently Christian meanings for pagan fables, even meanings which involve equations between characters in Ovidian stories and Christ, the Church, and the Blessed Virgin. Boccaccio in a few instances suggests that fables have meanings consonant with the four senses of Scripture. During the later Middle Ages, when fables became a common source of exemplary materials for preachers and expositors, a development of this kind was almost inevitable. The stories themselves became disassociated from their contexts and circulated as independent exemplary units. There is no law which restricts the application of an *exemplum*, so that the author who employed one had no qualms about using it in any way he saw fit. The *Ovide moralisé* presents in this respect a strange mixture of traditional academic interpretations of the *Metamorphoses* and exemplary expositions. However, certain interpretations of a theological nature had a very long history. Orpheus appears as a figure for Christ in the art of the catacombs, and there are very early associations between Christ and Hercules, or between Christ and Ulysses. In a sense, therefore, the growth of theological interpretations was supported by a very ancient tradition. But it is undoubtedly true that the increasing popularity of the *exemplum* during the thirteenth and fourteenth centuries tended to stimulate what modern scholars regard as "outrageous" interpretations of classical narratives. Meanwhile, the underlying logic of the four senses of Scripture became a habit of mind, and we find preachers like Brinton giving "mystical" or "spiritual" interpretations of materials which have no connection with the Scriptures whatsoever. It is not surprising that the same logic was sometimes applied to materials from classical sources. Genial spirits who found sacramental mysteries in the natural world around them could without difficulty find them also in stories from Ovid.

Among pagan poets who were widely read during the Middle Ages, perhaps none occasions more surprise among modern scholars than Ovid. Virgil, Juvenal, and even Horace are moral enough on the surface, but Ovid is the author of a poem which has been called "the most immoral work ever written by a man of genius." Yet the medieval *accessus* which introduced Ovid to monastic readers in the Middle Ages frequently call him an instructor in good manners or a teacher of legitimate love.[153] With reference to the later Middle Ages, Ghisalberti writes that "the high esteem in which this poet was held, particularly in the fourteenth and fifteenth centuries, caused his work to be much sought after and transcribed, commented in the schools, and paraphrased in the vulgar tongues of Europe. . . . The rich wealth of mythological lore presented by him in such vividly pagan coloring, was copiously drawn upon by allegorists and moralizers in the service of a world dominated by the Christian faith."[154] We should understand at the outset that the medieval world was predominantly rural, that the "facts of life" were not usually glossed over for the sake of an artificial parlor decorum, and that these "facts" were not considered inimical to piety on the one hand or to useful philosophical thought on the other. Bishop Bradwardine, although he was misled into thinking of the *De vetula* as an authentic work, considered Ovid to be a Platonic philosopher.[155] With reference to the *Ars amatoria*, a fourteenth-century introduction tells us that, although the work seems to encourage adultery and laxity, as a matter of fact the author detests lechery and lecherous love, and describes how we may love virtuously.[156] The poem is, in other words, ironic. Another says that the purpose of the poem is to attack the corruption of dissolute women.[157] A thirteenth-century MS informs us that the *Remedia amoris* is not contrary to the *Ars amatoria*; its purpose is to remove pernicious love.[158] Manuscripts of the *Heroides* which contain

[153] Cf. Jean Leclercq, *L'amour des lettres et le désir de dieu* (Paris, 1957), p. 113.

[154] F. Ghisalberti, "Mediaeval Biographies of Ovid," *JWCI*, ix (1946), 25.

[155] *De causa Dei* (London, 1618), pp. 94-95, 108.

[156] "Mediaeval Biographies of Ovid," p. 57.

[157] *Ibid.*, p. 13.   [158] *Ibid.*, p. 47.

prefatory material usually defend its moral purpose.[159] Salutati, who was probably here presenting traditional rather than original views, defends the moral purpose of both the *Amores* and the *Ars amatoria*.[160] In general, Ovid's amatory figures like the "militia Veneris" were taken as being humorously ironic rather than lustfully serious. Although Ovid was sometimes attacked during the Middle Ages, it is quite likely that many medieval readers would have agreed with the assertion of E. K. Rand that Ovid "left it for those who could detect his satire to find . . . that ridicule is the most potent enemy of love."[161] The sprightly tone and ironic humor of much vernacular literature after the first half of the twelfth century probably owes a great deal to Ovidian inspiration. What saved Ovid for Christian readers was thus *allegoria*, either in the form of irony or in allegorical exposition.

The history of medieval commentaries on the classics and manuals of mythography has yet to be written. Much material remains to be edited, and until this work is done it will be impossible to establish the literary relationships among the various commentaries or even, in some instances, to establish the authorship of some of the more important documents. A brief account of some useful works may be helpful, however, for those who wish to pursue the subject further.[162] Among the earliest of the commentaries on the classics which exerted a strong influence on the traditions of medieval allegory was that on the *Thebaid* attributed to Lactantius Placidus. This work, although it is not heavily allegorical, gathered accretions of an allegorical character as it was copied and recopied throughout the centuries. Another commentary on the *Thebaid*, of uncertain date and attribution, was printed by Helm among the works of Fulgentius, the first influential Christian mythographer. The rather fantastic commentary of Fulgentius on the *Aeneid* was supplanted in the twelfth century by that of Bernard Silvestris. His books on mythography, on the other hand, enjoyed a more lasting reputation, and were still being used in the Renaissance. Scattered remarks during Carolingian times, for example in the

---

[159] *Ibid.*, pp. 11, 44, 46.

[160] *De laboribus Herculis*, ed. B. L. Ullman (Zürich, 1951), I, 68.

[161] "Ovid and the Spirit of Metamorphosis," *Harvard Essays on Classical Subjects* (Cambridge, Mass., 1912), p. 229.

[162] Bibliographical material will be found in Seznec's *The Survival of the Pagan Gods*.

poem quoted earlier by Theodulf of Orléans and in the *Libri Caro-lini* recently attributed to the same author, show that the allegori-zation of myths was a current practice. Some useful materials ap-pear in the *Etymologiae* of Isidore of Seville and in the *De uni-verso* of Rabanus Maurus. Commentaries on Martianus Capella by Remigius of Auxerre, John the Scot, and Alexander Neckam re-veal a strong mythographic tradition. Remigius is also probably the author of a manual of mythography printed as the work of "Mythographus Vaticanus Secundus." In the twelfth century com-mentaries and manuals of mythography became more numerous. Among the commentaries on Ovid, those by Arnulf of Orléans were perhaps most important. His commentary on Lucan, recently published, although it is not rich in mythographical materials, fur-nishes a convenient guide to the manner in which classical texts were studied in an important academic center during the twelfth century. There is useful material in the encyclopedia of Alexander Neckam. Neckam may have been the author of the famous manual of the third Vatican Mythographer, although it has also been at-tributed to Albericus of London. Commentaries on the *Consola-tion* of Boethius, of which the most important for the later Middle Ages are those by Guillaume de Conches and Nicholas Trivet, are rich in mythographical materials. Neither, unfortunately, has been printed. John of Garland's *Integumenta ovidiana* presents an exposition of the *Metamorphoses* in highly condensed form. Most of the glosses on Ovid produced during the thirteenth and four-teenth centuries remain in manuscript, but we may assume that the *Ovide moralisé* contains, in its more restrained interpretations, much commonplace material. A Franciscan, John Ridewal, pro-duced a useful mythographical manual in the fourteenth century called *Fulgentius metaforalis*. Commentaries on Ovid by Gio-vanni del Vergilio and Berchorius have been printed, the latter in Renaissance editions, where it is attributed to Thomas Waleys. In England, Thomas of Walsingham produced a mythographical manual for the Prior of St. Albans which furnishes evidence for the increasing interest in mythological materials in that country during the later fourteenth century. Meanwhile, Boccaccio's *Gene-alogie deorum gentilium* became a standard manual, whose popu-larity lasted well into the Renaissance, and there is a great deal of allegorical material in the *De laboribus Herculis* of Coluccio

Salutati. As might be expected, these works vary a great deal in detail. There was no definitive interpretation of any myth or fable. On the other hand, the pagan deities and their attributes tended to form a more or less consistent iconological language in keeping with the conventionalizing tendencies of Gothic style; and certain of the more popular fables acquired fairly consistent meanings. If some of the French poets of the fourteenth century could create entirely new myths, without classical authority, their freedom in this respect was made possible only by a strong tradition of conventional exposition which could readily be applied to new material. The manuals and commentaries do not always furnish detailed material which can be applied mechanically in the interpretation of any given poem; they do furnish, however, conventional areas of meaning which are useful as guides, and a method which will usually elucidate the specific uses of myth in the contexts established by literary and artistic works.

It cannot be emphasized too strongly that the tradition of allegorizing classical material during the Middle Ages was essentially humanistic, and not simply an excuse which made an otherwise furtive taste for poetry respectable. Allegory was associated with works which appealed most strongly to the humanistic spirit, like the *Consolation* of Boethius.[163] This work was regarded not as a "history" or "autobiography" but as a fable consisting of a dialogue between two parts of the same person. Thus Trivet says that the two speakers are "the spirit suffering from the aggravation of the sensuality, and the reason offering consolation from the vigor of wisdom."[164] Again, the introduction to Chaucer's translation in a fifteenth-century manuscript says that the author "schewes him self as a persone withholde with wisdom and resoun that comes forth and bringes accordynge remedies and consolaciouns, and this dialoge in this oon persone as it were too, oon desolate and another full of confortht."[165] Not only is the work as a whole a fable, but it contains fables used morally as well as indirect expressions of philosophical ideas which could be, and were, explained *per in-*

---

[163] On the humanistic value of the *Consolation*, see Konrad Burdach, "Die humanistischen Wirkungen der Trostschrift des Boethius," *Deutsche Vierteljahrschrift*, XI (1933), 530-553. Medieval translations are surveyed by A. van de Vyver, *Humanisme et renaissance*, VI (1939).

[164] London, BM, MS Burney 131, fol. 3 verso.

[165] Oxford, Bodl. MS Auct. F. 3. 5, fols. 199 and 199 verso.

tegumentum. As time passed, this kind of "poetic" expression was also associated with Plato, to whose *Timaeus* the philosophers of the twelfth century busily applied the method of *integumentum.* Thus Trivet wrote, "In setting forth his philosophy in the manner of ancient theologians, Plato presented it *sub integumentis* and in figurative words, even though he had a firm understanding of what he wished to say. For it is the custom of poets to make use of fables and *integumenta* and to use figurative locutions frequently, so that Plato's method of speaking is harmonious with that of the poets."[166]

That this attitude toward Plato (and toward the nature of poetry) did not pass with the close of the Middle Ages we learn from Ficino, who wrote that "it was the custom among Pythagoras, Socrates, and Plato to conceal divine mysteries in figures and *involucris,* to conceal their wisdom modestly before the boasting of the Sophists, to joke seriously and to play most studiously."[167] Ficino's method of interpreting Plato was based on the method used in the allegorical interpretation of Scripture,[168] although he sometimes used the terminology of exegesis directly.[169] Moreover, he held that Plato exiled the poets only from the city, where the ignorant youth would not be able to interpret their allegories.[170] Similarly, Erasmus found allegory "in all the fictions of the ancient poets,"[171] and commended St. Augustine for having used a "Platonic" style consistent with that of the poets and of St. Paul.[172] The allegorical method, in spite of the abuse that has been heaped upon it in modern times, was dear to the hearts of some of the most intelligent and perspicacious thinkers of the Middle Ages and the early Renaissance. The literalists of the period, who, in the time of Ficino and Erasmus were for the most part Aristotelians, were generally anti-humanistic, detesting literature and the arts and embracing either materialistic philosophy or technical theology as the whole of human culture. The intense interest Erasmus showed in rhetoric and the techniques of persuasion was in part a

[166] MS Burney 131, fol. 46.
[167] *In Parmenidem, Opera* (Basel, 1576), II, 1137.   [168] *Opera,* II, 1370.
[169] E.g., *ibid.,* II, 1385: "The narrative of Socrates is allegorical and anagogical."
[170] *Opera,* II, 1315.
[171] *De rerum copia, Opera* (Leyden, 1703), I, 90-91.
[172] *Opera,* V, 82-83.

result of a desire on his part to prevent Christian philosophy from degenerating into a morass of empty technical verbiage.

The beginnings of a more "modern" attitude, but without any modern insistence on hedonistic aesthetics, may be found among the friars who attacked Mussato, Dante, Petrarch, Boccaccio, and Salutati, and, at the beginning of the Renaissance, in Jean Gerson. The controversy over the *Roman de la rose* affords an excellent means of describing the issues that were at stake in the defense of allegory as a humanistic device. It was precipitated by Christine de Pisan, who was an allegorist herself, but who steadfastly refused to admit the efficacy of any allegorical work which was not sufficiently pious on the surface to be fit for the ears of children. In a letter to Jean de Montreuil, she raised the following points: (1) Raison names the members of generation outright, (2) Raison says that it is better to deceive than to be deceived, (3) La Vieille and Jalousie are too severe in their treatment of women, (4) Genius encourages the work of Nature in everyone and recommends a lecherous garden, (5) Jean is generally too hard on women, (6) the end of the poem is horrible.[173] In evaluating these criticisms, we should remember that the art and exegesis of the Middle Ages show no qualms about the members of generation, so that Christine's stricture represents a change in taste and not an appeal to a universal principle. Her accusation against Raison refers to lines 4377ff., where the idea that it is better to deceive is attributed by Raison to lovers and certainly not advocated by Raison herself. La Vieille, Jalousie, and Genius all speak in character; no one of them represents the views of the author. Jean's attitude toward women is simply a traditional manner of expressing the evils of "effeminacy" or lack of virtue, and the end of the poem is, as we have seen, a vivid attack on idolatrous lechery. When Christine's strictures came to the attention of Gontier Col, secretary to the King, he penned a summary reply, accusing Christine of acting like a "passionate woman" (i.e., effeminately) and urging her to retract her hasty accusations. But Christine sent copies of the controversy to the Queen and to Guillaume de Tignonville, Provost of Paris. There resulted Gerson's first extended blast against the *Roman*.

[173] C. F. Ward, *The Epistles on the Romance of the Rose and other Documents in the Debate* (Chicago, 1911). Aside from references to Gerson's sermons, this brief summary is from the documents printed by Ward.

The *Tractatus contra romantium de rosa* is a very transparent allegory in which virtuous abstractions complain against the *Roman*. Thus Chastity holds that the teachings of La Vieille invite all to attack chastity; that Jean, the foolish lover, condemns matrimony altogether; that the poem says that those who enter religion violate nature; that the poem throws fiery words against chastity; that Raison speaks plainly and lasciviously; that the poem mixes the dissolute and the spiritual; that it promises Paradise to all who work carnally, especially outside of matrimony; that the poem mentions dishonest parts of the body and evil actions. Theology complains that Jean abused his learning by making rhymes; that he leads youth astray, as Ovid does; that he should have made devout and honest pictures; that he spreads perverse doctrines; that he has no right to say evil things through *personae*; that he urges all ladies to give themselves to men; that Genius urges everyone to work carnally; that Jean's Nature is a corruption of Nature in Alanus de Insulis. Gerson closes by saying that Raison should not have mentioned sinful members—obviously a sore point with him—because these members have been sinful since the Fall. The treatise ends with a long harangue against sin in general and Jean in particular. The direction of all of these complaints is obvious. A poem is, in the first place, an abuse of learning. Aside from that, evil things should not be said, even through *personae*. If the concept represented by Genius does represent something which urges everyone to "work carnally," then Genius has no place in a literary work. The surfaces should be kept clean at all costs. It will be seen at once that if these principles are maintained, much medieval poetry, including the works of Alanus, Chaucer, Petrarch, Boccaccio, and many others would have to be cast aside. Among classical authors Ovid especially would be forbidden. As a matter of fact, in a *Sermo contra luxuriam*, although he quotes Ovid against lechery in good medieval fashion, using the story of Pygmalion,[174] Gerson concludes by saying that those who own lecherous books like the works of Ovid or the *Roman* should be forced to burn them.[175] He alleges elsewhere that the *Roman* speaks of the violation of matrimony as a small sin,[176] urges that it is actually sinful, the *Roman* to the contrary notwithstanding, to mention the

---

[174] *Opera* (The Hague, 1728), III, col. 920.
[175] *Ibid.*, III, col. 923. [176] *Ibid.*, III, col. 929.

members of generation,[177] and asserts that if he had a unique copy of the *Roman* he would burn it, in spite of its monetary value.[178] It is easy to see how a man who assumes that the *Roman* is an autobiography and who attributes the views of all *personae* to the author would be horrified by the poem. In fact, most modern critics, tempering their horror with enlightened delight, have followed serenely in Gerson's footsteps.

The attacks of Christine and Gerson were answered elaborately and very sensibly by Pierre Col, who begins with the argument concerning members of generation. If the thing makes the word dishonest, he asks, how can you name the thing? If, moreover, the secret members were made sinful by Adam and Eve, then you should not mention Adam and Eve, for they sinned, not their members. Should the members of a baby be named? At what age do they become unmentionable? This incursion into the state of innocence was to bring an accusation of heresy down on Pierre's recalcitrant head. He points out further that Christine does not answer the arguments in favor of plain speaking advanced by Raison herself (lines 6943ff.); we might add that she does not account for the fact that the lover has very good worldly reasons for keeping his language "clean." Gerson, Pierre says, is wrong in identifying Jean de Meun with the foolish lover in the poem, especially since the poem condemns the lover as violently as Gerson does. When Jean calls the secret members "sanctuaries" or "relics" he does so to condemn the foolishness of the lover, since the foolish lover worships them as though they were deities. The secret members, moreover, are mentioned freely in the Bible. Pierre goes on to contrast the two gardens in the poem and to explain their significance very briefly. He shows that Christine's charge against Raison's doctrine of deception is taken out of context, and that La Vieille and Jalousie speak in character. The latter's abuse of women is intended especially to show the unreasonable passion of jealous men. In answer to Dame Chastity in Gerson's *Tractatus*, Pierre asserts that a careful reader of the poem will find in it "teachings to flee all vices and pursue all virtues." Jean blames men as much as women; if the ladies blush to read him, they blush at their own weaknesses. As for religion, Jean does not blame it, but the hypocrisy of false religion. Pierre insists that Jean does not recommend

---

[177] *Ibid.*, III, col. 930.   [178] *Ibid.*, III, col. 931.

"works of nature" outside of marriage. Jean shows, moreover, how chastity is guarded as well as how it is attacked. In this as in other matters, Pierre says, Jean follows Guillaume de Lorris. After a few more points in defense, Pierre asks why Theology has allowed the *Roman* to go without attack for a hundred years.

The documents in the controversy as they survive include further statements by Gerson and Christine. One was an irate woman and the other a zealous reformer, and they were not to be silenced by reason. Gerson accuses Pierre of Pelagian heresy with regard to the innocence of children! He remembers that in his youth he also read the sources of the *Roman*: Boethius, Terence, Juvenal, Alanus, William of St. Amour, Abelard "cum suo Heloyde," Martianus, and others. Now he realizes that a single small work, St. Bonaventura's *Mind's Road to God*, is worth ten such books. Needless to say, this is not a very humanistic attitude, and we may recall in the same connection that Gerson was the author of a *Consolation of Theology*, written in his later years to replace the more indirect work of Boethius. Christine repeats her frenzied observations on the members of generation, laments the "sanctuaries," and so on. She once more misreads what Raison has to say about deception. She recommends, finally, that one read Dante instead of Jean de Meun.

As an indication of a change in taste which took place in certain quarters after the death of Chaucer, this controversy is invaluable. From this time forward humanists would find themselves frequently put on the defensive by the attacks of the righteous. This is not to say that there were not earlier attacks of the same kind, but few had emanated from such influential circles or involved the attack of one poet on another. Gerson's contempt for Ovid, Boethius, Alanus, and Jean de Meun marks a most decisive break with the traditions of medieval humanism. A great deal of effort has been expended by certain scholars to show that Gerson was himself something of a humanist, but his use of classical materials is always obvious and literal, not to say a little dull. Basically, his attitude looks forward to the Reformation, and his motives differ little from those which led men to cover up or to destroy the more forthright wall paintings of the vices in medieval churches. He admired only obvious piety and was reluctant to engage in exposition to arrive at underlying truths. But Gerson was a sincere and zealous reformer, dedicated to the extirpation of the very glaring evils which confronted him in the Church and in society, so we should not make a Malvolio of him. The age in which pious monks and learned humanists could read Ovid and works based on Ovidian traditions with innocence, good will, optimism, and a genuine desire to mine Egyptian gold for the Lord was coming to a close; and a new and sterner age in which the Church was to divorce itself from art and literature was approaching. This does not mean that Gerson, the Puritans of the Renaissance, or those who finally succeeded in placing all moralizations of the classics on the *Index* were more sincerely devout than their predecessors. They were not. If anything, they had much less of that innocent faith in Providence which Rabelais has so charmingly and wittily described in the person of Judge Bridlegoose. Meanwhile, Gerson illustrates the possible alternative to the traditions of allegory and humanism in the late Middle Ages. There were no modern hedonists to provide a third alternative. Chaucer's obvious admiration for Ovid, for Boethius, and for Jean de Meun places him firmly in that tradition of "poetic philosophy" which extends from early glosses on Homer through the Fathers of the Church and down to the more sincerely Christian humanists of the Renaissance. If he sought, like Ficino's Plato, to "joke seriously and to play most studiously," he was only fulfilling the potentialities of the tradition in which he worked.

4. CHAUCER AND LITERARY ALLEGORY

There is plenty of evidence in his poetry to indicate that Chaucer was thoroughly familiar with the conventions of literary allegory and expected his audience to make use of them. In the Prologue to *The Canterbury Tales*, for example, the Host assures his companions that

> which of yow that bereth hym best of alle,
> That is to seyn, that telleth in this caas
> Tales of best sentence and moost solaas,
> Shal have a soper at oure aller cost.

With this arrangement before them, Chaucer's audience was led quite naturally to look for *sentence* in the tales as well as for more superficial attractions; and when, as the tales progress, it becomes apparent that the Host is deaf to the *sentence* of what he hears, the question of what kind of judgment he will make becomes more and more enticing. Again, the man of law refrains from describing the feast with which the Sultan welcomes Custance, saying, "The fruyt of this matiere is that I telle," with the implication that a detailed account of the festivities would add nothing to his *sentence*. The details of the marriage feast are slighted for the same reason:

> Me list nat of the chaf, ne of the stree,
> Maken so long a tale as of the corn.
> What sholde I tellen of the roialtee
> At mariage, or which cours goth biforn;
> Who bloweth in a trumpe or in an horn?
> The fruyt of every tale is for to seye.

This is not merely a device to save time; more importantly, it is an invitation to the audience to look for the grain beneath the chaff of the story and to determine whether or not the man of law does actually show any awareness of the "fruyt" of his tale. As we have seen, the wife of Bath insists so vociferously on the letter that we cannot help recalling the spirit which she is incapable of hearing in her own iteration; when she tells a tale, we are led to wonder whether or not she has misinterpreted it in the same way that she has misinterpreted other things. The blindness of the summoner in the Friar's Tale suggests the possibility that the friar may be blind to the implications of what he says as well; and the "glosynge" of the friar in the Summoner's Tale together with his misinterpretation of his own *exempla* alerts the audience to the deeper implications of the story. The clerk, whose speech is "short and quyk and ful of hy sentence" gives us a general indication of the *sentence* of his tale (1142ff.), but not enough to prevent the reader from recognizing for himself the pertinence of significant details like the "ox-stall" motif or the clothing imagery. When the merchant has finished a story which supposedly illustrates the wiles of women, and Harry Baily agrees with this interpretation, the fact that the interpretation does not fit the tale is so glaring that no one could refrain from wondering exactly what the tale does imply, in spite of its narrator. Again, a little reflection shows that no one in the Franklin's Tale is either very "fre" or very "gentil," so that we are led to consider the problem of just what the Franklin has actually said. The Pardoner's Tale is an *exemplum*, which is, by definition, a story with an implication. In the Melibee a key to the *sentence* is furnished by Dame Prudence (1409ff.), but the exact relation of that key to the conclusion of the tale is left to the reader. The nun's priest gives the audience an open warning at the close of his story, including a humanistic use of Rom. 15. 4:

> But ye that holden this tale a folye,
> As of a fox, or of a cok and hen,
> Taketh the moralite, goode men.
> For seint Paul seith that al that writen is,
> To oure doctrine it is ywrite, ywis.
> Taketh the fruyt, and lat the chaf be stille.

It is plain that the priest was not actually discussing barnyard matters. Since the tale of the second nun is a saint's legend, the medieval audience would naturally look for its abstract meaning. Even the remark at the close of the prologue to the Miller's Tale—"men shal nat maken ernest of game"—while serving, on the one hand, as a part of the auctorial apology, also smacks a little of antiphrasis; for had not medieval men been making "ernest of game" for centuries in Ovid's stories? And is this not what Ficino, who was being very conservative and traditional in this matter, did with Plato? These are only more obvious instances from the Tales which point to Chaucer's concern for his *sentence*.

Since comparisons between scriptural allegory and poetic allegory were common among poets and humanists in the fourteenth century, it would be strange if Chaucer did not make one too. As a matter of fact, he does, in the link between Sir Thopas and the Melibee, where the verb *write* (line 964) indicates that he is speaking in his own person as well as in the person of Chaucer the pilgrim to Canterbury. When Harry Baily puts a stop to Sir Thopas, Chaucer promises "a moral tale vertuous,"

> Al be it told somtyme in sondry wyse,
> Of sondry folk, as I shal yow devyse,
> As thus . . . .

But the "as thus" does not lead to an account of how the story of Melibeus was told by Albertanus of Brescia and later by various translators, nor is there any hint that it was ever told by anyone before in England. It is followed instead by a rather lengthy statement to show that although the four Evangelists tell somewhat different stories of the life of Christ, their "sentence is al oon." That is, when they are read spiritually rather than literally, they say the same thing. Chaucer is thus referring neither to his sources nor to any other versions of the Melibee whatsoever—there were no professors of English in his audience taking notes. He is saying that just as the Evangelists tell different stories on the surface with the same meaning after interpretation, so also "sondry folk" may express the same truth in various ways. The expression "sondry folk" is suggestively reminiscent of line 25 of the General Prologue, and, indeed, Chaucer goes on to suggest that the stories in his own collection agree in "sentence," even though they are very different on the surface:

> Therfore, lordynges alle, I yow biseche,
> If that yow thynke I varie as in my speche,
> As thus: though that I telle somwhat moore
> Of proverbes than ye han herd bifoore
> Comprehended in this litel tretys heere
> To enforce with th'effect of my mateere,
> And though I nat the same wordes seye
> As ye han herd, yet to yow alle I preye
> Blameth me nat; for as in my sentence,
> Shul ye nowher fynden difference
> Fro the sentence of this tretys lyte
> After the which this murye tale I write.

The word *tretys* here does not have its modern connotations. Thus Froissart's "Le paradys d'amour" is called a "trettié amourous"; "La prison amoureuse" is "uns traitiers": "Le joli buisson de jouece" is "un trettié amoureus"; and "Le temple d'amour" is "un trettié de moralité"; and so on. We may remember that Dante used a similar term for the *Commedia* in the letter to Can Grande. The word *treatise* in English was used to mean a "narration" and not necessarily a formal and systematic treatment of a subject. Thus "litel tretys" probably meant simply "little narrative" without the connotations of dullness which we associate with a treatise and also, mistakenly, with the Melibee. In the above passage, it is usually assumed that the "tretys" is the source of the Melibee, but there is no reason to assume that Chaucer's audience would have been so familiar with earlier versions of that story that this long explanation was called for. Moreover, Chaucer's version differs so slightly from Renaud's that there would have been little point in assuring everyone that the *sentence* remained unchanged in Chaucer's translation. The "tretys" is obviously *The Canterbury Tales* itself, insofar as it was complete at the time the Melibee was added to it; it is once more called a "litel tretys" in the "Retractions" at the end.[179] That is, Chaucer tells us that the Melibee, although it differs verbally from the other tales the audience has heard from the "sondry folk" who proceed toward Canterbury, and contains more proverbs than any of the others, after which it is now placed, it does not differ from them in *sentence*. But all this is a rather indirect and poetic way of saying something else: pay attention to the *sentence* of the Melibee because it affords a clue to the *sentence* of all the other tales which come before it. As Chaucer says elsewhere in an invocation to Apollo, the god of truth and the patron of poets,

> I do no diligence
> To showe craft, but o sentence.

What this *sentence* may be need not concern us here, but the link at the end of Sir Thopas reflects the current humanistic theory that poetic fables, like the Bible, are to be read for wisdom which lies beneath the surface.

As we have shown earlier, Chaucer's works contain numerous references to classical myth and an unmistakable reliance on the

---

[179] In five MSS the "Retractions" are preceded by the rubric, "Here taketh the makere of this book his leeve" and followed by the statement "Heere is ended the book of the tales of Caunterbury. . . ." The expression "this book" is thus a reference to the *Tales*, and it is to his collection of stories that Chaucer bids farewell. The text following the opening rubric begins, "Now preye I to hem alle that herkne this litel tretys or rede. . . ." The inference that the author of the rubric thought "this book" and the "litel tretys" to be one and the same is clear. The fact that "the tales of Caunterbury" appears in a formal list of titles which follows does not invalidate this conclusion, since (1) it does not appear at the beginning of the list where another reference to the "tretys" would be clear, and (2) only some of the tales—not the whole "tretys"—are retracted. We should note that in the Retractions the verse from Rom. 15 which appears at the end of the nun's priest's tale is used once more, "For oure book seith, 'Al that is writen is writen for oure doctrine.'" Chaucer adds, "and that is myn entente." This observation makes no sense as a reference to the Parson's Tale, which is transparently doctrinal.

mythographic tradition. It is not difficult to find in his descriptions obvious reflections of Fulgentius, Neckam (or Albericus), Berchorius, and Boccaccio. Since the literary history of the materials contained in mythological manuals and commentaries is obscure, it is frequently impossible to locate his exact sources. Walsingham mentions among his own sources Alexander (i.e., Neckam), Remigius, Rabanus, and Fulgentius; and there may have been other treatises or compilations like his, written earlier, which were available to Chaucer. Mythographical and fabulous material was also available in works of other kinds: in commentaries on Boethius, on *The City of God*, or on the Bible; in sermons and doctrinal treatises; and, finally, in the work of other poets like Jean de Meun or Machaut. The evidence indicates that there was an increasing interest in mythographic materials of all kinds during the second half of the fourteenth century, and it is probable that in using such materials so generously, especially in the Knight's Tale and in *Troilus*, Chaucer was answering a demand on the part of his courtly audience. Both the demand and the response, however, were manifestations of the force of the medieval humanistic tradition; they were not due to any spontaneous interest in the classics "for their own sakes." Chaucer's indebtedness to Ovid, who furnished him not only with material, but also with comic and ironic techniques, is especially noteworthy. He patently regarded himself as a poet of love, who was, like Ovid, a servant to the servants of love; and there are constant reflections of Ovid's text in his work. But Chaucer's Ovid was a medieval Ovid, not a modern Ovid. To regard the classical materials in Chaucer's poetry as being merely decorative, to think of them with their modern connotations, or to try to make them manifestations of Jungian psychology or Frazerian anthropology, or to disregard in any other way their obvious significance in the context of medieval traditions is simply to turn literary history into a fairy tale.

An interesting example of Chaucer's use of classical iconography is furnished by the Temple of Venus in the Knight's Tale. Conventional meanings for Venus are discussed above in Chapter II, but to these we may now add the observation of Boccaccio in his notes to *Teseida*, 7. 50ff., where the goddess is said to represent the concupiscible appetite, or, more specifically in this instance, illicit appetite, "per la quale ogni lascivia è desiderata." Whether Chaucer read these notes or not makes little difference, since here as else-where they are essentially conventional. Boccaccio's Venus differs not at all in implication from that described as "concupiscence of the flesh," or "the mother of all fornication." Chaucer confronts his reader at once with the natural results of such desire painted on the walls of the temple: broken sleeps, sighs, tears, lamenting, the fiery strokes of desire, and lover's oaths. There follow a series of personified abstractions: Plesaunce, Hope, Desir, Foolhardyness, Beautee, Youthe, Bauderie, Richesse, Charmes, Force, Lesynges, Flaterye, Despense, Bisynesse, Jalousye. Among these, beauty and youth sound attractive to the modern ear, but in this context beauty is the leporine beauty of mere physical attractiveness, and youth is a time of levity and irresponsibility. There follow

> Festes, instrumenz, caroles, daunces,
> Lust and Array, and alle the circumstaunces
> Of love.

As Boccaccio points out, feasts are places "ove donne sieno adu-nate," and music and dance form a fitting prelude to the act of Venus. As a *locus amoenus* Chaucer shows us next "al the mount of Citheroun," which, Boccaccio tells us, is a place near Thebes where the citizens offered "molti sacrifici ad onore di Venere." It has a temperate climate, he says, neither too hot nor too cold to inhibit lecherous activity. But Chaucer was not content to use only the details furnished by Boccaccio. To enrich the meaning of the "mount," he added "al the garden" with its porter "Idelnesse" and "Narcisus." In other words, the Garden of Deduit as it is de-scribed by Guillaume de Lorris becomes an iconographic attribute of the Temple of Venus. This garden is not, of course, "classical," in spite of the presence of a descendant of Ovid's *otia* and Narcissus. As we have seen, it acquires its general significance from the Bible. In view of the nature of medieval interpretations of the classics, there is nothing startling about this fact. Indeed, the garden is fol-lowed immediately by "the folye of kyng Salomon." As St. Au-gustine put it in *On Christian Doctrine* (3. 21. 31), "His begin-nings were redolent with the desire for wisdom; when he had ob-tained it through spiritual love, he lost it through carnal love." Medea and Circe, Turnus, and Cresus are added as further exam-ples to show that

> wysdom ne richesse,
> Beautee ne sleighte, strengthe ne hardynesse,
> Ne may with Venus holde champartie . . . .

In other words, he who seeks assistance from Venus almost inevitably suffers misfortune. The details so far do not speak well for the success of Palamon or for that of any other suppliant in this temple.

But to make this idea even more emphatic, Chaucer adds a picture of Venus derived ultimately from Fulgentius (*Mit.*, 2. 1). She is seen "naked, fletynge in the large see." The meaning of this configuration is that the "sailor" of Venus loses all of his possessions and suffers shipwreck. Mythographus Vaticanus Tertius comments further that the nakedness is appropriate because the crime of libido is difficult to conceal, because it is appropriate to the nude, or because it denudes its victim of counsel.[180] The roses Venus has are commonplace, and the explanation offered by Fulgentius is standard: they blush and prick with their thorns just as libido blushes with shame and pricks with the sting of sin. It is said also that like libido they quickly fade in time. Chaucer's Venus is also accompanied by doves, since those birds were thought to be "maxime in coitu fervidae." But Chaucer departs from his predecessors in one detail. Venus usually holds a conch shell in her hand; Chaucer shows her holding a "citole." An explanation for this fact has recently been advanced by John M. Steadman.[181] In his commentary on Ovid, Berchorius retains the conch, but he considers it to be a musical instrument which he associates with that of Is. 23. 10, 16: "Pass thy land as a river, O daughter of the sea, thou hast a girdle no more. . . . Take a harp, go about the city, thou harlot that hast been forgotten: sing well, sing many a song. . . ."

Venus was, of course, also a "daughter of the sea." Acting on the suggestion he found here and wishing to emphasize the musical idea, Chaucer, presumably, substituted a "citole" for the traditional shell. As we have seen, libido has its own "melody," so that an alteration of this kind is not difficult to understand. Finally, Chaucer

---

[180] See the discussion in Bode, *Scriptores rerum mythicarum* (Cellis, 1834), pp. 228-229, or what is practically the same material in A. Neckam, *Super Marcianum*, Oxford, Bodl. Lib., MS Digby 221, fol. 37.

[181] *Speculum*, XXXIV (1959), 620-624.

completes his picture by mentioning blind Cupid, whose significance needs no further comment here.

So far as the Knight's Tale is concerned, this temple is an appropriate enough place in which to vow perpetual warfare on chastity, as Palamon does, but its details neither comment favorably on the suppliant nor suggest that he will be successful. From the point of view of technique, we should notice that classical and scriptural materials are mingled freely so that their meanings reinforce each other. Moreover, all of the details are consistent with the traditional meanings attributed to Venus by medieval mythographers. It would be mere critical waywardness to consider the temple as a whole to be just so much decoration on the surface of a "story," or to regard it as a blind accumulation of detail without significance. Chaucer should obviously be considered as a representative of the medieval humanistic tradition.

Iconographic materials from the Bible also abound in Chaucer's poetry, where they afford a richness and depth of meaning which could not have been achieved in any other way. Among scriptural concepts which appear in *The Canterbury Tales*, the most important is the idea of pilgrimage. Any pilgrimage during the Middle Ages, whether it was made on the knees in a labyrinth set in a cathedral floor, or, more strenuously, to the Holy Land, was ideally a figure for the pilgrimage of the Christian soul through the world's wilderness toward the celestial Jerusalem. The pilgrimage of the soul was not in itself a journey from place to place, but an inner movement between the two cities so vividly described by St. Augustine, one founded on charity, and the other on cupidity. Love moved the pilgrim's feet and determined the direction of his journey. The *Tales* are set in a framework which emphasizes this journey and its implications. The opening in April, the month of Venus, under the sign of Taurus, the house of Venus, with its showers and singing birds, suggests the love which may move the pilgrims to Canterbury toward either one spiritual city or the other (Fig. 113). And as the journey draws to a close, with Libra's scales of justice hanging in the sky in a curious but irrelevant echo of Homer, the parson offers to show

the wey in this viage
Of thilke parfit glorious pilgrimage
That highte Jerusalem celestial.

The idea is reinforced from time to time in the prologue and tales. Thus the wife of Bath "koude muchel of wandrynge by the weye" both in the flesh and in the spirit; old Egeus in the Knight's Tale observes that "we been pilgrymes passynge to and fro"; Custance in the Man of Law's Tale undergoes a long pilgrimage from home; in the Pardoner's Tale the pilgrimage is seen as a quest for the death of death; and so on. The concept of the pilgrim and of the love which moves him "up a croked wey," or more directly to his home, provides a thematic background against which both Chaucer's pilgrims and the characters in their tales may be clearly seen and properly evaluated. The idea needed only to be suggested in the fourteenth century, when one of the most popular subjects for wall paintings, even in remote villages, was St. Christopher, the guide to man's spiritual voyage. As we visualize Chaucer's "folk" moving toward Canterbury, not winding through the soft intricacies of a landscape by Constable, but outlined against a background of gold leaf, we should do well to let the old words of St. Augustine echo in our ears: "Thus in this mortal life, wandering from God, if we wish to return to our native country where we can be blessed we should use this world and not enjoy it, so that the 'invisible things' of God 'being understood by the things that are made' may be seen, that is, so that by means of corporal and temporal things, we may comprehend the eternal and spiritual."

The solution to the problem of love, the force which directs the will, which is in turn the source of moral action, is, figuratively, marriage. The concept of marriage plays a large part in *The Canterbury Tales*, but to understand its significance it is necessary to know something of its wider implications. In the first place, every Christian of whatever condition should be "married." As Thomas Brinton put it, "Every soul is either an adulteress with the Devil or a spouse of Christ."[182] A man either preserves the marriage contracted at baptism,[183] or abuses it. When a man is properly "married" in this way, the "marriage" between the spirit and the flesh, or the reason and the sensuality within him, is preserved intact, and he is also a part of the "marriage" between Christ and the

---

[182] Ed. Devlin, I, 36.
[183] Cf. Odo Tusculanus, in Pitra, *op.cit.*, II, 247: "Licet animae omnium christianorum in baptismo desponsetur Christo, et cum eo contrahant matrimonium spirituale."

Church. In the Church, a bishop was solemnly "married" to his diocese, and a priest was regarded as the "husband" of his flock; for both inherited in the Apostolic tradition the place of Christ with reference to the Church. In the twelfth century, the Duke of Aquitaine "married" the church of Aquitaine.[184] Similarly, the idea that a prince should be a "husband" to his people gradually acquired the force of law in France during the later middle ages. A fourteenth-century commentator on Justinian wrote that "there is contracted a moral and political marriage between the prince and the *respublica*. Also, just as there is contracted a spiritual and divine marriage between a church and its prelate, so there is contracted a temporal and terrestrial marriage between the Prince and the State."[185] Jehan le Bel compares the "signerie" that a husband enjoys over his wife with that of a feudal lord over his subjects.[186] Marriage is thus a principle of order in the individual, in the church, and in lay society; in medieval terms, a well-ordered hierarchy of almost any kind may be thought of as a "marriage." It follows that there are various kinds of "adultery." When the sensuality or the lower reason rebels, the result is conventionally termed "adultery." As Berchorius puts it, any mortal sin is a kind of "adultery." Again, a prelate who abuses his office for personal gain is an "adulterer," and so on.[187] "Adultery" implies generally what Chaucer's parson describes as an "up-so-doun" condition in a hierarchy.

The theme of/marriage is developed first in the Knight's Tale, where order is represented initially by the marriage of Theseus and finally by the marriage of Palamon. Specifically, it appears here as a solution to the problems raised by the misdirected concupiscent passions, represented by Venus, and by the misdirected irascible passions, represented by Mars. The Miller's Tale which follows is a story of adultery in which a lecherous clerk, a vain clerk, and an avaricious old husband are amusingly shown to suffer the consequences of their abuses of "marriage," which include, incidentally, Nicolas' interest in judicial astrology and Absalon's refusal to accept offerings from the ladies, as well as the actions of

[184] See Mâle, *L'art rel. du XII* siècle (Paris, 1924), p. 198.
[185] Quoted by E. H. Kantorowicz, "Mysteries of State," *Harvard Theol. Rev.*, XLVIII (1955), 78.
[186] *Li ars d'amour*, II, 92.   [187] *Opera*, III, 97-98.

both with reference to Alisoun. In the Reeve's Tale we meet an "adulterous" priest, who neglects the "lineage" of the Apostolic succession in favor of his literal lineage—

> he wolde his hooly blood honoure,
> Though that he hooly chirche sholde devoure.

This "hooly blood" is pretty thoroughly put in jeopardy in the tale which follows. In the Man of Law's Tale Custance escapes marriage with a pagan Sultan whose mother scorns "this newe lawe," but she achieves a more proper marriage which she succeeds in preserving in the face of adversity. The wife exerts every effort to turn marriage "up-so-doun," and we meet the results of this kind of inversion in society in the persons of the blind summoner and the hypocritical friar, who abuse their offices in "adulterous" fashion. The clerk systematically restores the order inverted by the wife, calling attention specifically to the duties of the Christian soul as it is tested by its Spouse. There are, however, as he says, few "Grisildis," and in the Merchant's Tale the fool's paradise advocated by the wife in her tale is fully exposed for what it is when an old man seeks to make of marriage a lecherous paradise on earth. Although the theme of the Franklin's Tale is "gentilesse" rather than marriage specifically, the dangers of the kind of "headless" marriage dear to the Epicurean ideals of the middle class are fully revealed. Adultery appears again in three separate guises in the Shipman's Tale. In the Second Nun's Tale there is a literally chaste marriage which is a type of spiritual virginity under Christ. Again, in the Nun's Priest's Tale, the dangers of the service of Venus in marriage are once more shown, and in this instance the idea is applied by implication to the relationship between a priest and his flock. Finally, the pastoral theology of marriage is treated by the parson. Closely related to the theme of marriage is the theme of "multiplying," which is introduced by the wife and vividly developed in the character of the pardoner, in his prologue, and in the Canon's Yeoman's Tale, where a technical term in alchemy is so used that its wider implications in other contexts become unmistakable. If we look back over these developments—and I have mentioned only the more obvious of them—it is not difficult to see that Chaucer sets the marriage theme in humanistic terms in the Knight's Tale, suggesting the proper function of marriage as an ordering principle in the individual and in society, and develops its manifold implications in the subsequent tales. Once it is seen that the elaboration of the theme of marriage in the *Tales* is thematic rather than dramatic, the false problems raised by the old theory of the "marriage group" disappear.

The theme of marriage also has an important place in *The Parliament of Fowls* and in the Prologue to *The Legend of Good Women*. In the former, Nature, whose Law in the Middle Ages was thought to include an hierarchical arrangement in society as well as a hierarchy in marriage, presides over the "marriage" of people of various types, represented by birds, on St. Valentine's Day, which is a figure for the proper time either to choose a mate or to confirm a choice already made.[188] That is, it is not simply a day in the year, but a time which must come, sooner or later, in the life of any man (whether literally married or not), together with his subsequent "observance" of the event at whatever time. But in the poem a royal eagle instead of offering to be the husband of the formel wishes to serve her as his "soverayn lady" and not as his "fer" or mate. This action, whose significance is only obscured by rumblings about "courtly love," causes the lady to blush for shame, since she has been looking forward to marriage and not to extra-marital indulgence. It opens the way, moreover, for the other eagles to claim in turn that each loves the formel as hotly as the first and so deserves to "serve" her. The resulting argument, which has no solution, lasts all day, until, when she is given a choice, the formel decides that she will serve neither Venus nor Cupid "as yit"—that is, in spite of the pleadings of the silly eagles. What these events imply is that when nobility refuses the obligation of marriage in favor of lust,[189] a bad example is afforded the other birds, and the result is a dissension which affects the whole hierarchy of society. Moreover, the eagles, who have, as it were, entered the Temple of Venus, find there only Priapus, or frustration, and the sighs of "the bittere goddesse Jelosye," a fate presaged by Chaucer's description of the temple. If the eagles wanted the services of Venus, they should, perhaps, have consulted her

[188] See "The Complaint of Mars," lines 16-21 and Gower, "Balades," 35. 1. 1-5, ed. Macaulay, *Works* (Oxford, 1899-1902), 1, 365-366.

[189] Knighthood and lechery had long been considered incompatible. See John of Salisbury, *Policrat.*, 6. 11; *Carmen de bello Lewensi*, ed. Kingsford (Oxford, 1890), lines 165 ff. Deschamps was especially positive about this principle.

porter, Richesse, instead of pretending to follow Nature on St. Valentine's Day. The other birds, however, finally choose their mates, and the happy solution, when each gets the spouse "that sorest for hym syketh," is celebrated in a song to St. Valentine which promises for the "awakened" birds the passing of winter, or the adversity of temptation, and the darkness which is the absence of grace. The harmony of Nature's garden is restored in marriage. We may see these birds, who have escaped, as it were, from the Fowler, in Fig. 14. The eagles, meanwhile, are left in the unenviable position of the gentleman in Fig. 24. Again, the refusal of marriage in favor of an "up-so-doun" relationship brings disorder, and the consummation of marriage is a solution to the problems raised by Cupid and Venus.[190]

In the Prologue to the *Legend* Chaucer celebrates the daisy, a flower conventionally associated with Mary or with the concept of faithful espousal.[191] But the daisy is also Alceste, who, as Berchorius says, may be taken as typical of those "good women who love their husbands perfectly so that on account of their love they will if necessary expose themselves to death. They are worthy that Hercules, or Christ, rescue them from Hell, or Purgatory, because of the conjugal faith they maintain."[192] Alceste is also said to be typical of the "holy virgin" married to God who had rather die physically in martyrdom than that her husband should die spiritually in the hearts of men. But these two types are, after all, closely connected; for a woman of the first type is spiritually a woman of the second type. As Chaucer puts it, Alceste is an example especially of "wifhod the lyvynge." It is for this reason that she surpasses the figures from the Old Testament, pagan legend, and medieval story in the Balade. Dido and Iseut died for love, but not for conjugal fidelity. The reference to St. Valentine in conjunction with the "escaped birds" motif, the details in the description of the daisy and Alceste, the quarrel between Alceste and the God of Love who, although he is not blind and admires faith in love, has to be reminded that justice should be tempered with mercy, all point to the same concept: the Christian ideal of marriage. The

[190] The parliament as such in the poem is, of course, futile, since the difficulty raised by the eagles can be removed neither by Nature nor by reason, but only through grace.

[191] See above, Chapter III, note 128.

[192] *Studij romanzi*, XXIII, 101.

suggestion of Mary in phrases like "of alle floures flour" reinforces the theme, for Mary was frequently seen as the Sponsa in the Canticle of Canticles, and, in addition, her marriage to Joseph was a familiar type of ideal human marriage.[193] The use of Alceste also suggests morally the "marriage" of the reason and the sensuality,[194] so that both "allegorical" and "moral" implications emerge from the Prologue to serve as a background for evaluating the "saints" whose legends follow. The Prologue is, in effect, a very graceful and suggestive panegyric to an ideal which underlies a great deal of Chaucer's poetry. The fact that it is basically a Pauline concept with firmly established figurative applications made it easy for Chaucer to employ it in a wide variety of ways with very rich overtones of meaning.

Those who undertake their "pilgrimage" in a proper spirit love reasonably, are truly "married," and are "fruitful" in various commendable ways. They are also those who "put off the old" and "put on the new." They are "new" or "young" in spirit, not "old" with the frustrating burden of vice. A man may be literally "old" in years and at the same time "young" in spirit; and a "young" man in years may be, on the other hand, "old" in spirit. But from the point of view of art, either visual or literary, "oldness" of the spirit is most easily suggested by "oldness" of the flesh, and there were in the literary tradition, in addition to wise elders, many persons who could serve as models for spiritual "oldness": Dipsas, Maximian, La Vieille, and so on. It is not difficult to detect the difference between wise old persons like Egeus in the Knight's Tale and elderly fools like old John in the Miller's Tale or Januarie in the Merchant's Tale. The scriptural overtones of old age are first suggested in the Prologue to the Reeve's Tale. Brother "Osewold" is very angry with the Miller, but excuses himself on the grounds that he is too old to "pley." The subject of age seems to fascinate him, and he gives us an account of it. Old men like himself, he says, desire "folie" even when they cannot perform it, a fact of which we are reminded later by the parson with peculiarly medieval vividness. The "wyl" of the aged is green, Oswald says,

[193] Lombard, *Sententiae*, 4. 30. 2.
[194] See Holcot, *In librum sap.* (Basel, 1586), p. 682. Salutati, *De laboribus*, II, 612-613, makes Admetus the spirit and Alceste the flesh, which amounts to the same thing.

even though nothing else about them is very vigorous. When he has finished his little essay, the Host reprimands him:

"What! Shul we speke alday of hooly writ?"

The reeve has neither mentioned nor quoted the Bible. Harry's question is undoubtedly meant to call attention in a humorous way to his usual lack of perceptiveness, but it also reminds the audience of the Scriptures and of what they have to say about old age. As the reeve describes it, age, with its desire for folly, is very much like old age in St. Paul. Those who are "old" in spirit, it will be recalled, are associated with the old law or the law of the members and belong to the "lineage" of the bondwoman, described by St. Augustine as "the generation of Cain." When the reeve tells a tale about how this lineage, masquerading as "hooly chirches blood" is "bigiled," he is in a very real sense talking about himself and the fate of his own antiquity.

One of the most famous passages in *The Canterbury Tales* is the wife's disquisition on her lost youth:

> But Lord Crist! whan that it remembreth me
> Upon my yowthe, and on my jolitee,
> It tikleth me aboute myn herte roote.
> Unto this day it dooth myn herte boote
> That I have had my world as in my tyme.
> But age, allas! that al wol envenyme,
> Hath me biraft my beautee and my pith.
> Lat go! farewel! the devel go therwith!
> The flour is goon, ther is namoore to telle;
> The bren, as I best kan, now moste I selle.

The idea for this passage was undoubtedly suggested to Chaucer by a passage from a speech by one of the wife's literary ancestors, La Vieille (*RR*, 12932ff.):

> Par Deu! si me plaist il encores
> Quant je m'i sui bien pourpensee;
> Mout me delite en ma pensee
> E me rebaudissent li membre
> Quant de mon bon tens me remembre
> E de la joliete vie
> Don mes cueurs a si grant envie;

Tout me rejovenist le cors
Quant j'i pens e quant jou recors;
Touz les biens dou monde me fait
Quant me souvient de tout le fait,
Qu'au miens ai je ma joie eüe,
Combien qu'il m'aient deceüe.

Chaucer has added the significant word *pith* and expressed the thought of the last line in terms of *flour* and *bren* in order to emphasize the poetic significance of what "age" has done to Alisoun. But both passages contain a concept of rejuvenation or *renovatio*, explicit in the French and implied in the second sentence of the English. And this renewed youth is brought about by the memory of former joys. This is not, of course, in itself a scriptural concept, but it is an inversion of a very common idea. In Psalm 27. 7, we read, "The Lord is my helper and my protector: in him hath my heart confided, and I have been helped. And my flesh hath flourished again . . . ." The *Glossa major* takes this as a reference to Christ, who flourished when He was born without sin and again at the Resurrection.[195] The actions of Christ set a pattern for others to follow. Thus in Ps. 102. 5 we find another renewal: "Who satisfieth thy desire with good things: thy youth shall be renewed like the eagle's." This renewal, the *Glossa* says, is made possible by Christ,[196] and it naturally involves the removal of an "oldness." St. Paul urges us (Eph. 4. 22ff.) to "put off the old man" and "be renewed" so as to "put on the new man." When the wife, therefore, having invoked "Lord Crist," begins to talk about how good it feels to remember the "good things" of youth and then laments that age has bereft her of pith and "flour," leaving only bran, it is clearly and amusingly apparent that she has taken the name of Christ in vain and neglected her opportunity to "flourish again" in a true *renovatio*. The passage is neither sentimental, nor a lament on Chaucer's part for the joys of his lost youth; it is a jocular little complex of scriptural iconography designed to fill out the implications of the inversion represented by the wife. "Renewal" through the desires of the flesh must necessarily prove to be illusory, and it is this illusion that the wife holds out as a pros-

[195] *PL*, 191, col. 281.
[196] *PL*, 191, col. 920. The explanation is involved, but we need not be concerned here with its details.

pect of "parfit joye" in her tale, wherein a knight of strong carnal impulses allows an old hag who offers to satisfy his "worldly appetit" to win sovereignty over him so that she appears to him to be "fair and good." The wife's inverted *renovatio* sheds light on other "old" characters in the *Tales*. That old man the pardoner can, like Shakespeare's Falstaff, refer to "us yonge men," but we know that he, too, lacks "pith" and steadfastly refuses to be renewed. Januarie's abuse of marriage is another refusal of "youth," although Januarie tries very hard to regain the "youthful desires" of the "old man." The theme reaches its climax in the Pardoner's Tale, where the Old Man himself appears, knocking on the ground, his "mother's gate," and vainly seeking that death and that renewal which alone can restore his youth.

To the same general thematic complex belong the "old dance" and the various "melodies" which appear in Chaucer's work, and we may add to the important scriptural concepts developed there the elaboration of Matt. 5. 28 discussed in Chapter 11 above. In addition, there are various scriptural concepts which appear only sporadically, to furnish thematic coherence in a tale, or to lend significance to a narrative or description. For example, the theme of the three temptations, or of the three basic sins to which these temptations appeal, appears as a framework for the Miller's Tale. The classic statement of the concept may be found in one of the homilies of St. Gregory which is quoted by Lombard in the *Sententiae* (2. 21. 5): "The Ancient Enemy raised himself in three temptations against our first parents, for then he tempted them with gluttony, vainglory, and avarice. And in tempting he was triumphant, for he made them subject to him through consent. Indeed, he tempted them with gluttony, when he showed them the food of the forbidden tree and persuaded them to eat. He tempted them with vainglory when he said, 'you shall be as Gods' [Gen. 3. 5]. And, having advanced thus far, he tempted them through avarice when he said, 'knowing good and evil.' For avarice has as its object not only money, but also loftiness of station. That desire is rightly called avarice which seeks elation. . . . But in the same ways that he topped the first man, he lay subdued before the Second. He tempted Him with gluttony when he said, 'command that these stones be made bread' [Matt. 4. 3]. He tempted Him with vainglory when he said, 'If thou be the Son of God cast thyself down.' And with avarice for loftiness, he tempted Him when he showed him all the world, saying, 'All these things will I give thee if falling down thou wilt adore me.' "[197]

That is, the temptation of Adam and the temptation of Christ in the Wilderness were found to be parallel and to consist of an appeal to the same three weaknesses. Adam fell before these temptations, but Christ overcame them, paving the way for Christians to follow Him. This pattern of thought became quite fruitful in exegesis and theology.[198] In his commentary on Luke, Bede equates the three temptations with the excuses in the Parable of the Supper (Luke 14. 16ff.) and with the temptations of "the world" as they are described in 1 John 2. 16. That is, the excuse "I have married a wife" represents, as readers of this book should by now suspect, the temptation of the flesh, or gluttony, or "concupiscence of the flesh"; the excuse "I have bought a farm" represents avarice or "pride of life"; and the excuse "I have bought five yoke of oxen" represents vainglory or "concupiscence of the eyes."[199] Various other developments were explored. Thus Nicolas de Goran says that gluttony persuades to pleasure with respect to the concupiscible, pride persuades to ostentation with respect to the irascible, and avarice conduces to error with respect to the reasonable.[200] As we have seen, the same pattern was sometimes used in moralizations of the classics, so that the three temptations might be represented by the sirens or by the apples of Hippomenes. Trivet finds them in a passage from the *Consolation* of Boethius (1 m. 4) which Chaucer translated: "Whoso it be that is cleer of vertu, sad and wel oedynat of lyvynge, that hath put under fote the proude weerdes, and loketh upright, upon either fortune, he may holden his chere undesconfited. The rage ne menaces of the see, commoevynge or chasynge upward hete fro the botme, ne schal nat moeve that man. Ne the unstable mountaigne that highte Visevus, that writheth out thurw his brokene chemeneyes smokynge fieres, ne the wey of thonder-leit, that is wont to smyten hye toures, ne schal nat moeve that man." Trivet explains the imagery as follows: "First of all it is to be observed that the persecution of the wicked

[197] Cf. Bede on Matthew, *PL*, 92, cols. 19-20.
[198] It also appears in art. See Fig. 1.
[199] *PL*, 92, col. 370.
[200] *In quatuor Evang. comm.*, p. 23; cf. p. 64.

is designated in three ways, that is, by the rage of the sea, by the eruption of a certain mountain, and by the stroke of lightning. The reason for this is that the proud are found in three species according to the three kinds of sin which occupy the world as in 1 John 2. 16: 'For all that is in the world is concupiscence of the flesh, and the concupiscence of the eyes, and the pride of life.' Certain of the wicked are therefore lecherous, whose persecution is designated by the raging of the sea. . . . Others, indeed, are the avaricious whose persecution is designated by the fire from Mount Vesuvius. . . . Others are the proud whose persecution is designated by the flash of lightning."[201]

Again, Philippe de Mézières complained that in knighthood Rule, Discipline, Obedience, and Justice had been replaced by the three daughters of the Devil: "Orgueil, Convoitise, et Luxure."[202] It would be possible to cite further examples to show the commonplace nature of the concept in the late Middle Ages, but the material above will suffice to make its general implications clear. It does not matter especially whether we call the sins or temptations "gluttony, vainglory, and avarice" or "lechery, pride, and covetousness," or use some other combination with similar implications; moreover, as Trivet's remarks demonstrate, "the lecherous, the proud, and the avaricious" will do just as well, since we may think either of three sins within an individual or of three types of individuals who exhibit the sins.

The latter alternative is strongly suggested in the Miller's Tale, where three men center their attentions on a young Alisoun who urgently appeals to all of the senses. First, John, her husband is a "riche gnof" who is clearly among those who "trust in riches" (Mark 10. 24) and whose most prized treasure is Alisoun herself.[203] An avaricious, or, in the Biblical sense, a "rich" man is one

---

[201] MS Burney 131, fol. 9. Cf. the English commentary, Oxford, Bodl. MS Auct. F. 3. 5, fol. 210: "other thay are lechoures and thanne thay are understonde be the wodenes of the see or thay are couetoris, that is understandynge be the brennynge fire, or proude, that is understonde be the wastynge levenynge."

[202] N. Jorga, *Philippe de Mézières* (Paris, 1896), p. 500. The theme of the three temptations also appears in *Sir Gawain*. See Hans Schnyder, *Sir Gawain and the Green Knight* (Bern, 1961), pp. 55-66.

[203] The jealous husband became a type of the acquisitive or avaricious man during the later Middle Ages. See Paul Olson's unpublished dissertation, "*Le Jaloux" and History* (Princeton, 1957), pp. 46-65. The contempt with which jealous husbands were treated in the Middle Ages is well illustrated in Fig. 112, which could almost serve as an illustration for the Miller's Tale. The theme of the

who, as the parson says, "hath moore hope in his catel than in Jhesu Crist." When John thinks that a new Flood is coming, overlooking as a "lewed man" that "oonly his bileve kan" the promise of Gen. 9. 15, he can think of nothing but his most precious possession:

> "Allas, my wyf!
> And shal she drenche? Allas, myn Alisoun!"

The crowning temptation, which deprives him of his rational power, making him, as it were, "wood," as Nicolas de Goran suggested that it should and as the clerks at the end of the tale itself agree that it does, appeals to the same kind of avarice that Satan is said to have used in tempting Christ:

> "And thanne shul we be lordes al oure lyf
> Of al the world, as Noe and his wyf."

Nicolas engages in an iconographic action which very vividly and undeniably conveys the idea of lechery (Figs. 5, 59); and Absalon, as he looks over the ladies in church, is obviously guilty of "concupiscence of the eyes," as well as of more obvious forms of vainglory suggested by his clothing, his hair, his superior air with reference to farting, and by his playing Herod "upon a scaffold hye." The name *Herod*, as Huguccio of Pisa tells us in his popular encyclopedia, means "vainglorious."[204] In fourteenth-century illustration the Biblical Absalon, upon whom Chaucer's character is obviously modeled, is conventionally shown caught by his hair in a tree (Fig. 115). It is significant that this scene is used by Michelangelo in a medallion of the Sistine ceiling to exemplify the vice of pride. Absalon's vainglory leads, in Chaucer's tale, as we might expect it to from Nicolas de Goran's comment, to wrath. The false flood in this instance effects a purification, just as the original flood did, albeit on a very small scale:

> Thus swyved was this carpenteris wyf,
> For al his kepyng and his jalousye;

---

three temptations in the Miller's Tale is discussed further in forthcoming articles by Professor Olson and by W. Bolton. These articles contain alternative interpretations of some details of the story.

[204] Oxford, Bodl. MS Laud Misc. 626, fol. 82. Cf. Holcot, *In librum sap.* (Basel, 1586), p. 316, "Herod ... signifies those glorying in bodily appearance"; p. 520, "*Herod* is interpreted to mean 'glorying in clothing' and designates a person glorying in the beauty of the body."

And Absalon hath kist hir nether ye,
And Nicolas is scalded in the towte.

It should be emphasized that the scriptural ideas in this story in no way detract from its humor; on the contrary, the humorous as opposed to the merely farcical element in it is due entirely to its theological background. There are other scriptural echoes in the tale, like the echoes of the Canticle of Canticles in Absalon's love-making,[205] but these serve only to introduce ideas which contribute to the principal theme.

Chaucer not only uses concepts developed from the tradition of spiritual exegesis; he also uses a great deal of scriptural imagery which carries with it overtones of meaning from the exegetical tradition. Among the most fruitful complexes of related "things" in medieval poetry was that which concerned itself with gardens, like the garden of Deduit in the *Roman de la rose* discussed above in Chapter ii. There are significant gardens in works of all kinds— in saint's legends, in ribald comedies like the *Miles gloriosus*, in fabliaux, in romances, and so on. And most of them reflect, in one way or another, the gardens of the Bible: the Paradise of Genesis, the "garden enclosed" of the Canticle of Canticles, the grove of Priapus destroyed by Asa, or other gardens.[206] Generally they represent a Paradise of celestial delights or a false paradise of earthly delights, or on the other hand, a paradise which may be viewed as either of the foregoing, or which may be transformed, like that in the *Lai de l'oislet.*[207] By the fourteenth century, these gardens had acquired fairly consistent attributes. Usually, they included a central tree and a well, as in Fig. 89, or as in the tropological gardens described by John the Scot. They might also include singing birds, small animals, and groves of trees, which in the gardens of Deduit are arranged artificially with great regularity in such a way as to provide shade for the soft grass beneath. Chaucer was very fond

---

[205] See R. E. Kaske, "The Defense," in *Critical Approaches to Medieval Literature: Selected Papers from the English Institute, 1958-1959* (New York, 1960), pp. 52ff.

[206] For reflections of Susanna's garden in the Merchant's Tale, see A. L. Kellogg, "Susannah and the *Merchant's Tale*," *Speculum*, xxxv (1960), 275-279.

[207] The original of this story and its basic meaning are discussed by W. F. Bolton, "Parable, Allegory, and Romance in the Legend of Barlaam and Josaphat," *Traditio*, xiv (1958), 361-362, and p. 359, note 2.

of these gardens, and does not hesitate to use them to heighten the significance of his narrative.

In the Knight's Tale, for example, following the lead of the *Teseida*, Chaucer has Palamon and Arcite discover Emelye in what Boccaccio calls a "giardino amoroso," a walled garden which Chaucer fills with the atmosphere of May and with the melody of Emelye's voice—"as an aungel hevenysshly she soong." Appropriately the phantasy of Emelye enters the hearts of the young men as they see her in this paradise. Boccaccio emphasizes the idea by having Arcite exclaim, when he sees Emilia, "Quest'è di paradiso!" But the idea is clear enough in Chaucer's description. Perhaps the most elaborate garden of this kind in the *Tales* is that created by old Januarie, which is an iconographic realization of the paradise on earth he hopes to achieve in marriage. Chaucer deliberately recalls the garden of Guillaume de Lorris in this connection so that we need explain it no further. Januarie's peculiar use of it as a refuge was a mistake on his part, since Old Age cannot properly enjoy the garden. His "lewed" echo of the Canticle of Canticles as he invites May to enter it is a fitting prelude to the "fruit" which develops on the pear tree. And his reaction to the discovery of this "fruit" is a fitting comment on the illusory nature of the delights to be found in such gardens.

Another similar garden, again full of the atmosphere of May, appears in the Franklin's Tale:

> And this was on the sixte morwe of May,
> Which May hadde peynted with his softe shoures
> This gardyn ful of leves and of floures;
> And craft of mannes hand so curiously
> Arrayed hadde this gardyn, trewely,
> That nevere was ther gardyn of swich prys,
> But if it were the verray paradys.

It is in this setting, which is obviously another echo of the garden of Deduit, that Aurelius, "servant to Venus," makes his approach to Dorigen—"Have mercy, sweete, or ye wol do me deye!"—and receives her playful reply. The setting is, of course, not designed to afford "scenery" for the action but to act as a kind of commentary on its nature. It is significant also that Dorigen goes to keep her tryst with Aurelius in a garden. There is another "paradise" in *The Book of the Duchess*, where the Black Knight is discovered under an oak, like the Delyt that follows Cupid in *The Parliament of Fowls*. The latter poem contains a more elaborate garden of Nature, which includes, however, the well of Cupid and the Temple of Venus. In this garden, which is a parallel to the world as it is seen in the Dream of Scipio, one may follow either Nature or the deities of love so as to achieve either of the alternatives expressed in the poem. On the one hand, a man may come to

> that place deere
> That ful of blysse is and of soules cleere,

or, on the other hand, he may, if he is among those who may be called "likerous folk," "whirle aboute th'erthe alwey in peyne." In the more Christian language of the inscriptions on the gate of the garden, he may find

> that blysful place
> Of hertes hele and dedly woundes cure,

which includes a "welle of grace" and the eternal May of Paradise; or, on the other hand, he may arrive at a place of mortal spear strokes guided by Disdayn and Daunger, a world of dry trees and dry fish governed not by grace but by Venus, concerning whom Jean de Meun, Alanus, John of Salisbury (*Policrat.*, 8. 6), and St. Paul (1 Cor. 6. 18) had already observed, "Th'eschewing is only the remedye." Which place he discovers is his own affair. So far as the poem is concerned, the eagles choose the wrong one. It is in a "paleis gardyn, by a welle" that Troilus confesses his "sins" to the God of Love. Except for the garden of Nature in the *Parliament*, which may be either used or abused, all of these gardens carry, with individual variations, the connotations of the garden described by Guillaume de Lorris, and these connotations were made possible by a combination of signs developed in scriptural exegesis and figurative devices borrowed from the classics. The use of either Venus or Cupid or both to replace the serpent permitted an enrichment of the conceptual background which was not neglected by either medieval or Renaissance artists (cf. the serpent in Fig. 89 or Titian's painting of the Fall in the Prado).

Chaucer's poetry contains many casual and incidental reflections of scriptural imagery, but another volume as large as this one would be required to describe them and to indicate their signifi-cance.[208] Enough examples have been adduced in this and the previ-ous chapters to indicate something of the importance of this ma-terial, even though it has been necessary because of limitations of space to keep explanation to a minimum. In regard to the nature of medieval allegory, various conclusions may be drawn from our discussion. In the first place, the tradition of literary allegory is ancient and respectable, extending far into antiquity. The allegori-cal tradition during the Middle Ages, however, was strongly in-fluenced by the conventions of Pauline exegesis so that classical and other materials were shaped by scriptural concepts to suit the pur-poses of Christian humanism. A medieval poet had at his disposal various sources of figurative material: scriptural signs and concepts, moralized natural history from non-scriptural sources, and figura-tive materials derived from mythography or astrology and from commentaries on the classics. In addition, iconographic materials of various kinds which developed in the visual arts were sometimes used for literary purposes. During the later Middle Ages it is pos-sible to distinguish between what we may call "humanistic" al-legory, which is rich in classical materials and may, at times, be jocular or even "Rabelaisian" on the surface,[209] and "theological" allegory, which relies chiefly on the Scriptures and generally main-tains a solemn exterior. But if this distinction is made, we should remember that scriptural concepts frequently appear in allegoriza-tions of the classics and that the lessons derived from poets like Virgil and Ovid were not "pagan" or contrary to the philosophy of Christianity. Some poets, moreover, like Christine de Pisan, were capable of using classical materials in a very solemn and ladylike way. Chaucer quite clearly belongs to the tradition of "hu-manistic" allegory. When his poetry is seen in the light of this tra-dition it becomes infinitely more subtle and intellectually satis-fying than it can possibly be if it is read romantically and literally,

[208] For a striking example of the use of scriptural detail in iconographic por-traiture, see R. E. Kaske, "The Summoner's Garleek, Onyons, and eek Lekes," *MLN*, LXXIV (1959), 481-484. For an illustration of the manner in which scrip-tural ideas might enter literary tradition, see Alfred L. Kellogg, "On the Tradition of Troilus's Vision of the Little Earth," *Mediaeval Studies*, XXII (1960), 204-213.

[209] The nature of "Rabelaisian" comedy is beginning, at last, to be appreciated. See M. A. Screech, *The Rabelaisian Marriage* (London, 1958). However, there is nothing new about the kind of humor Screech describes.

or analyzed for "tensions," "ironical contrasts," "structural patterns," and so on. Details which seemed tedious and inept become meaningful and coherent. As we learn more about the literary iconography of Chaucer's work, we shall undoubtedly find that Chaucer was an artist whose subtlety, humor, and power fully justified his early reputation. Moreover, we shall come to appreciate more and more the fact that, in spite of the traditional and orthodox nature of his thought, his status as a philosopher is not to be taken lightly. It may be fairly easy to echo old thoughts and figurative materials, but the full implications of old concepts for one's own time are not easy to perceive, and the infusion of life and vigor into traditional figurative materials is a task which few artists since the eighteenth century have had the courage to face. Where Chaucer wished to lead his audience with these concepts and figures will be our concern in the next chapter.

V · SOME MEDIEVAL DOCTRINES
OF LOVE

I. "COURTLY LOVE" AND ANDREAS CAPELLANUS

𝕷𝖎𝖐𝖊 𝖒𝖚𝖈𝖍 medieval poetry written after the middle of the twelfth century, Chaucer's work shows a great deal of concern for the subject of love. In recent years, it has become fashionable to speak of almost all "secular" love in the literature of the later Middle Ages as "courtly love," and to assume that there existed at the time a "system" of love distinctive from and opposed to the "system" of Christian philosophy, either as a literary convention or as a feature of "gracious living" which found a reflection in literary texts. Unfortunately, there is little agreement among scholars as to the nature of this love, and still less agreement concerning its origin. Indeed, the connotations of the term *courtly love* are so vague and flexible that its utility for purposes of definition has become questionable. This situation is not improved by the fact that although a number of treatises about love were written during the Middle Ages, some of which are rather elaborate, the term *courtly love* was not then in common use. Perhaps we should do better to employ a number of the terms that were then current and to respect the distinctions which they implied rather than to seek too hastily a single all-embracing formula.

Theories concerning the origin of what is called "courtly love" vary enormously. They include reference to such matters as Bulgarian or Albigensian heresies, Pictish matriarchal customs, social conditions in the south of France, where there is said to have been a shortage of desirable women in feudal courts, the Cult of the Virgin, and the influence of the Arabs in Andalusia. An element of romantic exoticism may be detected without too much difficulty in some of these theories, and, although the theory of Arabic origins now enjoys considerable popularity, none of them has been demonstrated with any very great rigor. The relative importance of Latin and Arabic poetic forms in the development of European vernacular verse is still unsettled, and even if this question were decided in one way or another, it would still prove nothing about the matter of content. Most commonly, it is assumed that "courtly love," whatever its ultimate origin, was first celebrated by the troubadours, that it became popular at the court of Champagne under the Countess Marie, and that Marie and Eleanor of Aquitaine held "courts of love" at Poitiers where the doctrines of the new love were disseminated. However, the troubadours included men of very diverse types whose treatment of love was by no means uniform, and critics may at times have been too eager to find a common attitude toward love in their works. For example, "courtly love" has been seen in the poems of Marcabru, in spite of the fact that he himself said, on scriptural authority,

> Qui per sen de femna reigna
> Dreitz es que mals li·n aveigna.

Again, there has been an unmistakable tendency to romanticize the activities of the southern poets. Bernard of Ventadorn concluded one of his lyrics with the lines,

> Huguet, mos cortes messatgers,
> chantatz ma chanso volonters
> a la reïna dels Normans.

The Provençal biographers, on the basis of this and other hints in Bernard's poems, envisaged a love affair between the poet and the Queen. In spite of the fact that the speculations of the jongleurs concerning the composers of the songs they sang are notoriously inaccurate, the story has sometimes been given credence in modern times.

Literary activity at the court of Champagne has been studied very carefully by John F. Benton, in an article "The Court of Champagne as a Literary Center" (*Speculum*, xxxvi [1961], 551-591). There seems to be no evidence whatsoever for the presence of troubadours at Marie's court, and little real likelihood that Marie would have been seriously interested in what is now called "courtly love." Moreover, there is no firm basis for the assumption that Marie met Eleanor at Poitiers, much less that the two ladies held "courts of love" there. The supposition that they did so undoubtedly has a strong romantic appeal, it probably seems fascinating to tourists who visit Poitiers today, and it has been repeated uncritically by so many modern writers that it has an air of established truth. One has gone so far as to compose correspondence between Marie and Eleanor in which the meeting is anticipated and in which Eleanor asks Marie to bring her chaplain, Andreas, as though he were an extraordinarily fascinating Mr. Slope. But none of these facts makes either the meeting of the two women or their "courts" a matter of history. The presumed evidence for the "courts of love" as well as for a great deal else concerning "courtly love" appears in the treatise *De amore* by Andreas Capellanus. Since that work is usually acknowledged to be of considerable importance to an understanding of medieval love conventions, it will repay us to examine it in some detail. We shall also consider certain other works which have a bearing on the subject with a view to establishing some basis for an approach to Chaucer's treatment of love. But the literature of love is very extensive during the later Middle Ages, and only a very small part of it may be treated in a single chapter. In particular, German literature is not included in our discussion, and there may be works in German which should be thought of as exceptions to the generalizations here developed. However that may be, the relevance of German literature and its special peculiarities to the study of Chaucer has yet to be demonstrated. We have already considered the *Roman de la rose* and the work of some of Chaucer's French contemporaries in earlier chapters, and we shall seek to confirm and supplement here some of the conclusions already stated.

It is not certain that Andreas Capellanus, who calls himself a royal chaplain, wrote the *De amore* for Marie of Champagne. We have no knowledge of her reaction to it, if she saw it, and hence we can deduce nothing about her character from it. It is not certain that she could read Latin. Although tentative identifications have been made, we do not know who Andreas was and thus have no external evidence concerning his character and associations. But these facts, unfortunately, have not prevented some modern writers from suggesting that Marie helped Andreas with his book, composing the more ornate passages for him, supplying him with an official document containing her decision in a "love case," and seeing to it that he reflected her views on love and on the proper way to treat husbands like Henry the Liberal.

The *De amore* was ostensibly written neither for Marie nor for any other lady, but for a certain "Walter," about whom we know nothing, and who may have been either fictitious or so named to poke fun at an existing Walter. In any event, the language of Andreas' preface leaves no doubt about Walter's condition. He has recently been wounded by an "arrow" of Love (Cupid) and cannot manage his "horse's" reins. That is, he has been stimulated by a phantasy of beauty and cannot control his flesh with the reins of temperance as the gentleman does in Fig. 6. We may see some recalcitrant horses of this kind in Fig. 63. This, Andreas says, is a serious condition, for a servant of Venus can think of nothing except of how to enmesh himself further in his "chains" (cf. Figs. 24, 71, 100). That is, one who is enslaved to a desire for pleasure (Venus) simply cultivates the heat of his passion. This is clearly an unfortunate position for any man to get into, so that Andreas assures Walter that it is not proper for a prudent man, that is, a man who is able to distinguish between good and evil, to engage in this kind of "hunting." The "hunt" referred to here is the one celebrated later in the visual arts (Figs. 26, 61, 100). Having been requested to show how a state of love may be preserved on the one hand or terminated on the other, Andreas says that he cannot refuse; but he assures Walter that after he has learned about love he will be more "cautious." A popular florilegium of Andreas' day defines caution as the ability to discern the difference between "virtues and vices presenting the appearance of virtues,"[1] and it is probable that this is the ability Andreas wished to make possible to Walter in his treatise. Various inferences arise from these prefatory remarks. In the first place, whether "Walter" was fictitious or not, the condition ascribed to him was common among young men for centuries before the beginning of the Middle Ages. Amnon and Holofernes experience it in the Old Testament; Lucretius, Horace, Virgil, and Ovid all describe it; and indeed something very much like it may be observed among the lower animals:

> Omne adeo genus in terris hominumque ferarumque
> et genus aequoreum, pecudes pictaeque volucres,
> in furias ignemque ruunt: amor omnibus idem.

It is not a condition that suddenly blossomed forth among the youth of the late eleventh century for the first time. Again, it is

---

[1] *Moralium dogma philosophorum*, ed. J. Holmberg (Uppsala, 1929), p. 10. It seems likely that Andreas knew this work.

clear that Andreas does not regard this condition as something that ought to be cultivated. On the contrary, he suggests that what he has to say will make "Walter" and, by implication, other readers in the same condition, wary in their pursuit. If anything, the tone of the preface, with its "humanistic" language, suggests light mockery. The problem Andreas sets for himself, therefore, is to furnish instructions for the young man which will seem to help him toward his goal but will at the same time encourage him to be sensible about his problem. As we read the treatise, we should not forget that the problem of men who "in furias ignemque ruunt" had been fully treated by St. Paul, and that it was not something that had been completely overlooked in the "system" of Christian philosophy.

At the end of his work, Andreas seems to think that he has successfully carried out the purpose announced in the preface. He tells Walter that if he studies the work carefully, he will find it to have a double lesson (*duplicem sententiam*), that is, a lesson with two sides. Lessons of this kind, we may interject, were not uncommon: Chaucer attributes one to the Dream of Scipio in *The Parliament of Fowls*, and there is another one over the gate to the garden in the same poem. If Walter follows instructions, Andreas tells him, he will obtain the delights of the flesh, but, at the same time, he will lose the grace of God, worthy companionship, true friendship, his good name, and honor in the world. Moreover, he adds, "If you will study carefully this little treatise of ours and understand it completely and practice what it teaches, you will see clearly that no man ought to mis-spend his days in the pleasures of love."[2] The discouragement to the pursuit of love is thus something that runs through the whole work, not something confined to the last book.

Before we consider the techniques by means of which Andreas is able to keep his "double lesson" before the reader, we should recall that there are certain attitudes taken very seriously since the romantic movement which were not taken very seriously during the Middle Ages. Schlegel wrote that in romantic poetry "the impres-

[2] All English translations of the *De amore* in this discussion are from J. J. Parry, *The Art of Courtly Love* (New York, 1941). Paraphrases, however, are based directly on Trojel's Latin text. Occasionally these paraphrases may show some departure from Parry's translation.

sions of the senses are to be hallowed, as it were, by a mysterious connexion with higher feelings." In practice, this "mysterious connexion" is almost always achieved, both in literature and life, by an appeal to sentiment. But sentimentality was not, during the Middle Ages, a respectable method of appealing to the thinking public, that is, to the courtly audience. We shall find that Andreas' lovers are not sentimental; their appeal is an appeal to logic, and we should judge them on the same grounds, without allowing our sentimental inclinations to interfere with our comprehension of what they say. No one in the *De amore* may be said to anticipate in any way the attitudes so appealingly expressed in our popular *Indian Love Lyrics*. Again, so far as "gracious living" is concerned, there is nothing in the *De amore* which sounds in the least as though it might have been written by Vatsyayana, who treated the amorous aspects of that art thoroughly. Andreas was a twelfth-century clerk who probably had a pretty thorough training in the *trivium*. We should alert ourselves, therefore, neither for sentiment nor for refinements of amorous technique, but for logical and rhetorical devices playing against a background of scriptural and classical learning.

In the first chapter of his first book Andreas sets out at once to indicate the wider implications of his theme by using a definition of love which recalls the familiar pattern of thought surrounding Matt. 5. 28 which we discussed above in Chapter II. The *passio* of love results from "sight" followed by "excessive meditation," so that love is, in effect, typical of any sin as it develops within the individual in a pattern established by the Fall. This definition does not apply to the various animals affected by love in the passage from Virgil's *Georgics* we have just quoted; animals may share Walter's initial condition, but since they lack reason, they cannot develop a passion. Certainly, Andreas' definition is not encouraging to any Walters who may read it, since it strongly implies that the lover loses the grace of God. Meanwhile, Andreas insists that the lover is always fearful. He fears that he may not get what he wants, that someone may hear about his love (which is illicit and hence secret), that he may himself be too poor to bring it off, or too ugly, and so on. If his love is returned, Andreas says, the fear is even worse, since it is worse to lose something acquired than to lose something for which one merely hopes. The lover is thus doomed to a perpetual anxiety, which is bad enough. But a commonplace of theology taught that love and fear are the sources of all good and of all evil, depending on their objects.[3] It is clear that the love and fear described by Andreas are not, in these terms, the sources of all good, so that once more the prospective lover, if he reads carefully, will not find himself encouraged.[4] But are theological considerations of this kind relevant? Should we think of them at all in connection with Andreas? The answer to this hesitation is very simple. Andreas was himself a chaplain, his book is full of allusions to the Scriptures, including that in the definition itself, and it is quite probable that the theological idea was responsible in the first place for the coupling of love and fear in Andreas' discussion. If we reflect on the nature of the *De amore* as a whole, we can see without difficulty that it does not anticipate Frederick's *De arte venandi cum avibus* as an empirical record.

The succeeding chapters of the first book of the *De amore* are no more encouraging than the first. Chapter 2, which is somewhat miscellaneous in content, but unified in theme, begins by limiting love to opposite sexes, a feature which is consistent with the definition and the surface meaning of Matt. 5. 28.[5] The limitation is expressed in the *sententia*, "Whatever Nature forbids, love is ashamed to accept," a reminder of the fact that Venus, or the pleasure of love, has been natural in man since the Fall. Nature, however, had no intention of causing man to think about love continually or of urging him to place the act of love above everything else; and this is exactly what the lover does, as Andreas goes on to say. Can a man follow Nature and at the same time be unnatural? The idea that lechery is simply "natural" is an old one, and

---

[3] See St. Augustine, *PL*, 36, col. 1026; Peter Lombard, *PL*, 191, cols. 765-766; Hugh of St. Victor, *PL*, 176, col. 572; *Summa sententiarum, PL*, 176, col. 113, where Isidore of Seville is quoted.

[4] For later discussion of fear in "love for delight," see Jehan le Bel, *Li ars d'amour* (Brussels, 1876), I, 171. Cf. the treatment of fear in "mundane" love, *ibid.*, I, 174.

[5] Cf. Ovid's restriction, *Ars am.*, 2. 683-684. Andreas undoubtedly had this work in mind as he planned his own, but this does not mean, as some writers seem to think, that he was "naughty." On the restriction, Andreas differs sharply from Ibn Hazm, who, in *The Dove's Neck Ring*, exhibited the follies of sexual passion of all kinds. There are no specific parallels between Andreas and Ibn Hazm, and there is absolutely no reason to suppose that Andreas was familiar with this or any other Arabic treatise on love.

397

the lovers in a poem written about 1180 are made to rationalize by saying,

> n'est pechiez de luxure;
> de tot est humainne nature.[6]

But the medieval mind distinguished two "natures" with reference to man, one "nature" which made virtue natural before the Fall, and one which made vice natural thereafter.[7] It was thought to be the business of man to "restore nature" by following virtue, since vice is, with reference to Creation, "unnatural." The inference that arises from the statement about love and nature is clear: a man who puts the act of love above everything else is being "natural" in a vicious sense, or, in other words, unnatural. To show further the unnatural and imprudent behavior of lovers, Andreas says that "we see them despise death and fear no threats, scatter their wealth abroad, and come to great poverty." All this they do because of their delight in the act of love and their obsession with it. The principle described here is fully developed in the *Consolation* of Boethius, which is probably its source: he who pursues one partial good, like delight, loses not only the one he pursues, but all the others as well.[8] Certainly, this consideration should not encourage Walter to give his horse free rein. To confuse his young reader thoroughly, Andreas concludes by saying that since love is incompatible with both poverty and avarice, the lover should be generous, remembering at the same time that he will enjoy no favors from the lady except those given freely. Constant generosity for a dubious end without prodigality presents a ticklish problem, but the further problem of being generous without encouraging favors in return is even worse, for the lady's favors must be given freely and not in return for anything given to her. At the close of Chapter 2, therefore, Walter has learned that love is "natural," but that if he behaves in the way lovers usually do he will lose his love through poverty. In spite of this, he must give freely, although he cannot accept anything in return. We should add that generosity

---

[6] *De David li prophecie*, ed. Fuhrken (Halle, 1895), lines 1153ff.

[7] See Peter Lombard, *Sententiae*, 3. 20. 2; and the "Summarium" following the *Anticlaudianus* as printed by Bossuat (Paris, 1955), p. 199.

[8] 3 pr. 9. Cf. the discussion in Hans Liebeschütz, *Mediaeval Humanism in the Life and Writings of John of Salisbury* (London, 1950), p. 33.

in the twelfth century was a "natural" virtue,[9] but that such virtues are inconsistent with the aim of lovers as Andreas describes it. By this time it should be clear that the "system" presented to Walter is in danger of being consistently (and intentionally) self-contradictory.

Chapter 3 on the "name" of love does not improve Walter's prospects. Andreas, following Isidore of Seville, says that the name *amor* is derived from *amus*, "hook," because a man in love is captured in the chains of cupidity (*cupidinis vinculis*), and "wishes to capture someone else with his hook." Without further ado, the prospect of being caught in the chains of cupidity is not a pleasant one. But it is worthwhile to look a little more closely at Isidore's definition (*Etym.*, 10. 4-5): "The word *amicus* is as if to say by derivation *animi custos*, 'custodian of the soul.' In particular it is to say 'love of turpitude' because it is bent by sensual desire. Thus *amicus* is from *hamus*, that is, from the chain of love (*catena caritatis*), whence friends are called *hami*, 'hooks,' because they hold." The first derivation concerns true love or friendship and was used in discussions of that subject,[10] but the derivation based on the "hook" figure is used to describe exactly the unworthy kind of love described by Andreas, a love "bent by sensual desire." To make this unworthiness clear, Andreas has substituted *cupidinis vinculis* for *catena caritatis*. It is small wonder that later writers regarded Andreas' definition of love as a definition of cupidity, and we may assume that if this fact had not yet dawned on Walter, he was a dull boy.

Chapter 4 concerns the effects of love. In the first place, the lover cannot be degraded by avarice, for reasons we have seen. Second, love makes a rough man handsome. To understand this bit of magic, we have only to read Ovid's account of Polyphemus in love (*Met.*, 13. 744ff.) or the account in the *De amore* itself of how a lover's ugly legs and feet become a part of "divine nature" and hence above criticism. Love makes the proud humble, for, as Andreas has explained, the lover is always fearful of offending. It makes the lover perform "many services gracefully for everyone,"

---

[9] See Alanus, *De planctu naturae*, PL, 210, cols. 478-479.

[10] E.g., by St. Ailred, *De spirituali amicitia*, PL, 195, col. 663. This work became a standard source of medieval ideas of friendship. It was translated into French by Jean de Meun.

an effect we may see exemplified in Chaucer's Damyan (Merch. Tale, 2009ff.). "O what a wonderful thing is love," exclaims Andreas, "which makes a man shine with so many virtues, and teaches everyone, no matter who he is, so many good traits of character!" At this point we may assume that Drouart la Vache, who tells us that he sat laughing as he read the *De amore*,[11] probably began to chuckle in earnest. The "double lesson" of the work, up to this point, has been sufficiently apparent, but it is here reinforced by the familiar device of irony, the art of condemning something while seeming to praise it. Love is such a wonderful thing, Andreas says, that it actually confers the virtue of chastity, because a man devoted to one woman cannot think of embracing another. Since the object of love is the act of love, it is not difficult to see that this virtue will result only from the kind of success obtained by the lovers in the dialogues—none at all. Andreas assures us that in view of these wonderful effects of love, he would be a lover also, were it not for the fact that love carries unjust weights and often "leaves his sailors in the mighty waves." These rather cryptic remarks rest on two figures, one from the Bible and the other from mythography. In the Bible, the justice of God is several times expressed in terms of just weights.[12] In his popular commentary on Leviticus, Radulphus Flaviacensis tells us that to use just weights is to obey the law of God, or to act charitably.[13] Love, Andreas says in effect, does not do this, so that for this reason he avoids love. The figure of the shipwrecked sailors of love is from Fulgentius, who says of Venus that "they depict her swimming in the sea, for all things suffer shipwreck on account of lust, whence also Porphyrius says in an epigram, 'Nude, hungry, the shipwrecked sailor of Venus is in the seas.' "[14] Venus is still "naked, fletynge in the large see"

---

[11] See R. Bossuat, *Li livres d'amours de Drouart la Vache* (Paris, 1926), p. 2.

[12] Lev. 19. 35-37; Deut. 13. 16; Job 31. 5-6; Prov. 11. 1, 16. 11, 20. 23; Ez. 45. 9-11; Amos 8. 4-8; Mic. 6. 9-12. The Glossa, *PL*, 113, col. 353, treating the first of these passages, associates just weights with the laws of the Holy Scriptures.

[13] *MBP*, ed. 1677, 17, p. 177. For the popularity of this commentary, see C. Spicq, *Esquisse d'une histoire de l'exégèse latine* (Paris, 1944), p. 125.

[14] *Mit.*, ed. Helm, 2. 1; cf. Neckam, *Super Marcianum*, Oxford, Bodl., MS Digby 221, fol. 37: "In mari natat [Venus] quia libidinosorum substancie naufragium patiuntur." Cf. Myth. III in Bode, *Scriptores rerum mythicarum* (Cellis, 1834), p. 229: "Pingunt eam in mare natantem, quia libido rebus naufragia inferre non dubitatur. Unde Porphyrius. . . ."

in Chaucer's Knight's Tale for the same reason. That is, Love not only acts contrary to God's justice; it also leads to shipwreck in the world. Thus Andreas refuses to submit to love, adopting, perhaps, a "cautious" attitude toward Love's apparent virtues.

In Chapter 5, Andreas points out that age, blindness, and excessive lust may prevent love. Old men above sixty and women above fifty lack the necessary vigor to carry out Love's precepts, he says; and girls under twelve or boys under eighteen are also barred because they are inconstant. Boys and girls of these ages were excluded from marriage for the same reason,[15] and immature persons were thought also to be incapable of true friendship.[16] Blindness prevents love because a blind man cannot see something and then engage in an excessive meditation upon it. Finally, those who are too lustful seek the embraces of any woman and will not concentrate on one. The inference from all of these limitations is that love requires an idolatrous fixation of a kind necessary to generate a strong passion. The lustful are like animals, as Andreas says, and animals are incapable of passion since they have no reason to corrupt. The blind cannot form a phantasy to cherish in the memory; the young will not keep one there; and the old lack sufficient interest to do so.

With these preliminaries out of the way, Andreas is now ready, in Chapter 6, to introduce the subject of how love may be acquired, a subject illustrated by the celebrated dialogues between lovers. Before we consider the dialogues themselves, however, we should pay very careful attention to the manner in which they are introduced, so that we may know exactly what they are supposed to illustrate. At the outset, there are said to be five means of acquiring love: "a beautiful figure, excellence of character [*morum probitas*], extreme readiness of speech, great wealth, and the readiness with which one grants what is sought." Andreas dismisses the last two as unworthy at once for reasons he explains later (Chapters 9 and 10 of the first book). The first, a beautiful figure, is also dismissed,[17] since it appeals to the simple, arouses attention and suspicion, and hence creates a love which does not last long. When it is frustrated, moreover, love based on beauty increases enormously and torments

---

[15] Lombard, *Sententiae*, 4. 36. 4.

[16] St. Ailred, *De spirituali amicitia*, PL, 195, cols. 676-677.

[17] Cf. Ovid, *Ars am.*, 2. 113-116, and for a later discussion, Jehan le Bel, *Li ars d'amour*, II, 95.

the lovers, for, as Ovid indicates (*Amores*, 3. 4. 17), people strive for what they cannot get and want that which is denied them. We should notice that this restriction puts something of a damper on the kind of love defined at the outset, which arises from a meditation on "the beauty of the opposite sex." The discussion which follows leads us by degrees to the conclusion that the only legitimate means of acquiring love is *morum probitas*, "worth of character." First, it is said that a wise woman will prefer probity to a cultivated appearance, as Ovid indicated (*Her.*, 4. 75-76).[18] Women who use too much adornment, Andreas continues, frequently do so because of weakness of character, so that women should be sought, not for their adornment, but for *morum honestas*, or virtuous behavior.[19] Thus a well-taught lover will not hesitate to select an ugly companion if the person is wise. A wise man cannot "easily go astray" in love's path, and a woman who has such a lover can easily keep her love concealed. Excellence of character rather than beauty is the source of true nobility, for it is this which created class distinctions, although not all noblemen are now virtuous, and not all of the non-noble are vicious. The idea that true nobility consists of virtue and is not a matter of heredity is a commonplace,[20] and we should pay close attention to the manner in which the speakers in the dialogues exhibit their nobility and their *probitas*, which is the only ground for love.

The idea that affection should be based on *morum probitas* is one of the central theses of the *De amicitia* of Cicero (28-29), whence it became a part of the standard doctrine of friendship during the Middle Ages.[21] But unless Walter is very unobservant, he will realize that *probitas* is inconsistent, either in Ciceronian

[18] Cf. *Ars am.*, 1. 505-524, 3. 433-452. The passage cited by Andreas is an observation of Phaedra, whose love for the unadorned masculinity of Hippolytus is strong enough, but is admittedly contrary to *vetus pietas*, and it leads to the death of the young man.

[19] Cf. Ovid, *De medicamine faciei liber*, 43-50, where exactly the same point is made.

[20] Parry, p. 35, note 12, cites Seneca, *De beneficiis*, 3. 28, in this connection. The idea may also be found in Ovid, *Met.*, 13. 140-141; Cicero, *De off.*, 1. 34. 121; *Moralium dogma philosophorum*, p. 55; Walter of Châtillon, *Alex.*, 1. 104-105; Boethius, *De cons.*, 3, met. 6; Alanus de Insulis, *Summa de arte praed.*, *PL*, 210, col. 154.

[21] Cf. St. Ailred, *De spir. am.*, *PL*, 195, cols. 674, 675. For Andreas' use of the *De amicitia*, see Parry, p. 189.

terms or in medieval terms, with a concentration on the act of love as the highest good. Moreover, the reference to true nobility should suggest to him that the kind of love Andreas is describing is not very noble. However, Andreas leaves these little difficulties to Walter, and suggests that an "elaborate line of talk" may create a "presumption of the excellence of character of the speaker." And it is this line of talk, designed to give the impression of *probitas*, which is illustrated in the dialogues. It should be pointed out that the male speakers in the dialogues thus have a very difficult task before them. They must try to persuade their ladies to commit the act of love by extolling their own merits. Hence the general form of their arguments is this: "I am very noble and virtuous, and you are very noble and virtuous: therefore we should enjoy a little fornication (or adultery)." Needless to say, this argument presents grave difficulties, and no one of the lovers who is made to speak has any success in overcoming them. The more elaborate the arguments become, the more ridiculous and amusing they become at the same time. Meanwhile, it is well to emphasize again that the various approaches used by the lovers are logical in character, not what a nineteenth-century novelist would call "passionate." If we read them as passionate outbursts of sentiment, we shall simply misread them, or read into them things that are not there at all.

The "nobleman" of the first dialogue is a plebeian who addresses a lady of his own hereditary class. His behavior illustrates very well the fact that the aid of Faus Semblant is required in enterprises of this kind. He is advised to approach his business gradually, to avoid being tongue-tied, and to use a little indirect preliminary flattery on the grounds that some women, especially those in the plebeian class, are susceptible to praise. Noble ladies, presumably, are a little wiser. Following this general advice, the proper approach is illustrated: "When the Divine Being made you there was nothing that He left undone. I know that there is no defect in your beauty, none in your good sense, none in you at all except, it seems to me, that you have enriched no one by your love." Flattery, it should be remembered, had been satirized by Ovid and condemned by Cicero;[22] in the language of Psalm 140. 5, Chris-

---

[22] For Cicero's view, see *De amicitia*, 91: ". . . sic habendum est nullam in amicitiis pestem esse maiorem quam adulationem, blanditiam, adsentationem; quamvis enim multis nominibus est hoc vitium notandum levium hominum atque

tians regarded flattery as the *oleum peccatoris*, and it was widely condemned in the twelfth century.[23] The lover's opening is thus consistent neither with a Christian nor a classical concept of *probitas*, and this fact could hardly have escaped Walter. However, the lover is confident of his own good character and gives the lady frank assurances of it: "Now if I, by my merits, might be worthy of such an honor, no lover in the world could really be compared with me." Disregarding this self-anointing, the lady objects modestly that she has neither the beauty nor the wisdom attributed to her. The lover's reply should be considered in the light of his own observations concerning himself: "It is a habit of wise people never to admit with their own mouths their good looks or their good character, and by so doing they clearly show their character, because prudent people guard their words so carefully that no one may have reason to apply to them that common proverb which runs, 'All praise is filthy in one's own mouth.'" The implication is clear that the lover is, on the basis of standards to which he himself has called attention, not very prudent. The remainder of the lovers in the dialogues frequently involve themselves in the same difficulty: How can one show one's *probitas* and, at the same time, avoid self-praise? The dilemma as Andreas presents it is essentially amusing; it is not intended to provoke sighs about the odd but charming behavior of dear young men when subjected to the influence of that strange but wonderful force called, preferably with protracted sighing aspiration and a far-away look, "love."

The prudence of the lover does not improve as he progresses. After complimenting the lady for her modesty, he assures her that even if she is not beautiful, he thinks she is, for "love makes even an ugly woman seem beautiful to her lover." Just how this blindness, illustrated so vividly by a later writer in the person of Titania, reflects either the lover's *probitas* or the merits of his lady would be difficult to explain. As for the lady's plebeian status, the lover attributes to her a nobility arising from *morum probitas*, the

---

fallacium, ad voluntatem loquentium omnia, nihil ad veritatem." Cf. Seneca, *De ben.*, 6. 30. 5.

[23] See St. Augustine, *Enn. in Ps.*, in *Opera* (Gaume ed.), IV, 2237: "Falsa laus adulatio est; falsa laus adulatoris, hoc est oleum peccatoris." Cf. *ibid.*, cols. 28, 77, 97, etc. Twelfth-century sensitivity to the vice is well attested by the space devoted to it by Neckam, *De naturis rerum* (ed. Wright), pp. 316-320; John of Salisbury, *Policrat.*, 3, *passim*; Walter of Chatillon, *Alex.*, 10; etc.

only real index of class distinction. But this argument proves disastrous, since the lady deduces from it that she should then seek a noble lover to suit the nobility which has so conveniently been conferred upon her. To support this truly modest contention, she blithely misapplies a line from the *Metamorphoses* (2. 846-847): "Nobility and commonalty [*popularitas*] 'do not go well together or dwell in the same abode.' "[24] The lady's learning is suited to her station, for the two things Ovid refers to as being incompatible are "maiestas et amor," specifically in Jove, who laid aside his scepter and majesty to take the rather ignoble form of a bull that he might seduce Europa. The seduction, incidentally, had disastrous consequences.[25] The lady's "authority" thus contradicts her argument, since the quotation implies that the more noble she is, the less she will find love compatible with her station. We shall find that most of the "authorities" cited by lovers in the *De amore* have just this effect. But the lover, disregarding these implications, is quick to raise himself to that eminence to which he has already elevated the lady. She should not seek a nobleman for a lover, but, he assures her, a man like himself, whose nobility is of the better kind deriving from *morum probitas*. Just how serious all this would be to a courtly audience, either in Champagne or elsewhere, the reader should be able to imagine for himself. If he cannot imagine it, no amount of explanation will help him.

Andreas provides his lover with ammunition to use if the lady objects either to his advanced age or to his extreme youth. As we might expect, the arguments contradict each other. In answer to the objection against old age, the lover calls attention to the fact that his age is due to the divine power which set his nativity, so that he is not to blame for it. Thus exculpated, he asserts that he

---

[24] The translation omits the phrase *in diversis sexibus*.

[25] Jove's reputation on this account was not very good in classical times. Ovid, *Ars am.*, 3. 252, says that Europa was carried away "falso . . . bove." In *Her.*, 4. 53ff., Phaedra attributes her own unfortunate passion to the fact that Europa began her genealogy. In Horace, *Carm.*, 3. 27. 25-26, Europa entrusts herself "doloso . . . tauro." Statius, *Theb.*, 1. 5, refers to Jove's act as the beginning of an evil race. In its Christian context the story was taken as a warning against deceitful eloquence. See Arnulf of Orléans, ed. Ghisalberti (Milan, 1932), p. 207, where it is said that Jupiter lured Europa to the shore with his eloquence (Mercury) and then spirited her away on a ship either named *Bull* or adorned with a bull. For the background of this explanation, see Fulgentius, *Mit.*, 1. 20; Lactantius, *Div. inst.*, 1. 11.

has spent his time well: "I have done many praiseworthy deeds, extended many courtesies, offered numberless services to everybody I could, and done many other good things which no one would have been able to do in a short space of time, and so I deserve great rewards and should be honored with the greatest recompense." On the grounds of these great merits, to which the lover so bashfully calls attention, he certainly deserves something. But in spite of this advantage of age, the lover concludes by questioning his own antiquity: "It is not proper to assume that a man is old because his hair is white, for we constantly see many men grow white when they are not old. . . . Therefore, you should judge a man's age more by his heart than by his hair." He is old and therefore virtuous, but at the same time, he is not really old. To afford material for the opposite situation, in which the lover is rather young, Andreas has the lady object first that her suitor has not performed many good deeds, so that an older more praiseworthy lover would suit her better. At this, the argument becomes rather heated, for the lover begins to doubt his lady's much vaunted prudence: "If I didn't think that you said this in jest or to make me blush for modesty, I would say that your good sense had deserted you." If the lady's beauty is a product of the lover's blindness and her prudence is questionable, not much remains of those sterling virtues mentioned by the lover at the outset. In any event, the lover explains, with an argument directly contrary to that employed when he was in the guise of an old man, that a lady who bestows her gifts on account of good deeds has, as it were, sold them. This, incidentally, is a good principle to remember when we consider the *probitas* of subsequent lovers. But, our plebeian nobleman continues, a lady who shows her grace to an undeserving youth shows pure generosity. Moreover, the lady will do a very creditable thing if she will instruct him. In reply, the lady asserts that if this argument were true, good deeds would be harmful, but that according to a precept of Love, a man who performs good deeds deserves a reward. The lady simply advises the young man to go to Paris for instruction. At this, the lover's impatience overcomes him: "I marvel at your words and that you try so sophistically to find fault with what I said." The lady's "sophistical" argument very closely resembles the argument used by the lover as an

406

old man. Meanwhile, what has become of the lady's supreme prudence? And where is the lover's great *probitas*?

The lover's lengthy reply to the lady is no less sophistical. In the course of it he refers to Luke 15. 7, setting up a contrast between "Deus" and "mundus": "Just as there is more profit to God in the conversion of one sinner than in the improvement of the ninety-nine just, so society gains more [*ita maius fit mundo lucrum*] when one man who is not good is rendered excellent than when the worthy character of some good man is increased." Perhaps the lover has forgotten that his *probitas*, the basis of nobility, should be pleasing to God rather than to the world. As for his love, he reveals clearly what it is by dividing it into steps in accordance with the traditional stages of lechery.[26] For all of his pains, however, his only reward is to be told that he "will have to be exhausted by a great deal of labor" before he gets what he wants. The lover, at the end, reverses himself and looks forward to doing many good deeds. By the time he has finished these great enterprises, he will, of course, be in the position of the lover as an older man. Will he then, we may ask, try to buy favors with his reputation? If the first dialogue proves anything, it shows that neither a virtuous career nor a willingness to undertake a virtuous career is a sufficient basis for claiming the "rewards" of love. Meanwhile, the difficulty of claiming *probitas* while demanding something improper is also sufficiently illustrated.

The lover of the second dialogue, a plebeian who addresses a noble lady, fares no better, although his words exhibit more vanity and affectation than those of the lover, or lovers, in the first dialogue. This heightened hypocrisy is due to the fact that what he asks is not only a violation of his own *probitas*, but also a violation of the natural order of society. Andreas says that the approach of the first dialogue may be used if the lady is "simple," or foolish enough not to see through it, but that more subtlety is required if she is "wise and astute." But the subtle approach is illustrated. At the outset, the lover confesses that his heart has diverted his will "from its natural path," so that he may say something foolish.

---

[26] There are traditionally five stages rather than four, but the lover takes the first one, "sight," for granted. See Hieric, *Scholia in Horatium*, ed. J. Botschuyver (Amsterdam, 1942), p. 24; Alanus, *Summa de arte praed.*, *PL*, 210, col. 122; John of Salisbury, *Policrat.*, 4. 23, and Webb's note, 1, p. 64.

He does. The distinction between the "heart" and the "will" here is based on the discussion of the Old Law and the New in Romans 7, where to do something contrary to the will means to allow concupiscence to overcome the will "to accomplish that which is good." When the lover says, therefore, that his heart has diverted his will "from its natural path,"[27] he implies that his concupiscence is leading toward illicit and unnatural conduct. Nevertheless, he continues by appealing to Nature: "Love is a thing that copies Nature herself, and so lovers ought to make no more distinction between classes of men than Love himself does." The suppressed premise here is that Nature makes no distinctions between classes, a premise that it was just as well to suppress in view of the fact that throughout the Middle Ages the hierarchy in society was regarded as being established by Nature. However, the lover has, he says, an "unanswerable argument," and he insists that he can love any woman he chooses so long as he has "no depravity of character." His initial statement, however, has revealed a very definite "depravity of character," so that the invincible argument is more than a little hollow. Again, the effect on an aristocratic audience—the only kind of audience outside of the clergy who could understand Andreas' Latin—of this effort to transcend class distinctions on the grounds of concupiscence may well be imagined. We should do well to remember that Andreas had never read *The American* or anything like it and had no regard for democratic sentiments. The lover goes on to elaborate his *probitas* and *nobilitas* by modestly asserting that he is not an insufficient *miles amoris*. Since he makes a point of it, we might consider what a *miles amoris* might have meant to Andreas and his audience, who had never had the enviable privilege of reading "Ovid Understood."

The military triumph of Cupid, whose arrows have wounded Walter and all his kinsmen, is described as follows at the beginning of the *Amores* (i. 2. 31-38):

> Mens bona ducetur manibus post terga retortis,
>   et Pudor, et castris quidquid Amoris obest.
> omnia te metuent; ad te sua bracchia tendens
>   vulgus "io" magna voce "triumphe!" canet.

[27] Cf. the discussion in the Glossa, *PL*, 114, col. 493.

blanditiae comites tibi erunt Errorque Furorque,
    adsidue partes turba secuta tuas.
his tu militibus superas hominesque deosque;
    haec tibi si demas commoda, nudus eris.

To be a soldier of love may be pleasant, but it involves an association with Flattery, Error, and Furor, and a contempt for Mens Bona and Pudor. In *Amores* 1. 9, Ovid elaborates the theme "militat omnis amans." The effectiveness of this figure lies in the contrast between the stern virtues of the soldier and the ridiculous behavior of the lover, to whom the similarities adduced can be nothing but a mockery. Both find it necessary to rest on the ground, one at the door of his mistress, and one at the door of his officer in the field. Just as the soldier often rushes upon a sleeping enemy, so also the lover wields what Marlowe translates as his "swelling armes" while the husband sleeps, and so on. Achilles, Hector, Agamemnon, great soldiers all, all loved. The irony of these exemplars is sufficiently apparent in the treatment of Achilles:

Ergo desidiam quicumque vocabat amorem,
    desinat, ingenii est experientis amor.
ardet in abducta Briseide magnus Achilles—
    dum licet, Argivas frangite, Troes, opes!

Mars himself succumbed also. He is one of the soldiers of love in the *Ars amatoria* (2. 233-250; cf. 1. 36, 2. 674, 3. 1), where the connotations of his warfare are made plain (2. 563-564):

Mars pater, insano Veneris turbatus amore,
    De duce terribili factus amator erat.

What Ovid implies is that lecherous love, in spite of its ludicrous pretensions, is inconsistent with military virtue and with Roman *pietas*. We should be very careful not to confuse him with Algernon Swinburne. A very similar attitude is apparent in the *Aeneid*, where Aeneas and Dido are for a time "oblitos famae melioris amantis," and where Tarchon chides his horsemen for being interested "in Venerem segnes nocturnaque bella." The *miles amoris* fared no better in the Middle Ages. John of Salisbury explains that nothing is more contrary to knighthood than lechery, which disrupts all order.[28] Walter of Châtillon finds it especially dangerous among those who rule others (*Alex.*, 1. 164-169):

> sed non te emolliat intus
> Prodiga luxuries, nec fortia pectora frangat
> Mentis morbus amor, latebris et murmure gaudens.
> Si Baccho Venerique vacas, qui cetera subdis,
> Sub iuga venisti: periit delira vacantis
> Libertas animi, Veneris flagrante camino.

And Alanus, in the *Anticlaudianus* (1. 179-181), sums up the qualities of a "knight of Venus" in his description of Paris:

> Fractus amore Paris, Veneris decoctus in igne,
> Militat in Venerem; dum militis exuit actus,
> Damnose compensat in hac quod perdit in armis.

Andreas' lover thus cuts an extraordinarily ridiculous figure when he praises himself as a *miles amoris*, for he is not only a pretender to the interior nobility of *probitas* but also to an exterior knighthood which is contrary to *probitas*. His plaints that only the lady can cure his mortal wound do not add to his dignity.

The noble lady is quick to discern her suitor's departure from nature: "I am very much surprised—it is enough to surprise anyone—that in such a great upsetting of things the elements do not come to an end and the world itself fall into ruin." In other words, the lover has so loosened the reins of natural justice within himself that it is strange to find the harmony of things in general undisturbed, "nature's moulds" uncracked. She explains what she means by an example drawn from nature involving birds which should place her lover who "devotes all his efforts to the various gains of business" in his rightful position: "Did a buzzard [*lacertiva avis*] ever overcome a partridge or a pheasant by its courage? It is for falcons and hawks to capture this prey [cf. Figs. 9, 58, 60,

---

[28] *Policrat.*, 6. 11. The clergy are admonished here as well as the knights. Cf. The *Livre des manières*, ed. Kremer (Marburg, 1887), lines 585-588; Raoul de Houdenc, *Li romans des eles*, ed. Scheler, *Trouvères belges* (Louvain, 1897), p. 264; *Carmen de bello Lewensi*, ed. Kingsford, lines 165 ff. The conflict between the "militia" of love and that of chivalry is well illustrated in Chrétien's *Erec*. Cf. *Le chevaler Dé*, ed. K. Urwin, *RLR*, LXVIII (1937), lines 15 ff. A knight who forsakes his duty for the sake of amorous passion is said to be *recreant*, lines 395 ff.

62, 64], which should not be annoyed by cowardly kites." The
lacertiva avis mentioned here is probably a kestrel rather than a
buzzard,[29] and neither kestrels nor kites were thought to be very
admirable birds. The kestrel feeds on mice and beetles, and the
kite is a scavenger which was once considered to be excellent if
difficult quarry for hawks. The kestrel was associated with the
lowest order of society, and the kite was said to make false pretenses
of being a hawk.[30] These alternatives do not speak well for our
lover, although they seem to be apt enough. The lady continues
her argument on the basis of the "unequal weights" that Love
carries. In view of the nature of these weights, a woman accosted
by a lover is under no obligation to return his love. Nor is this unjust: "for he does not use them except when compelled by the best
of reasons [*nisi iustissima causa cogente*]." That is, it is just that

[29] The rendering "kestrel" is not based on any understanding of Andreas'
epithet, but on the French and Italian translations of the *De amore*. Drouart la
Vache has *cercele* at this point. Although Bossuat glosses this word "crécerelle,
petit oiseau de proie," there is even some doubt about this. OF *cercele, crecele* is
supposed to be derived from Latin *querquedula*, "teal," so that there is reason
for T. B. W. Reid's gloss "teal" for *cercele* in Chrétien's *Yvain* (Manchester,
1948), p. 225. However, ENE *kestrel* seems to be related to *cercele*, and Drouart
writes of it as though it were a small bird of prey. The rendering "kestrel" is
further supported by the Italian translation of the *De amore*, ed. S. Battaglia
(Rome, 1947), pp. 49, 55, where "l'uccello laniero" and "acertulo" are used.
Tommaseo and Bellini define *acertello* as *falco tinnunculus* (i.e., "kestrel"), and
concerning *laniere*, which also means "kestrel," they quote Brunetto Latini: "Fal-
coni sono de sette generazioni: il primo lignaggio sono lanieri, che sono siccome
villani infra gli altri." Transferred to men, the term has the connotation "*con-
trario di* Affabili *e di* Gentile." The evidence thus favors "kestrel," and the traditional etymology of OF *cercele* probably needs revision. However, Giraldus Cam-
brensis, London, BM, MS Royal 13 B. VIII, fol. 21, describes "cercellis" as water
birds.

[30] For the kestrel see *Yvain*, 3192-3195, where Yvain attacks Count Alier and
his followers: "Car li cortois, li preuz, li buens, / Mes sire Yvains, tot autressi /
Les fesoit venir a merci / Con li faucons fet les cerceles." On the association
between the kestrel and the lowest social order, see the preceding note. For what
it is worth, *kestrel* was a term of opprobrium in ENE, where it became associated
with *coistrel*. One revealing epithet for the bird was *windfucker*, derived possibly
from its manner of hovering with its head against the wind. The term is also
applied in various amusing ways to base persons. See the *NED*, s. v. *kestrel, windfucker*. The latter term has an exact counterpart in Italian. With reference to the
kite, Alanus, *De planctu nat.*, PL, 210, 435, wrote: "Illic venatoris induens per-
sonam milvus, veneratione furtiva, larvam gerebat accipitris." For later references
to the kite, see my article, "*Buzones*, an Alternative Etymology," *SP*, XLII (1945),
741-744.

Love's weights should be unjust, for otherwise ladies would have no freedom of choice but would have to submit to the attentions of low persons.[31] The lady concludes by saying, "your efforts are worse than useless, and when you finish you will see that you have spent your labor in vain." But the lover is not to be dismayed. Referring first to the "kindly and gentle" answer just quoted, he accuses the lady of error, since she has overlooked his *morum probitas*. His mercenary labors, which, as it were, set him off from birds of prey, reinforce his virtue: "if I did not concern myself with honest and legitimate gains, I would fall into obscure poverty, and so I could not do noble deeds, and my nobility of character would remain only an empty name, a kind of courtesy or nobility which men never put much faith in." It is clear that he has hit the nail on the head; his *probitas* is a mere name, for the idea that mercenary labor is either necessary to it or an adjunct to it would undoubtedly have struck a twelfth-century aristocratic audience as being ludicrous.[32] There is little hope that if the kestrel attends assiduously to his beetles and the kite to his carrion their energy and pertinacity will make hawks of them. The lover has not forgotten these birds, for he says that birds of prey are valued only for their bravery, so that if the kite or the kestrel is brave, it deserves the perch of the falcon or a place on the fist of the hunter. The picture of a knight carrying a kite or kestrel to the hunt does not add to the solemn cogency of this argument. Finally, the lover asserts that Love's weights are not really unjust because they give the lady freedom of choice, just as God gives man freedom of choice and rewards or punishes him in accordance with whether he has chosen

[31] On the inequity of love in Ovidian contexts, see E. Faral, *Recherches sur les sources latines des contes et romans courtois du moyen âge* (Paris, 1913), p. 148.

[32] It was widely recognized that *beneficentia* might involve either money or good deeds, but that involving good deeds was thought to be vastly superior. See Cicero, *De off.*, 2. 15. 52; *Moralium dogma phil.*, p. 20; *Policrat.*, 8. 4. Father Denomy, *Med. Stud.*, VIII, 116-117, associated the merchant's position with a proposition condemned by Bishop Tempier, "Quod pauper bonis fortunae non potest bene agere in moralibus." But Andreas shows small sympathy for the merchant. The proposition condemned by Tempier probably had its origin in some overenthusiastic secular attack on the doctrine of Evangelical poverty advanced by the friars. For example, see P. S. Clasen, ed., "Gerardi de Abbatsvilla contra adversarium," *Arch. franc. hist.*, XXXII (1939), pp. 188-189. Tempier's condemnation was hastily drawn up by a committee, and although there is a general attack on the *De amore*, it is doubtful that any of the specific doctrines condemned refer to Andreas' text.

to do good or evil. It follows from this, the lover asserts, that if a lover has done well and is meritorious, a lady should by no means refuse him unless she has other obligations. That is, her freedom of choice is an aspect of Love's justice, but if she refuses the deserving lover, she will be violating the principles of God's justice. But this desire to benefit from both types of justice, although typical of the middle-class feeling that one ought to have one's cake and eat it too, makes little impression on the lady, who accuses her suitor of "more than empty words." After defending the social hierarchy and asserting that men should seek love among those of their own class, she concludes with the rather bitter remark, "May God give you a reward suited to your effort." The lover in turn prays that his sails "may find a quiet haven," but, as we know from Andreas' remarks spoken in his own person earlier, the likelihood that the sailors of Venus will find such a haven is small. Walter must have learned from this dialogue that it is futile to attempt to upset the order of society on the basis of vain pretensions to *probitas* motivated by cupidity.

The theme is elaborated still further in the third dialogue between a man of the plebeian class and a woman of the higher nobility. The lady in this instance is appropriately wiser than those in the previous dialogues and is able to furnish her lover with some very good doctrine, although it is, from his point of view, entirely impractical. If it is foolhardy to try to make a hawk of a kestrel, it is even more foolish to try to make an eagle of him. To begin, Andreas explains that the probability of finding a plebeian who excels all available men in the two upper classes is very slight. Among kestrels, there are a few that capture partridges when very young, but this activity "goes beyond their nature," and it does not long endure. After much testing, Andreas says, the plebeian may use the approach suggested in the second dialogue, but, as we have seen, this suggestion does not afford much hope. Or, he continues, the lover may try another approach, which is illustrated. Our tested and virtuous merchant begins with some guarded references to the lady's famed probity and beauty, an humble prayer to God that he may please her, and the following obsequious nonsense: "I have in my heart a firm and fixed desire, not only to offer you my services, but on your behalf to offer them to everybody and to serve with an humble and acceptable spirit, since I have a

413

firm faith that my labor can never remain with you without the delightfulness of fruit. If my trouble should prove fruitless, I must, after many waves and tempests of death, suffer shipwreck unless my soul is guided by hope, even though it is a false one. For only a hope, even one granted with a deceitful mind, can keep the anchor of my support firmly fixed." We might well recall that it is the hope of illicit *fructus* that leads to shipwreck.[33] That the request for false hope is contrary to her well-known *probitas* does not escape the lady's attention. After thanking her suitor for his offer of services, but objecting that he seems to be hunting game that he is unworthy to take, she concludes, with reference to the request for hope, "To this I answer that the mere fact that you accuse me of clever deceit and falsehood shows that you are infected with this same failing and that you keep one idea in your mind and speak another with your deceitful tongue." He has clearly thought one thing and said another either when he spoke of the lady's *probitas* or when he asked her for false hope, and to have one thing in mind while expressing another is to lie.[34] Our tested plebeian has not begun very well. The lady adds that the giving of false hope is characteristic of prostitutes.[35]

But the lover carefully pays no attention to what she says and insists instead on his own *probitas*, the character of which he has just inadvertently revealed. Nature, he says, urges him beyond the limits of his class. We should have no difficulty in deciding what kind of nature this is, for he justifies his transcendent potentialities on the authority of St. Paul, who says that the law was not made for just men but for sinners. As a just man, he is, of course, above the law. But this inference is hardly supported in the text to which he refers. We need only to look at the context of the passage to see that our lover follows the usual pattern of adducing authority only to condemn himself (1 Tim. 1. 5-10): "Now the end of the commandment is charity, from a pure heart, and a good conscience, and an unfeigned faith. From which things some going astray, are turned aside unto vain babbling: Desiring to be teachers of the law, understanding neither the things they say, nor whereof they

[33] Cf. 1 Tim. 1. 19 and 6. 9-10; and *Scholia in Horatium*, p. 14, where the expression *naufragium meretricis* is used.
[34] For the standard definition of a lie, see St. Augustine, *De mendacio*, 3. 3.
[35] Cf. the character of Pyrrha in Horace, *Carm.*, 1. 5, and *Scholia*, p. 13.

affirm. But we know that the law is good, if a man use it lawfully: Knowing this, that the law is not made for the just man, but for the unjust and disobedient, for the ungodly, and for sinners, for the wicked and defiled, for murderers of fathers, and murderers of mothers, for manslayers. For fornicators, for them who defile themselves with mankind, for mensteakers, for liars, for perjured persons, and whatever other thing is contrary to sound doctrine." As a follower of Venus, he is clearly not among those who obey the law of charity, so that his "authority" puts him in very bad company indeed and specifically alludes to his "vain babbling." To modern readers unfamiliar with the Bible, the humor in passages such as this in the *De amore* is a little difficult to see, but that humor could hardly have escaped a twelfth-century Latin audience whose literary training was directed toward scriptural study. The lover concludes by saying that his suggestion that the lady might deceive him was not intended to belittle her character but to show his very great affection for her: in other words, to accuse her of a kind of fraud typical of prostitutes is to exhibit very great love. The lady acknowledges that although merit may ennoble a man, he cannot change his actual status without the authority of a prince. The specimen before her does not look very promising as a potential knight, for, as she points out, he has very fat calves and immense square feet. To this our virtuous plebeian replies that the lady should consider his *mores* rather than his calves; his calves and feet are above criticism since they are a part of "divine nature." That is, they are inevitably beautiful because God made them. This remarkable assertion is a good illustration of how love makes a man handsome. But when the lady does consider the gentleman's *mores*, she finds them to be intangible. His good deeds, whatever they may have been, have won him no fame. Indeed, he has not yet undertaken his virtuous career and is anxious to know how to begin. Like the virtues of the other lovers described by Andreas, his exist only in his own mouth.

The lady very graciously agrees to give her suitor some good advice. The instructions which follow are excellent, comprising a little *summa* of the virtues of a knight, in part derived from classical sources; but the actions recommended are good only so long as they are carried out by the right persons with the right motives. In the Middle Ages, men were very sensitive about class distinctions and the virtues proper to each class.[36] The lover is first advised to be generous, not in the manner satirized by Ovid, to the lady of his desire, but to everyone, especially to the noble and virtuous. However, he is not to neglect the poor and needy, for feeding the poor is regarded as a very courteous and generous action. The notion that the virtuous among rich and poor should be objects of generosity, probably derived from Cicero,[37] became a recognized chivalric ideal;[38] but a merchant whose welfare depended upon profit might have some difficulty in fulfilling it, unless he was very wealthy indeed.[39] The lover is advised to be humble, respectful to God and to His saints.[40] It should be noted that his boastful *probitas*, his references to the transcendent social aspirations, and his use of Biblical authority have not demonstrated much inclination toward these virtues. With reference to speech, he is urged never to disparage anyone. On the other hand, he should not praise the wicked, but should admonish them privately, or, if they persist in wickedness, abandon their company altogether.[41] And he should neither mock anyone nor beget quarrels.[42] Moderate laughter only should be indulged before women to avoid the appearance of foolishness,[43] for wise men avoid fools. As a lover,

[36] This sensitivity is evident, for example, in the *Livre d'Enanchet*, where separate sets of instructions are given for persons of various stations. It is noteworthy that each station was considered to have its peculiar vices as well as its virtues.

[37] *De off.*, 2. 20. 69-70. See also Parry's reference to Seneca, p. 59.

[38] In *Li romans des eles* "Largece" is the right wing of chivalry. The third "feather" of this wing, pp. 254-255, furnishes the principle described by Andreas. Cf. the *Livre d'Enanchet*, ed. Fiebig, pp. 18-20.

[39] The merchant would have done better to follow something like the "doctrine dou mercheant" in the *Livre d'Enanchet*, p. 11: "Se tu veuz estre cortois, il te covient estre veritable et no eser plains de mauvais paroles. . . . Apres doiztu aprendre randu, por qu'ele est lumere des merchent. Apres les monees, a ce que tu n'i soies deceu an autre terre, quant tu i seras."

[40] Loyalty to one's feudal superior and loyalty to God were not unrelated. See the *Livre d'Enanchet*, p. 20.

[41] On the admonition of the wicked, cf. John of Salisbury, *Policrat.*, 8. 4. Villainous speech was considered to be inconsistent with chivalry. See the sixth feather of Cortesie in *Li romans des eles*, lines 421-423. To judge from the insistent admonitions in the *Livre d'Enanchet*, p. 11, merchants were thought to be particularly given to scandalous speech.

[42] *Moralium dogma*, p. 50.

[43] On jokes and laughter, see Cicero, *De off.*, 1. 29. 103-104.

our hero will require a knowledge of the arts,[44] and should associate with great men.[45] Dice should be used only with moderation.[46] He should recall freely and retell the great deeds of great men,[47] and he should himself be courageous and hardy in battle.[48] Where the ladies are involved, our lover should be courteous to all for the sake of one. This advice finds a parallel in Raoul de Houdenc, who wrote:

> ki cortois est, il doit faire
> S'amur as dames si comune
> K'il les aint trestoutes por une.[49]

Scheler comments on this passage, "cette *une* est-elle la dame du chevalier ou la dame chère à tout le monde, Notre-Dame? J'opine pour la seconde interprétation."[50] It is possible that the noble lady refers also to the Blessed Virgin, but if she does not, the lady who is to be revered by the lover is probably intended to be treated in the manner recommended in the fourteenth century by Geoffroi de Charny. Continuing her instructions, the lady tells the merchant that he should be moderate in personal adornment,[51] and generally wise, tractable, and gentle. He should not lie, and he should be temperate in conversation.[52] He is instructed not to make false promises,[53] and to receive gifts courteously. If anyone is deceptive

[44] A similar idea is implied symbolically in Chrétien, *Erec*, lines 6736ff. Cf. "La doctrine des vaslet" in the *Livre d'Enanchet*, p. 23: "Au comencement doit lo valez aprendre letres, por ce qe sa vie en sera alumee tant com il vivra, por qu'il en saura meuz amer et conoistre deu, et mieuz lo droit dau tort."

[45] Cf. Cicero, *De off.*, 2. 13. 46.

[46] The author of the *Livre d'Enanchet* found merchants especially inclined to use dice. See p. 12. But addiction to games of chance was severely frowned upon among the nobility. See *Policrat.*, 1. 5.

[47] This activity was an aspect of medieval *pietas*. For its relation to chivalry, see "Coment vindrent li home de cort," in the *Livre d'Enanchet*, p. 19.

[48] Cf. Cicero, *De off.*, 2. 13. 45: "Prima est igitur adulescenti commendatio ad gloriam, si qua ex bellicis rebus comparari potest, in qua multi apud maiores nostros exstiterunt. . . ."

[49] *Li romans des eles*, lines 336-338.

[50] *Trouvères belges*, pp. 383-384. Cf. Baudouin de Condé, "Li contes dou baceler," lines 79-85, in *Dits et contes de Baudouin de Condé et de son fils Jean de Condé* (Brussels, 1866), 1, 48.

[51] Too much personal adornment was considered to be a manifestation of pride. Cf. Fig. 68.

[52] Cf. Cicero, *De off.*, 1. 37; *Li romans des eles*, lines 313-316.

[53] On promises, cf. *Li romans des eles*, lines 193ff.

or discourteous, he should continue to do good to him and to serve him until he acknowledges his fault.[54] He should be hospitable. He should attend church regularly and be respectful to the clergy.[55] Finally, he should be truthful and never envious.[56] The last admonition, we should note, eliminates jealousy as a feature of love. If sincerely observed, these strictures would remove the possibility of passion of the kind implied in Andreas' definition as well as the various techniques which are necessary to demonstrate *probitas* in a line of talk. The merchant expresses gratitude for this good advice and very foolishly asks for hope. But the lady courteously refuses it, so that the merchant can ask only that God may reward him as he deserves. If God is to distribute this reward, it is pretty clear that the best course open to our lover is to return to the way of life established by his ancestors and to abandon the pursuit of Venus.

The lady's instructions to the plebeian in the third dialogue serve as a set of standards by means of which we may judge the lovers in the fourth and subsequent dialogues in which the lovers are noblemen. Structurally, they afford a thematic transition to the material that follows. If "Walter" happens to belong to the middle class, the first three dialogues show him how he may seek to demonstrate his *probitas* to ladies of his own class and to those in higher classes. If he happens to be a nobleman, the subsequent dialogues illustrate appropriate lines of approach for him. There is a sense in which "Walter" is any potential lover who is not a serf, and the ladies are used simply as foils to demonstrate the hollowness of any arguments that a lover may advance. In the fourth dialogue a nobleman approaches a woman of the middle class. Although he has the advantage of social superiority, the noble lover is no more successful than are his plebeian predecessors. He is told first that he may sit beside the lady of lower rank without first asking permission. We may be sure, however, that in spite of this liberty of behavior, the lover will soon be praising the lady for her nobility based on *probitas*. He will, that is, act in one way and speak in another. He begins by proposing a question which he

[54] Cf. Seneca, *De ben.*, 1. 2. 5, and 8. 31-32; *Moralium dogma*, pp. 15-16; and, generally, *Li romans des eles*, lines 227ff.

[55] Cf. the first feather of courtesy in the *Romans des eles*, lines 276-292.

[56] Cf. *ibid.*, lines 339ff.

brings as a messenger from Love's court: "In which woman does a good character deserve more praise—in a woman of noble blood, or in one who is known to have no nobility of family?" Obviously, he expects her to fall into the trap thus laid and praise her own nobility of character. But the lady, feeling that noble ladies should be naturally virtuous, replies that *probitas* is more fitting to one of noble blood. The lover objects in effect that since *probitas* is unexpected in a lady of the middle class, it is more to be admired in her than in a noble lady. At this, the lady finds that he is deprecating his own nobility: "Although you are of noble blood and well-born, you are openly trying to belittle nobility and to plead against your own rights. And you make such a reasonable defense of your position that I am inclined to believe we should consider that good character deserves more credit in a plebeian than in a noblewoman, because no one has any doubt that the rarer a good thing is the more dearly it is prized." Having got her around to the position he sought in the first place, although at some expense, the nobleman declares that in the lady before him the plebeian class is exalted by *probitas*, so that he is determined to persuade her to accept his service. That is, since she is more virtuous than the usual run of her class, she should be eager for the act of love with him. But the lady concludes that he is himself not very virtuous, since he has failed to win the love of a noble lady. He has not, we may observe, succeeded in conveying to her much respectful admiration for his great *probitas*. But now the lover shifts his ground and calls attention to the irrational character of love: "Neither excellence of birth nor beauty of person has much to do with the loosing of Love's arrow, but it is love alone that impels men's hearts to love, and very often it strongly compels lovers to claim the love of a stranger woman [*alienigenae*; cf. 3 Kings 11. 1]—that is, to throw aside all equality of rank and beauty. For love often makes a man think that a base and ugly woman is noble and beautiful and makes him class her above all other women in nobility and beauty." For this reason, the lover says, somewhat incautiously, he prizes the "dazzling beauty" and "excellent character" of the lady before him. It follows, he says, that the lady cannot reject his love if his character corresponds with his birth.

If she loves him, as he has just explained, his character is a matter of little moment, since she will admire it no matter what it may be. But the lady prudently disregards the description of irrational love, which is obviously not very complimentary either to her lover or to herself. Returning to more rational ground, she points out that if good character is more noteworthy in a plebeian than in a nobleman, as her lover has so painfully tried to convince her, she would do better to love a plebeian of perfect character rather than a nobleman. As usual, the lover's sophistry has succeeded in doing nothing except to pull the rug out from under his own feet. He makes a frantic but not very fruitful effort to modify his position. If the plebeian is more worthy than the noble lady, she should be chosen, he says. If the two ladies are of equal merit, one is free to choose either of them according to the authority of Queen Eleanor of England.[57] But he feels himself that the plebeian is preferable, so that if the lady finds a plebeian nobler than himself, she has a right to choose him. After pointing out that the suitor's argument goes backwards, like a crab, the lady agrees to accept her freedom of choice and to deliberate long and carefully on the selection of a man of good character. But the prospect of long deliberation does not please the lover, who fears that the lady may be wise as well as simple. This fear is expressed in an amusing and suggestive figure: "If there weren't a snake here hidden in the grass, and if you were not asking for a chance to think the matter over only as a clever pretext, such a deliberation would be very sweet and pleasant to me."[58] Perhaps because of a certain physical discomfort, the lover fears that he will die if the lady delays without giving him hope. Although the lady has no wish to kill him, all she will say is that if she ever decides to devote herself to love, she will choose a suitable man. The nobleman expresses a determination to serve her and everyone else on her account. This is, of course, a reflection of the advice given the plebeian in the previous dialogue, but the service falls short of disinterested benevolence, so that the lady replies quite properly that if he performs such services, he will certainly be rewarded by someone.

[57] No love decision to this effect is adduced in the later pages of the *De amore*. But this reference to Eleanor is a rather obvious thrust at that lady's widely alleged "freedom of choice."

[58] Cf. Virgil, *Ec.*, 3. 92-93: "Qui legitis flores et humi nascentia fraga, / frigidus, o pueri, fugite hinc, latet anguis in herba." Cf. Ovid, *Met.*, 10. 8-10, and the references above in Chapter II, note 97.

A nobleman addresses himself to a noble lady in the fifth dialogue, beginning by stating that in the presence of his prudent lady
he may freely express those things he has in his heart. Having
been encouraged to proceed, he declares his great faith: "How
faithful I am to you and with what devotion I am drawn to you
no words of mine can tell. For it seems that if the fidelities of every
living soul could be gathered together in a single person, the total
would not be so great, by far, as the faith that prompts me to serve
you, and there is nothing so unalterable in my heart as the intention of serving your glory." In spite of this faith, however, the
lover has as recompense only the "deceitful visions" of dreams;
for he sees the lady very seldom. When the lady cheerfully grants
him the privilege of looking at her, since she does not wish to kill
him by denying it, the lover confesses that he needs something
else: hope. But the lady has no wish to submit to what she calls
"the servitude of Venus," although she will not deny her suitor
or any other man the privilege of serving her. Disturbed by this
reluctance, the nobleman insists that good deeds arise only from
love, so that the lady should enter Love's court. The lady, still
reluctant, compares it with "the court of hell," for once a person
enters it, there is no escape. The lover then threatens her with
torments, which he describes in figurative terms. Love's palace, he
says, has four sides, each with a gate. Love keeps the eastern gate
himself. At the southern gate are ladies who admit men only after
diligent inquiry; at the western gate are loose ladies who admit
everyone indiscriminately; and at the northern gate are ladies who,
so to speak, never open the door. When the lady of the dialogue
says that she prefers a position at the northern gate of this edifice,
which, we may interject, bears a certain thematic resemblance to
Gottfried's grotto, the lover replies with a long fabulous narrative
involving the garden of love. This garden, designed to show the
rewards reaped by ladies in the afterlife but actually indicative of
more immediate circumstances, has three concentric sections. The
central part, called *Amoenitas*, is shaded by the branches of a tall
tree bearing all kinds of fruit, and beneath it is a fountain of clear
and delightful water which flows in little streams around the garden. Thrones for the King and Queen of Love stand beneath the
tree, and there are couches for knights and ladies who "while they
were alive knew how to conduct themselves wisely toward the sol-

diers of love, to show every favor to those who wished to love, and to give appropriate answers to those who under pretense of love sought love falsely." Here everything is pleasant, and the knights and ladies are entertained by jongleurs and musicians. The second area, *Humiditas*, is soggy and marshy with very cold water but unshaded from the hot sun, and here common women suffer extreme discomfort attended by many persons whose services are converted into their "harmful opposites." Since these services parallel the indiscriminate services accepted by these ladies in life, the prospect is a little appalling. On the outside is the area called *Ariditas* where the sun is very hot and dry indeed and where ladies who never opened their doors to lovers sit on bundles of thorns held on poles by strong men, two for each pole, who revolve them beneath the ladies. *Amoenitas* is a forerunner of the garden of Deduit, with the familiar tree, fountain, streams, music, and so on, and its rather illusory shade. The torments of *Humiditas* and *Ariditas* are fairly obvious illustrations of the plights of the simply lustful and indiscriminate on the one hand and the lustful but reluctant on the other. The lover does not suggest the possibility that the lady might avoid following the King of Love into this garden at all or along the broad road that leads to the center. But the lady wisely disdains to pass through *Humiditas* and decides to move from the northern to the southern gate of Love's palace without lingering at the western entrance. "I shall try," she says, "to find out who is worthy to enter, and having tried him and known him, I shall receive him in good faith." The lover, who is practically unknown to the lady, can only refer to his merits and pray that God may give him hope. What God might give him is conjectural, but he gets no hope from the lady.

At the beginning of the sixth dialogue a man of the higher nobility who valiantly presents himself to a woman of the middle class is told that he may use the approach of the fourth dialogue, which, as we have seen, was fruitless, or an alternative approach here set forth, which is a little more subtle and involves a touch of theology. The lover begins very gracefully and elegantly, affirming in effect that he values the lady's person above everything else in the world, that he is poor without her, that he will die if he lacks hope of possessing her, and that it would be a shame for anyone with her beauty and *probitas* to accept another of the same class. The lady is not much impressed by all this, and discerns a violation of nature in what confronts her; it would be about as commendable, she says, for her suitor, who is a count, to pursue her as it would be for a tercel to pursue sparrows and chickens. She fears that he lacks magnanimity so that he would probably make a poor lover. Magnanimity is a branch of fortitude, conventionally defined as "a willing and reasonable attack on difficult things."[59] In attacking a lady of the middle class, that is, the lover has not engaged in a matter of great difficulty. For her own part, she asserts that love is not natural to her class,[60] so that they would make an ill-assorted pair. The lover explains that love arises "from pleasure and delight in the beauty of some woman" rather than from considerations of rank, and that all in love's court are equal. But the lady fears that the union he envisages would draw her beyond the limits of her nature and that her rank would eventually bring the lover to despise her, especially if anyone knew of the affair. The lover explains that love is always secret, so that no one would know of it, and that even if it became known, the lady would not take malicious gossip very seriously. Moreover, she should judge his character by his deeds, since only God knows the secrets of the heart: "But neither I nor anyone else can fully convince you of the good faith and lawfulness of my love, because God Himself is the only searcher and beholder of the human heart." This assertion reflects Psalm 7. 10: "The wickedness of sinners shall be brought to nought: and thou shalt direct the just: the searcher of hearts and reins is God." Our lover omits *reins*, which conventionally signify "delights."[61] The pleasures the lover seeks are obvious, and it is equally obvious that they are a part of "the wickedness of sinners." The lady replies with a humorous figure, saying that although it is true that the good should not be impeded by the

---

[59] *Moralium dogma*, p. 30.

[60] The point that love is not "natural" to the middle class does not mean that persons in that class are not subject to lecherous inclinations. It does mean that they were not then inclined to the kind of idolatry the lover proposes, the reason being simply that one could not engage in business and devote all of his energies to love at the same time.

[61] See St. Augustine, *Enn. in Ps. 7, Opera*, IV, 48-49: "Videt igitur curas nostras, qui scrutatur cor: videt autem fines curarum, id est dilectiones, qui perscrutatur renes. . . . Opera enim nostra, quae factis et dictis operamur, possunt esse nota hominibus; sed quo animo fiant, et quo per illa pervenire cupiamus, solus ille novit, qui scrutatur corda et renes Deus."

wicked, "still, it does not follow that the anchor of good men should always find bottom." She does no evil, she says, to refuse a request. When the lover demands a definite answer, she replies, "I shall refuse to love you."

At this, the worthy gentleman undertakes to prove by logic that she can not refuse him in this way. Simplifying what he says a little, the argument runs something like this: (a) Love is a good thing and the source of good deeds. Therefore a good man or woman must love. (b) You must love a good man rather than an evil one. Therefore you must love me. But this academic display properly fails to impress the lady. It is true, she says, that one must love the good, but in this matter she should have freedom of choice, especially, we infer, where the anchor is concerned. The lover seeks to circumvent this freedom by claiming priority; he should have her, he alleges, just as a man who starts a wild beast from its lair while hunting has priority over a man who later captures the beast. The lady replies that although her will is ready to love, her heart remains unmoved; that is, she may desire "to accomplish that which is good," but her concupiscence is not operating in the lover's direction. She decides, in fact, not to devote herself to love at all, but to see whether "a sinful maiden has conceived and a gentle hen given birth to a serpent." She will, that is, wait.

The lover attempts to inspire the lady's concupiscence by drawing an analogy between the grace of God and the grace of Love: "Shall a sinner remain excused of God because God has not poured grace upon him? By no means; he shall be delivered over to everlasting torments. Therefore, if you wish to escape Love's wrath and desire to be inflamed by his breath, you must render yourself fit and worthy to receive Love's grace."

The lady, whose theology is better than her lover's, replies with a reference to the most famous discussion of charity in the Bible (1 Cor. 13): "No matter how much good a man does in this world, it is of no profit to him in attaining the rewards of eternal blessedness unless he is prompted by love [caritas]. For the same reason, no matter how much I may strive to serve the King of Love by my deeds and my works, unless these proceed from the affection of the heart and are derived from the impulse of love, they cannot profit me toward obtaining the rewards of love [amor]. There-

424

fore until Love's arrow strikes me you cannot obtain the grant of my love."

The lady is obviously aware of the emptiness of what seem to be good deeds performed for the wrong reasons, and she is clearly not interested in the "rewards" of love. Confronted by the contrast between what he has been expressing and charity, the lover can only say, "I shall ever pray to God on bended knees to make you love what you should and what will clearly profit Your Highness."

The seventh dialogue, between a man of the higher nobility and a woman of the simple nobility, is phrased in such elaborate and florid language that a detailed summary would lengthen our discussion immoderately. The language conveys an impression of the pretentiousness of the nobleman, whose affectation is remarkably airy. He begins very piously, with thanks to God for answering his prayers and allowing him to see the wonderful creature before him. His piety becomes a little suspect, however, when he cites Donatus falsely to show that "the human will is so very free that no one's efforts can divert it from a purpose firmly formed." His will is so free, in other words, that it has become a slave to a single desire.[62] He is a little slow, out of "courtesy," to reveal what this desire is, but it finally appears accompanied by a familiar metaphor: "It is your love that I seek, in order to restore my health, and which I desire to get by my hunting." After some discussion concerning the problem of whether he has been too hasty in his revelation and of the further problem of whether the two live at too great a distance from each other to manage a love affair conveniently, the real subject of the dialogue appears. The lady is married, she says, to a man who loves her, so that the laws forbid her to love another. This fact brings up the question, much discussed in modern treatments of "courtly love," as to whether love and marriage are compatible. We might observe, by way of background, that the kind of love defined by Andreas, a passion involving a corruption of the reason, was thought to be a manifestation of the weakness of original sin; and marriage, with its sacramental hierarchy, was thought to be a means of preventing that passion, which causes its victims to put the act of love above everything else, from developing. Hence no one would have claimed that love in

[62] This kind of servitude was a theological commonplace based on Jo. 8. 34. See Lombard, *Sententiae*, 2. 25. 4.

the sense used by Andreas is compatible with marriage. On the other hand, a man was expected to love his wife, but not in this extreme way.

The lover objects to the idea that love may exist between husband and wife on the grounds that although the affection involved may be extreme and immoderate, it does not fall under the definition of love, which is "an inordinate desire to receive passionately a furtive and hidden embrace." But the embraces of husband and wife are not "furtive." The principle is supported in terms of a little social satire: "Besides, that most excellent doctrine of princes shows that nobody can make furtive use of that which belongs to him." As a matter of fact, neither political sovereignty nor marital sovereignty was a suitable excuse for unbridled license, and the lover's main point about marriage is no better than his analogy. The lover calls attention to certain restrictions in married love later on in his argument. Here he adduces another analogy from friendship. Father and son feel an affection for each other, but "as Cicero tells us," this is not true friendship.[63] In the same way, a man and his wife have affection for each other, but this is not love. To understand this argument, we must consider certain twelfth-century theories of the relationship between affection and love. Generally, "natural affection" was said to exist between parent and child, or between brothers, and also between husband and wife.[64] And this affection, like affection of other kinds, is not love, but the root of love.[65] The distinction between natural affection and friendship rests on the fact that friendship is based on reason as well as on affection.[66] But there is nothing to prevent natural affection from developing into rational love; indeed, those who are moved by it are under an obligation to develop it in this way. Thus St. Ailred says, "It is natural that a man should have affection for himself and for his own, but he should not have love according to this affection;

---

[63] Although Cicero does not make this point explicitly in the De amicitia, it is clear that he does not consider friendship and natural affection to be the same thing. For a discussion of natural affection, see Ailred, Speculum charitatis, 3. 14, PL, 195, 589-590.

[64] See Peter of Blois, De amicitia Christiana, ed. Davy (Paris, 1932), p. 502. "Est etiam naturalis affectus viri ad conjugem, matris ad filium," etc.

[65] See St. Ailred, Speculum charitatis, 3. 16, col. 590; Peter of Blois, p. 510.

[66] Speculum charitatis, 3. 12, col. 588: "Rationalis affectus est, qui ex consideratione aliene virtutis oboritur. . . . Hic affectus inter David et Jonathan sacratissimi amoris primitias consecravit. . . ."

rather he should have it according to reason."[67] Our lover, who is moved neither by natural affection nor by rational love, but by what was called "carnal affection," wishes to remove the possibility of the lady's reasonable satisfaction and to substitute carnal affection for the love she bears her husband. It is affection of this kind, as St. Ailred points out, which brought about the idolatry of Solomon.[68] The lover in the dialogue seeks to satisfy his carnal affection on the grounds that it resembles true friendship, which is, of course, ridiculous.

The lady answers quite properly that a husband and wife may engage in "hidden" embraces if they wish to do so, and that those which may be enjoyed securely and regularly without crime in marriage are to be preferred. Taking her companion's conception of love, she says, it is "nothing but a great desire to enjoy carnal pleasure with someone, and nothing prevents this feeling existing between husband and wife." But the lover has also introduced a point about jealousy, which, he says, "is always welcome as the mother and nurse of love." The lady, however, replies, "Who can rightly commend envious jealousy or speak in favor of it, since jealousy is nothing but a shameful and evil suspicion of a woman?" Before considering the lover's further arguments in favor of jealousy, we should recall the fact that jealousy had, in the twelfth century, long been regarded as an inevitable adjunct of carnal love. Thus St. Augustine wrote, "Whoever loves carnally must necessarily love with a pestiferous jealousy; if he regards it as a very great thing that he may see the one he loves with a pestiferous love nude, does he wish that another may see her also? It is necessary that he be wounded with jealousy and envy if another sees her."[69] But our lover makes a distinction between jealousy in love and jealousy in marriage. The latter, he says, is false and is universally condemned. But jealousy in love is a "true passion of the mind." There are, he says, three manifestations of jealousy: (1) the fear that one's services are insufficient to retain love, (2) the fear that love is not returned, and (3) the fear that the beloved loves another. But the husband cannot indulge in the last manifestation,

[67] *Speculum charitatis*, 3. 26, col. 599. Cf. 1 Tim. 5. 8, which St. Ailred quotes in his discussion.

[68] *Speculum charitatis*, 3. 15, col. 590. Cf. *De amicitia Christiana*, pp. 506, 508.

[69] *Enn. in Ps. 33*, *Opera*, IV, 310.

"for a husband cannot suspect his wife without the thought that such conduct on her part is shameful." His thoughts are clouded by evil, just as almsgiving may be clouded by thoughts of vainglory. A lover, on the other hand, can think of a rival, and although the thought produces great anxiety in him, it does not produce any shameful condemnation of the lady. Andreas does not explain why this is true, but the reason is fairly obvious: if a lover has persuaded a lady to commit fornication or adultery, he cannot regard it as an evil if someone else does the same thing.

The discussion of sin in this dialogue has led to some rather startling historical conclusions. For example, a widely used and otherwise excellent manual for students of medieval history contains the following observations: "This conviction on the part of its devotees that courtly love was new and different led to an interesting conception, that of the incompatibility of love and marriage. A wife had to perform her marital duties, and love could never come through compulsion. This they cheerily support by citing the ancient doctrine of the church that intercourse in marriage was justified only when there was a desire to beget children, not for mere entertainment." Spice has been added to a great many elementary courses in medieval history by sage professorial remarks to the effect that in the twelfth century men did not love their own wives but wives of other men instead. "Curiously enough, among our quaint medieval ancestors, it was the custom, etc." Returning to our historical statement, we find that three objections may be raised to it: (1) no one in the Middle Ages ever said anything about new doctrines of "courtly love"; (2) the idea that marriage is incompatible with irrational passion was very old in the twelfth century; and (3) there is no such "ancient doctrine of the church" as the one described. With reference to this last point, the lover in the dialogue is more accurate than the historian, that is, if one does not take the "sacred thing" he mentions in its most amusing sense: "For whatever solaces married people extend to each other beyond what are inspired for the desire for offspring or the payment of the marriage debt [1 Cor. 7. 1-5], cannot be free from sin [*crimen*], and the punishment is always greater when the use of a holy thing is perverted by misuse [*si sacrae rei usum deformet abusus*] than if we practice the ordinary abuses. It is a more serious offense in a wife than in another woman, for the too

428

ardent lover, as we are taught by apostolic law, is considered an adulterer with his own wife."

In substance, this is more or less correct, but it does not contradict the lady's statement that she may enjoy carnal intercourse with her husband "sine crimine," without grave sin. A *crimen* is not any sin, but a grave and mortal sin.[70] In marriage, carnal intercourse for the sake of children alone, without regard to pleasure, was said to be without guilt. However, the fact that this kind of activity borders on the impossible was recognized by the theologians of the period. Peter Lombard, for example, says, "There may hardly be found now persons experiencing carnal intercourse who do not sometimes come together without the intention of generating offspring."[71] When such intercourse was undertaken for the satisfaction of concupiscence, or, in the phrase of our historian, "for entertainment," it was thought to be a safeguard to marital faith which involved venial sin only. As a venial sin, the pleasure involved ranks with minor daily transgressions "without which this life may not be led,"[72] and like other sins of its type, it was taken care of in the daily recitation of the Paternoster.[73] The lady may thus enjoy the fruits of carnal love with her husband in order to prevent his concupiscence and hers from developing into a *passio*, thus preserving the faith of marriage. But the faith between her and her husband is the last thing the lover wishes to preserve. He tells her, therefore, correctly, that sexual acts which have nothing to do either with procreation (in the minds of the participants) or with the faith which is preserved in the payment of the marriage debt are criminal. In the words of Peter Lombard, "Where these goods are lacking, that is, faith and children, coitus may not properly be defended from the charge of crime."[74] The lover warns further that the over-ardent husband is, in effect, an adulterer. That is, if the husband insists on treating his wife simply as an object of "carnal affection" without reason, he is on the same plane as the lover himself. For this reason, St. Jerome had long since warned husbands that "nothing is more foul than to love a wife as though she were an adulteress."[75] To develop a *passio* in

[70] See St. Augustine, *In Jo. Evang.*, 41. 9, and *Contra duas epistolas Pelag.*, I. 14. 28.

[71] *Sententiae*, 4. 31. 8.   [72] See St. Augustine, *Enchiridion*, 70. 19.

[73] *Sententiae*, 4. 31. 5.   [74] *Loc.cit.*

[75] *Loc.cit.* Cf. *Adv. Jov., PL,* 23, col. 293. As Parry indicates, Andreas seems

marriage, as Chaucer's Januarie seeks to do, for example, is to destroy the marriage so that it becomes a vehicle for original sin rather than a remedy for it; it is, in the language of St. Augustine, which is reflected in the lover's argument, to abuse marriage rather than to use it. If we have these matters sufficiently clear in our minds, we are now in a position to see what the lover is trying to do. The act of adultery he desires is the very crime against which he is warning the lady. To quote Lombard once more, "To pay the marriage debt is no crime at all; to demand it beyond the necessity for generation is a venial trangression; but either fornication or adultery is to be punished as a crime."[76] Like the arguments of his predecessors, the argument of our nobleman simply serves to condemn himself.

The lady very naturally remains unconvinced by what her suitor has to say about love between married persons and jealousy, and the two decide to present their problem to the Countess of Champagne, who is made to reply in a very famous epistle. There is no reason to suppose that this epistle is any more reliable as an historical document than are the dialogues themselves. However, even though the decisions of the Countess may seem a little scandalous on the surface, they are actually quite orthodox. Her first decision runs, "We declare and we hold as firmly established that love cannot exert its powers between two people who are married to each other. For lovers give each other everything freely, under no compulsion of necessity, but married people are in duty bound to give in to each other's desires and to deny themselves to each other in nothing." If we take "love" here to mean carnal love, this statement would have won the wholehearted approval of both St. Jerome and the Master of the Sentences. If there is any heresy in the statement at all, it is a heresy against Love, for Andreas tells us in his second book that "all lovers are bound, when practicing love's solaces, to be mutually obedient to each other's desires," and again that "Love can deny nothing to love." The Countess, or Andreas speaking for the Countess, adds, "Besides, how does it increase a husband's honor if after the manner of lovers he enjoys the embraces of his wife, since the worth of character of

---

to be following the discussion in Alanus, *Summa de arte praedicatoria*. For a later treatment, see Jehan le Bel, *op.cit.*, II, 95-96.

[76] *Sententiae*, 4. 32. 1.

neither can be increased thereby, and they seem to have done nothing more than they already had a right to?" To this question we may reply, as the tone of the question implies, that such activity does not necessarily increase a husband's honor. But we may add also without stretching our areas of implication, that it does not increase anyone's *probitas* to take something he has no right to. Nor does the Countess imply that it does. A third reason follows: "And we say the same thing for still another reason, which is that a precept of love tells us that no woman, even if she is married, can be crowned with the reward of the King of Love unless she is seen to be enlisted in the service of Love himself outside the bonds of wedlock." The bonds of wedlock were designed to prevent just this glorious coronation from taking place and to facilitate a rather different coronation. The Countess continues, "But another rule of Love teaches that no one can be in love with two men. Rightly, therefore, love cannot acknowledge any rights between husband and wife." Since love involves an idolatrous concentration on a single object of a kind which is destroyed by the hierarchy of marriage, the justice of these remarks is obvious. With reference to jealousy, the Countess concludes, "But there is still another argument which seems to stand in the way of this, which is that between them there can be no true jealousy, and without it true love may not exist, according to the rule of Love himself, which says, 'He who is not jealous cannot love.'" As we have seen, in making jealousy an adjunct of carnal love, the Countess is here simply following St. Augustine, who is a pretty good authority, and the predicament of "true" jealousy has already been described. It is true, of course, that if we read "romantic love" where the Countess is made to say "love," the epistle looks strange, but if we do this we are reading it out of context. If Walter was very astute, what he learned from this dialogue must have been that carnal love leads to crime unless it is checked by marriage. As Andreas says more openly in his third book, which does not actually contradict anything said in the first two, "with a wife we overcome our passion without sinning [*sine crimine*], and we do away with the incentives to wantonness without staining our souls."

The eighth dialogue between two persons of the higher nobility contains a certain amount of recapitulation and several interesting new concepts, including the fascinating notion of "pure" love. In technique this dialogue does not differ essentially from the earlier dialogues. The lady assumes various conditions of life—youth, age, maidenhood, widowhood, for example—to afford a variety of approaches, and the result is what we should by this time expect: contradictions in the lover's "line." At the same time, the lover changes, so that, for example, in one part he is a soldier and in another a priest. But in none of the situations adduced is the lover successful either in achieving his goal or in creating a very strong impression of *morum probitas*. As usual, his vanity and hypocrisy only serve to make him ridiculous. We have already seen, in the third dialogue, that a woman of the higher nobility is likely to be astute. Recognizing this fact, Andreas warns his prospective lover at the beginning that "a noble woman or a woman of the higher nobility is found to be very ready and bold in censuring the deeds and the words of a man of the higher nobility, and she is very glad if she has a good opportunity to say something to ridicule him." The lover begins piously and verbosely, arguing that God has given ladies an opportunity to promote good deeds and that therefore the lady should not keep away from the court of Love where she can act as a stimulus to good man. The lady replies very appropriately that love brings great tribulations to lovers and is, moreover, an injury to one's neighbor offensive to God. It is, in other words, a violation of the law of charity. Her statement to this effect sets the theme for the entire dialogue, which has the function of bringing clearly before Walter the theological implications of the definition of love at the beginning of the treatise. She goes on to say that although love makes men courteous, it is followed by great inconveniences and is a thing "which no wise man should choose and should be especially hated by soldiers. For those who seem to be every day in peril of death from some chance of battle ought to be especially careful not to do anything that might be considered offensive to the King of the Heavenly Country." In her discussion she opposes the King of the Celestial Country (God) to the King of Love, with the implication that, as Andreas says in the third book, "the Devil is really the author of love and lechery." The lady says that she herself has had no experience in love, but knows about it only from what she has heard.

At this, the lover berates the lady for being courteous to him in order to make him courteous. Like all lovers, he is interested in courtesy only as a means to something more concrete. Feeling that the lady's courtesy is a matter of hypocrisy unlike his own "true" courtesy, he compares her, not very courteously, with a Pharisaical priest "who by pretending to do many good deeds and by urging upon others the works of eternal life condemns himself by his own judgment, while he shows others how to obtain heavenly reward." Although this is grossly unfair to the lady, who has shown no inclination to speak in one way and to act in another, it is true that the lover himself has been condemning himself "by his own judgment." We shall meet a priest of exactly the type described, incidentally, later in the dialogue. The hypocrisy our lover refers to is the hypocrisy typical of lovers as the following laughable argument fully demonstrates: "Your statement that God is offended by love cannot keep you from it; it seems to be generally agreed that to serve God is a very great and an extraordinary good thing, but those who desire to serve Him perfectly ought to devote themselves wholly to His service, and according to the opinion of Paul [1 Cor. 7. 32ff.] they should engage in no worldly business. Therefore, if you choose to serve God alone, you must give up all worldly things and contemplate only the mysteries of the Heavenly Country, for God has not wished that anybody should keep his right foot on earth and his left foot in heaven, since no one can properly devote himself to the service of two masters [Matt. 6. 24]. Now since it is clear that you have one foot on earth from the fact that you receive with a joyful countenance those who come to you and that you exchange courteous words with them and persuade them to do the works of love, I believe that you would do better to enjoy love thoroughly than to lie to God under cloak of some pretense."

There is no reason why the lady should seek the perfection of counsel simply because she does not wish to commit fornication. If this argument were valid, the world would contain only whores and nuns. What St. Paul implies in 1 Cor. 7. 32ff. is not that marriage is an evil, but that although it is a good, virginity is better.[77] And the lady's courtesy is certainly no indication that she has her "right foot on earth" while her "left foot" is in heaven. On the contrary, it is the lover, not the lady, who is trying to serve two masters: the King of Heaven, whose Law he cites, and the King

[77] Cf. Lombard, *Coll. in Epist. d. Pauli, PL,* 191, col. 1599.

of Love, whose precepts he wishes to fulfill. To the above statement, he adds the old argument that love is "natural," without,
however, adding the obvious fact that all other sins are "natural"
in the same way. The act which he contemplates, he says, produces
"the highest good in this life," and he sees no reason for thinking
that anything leading up to this great ultimate is a sin.

This argument is supported with a theological discussion based
on Matt. 7. 12 and Tob. 4. 16, both of which are descriptions of
charity: "Again, one's neighbor feels no injury from love—that is,
he should feel none—because whatever one person asks of another
—that is, whatever he should ask [*exigere debet*]—he is bound to
suffer freely when another asks it of him. Many, however, include
among their wrongs things which seem to contain no wrong. And
let it not seem to you absurd that I have explained it to you in
this way: 'he asks—that is, he should ask [*exigere debet*]'—since
we are taught to explain in the same way a certain word in the
Gospel law upon which dependeth the whole law and the prophets
[Matt. 22. 40]. For we say, 'What you do not wish others to do
to you—that is, what you should not wish—do not do to others.' "

If cupidinous love is a good thing, there is nothing wrong with
this reasoning except the authority used for it, but that authority
is used in such a way that Walter or any other reader cannot help
having his attention called to the fact that it is inverted. This effect is reinforced by the repetition of *"exigere debet."* The same
phrase (with a difference in person and number) is used by Peter
Lombard to imply exactly the opposite of what the lover has in
mind: *"Omnia quaecumque vultis, ut faciant vobis homines,* etc.,
de bonis accipiendum est, quae nobis invicem exhibere debemus."[78]
St. Gregory's comment on the passage is illuminating also: "If
anyone loves another, but does not love that person on account
of God, he has no charity but thinks he has."[79] Meanwhile, it is
worth noting that St. Augustine had used a similar variant of Tob.
4. 16 in his great sermon "De decem chordis" as a warning against
fornication.[80] It is clear that what the lover is asking for is not
"what he should ask" and that it is, on the other hand, a thing
"by which the Heavenly Bridegroom is offended and one's neighbor is injured." His argument, in other words, contradicts itself.

[78] *Sententiae,* 3. 37. 5.   [79] *Hom. in Evang.,* 2. 38, *PL,* 176, col. 1289.
[80] *Opera,* v, 85.

The lover continues by saying that no one is more worthy of the lady's love than he is, an assertion which moves the lady to refer to a proverb according to which self-praise vanishes away. She also wonders when her suitor is going to exercise his great generosity by giving away the old clothes he is wearing. As a nobleman, he is bolder than his plebeian predecessors, for he asserts that a lover is free from the obligation not to praise himself. We have seen plenty of evidence of this freedom. In love, he says, all men are envious of all other men, and a lover hardly ever praises the good character of a friend before a woman. This statement not only shows his profound understanding of the Golden Rule; it also illustrates the manner in which lovers may be expected to apply it. And it demonstrates that love is inconsistent either with friendship or with the kind of courteous behavior recommended by the noble lady of the third dialogue. As for his clothes, our twelfth-century Hippolytus says that he put them on to test the lady's discernment. He wishes to know whether she honors his character or his clothes, and he intimates that she is ill-bred because she has not discerned his great worth beneath his shabby appearance. With the remarkable consistency of lovers, he implies also that his generosity has been so great that he has nothing else to wear except his old clothes. There is clearly a lie lurking somewhere in this very courteous and noble self-justification.

At this point the lady's situation changes. Our new lady suffers from concealed griefs and has previously been accosted by another man. The question of priority arises again, but this time the argument of the lover directly contradicts that advanced by the man of the higher nobility in the sixth dialogue, who said, "Nor can you defend yourself by giving your love to some man who asked for it after I did, for it is dishonorable to deny one's love to the first worthy man who asks for it and not very honorable to give it to a later suitor, since Love does not want one of his servants to be benefited at the expense of another." To support the principle of delay for a better choice like himself, our present lover cites the example of the son of Priam who rejected the gift of Pallas and Juno to accept that of Venus. Since the choice in this example was plainly unwise, the example is not very reassuring. Concerning it, Ovid said (*Her.* 16. 49), "arsurum Paridis vates canit Ilion igni,"

435

and again (*Fasti*, 6. 99-100), "perierunt iudice formae Pergama."
In the words of Horace (*Epist.* 1. 2. 10-11),

> quid Paris? ut salvus regnet vivatque beatus
> cogi posse negat.

The comments of medieval authorities were even stronger, since they felt that Paris gave up both active and contemplative virtues in favor of physical pleasure.[81] Andreas again shifts the situation by giving the lover a fair wife. Under this circumstance, the lover is advised to use the arguments of the previous dialogue, so that we are fortunately spared what he might have said about his wife. In another shift, the lady becomes a widow, too old, she says, for love. Now the lover maintains that her outward appearance, which is youthful, indicates that she is actually youthful underneath. For, he says, "the outward appearance shows clearly what was the disposition of the mind within," directly contradicting the lover's earlier remarks about his worn clothing. After the lady has successfully defended her widowhood, the scene shifts again, and the lady becomes a young maiden, without sufficient years, as she so charmingly phrases it, to "manage love's anchor with the proper diligence." Her figure of speech, which is worthy of Boccaccio, provokes a physiological argument to show that women are capable of constancy at the age of twelve. But the young maiden is shy and is afraid of deceptions which she lacks the necessary prudence to discern. To "help" her in this predicament, her suitor recommends that she test his character, deceiving him with false promises. If he still remains faithful, he may be assumed to have a good character.

It is here that the foundation is laid for that profound metaphysical concept which has so moved the hearts of modern academicians: "pure" love. It cannot be properly understood, however, outside of its context. Our coy young maiden argues correctly that her companion is no friend, since he is interested only in himself and has no concern for her welfare. As a maiden, she would be unwise to love, she says, for if she were to decide to marry later,

---

[81] See Bernard Silvestris, *Comm. super sex libros Eneidos Virgilii*, ed. Riedel, p. 46. Cf. S. Skimina, "De Bernardo Silvestri Vergilii interprete," in *Commentationes Vergilianae* (Cracow, 1930), pp. 227-228. Similar explanations appear in *Myth.* III, in Bode, *Scriptores rerum mythicarum*, p. 241, and (very elaborately) in Neckam, *Super Marcianum*, Oxford, Bodl. MS Digby 221, fols. 45 verso-46.

her husband would discover that she had been seduced and she would be disgraced. The lover first cites some instances from romances, which are not very convincing, to show that maidens may love. Next he argues that a good husband would appreciate the fact that she had learned something about love, but that a bad husband, or a husband who did not react in this way, would be better without affection anyhow. But these arguments are not successful, and the lover hits upon the brilliant idea of "pure" love. Essentially, "pure" love consists of the kiss, the embrace, and contact with the nude beloved, but with the final solace omitted. If the maidenly lady practices this love, her future husband can have no very clear evidence of it, and she will not be disgraced. Moreover, it has other advantages: "This is the kind that anyone who is intent upon love ought to embrace with all his might, for this love goes on increasing without end, and we know that no one ever regretted practicing it, and the more of it one has the more one wants. This love is distinguished by being of such virtue that from it arises all excellence of character, and no injury comes from it, and God sees very little offense in it. No maiden can ever be corrupted by such a love, nor can a widow or a wife receive any harm or suffer any injury to her reputation."

As Andreas explained in his sixth chapter, "when love cannot have its solaces, it increases beyond all measure and drives the lovers into lamenting their terrible torments." Our present lover, of course, has no real intention of allowing these torments to last too long, knowing, as Andreas says at the end of the sixth chapter of his second book, that "all lovers are bound, when practicing love's solaces, to be mutually obedient to each other's desires." It is possible that the word *purus* may have led some modern writers to connect this love with an elevated concept of some sort; but *purus* is a conventional antonym for *mixtus*, the participle of *misceo*, which, among other things, may be used to designate the act of sexual intercourse.[82]

The lover is amusingly certain that he can make this virtuous activity, which, incidentally, as a lover's gambit probably antedates the twelfth century by many hundreds of years, attractive to the bashful young maiden who is fearful for her virginity. In his enthusiasm he contradicts the earlier arguments of lovers concerning

[82] See Ovid, *Met.*, 13. 866.

the theological virtue of "mixed" love: "by it one's neighbor is injured," he says, "and the Heavenly King is offended." This is not really to condemn it, he says, for it is "praiseworthy," but pure love is better. Knowing these things, the little lady can now "put aside all fear of deception" and choose between the two kinds of love. Unfortunately, the girl still has little inclination toward either variety, and she expresses a becoming scepticism concerning "pure" love in terms that echo the condemnation of adultery in Prov. 6. 24-35: "Everybody would think it miraculous if a man could be placed in a fire and not be burned." It is certainly true that "pure" love is a very warm business. But as her discussion progresses, her lover becomes a clerk, who, she says, should "avoid all desires of the flesh" and "keep his body unspotted for the Lord" [Jas. 1. 27]. In reply, the new lover tries to argue that a clerk is "human" like anyone else and is under no greater obligation to keep himself cleaner than a layman. It should be observed that this argument has the effect of nullifying counsel and thus contradicts the argument advanced earlier that a lady should either follow counsel or commit fornication.

In considering the clerk's theological defence of his position, we should remember that for good scriptural reasons the word "Pharisee" was a standard epithet in the Middle Ages for a hypocritical priest. We should notice further the resemblance between the priest's description of himself and the description of the evil priest earlier in the dialogue: "This is what the authority of the Gospel proclaims; for the Lord, seeing His clergy, in accordance with the frailty of human nature, about to fall into various excesses, said in the Gospel, 'The scribes and the Pharisees have sitten on the chair of Moses. All things whatsoever they shall say to you, observe and do: but according to their works do ye not,' just as though he said, 'You must believe what the clergy say, because they are God's deputies; but because they are subject to the temptation of the flesh like other men, you must not regard their works if they happen to go astray in anything.' Therefore it is enough for me if, when I stand by the altar, I devote myself to proclaiming the word of God to my people. So if I ask any woman to love me, she cannot refuse me on the pretext that I am a clerk."

Needless to say, in Matt. 23 Christ warns his disciples not to imitate the Scribes and the Pharisees. Our lover's use of the Scriptures in this connection is not only hypocritical itself, but it points directly to his own hypocrisy. We should notice, moreover, that our clerical lover does not recognize the condemnation of the Pharisees and defy it, as though he were setting up some new doctrine opposed to scriptural authority. Instead, he makes a show of piety. Is it necessary to add that his words result in a humorous effect?

The lady insists that a sin in a clerk is more grave than the same sin in others and that a clerk can neither dress, practise generosity, nor fight in battle as a lover should. Andreas uses her remarks for purposes of a little satire oh his own order, making her say that a clerk is "given up to continual indolence and devoted only to serving his belly." A woman should make a clerk ashamed if he seeks her love, "for many people abstain from things that are forbidden and wicked more because of the disgrace in this world than to avoid the torments of the everlasting death." Her rather cynical observation has no effect, for the lover is too ardent to be ashamed in any way. Exactly inverting the truth, he says that for certain reasons he does not wish to reveal, a great man's sins are no greater than those of a lesser man before God, but only in the eyes of the vulgar. After some excuses for his dress, which the lady has characterized as "women's garments," and for his unwarlike behavior, he proceeds to identify himself not only with the Scribes and the Pharisees, but also with those who (Rom. 16. 18) "serve not Christ our Lord, but their own belly; and by pleasing speeches and good words, seduce the hearts of the innocent." He says, "As for what you say about serving the belly, that can in no way harm me, because you cannot find anyone, clerk or layman, man or woman, young or old, who does not gladly devote himself to the services of the belly. But if anyone is too much inclined in that way, it is clear before God and all men that this is just as harmful to a layman as to a clerk, and it deserves every reprehension."

He goes on to say that women are worse in this respect than clerks, since Eve served her belly first, transgressing the commandment of God and setting a precedent for men like himself to follow. This is nothing more than the hollow excuse of Adam (Gen. 3. 12): "The woman, whom thou gavest me to be my companion, gave me of the tree, and I did eat." The two dispute for a while on the subject of why the serpent tempted Eve first, but the lover makes no progress. His argument, however, has led him finally to the heart of the matter and the origin of the love described by Andreas: the Fall of Man.

Once more the scene shifts and we find that our lady has a second lover and that the lover before her is no longer a clerk. The second lover, who does not appear in person, is one who serves his lady by deeds rather than by words. His *morum probitas* is apparent in his actions. The noble suitor tries to convince her that she should value his words more than the other man's deeds, but in vain. His ill success is a kind of final comment on the futility of the task all of the lovers in the dialogues have set for themselves: to create a presumption of *morum probitas* through eloquence. To make the defeat of this final lover more decisive, Andreas has him render judgment on two questions of love in a way which makes his case at first dubious and finally hopeless. The first question proposed by the lady concerns the relative merits of the upper and lower parts of the body in love's solaces. The discussion of this problem constitutes one of the most hilarious passages in the *De amore*, although it is difficult to convey this fact in a summary. Before beginning his argument the lover says that he will answer the question in such a way as to nullify the lady's excuse for not loving him. Unfortunately, the verbose lover decides in favor of the upper part, giving reasons for this decision very much like those advanced by the advocate of "pure" love. The solaces of the lower part, he says, are enjoyed by men and beasts alike. But those of the upper part are peculiar to the nature of man, so that he who chooses the lower part "should be driven out from love just as though he were a dog." This decision eliminates all of our previous lovers and leaves Walter in a somewhat uneasy position. He who chooses the upper part, our lover says, "should be accepted as one who honors nature." Perhaps no comment is needed on the subject of how "natural" this restriction is. The lover adds: "Besides this, no man has ever been found who was tired of the solaces of the upper part, or satiated by practicing them, but the delight of the lower part quickly palls upon those who practice it, and it makes them repent of what they have done." This opinion puts the ambitions of all our previous lovers in a gloomy light, and we may well imagine the unpleasant physiological consequences of prolonged concentration on the upper part.

The lady, perhaps feeling that her lover's opinion leaves something to be desired, objects heatedly, pointing out that the lower part is of fundamental importance. Her argument resembles the theme of the *Lai dou lecheor*, and has much the same ironic force: "the delight of the upper part would be absolutely nothing unless it were indulged in with an eye to the lower and were kept alive by contemplation of it." Moreover, she says, the solaces of the lower part are more natural than those of the upper. The lower should be preferred just as one prefers nourishing food to food which "stuffs the body without nourishing it and fills the bowels with discomfort." She pursues the argument with instances of other things in which the lower parts are preferable. In his reply, the lover modifies his position a little, suggesting that one should at least begin with the upper part. But he nevertheless concludes that a man who chooses the upper part, like himself, should be preferred. At this point the lady suddenly agrees, thus depriving her poor suitor of anything except a little preliminary excitement. She is not yet ready to grant even that, however, for she has another question. If a lady thinks that her lover is dead and takes a second, what should she do in the event that the first returns? In answering this question our verbose lover states a principle which deprives him of any possible opportunity to replace his rival, the man of deeds. Having made the assertion that a rule of love is not valid if one presents it in his own defense—a principle rather damaging to the arguments of many of our lovers—he says, "Therefore it cannot rightly follow, as you said it did, that a woman may spurn the love of one man and accept that of another if she is driven to do so by love's remorse; but if any man attempts to undermine her good faith, she must try to turn him away politely, and if he is too insistent she must finally tell him that she is already in love with someone else, that she ought not incline her heart to his words or remember what he tells her, or keep his image in her mind, or even think about him very often lest because women are weak she might open the way for some spark of love to enter and might direct her mind toward him. For if a woman does not begin to fall in love by thinking about a man immoderately or by imagining the acts of delight, she will never care to seek a new love with any man." The lady proceeds to turn him away politely.

But the lover has one final question: whether a lover who approaches a second woman with no intention of forgetting the first or of giving up her love should be punished by loss of his first lady. The lady thinks he should be punished. The suitor wishes further elucidation. Suppose the second affair is unsuccessful. Should the first lady still reject him? The lady replies that the lover should be punished unless he repents spontaneously and gives every proof of faith. There is, of course, a sense in which all the ladies in these dialogues are "second" ladies. The concluding remark of the lady, which ends the dialogues, is an excellent comment on all of the lovers whose artifices we have followed. It is, so to speak, Walter's final reward for trying to demonstrate verbally his *probitas* while seeking an unworthy end: "It does not seem to be in accordance with Love's precept to keep oneself chaste for a lover whose shameless attempt betrays a shameless mind."

If we look back over the dialogues, we shall find that a number of conclusions present themselves. First, as Walter pursues his hunt, he will find it very difficult to persuade any lady that he is a person of great *probitas* through eloquence. In fact, the harder he tries, the more apparent his lack of *probitas* will become. His only hope seems to be to find a lady who is very stupid. Now looking at the dialogues more particularly, we can see readily that no lover says anything of consequence that is not either (a) patently ludicrous, (b) self-contradictory, (c) contrary to something he has said elsewhere, or (d) contrary to something some other lover says. It follows that it is injudicious to attribute the statements of any lover to Andreas himself. The lovers are *personae*, not vehicles for auctorial opinion. To treat them as "authorities" on twelfth-century love theory, as some scholars have done, is to exhibit, perhaps, a certain naïveté in the handling of texts. Should we conclude, for example, that in the twelfth century men loved only the solaces of the upper parts of other men's wives? Finally, the pretensions of the lovers as they seek to elevate themselves for an ulterior purpose are comic. The humor of the dialogues is not modern humor; it depends for its effectiveness on an assumed scale of values which is not at all like the assumed scale of values which modern readers bring to texts and situations. The values involved are theological values derived from the Scriptures and moral values derived from classical literature. There are enough direct and indirect reflections of these sources in the text to make this fact beyond dispute. If we assume, for purposes of our reading, some of these values, the humor of the text will appear. It is not conveyed very well in the present summary in which some of the more important relevant background ideas are introduced. These ideas are not in themselves humorous, and the explanation ruins the joke. Moreover, our account has missed many details. But if those interested will read the Latin text, which carries nuances of meaning that cannot be conveyed in any translation, however skilful, with some of the common values of twelfth-century clerical culture in mind, and with their attention alerted for the ludicrous, they will not be disappointed.

Turning now to the remainder of Andreas' book, Chapter 7 on the love of the clergy supports very well the reasoning of the noble lady who defended herself from the attentions of a priest. It is explained, on scriptural authority, that a clerk should put aside all fleshly delights. His nobility comes neither from his ancestors nor from secular authority, but from God. Love is inconsistent with this nobility, so that if he becomes a lover he should be deprived of it. Since clerks, as the lady also said, lead an idle life with plenty of food and are thus subject to temptation, it may happen that a clerk may wish to love. If he does, he should enter the service of love "in accordance with the rank or standing of his parents." That is, a clerical lover should put aside his God-given nobility. Then, Andreas says, he may follow the procedures outlined in Chapter 6. The results he may expect are sufficiently clear in the dialogues.

Andreas is more vehement in Chapter 8, where he attacks the love of nuns. To love a nun is to violate both the laws of Heaven and the laws of the world, so that the solaces of nuns should be studiously avoided. Even private conversation with nuns is dangerous, a fact which Andreas supports with what purports to be a personal experience. If a man approaches a nun in a secluded place, he can "hardly escape the worst of crimes, engaging in the work of Venus." Since nuns are dangerous even to clerks who know the art of love well, they are even more dangerous to young men who are not clerks. Chapters 9 and 10 eliminate love acquired by money or gifts and love freely given for praise or fleshly desire, leaving, we may notice, very little room to acquire love at all; and Chapter 12 eliminates the love of prostitutes. In Chapter 11 we are told that peasants love naturally, so that if one is so imprudent as to fall in love with one of them, the usual flattery is not quite enough, and it may be necessary to use a little force in addition. Although this doctrine is actually complimentary to the peasant girls, it should not be overlooked that Andreas says that it is improvident to love one. And there is nothing in what he says that implies any kind of license to rape peasants.[83] If all of these strictures are considered carefully, it will be seen that there is nothing much left for Walter to do except to curb his horse severely or get married. The dialogues offer him little hope of maintaining his *probitas* and following Venus with a free rein at the same time. In the first book of the *De amore*, therefore, Andreas reinforces, in an elaborate way, what he said in the preface: A prudent man will not engage in the hunt of Venus.

The second book is rather miscellaneous in character. The opening chapters on the retention of love, the increasing of love, the decreasing of love, the termination of love, and the indications that love is returned contain little that is not obvious in the light of the dialogues. But the emphasis on secrecy, wealth, good reputation, and a good appearance make it plain, first, that love was not greeted with much social approval in Andreas' time, and, second, that it is, as he describes it, closely allied with Fortune. The predicament of the lover, who has to maintain a fine reputation while doing something that would ruin it, is not only precarious but also hypocritical. Chapter 6 emphasizes the necessity for faith in love, but it contains two principles that are of especial interest with reference to the "system" as a whole. First, Andreas assures us that "pure" and "mixed" love are essentially the same thing. Hence, we have no excuse for making something mysterious or "metaphysical" of "pure" love. Again, Andreas tells us that if lovers have been engaging in "pure" love and one of them wishes to change to "mixed" love, the other cannot refuse, because "all lovers are bound, when practicing love's solaces, to be mutually obedient to each other's desires." The celebrated "freedom from compulsion" said to characterize "courtly love" here vanishes into thin air. It is not assisted by the further principle that if a woman grants a man hope, she is bound to grant him her love.

Chapter 7 contains the "love decisions" which have sent Marie of Champagne to Poitiers to join Eleanor of Aquitaine, although

---

[83] See G. H. Gerould, *Chaucerian Essays* (Princeton, 1952), p. 75. As Professor Gerould observed, what Andreas describes is seduction rather than rape.

no other "evidence" supports this conjunction. Our knowledge of the private lives of Marie, Eleanor, and the other ladies mentioned by Andreas is not detailed enough for us to know in every instance what their decisions may imply, but, as John F. Benton suggests, at times Andreas' satiric intention is clear. In the sixth "case" a worthless youth and an older man of good character are said to have sought the love of the same woman, the younger arguing that through love he might acquire excellent character and thus bring credit to the lady. The situation, in other words, resembles that in the first dialogue. Queen Eleanor renders the following decision in this case: "Although the young man may show that by receiving love he might rise to be a worthy man, a woman does not do very wisely if she chooses to love an unworthy man, especially when a good and eminently worthy one seeks her love. It might happen that because of the faults of the unworthy man his character would not be improved even if he did receive the good things he was hoping for, since the seeds which we sow do not always produce a crop."

In 1152, as was well known, Eleanor had divorced Louis VII of France, who was 32, and married Henry, who was 19. At the time Andreas wrote, Eleanor was being kept in custody by her husband, who had long since sought the solaces of love elsewhere. Her seeds very obviously failed to "produce a crop." In the seventh case, a man became the lover of a woman whom he later found to be related to him. He then wished to abandon the lady, who objected. Queen Eleanor reached the following decision: "A woman who under the excuse of a mistake of any kind seeks to preserve an incestuous love is clearly going contrary to what is right and proper. We are always bound to oppose any of those incestuous and damnable actions which we know even human laws punish by very heavy penalties."

Everyone knew that Eleanor divorced Louis on grounds of consanguinity and three months later married Henry, who was almost as closely related to her as was Louis. Her "decisions" as devised by Andreas thus constitute in these instances rather amusing bits of self-criticism. They are far from being the kind of thing that Eleanor herself, who was certainly a very astute person, would have been likely to say in public. It is possible that research into the lives of the other ladies whose "decisions" Andreas renders might uncover other satirical digs of the same kind.

The final chapter of the second book contains a fable which explains how a knight of Britain obtained the "Rules of Love." We need not concern ourselves here with an interpretation of the fable, in which the amorous knight acquires the hawk, which was to become a piece of conventional Gothic iconography, as well as the rules. Suffice it to say that Andreas was careful to have these rules emanate, not from France, which was his native country, and not from Andalusia, about which he probably knew very little, but from England. It is not surprising that the British have never on this account attempted to claim the laurels of France for showing the world how women should be cultivated and revered, for the English origin of the rules constitutes a very dubious compliment. The rules themselves are a sort of summary of what has been said previously, and their meanings within the "system" of Andreas' work are clear. To make the whole matter ridiculous, Andreas suggests that written copies of these rules were circulated so that every lover everywhere received one. We can imagine a lover studying his copy and trying to comply with the rules. He learns, for example, (5) that "that which a lover takes against the will of his beloved has no relish," which is a little awkward, but he is soon consoled to find (8) that "no one should be deprived of love without the very best of reasons," and (26) that "Love can deny nothing to love." As for his own behavior, he finds that (2) he must be jealous, and that (28) "a slight presumption" is enough to make him suspect his beloved of infidelity. He must (15) regularly turn pale when he is with his beloved, and (16) his heart must palpitate when he sees her. He must (23) eat and sleep very little, always be apprehensive (20), think always of his beloved (24, 30), and (27) never tire of her solaces. Although (1) "marriage is no real excuse for not loving," the lover (18) is made worthy of love only by good character. The chances of our lover's failing to make a fool of himself in trying to follow these rules are very slim indeed. And that is exactly the reason for their being set up as an artificial system of rules. What Andreas is saying, in effect, is that the behavior of lovers is about as rational as if they all went cross-gartered in yellow stockings.

However, in the event that Walter might still be inclined to gape in incomprehension, Andreas added the third book, not to contradict what he had said before, but to make the implications of what he had already said explicit. There he explained that no man can devote himself to love and at the same time please God by doing anything else, since God detests the acts of Venus or fornication and instituted marriage so that his people might multiply. Love not only offends God, but it also injures one's neighbor, so that it is inimical to charity. Love is also inimical to friendship, which is a reasonable relationship. It injures both body and soul. The fear and jealousy of love constitute a miserable servitude. Again, the "generosity" of love is actually prodigality, and this is not only a mortal sin, but it leads to poverty and crime. Although love torments men while they live, it brings even greater torments later. The virtue of chastity is violated in love, and this violation leads to loss of reputation and blasphemy. Love ruins a woman's good name, "even if she is loved by one of royal race." Love leads to criminal excesses of all kinds, and to idolatry. The delight of the flesh is not a great good but a sin which causes loss of reputation and inattention to duty. The author of love is really the devil, who promises much but gives bitter payment. Love, moreover, leads to warfare, breaks up marriages, and is the source of untold evils, including a loss of wisdom. Andreas concludes with a lengthy diatribe against women regarded as objects of desire, which is certainly very far from placing them on a pedestal.

It is significant that what Andreas condemns in his last book is not some romantic conception of "courtly love" wherein, because of a shortage of women, or for any other reason, men engage in Albigensian, Neoplatonic, Andalusian, Pictish, or other heresies in order to evade the Christian "system." He condemns instead the foolishness and vice to which unbridled concupiscence leads. Concupiscence is something we all inherit, a thing which since the Fall we have had in common with wild beasts, fish, cattle, and birds. When the bridle begins to slacken and we feel that the horse is running away with us, what will happen if we let it go? This is the problem with which Andreas concerned himself. Can we give the horse its rein and avoid offending and injuring our neighbors in society on the one hand and God on the other, keeping all the while our probity? The answer to this is "no." The "no" is implied from the start, in the definition of love which identifies it with cu-

447

pidity and indicates that its development is simply the development of sin. It is implied again in the foolish and hypocritical behavior of the lovers in the dialogues and once more in the decisions of the ladies regarding problems of love. The last book simply states the same answer to the same problem openly. The work as a whole is studded with material from the Bible, from the classics, and from the doctrinal literature of medieval Christianity. There is absolutely no reason to look for exotic sources elsewhere, to doubt Andreas' orthodoxy or probity, to question his psychological stability, or to feel that he had any sympathy for poor distracted persons in "the human condition," wavering uncertainly between Venus and Christ. He undoubtedly acquired his taste for humorous mockery from Ovid. Because of it, and because of his skillful and perceptive handling of his themes, he belongs to the tradition of Christian humanistic literature which includes such writers as Jean de Meun, Boccaccio, Chaucer, and Rabelais. The fact that modern scholars have failed to see his humor is nothing in his disfavor. They have also turned Ovid into a dandified parlor pagan who wrote "immoral" poetry; they have assured us that Jean de Meun was a "sensualistic naturalist," that Boccaccio was not a Christian, that Chaucer was a sceptic, that Ficino was a pagan, that Rabelais was an atheist, and so on. In spite of anything said in this book, most scholars will probably continue to shake their heads over the strange doctrines which, curiously enough, permeated the *mores* and *amores* of the twelfth century.

2. "COURTLY LOVE" AND COURTESY

The atmosphere of the *De amore* is not systematically courtly; the first dialogue, in fact, involves persons of the middle· class and is not courtly at all. A more courtly treatment of the themes developed by Andreas appears in the *Chevalier de la charrete* of Chrétien de Troyes. The analysis of a twelfth-century narrative, written prior to the establishment of the conventions of Gothic iconography, is difficult; but a few points may suffice to show that Chrétien was not, actually, advocating any new doctrines of love. Lancelot begins his little pilgrimage in quest of Guinevere, whom Arthur has foolishly allowed to be taken to the land of Gorre, by mounting a cart used, like a pillory, for criminals. Professor Urban T. Holmes has suggested that the name *Gorre* meant "vanity" and that the capital of that country has a name, *Bade*, which meant "that which is worthless."[84] Although the word *gorre* does not appear elsewhere as a common noun until much later, this fact is not necessarily decisive evidence for rejecting Professor Holmes' interpretation. It is certainly true, as we saw earlier in a discussion of the illustration for Psalm 118 in the St. Alban's Psalter, that vanity could be thought of as including a proclivity to love of a certain kind. In any event, as Lancelot mounts his cart, a love which is not altogether admirable overcomes reason:

> Mes Reisons, qui d'Amors se part,
> li dit que del monter se gart,
> si le chastie et si l'anseigne
> que rien ne face ne anpreigne
> dom il ait honte ne reproche.
> N'est pas al cuer, mes an la boche,
> Reisons qui ce dire li ose;
> mes Amors est el cuer anclose
> qui li comande et semont
> que tost an la charrete mont.
> Amors le vialt et il i saut,
> que de la honte ne li chaut
> puis qu' Amors le comande et vialt.

The dwarf turns to Gawain, and says,

> "Se tu tant te hez
> con cist chevaliers qui ci siet,
> monte avoec lui . . . ."

But Gawain regards Lancelot's action as "molt grant folie." Reason is, as usual, the power which guards man from folly, but Lancelot's condition is such that he keeps reason only "an la boche." Love, on the other hand, is a function of the sensuality unless it is reasonably directed. If Lancelot allows unreasonable love to triumph over reason so that he shamelessly enters a cart suitable for criminals, the inference for the theme of the romance is obvious: Lancelot will join Guinevere in Gorre through shameless criminal action.

[84] See Urban T. Holmes, Jr., and Sister M. Amelia Klenke, o.p., *Chrétien, Troyes, and the Grail* (Chapel Hill, 1959), p. 46. Professor Holmes, however, considers Lancelot to be a "true and worthy knight."

The romantically inclined will object at once that Chrétien did not regard Lancelot's affair with Guinevere as criminal. But the text of the romance hardly supports this view. When the Queen is accused of entertaining Sir Kay in her bed, she replies,

> "Se Dex m'aït,
> onques ne fu, neïs de songe,
> contee si male mançonge
> Je cuit que Kex li seneschax
> est si cortois et si leax
> que il n'an fet mie a mescroire;
> et je ne regiet mie an foire
> mon cors, ne n'an faz livreison."

For Kay to have tupped her, she says, would have been contrary to loyalty and courtesy. Kay himself says,

> "Ja Dex, quant de cest siegle irai,
> ne me face pardon a l'ame,
> se onques jui avoec ma dame.
> Certes, mialz voldroie estre morz
> que tex leidure ne tiex torz
> fust par moi quis vers mon seignor. . . ."

Adultery was a crime both in the theology and in the feudal *mores* of the period, and there is absolutely no reason to assume that Chrétien wished to contest this fact. Clearly, it is no more courteous, loyal, and just for Lancelot to lie with the Queen than it would have been for Kay to do so, and Chrétien undoubtedly included the above passages in his romance to emphasize exactly this point.

The relationship between Lancelot and Guinevere, consummated in the Land of Gorre, is based on exactly the same kind of idolatrous passion that is described by Andreas and examined in detail later by Jean de Meun. Having allowed reason to be overcome by love, Lancelot sleeps in a perilous bed. As he lies in it a blazing lance descends from above, sets the bed on fire, and wounds him in the thigh. The fire that starts in the bed is a familiar figure for lecherous desire which was still being used by Chaucer, and the thigh wound also had very familiar connotations in the Middle Ages. It is a scriptural figure, but a passage from St. Jerome's letter to Eustochium will serve as well as a series of citations from commentaries to explain it (22. 11): "Job was dear to God and was by His testimony immaculate and simple. But hear how the Devil was mistrusted by God: 'His strength was in his loins and his force is in the navel of his belly' [Job 40. 11]. The genitals of men and women are here given altered names for decency [cf. Figs. 38, 39 (bottom left), 49, 64 (bottom left)]. Whence also he who is from the 'loins' of David is promised a seat on his throne. And it is said of the seventy-five souls who entered Egypt that they came from the 'thigh' of Jacob. And after his wrestling with God, the size of Jacob's 'thigh' shrunk and he ceased to father children. And he who is to celebrate the Passover is warned to do so with bound and mortified 'loins.' And God says to Job [Job 38. 3], 'Gird up thy loins like a man.' And John the Baptist is bound with a girdle of skin. And the Apostles are ordered to have in hand the lamps of the Gospel with girded 'loins.' "

It is possible to be "wounded" in the "thigh" in two ways, either as Jacob was wounded, or as those who neglect to "gird up their loins" are wounded. Lancelot's wound in a fiery bed is an indication of the heat and vigor of his passion, not to mention being, at the same time, an indication of its origin. We may recall that Erec and Tristran receive similar wounds.

As Lancelot progresses, we see him engaging in excessive meditation, maintaining the "chastity" of love, and developing the idolatry necessary to make him swoon over a wisp of Guinevere's hair. At the same time, however, he takes on the characteristics of a Redeemer. He removes a stone from his tomb, albeit from the outside, receives *stigmata* at the sword bridge, and eventually releases the captives in Gorre. Chrétien uses much the same kind of material that Jean de Meun used later to show the nature of his passion. When he approaches the bed of the Queen,

> si l'aore et se li ancline,
> car an nul cors saint ne croit tant.

At his departure, however, he suffers martyrdom:

> Au lever fu il droiz martirs,
> tant li fu griés li departirs . . . .

And as he leaves, he bows as before an altar:

451

> Au departir a soploié
> a la chanbre, et fet tot autel
> con s'il fust devant un autel.

It would be difficult to make the idea of idolatry any clearer. But the great achievement of Lancelot is that he is able to go to Gorre (perhaps give himself up to Vanity), consummate his criminal love, and return (maintain his place in society). In this sense, he is an inverted Redeemer who shows others how to live vainly without incurring social ostracism. His actions demonstrate that

> ne puet mie tant proesce,
> con fet malvestiez et peresce.

His secret is that he can cause Bien Celer to vanquish Honte, as Jean de Meun put it, and teach others to use the same device. It is for this reason that Gower was able to write of Lancelot (*Traitié*, 15. 1. 1-7):

> Comunes sont la cronique et l'istoire
> De Lancelot et Tristrans ensement;
> Enquore maint leur sotie en memoire,
> Pour ensampler les autres de present:
> Cil q'est guarni et nulle garde prent,
> Droit est qu'il porte mesmes sa folie.

Our own difficulties with Chrétien's romance arise from the fact that we insist on reading it "as a story," so that we become vicariously involved in the hero's "adventures" and so lose the exemplary force of the narrative. Meanwhile, we are very anxious, for romantic reasons, to miss the purport of the religious imagery in the poem, which is not designed to set up a "system" opposed to Christianity, but to make the significance of Lancelot's misdeeds apparent and to emphasize the extent of the inversion to which a submission of the reason to the sensuality may lead. That is, the religious materials in the romance have the same function as the scriptural citations produced by the lovers in the dialogues of the *De amore*.

Chrétien's romances form a part of an enormous efflorescence of literary interest in love during the twelfth century. Theologians as well as poets devoted a great deal of attention to the subject,[85] and

---

[85] See E. Gilson, *La théologie mystique de S. Bernard* (Paris, 1934), pp. 14-16. Richard of St. Victor's *De IV gradibus violentae caritatis*, recently edited by G.

it is undoubtedly true that there was a similar interest in courtly society. A kind of love developed there which we might call "courtly" or "courteous" love, although it has no relevance to anything in the *De amore* except to the instructions of the noble lady in the third dialogue, and it has no relation to heretical doctrines or to alien systems of metaphysics. In the feudal system, if something as loose as feudalism may be called a "system," a nobleman was bound theoretically to his overlord by a tie of love. The love he bore for his lord extended to the members of his family, including any ladies it might contain. Meanwhile, as noble ladies acquired more prominence, sharing in the administration of their dominions or at times actually acting as lords themselves, efforts were made to refine court manners and to develop standards of courtesy, especially where ladies were concerned. The ladies were "loved" by all of their more prominent subjects as well as by any noble visitors who wished to make a good impression. Love was the commonly accepted basis for noble behavior, either with reference to a friend, lord, or vassal of the same sex or with reference to a lady. In a Christian society, where love was thought to be the determining factor in motivation and an aspect of universal harmony, such a development was not unnatural. Our medieval ancestors lacked both our squeamishness about the subject and our more recent frankness before the unfortunate psychological facts, which is simply the other side of the squeamishness.

It may be true that young men who vied with one another in an effort to be courteous and amorous may have sometimes abused their graces in a quest for physical satisfaction. This possibility occurs to old Archambaut in the Provençal *Roman de Flamenca*; he is afraid that some unscrupulous man will approach his wife and simulate "amor cortes," without knowing what love is, and cause her to do folly (lines 1204-1207). It should be noted that "courteous love" is not in itself a sufficient cause for jealousy and does not lead to the "folly" which Archambaut fears. An illustration of it appears in the same romance when the King of France devotes courteous attention to Flamenca. His gestures are at one point a little extreme, but they do not imply a passion for the lady; that is, his courtesy, however direct, does not serve as an ulterior dis-

---

Dumièges (Paris, 1955), contains an interesting account of parallels between human and divine love.

guise for something else. It is not surprising that works like the *Lai dou lecheor* were written to satirize false courtesy as opposed to "true" or disinterested courtesy.

By the first half of the fourteenth century it became fashionable for a noble knight to have a "lady" on whose behalf he was courteous and valiant. She might well be someone whom he seldom saw and in whom he had no very intimate personal interest. Oton de Grandson's affection for the Queen of France, for whom he wrote love poems, may be taken as a good illustration of this custom. On the other hand, ladies were encouraged to promote worthy deeds in those who loved them "par amours." It is doubtful that love "par amours" had any very rigorous meaning at the time. Jehan le Bel describes it in his *Ars d'amour*[86] as a love for the sight of the beloved, something like the love described with some misgivings in the *Livre du Duc des vrais amans* of Christine de Pisan. Its basis, Jehan says, is the "natural" love which arises from difference in sex,[87] but although it may lead to a kiss or a chaste (not nude) embrace,[88] its chief satisfaction arises from the contemplation of the beauty of the beloved. Lovers "par amours" turn pale, tremble, and grow ill like lovers who seek more active delights, for the mutability of the object loved causes uneasiness.[89] They may be moved to perform seemingly virtuous actions by their love, but these actions are not truly virtuous because such lovers are interested in the impression they make on their ladies, and not in "the good, the right, and the reason" which truly virtuous action entails. Thus they may resemble true lovers, but the resemblance is superficial.[90] Moreover, many who are moved by "natural" love or carnal affection feign love "par amours," but carnal affection is inimical to true amity.[91] A true lover loves virtue, so that his love cannot lead him to perform an evil action.[92] On the other hand, those who are moved by nature to love "for delight" place that delight above everything else so that they fail to do what they should do and ultimately achieve only sadness.[93] They subject

---

[86] I, 149.

[87] For "natural" love, see *ibid.*, I, 19, 135-136. Cf. Arnaldus of Villanova, "De coitu," *Opera* (Basel, 1585), col. 839.

[88] *Li ars d'amour*, I, 164.

[89] *Ibid.*, I, 167-170. Jehan thought women to be by nature changeable, like water, *ibid.*, I, 48-49.

[90] *Ibid.*, I, 158.   [91] *Ibid.*, I, 166.   [92] *Ibid.*, I, 53.   [93] *Ibid.*, I, 136.

themselves to the whims of a woman, and a man who does this becomes a "très malvaise chétif" because "einsi con li cors sur l'ame seignerist, ensi est-il quant la feme a sour l'omme signourie."[94] The remedy for this kind of love, we are told, is to flee the occasion for it. When it dominates a man, nature has overcome reason in him, and reason should be the "dame et governesse" of the movements of nature. When the two are inverted, the result is sorrow. But in true love, reason and love are harmonious.[95] Jehan's concept of jealousy is somewhat different from that advanced by the lover in the *De amore*. He says that in love for delight, the jealous lover believes that his love has done wrong, so that his jealousy is an evil. In true love, however, the lover desires only the welfare of the beloved, so that he becomes jealous against all those who would injure that welfare.[96] Jehan concludes his work by explaining that true happiness resides in charity, or, that is, in loving well.[97] There is little doubt that knights and noblemen were encouraged to love in accordance with what Jehan describes as "true" love in the later Middle Ages. It may be that many of them failed to do so, but we should not allow our own assumed sophistication to blind us to the fact that there were undoubtedly some who did.

Geoffroi de Charny begins his *Livre de chevalerie* with an account of various kinds of "gens d'armes" who are praiseworthy. Among them are some who at first knew nothing of the honor they might acquire through arms, but when they set their hearts on "amer par amours," their ladies, not wishing them to waste their time, advised and commanded them to go out and seek the great goods and honors that arms can bring. Having discovered these things, they became good knights, to the great honor of the ladies who advised them.[98] Those who seek to become knights, Geoffroi says, should, moreover, learn to speak, to dance, and to sing honorably in the company of ladies.[99] Good men at arms should, in fact, "amer par amours" honorably, "car l'est li droit estat de ceulx qui cel honour veulent acquérir." But the honor of the ladies should

---

[94] *Ibid.*, I, 137.
[95] *Ibid.*, I, 139.
[96] *Ibid.*, I, 171.
[97] *Ibid.*, II, 383-386.
[98] The treatise is printed in the second part of the first volume of Kervyn de Lettenhove's edition of Froissart (Brussels, 1875), 463ff. For the above point, see p. 469.
[99] *Ibid.*, p. 480.

be protected above all else, and the lover should not boast about his love. The ladies, moreover, should honor and love the knights they inspire.[100] In view of Geoffroi's obvious piety, his firm Boethian contempt for Fortune and its gifts, and his inclusion of chastity among the chivalric virtues, we may assume that love "par amours" is here not the same thing that is described by Jehan le Bel, but a form of "courteous" love.

Again, the little poem "Instructio patris regis ad filium Edwardum," thought by its editor to have been written by Edward III for the boy who became the Black Prince,[101] is largely devoted to instruction on how to behave in a manner consistent with the love of God. But it contains the following advice concerning the ladies:

> Dames et puceles amés
> Et les servés et honurés
> En parole, en fet, en samblant;
> A dames seiés bien voillant.
> Des femes venent les proesces,
> Et les honours et les hautesces.
> Qui de femes s'est fait haier,
> Ja ne verres bien acheveir.
> El monde n'a plus cher aveir
> Que bone femme, sachés de veir.
> A paine verrés nul home vaillant
> Qu'il n'aime ou ait aimé avant.
> Partot lur dois honnour porter.
> Si tu voes à haut pris munter,
> Portés-lur bone compaignie:
> C'est une trèble curtesie.

The poem closes with a little prayer to be said after dinner which contains the lines,

> Uncore pri-jeo le fils Marie
> Qu'il me doint joie de m'amie
> Et bone feme et beaus enfauns,
> Cortois et sages et vailliauns.

It is obvious that neither Geoffroi nor the author of this poem was

---

[100] *Ibid.*, pp. 485-486.
[101] Printed in the first part of the first volume of the same edition of Froissart, pp. 541-553.

advising anyone to emulate Sir Lancelot or the kind of lover described by Andreas Capellanus. If we wish to speak of this love as "courtly love," which it certainly was, we shall not be abusing the term. Love of this kind presupposes a Christian feudal society, so that it is a peculiarly medieval phenomenon. On the other hand, it does not involve any profound "revolution in love," and it is a far cry from the romantic love celebrated by poets in the nineteenth century. The ideal of reasonable love for a woman based on a love of virtue is a Christian extension of the classical ideal of friendship which owes its inspiration in part to the *De amicitia* of Cicero and in part to Christian charity. It is this love as it expressed itself in terms of the feudal conventions of medieval society which constitutes the major contribution of the Middle Ages to the theory of love.

True or virtuous love was sometimes contrasted with "heroic" love, as it is, for example, in Philippe de Vitry's *Virtutibus laudabilis*, where true love is represented by love for the Blessed Virgin.[102] But "heroic" love is simply a "medical" variant of the same kind of love that is described by Andreas and illustrated in Chrétien's Lancelot, or in the foolish lover of the *Roman de la rose*. Arnaldus of Villanova says that such love is called "heroic," not because only lords have it, but "either because it dominates, subjecting the spirit and heart of man to its rule, or because the acts of such lovers with respect to the thing loved are similar to the actions of subjects in relation to their lords; they fear to offend the majesty of their lords and seek to aid them in faithful subjection so that they may obtain peace and favor."[103] In the treatise *De parte operative* attributed to the same author, heroic love is taken up under "Alienatio," where it is said to corrupt the reasoning process and to be called "heroic" because it is immense and irrational.[104] The remedy for love is to avoid immoderate thought about the lady and the hope of attaining her favors. To this end, Arnaldus recommends as distractions temperate baths, pleasant conversation, the sight of beautiful and lovable persons, foreign travel, and sexual intercourse with young and delightful girls.[105]

[102] Leo Schrade, *Polyphonic Music of the Fourteenth Century* (Monaco, 1958), I, 91-96.
[103] "De amore heroico," *Opera*, col. 1528.   [104] *Opera*, cols. 270-271.
[105] "De amore heroico," *Opera*, col. 1530.

The last is a deliberate avoidance of the chastity mentioned by Andreas and illustrated by Lancelot's treatment of the hospitable lady who insists on sleeping in the same bed with him. As we have seen, the general pattern of the description of love given by Arnaldus follows the pattern of Andreas' definition.

In the popular *Lilium medicinae* of the fourteenth-century physician Bernard of Gordon, heroic love is described as follows: "That love which is called 'heroes' is a melancholy solicitude arising from the love of a woman. The cause of this passion is a corruption of the *virtus aestimativa* on account of a firmly fixed form and figure. Thus when anyone is overcome by love [*philocaptus*], with reference to any woman, he so conceives her beauty and figure and manner that he thinks and believes that she is more beautiful, more venerable, more attractive, and more gifted in nature and conduct than any other; and thus he ardently desires her without method or measure, thinking that if he could attain his end it would be his felicity and blessedness. And the judgment of the reason is corrupted to such an extent that the lover continually thinks of her and neglects his natural operations, so that if anyone speaks to him, he hardly understands anything else. And because he is in a continuous meditation, he is said to have a melancholy solicitude."[106]

Bernard goes on to say that the lover may be so overcome that he becomes insane, like the one described by Ovid (*Rem. am.*, 118) who "Hung, a sorrowful burden, from a lofty beam." To illustrate the corrupted judgment of the lover Bernard quotes the verses,

> All lovers are blind; love is no just arbiter
> For it thinks a deformed breast to be beautiful.

Again, "Whoever loves a frog thinks the frog to be Diana."

He explains that the *virtus aestimativa* controls the *virtus imaginativa*, which in turn controls the concupiscible function. The concupiscible controls the irascible, and the irascible the motion of the muscles. Hence, when the first is corrupted, the whole action of the body is "in contempt of the order of reason." Therefore the lover is willing to suffer heat, cold, and other unpleasant things,

[106] For this and the following passages see the edition of Lyons, 1574, pp. 216-219.

thinking them pleasant with reference to what he has in mind, just as a ribald is willing to go naked and sleep on the ground for the sake of his pleasure in gambling and drinking in the tavern on which he squanders his wealth. Among the symptoms, Bernard lists neglect of food and drink, secret thoughts and profound sighs, and an irregular pulse. In connection with the last, he describes an "association test" for determining the name of the beloved. The prognosis is that lovers who are not cured "either fall into a mania or die."

Bernard's cures are somewhat more elaborate than those described by Arnaldus. In the first place, the nature of the cure should be adapted to the nature of the victim. If the patient is reasonable, "he should be separated from his false imagination by a man whom he fears and by whom he may be shamed with words and admonitions showing the perils of the world, the Day of Judgment, and the joys of Paradise." If he is a youth, he should be beaten. Either very sorrowful or very joyful tidings may be of assistance. Idleness should be avoided on the authority of Ovid (*Rem. am.*, 139), "If you take away idleness, Cupid's bow is broken."

Active occupation of the kind Ovid suggests (*Rem. am.*, 150), travel (*Rem. am.*, 152), or the love of other women (*Rem. am.*, 441-442) are also useful. Pleasant sights, places, and music may be helpful. But if none of these things is of avail, more strenuous measures must be taken. These are, from a modern point of view, rather startling, but they certainly indicate that the physician of the Middle Ages had no more respect for the passionate lover than had the theologian: "Finally, however, when we have no other counsel, let us employ the counsel of old women, who may slander and defame the girl as much as they can, for they are more sagacious in this than are men. However, Avicenna says that there are some who delight in hearing smelly and illicit things. Let there be sought a most horrible-looking old woman with great teeth, a beard, and evil and vile clothing who carries a menstruous napkin in her lap. And, approaching the lover, let her begin to pull up her dress, explaining that she is bony and drunken, that she urinates in bed, that she is epileptic and shameless, that there are great stinking excrescences on her body, and other enormities concerning which old women are well instructed. If the lover will not relent on account of this persuasion, let her suddenly take out the menstruous napkin before his face and bear it aloft saying with a loud cry, 'Such is your love, such!' If he doesn't relent on account of these things, he is a devil incarnate. His fatuousness will be with him finally in perdition." After some miscellaneous observations, Bernard concludes with a variation on a popular verse, which, in his Latin, runs,

> Amor est mentis insania
> Quia animus vagatur per maniam
> Cerebri, doloribus miscens pauca gaudia.[107]

The rather extensive use of the *Remedia amoris* in this discussion indicates that Bernard did not think that he was describing something which originated in the Middle Ages. When a literary character says that he will die if his love is not satisfied, we may conclude that the love he refers to is "heroic" love, which, since it is not based on virtue, is not very admirable.

At the close of the Middle Ages courteous love, like chivalry itself, became a somewhat artificial cult. Although Christine de Pisan was scandalized by the *Roman de la rose*, in her own *Dit de la rose*, she describes the founding of an "order" of the rose devoted to the celebration of loyal love, which was not, of course, love for what the rose represented in the *Roman*. A similar order, the *Cour amoureuse*, was founded on January 6, 1401, at a council presided over by Charles VI. It was established "principaument soubz la conduite, force et seurté d'icelles très loés vertus, c'est assavoir humilité, et léauté a l'honneur, louenge et recommandacion et service de toutes dames et damoiselles."[108] The honor offered the ladies by this institution was chiefly in the form of verse. A more chivalric organization was the order of the "Dame Blanche" described in the *Livre des faits de Boucicaut*, where love is made the source of loyalty, courage, and honor. These efforts to maintain something of the chivalric atmosphere of the first half of the century were, however, French. French prestige had increased steadily during the second half of the fourteenth century,

---

[107] For the standard version of this piece, see Carleton Brown, *English Lyrics of the Thirteenth Century* (Oxford, 1932), p. 14.

[108] From the charter, excerpts from which are printed by Marie-Josèphe Pinet, *Christine de Pisan* (Paris, 1927), p. 84.

so that by 1400 it was greater than it had been at any time since the days of Saint Louis.[109] Meanwhile, in England Edward III had reached the height of his military reputation by the end of 1360. His splendid court was the center of European chivalric activity for a brief period, but the gaiety and exuberance of the English court gave way in the face of widespread political unrest, and Edward himself fell under the influence of Alice Perrers, a lady whose character and actions were not of a kind to encourage widespread idealism concerning women and love. In fact, Edward's submission to Alice afforded an excellent example of the evils which might be expected to result from the kind of feminine domination that had long been condemned by both moralists and poets. By the close of the century, England was in a state of political exhaustion, a condition conducive to reminders of bygone glories, pessimism concerning the present, and satirical criticism in literature. The pessimism concerning society which we find in *Piers Plowman, Vox clamantis,* and "Lak of Stedfastnesse" was hardly conducive to idealistic glorifications of courteous love. Although King Richard sought to maintain chivalric ideals as a standard of conduct, he was not eminently successful in exhibiting them in himself.

Chaucer's major works, except for *The Book of the Duchess,* were thus written in an atmosphere of social decline when the present seemed but a pale reflection of the past, and the problems of society were pressing. The poet's untroubled faith, most clearly expressed in "Truth," and a concomitant sense of humor saved him from the surface bitterness which characterizes the work of many of his contemporaries. The little poem of instruction to a young man quoted above contains the lines,

> Seiés jolis devant la gent
> Et servés Dieu privéement;
> Chantés et volunters jués,
> Que papelard ne resemblés.

Chaucer, who had probably received similar instructions in his early courtly associations and found them peculiarly suited to his personality, never resembles a "papelard." But the seriousness of the religious, social, and moral problems of his society must

---

[109] See E. Perroy, *The Hundred Years' War* (New York, 1951), p. 206.

461

have nevertheless made a deep impression on him. He undoubtedly admired real courtesy, but his treatment of the problems of love shows far more interest in an analysis of the vagaries of cupidinous love than in the idealization of courteous love. Like most medieval men, he regarded political and social problems as moral problems, not as difficulties to be overcome by reorganization and legislation. And moral problems in a Christian society were essentially problems of love.

Glancing back over the types of love discussed by medieval authors, we can see that none of them, except that carnal impulse which, as Virgil says, we share with the animals, has any real counterpart in modern society. Certain aspects of "human nature," it is true, do not change; but the behavior patterns which human impulses produce vary enormously with changes in social structure, and, at the same time, customary attitudes toward common human impulses, which constitute their "meanings," change also. The Ciceronian ideal of *probitas* as a basis for friendship was a matter of grave importance in a society whose structure depended largely on personal relationships. With the development of written contracts, a monetary economy, and the substitution of a complex of written laws for inherited customs, the ideal became less significant. Again, in the course of time, Christian teaching came to emphasize righteousness rather than charity. With these developments, the foundations of courteous love disappeared. Today, when virtue is neither taught as an ideal in our educational system nor commended when it conflicts with personal or social adjustment, there is no place for courteous love in our society, and our natural impulse is to regard it with cynical incredulity. This incredulity has not been lessened by the teachings of psychiatry. Meanwhile, the kind of idolatrous passion for a member of the opposite sex which is satirized by Andreas and Jean de Meun, exemplified in the foolish behavior of protagonists like Tristran, Lancelot, and Troilus, and regarded as a malady by medieval physicians, has been modified in such a way as to make it generally acceptable. It began to be surrounded with an aura of sentiment in the middle-class literature of the late Middle Ages and the Renaissance, an aura which reached its full splendor with the literature of romanticism. Romantic sentiment, like other features of romantic style, has been considerably toned down in more recent

462

times; but the basic pattern of romantic love survives as a literary ideal. In George Orwell's *Nineteen Eighty-Four*, for example, it is the only force envisaged as being strong enough to resist the regimentation of society which is there depicted in such vivid terms; and the emotional force of the book arises from the fact that it is crushed. From a medieval point of view, this fact might well be more terrifying than Orwell's picture of external oppression. On the other hand, the medieval attitude toward passion, which no longer strikes us as being "idolatrous," may well seem inhumane and illiberal. But we should remember that love of this kind had not yet been sanctified by sentimental, aesthetic, or psychological considerations. Its connotations were unlike any connotations romantic love may have today, and we will only be guilty of injustice if we read our own amorous *mores* into medieval texts.

3. MEDIEVAL LOVE IN CHAUCER

The conventions of courteous love appear in fully developed form only once in Chaucer's major works, in *The Book of the Duchess*, written shortly after the death of Blanche of Lancaster in 1369; and even here, the poet is careful to indicate a transition from love "for delight" to courteous love in such a way that the former is eliminated. The usual interpretation of this poem involves certain assumptions that are open to serious criticism. To begin with, the hypothesis that the Black Knight is John of Gaunt leaves much to be desired. The account of how the knight played a game with Fortune, gave himself up to Love, allowed himself to be governed by "Yowthe" in "idelnesse," and made his first awkward approach to Blanche is not very complimentary and would hardly have pleased John of Gaunt. Nor would the observation that he had "upon his berd but lytel her" have been tactful. The age, twenty-four, is also wrong, for John would have been twenty-nine. On the other hand, if the "foure and twenty" is a scribal error, the scanty beard is even more incongruous, for a man of twenty-nine should certainly be able to acquire a substantial growth. Again, the ceremony of the ring near the close of the poem might indicate some kind of feudal investiture, but not the investiture of marriage in which the man gives the woman the ring. The further assumption that the description of the "malady" at the beginning of the poem is a record of some love affair in

463

which Chaucer had been engaged for eight years introduces a strange irrelevancy at the point where we would expect instead some sort of thematic statement. As a matter of fact, the malady probably represents the *tristitia* felt by the poet at the loss of Blanche, the nature of which rather than its literal duration is suggested by the eight years.[110] The symptoms described parallel those of the Black Knight when he is mourning, as his little tuneless song indicates, for the death of Blanche.

There are, in a Christian society, two ways to mourn for the death of a loved one: either the bereavement represents the loss of a purely physical object, taken away by blind Fortune, or the deceased may be regarded as having been most attractive for virtue, so that ideas of Resurrection, hope, and inspiration are suggested. The first attitude, which may be expected to occur spontaneously, leads to sloth and despair if it is maintained. The second, illustrated in Fig. 92, leads ultimately to a recognition of the providential order. At the beginning of his little confession the Black Knight reveals an inclination to take Blanche merely as a gift of Fortune. By the time he has finished describing her virtues, symbolically in the physical description which contains echoes of the Canticle of Canticles and its commentaries, and literally thereafter, and has, moreover, described his two efforts to gain her favor, the first awkward and self-conscious, but the second innocent and honorable, it becomes evident that Blanche was lovable for her virtues rather than simply for her person. With this realization, the Knight can understand the words of Seys to Alcione:

> Awake! let be your sorwful lyf!
> For in your sorwe there lyeth no red.
> For certes, swete, I nam but ded.

Alcione looks up and sees nothing, but at the close of the poem, after the Knight has said, "She ys ded," and the "hart-huntyng" is, in consequence, over, the dreamer looks up and sees "Octovyen" riding up to

> A long castel with walles white,
> By seynt Johan!

[110] Professor B. F. Huppé is preparing an interpretation of this poem in which such details are explained. For the eight years' malady, see Acts 9. 32-34, and the Glossa, *PL*, 114, col. 449.

The resemblance between the poet at the opening of the poem and the Black Knight suggests the clue to the latter's identity: the dreamer and the Knight are both aspects of the poet. The separation comes when the dreamer says, "I was go walked fro my tree." The tree in question is the same tree under which he finds the Knight, "an ook, an huge tree," symbolizing the despair which follows the joys of an earthly paradise. The *Consolation* of Boethius was a sufficient literary precedent for devising a dialogue between two parts of the same person, but if further precedent were needed, Chaucer might have found it in Dante's *Vita nuova* (38). The fact that the Knight is a knight presents no difficulty, for every Christian after confirmation was a *miles Christi*. The "dreamer" interrogates the Knight, not because he does not know what is the matter with him, but because he wishes fully to realize the implications of what has happened. The Knight is the will or the heart of the poet which sees the death of Blanche at first as a loss to Fortune. The dreamer is the reason. The poem becomes a meditation on the death of a lady universally admired by the chivalry of England, a "hunt" for the erring heart which fails to see that her beauty in death is, like that of Beatrice, even greater than it had been in life.

With reference to the courteous love in it, we should notice that the first approach of the Knight to his lady is typical of that of lovers "for delight." He is afraid to speak out for fear of offending the lady, so that, like the squire in the Franklin's Tale, he makes songs about his love. He is ashamed and can say only, "mercy!" When she at last hears his plea, this lady, who loves only "goode folk" and whose sweet looks were mistaken for coquetry only by "fooles," says, "nay." But when the Knight returns "another yere" and she understands that he desires nothing except to "kepe hir name," and "drede hir shame," the lady grants her request and give him a ring so that he becomes one "in hir governaunce." Whether or not Chaucer was actually attached to the household of John of Gaunt at the time of Blanche's death we do not know. But that fact makes little difference. Blanche was known and loved by many as one of the most attractive woman of her time, and it is quite possible that the young poet and diplomat had found occasion to serve her in some way. King Edward was soon to fall completely under the domination of Alice Perrers, and John of

Gaunt himself undertook a marriage for the sole purpose of fulfilling his political ambitions. Chaucer would never again write of
a man in the "governaunce" of a woman without reflecting the
traditional mockery of Andreas, Chrétien, and Jean de Meun.

In *The Canterbury Tales* the effects of cupidinous love are first
set forth in the Knight's Tale. Palamon becomes a worshiper of
Venus, bent on a perpetual war against chastity, and Arcite a worshiper of Mars, in whom wrath becomes so strong that it leads to
self-destruction (cf. Fig. 68). Since Palamon is more "reasonable," Duke Theseus is able to direct him toward a cure for his
trouble, marriage, with a long speech on Divine Providence.
Neither Palamon nor Arcite engages in any form of courteous love.
The treatment of the lovers is mocking and humorous. When
Palamon first sees Emelye, he cries out "A," as though he "stongen
were unto the herte." Arcite, who does not understand what has
happened, delivers an unctuous little sermon on patience:

> "Cosyn myn, what eyleth thee,
> That art so pale and deedly on to see?
> Why cridestow? Who hath thee doon offense?
> For Goddes love, taak al in pacience
> Oure prisoun, for it may noon oother be . . . ."

This friendly and charitable concern vanishes like the shadow it is
as soon as Arcite sees the girl for himself. If the friendship of the
two sworn brothers cannot survive the mere sight of a girl from
a prison window, when neither of the friends has any prospect of
approaching her, that friendship does not amount to much, and
there is no hope that either "friend" has any potentiality for true
love. The pair fall into a heated and futile argument, the seriousness of which is not deepened by Arcite's very transparent sophistry. The whole scene is, in fact, comic. One has only to read it
aloud with some expression and a little of the intonation of English colloquial (not "school") speech to see that rhetorically it is
comic. As for the content, neither Chaucer nor his contemporaries
had sufficient training in nineteenth-century attitudes to regard it
with sympathetic seriousness. Arcite's malady adds nothing to his
dignity. If there is a point in the narrative where sentiment might
have intervened, it is at the death of Arcite. But the Knight's remarks about his fate are not very propitious:

His spirit chaunged hous and wente ther
As I cam nevere; I kan nat tellen wher.
Therfore I stynte. I nam no divinistre.
Of soules fynde I nat in this registre;
Ne me ne list thilke opinions to telle
Of hem, though that they writen wher they dwelle.
Arcite is coold, ther Mars his soule gye!

This elaborate restraint from Dantean speculation can only lead
the reader to wonder what kind of guide Mars might make; his
temple does not look very promising. Nor is the sudden noise of
the mourners entirely convincing:

Shrighte Emelye, and howleth Palamon,
And Theseus his suster took anon
Swownynge . . . .

To think of the shriek, the howl, and the swoon as quaint medieval
ways of expressing strong passion roughly equivalent to

Oh, lift me from the grass!
I die! I faint! I fail!

is to transfer Chaucer to the nineteenth century. Shelley flourished
in an entirely different environment where expressions of this kind
could be taken with respectful seriousness. And the seriousness of
Chaucer's scene is not heightened by the hyperbolic comparison
with the lament of the Trojans for Hector. But any sentiment we
might still feel is punctured finally, or should be, by the ridiculous
practicality of the women:

"Why woldestow be ded," thise wommen crye,
"And haddest gold ynough, and Emelye?"

This behavior illustrates well the remark made concerning Emelye's attitude toward the tournament:

For wommen, as to speken in commune,
Thei folwen alle the favour of Fortune.

Arcite has very little dignity even in death, in spite of the very
courteous efforts of Theseus on his behalf. Theseus himself, who
is treated with much more seriousness, shows a certain susceptibil-
ity to the courteous form of chivalric love, first when he takes pity

467

on the women before Thebes and again when he heeds the pleas of the Queen and Emelye for the lovers when they are caught fighting in the grove. Distressed ladies are not treated lightly by Chaucer's wise and noble Athenian, but the young lovers never exhibit what the eighteenth century would call "disinterested benevolence" or what the fourteenth knew as charity.

In the Miller's Tale the love that moves Nicolas is undisguised carnal affection. But the approach of vain Absalon is more elaborate. He falls into a "love-longynge" so profound

> That of no wyf took he noon offrynge.
> For curteisie, he seyde, he wolde noon.

Needless to say, this is a ridiculous kind of "courtesy." He sings before Alisoun's window and sends her gifts on the theory that town girls require generosity. On the "fateful night," his approach, with its scriptural echoes and inflated language, is an amusing comment on his vanity:

> "What do ye, hony-comb, sweete Alisoun,
> My faire bryd, my sweete cynamome?
> Awaketh, lemman myn, and speketh to me!
> Wel litel thynken ye upon my wo,
> That, for youre love, I swete ther I go.
> No wonder is thogh that I swelte and swete—
> I moorne as dooth a lamb after the tete.
> Ywis, lemman, I have swich love-longynge,
> That lik a turtel trewe is my moornynge.
> I may nat ete na moore than a mayde."

If we compare this address with that of the first lover in the dialogues of the *De amore*, we may notice a significant difference. Andreas' lovers do not, for the most part, dwell on their feelings except to make occasionally the usual threat to die if they are frustrated. But Absalon suggests that he is in a state of melancholy frustration accompanied by a loss of appetite for food. In part, this is a stylistic difference; feelings were more liberally used in the art of the fourteenth century than they had been in the art of the twelfth century. Nevertheless, fourteenth-century feeling was just as susceptible to analysis and criticism as was twelfth-century logic. That is, there were reasonable and unreasonable emotions as well as reasonable and unreasonable inferences. In the present instance, Absalon indicates that he has certain symptoms of the lover's malady. He has dressed these symptoms up in what he apparently thinks of as elegant language in order to appeal to the lady's "pity." But the lover's malady is, as we have seen, not something very admirable, and this effort to make it appealing produces an effect of the ludicrous, just as the efforts of Andreas' lovers to conceal their lack of virtue with flattery, self-flattery, and sophistry produces an effect of the ludicrous. In other words, even if Chaucer had omitted the sweating and the hungry lamb, the general effect of Absalon's speech would still be ridiculous. The "cure" the lover receives is amusingly reminiscent of that advocated by Bernard of Gordon for unreasonable lovers:

> For fro that tyme that he hadde kist hir ers,
> Of paramours he sette nat a kers,
> For he was heeled of his maladie.

Although Arcite actually falls into the lover's malady, whereas Absalon only pretends to do so, there is no real difference between the love expressed by Palamon and Arcite on the one hand and that expressed by Nicolas and Absalon on the other. It is, in all of these instances, love "for delight." Chaucer has, as it were, played the same "melodie" in two different keys in the two opening tales of his collection.

The song continues with still further variations in the Reeve's Tale. Here the little *aube* to which Professor Kaske has called attention is an amusing comment on the lovers. Inflated courtly language is not uncommon among the lovers of the fabliaux, but this is an extremely fine example of the technique. Aleyn's initial motivation has nothing to do either with his lady's beauty or with any other attractions she may have; he is concerned only with revenge. But early in the dawn, having "swonken al the longe nyght," Aleyn wearily takes his leave, swearing to be Malyne's "awen clerk." She, evidently favorably impressed by his efforts, returns his farewell, tells him of the cake, and blesses him. Here the elevated form of the *aube* points to the ridiculousness of the sentiments by inflating the language in which they are expressed. The intention is probably neither to satirize the lower classes nor to engage in parody of a literary nature, but to comment on the lovers. Professor Kaske asserts that the *aube* expresses "at least an aesthetic judgment" on their activities. If, however, as some scholars have suggested, the popularity of the *aube* form in the Middle Ages was due to a background of ideas from St. Paul (Rom. 13. 11-14, 1 Cor. 15. 34, Eph. 5. 14, 1 Thess. 5. 6-7) and from the liturgy of Advent, this criticism was more than "aesthetic." In any event, the activities of Aleyn and his companion typify the "lineage" to which the proud miller actually belongs.

Arveragus in the Franklin's Tale has frequently won the acclaim of modern critics as a lover and a husband. But he shows no traces of what medieval writers called "true" love, and, indeed, very little courtesy. He exerts himself with "many a labour, and many a greet emprise," not for the sake of virtue, but to make an impression on the lady. The theme had already been set in the Merchant's Tale, where Damyan

> kembeth hym, he preyneth hym and pyketh,
> He dooth al that his lady lust and lyketh;
> And eek to Januarie he gooth as lowe
> As evere dide a dogge for the bowe.
> He is so plesant unto every man
> (For craft is al, whoso that do it kan)
> That every wight is fayn to speke hym good;
> And fully in his lady grace he stood.

Dorigen is of so "heigh kynrede," however, that her lover is afraid to speak out. But she is finally impressed by his "worthynesse," especially insofar as it consists of "meke obeysance" to her and "penance" on her behalf, and consequently takes pity on him. Meanwhile, he promises her not to assume any "maistrie,"

> Save that the name of soveraynetee,
> That wolde he have for shame of his degree.

That is, he will actually be what Jehan le Bel calls a "très malvaise chétif," but he will carefully conceal this fact for shame. The Franklin, with the irrepressible Epicurean optimism of his class, is at some pains to explain how this delightful arrangement works.

In the first place, he says that love and "maistrie" are incompatible, echoing faintly Ovid's famous dictum about love and majesty (Met. 2. 846-847). As he puts it,

> When maistrie comth, the God of Love anon
> Beteth his wynges, and farwel! he is gon!
> Love is a thyng as any spirit free.
> Women, of kynde, desiren libertee,
> And nat to ben constreyned as a thral;
> And so doon men, if I sooth seyen shal.

The first part of this statement is true. The hierarchy of marriage with its "maistrie" is inimical to the activities of the God of·Love, and that, in fact, was the chief reason for its establishment. The fact that the Franklin wishes to maintain the delights of the God of Love in marriage puts him in the same class with Januarie and the wife of Bath. The statement about the "freedom" of love is pleasant to the romantic ear, but in the Middle Ages passionate love as inspired by Cupid is traditionally described in terms of chains, thralldom, servitude, and so on. The "meke obeysance" of Arveragus before his marriage is hardly a kind of freedom. The first woman to desire liberty was Eve, who may be supposed to have had many descendants in the spirit as well as in the flesh in the fourteenth century. One may think of that "free spirit" Alice Perrers, for example. As the Franklin seeks to describe his hero's position more particularly, its ambiguity becomes only more apparent:

> Heere may men seen an humble, wys accord.
> Thus hath she take hir servant and hir lord—
> Servant in love, and lord in mariage:
> Thanne was he bothe in lordshipe and servage.
> Servage? nay, but in lordshipe above,
> Sith he hath bothe his lady and his love—
> His lady, certes, and his wyf also,
> The which that lawe of love accordeth to.

1t is clearly impossible to be "servant" in love and "lord" in marriage at the same time except under conditions like those arranged in this instance, where the husband keeps only the "name" of lordship. As for the law of love, the Franklin has just explained that the God of Love flees when lordship is established, or, to put it in the words attributed to Marie of Champagne, "no woman . . . can be crowned with the reward of the King of Love unless she is seen to be enlisted in the service of Love himself outside the bonds of wedlock." Looked at from the point of view of another "lawe of love," what the Franklin actually wants is a marriage which avoids the image of the sacrament, like those sought by Alisoun of Bath and Januarie. The fact that the Franklin desires such an arrangement is consistent with his class outlook and his Epicureanism, and these factors also account for the "modernity" of his views. But Chaucer had no way of knowing that the spiritual descendants of the Franklin would one day rule the world. When the time comes in the Franklin's story for Arveragus to assert his husbandly authority, all he can do is to advise his wife to go ahead and commit adultery. As a lover, he can have, as Andreas implied, no real objection to this action. He is, at the same time, only enough of a husband to threaten his lady to be quiet about what she does "up peyne of deeth." And that is not to be much of a husband.

Chaucer's most famous love story, the tragedy of *Troilus and Criseyde*, is neither a tale of true love, of what Jehan le Bel called love "par amours," nor of courteous love. It is, rather, a tale of passionate love set against a background of Boethian philosophy. Those familiar with the *Consolation* and its major themes will realize at once that it is impossible to idealize passionate love for a gift of Fortune in Boethian terms. In the fourteenth century, Boethius was widely regarded as a saint. Iconographic devices inspired by his work, like the Wheel of Fortune, decorated churches and cathedrals throughout England, and the *Consolation* itself was widely read. Froissart tells us that Baudouin le Courageux, Count of Hainaut, could recite it by heart. The Boethian elements in *Troilus* and their implications were thus easily recognizable to the members of Chaucer's audience. And no one reminded of the doctrines of Fortune and Providence, fate and free will, the love of God and the love of worldly goods, or the Herculean nobility and heroism of virtue, could possibly regard passionate love for a fickle woman with anything but disfavor. This disfavor might appear either as amusement at the antics of the lover or as pity of the kind that one should, from a Boethian point of view, bestow on any sinner. If Chaucer had shown any inclination to doubt the wisdom of his philosophical master, we might have reason to approach his poem with something like a romantic point of view. But such doubt would have been strange indeed in fourteenth-century

English court circles, and the poem itself is one of the most moving exemplifications of Boethian ideas ever written.

It is, in the first place, a tragedy, a work, that is, as Radulphus de Longo Campo said, "altogether in contempt of Fortune." In Chaucer's translation of Boethius, Lady Philosophy is made to say (2 pr. 2), "What other thyng bywaylen the cryinges of tragedyes but oonly the dedes of Fortune, that with unwar strook overtuneth the realmes of greet nobleye?"

Fortune is, as Boethius explains, no menace to the virtuous, but only to those who subject themselves to it by setting their hearts on a mutable rather than an immutable good. Such persons are those who abandon reason for the sake of false goals, in the pursuit of which they engage in criminal behavior. Hence Trivet in commenting on the above passage says that "a tragedy is a song of great iniquities beginning in prosperity and terminating in adversity."[111] In his commentary on Seneca's tragedies, he explains that Virgil in the *Aeneid*, Lucan, and Ovid in the *Metamorphoses* may be said to have written in the tragic manner, since they described the downfall of kings. A comedy, on the other hand, deals with private persons, and the plots of comedy are concerned with things like "the debauching of virgins and the love of prostitutes." Either mode may appear in three forms: in the form of narration, in which the poet speaks; in the form of drama (*dragmatico*), in which the poet does not speak, but only the persons introduced; and in a "mixed" form, in which the poet and the persons introduced all speak. The *Aeneid* is said to illustrate the last form.[112] In these terms, Chaucer's *Troilus* is a mixed tragedy which properly belongs, as he says it does, beside the works of "Virgile, Ovide, Omer, Lucan and Stace." This is not simply a conventional list of poets, but a list of what an educated man of Chaucer's time would have thought of as tragic poets. His own tragedy involves the fall of a prince who subjects himself to Fortune through an unworthy love. Medieval tragedy is, of course, very different from modern tragedy, in which the suffering protagonist becomes an emblem of humanity crushed by the mysterious iniquities of a strangely recalcitrant world. But to the medieval mind, that hostile world of fortuitous events was an illusion generated by misdirected love, and

[111] London, BM, MS Burney 131, fol. 20 verso.
[112] Oxford, Bodl., MS Bodl. 292, fol. 1.

473

this, indeed, is one of the great themes of the *Consolation*. Unless we realize that this conception is just as susceptible to profound elaboration and just as provocative of rich emotional implication as is the more modern conception, we shall have little opportunity to appreciate the force and coherence of Chaucer's poem. To attribute a modern conception of tragedy to Chaucer would be to deny his faith in the Providential order and to make him, in his cultural environment, a shallow fool. And to criticize him for not sharing our modern views on the subject would be a little like criticizing him for not making use of the latest photographs from Mount Palomar in his treatise on the astrolabe.

Chaucer begins his poem appropriately by invoking one of the furies, Thesiphone. Something of what this invocation implies may be gathered from the fact that in the *Anticlaudianus* (8. 147ff.) Alanus makes the furies leaders of all the vices that attack the New Man. Trivet tells us, in his commentary on Boethius, that the furies are three women with serpentine hair who are so named because of "three passions which produce many perturbations in the hearts of men, and at the same time make them transgress in such a way that they are not permitted to take any regard either for their fame or for any dangers that beset them. These are wrath, which desires vengeance, cupidity, which desires wealth, and libido, which desires pleasures. Hence they are called 'avengers of crimes' because crimes are always accompanied by mental pain. And they may be ordered according to their etymologies, for *Alecto* means 'incessant,' and signifies cupidity; *Thesiphone* means 'voice,' and signifies libido; *Megara* means 'great contention,' and signifies wrath."[113]

The wrathful fury which destroys Arcite in the Knight's Tale may be seen in Fig. 116 urging Eteocles and Polynices to become "pares in vulnere fratres." It is, in effect, this same fury which sends Troilus out in the field seeking Diomede in the fifth book of *Troilus*. But Megara takes him from her sister Thesiphone, just as she does Arcite, and the language of Chaucer's invocation becomes clear if we remember Thesiphone's identity:

---

[113] London, BM, MS Burney, 131, fol. 39 verso. The same explanation appears in the commentary on Seneca, fol. 3. A study of the classical imagery in *Troilus* is being prepared by John P. McCall.

> Thow cruel furie sorwynge evere yn peyne,
> Help me that am the sorwful instrument
> That helpeth lovers, as I kan, to pleyne.

The invocation makes it obvious that the kind of love with which
Chaucer is to concern himself is that which leads to tragic action.
He is himself, he says, not a lover; but he calls upon all lovers to
take pity on those who are "in the cas of Troilus." As for himself,
he explains,

> For so hope I my soule best avaunce
> To preye for hem that loves servauntes be,
> And write hire wo, and lyve in charite,
> And for to have of hem compassioun,
> As though I were hire owne brother dere.

In other words, he wishes to maintain in himself a charitable attitude toward the servants of love. Charity is also a kind of love,
but not the kind that leads to the "wo" of Thesiphone, from which
Chaucer maintains a studied detachment. He is, in this respect,
departing from the custom of Boccaccio, who, in harmony with the
greater personal involvement of Italian art generally, liked to
identify himself with his heroes, or at least to pretend to do so.
Chaucer's detachment is more "Gothic" in tone, and it permits a
more deliberately philosophical attitude on the part of the author.
In the present instance, it serves to set off the love about to be
described from charitable love and thus to suggest the major theme
of the poem in unmistakable fashion.

With reference to the matter of types of love in the poem, the
only character who shows any inclination toward courteous love is
Hector, who, when Calkas deserts to the Greek camp, takes pity
on Criseyde as she kneels before him asking protection:

> Now was this Ector pitous of nature,
> And saugh that she was sorwfully bigon,
> And that she was so fair a creature;
> Of his goodnesse he gladede hire anon,
> And seyde, "lat youre fadres treson gon
> Forth with meschaunce, and ye youre self in joie
> Dwelleth with us, whil yow good list, in Troie;

> And al thonour that men may don yow have,
> As ferforth as youre fader dwelled here,
> Ye shul have, and your body shal men save,
> As fer as I may ought enquere or here."

This chivalric promise of security is maintained, without any desire for anything in return, when it is suggested that Criseyde be exchanged for Antenor:

> "Sires, she nys no prisoner," he seyde.
> "I not on yow who this charge leyde,
> But, on my part, ye may eftsone hem telle,
> We usen here no wommen for to selle."

But even the might of Hector cannot withstand the "noyse of peple" who inquire, "what goost may yow enspire this womman thus to shilde?" The "goost" is not one concerning which the commons can be expected to have much understanding, and Troilus himself is prevented by the shame of his illicit passion from seconding the courtesy of Hector.

When we first meet Troilus, he is, so to speak, daring Thesiphone by spending his time at the festival of the goddess of wisdom "byholding ay the ladyes of the town," and proudly jesting about the blind foolishness of lovers.[114] The lovers are not the only blind ones, however, for as Chaucer observes, blind pride and presumption often precede a fall, and in the same way Troilus will have to descend from his height. It may be of some relevance to notice in this connection that pride is conventionally represented in Gothic iconography as a rider falling from his horse. Chaucer, perhaps taking a hint from the kind of equine imagery that appears in the preface to the *De amore* and in representations like those in Figs. 7, 8, 61, and 63, compares Troilus with a horse. Just as a horse must obey "horses lawe," so Troilus will succumb to the "lawe of kynde" which dominates the fleshly or "horsy" aspect of man. But this is an eventuality to be commended, Chaucer says, for love frequently makes worthy men worthier and causes them to dread vice and shame, so that it is best to submit to love, which, in any event, can hardly be resisted. This is very good advice, so long, that is, as the love acquired is properly channeled

---

[114] The following account of the *Troilus* is a modified version of the author's "Chaucerian Tragedy," ELH, XIX (1952), 1ff.

so that the virtues it inspires are real virtues and not vices masquerading as virtues. But Troilus does not begin his amorous career very well. Among the ladies at the feast he sees Criseyde:

> And sodeynly he wax therwith astoned,
> And gan hir bet beholde in thrifty wise.
> "O mercy God!" thoughte he, "wher hastow woned
> That art so fair and goodly to devise?"

Instead of approaching her to discover what she is like, however, Troilus is overcome by the fact that Criseyde is "fair to the eyes and delightful to behold." He receives a "fixe and depe impressioun" and retires hastily to his chamber, where he begins to

> make a mirour of his mynde,
> In which he saugh al holly hire figure . . . .

The pattern of these actions is familiar enough, and it is not one which Chaucer's contemporary audience would have been likely to miss. Troilus has fixed a phantasy of Criseyde in his memory and has begun to meditate on it; he has proceeded from "suggestion" to "delightful thought," or from "sight" to the beginnings of "immoderate thought." These are the initial steps which lead to an inner repetition of the Fall, to *passio*, or to mania and death. Cupid's arrow has struck Troilus with full force. The implications of these facts are not calculated to elevate Troilus in the minds of Chaucer's readers, nor to invite in them much vicarious sympathy for his predicament. On the other hand, the processes involved were a familiar part of everyday experience, for no one escapes from sin in one form or another, so that Troilus' behavior would have been familiar in a practical as well as in a theoretical sense. The underlying theory, in other words, did not make the situation purely academic.

The song Troilus sings in his chamber is a foreshadowing of the course of his love, typical of those who abandon reason for Fortune. His torments seem to him "savory," just as Bernard of Gordon says they are in such cases. The more he drinks the more he thirsts, for he has begun to experience something which we may call either the curse of Dipsas in classical terms or the unquenchable thirst generated by the water of the well of the Samaritan in Christian terms. Love seems to him a thing of clashing contraries—a "quike deth," a "swete harm so queynte"—like the realm of Fortune itself, a suburb of which is that realm of illogical consonances which Matthew of Vendôme had long since ascribed to lovers. Troilus is "al steereles within a boot," an image which derives ultimately from Prov. 23. 33-34: "Thy eyes shall behold strange women, and thy heart shall utter perverse things. And thou shalt be as one sleeping in the midst of the sea, and as a pilot fast asleep when the stern [i.e., "rudder"] is lost." The perverse doctrines appear at once in the last two stanzas of the song. Troilus gives himself up to the God of Love (cf. Fig. 27) and regards his lady as a "goddess" (cf. Fig. 25). He is ready, therefore, to resign his "estat roial" to her, since love and majesty "non bene conveniunt nec in una sede morantur."

This is the neglect of duty which leads to the tragedy. Troilus is a "public figure," a prince whose obligations to his country are not inconsiderable, especially in time of war. But his external submission to Criseyde is based on an inner submission of the reason to the sensuality, for, in the words of Jehan le Bel, "einsi con li cors sur l'ame seignerist, ensi est-il quant la feme a sour l'omme signourie." And when sensuality rules him, he can no longer fulfill the chivalric obligations of his station. To stress this fact, Chaucer tells us that Troilus fears nothing except the loss of Criseyde. He has submitted, in other words, to that fear which can lead to no real good which Andreas describes at the beginning of the *De amore*. The "fire" which burns in the Book of Ecclesiasticus (9. 9), in the description of Libido in the *Psychomachia* of Prudentius, in Lancelot's perilous bed, and in the torch of Venus in the *Roman de la rose* now burns him (lines 436, 445, 449, 490); and he finds himself in the "snare" or "cheyne" which had held Holofernes (Judith 10. 5), Mars (cf. Fig. 71), "Walter," and Guillaume's foolish lover (cf. Fig. 24). Although he seeks renown on the battlefield, he does so

> for non hate he to the Grekes hadde,
> Ne also for the rescous of the town,

but only to make an impression on Criseyde. His virtuous behavior should thus be regarded with what was called "caution." But it offers him little consolation, and he is soon complaining about "destine" and seeking death:

"God wolde I were aryved in the port
Of deth, to which my sorwe wol me lede."

It does lead him there, but not without the aid of Pandarus. All of this woe, we should remember, arises from a mere phantasy in Troilus' mind. He has never talked to Criseyde, knows nothing of her character and manners, and has no idea whether she is a lovable person, a moral weakling, or a shrew. That is, there are very clearly no grounds for true love in Troilus' passion.

The character of Pandarus is a masterpiece of medieval irony. On the surface, he is an attractive little man, wise, witty, and generous. But his wisdom is not of the kind that Lady Philosophy would approve, and his generosity is of the type which supplies gold to the avaricious and dainties to the glutton. His prototype is Jonadab, a "very wise man," and the device he uses to bring the two lovers together is strikingly like that of his Biblical predecessor (2 Kings 13; cf. Figs. 93-95, 108). Beneath his superficially attractive surface, this little grotesque has as his real function that of intermediary between a victim of foolish love and the object of his love. As an intermediary of this kind, he acquires something of the characteristics of a priest. Indeed, there is more than a suggestion in the poem that Pandarus is a blind leader of the blind, a priest of Satan (1. 625-630). It is true that he is not a Mephistophelian figure, for the Devil had not been romanticized when he was created; he is externally pleasant, somewhat commonplace, and a little unctuous. This "devel," as Troilus once jokingly calls him (1. 623),[115] is convincingly decked out in sheep's clothing. His "wit" is no better than his wisdom or his generosity. When we first meet him, his remarks reveal a witty contempt for "remors of conscience," "devocioun," and "holynesse" (1. 551-560). And when Troilus, with the blind unreasonableness of a typical tragic protagonist, complains against Fortune (1. 837), Pandarus can reply only that everyone is subject to Fortune and that she is by nature fickle (1. 844-854). Neither here nor elsewhere does he ever suggest that it is possible to rise above Fortune. He is so "friendly" and so full of pity for Troilus and natural generosity that he offers to get anyone for him if necessary, even his own

[115] Root's punctuation. Pandarus is neither a devil nor a man, but an element in a poem; as a part of a poetic configuration, his actions sometimes suggest those of a devil.

sister (1. 860-861). Much has been made of Pandarus as a "true friend," but friendship in Cicero, Boethius, St. Ailred, Andreas, Jean de Meun, Jehan le Bel, and, in fact, in almost any medieval account of the subject, is based on virtue and cannot lead to vice. Pandarus' offer of his sister is thus an unmistakable clue to his real nature and to the nature of his relationship with Troilus. He has no "psychological" motivation for what he does, and such motivation should not be sought; his actions depend upon the moral structure of his person.

When Pandarus discovers that Criseyde is the object of Troilus' desire, he gives him a little sermon, emphasizing Criseyde's "pitee":

> "And also thynk, and therwith glade the,
> That sith thy lady vertuous is al,
> So foloweth it that there is som pitee
> Amonges al thise other in general;
> And forthi se that thow in special
> Requere nat that is ayeyns hyre name,
> For vertu streccheth nat hym self to shame."

Virtue may "stretch itself" to the kind of "pity" May shows for Damyan, and in Pandarus' view it will not reach the point of "shame" unless someone else finds out about it. Like Lancelot before him, Pandarus has great confidence in Bien Celer. Again, if Criseyde's other "virtues" are like this one, and, indeed, they turn out to be so, they are not very admirable. Pandarus closes his series of admonitions by urging Troilus to repent his earlier remarks about the foolishness of lovers. Like a good priest, he leads his sinner in confession:

> "Now beet thi brest, and sey to god of love:
> 'Thy grace, lord; for now I me repente
> If I mysspak, for now my self I love';
> Thus sey with al thyn herte in good entente."
> Quod Troilus, "A, lord! I me consente,
> And preye to the my japes thow foryive,
> And I shal nevere more whil I live."

Pandarus further admonishes perseverance and devotion, asserting that Criseyde will certainly not devote herself to celestial love:

"Was nevere man nor womman yit bigete
That was unapt to suffren loves hete,
Celestial, or elles love of kynde.
Forthy som grace I hope in here to fynde.

"And for to speken of hire in specyal,
Hire beaute to bithynken, and hire youthe,
It sit hir naught to ben celestial
As yit, though that hire liste bothe and kowthe;
But, trewely, it sate hire wel right nowthe
A worthi knyght to loven and cherice,
And but she do, I holde it for a vice."

The assertion that celestial love would be vicious in a woman so young and beautiful hardly enhances Pandarus' character; in fact, it again suggests its "diabolical" nature. He goes on to say, rather amusingly, that Troilus will serve the God of Love well, and, in fact, be "the beste post . . . of al his lay." When Troilus protests that he means no "harm" or "vilenye," but only what will "sownen into goode," Pandarus laughs at his touch of courtesy, saying, "Am I thy borugh? Fy! No wight doth but so." That is what they all say. Pandarus is perfectly aware that Troilus is not simply interested in what Jehan le Bel called love "par amours"; he knows what Troilus wants and is anxious to get it for him. As for Troilus, he falls on his knees, embraces Pandarus, and submits to him completely. "My lif, my deth, hool in thyn honde I ley," he says. Pandarus, full of worldly wisdom, begins to plan his attack. Troilus plays the lion on the battlefield and, like Damyan, becomes very virtuous,

For he bicome the frendlieste wight,
The gentileste, and eek the moste fre,
The thriftieste, and oon the beste knyght
That in his tyme was, or myghte be.

This is one way in which love can make a man who is "worthy" even "worthier."

At the close of Book 1, Troilus has been struck by the phantasy of Criseyde's beauty, has lodged it firmly in his memory, and, encouraged by Pandarus to hope, has begun the immoderate thought necessary to passion. Wishing to make an impression on Criseyde, he has begun to be "virtuous," without, however, manifesting any real interest either in Criseyde's virtues or in the condition of the city which he is supposed to be defending. Poetically speaking, he defends neither his own heritage nor the "reign" of his mind, which is now beginning to assume the "up-so-doun" condition symbolized in late medieval art by representations of Aristotle with the *pucele* on his back, or by grotesques carrying female companions to the tune of bagpipes (Fig. 117). He has not yet begun to dance, but the dance is arranged for him in Book II, which is a study in false "curtesie," the Curtesie that leads the lover to the dance and finally overcomes the lady's scruples in the *Roman de la rose* or that accompanies Aray and Lust in *The Parliament of Fowls*. This courtesy has nothing to do either with the courtesy of Hector or with the courtesy recommended in the "Instructio regis ad filium Edwardum"; it is, rather, the activity of the unguided lower reason operating with its worldly wisdom in a sophisticated society. To speak of it as "courtly love" would be to take a very small-minded and cynical view indeed of the *mores* of our chivalric ancestors. The book furnishes us with a vivid picture of "manners," but they are the manners of the less noble of Chaucer's noble contemporaries, and are by no means intended as a model to be followed. The activities in the parlor, in the garden, and in the bedchamber combine, in fact, to form one of the first comedies of manners in English. The action opens on May 3, a significant day for lovers.[116] Pandarus, who is doomed to perpetual frustration, is especially downcast on that day. He can lead others down the road to *Amoenitas*, but he can never reach that happy land himself. With many an elegant flourish, he proceeds to guide Criseyde, although, as it turns out, she actually needs little assistance.

The meeting between Pandarus and Criseyde is characterized by a meticulous attention to the social graces. Pandarus finds her with two other ladies, listening to the Tale of Thebes. The story has reached the point where "Amphiorax fil thorugh the ground to helle," an event brought about by the fact that his wife coveted the brooch of Thebes, which, as we learn in "The Complaint of Mars" is a kind of emblem for that which attracts lovers. Pandarus hastily professes a full knowledge of these matters, since it is prob-

---

[116] See John P. McCall, "Chaucer's May 3," *MLN*, LXXVI (1961), 201-205.

able that he has no wish to dwell on their implications. "Lat us daunce," he says, and "don to May some observance." But Criseyde is perfectly aware of the obligations of her status, and knows that it is, or should be, inconsistent with the *amoenitas* of May and the dance of the garden of delight (Fig. 42). "Is that a widewes lif?" she asks.

> "It satte me wel bet ay in a cave
> To bidde, and rede on holy seyntes lyves;
> Lat maydens gon to daunce, and yonge wyves."

The underlying principle in this assertion is from St. Paul, who said (1 Tim. 5. 5-6), "But she that is a widow indeed, and desolate, let her trust in God, and continue in supplications and prayers night and day. For she that liveth in pleasures, is dead while she is living." It was elaborated in St. Augustine's *De bono viduitatis* and became a recognized bit of standard doctrine. At the same time, however, in pastoral theology, a widow was thought to be not altogether responsible, having, presumably, lost the wise guidance of a husband.[117] What St. James describes as "religion clean and undefiled" (James 1. 27), that is, "to visit the fatherless and widows in their tribulation: and to keep one's self unspotted from the world," became a feature of the late medieval chivalric ideal. On the other hand, widows are attractive to lovers whose interests are selfish rather than chivalric; and Criseyde, who is not only a widow but also beautiful, lonely, and fearful, is a peculiarly fetching possibility. With no chivalric motives whatsoever, Pandarus sets about the business of taking advantage of her vulnerable position and her fear, which at this point envisages the dangers of "Grekes." Her fear, it should be noticed, is always self-centered and never actually involves the fear of violating any higher principles, in spite of the fact that she is quick to allude to such principles, as she does in the above instance. Pandarus, playing on her fear of the Greeks, finds an opportunity to praise Troilus at some length, preparing the way for his message. Finally, he cleverly offers to leave without telling her the "good news" he has hinted at, and at the same time repeating his invitation to dance: "let us daunce, and cast youre widwes habit to mischaunce." Whatever May dances he may have

[117] See D. W. Robertson, Jr., and B. F. Huppé, *"Piers Plowman" and Scriptural Tradition* (Princeton, 1951), p. 111.

in mind at the moment, the dance he has in mind ultimately is the "old dance" at which he, although he does not·practise it himself, is an expert.

Criseyde, overcome by feminine curiosity, will not let him leave. He plans very carefully his next Polonius-like bit of strategy (2. 267-273), opening this time with some remarks about good fortune. He who does not make the most of it when it comes, he says, is foolish, seeking to tempt Criseyde with rumors of prosperity. She remains fearful, so that he can reveal his message safely. When he does so, he repeats the familiar line that Troilus will die if he does not get her. Indeed, he will cut his own throat too. "With that, the teris burste out of his eyen." All of this is obviously a carefully prepared bit of acting. It is followed by a long sentimental lament, which has the desired effect of increasing Criseyde's fear. He is, he asserts, not a "baude," although it is perfectly obvious that that is exactly what he is. All he wants, he says, is "love of frendshipe," a "lyne" which Diomede uses with great success later on (5. 185). We may recall the same stratagem in the dialogues of the *De amore*. Friendship, as Raison explains in the *Roman de la rose*, has nothing to do with the pleasurable satisfactions of the flesh, but Criseyde is very much aware of what Pandarus and Troilus are actually after: "I shal felen what ye mene, ywis." But after Pandarus has driven his point home with a little false philosophy from Wisdom 2, which is highly irrelevant to the subject of "friendship," Criseyde feigns shock and astonishment. At this, Pandarus pretends to be hurt by her suspicions and offers to go, but she catches his garment and agrees to "save" Troilus provided that she can also save her "honor." Like Fenice in Chrétien's *Cligés*, Criseyde has a great deal to say on this subject, but the "honor" she seeks to preserve is the honor of appearances, a middle-class virtue dear to the heart of the Franklin's hero Arveragus, but not altogether harmonious with the "aristocratic" qualities some modern critics have wished to see in her behavior. It is simply the hollow "reputation" cherished by the lovers in the *De amore* which Lancelot was so spectacularly successful at maintaining.

But to reassure Criseyde, Pandarus offers a little picture of Troilus as he expresses his love. In a "gardyn," which is thematic rather than scenic, Troilus is depicted "by a welle" confessing his sins to Cupid:

484

> "Lord, have routhe upon my peyne.
> Al have I ben rebell in myn entente,
> Now *mea culpa*, Lord, I me repente...."

Clearly, if Troilus has gone this far, he will not easily be disengaged, but if Criseyde had been a careful reader of the *Roman de la rose*, she might have recognized the little scene described for her as the beginning of a nightmare. Again, Troilus is depicted lamenting in bed. Pandarus assures Criseyde that his "entente is clene," and then, almost immediately, observes,

> "Ther were nevere two so wel ymet,
> Whan ye ben his al hool, as he is youre.
> Ther myghty god yit graunte us see that houre."

Criseyde understands what this implies, and pretends shock. But Pandarus is able to gloss over what he has said with little effort:

> "Nay! Thereof spak I nought, a ha!" quod she—
> "As helpe me god, ye shenden every deel."
> "A, mercy! dere nece," anon quod he,
> "What so I spak, I mente nat but wel,
> By Mars, the god that helmed is of steel.
> Now beth nat wroth, my blood, my nece dere."
> "Now wel," quod she, "foryeven be it here."

What Pandarus means by "meaning well" has long since been apparent. Criseyde's forgiveness is also interesting in view of the fact that she has never seen Troilus to know him. When she does see him, shortly thereafter, the serpent lifts its head again, this time in a somewhat more calculating way than it did when Troilus saw Criseyde. The lady's eyes betray her:

> Criseyda gan al his chere aspien,
> And leet it so softe in hire herte synke,
> That to hire self she seyde, "Who yaf me drynke?"

When Troilus saw Criseyde, he thought only of her "figure." In addition to his shape, however, she considers his prowess, estate, reputation, wit, and lineage. These things all contribute to a vast self-satisfaction:

> But moost hire favour was, for his distresse
> Was al for hire . . . .

Ultimately, her love is a self-love that seeks the favor of Fortune. The stars have something to do with it (2. 680-686). Criseyde will always be true to herself; she will always seek to escape from the fear of misfortune, no matter what effects her actions may have on others. If Troilus wishes to turn the order of things "up-so-doun" by submitting to her, she is equally determined that no husband will rule her:

> "Shal noon housbonde seyn to me 'chek mat';
> For either they ben ful of jalousie,
> Or maisterful, or loven novelrye."

The mastery of a man like Troilus, a man of prowess and renown, a prince, and a handsome prince at that, would be quite an achievement.

In the remainder of Book II we are given some lessons in "Messagerie," which accompanies "Foolhardinesse," "Flaterye," "Desyr," and "Meede" in the Temple of Venus (*PF*, 227-228). Pandarus instructs Troilus carefully in the art of writing an effective love-letter in which one says not necessarily what one thinks or feels, but what will have the desired effect on the recipient. Among effective objective correlatives, a few tears shed in the right places may help. Criseyde, having reluctantly, or coyly, permitted Pandarus to thrust Troilus' literary efforts into her bosom, knows well enough how to write an artfully ambiguous reply. When she sees Troilus again, she again reacts to externals:

> To telle in short, hire liked al in fere
> His person, his aray, his look, his chere.

Meanwhile, the increased hope inspired by Criseyde's letter makes the "fir" of Troilus' desire hotter than ever. And Pandarus arranges his little plot to bring the young lovers together. The plot involves lying to Deiphebus, to Hector, to Helen, and to Paris, not to mention lying a little also to Criseyde, preying on her fear with a tale about "false Poliphete." Having made these very "honorable" arrangements, Pandarus informs Troilus about them, urging him to keep faith with an echo of Christ's words in the Gospels (Luke 8. 48, 18. 42): "Thou shalt be saved by thy feythe in trouthe." Needless to say, no one in Chaucer's audience would have needed to be reminded of the Augustinian principle that "If

486

anyone engages his faith to commit a sin, it is not faith." There is little possibility that the Franklin of *The Canterbury Tales* was in his audience. In any event, Troilus, in whom desire has overcome rational perspective, is overjoyed—"so glad was he never in al his lyve." He is quite willing to feign sickness like his illustrious predecessor Amnon so that he and Criseyde may come together, like Adam and Eve still earlier, "under cover of lies."[118] When the company is assembled with Deiphebus, and Troilus' "illness" is being discussed, Criseyde once more reveals the pride and self-love upon which her "love" for Troilus is based:

> For which with sobre chiere hire herte lough;
> For who is that nolde hire glorifie,
> To mowen swiche a knight don lyve or dye?

She shows no real sympathy for the poor boy at all. This is the love for which Troilus meets his death, the lady for whom he sacrifices his wisdom, his honor, and his obligation to his country. As Pandarus leads Criseyde toward the chamber where Troilus lies, he preaches her a little sermon containing a *sententia* which might well serve as the motto of Book II, and, at the same time, as an emblem for Pandarus himself: "Whil folk is blent, lo! al the tyme is wonne." Whose doctrine is this?

In Book III there is a great deal of religious imagery. Literary historians are apt to say that it is "conventional" and that it reflects the traditions of "courtly love." No one in the book, however, uses religion as an adjunct to courtesy. And Chaucer certainly does not "accept" the behavior of Troilus. The religious imagery serves exactly the same function it serves in Chrétien's *Chevalier de la charrete*: to suggest the values which the hero inverts and, at the same time, to furnish opportunity for ironic humor. Specifically, the religious imagery serves to show the corruption of the higher reason in Troilus as it submits completely to the wiles of the lower reason in pursuit of sensual satisfaction. When Troilus comes to regard the "grace" of Criseyde as a kind of divine Providence, his fall is complete. In the opening scene, both the religion and the humor are displayed. Troilus is busy concocting proper speeches to use when Criseyde approaches, but when Criseyde arrives, thinking

[118] See "The Doctrine of Charity in Medieval Literary Gardens," *Speculum,* XXVI (1951), pp. 25-26.

of the avowed purpose of her visit, she asks him for "continuance" of his "lordshipe." Troilus is no Hector, and "lordshipe" is the last thing he wants to hold over her; indeed, it is the last thing she wishes him to have, so that the request puts the poor man in some confusion. All he can do is finally to mumble, "mercy, mercy, swete herte!" When he regains a little composure, he asks her, in effect, for "ladyship," and concludes by saying that since he has spoken to her, he can do no more: "Now recche I never how soone that I deye." This "manly sorwe," of what might better be called an "unseemly woman in a seeming man," impresses Pandarus, who, shedding some well-timed tears, digs Criseyde persistently in the ribs:

> And Pandare wep as he to water wolde,
> And poked evere his nece newe and newe,
> And seyde: "Wo bigon ben hertes trewe!
> For love of god, make of this thing an ende,
> Or sle us bothe at ones, or ye wende."

Criseyde pretends prettily not to understand. But after some pre-liminaries in which Troilus promises to put himself, of all places, under her "yerde," and Criseyde stipulates that she will keep her "honour sauf," retaining, at the same time, in spite of her earlier request, the "sovereignete," she assures Troilus that he will for every woe "recovere a blisse." She then takes him in her arms and kisses him. This is a triumph for Pandarus, an event of truly litur-gical significance for our little priest, the *elevatio* of his mass for which the bells all ring:

> Fil Pandarus on knees, and up his eyen
> To hevene threw, and held his hondes hye.
> "Immortal god," quod he, "that mayst nat dyen—
> Cupide, I mene—of this mayst glorifie.
> And Venus, thow mayst maken melodie.
> Withouten hond, me semeth that in towne,
> For this miracle, ich here ech belle sowne."

God, or at least Cupid, is rapidly drawing matters to what Alisoun of Bath would call a "fruitful" eventuality. This is the "miracle" Pandarus has hoped for; soon, perhaps, he can prepare the way for his communion, a "revel" accompanied by the old "melodie" of Venus:

"But I conjure the, Criseyde, and oon,
And two, thow, Troilus, whan thow mayst goon,
That at myn hous ye ben at my warnynge,
For I ful wel shall shape youre comynge."

Criseyde's "honour sauf" through the good offices of Bien Celer, the two young people will, of course, engage in a little light conversation:

"And eseth there youre hertes right ynough.
And lat se which of yow shal bere the belle
To speke of love aright"—therwith he lough.

Troilus is now quite ready to walk, perhaps even to dance, and very anxious to talk—"How longe shal I dwelle, or this be don?" Evidently the few words spoken earlier were not really enough before death takes him, after all. But Eleyne and Deiphebus approach, so that Troilus, to keep his "honour sauf," falls to groaning, "his brother and his suster for to blende." He is a king's son; his country is in danger of destruction by a foreign enemy. But he has a fiddle, or bagpipe, to play too.

When Pandarus and Troilus are alone again, Pandarus decides to confess openly what he has been doing all along. Troilus will not now object. He has become, he says, "bitwixen game and ernest" a "meene" between a man and a woman. This sentimental statement has won for Pandarus many adherents in addition to the one being addressed. But the "game," as Book II abundantly illustrates, was always simply a pleasant and clever device to ameliorate his real intention, to put a "witty" and hence "harmless" face on the matter; and the "ernest," involving such matters as his priestly services for Cupid, could have been directed toward no other end than the one now contemplated. He admonishes Troilus seriously and at length to keep counsel, to treasure Criseyde's reputation. A boasting lover is a liar, he explains, and we know that Pandarus detests lies and liars. Troilus returns a solemn promise. The surfaces must be kept clean. As for Pandarus' pandering, in Troilus' mind it was only "gentilesse," "compassioun," "felawship," and "trist." To show that he too has these noble virtues, which are typical of those fostered by Cupid and are best regarded "cautiously," Troilus says that he will be glad to do the same for Pandarus. His sisters, for example, or Helen, might please that gentleman:

"I have my faire suster, Polixene,
Cassandre, Eleyne, or any of the frape.
Be she nevere so faire or wel yshape,
Tel me which thow wilt of everychone
To han for thyn, and lat me thanne allone.

Whether any of the "frape" are suitable or not—and their suitabil-
ity seems to be a matter of shapeliness—Troilus is anxious to finish
his business. He is thirstier than ever: "Parforme it out, for now
is most nede." Those in Chaucer's audience who remembered
Polixene's moving defense of her virginity as she was about to be
sacrificed upon the grave of Achilles—"scilicet haud ulli servire
Polixena vellet!"—might have detected perhaps a touch of dis-
courtesy in Troilus' "courtly" offer. But the modern reader may
be inclined to echo literally the wonderment of Andreas: "O what
a wonderful thing is love, which makes a man shine with so many
virtues and teaches everyone, no matter who he is, so many good
traits of character!" Nobility, compassion, fellowship, and trust
are certainly not to be sneezed at, especially when they are mentioned openly in the text so that their presence is incontrovertible.

After the first exchange of courtesies at Deiphebus' house, Pandarus keeps at his task, "evere ylike prest and diligent" to "quicke
alwey the fir." He is no man to put the fire out, as should a true
priest or a true friend, moved by a certain Boethian pity. In his
"messagerie" he is very busy, arranging the proposed conversation
at his house. Troilus devises an excuse to explain any absences from
his usual haunts. He will be at the Temple of Apollo watching the
"holy laurer." The chaste laurel, as Neckam tells us, is placed in
the Temple of Apollo "to show that wisdom is imperishable."[119]
But Troilus seems to have no real interest either in wisdom or in
abstract truth, and Criseyde is no Laura. When Pandarus finally
invites Criseyde to "supper," he swears that Troilus is not there,
although he knows full well that Troilus is waiting in his little
"stuwe." There is a very hard rain, encouraged by a sign of disas-
ter in the heavens. Criseyde can make her way through it to Pandarus' house, but not back again. She "koude as muche good as
half a world."

[119] *Super Marcianum*, Oxford, Bodl., MS Digby 221, fol. 61 verso. Holcot,
Super librum ecclesiastici (Venice, 1509), pp. 9 recto and verso, explains in detail that the crown of Apollo is the crown of wisdom. Apollo was generally associated with wisdom or truth.

Pandarus gets her safely bedded and goes after Troilus. Still unmindful of Pallas, and not actually very much concerned about the laurel of Apollo, Troilus says a little prayer to "Seint Venus," whose energies he will need in "hevene blisse." But before the lovers may be united, yet one more ruse is needed, another lie to get Troilus "honorably" into Criseyde's chamber. Never at a loss in such matters, Pandarus devises a little story of jealousy by means of which he finally, after a great deal of dissimulated hesitation on Criseyde's part, manages to arouse the lady's "pitee," so that she agrees to see her lover. But unfortunately the two find it necessary to engage in considerable talk, to "speke of love," as Pandarus had promised. They are impeded further by Troilus' confusion brought about by his own lies. He is so troubled that he falls "a-swowne." Pandarus, ever ready with a sentimental remedy, tosses him in bed and disrobes him "al to his bare sherte," admonishing Criseyde to "pullen out the thorn." But even after Troilus recovers, more talk ensues before Troilus, "sodeynly avysed," embraces his lady. Pandarus, at last satisfied that his services are no longer needed, since, after all, Faus Semblant may be abandoned when the goal is obvious to everyone concerned, offers a bit of parting counsel: "swouneth nat now." When Troilus tells Criseyde that she must yield, she replies,

> "Ne hadde I or now, my swete herte deere,
> Ben yolde, I were now nat here."

As Diomede later demonstrates, the very elaborate efforts of Pandarus were not really necessary. As the two enter their bliss, Chaucer warns the ladies in his audience,

> For love of god, take every woman heede
> To werken thus, when it comth to the neede.

When the "need" arises will depend, of course, on which god one loves. Criseyde, perceiving what strikes her as his "trouthe and clene entente," makes Troilus a joyful "feste." In the resulting "hevene," at a feast which is not exactly the Feast of the Lamb, Troilus appropriately sings a hymn. This hymn is in part a paraphrase of St. Bernard's prayer to the Virgin in the last canto of Dante's *Paradise*, in the original an aspect of the New Song of Jerusalem, but in Troilus' version a song to Cupid, ironically called

"Charite." It is the grace of Cupid which Troilus praises, a grace to which at this time he can offer only "laude and reverence," but which will appear to him later in all of its bitterness. He has lost sight of Providence and turned instead to the "grace" of Fortune. He is no longer a free agent, no longer a man. He is a pawn to Fortune, a star-crossed lover, Fortune's fool. The priest of Satan has led him to his highest sacrament. But the "unequal weights" of the God of Love will soon make themselves apparent, and the follower of Venus will find himself naked in the sea.

The "hevene" in which Troilus finds himself is not without its qualms, the "doutances" which he foresaw before his eye fell upon Criseyde. The blessed are afraid in the midst of their bliss, as Andreas tells us they should be; they find

> That ech from other wende ben biraft,
> Or elles, lo! this was hir mooste feere,
> Lest al this thyng but nyce dremes were.

Indeed, joys of this kind are dreams, revels soon ended and rounded with a sleep. The lovers are disturbed by the parting of the night, a necessary adjunct to the deed of darkness; and they curse the light of day, that "candel of jelosye," as the sun is called in "The Complaint of Mars," which follows Venus over the horizon and puts every degenerate Mars to shame. This love cannot withstand the light of truth and reason. Parting is torture for the lovers, especially for the fearful Troilus (3. 1472-1491). Although he treasures Criseyde's solaces more than "thise worldes tweyne," after he has left her he is far from being satisfied. If he was tormented by desire before, he is tormented more than ever now. As one old moralist put it, "And just as the fire does not diminish as long as the fuel is applied, but rather becomes hotter and more fervent when more fuel is cast upon it, so also the sin of lechery burns more fiercely the more it is exercised."[120] Pandarus brings the lovers together occasionally,

> And thus Fortune a tyme ledde in joie
> Criseyde and ek this kinges sone of Troie.

This is the uncertain bliss, the fearful joy, for which Troilus has relinquished his "estat roial." To protect himself, he makes his

[120] Gerard of Liège, ed. Wilmart, *Analecta reginensia* (Vatican, 1933), p. 201.

own feeling a cosmic force, this time paraphrasing Boethius on Divine Love, for which he substitutes a generalization of his own idolatrous lust (3. 1744-1771). The pleasure he finds in Criseyde's bed has become the center of his universe, a center that actually rests within himself.

"But al to litel," as Chaucer says at the beginning of Book IV, "lasteth swich joie, ythonked be Fortune." Fortune can "to fooles so hire song entune" that they become, as it were, asses to the harp of Philosophy's harmonies. Troilus is one of these fools. If he called for night and cursed the day, Night's daughters "that endeles compleynen evere in peyne" control him. As events progress, cupidity with its jealousy, and wrath with its desire for vengeance join libido. Specifically, the "unwar strook" which unsettles his proud realm appears when he learns that Criseyde is to join the Greek camp in exchange for Antenor. Thinking of her "honour," Troilus can do nothing to arrest the transaction. In despair he is like a bare tree (4. 225-231), for the false words of his idolatry no longer protect him. As he mourns alone in his chamber, he is like a "wylde bole," whose wild acts "denote the unreasonable fury of a beast." He complains bitterly against Fortune, asking, "is there no grace?" He has honored Fortune, he says, above all other gods always; his subjection is complete and self-confessed. He also blames "the verrey lord of love," Cupid, whose "grace" but a short time ago was all-pervasive. Actually, his difficulty is of his own making. "Nothyng is wrecchid but whan thou wenest it," said Boethius, but Troilus has made of himself a prisoner. Nothing destined him to subject himself to Fortune or to Cupid, but his reason has lost "the lordshipe that it sholde have over the sensualitee," and he is a hopeless thrall in the chains of Venus. Pandarus can offer no real comfort. No person, he says, can "fynden in Fortune ay proprietee." He knows that Fortune is fickle and recommends expediency: he can find Troilus another. But Troilus is no mere sinner in the flesh, and Ovid's remedies will not help him. The only feasible solution seems to him to be suicide, the final act of despair and the ultimate sin against the true love for which he has substituted a false one. Criseyde's condition is almost as bad. With a touch of the comedy of manners developed in Book II, Chaucer shows her beset by her familiar companions, a group of chattering women, full of the gossip of her departure. She thinks of herself "born in cursed constellacioun," subject to the stars. She will do herself to death. Pandarus finds her with her "sonnysh heeris" falling untended about her ears, like *Tristitia* in a picture (Fig. 118), a condition which indicates in her a desire for martyrdom.

In the process of arranging another meeting between the two lovers, Pandarus discovers Troilus despairing in a temple. The frustrated prince laments that "al that comth, comth by necessite" and that to be lost is his "destinee." This conclusion is followed by a long supporting discussion based on Boethius in which Troilus confuses "absolute" and "conditional" necessity in a way that would have taxed the patience of Lady Philosophy and astonished Bishop Bradwardine, who was not quite so unorthodox on this matter as a recent study seeks to make him. The purpose of the discussion is to show that Troilus has so far abandoned reason that he has practically no free will left. He has become a slave to his desire, a victim of Cupid, prepared for his position painted on the wall of Venus' Temple, along with Tristan, Achilles, Paris, and other worthies of his cause. When his love fails, "chaos is come again," a chaos in his own mind resulting from the universalization of a selfish passion. If he has so far abandoned reason that he can no longer choose, destiny, which controls the operation of Providence in particular instances among unreasoning creatures, will envelop him. Again, Pandarus is of little help. His "wise" philosophy is mere shallow Stoicism:[121]

> "Lat be, and thynk right thus in thi disese:
> That in the dees right as ther fallen chaunces,
> Right so in love ther come and gon plesaunces."

The old doctrine of "happes aventurous" can afford no real help to Troilus, just as it cannot help Boethius in the *Consolation*.

The lovers meet once more. Criseyde is so overcome that she swoons. Thinking her dead, Troilus offers to kill himself in Prome-

[121] The Stoicism of Pandarus should be distinguished sharply from the philosophy of Boethius, whose lady complains (1 pr. 3) that the Stoics and Epicureans have torn shreds and patches from her garment. Pandarus is an Epicurean with respect to pleasure and a Stoic with respect to pain—a position that is hardly unusual. He seeks, in other words, to harden himself against what Boethius regarded as the lessons of both good and bad fortune. For further discussion, see Alan Gaylord, "Uncle Pandarus as Lady Philosophy," *Papers of the Michigan Academy*, XLVI (1961), 571-595.

thean defiance (4. 1192ff.). He will conquer Fortune by committing suicide, a device attempted by Nero in the Monk's Tale, "Of
which Fortune lough, and hadde a game." Since neither Jove nor
Fortune is responsible for his plight, Troilus' defiance is a little
hollow. It is especially hollow when we consider the character of
the lady whose pleasant capabilities with reference to himself he
finds more important than either his country or life itself. When
she awakens, she finds a characteristic solution to their mutual problem. If reason fails, something else might help:

> "But hoo, for we han right ynough of this,
> And lat us rise and streight to bedde go,
> And there lat us speken of oure wo."

But there is no king in this bed of justice. When Troilus suggests
that they "stele awey," Criseyde replies that if they did so, people
would accuse them of "lust voluptuous and coward drede," weaknesses, naturally, of which Troilus would never be guilty. Moreover, she herself would lose her "honeste." She engages in a long
and verbose promise of fidelity connected with that ancient symbol
of fickle Fortune, the moon. Her doctrine is considerably better
than that offered by Pandarus:

> "And forthi sle with resoun al this hete;
> Men seyn, 'the suffrant overcomth,' pardee;
> Ek, 'whoso wol han lief, he lief mot lete'.
> Thus maketh vertu of necessite
> By pacience, and thynk that lord is he
> Of Fortune ay, that naught wol of hire recche;
> And she ne daunteth no wight but a wrecche."

Criseyde can paraphrase Boethius and mean what she says, but
since she has no notion of how to apply her words, they become,
as Andreas' lady puts it, "more than empty." There is no stopping
the heat of the fire lighted at the festival of Pallas now, and Criseyde's bed is no place to slay heat with reason. Neither Troilus
nor Criseyde actually has any notion of how to become "lord of
Fortune." She knows also that "love is a thyng ay ful of bisy
drede," but this fact is adduced as a reason for Troilus to remain faithful, not as something to discourage him from being a

"wrecche." The book closes with one final touch of irony. Criseyde explains her love for Troilus:

> "For trusteth wel, that youre estat roial,
> Ne veyn delit, nor only worthinesse
> Of yow in werre or torney marcial,
> Ne pomp, array, nobleye, or ek richesse,
> Ne made me to rewe on youre distresse;
> But moral vertu, grounded upon trouthe,
> That was the cause I first hadde on yow routhe.
>
> "Ek gentil herte and manhood that ye hadde,
> And that ye hadde, as me thoughte, in despit
> Every thyng that souned into badde,
> As rudenesse and poeplissh appetit,
> And that youre resoun bridlede youre delit,—
> This made, aboven every creature,
> That I was youre, and shal, whil I may dure."

If this had been true, the lovers would not now be in difficulty— if Troilus had used his reason from the beginning and loved Criseyde for something more than her pleasing "figure" and surpassing competence in bed. This might have been true if Criseyde had actually been interested in "vertu" rather than in Troilus' "persone, his aray, his look, his chere," and in the further fact that the woe of this man of great estate was all for her. But as it stands, this little picture could not be more false, more distant from the furtive actions that Chaucer has described. Troilus' courtship was grounded on a tissue of lies rather than on "trouthe." Both he and Criseyde insisted on an "up-so-doun" relationship directly contrary to reason and honor. And Troilus very carefully renounced, under the direction of Pandarus, his denunciations of "poeplissh appetit." Criseyde can always think of some elevated doctrine to rationalize her situation, but she perverts it into so much idle talk. And idle talk cannot now save Troilus from pains "that passen every torment down in helle."

Book v is a picture of Hell on earth, the Hell which results from trying to make earth a heaven in its own right. In medieval terms, when the human heart is turned toward God and the reason is adjusted to discern the action of Providence beneath the apparently fortuitous events of daily life, the result is the City of Jerusalem, radiant and harmonious within the spirit. But when the will desires its own satisfaction in the world alone, the reason can perceive only the deceptive mutability of Fortune. And the result, as one cloud-capp'd tower after another fades away, is the confusion and chaos of Babylon, the world without Christ so mercilessly described in Innocent's *De miseria humane conditionis.* Troilus has defied the gods and placed Criseyde above them. When adversity strikes, he becomes the "aimlessly drifting megalopolitan man" of the modern philosophers, the frustrated, neurotic, and maladjusted hero of modern fiction, an existentialist for whom Being itself, which he has concentrated in his own person, becomes dubious. He is hypersensitive, sentimental, a romantic hopelessly involved in a lost cause. These are, however, the results of a moral process, not the operations of a psychology. Cupidity not only isolates a man from God; it also isolates him from the free society of his fellows, who can no longer afford him any satisfactions when the idol of his lust has vanished away. In this last Book, as the Parcae dominate the unreasoning creature that Troilus has become,[122] Chaucer's ironic humor becomes bitter and the pathos of the tragedy profound.

It is Troilus who leads Criseyde out of town to meet the Greek convoy. All he can do, in spite of dreams of violence, is to mutter, "Now hold youre day, and do me nat to deye." Diomede recognizes the general features of the situation at once, being an old hand at love's stratagems. He takes Criseyde by the "reyne," and for a short time the little filly will be his, but she has no bridle that will hold her to "any certayn ende." Like Polonius or Iago, Diomede is a man true to himself: "He is a fool that wol foryete hym selve." Since he has nothing to lose but words, he begins the old game played by Pandarus in Book II, but without circuitous preliminaries. Just as Pandarus requested at first love of "frendshipe," Diomede asks to be treated as a "brother" and to have his friendship accepted. He will be hers, he says, "aboven every creature," a thing he has said to no woman before. This is the first time. This is different. And sure enough, by the time they reach the Greek

[122] The Parcae, invoked at the beginning of Book v, are said by Neckam, *Super Marcianum*, Oxford, Bodl., MS Digby 221, fol. 40 verso, to represent the "operations of Providence in worldly affairs."

camp, Criseyde grants him her "frendshipe." She has nothing to lose either and can be thoroughly depended upon to be to her own self true. In the Greek camp, Diomede does not neglect his opportunity. "To fisshen hire, he leyde out hook and lyne." On her "day," when she was supposed to return to Troilus, she welcomes Diomede as a "frend," and is soon lying to save appearances again:

> "I hadde a lord, to whom I wedded was,
> The whos myn herte al was til that he deyde;
> And other love, as help me now Pallas,
> Ther in myn herte nys, ne nevere was."

She allows Pallas to be of small assistance, for at the close of her conversation she gives Diomede her glove. Her fear helps Diomede, just as it had helped Pandarus. Moreover, Diomede is a man of "grete estat," a conquest to please her vanity. That night she goes to bed

> Retornyng in hire soule ay up and down
> The wordes of this sodeyn Diomede,
> His grete estat, the peril of the town,
> And that she was allone and hadde nede
> Of frendes help. And thus bygan to brede
> The cause whi, the sothe for to telle
> That she took fully purpos for to dwelle.

"Wo hym that is allone." These are the same causes that led her to succumb to Troilus, for she was also fearful and alone in Troy, and Troilus was a man of "estat roial." Clearly, "moral vertu, grounded upon trouthe" has nothing to do with either affair. Criseyde has not changed at all. She is beautiful and socially graceful, but fearful, susceptible to sentimental pity, and "slydynge of corage." When the die is cast, and Diomede has what he wants, she says, "To Diomede algate I wol be trewe." She meant to be true to Troilus too, but she is actually faithful only to her own selfish desires of the moment. Her beauty is the sensuous beauty of the world, and her fickleness is the fickleness of Fortune; but she is, at the same time, a sort of feminine Everyman. The world's poor sinners seldom go as far in idolatry as does Troilus or have the enterprise of "sodeyn Diomede." But the average man or woman can very sincerely say all the right things while pursuing selfish ends. This is the reason that Chaucer warns his readers not to condemn Criseyde. She is no gay deceiver, no strumpet, and no mere graceless wench. But her conception of honor is pitifully inadequate, as is her understanding of virtue and truth. In the fourteenth century "sincerity" had not yet been elevated to its present eminence, so that it does not palliate her misdeeds; but it does make Criseyde a pitiable creature whom we can look upon with that compassion which Chaucer recommends to us at the beginning of his poem. Neither Criseyde nor Diomede, both of whom seek momentary footholds on the slippery way of the world, is capable of the idolatry of which Troilus is guilty, or of the depths to which he descends.

Left alone in Troy, Troilus curses all the gods together, including Cupid and Venus. But he is still a slave to his cupidity, a "great natural," who has no place to hide his bauble. In bed he wallows and turns like "Ixion in helle," for he has nothing but a pillow to embrace.[123] His "lode sterre," which has turned out to be no *Stella Maris*, has gone. In sleep, he is beset by nightmares. He dreams that he is alone in a horrible place, that he has fallen among his enemies, that he has fallen from a high place. These are symbolic revelations of his actual situation, and Troilus receives small comfort from the Pertelote-like scorn that Pandarus casts upon them. Pandarus gets him off "to Sarpedoun," who provides singing and dancing, but there is no "melodie" left for Troilus without Criseyde. The celestial source of the world's harmony, is, as it were, entertaining Diomede in the Greek camp. Troilus spends his time, like a jilted schoolboy, moping over his beloved's old letters. Hastening back to Troy, he hopes to find his lady there, but in vain. The places where he has seen or enjoyed Criseyde have a perverse fascination for him. First, having found an excuse to go into town, he visits her house. When he sees it, he exclaims,

> "O paleys desolat,
> O hous of houses whilom best ihight,
> O paleys empty and disconsolat,
> O thow lanterne of which queynt is the light,
> O paleys, whilom day, that now art nyght!"

[123] Trivet, London, BM, MS Burney 131, fol. 49 verso, explains that Ixion sought the love of Juno. That is, he sought libidinous delight in the active life. He revolves on a wheel because a man dedicated to temporal affairs is "continually elevated by prosperity and cast down by adversity."

The ironic pun on "queynt" is a bitter comment on what it is that
Troilus actually misses, and the change from day to night is, ironically again, the fulfillment of his wish in Book III. The house is
a shrine "of which the seynt is oute," the empty inverted church
of Troilus' love. Everywhere he goes, he finds memories of Criseyde. He becomes intensely self-conscious, aware of the eye of
every passing stranger on the street. Everyone sees his woe:

> Another tyme ymaginen he wolde,
> That every wight that wente by the weye
> Hadde of him routhe, and that they seyn sholde:
> "I am right sorry Troilus wol deye."

His spirit is the painful focus of creation, protected neither by the
"harde grace" of Cupid, nor by his empty hopes that Criseyde
may return. Each new rationalization leads only to more bitter frustration. On the walls of the city the very wind itself blows from
Criseyde straight to him, and as it blows it sighs, "Allas, why
twynned be we tweyne?" Criseyde lurks in the form of every
distant traveller, even in a "fare-cart." At last, jealousy adds to
Troilus' discomfort, and with it comes another nightmare. He
tries an exchange of letters, but the artfulness of Criseyde's epis-
tolary style is now painfully apparent. One day he sees the brooch
he gave her on parting on Diomede's armor. Now his worst fears
are confirmed: "Of Diomede have ye al this feste?" The jealousy
of carnal love overcomes Troilus completely, and the furies dominate his heart. Pandarus' shallow reaction—"I hate, ywis, Criseyde!"—is no comfort, and in the depths of despair Troilus goes
out to seek Diomede in vengeance and his own death on the battlefield. His is no heroic defense of the city, no fulfillment of his
political obligations, but a quest for Megara's vengeance and his
own destruction. This is the ultimate loneliness, a loneliness he has
brought upon himself. So far as vengeance is concerned, Troilus
fails, fortunately for Criseyde, but "Ful pitously him slough the
fierce Achille."

If Fortune "lough" at the self-destruction of Nero in the
Monk's Tale, Troilus can, in spirit, share that laughter as he rises
through the spheres above Fortune's realm toward a destiny of
which his own last acts are a sufficient indication. When the flesh
with its cumbersome desires has been left behind, he sees the fool-

ishness of his earthly plight. There, the "jugement is more cleere, the wil nat icorrumped":

> And in hym self he lough right at the wo
> Of hem that wepten for his deth so faste,
> And dampned al oure werk that folweth so
> The blynde lust, the which that may nat laste;
> And sholden al oure herte on heven caste.

The laughter is the ironic laughter with which Chaucer depicts Troilus' "wo" from the beginning, a laughter which he, and Troilus from his celestial vantage point, would bestow on all those who take a sentimental attitude toward such love as that between Troilus and Criseyde. If, in the course of the poem, the plight of Troilus has moved us to compassion, we too can laugh, partly at ourselves.

Toward the end of *Troilus and Criseyde* Chaucer includes two stanzas in what St. Augustine would have called "high style":

> O yonge fresshe folkes, he or she,
> In which that love up groweth with youre age,
> Repeyreth hom fro worldly vanyte,
> And of youre herte up casteth the visage
> To thilke god that after his ymage
> Yow made, and thynketh al nys but a faire
> This world, that passeth soone as floures faire.

> And loveth hym which that right for love
> Upon a cros, oure soules for to beye,
> First starf, and roos, and sit in hevene above;
> For he nyl falsen no wight, dar I seye,
> That wol his herte al holly on hym leye.
> And syn he best to love is, and most meke,
> What nedeth feyned loves for to seke?

This, in effect, is what Chaucer has to tell us about love, not only here but in *The Canterbury Tales* and in the major allegories as well. It is his "o sentence." It is, of course, also the message of the Bible, of the *Consolation of Philosophy*, of Andreas Capellanus, of Chrétien de Troyes, and of a great many other medieval writers. The idea, indeed, was a part of the normal expectation of the medieval reader, and to say that an author intends it is simply to say that he is a Christian. The artist or poet, knowing that if left to itself in its abstract form it might become as empty as Criseyde's moral philosophy, sought to get at it indirectly, at the same time giving it a renewed vigor, incisiveness, and applicability in terms that a given audience could understand. To appreciate the value of Chaucer's artistry, we must seek to comprehend, insofar as our historical knowledge permits, the reasons why that artistry appealed strongly to his contemporaries. It does not stand alone, but depends for its effectiveness, like the artistry of any other period, on what the audience brings to it. No art reproduces nature or conveys ideas with absolute fullness; it simply affords hints which the observer rounds out in his own mind. The fact that our minds are conditioned to respond to the hints and stratagems of art in very different ways from those with which court audiences of the late fourteenth century responded to them makes the task of recovering Chaucer's art extremely difficult. If Troilus standing on the windy walls saw Criseyde in the form of a cart, we also, with the predispositions supplied to us by modern poetry, fiction, and music, may be likely to see Chaucer's poem as a celebration of the tragic potentialities in a relatively innocent romantic love affair. But it is improbable that Chaucer wrote either to titillate the young or to supply pap for the fancied appetites of the aged. He had instead a philosophical message of some profundity to impart, a message which, if properly elaborated, could be just as moving as any celebration of romantic love. It was not original with him; but the peculiar luminosity with which he presented it was his own achievement.

How does Chaucer develop his *sentence* in *The Canterbury Tales?* Since the collection is incomplete, and the final arrangement unsettled, this question has no precise answer. But the Prologue opens in April with the sun in Taurus, when nature moves her creatures to love (Fig. 113) and the renewal of the earth suggests the renewal of the spirit. The character of the pilgrimage as it is carried out by the individual pilgrims depends on how they love; their tales, the revelations of human will and motive in speech, are manifestations of the love of the speakers. The aberrations of love and the solutions to the problems they give rise to are kept constantly before the audience. Everyone, in one way or another, through the promptings of Venus or Mars or some other "deity," is a Melibeus who drinks too deeply of the world and loses that innocence which shines from the tale of the prioress as if in answer to her prayer. There are few Custances, Griseldas, or St. Cecelias in the world, and it is difficult for most of us to keep our hierarchies right side up. When they are overturned, our only solution is penance, and there are not enough pardoners among us to make it impractical. Hence the collection ends appropriately with a sermon on the subject. Penance undertaken to "spare heaven as we love it," not "as we stand in fear," releases the floods of God's love for mankind and leads to peace on earth for those who seek it with good will. In Chaucer's world not many sought it, and his problem as an artist was to encourage their thirst for it. It may be that many of us cannot look upon ideas such as these without cynicism. They are, we may suspect, mere chimaeras

> de cette heure où l'homme épouvanté,
> Sous le ciel sans espoir et têtu de la Grace,
> Clamait: "Gloire au Très-Bon," et maudissait sa race!

In our own society, although a few poets like Mr. Eliot continue to emphasize the value of love in Christian terms, the urgent need for a love that is neither lust nor avarice has now become the affair of psychologists and sociologists. So far as Chaucer is concerned, we may as well recognize the fact that he was a Christian poet. Not much has been said in this book about his artistry, except in passing. But if we consider the aesthetic presuppositions of his time, the stylistic limitations of his work, and the literary techniques he inherited from the classical tradition and from St. Paul, we should be in a position to judge the artistry with which he presented what he had to say to his own audience. That, however, is a subject for another volume.

INDEX

INDEX

Names of post-classical literary characters are not included in this index. References to them should be sought under appropriate titles or authors. Medieval names are listed under what are presumed to be their more familiar forms. Thus the reader will find GUILLAUME DE Conches but WILLIAM OF Auvergne. References to the Scriptures under BIBLE are to the Douay version.

PLATES

1. *Très riches heures de Jean de France*. Chantilly. Fol. 161 verso. Photo Giraudon

2. Vézelay. La basilique
de la Madeleine.
Photo N. D. Giraudon

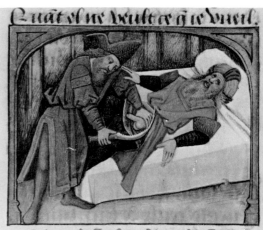

3. *Roman de la rose* (French, 15 c.).
Oxford. Bodleian Library.
MS Douce 195, fol. 76 verso

4. Exeter Cathedral.
NBR photo, reproduced by
permission of the estate of
the late C. J. P. Cave

5. "Taymouth Hours" (14 c.). London. British Museum. MS Yates Thompson 13, fol. 177

7. *Roman de Fauvel* (French, 14 c.). Paris. Bibl. Nat. ms Fr. 146, fol. 3 verso

8, 9. Horae (Flemish, ca. 1300). London. British Museum. ms Stowe 17, fols. 106, 59

10. *Roman de la rose* (French, ca. 1400). Oxford.

11. Horae (14 c.). Cambridge. University Library.

13. *Roman de la rose* (French, 14 c.). Oxford. Bodleian Library. MS Selden supra 57, fol. 10

12. *Roman de la rose* (French, 15 c.). Paris. Bibl. Nat. MS Fr. 24392, fol. 163

Dmine labia mea apm
es er os meum annunci
abir landem tuam

14. Horae (Flemish, 14 c.).
London. British Museum.
MS Add. 24681, fol. 20

15. Psalter (Flemish, ca. 1300). Oxford.
Bodleian Library. MS Douce 5, fol. 42

uos quemadmodum sperauim
in te.

In te domine sperani non co
fundar in eternum. v. Sperala sca
es et suauis. R. In delicis tuis sancta dei
genitrix.

In laudibus.

16. Horae (French, 14 c.). Oxford. Bodleian Library. MS Douce 62, fol. 51

Puis aduise com bonc archicre.
Par vnc petite archiere

17. *Roman de la rose* (French, 15 c.).
Oxford. Bodleian Library. MS Douce 195,
fol. 148 verso

18. *Roman de la rose*
(French, ca. 1400). Oxford.
Bodleian Library.
MS Douce 364, fol. 153 verso

Comme pymalion para symage .
Ainsi pymalion estuie
Na son estoil na zanc ne trme

21. Falconet. "Pygmalion." Baltimore, Md. Walters Art Gallery

22. "Hours of St. Omer" (Flemish, 14 c.). London. British Museum. MS Add. 36684, fol. 1 verso

23

24

23-28. Psalter (Flemish, ca. 1300). Oxford. Bodleian Library. MS Douce 6, fols. 79 verso-80, 83 verso, 89, 125 verso-126, 159 verso, 160 verso-161

25

26

23-28. Psalter (Flemish, ca. 1300). Oxford. Bodleian Library. MS Douce 6,
fols. 79 verso-80, 83 verso, 89, 125 verso-126, 159 verso, 160 verso-161

23-28. Psalter (Flemish, ca. 1300). Oxford. Bodleian Library. MS Douce 6, fols. 79 verso-80, 83 verso, 89, 125 verso-126, 159 verso, 160 verso-161

29, 30. Psalter from the Abbey of St. Remigius, Reims (12 c.). Cambridge. St. John's College. MS B 18, fols. 1, 182. Reproduced by permission of the Master and Fellows of St. John's College, Cambridge

29, 30. Psalter from the Abbey of St. Remigius, Reims (12 c.). Cambridge. St. John's College. MS B 18, fols. 1, 182. Reproduced by permission of the Master and Fellows of St. John's College, Cambridge

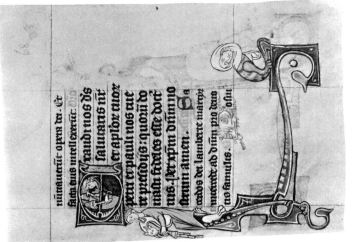

32. Horae (Flemish, ca. 1300). London. British Museum. MS Stowe 17, fol. 68

31. Psalter (Flemish, ca. 1300). Oxford. Bodleian Library. MS Douce 6, fol. 1

33. Psalter (Flemish, ca. 1300). Oxford. Bodleian Library. MS Douce 5, fol. 17

34. Guido Faba, *Summa de viciis*. Paris Bibl. Nat.
MS Lat. 8652A, fol. 51 verso

35. Monastic breviary from near Ghent (14 c.).
London. British Museum. MS Add. 29253, fol. 345

36. "Arundel Psalter" (14 c.). London, British Museum. ms Arundel 83, fol. 63 verso

Antate do
mmo can
ticum no
uum: quia
mirabilia
fecit. Salua
uit tibi dex
tera eius 7
brachium

sanctum eius.

Notum fecit dominus salutare suum: in con
spectu gencium reuelauit iusticiam suam.

Recordatus est misericordie sue: et ueritatis
sue domui istrael.

Viderunt omnes termini terre salutare dei
nostri: iubilate deo omnis terra cantate 7 exulta
te et psallite.

Psallite domino in cithara in cithara 7 uo
ce psalmi in tubis ductilibus et uoce tube corne
corne

Iubilate in conspectu regis domini: moue
atur mare 7 plenitudo eius orbis terrar: 7 qui ha

37. Psalter (14 c.). Vienna. Nationalbibliothek. Cod. 1826*, fol. 85 verso

38. Horae (French, 14 c.). Oxford. Bodleian Library. MS Douce 62, fol. 40

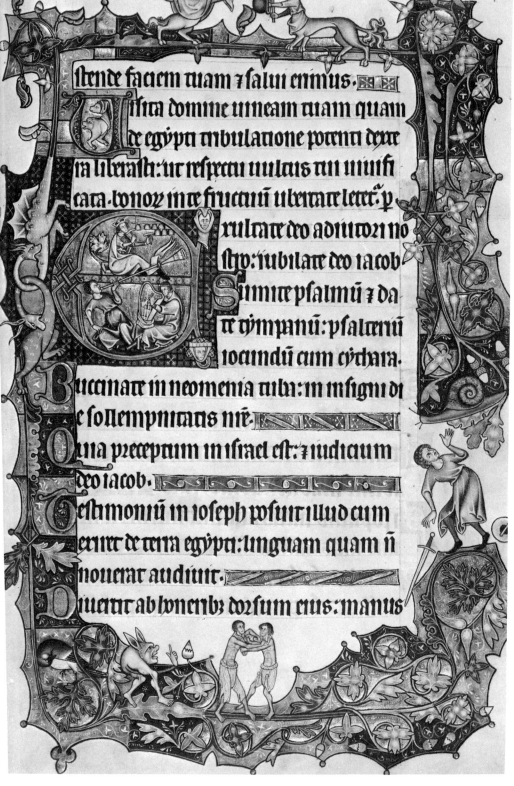

stende faciem tuam 7 salui erimus ·

Uisita domine uineam tuam quam
de egypti tribulatione potenti dexte
ra liberasti: ut respectu uultus tui uinifi
cata · bonoz in te fructuu ubertate letet̃ · p

rultate deo adiutori no
stro: iubilate deo iacob

umite psalmũ 7 da
te tympanũ: psalteriũ
iocundũ cum cythara ·

uccinate in neomenia tuba: in insigni di
e sollempnitatis nr̃e ·

uia preceptum in israel est: 7 iudicium
deo iacob ·

estimoniũ in ioseph posuit illud cum
exiret de terra egypti: linguam quam ñ
nouerat audiuit ·

iuertit ab oneribz dorsum eius: manus

40

41

40, 41. "Queen Mary's Psalter" (14 c.). London. British Museum.
MS Royal 2 B. VII, fols. 229, 196 verso-197

42. *Roman de la rose* (14 c.). Oxford.
Bodleian Library. MS e Mus. 65, fol. 3 verso

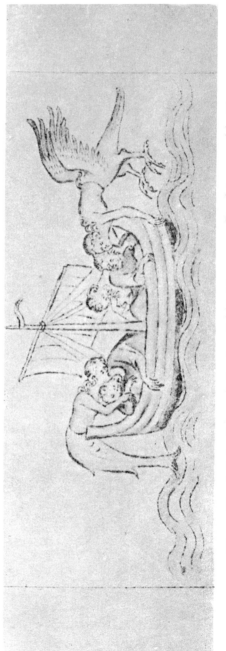

43, 44. "Queen Mary's Psalter" (14 c.). London. British Museum. MS Royal 2 B. VII, fols. 96 verso-97

45. Etruscan cinerary urn (2 c. B.C.). Oxford. Ashmolean Museum

46. "Shaftesbury Psalter" (12 c.). London. British Museum.
MS Lansd. 383, fol. 165 verso

47. Ivory. London. Victoria and Albert
Museum. Crown copyright

48. Psalter from the Abbey of St. Remigius, Reims (12 c.). Cambridge. St. John's College. MS B. 18, fol. 86. Reproduced by permission of the Master and Fellows of St. John's College, Cambridge

49. Horae (French, 14 c.). Oxford. Bodleian Library. MS Douce 62, fol. 43

50. Chartres Cathedral

51. Chartres Cathedral

52. Amiens Cathedral

53. "Amesbury Psalter" (13 c.). Oxford.
All Souls College. MS 6, fol. 3

54. Strassburg Cathedral. Photo Giraudon

55. Strassburg Cathedral. Photo Giraudon

56. Paris Cathedral

57. Amiens Cathedral

58. Amiens Cathedral

59. Ivory mirror case. Victoria and Albert Museum. Crown copyright

60. Ivory mirror case. Victoria and Albert Museum. Crown copyright

61. Ivory mirror case. Victoria and Albert Museum. Crown copyright

62. Ivory mirror case. Cambridge. Fitzwilliam Museum. Reproduced by permission of the Syndics of the Fitzwilliam Museum, Cambridge

63. Ivory mirror case. Victoria and Albert Museum. Crown copyright

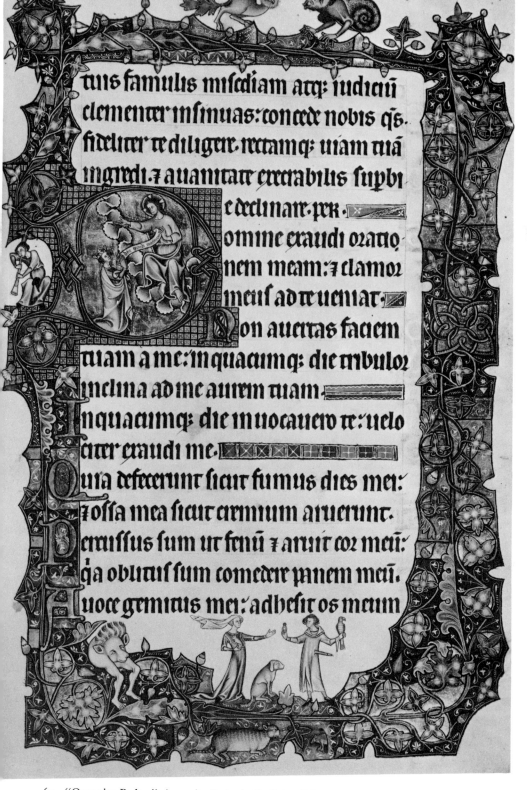

tuis famulis misediam atq; iudiciu
clementer insinuas: concede nobis qs.
fideliter te diligere. rectamq; uiam tua
ingredi. 7 auanitate erecrabilis supbi
e declinare. per.
omine exaudi oratio
nem meam: 7 clamor
meus ad te ueniat.
on auertas faciem
tuam a me: in quacumq; die tribulor
inclina ad me aurem tuam.
in quacumq; die inuocauero te: uelo
citer exaudi me.
Quia defecerunt sicut fumus dies mei:
7 ossa mea sicut crinium aruerunt.
ercussus sum ut fenu 7 aruit cor meu:
qa oblitus sum comedere panem meu.
uoce gemitus mei: adhesit os meum

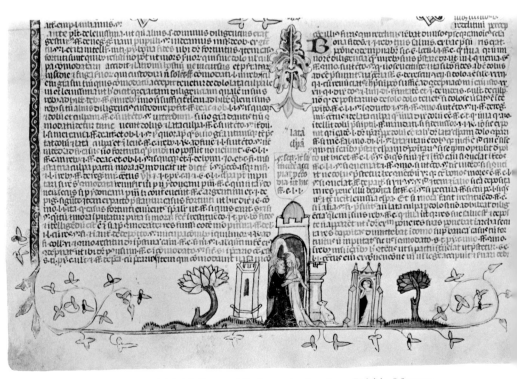

65, 66. "Smithfield Decretals" (14 c.). London. British Museum.
MS Royal 10 E. IV, fols. 185-185 verso

67. Psalter (ca. 1300). Oxford. Bodleian Library. MS Douce 131, fol. 96 verso

68. *Roman de la rose* (French, 14 c.). London. British Museum. MS Yates Thompson 21, fol. 165

69. *Roman de la rose* (French, ca. 1400). Oxford.
Bodleian Library. MS Douce 364, fol. 124 verso

70. Amiens Cathedral

71. *Roman de la rose* (French, 15 c.). Oxford.
Bodleian Library. MS Douce 195, fol. 99

72. *Roman de la rose* (French, ca. 1400). Oxford.
Bodleian Library. MS Douce 364, fol. 3 verso

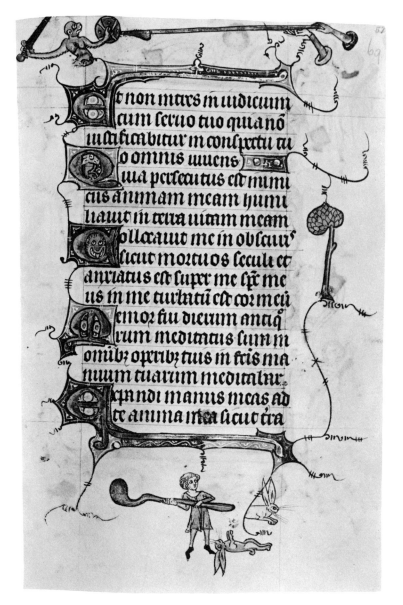

t non mors in iudicium
cum servo tuo quia nõ
iustificabitur in conspectu tu
o omnis viuens
quia persecutus est inimi
cus animam meam humi
liauit in terra vitam meam
collocauit me in obscuris
sicut mortuos seculi et
anxiatus est super me sps me
us in me turbatum est cor meu
memor fui dierum antiq
uorum meditatus sum in
omnibz operibz tuis in fcis ma
nuum tuarum meditabar.
expandi manus meas ad
te anima mea sicut tra

73. "Hours of St. Omer" (Flemish, 14 c.). London. British Museum.
MS Add. 36684, fol. 69

74. Amiens Cathedral. Photo Marburg

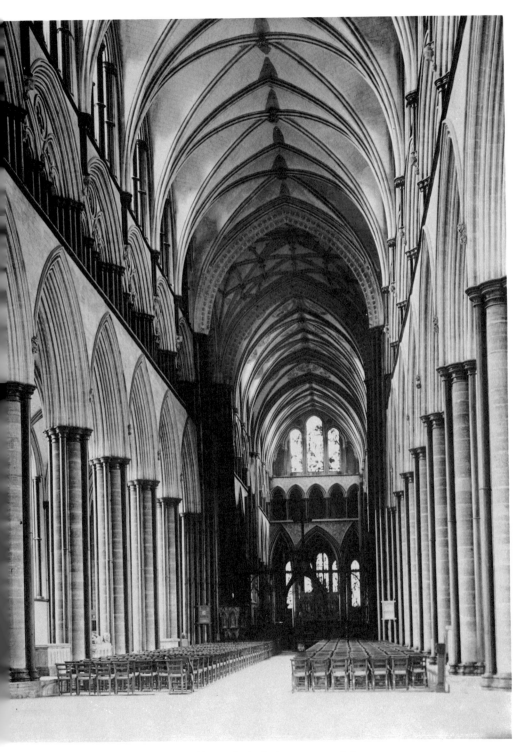

75. Salisbury Cathedral. NBR copyright

76. Wells Cathedral. Copyright Leo Herbert-Felton

77. Beverley Minster. NBR copyright

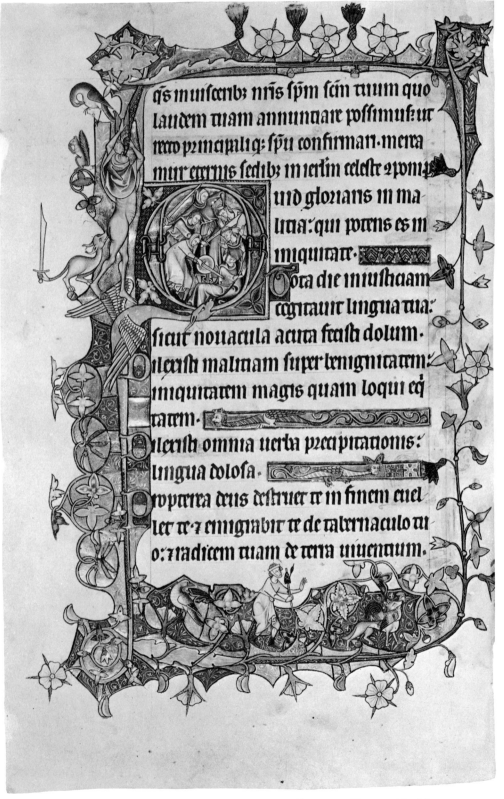

78. "Ormesby Psalter" (14 c.). Oxford. Bodleian Library. MS Douce 366, fol. 71 verso

79. *Somme le roi* (French). London. British Museum. MS Add. 28162, fol. 7 verso

80. "Taymouth Hours" (14 c.). London. British Museum.
MS Yates Thompson 13, fol. 120 verso

81. Horae (French, late 14 c.). London. British Museum. MS Add. 23145, fol. 168

83. Horae (Netherlandish, ca. 1394). Oxford. Bodleian Library.

82. "Taymouth Hours" (14 c.). London. British Museum.

84. "Arundel Psalter" (14 c.). London. British Museum. MS Arundel 83, fol. 131 verso.

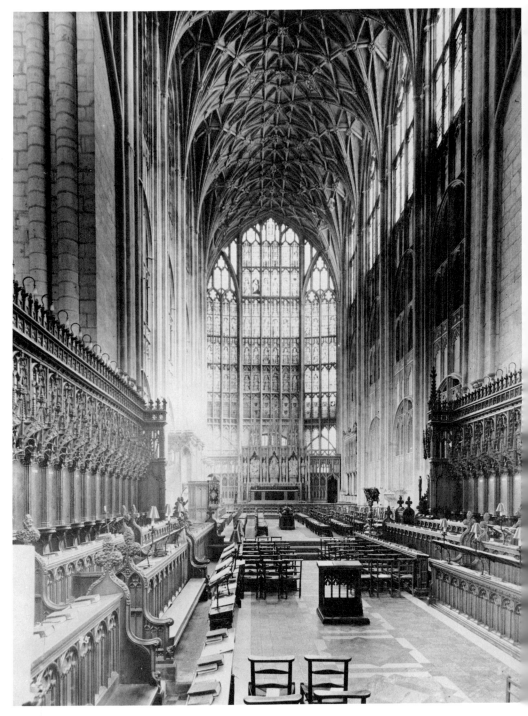

85. Gloucester Cathedral. NBR copyright

86. Durham Cathedral. Neville Screen (at right). Photo Walter Scott

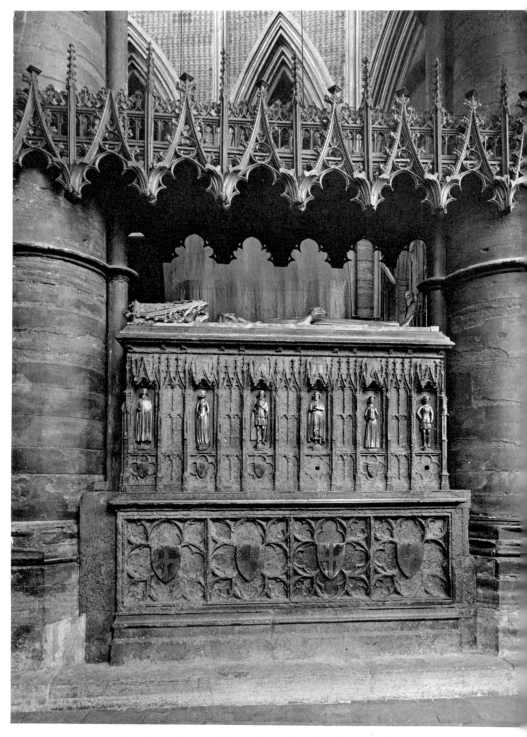

87. Westminster Abbey. Copyright Leo Herbert-Felton

88. Westminster Hall. Photo A. F. Kersting

89. *Très riches heures de Jean de France*. Chantilly. Fol. 25. Photo Giraudon

90. Canterbury Cathedral. Copyright Leo Herbert-Felton

91. Psalter (14 c.). Oxford. Exeter College. MS 47, fol. 34

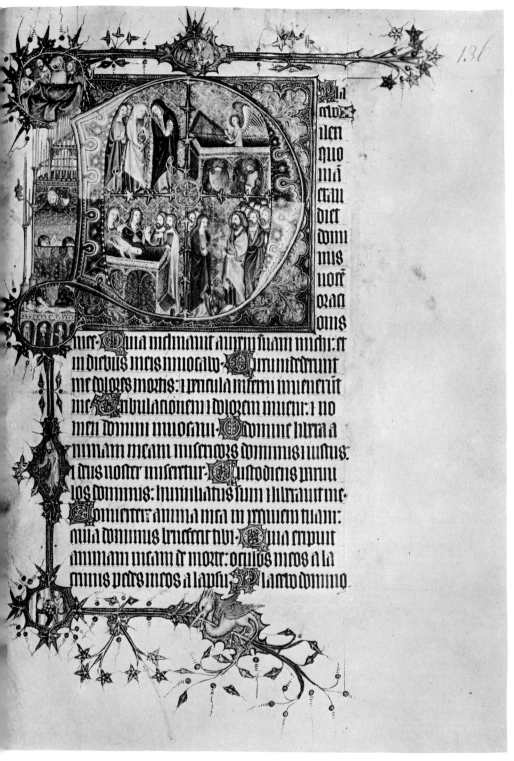

92-95. Psalter and Horae (after 1380). London. British Museum.

MS Egerton 3277, fols. 142, 61, 62 verso, 63 verso

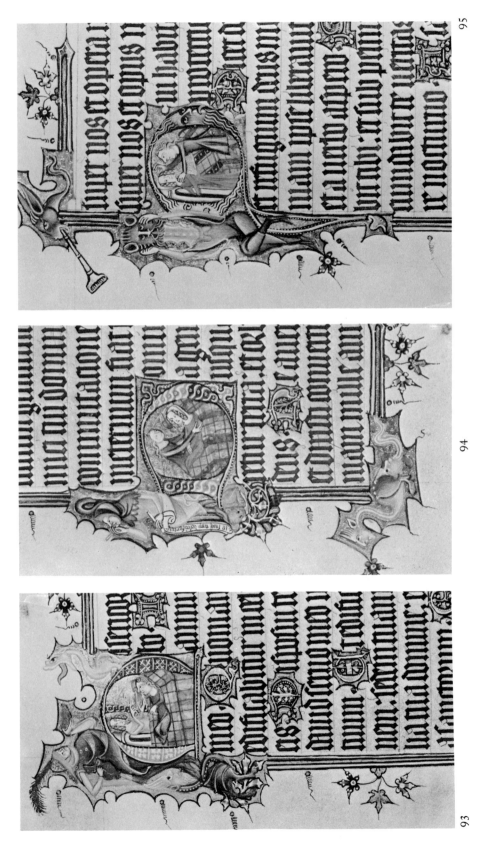

95

94

93

92–95. Psalter and Horae (after 1380). London. British Museum. MS Egerton 3277, fols. 142, 61, 62 verso, 63 verso

96. Virgin of the Outer Gate. Winchester College. Reproduced by permission of
the Warden and Fellows of Winchester College

97. Wilton Diptych. Reproduced by courtesy of the Trustees,
The National Gallery, London

98. Wilton Diptych. Reproduced by courtesy of the Trustees,
The National Gallery, London

99. Psalter (Netherlandish, 14 c.). Oxford. Bodleian Library.
MS Canon Liturg. 126, fols. 70 verso-71

100. "Smithfield Decretals" (14 c.). London. British Museum. MS Royal 10 E. IV, fol. 159

te marie unginita scamda hu
mano genen premia prestristi: ar
buc qs ut ipam pro nobis inter
cedit seruaamus per quam me
ruimus auctorem uite susaper
dium nrm ihm xpm. alia ord
[E]cclam tuam quesumus
domine benignus illu
stra ut beati iohannis apostoli
tui et euangeliste illuminata
doctrinis ad dona preueniat sem
piterna. per dominum nrm ihm
xpm filium tuum. Qui tecum
uiuit et regnat. ad uespas

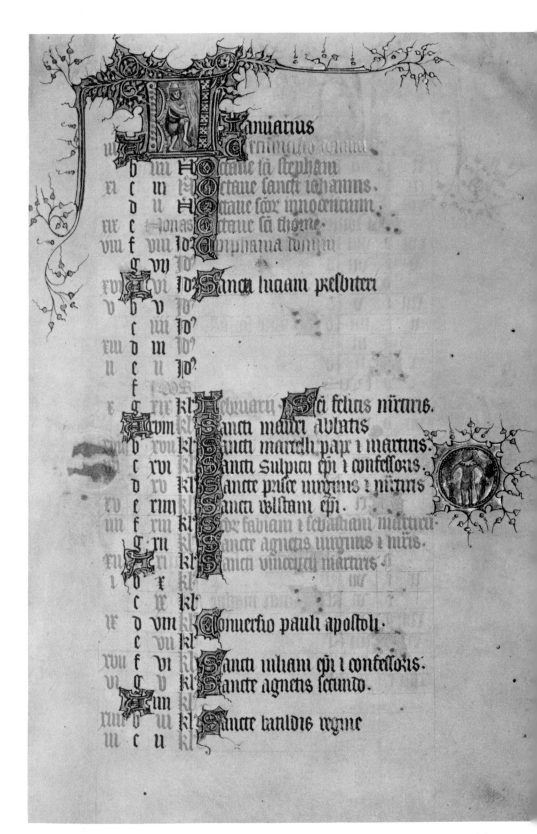

102. "Taymouth Hours" (14 c.). London. British Museum. MS Yates Thompson 13, fol. 177

103. *Roman de la rose* (French, 14 c.). London. British Museum.
MS Royal 19 B. 13, fol. 7 verso

104. Psalter (14 c.). Oxford. Exeter College.
MS 47, fol. 66 verso

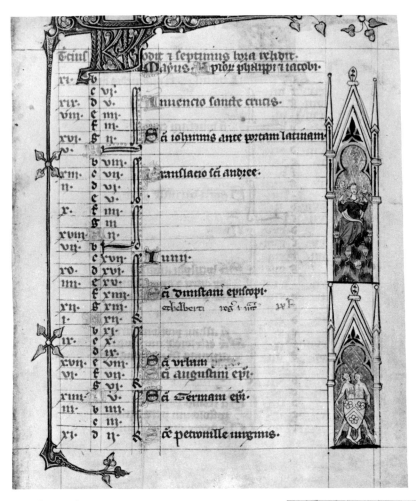

105. Horae (French, 14 c.). Cambridge.
University Library. MS Dd. 4. 17, fol. 15

106. Horae (Flemish, ca. 1300).
London. British Museum. MS Stowe 17, fol. 7

107. Horae (French, 14 c.). Oxford. Bodleian Library. MS Douce 62, fol. 7

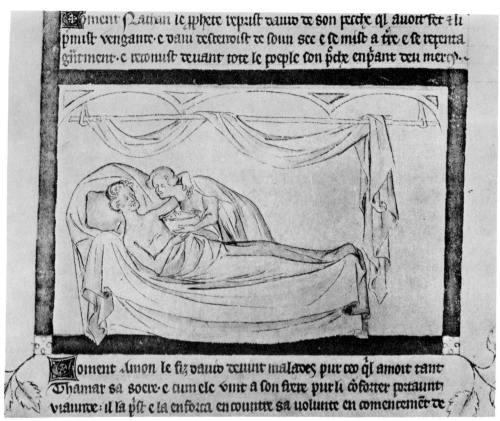

108. "Queen Mary's Psalter" (14 c.). London. British Museum. MS Royal 2 B. VII, fol. 58

109. *Roman de la rose*. London. British Museum.
MS Egerton 881, fol. 123

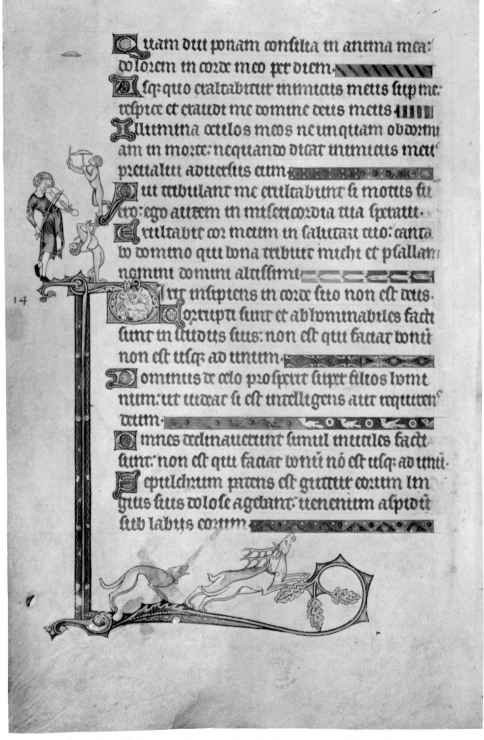

110. "Tenison Psalter" (13 c.). London. British Museum. MS Add. 24686, fol. 17 verso

111. Vézelay. La basilique de la Madeleine. Photo N. D. Giraudon

Q uil luy dit aſſe eſt nice ⁊ folle.

112. *Roman de la rose* (French, 15 c.).
Oxford. Bodleian Library. MS Douce 195, fol. 60 verso

113. *Très riches heures de Jean de France*. Chantilly. Fol. 4 verso. Photo Giraudon

114. Poitiers. Notre Dame la Grande

Omient abfolon sen fuit + puro p les dictus te son thief te sue vne bn

115. "Queen Mary's Psalter" (14 c.). London. British Museum.
MS Royal 2 B. VII, fol. 60 verso

D ua trabit magno ge fugit questura tonanti:

τ uuc uew actuise stuuulis maiorib; ue

116. Statius, *Thebaid*. London. British Museum.
MS Burney 257, fol. 187 verso

117. Horae (Flemish, ca. 1300). London.
British Museum. MS Stowe 17, fol. 31

118. Roman de la rose
(French, ca. 1400).
Oxford. Bodleian Library.
MS Douce 364, fol. 4